FANTASY

The Definitive Illustrated Guide

THIS IS A CARLTON BOOK

First published in 1998 by Carlton Books Limited

This updated edition published in 2002 by Carlton Books Ltd
20 Mortimer Street
London
W1T 3JW

10 9 8 7 6 5 4 3 2 1

A CIP catalogue record for this book is available from the British Library

ISBN 1 84222 747 5

PROJECT EDITOR: Roland Hall
ART DIRECTION: Diane Spender
DESIGNER: Simon Balley
PICTURE RESEARCH: Lorna Ainger
PRODUCTION: Alexia Turner

Printed and bound in Dubai

General Editor

David Pringle is best known as editor, publisher and co-founder of the internationally-acclaimed, Hugo Award-winning fantasy and science fiction magazine *Interzone*. He has also written several fantasy and science fiction studies, including *Imaginary People: A Who's Who of Fictional Characters from the 18th Century to the Present Day*, the *St James Guide to Fantasy Writers*, *Modern Fantasy: The Hundred Best Novels 1946–1987* and *Science Fiction: The 100 Best Novels 1949–1984*. He was general editor for the popular *Ultimate Encyclopedia of Science Fiction* (Carlton Books).

Contributors' Details

David Langford is a freelance author. He has written three novels and several non-fiction books, including *The Third Millennium*. He is an eleven times Hugo award-winner for best science-fiction fan writer and best fanzine.

Brian Stableford is a novelist and critic of distinction in the science fiction and fantasy fields. His many novels include *Cradle of the Sun*, *The Realms of Tartarus*, *The Empire of Fear*, *The Werewolves of London* and *Serpent's Blood*. His non-fiction works include *The Third Millennium* (with David Langford), *Scientific Romance In Britain 1890–1950* and *The Way to Write Science Fiction*.

Tim Dedopulos is a freelance author, editor and games designer living in southern England. He has worked for a number of games companies, including Wizards of the Coast, and has been a dedicated gamer since the first edition of *Dungeons & Dragons*. His previous works for Carlton Books include *Wizards*, the *Official Magic: The Gathering Deckbuilders' Guide* and the *Official Magic: The Gathering Advanced Strategy Guide* .

FANTASY
The Definitive Illustrated Guide

Foreword by Terry Pratchett • General Editor David Pringle

CARLTON
BOOKS

CONTENTS

FOREWORD

Welcome To The Thunderstorm Cave. Our ability to make other worlds made us human. Lots of animals are bright, but as far as we can tell they've never come up with any ideas about who makes the thunder.

A proto-human did, in some rain-lashed cave. It must have struck him like a bolt from above. Perhaps it was a bolt from above. Suddenly... inside his head there were people in the sky, and suddenly there was somewhere that people went when they died... and suddenly there was this huge ghost world behind this one where all the colours were brighter.

As time went on, our proto-human found that his daydreams were not only providing explanations, they'd opened a way to a good job in the warm and all the nice bits of mammoth he could eat. He'd got hold of something worth more than food. The news spread. The world's second oldest profession became a growth industry (the oldest is "flint knapper", no matter what you may have heard).

It used an invisible invention that sent mankind on the path to... well, humanity, because before you can change the world you have to be able to form a picture of the world being other than it appears. Imagination, not intelligence, made us human. Squirrels are quite intelligent when it comes to nuts, but as far as we can tell they have never told stories about a hero who stole nuts from the gods.

That ability has given us all our fiction and our mythology. Most of our religions, too, because following the success of "What Thunder Is" and its sequel "How We Got Fire", which was breaking pile-of-juicy-mammoth-ribs records all along the valley, some bright apprentice with a forehead like a balcony came up with the incredible "We Can Stop The Thunderer Hurting Us If We Do These Special Things" followed by "We Are The True People And We're Better Than Those People In The Next Valley Because We Do These Special Things'". Suddenly, life was a lot more exciting although, for the people in the next valley, it was going to be somewhat shorter.

Suddenly, the world was a story. Homo Sapiens became Homo Narrans, "Story-telling Man"; the rest was, literally, history.

We are creatures of fantasy. We spend a lot of time in that huge ghost world with the bright colours, and one part of it is now called "civilization". The mental muscles swollen on the aerobics of gods and heroes have gone on to invent new fantasies "natural justice", "eminent domain", "human rights" which have given something approaching solid form. A raft of fantasies, "made-up things", floats us through the cold dark universe.

It's odd, then, that unashamed fantasy still trails clouds of disapproval. But some of the reasons are easy to see, even in these pages. The sheer torrent of the stuff, for one thing. The telling and retelling. All those new worlds and eternal heroes. And the suggestion that the world could be completely other than it is always annoys those who are content with the way things are. Stories of imagination tend to upset those without one. Rulers are suspicious of new worlds where their writ does not run. Jailers don't like escapism. Probably the man in the cave got the occasional wallop from the clan leaders. Telling stories can be dangerous.

And now, welcome to the map of invisible places...

And pass the mammoth ribs, please.

Terry Pratchett.

INTRODUCTION

Fulfilling the Heart's Desire

Fantasy is the fiction of the heart's desire. This description might seem vague, as do most brief definitions of literary categories, but it may have its uses. Other fictions of the fantastic are named for their subject-matter, or for the emotions they arouse. Thus, science fiction has something to do with science – that is, "knowledge" – and is therefore a fiction of ideas, rooted in empiricism and the modern scientific world-view. Horror stories are intended to evoke the feeling they are named for – horror, with its kindred emotions such as terror, revulsion and, at times, a sense of the fearful "sublime". Magic-realist fiction is what the phrase implies, a form of realism with its eye mainly on the actual daily world around us, but lightly dusted with the magical – those hints of the inexplicable which may heighten our sense of the real. All these forms – sf, horror, magic realism – overlap to some extent, and all are examples of the fantastic, but none of them is quite what we mean by fantasy proper. Pure fantasy, or what the critic John Clute calls "full fantasy", seems to deal in the fulfilment of desire – not in the simple carnal sense (although it can pander to that too) but in the sense of the yearning of the human heart for a kinder world, a better self, a wholer experience, a sense of truly belonging. To use the ancient metaphor (but then most things about this genre are ancient, going back to the beginnings of our humanity), fantasy seeks to heal the waste land.

So, unlike science fiction, which appeals to the intellect, but like horror, which produces gut-reactions, fantasy makes its play primarily to the emotions. However, the emotions it deals in are more complex, if on the whole much more "positive", than those that horror plays with. Desire, wonder, yearning and nostalgia all have their places here, as does laughter. We can see sharply different aspects of the workings of the Heart's Desire in two of the most primal forms of fantasy, fairy tale and heroic epic. In fairy tales – deriving from oral folk stories or "old wives' tales", and long associated with women and children – we see the movements of perennial human desire at their most straightforward, through the creation of worlds where every boy is a potential prince, every girl a potential princess, and every ending a happily-ever-after. In heroic epics – deriving from the songs that hunters and warriors sang to each other to boost their courage, and long associated with men as opposed to women and youngsters – we see the movements of human desires of the more violent and selfish sort, through the creation of worlds were heroic selves prevail in bloody conflict, monsters are slain, and pride and status and honour are gained. These two kinds of fantasy-of-desire intermingle: fairy tales often contain violence, and epics usually encompass the romance of sexual love as well as of manly action. Both forms channel desire towards a kind of social fulfilment, where love and pride and a cluster of other positive emotions combine to create the best of all possible worlds, the waste land healed.

There is also an ancient religious element to fantasy, which may underlie both fairy tale and heroic epic. The human heart desires more than bodily and egoistic and social satisfactions: it yearns for a larger sense of belonging in the universe as a whole, a sense of worship, and peace with whatever powers there may be. We need to know about the ways of God (or the Goddess, or the gods), about the reasons for our being, and about the beginnings and endings of things. All societies, even recent secular ones, have their shared belief-structures, and stories which embody widespread beliefs are called "myths". Today we are accustomed to the imprecise use of the words myth and mythology to mean untruths or downright lies, but the essence of all myth is that once upon a time it was *believed*, in a literal way; and so a distinction needs to be made between those bodies of stories from the past that we label mythologies, which are in effect the relics of dead religions, and those others, such as fairy tales, which have always been regarded as mere fictions concocted for people's entertainment. Modern fantasy obviously takes its place with the latter – it is avowedly fictional – but, like folk tale and epic, it may draw upon mythology for its subject-matter – and for a good deal of its hidden power.

The principal mythologies which underlie modern fantasy fiction include those of the ancient Greeks, the pantheon which comprises the gods Zeus, Hera, Apollo, Aphrodite, Dionysus, Athene, Poseidon and many others, as well as the demi-gods or half-human heroes such as Heracles and Perseus; those of the Celtic, and particularly Irish, cultures, including the tales of Cuchulain and Finn Mac Cool; those of the Germanic, Old Norse and Icelandic peoples, comprising the stories of the gods Odin, Thor, Loki, Tyr and Freya, and heroes such as Sigurd (Siegfried); and, of course, those of the Judaeo-Christian tradition as recorded in the Holy Bible and its Apocrypha. With the last-named, we come within the reaches of still-living faiths which have millions of adherents worldwide (as do other major religions like Islam, Buddhism and Hinduism), and so many people might regard them as inappropriate sources for fantasy

ANCIENT GODS SUCH AS NEPTUNE – ROMAN EQUIVALENT OF THE GREEK POSEIDON – WERE SOME OF THE FIRST FANTASY FIGURES

fiction – despite which, much fantasy (including works by J. R. R. Tolkien and C. S. Lewis) could be said to be Christian in its inspiration. Other mythologies, both "dead" and living, have been ransacked by fantasy writers, including those of ancient Mesopotamia, Egypt, India, Persia, Arabia, China, Japan, Finland, sub-Saharan Africa, Native America, Polynesia and Australia.

From its origins in religious mythology, folk wonder-tale and heroic song, fantasy has developed in multitudinous forms throughout the history of world literature. It is continuously present since the invention of writing, some 5,000 years ago. There are fantastic tales from ancient Egypt, such as the imaginary-voyage story of "The Shipwrecked Sailor", and from Babylonia – most famously *The Epic of Gilgamesh* (c. 1500 BC), in which the legendary king of the title allies with the wild man Enkidu to defeat various monsters and then, after Enkidu's death, searches for the secret of eternal life. In the beginning, there was little distinction between "story" and "history", and so much tale-telling was based on legend (a word which could be defined, from our point of view, as "history retold as fantasy"). Actual historical events were commemorated – and fantasticated – in cycles of oral stories and songs: *Gilgamesh* may have begun in that way, along with many other epics now lost. Most famous and influential of these cycles was the body of early Greek stories which accreted around the siege of the city of Troy, in Asia Minor, tales which centuries later were reworked into the two most perfect of heroic epics, Homer's *Iliad* and *Odyssey* (c. 750 BC). Both deal with gods and men, but the second poem, in particular, describing Odysseus's amazing voyage home from Troy, has become a kind of template for a great deal of later fantasy – ranging from the medieval Arabic "Seven Voyages of Sinbad" to many of the quest-fantasy novels of today.

Other celebrated epics include *The Argonautica* of Apollonius Rhodius (c. 250 BC), retelling the voyage of Jason and the Argonauts, and the greatest of Roman works, Virgil's *Aeneid* (19 BC), which deals with the *Odyssey*-like adventures of the Trojan hero Aeneas. Much early Greek literature is in verse, including the comic fantasy plays of Aristophanes and the myth-based tragedies of his great contemporaries such as Aeschylus and Sophocles; but by late Greek times, as the Roman Empire was beginning to take over the Mediterranean, prose fiction had become firmly established as the entertainment reading of a wide class of literate people. These prose works, usually referred to as "romances", contained strong elements of fantasy. Although most were written in Greek, the best-known single example is a late Latin work, *The Golden Ass* by Lucius Apuleius (c. 180 AD). This picaresque adventure concerns a young man who drinks a magic potion which turns him into an ass, and it also includes, as an embedded story, one of the world's finest fairy tales, "Cupid and Psyche". An earlier major Roman work concerning magical transformations, *The Metamorphoses* by Ovid (17 AD), is also a fantasy masterpiece, although written in verse: it retells many of the Greek myths in a fashion designed to entertain sophisticated urban readers. By Ovid's time those myths were no longer believed: they were regarded as beautiful stories, and fit matter for a conscious work of fantasy.

Throughout post-Classical times, in the so-called Dark Ages, fantasy fiction continued to thrive, though much of it took oral form and is now lost to us. Works that survive in written versions include the Anglo-Saxon epic of *Beowulf* (c. 725), based on heroic Danish legend, and the prose *Alexander Romance* by Leo of Naples (952), which retells the exploits of the Macedonian world-conqueror Alexander the Great with much fantastic embellishment. The latter was to inspire many medieval imitations. Another common form of "Dark Age" fiction was the Saint's Life, a type of tale again based on history and biography but tricked out with the motifs of fantasy; an

CHRISTIAN NOTIONS OF THE AFTERLIFE, AS IN DANTE'S *INFERNO* (PART OF HIS GREAT 14TH-CENTURY POEM *THE DIVINE COMEDY*), HAVE ALSO ENRICHED THE TRADITION OF FANTASY

interesting example is the *Voyage of St Brendan* (c. 850), written in Latin prose, which tells of the Irish saint's sea-journey to the mythical Island of Promise.

Throughout this period in Western Europe, other great cycles of secular oral tales were accumulating, in a fashion similar to the Classical "Matter of Troy" – chief among them the stories concerning the feats of the Emperor Charlemagne's paladins, especially the hero Roland who fell at the Battle of Roncesvalles, and the stories about an obscure British war-leader called Arthur and his supposed mentor, the Welsh wizard Merlin (originally "Myrddin" – it is said that the "l" spelling was introduced so that French readers, then the dominant group, would not be offended by a name which reminded them of the swear-word *merde*).

The "Matter of Britain" was to inspire much of the greatest medieval fantasy, and has remained potent to the present day. Somehow, the quasi-historical tales of King Arthur, Queen Guinevere, Merlin and the Knights of the Round Table attracted to them a body of deeper, religious myth – the stories of the various knights' quests for the Holy Grail. Christianized versions of Celtic mythology, the Grail romances are our prime source for the notion of the healing of the waste land, alluded to above.

Besides these romances, numerous other works of fantasy remain to us from the medieval period, ranging from animal fables, such as the cycle about Reynard the Fox, to that supreme Italian masterpiece of the Christian afterlife, Dante's *The Divine Comedy* (1321). In the wake of Dante, other Italian writers were to produce more secular poetic fantasies during the Renaissance period, chief among them Ludovico Ariosto, whose *Orlando Furioso* (1532), retelling the story of Roland, has been praised memorably by C. S. Lewis in his book *The Allegory of Love* (1936) and was considered sufficiently close to modern generic fantasy for Lin Carter to include a prose rendition of it in his Ballantine Adult Fantasy series of paperbacks (1973).

Most of the foregoing works, especially the Italian epics and such English "imitations" as Edmund Spenser's *The Faerie Queene* (1590–1596) were in verse, but the 16th century also saw a significant flowering of lengthy tales of fantasy in prose form – the direct ancestors of the modern fantasy novel. These were the so-called Chivalric Romances, beginning in Spain with Garcia Ordonez de Montalvo's *Amadis of Gaul* (1508), and continuing through countless sequels, variations and imitations in all the major European languages over the next century and more.

The chivalric romances were unabashedly fictional, owing little or nothing to historical legend or religious mythology (although inevitably elements from those sources were to creep in, as they continue to do in the successor works of our own time). Lengthy fantastical yarns of knightly heroes and lovely heroines pitted against ogres and giants and sorceresses in the settings of enchanted castles and mysterious islands, these have all the feel of fantasy for fantasy's sake.

Although the fashion for them passed away during the 17th and 18th centuries – an Age of Reason, and the great period for the growth of modern science and its attendant form of fantastic fiction, the utopian tradition of proto-science fiction – the chivalric romances were never entirely forgotten, and repeated attempts to revive them (or something very like them) were made by 19th-century writers, including the German Friedrich de la Motte Fouque, in his novels *The Magic Ring* (1813) and *Sintram and His Companions* (1815), and the Englishman William Morris, in his *The Wood Beyond the World* (1894), *The Well at the World's End* (1896) and many other works. And with Morris we arrive at the beginnings of fantasy fiction in the fully modern sense: he was to be a direct influence on all those 20th-century writers, including Lord Dunsany, E. R. Eddison, C. S. Lewis and J. R. R. Tolkien, whose books have defined the fantasy of recent decades.

Meanwhile, even though it was an age whose fiction was dominated by realism, other forms of fantasy flourished in the 18th and 19th centuries – the literary fairy tale, whose vogue was initiated in France by Madame d'Aulnoy and Charles Perrault and much strengthened by the German researches of the Brothers Grimm; the exotic "Eastern" fantasy, inspired by Antoine Galland's translation of *The Arabian Nights* (1704–17), which produced many examples – see the useful anthology *Oriental Tales* edited by Robert L. Mack (Oxford World Classics, 1992); the American pseudo-folk tales of Washington Irving, most famously "Rip Van Winkle" (1819), and the fantastic moralities of Charles Dickens, especially *A Christmas Carol* (1843); the children's fairy tales of Hans Christian Andersen (beginning in the 1830s), Charles Kingsley (*The Water-Babies*, 1863), Lewis Carroll (the "Alice" books, 1865–71), George MacDonald (*At the Back of the North Wind*, 1871), Carlo Collodi (*The Adventures of Pinocchio*, 1883) and E. Nesbit (*The Book of Dragons*, 1899); the humorous fantasies of Thomas Love Peacock (*The Misfortunes of Elphin*, 1829), Douglas Jerrold (*A Man Made of Money*, 1849), George Meredith (*The Shaving of Shagpat*, 1855), F. Anstey (*Vice-Versa*, 1882), Mark Twain (*A Connecticut Yankee in King Arthur's Court*, 1889) and John Kendrick Bangs (*A House-Boat on the Styx*, 1896); the lost-race fantasies of H. Rider Haggard (*She*, 1886) and his legion of imitators; and, towards the Victorian period's close and well into the 20th-century, a host of occult fantasies, "karmic romances" and fantastic thrillers – often involving serial reincarnation, revived Egyptian mummies or bizarre villains bent on world-domination, and sometimes verging on outright horror fiction – by Edgar Lee (*Pharaoh's Daughter*, 1889), Edwin Lester Arnold (*The Wonderful Adventures of Phra the Phoenician*, 1890), Guy Boothby (*A Bid for Fortune, or Dr Nikola's Vendetta*, 1895), C. J. Cutcliffe Hyne (*The Lost Continent*, 1900), Bram Stoker (*The Jewel of Seven Stars*, 1903), Sax Rohmer (*The Mystery of Dr Fu Manchu*, 1913, and *Brood of the Witch-Queen*, 1918) and Robert W. Chambers (*The Slayer of Souls*, 1920).

THE AGE OF THE STORYTELLERS

With those last two sub-categories, the lost-race story and the fantasy thriller, we arrive at the phenomenon of the pulp magazines. Of course, fiction had appeared in magazines of various kinds long before the arrival of pulp-paper monthlies (the first of which was the American publisher Frank A. Munsey's *The Argosy*, from 1896), but it was the pulps which were to be essential to the further evolution of fantasy – and of modern popular-fiction genres in general, including crime fiction, Westerns, adventure stories, horror and science fiction. The early pulps were standard-sized magazines, large and thick and printed on coarse paper, with lurid colour covers (from about 1905 onwards), specializing in fiction of any sensational or sentimental sort. They took their example and their varied inspiration from two prime sources – partly from the 19th-century lower-class story papers, dime novels and five-cent weekly "libraries" which had been aimed mainly at a youthful readership, and, more importantly, from the turn-of-the-century middle-class standard magazines (and large-format illustrated weeklies) which had arisen in the 1880s and 1890s as a result of extended literacy, growing social aspirations, new printing technologies and the enormous expansion of popular journalism. (It was an epoch of robber-baron publishing, represented by individuals like Frank Munsey in America, and George Newnes, C. Arthur Pearson and Alfred Harmsworth in Britain, men who became millionaires many times over through the peddling of dreams to that newly conceived entity – the "mass" public.)

The late-Victorian and Edwardian monthlies, such as *The Strand Magazine* and *Pearson's Magazine* (or *Harper's Monthly* and *Munsey's Magazine* in America), were the same size as the later pulps, but printed on book-quality paper and not exclusively devoted to fiction, though fiction was their predominant ingredient; the illustrated weeklies, like *Tit-Bits* and *Pearson's Weekly* (or *Harper's Weekly* and *Collier's Once-a-Week*), which were also common at that time, were larger in size, and shaped more like tabloid newspapers. These publications dominated a period which the critic Roger Lancelyn Green (writing in another context) has called "The Age of the Storytellers". The period in question lasted from the early 1880s, when Robert Louis Stevenson published *Treasure Island*, until about 1914. It was a time of synthesis and synchronicity, when readerships were rising, journalism was booming, and a large group of talented new writers suddenly emerged to cater for the age's imaginative needs. At their best, what these writers did was marry the "popular" to the "artistic" – they took the vulgar but lively influences of the penny dreadfuls, boys' papers and dime novels they had read in their youth and merged them with the more literary traditions of the High Victorian novel in general, creating an exciting new synthesis.

Their work took the form of short stories, novellas and short novels (as opposed to the ponderous Victorian "three-deckers") for which they found eager audiences in the magazines. Their novels did not appear solely in magazines – Rider Haggard's first success, *King Solomon's Mines*, for example was published straight into book form in 1885, though thereafter almost everything he wrote was serialized first – but the magazines made these writers' careers possible, for in that pre-cinema, pre-radio and pre-television world it was these periodicals which were the leading entertainment medium.

Many writers helped create the Age of the Storytellers, which was mainly a British phenomenon (the USA seems not to have had talented writers in sufficient numbers in the 1880s and 1890s, with honourable exceptions such as Mark Twain). Of those many writers one can argue that the "Big Five" were:

Robert Louis Stevenson (born 1850)
H. Rider Haggard (born 1856)
A. Conan Doyle (born 1859)
Rudyard Kipling (born 1865)
H. G. Wells (born 1866)

Of course, there were other popular middlebrow authors – Bram Stoker, Oscar Wilde, Stanley J. Weyman, F. Anstey, Edwin Lester Arnold, J. Meade Falkner, E. Nesbit, Kenneth Grahame, J. M. Barrie, Jerome K. Jerome, R. Austin Freeman, M. R. James, Anthony Hope, W. W. Jacobs, Arthur Machen, Arthur Morrison, Barry Pain, C. J. Cutcliffe Hyne, A. E. W. Mason, M. P. Shiel, E. W. Hornung, E. F. Benson, Guy Boothby, Ernest Bramah, Algernon Blackwood, etc. mostly born in the 1850s and 1860s, all coming of age as writers after 1880, plus a group of slightly younger people arriving after them in the 1900s, including Saki (H. H. Munro), G. K. Chesterton, John Buchan, Edgar Wallace, William Hope Hodgson, P. G. Wodehouse, Rafael Sabatini and Sax Rohmer. (Most of these wrote at least some fantasy, and several of them wrote a great deal.) At least two literary giants, Henry James and Joseph Conrad, were also active contributors to the magazines with their ghost stories and sea stories. But it is arguable that the Big Five listed separately above were the crucial influences; between them, they–and their literary offspring dominated the turn-of-the-century maga-

"IWAN AUF GRAVEN WOLF" (1889)
BY VIKTOR MICHAILOWITSCH WASNEZOW

zines, and were equally important for the pulps that came afterwards. However, only one of the Big Five, Rider Haggard, actually published in the pulps to any significant degree; the others, those who lived long enough into the 20th century, ended up in the slick magazines.

Where would the pulp-magazine adventure story have been without the examples of Stevenson, Haggard and Kipling? More specifically, where would the pulp lost-race fantasy have been without Haggard; and where would Edgar Rice Burroughs's Tarzan have been without the example not only of Haggard but of Kipling's Mowgli? Where would pulp science fiction have been without Wells? Most obviously, where would the whole genre of detective fiction have been without Conan Doyle's Sherlock Holmes? These were the writers who set the imaginative parameters for the next couple of generations. They also created the forms: the series short story was essentially invented by Doyle, in 1891, in *The Strand Magazine*, with his first Holmes series. (He had a few pointers from the long-dead Edgar Allan Poe, but the Chevalier Dupin trilogy of stories of the 1840s had been an abortive "near-series", appearing in three different magazines over a period of several years, rather than a series proper.) The Doyle-invented magazine short-story series was so explosively popular that literally scores of writers immediately emulated it – not only in detective fiction but in other genres too: a few examples are Cutcliffe Hyne with his Captain Kettle adventures, Hesketh Prichard with his Don Q capers, Baroness Orczy with her Scarlet Pimpernel historicals, Wodehouse with his Jeeves-and-Wooster comedies, etc. – or, to choose one of the few American examples of the period, Owen Wister with his Virginian Westerns in *Harper's Monthly* (his famous book *The Virginian* [1902] was a "fix-up" novel, built out of magazine short stories which had appeared over the preceding decade). Where would the later pulp-magazine story-series have been without all this background – without the examples of Holmes and Mowgli and Allan Quatermain, without Raffles and Stingaree and Kai Lung and the Old Man in the Corner and Father Brown and a hundred others?

So the most important precursors, the immediate parents, of the pulp magazines were not so much the story papers and dime novels as the late-Victorian/Edwardian popular magazines, mainly British – magazines not in themselves "pulp ", but the midwives of pulpdom. The pulps, as they emerged after 1900, were in the main cheapened versions of the earlier magazines such as *The Strand*, *The Idler*, *Pearson's*, *Harper's*, *McClure's*, *Munsey's* and so on; this is very evident in Britain, where the first pulp, *The Grand Magazine* (from January 1905), was a sister publication of the more prestigious *Strand Magazine* – both were published by Newnes (British magazine-expert Jack Adrian has described *The Grand* as "*The Strand Magazine*'s dustbin"). And of the Big Five authors who did so much

RIDER HAGGARD'S LONG-LIVED *SHE WHO MUST BE OBEYED* IS BEST KNOWN TO MODERN VIEWERS AS PORTRAYED BY URSULA ANDRESS IN THE 1965 PRODUCTION BASED ON THE NOVEL

to sustain those periodicals, the most important for fantasy – and arguably the most significant for pulp fiction as a whole – was Rider Haggard. As mentioned above, Haggard did in fact become a pulp writer, if unwittingly: from *Ayesha: The Return of She* (1905) onwards, much of his fiction was serialized in pulp magazines before book publication, that particular novel appearing in the second American pulp, Street & Smith's *The Popular Magazine* (January-August 1905; it also appeared in Britain's *Windsor Magazine* – not a pulp – at the same time, but the serialization was in bigger chunks and ended sooner, so *The Popular*'s readers had the complete text in their hands first: on such hair-splittings whole theses can be built). The February 1914 issue of another Street & Smith pulp, *The New Story*, has a cover which advertises three wellknown authors, among others: Rider Haggard, Edgar Rice Burroughs and Edgar Wallace. So Haggard not only influenced Burroughs, but they actually rubbed shoulders in the same pulp. The Haggard serialization in that case was of his novel *Allan and the Holy Flower*; other Haggard yarns which appeared in pulps prior to book publication included

Morning Star (*Cavalier*, 1909-1910), *The Ivory Child* (*Blue Book*, 1915) and *Finished* (*Adventure*, 1917). In Britain, his late serial "She Meets Allan" appeared in the pulp *Hutchinson's Story Magazine* (1919-20) a long time before its publication in book form as *She and Allan* (1921).

Haggard's great contribution, not just to the pulps but to the fantasy genre as a whole, was the lost-race/lost-world motif (which was to spawn many cousins, or similar sub-genres, in popular fiction – tales of forbidden enclaves, Ruritanias, planetary romance, prehistoric neverworlds, fantasy-lands accessed by "portals" etc). He did not quite invent the lost-land story – there had been prior hints of it in various utopian fictions and in the novels of Jules Verne and Bulwer Lytton – but he remade it as new, by combining many realistic touches based on his South African experiences with his powerful and at times grotesque imagination and his marvellous ability to handle violent action. Nobody wrote better battle scenes than Rider Haggard, and nobody created more memorable warriors. The supernatural themes which recurred in his stories – particularly the notion of reincarnation, and of doomed loves crossing the ages – appealed strongly to women (versions of them turn up in the bad but best-selling occult fantasies of his contemporary Marie Corelli, and in other women's fiction of the day) as well as to men, and so he succeeded in reaching a vast audience. His early novels, *King Solomon's Mines* and *She*, have never been out of print, and have been filmed many times. A new paperback edition of another of his lost-race novels, *The People of the Mist* (first serialized in Newnes's *Tit-Bits*, 1893-94), has just appeared in Britain in 1998, from a publishing company calling itself, appropriately enough, "Pulp Fictions".

For it is via the pulps that Haggard's main legacy can be traced. As a writer of historical novels and colonial romances (along with Stevenson and Kipling), he influenced the whole *Adventure*-magazine school of pulpsters – writers like Harold Lamb, Talbot Mundy, Arthur O. Friel and H. Bedford-Jones – and as a lost-race fantasist he influenced many of those who wrote for *Argosy, All-Story* and other titles – pre-eminent among them Edgar Rice Burroughs, whose "Tarzan" series began to appear in 1912, but also A. Merritt, James Francis Dwyer, Charles B. Stilson, William L. Chester and numerous others, extending to various contributors to the science-fiction magazines such as Philip José Farmer and Marion Zimmer Bradley. By way of both these streams, which might be identified with the magazines *Adventure* and *All-Story* although they cropped up in most pulps, he was a prime influence on Robert E. Howard, the creator of such fantasy adventurers as King Kull, Solomon Kane and Conan the Barbarian for *Weird Tales* magazine. When we come across a passage such as this in Howard, we are reading pure Haggard:

> "He emerged into a vast domed chamber... It was octagonal in shape... At the farther side of the great room there rose a dais with broad lapis-lazuli steps leading up to it, and on that dais there stood a massive chair with ornate arms and a high back... Behind the throne there was a narrow arched doorway..."
>
> ROBERT E. HOWARD, "JEWELS OF GWAHLUR", *WEIRD TALES*, MARCH 1935

Compare Burroughs:

> "Tarzan found himself upon the threshold of an enormous chamber, the walls of which converged toward the opposite end, where a throne stood upon a dais... The room was vacant except for two warriors who stood before the doors that flanked the throne dais..."
>
> EDGAR RICE BURROUGHS, "TARZAN AND THE ANT MEN", *ARGOSY ALL-STORY*, FEBRUARY–MARCH 1924

Compare Haggard:

> "At last we came to the head of the cave, where there was a rock dais... On either side of this dais were passages leading, Billali informed me, to other caves full of dead bodies... On the dais was a rude chair of black wood inlaid with ivory... Suddenly there was a cry of "Hiya! Hiya!" ("She! She!"), and thereupon the entire crowd of spectators instantly precipitated itself upon the ground, and lay still... A long string of guards began to defile from a passage to the left, and ranged themselves on either side of the dais. Then followed about a score of male mutes, then as many women mutes bearing lamps, and then a tall white figure, swathed from head to foot, in whom I recognized She herself. She mounted the dais and sat down upon the chair".
>
> H. RIDER HAGGARD, *SHE: A HISTORY OF ADVENTURE, THE GRAPHIC*, OCTOBER 1886–JANUARY 1887

(For those who may be curious about an uncommon word which occurs in all three of those passages, *dais,* pronounced "day-iss", means a "raised platform, esp. at end of hall for high table, throne, etc.," according to *The Concise Oxford Dictionary*) Haggard is the spiritual father of Sword & Sorcery – and not solely because he happened to write a novel, *Eric Brighteyes* (1891), which specifically prefigures that sub-genre.

Howard, along with many of his co-contributors to *Weird Tales* and the later magazine *Unknown*, established Sword & Sorcery, and thus became a prime mover – together with Edgar Rice Burroughs – in the eventual establishment of modern fantasy as a book-publishing category well after World War Two (and well after the deaths of both authors).

Prior to the late 1960s, there was little consciousness on the part of publishers, critics and the reading public of "fantasy" as a mass-market paperback genre. It is said that the great fantasy boom began in the summer of 1965 with the American release by Ace Books of their "pirate" paperback edition of Tolkien's *The Lord of the Rings* (see Humphrey Carpenter's biography of Tolkien for more details). Some months later, Ballantine Books issued an official edition of Tolkien's masterpiece, and by the end of 1966 a million copies of the latter edition had been sold (plus 100,000 of the Ace edition, which was then withdrawn from the market).

An interesting aspect of this well publicized disagreement between two leading paperback houses is that the whole tussle had been prefigured in 1962–63 by a similar dispute over the paperback rights to Edgar Rice Burroughs's novels. Discovering that certain Burroughs titles were technically out of copyright, Ace rushed out editions of *At the Earth's Core* and other books in late 1962; as in the later Tolkien case, their rivals Ballantine came up with "official" editions, beginning in 1963 and including the whole of the Tarzan series (see Richard Lupoff's *Edgar Rice Burroughs: Master of Adventure* for more details). In the several years following, many millions of copies of Burroughs's books were issued in paperback editions, and helped, along with Tolkien, to form the tastes of a new generation of readers. And, no doubt inspired by both the Burroughs and the Tolkien booms, Lancer Books began reissuing the works of Robert E. Howard (as edited by L. Sprague de Camp) in 1966, soon achieving hundreds of thousands of sales to a largely young audience. The rest is history: fantasy of the heroic sort had finally arrived as a high-profile, best-selling, non-juvenile publishing category.

Rider Haggard, one may claim, was the great initiator – and not only because he influenced Burroughs and Howard. There is also the strong likelihood that he influenced J. R. R. Tolkien. At first sight, no lineages could seem more different than these two streams which combined to create the modern fantasy field – the British tradition of scholarly fantasy stemming from William Morris, and the American tradition of fantastic adventure fiction sprung from the pulp magazines – but in fact, if one traces them back far enough, Haggard stands at the point where they overlap (or rather, at the point where the "pulp" stream diverges: the Morris/Tolkien stream goes back a great deal farther into the main course of Western literature).

Like most Edwardian boys, Tolkien read Haggard in his youth – and of course Tolkien's friend and fellow "Inkling", C. S. Lewis, doted on Haggard, as he testified in several essays. Robert Giddings and Elizabeth Holland devote much of their book *J. R. R. Tolkien: The Shores of Middle-Earth* (1981) to a detailed analysis of plot similarities between *The Lord of the Rings* and *King Solomon's Mines* (and many other points of detail, they also assert, which bear a similarity to Haggard's follow-up novel, *Allan Quatermain*). Whether or not one accepts these critics' thesis in full, it is true that for some readers – including the present writer, who first read Haggard when he was 10 but did not tackle *The Lord of the Rings* until he was in his 20s – there is a shock of recognition which comes upon encountering Tolkien, particularly his action scenes, his landscape descriptions, the atmosphere of his Mines of Moria, the characterization of his dwarves and his use of the "hidden king" figure of Aragorn: "why, this is all very like Haggard!"

Today, Haggard seems curiously underrated as a progenitor of modern fantasy, which is why he has been given considerable emphasis here. Moreover, his key theme of the lost land or lost race could be seen as a way into an understanding of the meaning of fantasy as a whole. If fantasy is the fiction of the Heart's Desire, it may be that one of the principal desires it embodies is the wish to retrieve the lost – an urge which can be seen every bit as strongly in Tolkien's fiction as in Haggard's. Perhaps the entire vogue for fantasy over the past century, and especially in the last few decades, is due precisely to the fact that we have "lost" so much, to the fact that the world as a whole has become dis-enchanted. Much of the charm of J.K. Rowling's masterful Harry Potter series could be said to come from its evocation of long-gone, gentle Enid Blyton childhoods, although Hogwarts School is an enchanting lost land in its own right. There is a phrase in the last line of Haggard's preface to *The People of the Mist* which is rather haunting – his reference to "this small and trodden world". It is a phrase that expresses the essential pathos of the lost-race tale, a pathos evident to Haggard himself as early as 1894, and which implies that fictions such as his own were a sort of last-ditch stand against a modern world which had just lately become demystified, thanks to the great voyages of discovery which had borne magnificent fruit in terms of the extension of human knowledge but which had also pumped this poor old globe dry of all wonder.

Perhaps there is a need in the human heart for mystery and magic, for a feeling that on the other side of the hill or on the far shore of the ocean, under the earth or up in the sky, there are lands which are substantially different from those we live in and there are beings who have powers (and perhaps virtues) superior to our own. Call such lands lost kingdoms if you will, or call them Faerie, regard them as possible or impossible, the fact is that they are lands of the Heart's Desire.

Throughout most of human history and prehistory that quality of "unknownness" existed for most people, most of the time; it was a simple fact of life in a world where few people travelled more than a few miles from home.

TRADITIONAL MOTIFS OF HEROIC FANTASY ARE PERPETUATED ON THE COVERS OF RECENT NOVELS: JORDAN'S *THE GREAT HUNT*

Today, although we have gained in so many ways from the advances of modern science, modern medicine, modern transportation and modern communications, we have lost that feeling of otherness, that sense of mystery which sustains the human imagination. Tarmac and steel spread everywhere, and the forests of mystery shrink; when we disembark from our airliners we find people much like ourselves leading lives much like our own.

In taming the world, and making it over in our own image, maybe we have created a wasteland of the imagination, a land which cries out for regeneration. Backward-looking though they may be, fantasy is a form which speaks to these ancient and fundamental needs and longings.

TYPES OF FANTASY

Fairy Tales, Animal Fantasies, Arthuriana, Arabian Nights Tales, Chinoiserie, Lost-Race Fantasies, Humorous Fantasies, Sword & Sorcery, Heroic or "High" Fantasy – these are just some of the sub-types of the genre, described in the following pages in approximate chronological order of their emergence

We can divide the field of fantasy fiction into as many categories as we want, across as long a period of time as we wish, from Medieval Dream Allegory or Renaissance Chivalric Romance to present-day sub-types as variously fashionable as Magic Realism or Urban Fantasy. However, not all potential divisions are equally useful or enlightening. This chapter takes nine categories, from Fairy Tale to Heroic Fantasy, and endeavours to describe their histories and characteristics in some detail. Categories overlap, and terminology changes over time, so none of these divisions should be regarded as watertight: they are presented here as possibly useful approaches to the subject of fantasy from a reader's and critic's point of view. They are meant to be descriptive of what has been, not prescriptive of what should be. Creative writers will always endeavour to break through the boundaries perceived by critics and historians: they will mix and match, blend sub-genres, come up with new types of fantasy – and so they should do: all strength to them.

BOY MEETS GIRL: SLEEPING BEAUTY…

One of the problems in any discussion of fantasy is to decide just where "realistic" fiction ends and fantasy begins. Is Magic Realism, as practised, for example, by Latin American novelists such as the Nobel Prize-winning Gabriel Garcia Marquez, to be accounted a form of realism or a form of fantasy? Clearly, it has elements of both, but our judgment is that it belongs more to the tradition of realism than to fantasy in any generic sense. The same is true of a great deal of other modern writing – Absurdist fictions, Post-Modern "fabulations," psychological allegories, latter-day Menippean satires, and so forth. The subject of this book would become very unwieldy were we to try to describe and account for all these. It is not surprising that the critic Rosemary Jackson has remarked, in her study *Fantasy: The Literature of Subversion*: "As a critical term, 'fantasy' has been applied rather indiscriminately to any literature which does not give priority to realistic representation: myths, legends, folk and fairy tales, utopian allegories, dream visions, surrealist texts, science fiction, horror stories…"

… AND "UNDINE" (LEFT), ARE AMONG THE MOST POTENT OF ALL FAIRY TALES

We have attempted to find our way through this welter of discrimination (and indiscrimination) by concentrating on the popular, on those kinds of fantasy – other than science fiction and supernatural horror, each of them a large subject meriting a book in its own right – which have been the most recognizable, and have meant the most, to most people. Popular fantasy, a body of stories that deals in the marvellous, the magical and the otherworldly – what could be summarized as "tales of impossible things" – is, as we argued in the Introduction, a fiction of the Heart's Desire. Its primary purpose is not to moralize or to instruct, to politically arouse or to aesthetically elevate (even if some of those things may be achieved along the way), but to transport the common reader into new realms of imaginative (im)possibility and to provide him or her with heartfelt delights.

FAIRY TALE

Fairy tales, marvellous stories set in the magical realm of "once upon a time," have their roots in folk tales. In particular, they stem from that kind of short oral narrative known to folklorists as the "wonder tale". It is important to draw a distinction between the original wonder tales themselves, which date from time immemorial and were passed down from generation to generation by word of mouth – constantly changing in the process, and hence irretrievable to us in any "pure" form – and fairy tales as we now have them in books. The latter are obviously a *written* form, the products of individual authors whose names we usually know; they are a part of literature. The fairy tale was perhaps the first type of fantasy to become a "commercial genre", written and published as prose for the entertainment of modern readers.

That process of commercialization, of folk tales becoming a marketplace literature, began during the Renaissance in Italy, although there are scattered examples from Classical and Medieval times, such as Apuleius's famous tale of "Cupid and Psyche", embedded in his book *The Golden Ass*. Early Italian compilations of fairy tales include Giovanni Straparola's *The Delectable Nights* (1550) and Giambattista Basile's *The Pentameron* (1634), but more important than these for the later development of the form were the writings of certain French authors in the late 17th century. It was in France, from about 1690, that the fairy tale gained its name as a self-conscious literary form. These stories were originally known as "*contes des fées*" – translated into English as "fairy tales" – even though many did not literally concern fairies. The tales became a high fashion, read aloud in Parisian salons, and among their leading practitioners were Marie-Catherine d'Aulnoy, author of the collection which gave the genre its name, *Les Contes des Fees* (1696–1698) containing "The Blue Bird", "The Yellow Dwarf" and others – and Charles Perrault, author of *Histoires ou contes du temps passé* (1697; often known in English as *Mother Goose Tales*) – containing "Sleeping Beauty", "Little Red Riding Hood", "Cinderella" and others. Although based on folklore, these were polished works meant for the amusement of the upper classes.

Before long, the tales of Perrault and Madame d'Aulnoy were reissued in inexpensive chapbooks and translated into other languages, and so began the process of transforming them into nursery stories – the special literature of children. By the 19th century they had permeated western culture. It was in Germany, a hundred years after Perrault, that the next great burst of creativity occurred. It took two main forms. The first was the renewed search for authentic folk tales, identified with the brothers Wilhelm and Jakob Grimm (their famous book, *Household Tales* – universally known as *Grimms' Fairy Tales* – first appeared in 1812, although it continued to be enlarged in many later editions). The second was the cultivation of "art fairy tales", self-consciously made-up and literary examples of the form, often written at novella length.

The best-known example of this second type was the Baron De La Motte Fouque's *Undine* (1811), about a water-nymph, although there were many others.

The German tales inspired writers of other nationalities, of whom the most celebrated was a Dane named Hans Christian Andersen. His newly invented stories, published between the 1830s and the 1870s, included such small masterpieces as "The Little Mermaid", "The Emperor's New Clothes" and "The Snow Queen". At the same time, many British writers began to use the fairy-tale form, notable among them George MacDonald with stories such as "The Golden Key" (1867) and, later, Oscar Wilde with beautifully written pieces like "The Fisherman and His Soul" (1891). In the USA, L. Frank Baum strove to produce a specifically American form of fairy tale which did not depend so much on the traditional European lore (one of his books is actually called *American Fairy Tales*), and he succeeded when he created the well-loved children's fantasy *The Wonderful Wizard of Oz* (1900).

Since the turn of the century, numerous writers have produced new fairy tales (or retold the old ones, often with startling new twists, as did the late Angela Carter in her rather frightening book *The Bloody Chamber*, 1979). Fantasists who have made very specific use of fairy-tale motifs in novels or short stories include Robin McKinley (*Beauty*, 1978); Tanith Lee (*Red as Blood; or, Tales from the Sisters Grimmer*, 1983); Jane Yolen (*Tales of Wonder*, 1983); David Henry Wilson (*The Coachman Rat*, 1985); and Ellen Kushner (*Thomas the Rhymer*, 1990). Two splendid modern anthologies are *Spells of Enchantment: The Wondrous Fairy Tales of Western Culture* edited by Jack Zipes (1991) and *The Mammoth Book of Fairy Tales* edited by Mike Ashley (1997).

ANIMAL FANTASY

Fantasies about animals, and especially talking animals, also have ancient roots. They can be traced back to the beast fables of Aesop, and probably have their origins in deepest prehistory. Aesop himself is a semi-mythical figure, a Greek slave who supposedly lived around 600 BC. The collection of fables published in his name is one of the enduring works of world literature, and it has counterparts in fable collections from other languages, such as those of India. A much more modern equivalent can be found in the 19th-century

THE BEST FAIRY TALES EVOKE FEAR AND MAGIC – "LITTLE RED RIDING HOOD," WHERE A WOLF LURKS IN THE BACKGROUND

COMIC ANIMAL FANTASY: KENNETH GRAHAME'S *THE WIND IN THE WILLOWS* (HERE ILLUSTRATED BY ARTHUR RACKHAM)

plantation tales of the American writer Joel Chandler Harris, based on the black folklore of former US slaves (Harris himself was white). These fables of "Brer Rabbit" and "Brer Fox", like those attributed to Aesop, use animal characters to make sly statements about human nature and human behaviour.

Talking animals have appeared in an enormous range of literature ever since the Greeks. Medieval writers, with their fondness for allegory, were particularly apt to use beasts as "spokespeople". Well-known examples include the cycle of stories about Reynard the Fox (originating in France) and Geoffrey Chaucer's *The Parliament of Fowls* and "The Nun's Priest's Tale" (about Chanticleer the cock). Animals also feature prominently in the satirical tradition, from Lucian of Samosata's "The Cock" and "The Ass" (2nd century AD) to Jonathan Swift's wise horses, the Houyhnhnms, in *Gulliver's Travels* (1726). George Orwell's *Animal Farm* (1945) and Scott Bradfield's *Animal Planet* (1995) are latter-day equivalents. Children's literature of the past two centuries is densely populated with loquacious animals, in works ranging in sophistication from Lewis Carroll's complex *Alice in Wonderland* (1865) and *Through the Looking Glass* (1871) to Beatrix Potter's simple nursery tales, which commenced with *The Tale of Peter Rabbit* (1901).

Broadly speaking, modern animal stories have been of two types – the realistic and the fantastic. In the latter, beasts may speak with human voices, dress like humans, and participate in supernatural adventures. Tales of metamorphosis, from human to animal and back again, also belong here. In the former, a serious attempt is made to depict animals "as they are". Even here though, in a realistic book such as Anna Sewell's *Black Beauty* (1877), an element of fantasy inevitably creeps in, to the extent that the autobiographical horse is endowed with a human-like consciousness and is able to hold conversations with its fellow beasts of burden. As an aside, we may also note that a novel like *Black Beauty* owes much to the tradition of "inanimate-object fantasy" – first-person tales supposedly told by coins, thimbles, or three-guinea watches which pass from hand to human hand.

Among the many fantasies which employ animal characters, two of the most distinguished of modern times have been Rudyard Kipling's *The Jungle Book* (1894, followed by *The Second Jungle Book*, 1895) and Kenneth Grahame's *The Wind in the Willows* (1908). Both have frequently been filmed and otherwise adapted. The former has influenced subsequent adventure fantasy about feral children, for example *Jungle Tales of Tarzan by Edgar Rice Burroughs* (1919), while the latter has been sequelized by later fantasy writers like William Horwood in books such as *The Willows in Winter* (1993 – it features Toad of Toad Hall as an aviator rather than a motorist).

A comparatively recent development, following the rise in popularity of the secondary-world heroic fantasy, has been the large-scale fantasy which utilizes animals instead of humans in the unfolding of a quest narrative or tale of an epic struggle, often supernaturally tinged. The most influential novel of this type is Richard Adams's *Watership Down* (1972). Like Tolkien's *The Lord of the Rings*, Adams's book was a "sleeper", an unknown author's eccentric work which went on to confound its publishers' expectations. It sold in huge quantities, appealing to the ecologically aware generation of the early 1970s – much the same group of people who had turned Tolkien into a belated bestseller just a few years earlier. It is a long novel, full of loving detail and narrated in epic style. The central characters are a courageous young rabbit named Hazel, and his second-sighted brother, Fiver. They live in a crowded warren which is run in dictatorial fashion by the Chief Rabbit and his Owsla, a "group of strong or clever rabbits – second-year or older – surrounding the Chief Rabbit".The book is full of such invented terms. Nervous little Fiver has a scary premonition that doom is about to be visited upon the warren, and at first only his brother Hazel is inclined to believe him. They attempt to persuade the Chief Rabbit of the need for action, but he brushes them off. A notice board has been erected at the foot of the hill which houses the warren, and the reader is told its message – "This ideally situated estate... is to be developed with high class modern residences" – confirming Fiver's far-sightedness.

Hazel decides to lead Fiver and a group of discontented young rabbits away from the warren. These companions have names such as Bigwig, Dandelion and Pipkin. With difficulty, they evade the patrolling Owsla and make their escape by night. They have embarked on a vast journey (in reality, a distance of just a few miles across the Berkshire countryside) which is fraught with terrifying dangers. Along the way, they hearten themselves with tales of El-ahrairah, the mythical rabbit hero. They encounter human beings, predatory animals, fast-flowing streams and many other perils, including other colonies of rabbits. But eventually, thanks to Hazel's wise leadership, they reach the pastoral haven of Watership Down, where – in time, after they have won a great battle against the minions of General Woundwort (a sort of rabbit Hitler) – they found a new warren.

It is easy to mock *Watership Down* for being an over-inflated children's novel. It was Adams's book which provoked Michael Moorcock's quip: "if the bulk of American SF could be said to be written by robots, about robots, for robots, then the bulk of English fantasy seems to be written by rabbits, about rabbits and for rabbits" (repeated in his *Wizardry and Wild Romance*, 1987). Nevertheless it is a novel which pleased millions of readers, and it is not difficult to see why – it is a very accomplished quest narrative (and war story), combined with a moving tract on behalf of nature conservation. The many books which have followed in its wake include *The Book of the Dun Cow* by Walter Wangerin (1978), about farm animals; *Duncton Wood* by William Horwood (1980), about moles; *The Song of Pentecost* by W. J. Corbett (1982), about harvest mice; *Tailchaser's Song* by Tad Williams (1985), about cats; *Redwall* by Brian Jacques (1986), about mice; *Nightworld* by Brian Carter (1987) and *The Cold Moons* by Aeron Clement (1987), both about badgers; *Marshworld* by A. R. Lloyd (1988), about weasels; *The Heavenly Horse from the Outermost West* by Mary Stanton (1988), about horses; *An Ancient Solitary Reign* by Martin Hocke (1989), about owls; *Hunter's Moon* by Garry Kilworth (1989), about foxes; *The Wild Road* by Gabriel King (1997), about cats – and so on, through the menagerie. Most of these have been best-sellers and have trailed sequels, proving that the animal story as a whole remains very much a "live" sub-genre of fantasy.

ARTHURIAN FANTASY

The origins of the "real" King Arthur and his Knights of the Round Table are shrouded in a historical mist. There are brief mentions of an important Dark-Age British war-leader in old chronicles covering the 5th century and later, but they are tantalizingly slight and much argued over. Whatever historical truth they point to may bear little resemblance to the King Arthur we know from poetry, novels and films. However, there is no dispute as to the literary origin of the Arthur story – it first appeared in a book that began to be distributed in manuscript form in the year 1136, *Historia Regum Britanniae* (*The History of the Kings of Britain*) by Geoffrey of Monmouth. This was a prose narrative, written in Latin as was normal in those days, giving a highly coloured account of the supposed history of Britain's monarchs – from the legendary founder King Brutus through King Lear to King Arthur and beyond. The

ARTHURIAN FANTASY IS FULL OF WONDERFUL MOMENTS, NOT LEAST THIS ONE, AS A FEMALE ARM RISES FROM THE WATERS OF THE LAKE TO GRASP THE SWORD EXCALIBUR

story of Arthur and his queen Guinevere, entwined with those of the traitor Mordred and the magician Merlin, takes up a large part of the text. Full of marvels, it reads like a work of fiction rather than a genuine historical chronicle, and it is possible that Geoffrey invented much of it out of thin air. However, Geoffrey claimed to have taken his facts from "an old Welsh book", which may have existed even if later scholars cannot find the slightest mention of it elsewhere. Undoubtedly there were oral Welsh tales in circulation – the originals of those collected centuries later in manuscript form and known to us as *The Mabinogion* – and it is quite likely that Geoffrey grew up with a knowledge of these tales and was influenced by them when he came to create his King Arthur narrative.

Whatever its origins and nature – either pure fiction or a transcription of old legends containing some grains of historical fact – Geoffrey's book delighted 12th-century readers. It was a great success with the French-speaking upper classes of England, and soon spread from them back to France, where it was to bear exotic fruit as the inspiration of many "romances", both in prose and in verse. The romance, an elaborate tale of chivalry and courtly love – and frequently of magic – was the principal long form in medieval secular literature, and usually took as its subject matter either garbled versions of Greek and Roman history (especially the story of Alexander the Great) or equally garbled versions of more recent European history (especially the feats of the Emperor Charlemagne's knights and in particular the hero known as Roland). The Arthur story, or "the Matter of Britain" as it came to be known, provided the medieval romancers with a wonderful new subject and a whole new cast of characters.

The principal romances included Robert Wace's *Le Roman de Brut* (1155), which elaborated many details and first gave us the motif of the Round Table, and Chretien de Troyes' *Lancelot* and *Perceval* (1170–1182), which introduced the character of Sir Lancelot and the motif of the quest for the Holy Grail. Robert de Boron's *Joseph d'Aramathie*, *Merlin* and *Perceval* (1190–1202) elaborated the stories of the Holy Grail and of Merlin as Arthur's mentor, introducing the motif of the sword in the stone. The so-called Vulgate Cycle, by authors unknown, was immensely lengthy and detailed, and the first (since Geoffrey) to be written in prose – *Estoire del Graal, Estoire de Merlin, Lancelot, Queste del Saint Graal* and *Mort Artu* (1210–1225). In the 13th century, the Arthurian torch was passed to the German writers Gottfried von Strassburg and Wolfram von Eschenbach, who embroidered the tales in substantial works such as *Tristan* and *Parzival* (dates uncertain). Two centuries later, most of these were drawn upon by Thomas Malory when he wrote his prose compilation *Le Morte D'Arthur* (circa 1470) – which, despite its French title, remains the most famous Arthurian book in English.

Although it went in and out of fashion, the Matter of Britain

THE KNIGHTS OF THE ROUND TABLE ARE VOUCHSAFED A VISION OF THE HOLY GRAIL IN THIS MEDIEVAL "ILLUMINATED" MANUSCRIPT

was never forgotten. There are many references to it in English literature, culminating in the great revival of the 19th century when it was most famously enshrined by Alfred, Lord Tennyson, in his poem cycle *Idylls of the King* (1859). He was not alone – Bulwer Lytton produced an epic *King Arthur* (1848), and poets like Morris and Swinburne did similar work. There have been recent attempts at verse Arthuriana, too, one example being *Artorius: An Heroic Poem* by

John Heath-Stubbs (1973). But it is the use of Arthur and his knights in prose fiction which is of most interest to us here, and in fact there has been an unending stream of Arthurian novels over the past hundred years and more. Many of these have been "realistic" attempts to historicize Arthur in the light of modern archaeological evidence, but most have been fantasies, drawing freely on Malory. An early high-point was a darkly humorous novel by an American writer, Mark Twain's *A Connecticut Yankee in King Arthur's Court* (1889).

Among modern Arthuriana, one of the greatest works is T. H. White's *The Once and Future King* (1958), consisting of three linked novels, *The Sword in the Stone*, *The Queen of Air and Darkness* and *The Ill-Made Knight*, originally published in 1938–40, and a fourth, *The Candle in the Wind*, published in this volume for the first time. It retells the story of Arthur, beginning with his education at the hands of Merlyn (so-spelled). There have been countless Arthurian novels, but few which have inspired such devotion as this humorous and imaginative work. It became a bestseller when published in its final form, and inspired a Broadway musical, *Camelot*, as well as two films. In his book *Imaginary Worlds* (1972), Lin Carter states: "the single finest fantasy novel written in our time, or for that matter, ever written, is, must be, by any conceivable standard, T. H. White's *The Once and Future King*".

It is by no means a straight rendition of the time-hallowed tale. Although he sets the narrative in the high Middle Ages, White uses deliberate anachronisms – usually to charming effect, although sometimes the "modern" references have dated: "Lancelot ended by being the greatest knight King Arthur had. He was a sort of Bradman, top of the battling averages". He also introduces many supernatural elements, over and above those which are traditional. Young Arthur, or "the Wart" as he is known, is transformed by Merlyn into various beasts of the field, and is able to fly as a bird or swim as a fish. But the book's main qualities are its realism – White shows remarkable knowledge of sports such as hawking as well as medieval techniques of hunting, agriculture and warfare – and its strongly expressed feeling for nature. All this is combined with a powerful visual imagination. The book is also notable for its comic characterizations. Particularly rich in humour is the portrayal of the brilliant but forgetful Merlyn, who is so intent on foretelling the future that he has almost no knowledge of the past. Matters darken in the later episodes, which deal with Arthur's adulthood and his attempts to rule wisely, and also recount the tragic love of the Queen for Sir Lancelot. But the magic of the author's light touch remains potent throughout.

More recent fantasies that have employed some of the same material include *To the Chapel Perilous* by Naomi Mitchison (1955), *The Crystal Cave* by Mary Stewart (1970), the "Three Damosels" trilogy by Vera Chapman (1975–76), *Arthur Rex* by Thomas Berger (1978), *The Dragon Lord* by David Drake (1979), *Firelord* by Parke Godwin (1980), the "Guinevere" trilogy by Sharan Newman (1981–85), *The Mists of Avalon* by Marion Zimmer Bradley (1982), the "Pendragon Cycle" by Stephen Lawhead (1987–97), *The Coming of the King* by Nikolai Tolstoy (1988), *Any Old Iron* by Anthony Burgess (1989), the "Daughter of Tintagel" sequence by Fay Sampson (1989–92), *Kingdom of the Grail* by A. A. Attanasio (1992), *Merlin and the Last Trump* by Collin Webber (1993), the "Mordred Cycle" by Haydn Middleton (1995–97) and *Albion: The Last Companion* by Patrick McCormack (1997). These books, and many more like them, range widely in tone from light satire to darkest tragedy, and give proof – along with many recent films – that the Arthurian subject matter is still sufficiently relevant and flexible to fascinate a range of modern audiences.

ARABIAN NIGHTS FANTASY

The book called *Alf Layla wa-Layla* (Arabic for *A Thousand Nights and a Night*), popularly known in English as *The Arabian Nights*, is one of the world's greatest compendiums of stories. It consists of an immense cycle of tales supposedly told on a nightly basis by Scheherazade to her cruel husband, the King, in order to spellbind him into sparing her threatened life. The contents are varied in origin, some tales coming from Persia and probably even from India, and there is much dispute as to exactly when they took their "final" form. Between about 900 AD and the year 1400 seems to be the rough consensus, although a good deal may have been added later. Arabic culture of the Middle Ages was highly civilized and highly literate, so it is by no means certain that all the stories originated as oral folk tales. Some of them may have been the self-conscious products of professional writers. Of the many which probably were folk tales, not all are of the "wonder tale" (or fairy tale) type: some are bawdy stories, low-life anecdotes or moral homilies. But it is for its wonder tales, in other words for its fantasies, that *The Arabian Nights* has always been most prized in Europe. Most selections (all single-volume editions are necessarily selections because the original is very large) concentrate on the fantasies – the well-loved stories of "Aladdin and His Magic Lamp", "The Ebony Horse", "The Seven Voyages of Sinbad", "The City of Brass", "Ali Baba and the Forty Thieves", "Julnar the Sea-Born" and numerous others.

Prior to the book's first appearance in France as *Les Mille et une nuits* (1704–17), in 12 volumes translated and edited by Antoine Galland, there had been no printed editions. Galland, a Frenchman with a good knowledge of Arabic, claimed to be working from an original manuscript he had brought back from the Middle East. Such a manuscript does exist in a Paris library, but it is very far from complete, and later scholars have ascertained that Galland obtained

much of his material from an oral tale-teller. They have also raised the possibility that he made up some of the stories himself. Whether or not there is any truth in that suspicion, it is certain that he embellished and polished and generally made the stories suitable for 18th-century European tastes. In the centuries since Galland's death, other translators (French, German, English) have gone back to the East in search of "the original", but the only reasonably full manuscripts they have succeeded in finding are ones which post-date Galland. The first printed Arabic text was not published until 1814–18, a hundred years after Galland's time. It is astonishing to learn that some of the best-known stories, including both "Aladdin" and "Ali Baba", simply do not exist in any written form prior to Galland – leaving open the question of just how much the Frenchman invented or imported from other sources.

Whatever the case, it is *The Arabian Nights* as we have them, in French and other European languages, which have exerted the greatest influence on western fantasy. Galland's work began the whole vogue for "Orientalism" in popular literature. There were many French examples, including Voltaire's *Zadig* (1747), but in English two notable fantasy novellas also produced by that vogue were *Rasselas* by Samuel Johnson (1759) and *Vathek* by William Beckford (1786) – each in its exotic way a masterwork which has endured. Nineteenth-century fantasies which show the mark of the *Nights* include *The Shaving of Shagpat* by George Meredith (1855) and *Khaled: A Tale of Arabia* by F. Marion Crawford (1891). The influence of the great story collection upon literature in general has remained strong right down to various present-day works by novelists like John Barth and Salman Rushdie. It has also inspired numerous films, of which the most famous is probably *The Thief of Bagdad* (1940) and the best is perhaps the Italian version of *The Arabian Nights* directed by Pier-Paolo Pasolini (1974). In generic fantasy, one can point to the existence of a 1930s pulp magazine called *Magic Carpet* (formerly *Oriental Stories*), which published tales by E. Hoffmann Price and others with titles like "Ismeddin and the Holy Carpet" (January 1933).

Recent fantasy novels, or series of novels, which rework the matter of the *Nights* include Ian Dennis's *Bagdad* (1985) and *The Prince of Stars* (1987); Esther Friesner's humorous "Twelve Kingdoms" sequence beginning with *Mustapha and His Wise Dog* (1985); Seamus Cullen's *A Noose of Light* and *The Sultan's Turret* (both 1986); Craig Shaw Gardner's farcical "Arabian Nights" series beginning with *The Other Sinbad* (1991); and the novella *Child of an Ancient City* by Tad Williams and Nina Kiriki Hoffman (1992).

ALADDIN, BRAVING THE UNDERGROUND TREASURE-CAVE, MEETS THE GENIE OF THE LAMP, IN THIS 19TH-CENTURY ILLUSTRATION

THE MOST FAMOUS GENIE IN FILM, REX INGRAM, DANGLES ALADDIN IN *A THOUSAND AND ONE NIGHTS* (1945)

Possibly the most interesting work has been Tanith Lee's "Flat Earth" sequence, which commenced with *Night's Master* (1978) – this has much of the feel of the *Nights*, even though it evokes a fantastic world far removed from medieval Araby. The talented Lee is an author who also figures prominently in Susan Swhartz's pair of latter-day *Arabian Nights* anthologies, *Arabesques* (1988) and *Arabesques 2* (1989).

CHINOISERIE

One of the most famous stories from *The Arabian Nights* (or rather, from the *Nights'* "apocrypha", since no true Arabic original has been traced) is "Aladdin and His Magic Lamp", which is actually set in China – despite the recent Disney animated film, *Aladdin* (1992), which transfers the action back to an imaginary Araby. Long before Disney, "Aladdin" formed the basis of numerous pantomimes and other adaptations, most of which preserved the Chinese setting.

However, it is a fantasy China that these evoke – a land of pagodas and pigtails and dragons, a fabled land more familiar from works of fiction, popular stage dramas such as *Chu Chin Chow*, and comic strips like *Terry and the Pirates*, than any actual Far-Eastern country which can be found in mere grey reality.

Of course, the real China has produced its own works of fantasy, some of which – if to a very limited extent – have influenced the "myth" of China that westerners hold in their minds. The best-known example is the novel *Journey to the West* by Wu Ch'eng-en (1592), translated by Arthur Waley as *Monkey* (1942), and also known as a television series under the latter title (1979–81). The eponymous Monkey is a trickster hero with amazing powers whose adventures pit him against various magicians and monsters. Much less well known, but interesting and lively, is a 20th-century example of the same genre, *Blades from the Willows* by Li Shanji (1946; the author used the pseudonym Huanzhulouzhu, "Master of the Pearl-Rimmed Tower"). Translated into English in 1991, this is a sample of Chinese pulp fiction, a type of hugely extended newspaper serial which formed the staple reading matter for millions of readers in the mid-century. It bears a resemblance to western Sword & Sorcery fantasy, and clearly it also provides a literary origin for many of the martial-arts movies which have spilled out of Hong Kong and other parts of the East in more recent decades.

A few Chinese-American writers of fantasy have attempted to use authentic Chinese materials, notably Laurence Yep in his *Dragon of the Lost Sea* (1982) and its sequels and in his volumes of traditional tales such as *Tongues of Jade* (1991), and M. Lucie Chin in her single novel *The Fairy of Ku-She* (1988). But it was their own version of a mythical China, stemming from the 18th-century vogue for Orientalism in the arts, which most western writers used to create fantasies in what may be termed the tradition of Willow-Pattern Chinoiserie. Most successful of these was the English author Ernest Bramah, who, in books such as *The Wallet of Kai Lung* (1900) and *Kai Lung's Golden Hours* (1922), created an endearing series character who narrates tall tales in the amusingly ornate language of a well-mannered mandarin. Some critics regard the Kai Lung stories as minor masterpieces of humorous fantasy.

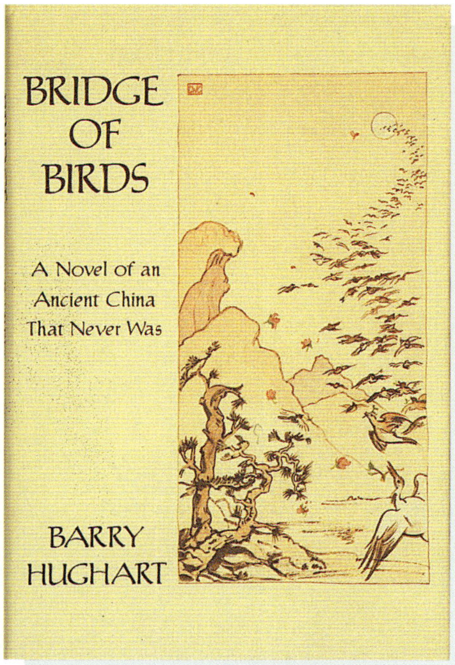

HUGHART'S NOVEL IS AN EVOCATION OF LEGENDARY FANTASTIC CHINA

An American writer who comes close to matching Bramah in his facility with this kind of material is Barry Hughart, whose three novels featuring Master Li Kao and

OWEN'S COLLECTION OF STORIES DELVES INTO THE SAME MAGICAL WORLD

Number Ten Ox – *Bridge of Birds* (1984), *The Story of the Stone* (1988) and *Eight Skilled Gentlemen* (1991) – are fantasy-comedy-mysteries of a high level of invention. Other fantasy authors who have revelled in Chinoiserie, or at least touched on Chinese themes, include Frank Owen (many stories in *Weird Tales*, some of them collected in *The Porcelain Magician*, 1948); E. Hoffmann Price (*The Devil Wives of Li Fong*, 1979, and *The Jade Enchantress*, 1982); R. A. MacAvoy (in her *Tea with the Black Dragon*, 1983); Jessica Amanda Salmonson (*Ou Lu Khen and the Beautiful Madwoman*, 1985); Avram Davidson and Grania Davis (*Marco Polo and the Sleeping Beauty*, 1988); Stephen Marley (the trilogy beginning with *Spirit Mirror*, 1988); and Molly Brown (in her long story "The Vengeance of Grandmother Wu", *Interzone*, July 1992). Like Arabian Nights fantasias, it seems Chinoiserie has become a perennial part of the fantasy writer's repertoire.

LOST RACE FANTASY

Fantastic stories about lost races or strange peoples – featuring lost cities, lost lands, undersea or underground worlds, forgotten civilizations, hidden valleys or forbidden enclaves, and all manner of combinations of these motifs – first gained huge popularity when H. Rider Haggard published his novels *King Solomon's Mines* (1885), *She* (1886) and *Allan Quatermain* (1887). There had been earlier examples – the *Arabian Nights* story called "The City of Many-Columned Iram" is one. From the 1880s to the 1930s, an enormous number of novels of this type were serialized in young people's story-papers or adult magazines, and many were reprinted in book form. Haggard's early tales were set in unexplored parts of Africa, but his later books (and those of his countless imitators) were set in any part of the world where exotic mysteries might yet be hidden. South America and Central Asia were two favourite locales, as were the North and South Polar regions. Alas, few forms of fiction dated more quickly, since the last "unknown" parts of the globe were being mapped (and, usually, annexed by European empires) at a very rapid pace. What was still mysterious in 1885 might well be familiar territory by 1895, and new transport technologies such as the internal combustion engine, the airship and the aeroplane were soon to banish all geographical mysteries.

Although a number of lost-race stories, including some of the best-known like Conan Doyle's *The Lost World* (1912), may be claimed as science fiction, the bulk of the sub-genre belongs more properly to fantasy. Many examples, notably Haggard's *She*, feature supernatural ideas and events, such as the Flame of Life in which the white African queen Ayesha bathes herself, and the whole notion of serial reincarnation and doomed love-affairs persisting down the ages. Most lost-race tales, even if they contain nothing so overtly supernatural, depict backward and hierarchical societies which have small awareness of science or the possibilities of technological progress and which therefore have all the "feel" of the fantastic for modern readers. The resemblance of these stories to later fantasies of the Sword & Sorcery type is obvious.

Following Haggard, lost-race novels included direct pastiches of the master such as *He* (1887), *It* (1887) and *King Solomon's Treasures* (1887), all by the American writer John De Morgan, as well as slightly more original variations on the theme: *The Cavern of Fire* by Francis W. Doughty (1888), *Beneath Your Very Boots* by C. J. Cutcliffe Hyne (1889), *The Aztec Treasure House: A Romance of Contemporaneous Antiquity* by Thomas A. Janvier (1890), *The Goddess of Atvatabar* by William R. Bradshaw (1892), *The Lost Valley of the Toltecs* by Charles S. Seeley (1893), *The Wonderful City* by J. S. Fletcher (1894), *The Land of the Changing Sun* by Will N. Harben (1894), *Devil-Tree of El Dorado: A Romance of British Guiana* by Frank Aubrey (1896), *The Great White Queen: A Tale of Treasure and Treason* by William Le Queux (1896), *The City of Gold* by Edward Markwick (1896), *The Eye of Istar: A Romance of the Land of No Return* by William Le Queux (1897), *A Queen of Atlantis: A Romance of the Caribbean* by Frank Aubrey (1898), *The White Princess of the Hidden City* by D. Lawson Johnstone (1898), *Thyra: A Romance of the Polar Pit* by Robert Ames Bennet (1901), *The Great White Way* by Albert Bigelow Paine (1901), *The Sunless City* by Joyce E. Preston Muddock (1905), *By the Gods Beloved* by Baroness Orczy (1905; republished as *The Gates of Kamt*) and *The Smoky God, or A Voyage to the Inner World* by Willis George Emerson (1908). The very titles of these books, which now read like a nostalgic litany, indicate the spread of motifs and geographical settings. White queens abound, as do inner worlds, secret valleys, hidden cities and the ever-enticing promise of long-lost treasures.

THIS MODERN ILLUSTRATION CAPTURES SOMETHING OF THE MYSTERY OF AYESHA (SHE)

The next major name to emerge in the sub-genre was that of Edgar Rice Burroughs, who was to prove Haggard's most popular and influential successor. His *The Return of Tarzan* (1915), the second volume in his 24-book Tarzan series, features the lost African city of Opar, founded by survivors from ancient Atlantis and ruled by (who else?) a white high-priestess known as La. Burroughs was to write dozens more lost-race tales, both within his best-known series and outside it. For example, the jungle hero stumbles upon the lost world of Pal-ul-Don, where men have tails and dinosaurs still roam (*Tarzan the Terrible*, 1921); he encounters a race of matriarchal "giants" and an elf-like race of "ant-men", who proceed to shrink him down to 18 inches in height for the duration of the adventure in question (*Tarzan and the Ant Men*, 1924); he visits, by airship through a polar opening, the land of Pellucidar which lies deep beneath the Earth's crust (*Tarzan at the Earth's Core*, 1930); he finds other lost lands and lost races galore, and in a handful of unashamedly supernatural episodes he has brushes with sundry witch-doctors, magicians and magical jewels (see, for example, *Tarzan the Magnificent*, 1939); and, as a result of one of those encounters, he enjoys the boon of eternal youth.

Foreign-language writers, as well as British and American ones, worked in the lost-race sub-genre: Gaston Leroux's *The Bride of the Sun* (1913), Pierre Benoit's frequently filmed *L'Atlantide* (1919) and J.-H. Rosny's *The Astonishing Journey of Hareton Ironcastle* (1919) are some French examples. But it was mainly in the American pulp magazines that the tradition thrived in the years during and after the First World War. Aside from the works of Burroughs, examples include *Under the Andes* by Rex Stout (*All-Story* magazine, 1914), *The Seal of John Solomon* by H. Bedford-Jones (*Argosy*, 1915), *Polaris of the Snows* by Charles B. Stilson (*All-Story*, 1915), *The Bowl of Baal* by Robert Ames Bennet (*All-Around*, 1916–17), *The Citadel of Fear* by Francis Stevens (*Argosy*, 1918) and *The Moon Pool* by A. Merritt (*All-Story*, 1918–19). The last-named, Abraham Merritt, became one of the

HUGH CONWAY (RONALD COLMAN) MEETS THE AGED HIGH LAMA (SAM JAFFE) IN CAPRA'S FINE MOVIE OF *LOST HORIZON* (1937)

most popular writers of this kind of fiction, with a sequence of highly coloured fantastic romances that ranged from *The Metal Monster* (*Argosy All-Story*, 1920), through *The Face in the Abyss* (*Argosy All-Story*, 1923) and its sequel *The Snake Mother* (*Argosy*, 1930) to *The Dwellers in the Mirage* (*Argosy*, 1932). Merritt's tales were lush and extravagant, representative of the lost-race adventure entering its late, "decadent" phase. No longer could such works make much of a bid for real-world credibility; they had become out-and-out fantasies which might as well have been placed in a series of parallel neverworlds.

Despite the increasing implausibility of lost-world stories in the days of international air travel, stories of the familiar type continued to appear throughout the interwar period and even into the war-torn 1940s. Some of the more notable were *Marching Sands* by Harold Lamb (1920), *The Temple of the Ten* by H. Bedford-Jones and W. C. Robertson (1921), *The Garden of Eden* by Max Brand (i.e. Frederick Faust, 1922), *The Pathless Trail* by Arthur O. Friel (1922), *City of Wonder* by E. Charles Vivian (1922), *Om: The Secret of Ahbor Valley* by Talbot Mundy (1924), *The Glory of Egypt* by Louis Moresby (i.e. Lily Adams Beck, 1926), *The City in the Sea* by H. De Vere Stacpoole (1926), *The Moon Gods* by Edgar Jepson (1930), *Beyond the Rim* by S. Fowler Wright (1932), *Golden Blood* by Jack Williamson (1933), *Lost City of Light* by F. A. M. Webster (1934), *The Secret People* by John Beynon (also known as John Wyndham, 1935), *Hidden World* by Stanton A. Coblentz (1935), *Queen of the Andes* by Barbara Gilson (i.e. Charles Gilson, 1935), *Dian of the Lost Land* by Edison Marshall (1935), *Hawk of the Wilderness* by William L. Chester (1936), *The Smoking Land* by Max Brand (1937), *The City of Cobras* by James Francis Dwyer (1938), *Jongor of Lost Land* by Robert Moore Williams (1940), *The Man Who Missed the War* by Dennis Wheatley (1945) and *The City of Frozen Fire* by Vaughan Wilkins (1950).

Most famous of them all was *Lost Horizon* by James Hilton (1933), beautifully filmed by Frank Capra in 1937. In this, an

English adventurer visits the peaceful valley of Shangri-La, somewhere to the north of the Himalayas, where he meets a mysterious High Lama who is hundreds of years old. The name "Shangri-La" has even entered the English language, to denote a tranquil haven far from the anxiety and violence of 20th-century life. The dream of such places may have endured, but by the 1950s fictional lost worlds seemed to have been mined out, even if they still made occasional appearances, mainly in juvenile novels. A well-known late example is *The Island at the Top of the World* by Ian Cameron (1961). However, the 1960s and 1970s saw a small revival in lost-race fiction, principally in the form of nostalgic pastiche following the posthumous surge in the popularity of Edgar Rice Burroughs in paperback reprints. Latter-day examples inspired by Burroughs include *Journey to the Underground World* (1979) and its sequels by Lin Carter. Other recent examples include *Congo* by Michael Crichton (1980), *The Undying Land* by William Gilmour (1985), *Kala* by Nicholas Luard (1990), *The Mountain Made of Light* by Edward Myers (1992), *Down to Heaven* by Mark Canter (1997), and various series pastiches such as *Indiana Jones and the Seven Veils* by Rob MacGregor (1991) and *Python Isle*, a "Doc Savage" adventure by Kenneth Robeson (i.e. Will Murray, 1991). Mention of George Lucas's movie hero Indiana Jones should also remind us that the "lost" motif – extending to lost temples, lost arks, lost grails – still retains a presence in late – 20th-century cinema.

HUMOROUS FANTASY

Most traditional fantasy – from the Arthurian romances to the Brothers Grimm – is not noted for its humour, although Aesopian animal fables frequently may be read as pointed jokes. Perhaps there is a necessary link between humour and high civilization, because Classical Greek literature after Aesop did in fact contain a good deal of humorous fantasy, a tradition of irreverence and knockabout satire which seems to have become lost in much of the surviving fantasy of later times. The Greek Old Comedy – that is to say, the non-tragic drama written before about 400 BC – was in essence a theatre of fantasy. The so-called New Comedy of the 4th century BC and later was largely mundane, and this is the form of comedy which has been the main influence on western theatre ever since, through Shakespeare and Moliére, right down to Hollywood movies of the "romantic comedy" type. The Old Comedy was a very different kettle of fish, in sharp contrast both to the great tragedies which were staged alongside it and to the later, much more realistic, New Comedies.

Fifth-century Old Comedians like Cratinus, Crates and Eupolis, most of whose works are now lost to us but are partially retrievable from surviving fragments and other writers' descriptions, filled their plays with fantasy. For example, Crates' *Theria* (*The Beasts*) "portrayed a meatless Golden Age, where food served itself" and Eupolis' *Demoi* featured "the resurrection of four great statesmen and their treatment of current problems" (both quotations are from *Cassell's Encyclopaedia of World Literature*). Humorous utopias and the reawakening of the famous dead – and other, similar, motifs such as imaginary tours of the afterlife – were fantastic themes that carried a satirical bite. Their purpose was not only to provoke laughs, but to comment on the failings of the contemporary world. Unlike the supernatural elements of the great tragedies, which in general were taken directly from mythology and legend – the time-honoured tales of gods and men – the fantasy elements in Old Comedy seem to have been minted as new, although no doubt their authors borrowed some motifs from folk tales. In effect, the Old Comedians invented whatever fantastic elements seemed necessary or desirable to them in order to make a series of sharp points. In these respects, in its "edge" and its novelty, Old Comedy is perhaps more ancestral

THE DISCWORLD BEGAN HERE: THE ORIGINAL COVER OF THE FIRST EDITION OF PRATCHETT'S FAMOUS COMIC FANTASY

to modern science fiction than it is to most recent fantasy.

Most famous of the Old Comedians, and the one for whom we still have a substantial body of complete plays (almost a dozen), is Aristophanes. His finest fantasy play, *Ornithes* (*The Birds*; 414 BC), concerns the building of an airborne city, Nephelococcygia – which translates beautifully into English as "Cloudcuckooland". Others of Aristophanes' comedies contain fantasy aplenty, for example *Batrachoi* (*The Frogs*; 405 BC), which is set in the underworld of the dead. These plays, with their bawdy elements and their *ad hominem* attacks on leading Athenian citizens, may have lost some of their immediate satirical relevance but nevertheless live on as great comedy – and as great fantasy. A present-day humorous fantasy writer who resembles Aristophanes in his procedures (for example, introducing gods and mythical heroes into low-life contemporary settings) is Tom Holt. Indeed, Holt has written directly about Aristophanes in his pair of historical novels, *Goatsong* (1989) and *The Walled Orchard* (1990). One is also reminded of a still more successful humorist of our time, though – it is tempting to think of the Old Greek as Terrypratchettes.

CLOWNING IT UP IN A RECENT STAGE PRODUCTION BASED ON RABELAIS'S BAWDY 16TH-CENTURY FANTASY *GARGANTUA*

There was a later Greek writer who may also remind us of Holt and Pratchett. More than 500 years after Aristophanes, the Syrian-born Lucian of Samosata combined much of the attitude and approach of Old Comedy with the prose form of Plato's philosophical dialogues (not notable for their humour!) to create a new type of writing that has been called the "Lucianic dialogue". These marvellously witty conversations – not plays but nevertheless designed for public reading – contain accounts of flights to the moon and to Mount Olympus on birds' wings; several tours of the underworld; the story of Charon, ferryman to the dead, leaving his duties on the River Styx in order to explore the world of the living (rather like Death in Pratchett's *Reaper Man*, 1991); and so on and on in a profusion of comical-fantastical invention. Lucian also wrote the prose tale known to us as The *True History*, about a shipful of explorers who are carried to the moon on a waterspout, and then later find themselves in the belly of a whale. A parody of now-lost "imaginary voyage" fictions of Lucian's own day, this is often regarded as an ancestral work of science fiction, although these days it reads more like humorous fantasy – Pratchettian fantasy.

Although it may have influenced certain Roman writers such as Apuleius (author of the entertaining 2nd-century AD fantasy *The Golden Ass*), the example of Lucianic satire lay dormant for over a thousand years, during the rise of Christianity (when Lucian's works were often condemned as irreligious), and throughout the Dark Ages and the Middle Ages, to eventually exert its greatest influence on Northern European literature at the time of the Renaissance and the centuries immediately following. Among numerous writers who prized Lucian and gloried in his example were Francois Rabelais, author of the massive ribald fantasy *Gargantua and Pantagruel* (1532–64); Jonathan Swift, author of the great satire *Gulliver's Travels* (1726); Henry Fielding, best known for his comic realistic novels but also the author of an afterlife fantasy entitled *A Journey From This World to the Next* (1743); and Voltaire, author of several 18th-century philosophical tales which tended to the humorous and the fantastic.

None of the foregoing were generic fantasies in the modern sense. As the fantasy genre grew in the 19th century, it was mainly under the twin influences of fairy tales and medieval romances – and mainly solemn. However, humour began to be employed as a regular device by some of the Victorian writers of "art fairy tales" and children's stories, beginning (perhaps) with Hans Christian Andersen and Charles Dickens, and producing a couple of glorious, oddball masterpieces in Lewis Carroll's "Alice" books (1865–71). The first writer to specialize in humorous fantasy was F. Anstey (Thomas Anstey Guthrie), who produced a number of delightful novels, beginning with *Vice Versa* (1882), in which magic – in the form of personality swaps, animated statues, or genies from old bottles – interrupted the lives of the staid Victorian middle classes. So appealing was Anstey's brand of lightly satirical humour that it inspired several imitators, the most successful of whom was E. Nesbit (Edith Bland), whose children's novels such as *The Phoenix and the Carpet* (1904) and *The Story of the Amulet* (1906) follow similar patterns to

SMITH WAS A MASTER OF HUMOROUS FANTASY, AND BEST KNOWN FOR *TOPPER* – SEEN HERE IN ITS RETITLED BRITISH EDITION

Anstey's and make very enjoyable reading for adults as well as kids.

The most important name in humorous fantasy after Anstey and Nesbit was that of an American writer, Thorne Smith. He took the by-now familiar formulae – genial ghosts, body-switches, living statues, domesticated witches – and spiced them up in a manner suitable for the Prohibition-era USA. Many of his novels, including *Topper* (1926) and *Turnabout* (1931), were filmed in Hollywood. Something akin to the Thorne Smith brand of humour and fantasy was achieved in the pulp magazine *Unknown* (1939–1943). Its most prominent contributors included the writing team of L. Sprague de Camp and Fletcher Pratt, who produced tales with titles like "The Mathematics of Magic" (later incorporated into the book *The Incompleat Enchanter*, 1942) in which a young maths teacher finds himself plunged into a fantastic world, with comical results. *Unknown* may have been short-lived, but its inspiration endured in occasional postwar novels such as Poul Anderson's amusing *Three Hearts and Three Lions* (1961), and eventually – at a considerable remove – it was to inspire a whole new school of American comic fantasy which included the series (both reliant on bad puns, but very popular for all that) by Piers Anthony and Robert Asprin that began, respectively, with their novels *A Spell for Chameleon* (1977) and *Another Fine Myth* (1978).

The British revival in funny fantasy was led by the brilliant Terry Pratchett, whose first "Discworld" novel, *The Colour of Magic* (1983), was in the main a parody of Fritz Leiber's Sword & Sorcery tales – although Leiber himself, a one-time contributor to *Unknown*, had been more than capable of a mean streak of humour. Pratchett's manic world soon took on a life of its own, becoming an all-purpose setting for a seemingly infinite variety of slapstick tales, some of which have surprisingly serious undertones. His command of language and comic characterization, his irrepressible invention and the way in which his work has improved over the years have led to Pratchett being compared to the English master of humorous fiction, P. G. Wodehouse, who himself wrote one comic fantasy in the Ansteyan style, *Laughing Gas* (1936). It is an accolade which does not seem unwarranted. Pratchett may well be remembered as the finest humorist of the late 20th century, both a new Wodehouse and a new Lucian of Samosata.

SWORD & SORCERY

The term Sword & Sorcery was invented in the early 1960s by Fritz Leiber, but the type of fiction it described had existed for several decades. It is associated primarily with the work of the Texan writer Robert E. Howard, and in particular his swashbuckling stories about Conan the Barbarian, first published in *Weird Tales* magazine in the 1930s. Conan, a mighty-thewed warrior from the ancient land of Cimmeria, has become one of the myth figures of our time, portrayed on paperback covers by the popular artist Frank Frazetta, in Marvel Comics titles (*The Savage Sword of Conan*, etc.) by numerous other artists, and, not least, on the cinema screen by the bodybuilder Arnold Schwarzenegger. Conan's success as a cultural icon is remarkable, especially when one remembers that his creator died by his own hand some ten years before his first book was published. Howard's hero had battled his gory way through various short stories and novellas before starring in his first (and only) full-length yarn, *The Hour of the Dragon* (serialized 1935–36; published in book form as *Conan the Conqueror*, 1950).

The action of the novel concerns a villainous 3,000-year-old sorcerer, Xaltotun, who has been brought back to life by a group of conspirators in order to help depose Conan from the throne of Aquilonia. Conan, although a rude northern barbarian and the son of a blacksmith, has succeeded in fighting his way to a kingship, and now jealous forces are marshalling against him. Our hero is a formidable man, described as "mightily shouldered and deep of chest, with a massive corded neck and heavily muscled limbs", and he commands a huge army, so it is evident to his enemies that only black magic can defeat him. Xaltotun duly immobilizes Conan by sorcerous means, defeats his army, and throws the deposed king into a dungeon. But a seraglio girl helps Conan escape; he slays an enormous ape which

CONAN THE BARBARIAN, AS PORTRAYED IN 1981 BY A CERTAIN WELL-KNOWN AUSTRIAN BODYBUILDER

prowls the cells, then hacks his way to freedom and begins the long task of winning back his kingdom. Gradually he draws together his allies, learns his enemies' weaknesses, and gains the magical assistance which will enable him to crush Xaltotun. Needless to say, he succeeds – but the body-count is high. *Conan the Conqueror* is a vigorous novel of bloody action, written in true pulp-magazine style by a writer who had a flair for the macabre. It moves along well, and never fails to deliver the excitements one might expect.

This was the original, unadulterated work of Sword & Sorcery, and as such it has been extremely influential. Howard's own inspirations included the pulp-magazine historical yarns of Harold Lamb, Talbot Mundy and H. Bedford-Jones, as well as the Tarzan adventures of Edgar Rice Burroughs and (probably) the lost-race novels of Rider Haggard; in fact, Haggard wrote one novel, *Eric Brighteyes* (1891) – not a lost-race story but a mock-Icelandic saga – which in many ways resembles a Sword & Sorcery epic before its time. But Howard brought a new flair and conviction to this kind of action story, turning it from mainly historical or exotic adventure into the purest fantasy, set in a neverworld of monsters and magicians where all women are beautiful and all men are dangerous. The author's early death robbed this new sub-genre of its prime mover, but others soon attempted to emulate him (among them at least one woman, C. L. Moore, with her tales of the heroine Jirel of Joiry) – and the most effective of these was Fritz Leiber.

Leiber began writing his good-humoured, roistering tales of the barbarian Fafhrd and the sneak-thief known as the Gray Mouser in the late 1930s, though the first volume of the heroes' exploits, *Two Sought Adventure*, did not appear until 1957. It was later expanded, and retitled *Swords Against Death*. Several more books followed, but only one of them, *The Swords of Lankhmar* (1968), is a full-length novel. Here the city of Lankhmar is suffering from a plague of rats. Fafhrd and the Gray Mouser are commissioned by a dissolute overlord to guard a grain-ship which bears gifts to another town. They are almost overcome by a rebellion of the rats aboard their vessel, before a two-headed sea-monster inadvertently comes to their rescue. Back in the city once more, after successfully completing their voyage, they find that the rodent plague has taken a firmer hold... and much magical adventure is to come before our ingenious heroes are able to defeat the gruesome curse. They have to call on sorcerous help from Sheelba of the Eyeless Face and Ningauble the Seven-Eyed Wizard; the Mouser must shrink in size, and descend into the rat's underground maze; and Fafhrd must learn how to unleash the dreaded War Cats. The tale builds to a satisfactory climax, and is extravagant fun all the way. Everything is narrated in a rich descriptive prose, amusing and sometimes erotically spicy.

Another writer who took the Howard formula and endowed it with greater literary sophistication – but in a rather different manner from Leiber – was the British writer Michael Moorcock, who invented the red-eyed, albino warrior Elric of Melnibone for *Science Fantasy* magazine in 1961. A collection of Elric's adventures appeared in book form as *The Stealer of Souls* (1963), to be followed by the novel *Stormbringer* (1965) and several more volumes. Moorcock's brand of Sword & Sorcery is heavily ironic and moody. Elric is a comparative weakling without his sword – the half-sentient "runeblade" Stormbringer – which drinks the life-force from its victims, conferring tremendous strength and vitality to Elric. This does not make the hero happy: he hates his weapon (as it apparently hates him), yet the two are inseparable. At the beginning of the novel *Stormbringer,* Elric has put the sword aside, and is attempting to rule his kingdom in peace. However, the supernatural minions of an evil master kidnap his wife, Zarozinia, and Elric is obliged to grasp his weapon once more. He becomes involved in world-shaking events. The forces of Chaos have broken loose, and everything is about to fall into wrack and ruin. With his faithful henchman Moonglum, Elric travels far and wide, encountering one terrible foe after another. All this is narrated speedily, and with great relish, and the story mounts from one climax to another, each surpassing the preceding one in sound and fury. Elric tackles the Counts of Hell, and eventually finds Zarozinia – only to lose her again. She is transformed into a wormlike creature, and, in a memorably horrid scene, she impales herself on her husband's magic blade, feeding her soul to him. Events move on to a final grandiose climax.

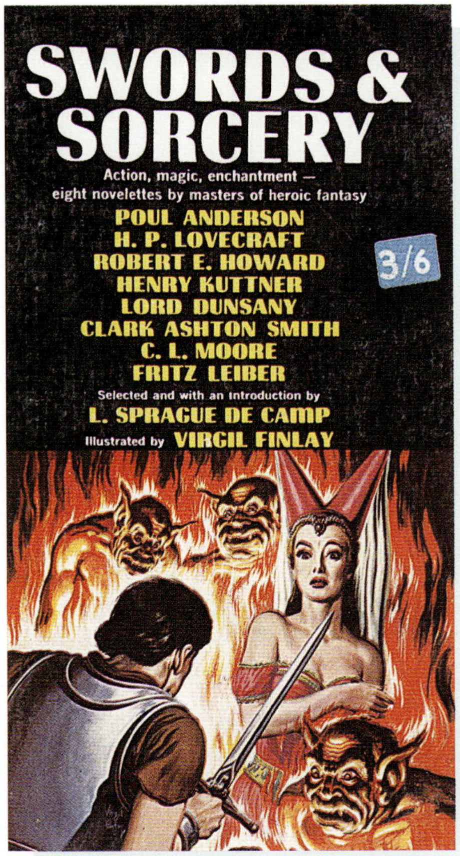

L. SPRAGUE DE CAMP DID MUCH TO ESTABLISH THE POPULARITY OF FANTASY IN PAPERBACK

Other writers, such as the late Karl Edward Wagner, contributed to Sword & Sorcery, but none did so as memorably as the above three. The popularity of the sub-genre peaked around 1970 (but its influence on the movies did not become fully apparent until the early 1980s), and since then it has faded away – or, rather, it has been absorbed into the general run of post-Tolkien heroic fantasy. A long series of Conan pastiches has continued to appear to the present day, however; the best of these have been written by Robert Jordan.

Sword & Sorcery owed absolutely nothing to J. R. R. Tolkien. It was essentially a pulp-magazine form, at ease in shorter lengths, and it appealed for the most part to male readers. As a genre, it was accused of fascism, sexism and all manner of sins, but in the hands of its best practitioners it had wit, imagination, an interesting darkness, and above all excitement.

HEROIC FANTASY

Heroic Fantasy is a broader term than Sword & Sorcery, though sometimes it is taken to mean much the same thing – that is, fantasy about a hero, or heroine, who has sundry adventures in an imaginary world where magic and the supernatural are often encountered. Perhaps, however, the word "heroic" should be understood in a wider sense – as not just pertaining to an individual hero, but to a cast of characters, a set of actions, a body of invention and a whole world conceived on a heroic scale. Terms like High Fantasy and Epic Fantasy have also been used to denote this kind of large-scale fiction, which, unlike Sword & Sorcery, usually comes in big packages – novels of 500 pages and more, and frequently in the form of trilogies, or even open-ended series of long novels. Sometimes works which appear, on the outside, to be unending series actually have a more complex structure. They may well consist of a core trilogy which the author enlarges by writing a sequel trilogy and then elaborates by going backwards in the chronology to write a "prequel" trilogy, or even a "sidebar" trilogy.

Invariably, though, heroically scaled works of this sort, whatever their actual length, have as their chief characteristic the fact that they are set in a wholly imaginary world – not in a version of our own everyday world into which magic has intruded (although much fantasy, particularly of the humorous type, takes that form), nor in a fantastic version of our past (such as the fabled Middle Ages of Arthurian romance, or the legendary worlds of Chinoiserie and the Arabian Nights). In Heroic Fantasy, the invented world – what J. R. R. Tolkien termed a "Secondary World" – is of more importance, both to writer and to readers, than any individual hero. In fact, the heroes, or viewpoint characters, of Heroic Fantasy often change:

the next chapter, or the next volume, may follow a different character or set of characters. What matters most, and what gives the work its unity and consistency, is the world, and that is why it is typical for books of this kind to open with a map, or a whole set of maps. Other common features include glossaries, mini-gazetteers, lists of *dramatis personae*, genealogies, and explanatory pseudo-historical appendices. These features can be very beguiling to the lovers of High Fantasy, but they can also be off-putting to the uninitiated.

The father of secondary-world fantasy is generally agreed to be William Morris, and his "big book" is *The Well at the World's End* (1896; 562 pages in the Ballantine paperback edition of 1975). A pseudo-medieval quest-romance written in archaic style (a prose which reads smoothly and beautifully once the reader becomes accustomed to it), it was not widely popular in its day, although it succeeded in inspiring the passionate devotion of a few much younger writers who read it in the succeeding decades – people like Lord Dunsany, E. R. Eddison, C. S. Lewis and J. R. R. Tolkien. The seed was sown, even if the tradition of Heroic Fantasy stemming from Morris was to remain semi-underground, almost invisible, for the next half century and more. Another landmark novel is Eddison's *The Worm Ouroboros* (1922; 520 pages in the Ballantine paperback). Set in a gorgeously evoked secondary world – supposedly the planet Mercury, but everyone soon forgets that unimportant framing device – it too is written in a deliberately archaic style which has its undeniable beauties and is no bar to readability when one has adjusted to it. It also contains a stronger, or at any rate more action-packed, story than Morris's masterpiece.

These were among the works which prepared the ground for the century's greatest fantasy novel, Tolkien's *The Lord of the Rings* (published 1954–55, but written in the main over a 12-year period from 1937 to 1949). It was first released in three volumes, *The Fellowship of the Ring*, *The Two Towers* and *The Return of the King*, but despite this it is not so much a trilogy as one long, continuous novel. At first seemingly destined for the same sort of obscurity as Morris's and Eddison's romances, it took over 10 years to gain wide acceptance. It was with the publication of American paperback editions, in 1965, that *The Lord of the Rings* finally took off and became one of the soaring bestsellers of 20th-century fiction. To what did it owe its immense success? The first chapter, which describes the "eleventy-first" birthday party of the hobbit Bilbo Baggins, is juvenile in tone – and in fact it is a direct sequel to Tolkien's novel for children, *The Hobbit*, or *There and Back Again* (1937). For some, that opening chapter, with its little furry characters and cosy rural setting, its "Bag End" and "Hobbiton", and its tone so redolent of English nursery-tale humour, was a deterrent to further reading. But those who read on soon found themselves succumbing to the spell of the grander narrative. As Bilbo's young kinsman, Frodo Baggins, sets out on his great journey at the behest of Gandalf, the wizard, the reader is drawn deep into the wonderful territory of Tolkien's richly detailed Middle-Earth. Like any novel, *The Lord of the Rings* brings with it its baggage of "content", its social attitudes whether overtly expressed or merely implied, but there are few examples in the whole of literature where that baggage counts for less when weighed against the book's central attraction – as near as is possible, Tolkien's masterpiece is pure *story*.

It is as a timeless quest tale that the book succeeds. The mysterious portents, the hard travelling, the varied landscapes, the good companionship, the encircling foes, the urgency of the task in hand, the magical revelations – all are handled with a superb sense of story-telling rhythm. It is a slow rhythm, for it is a very long novel, but in its leisurely way it builds a kind of tidal power. The prose is less rich than that of Morris or Eddison, but the cumulative power of Tolkien's huge tale is undeniable. The atmospheric decorations which all Tolkien fans find so intriguing – the interpolated verses, the invented languages, the complex genealogies and mythologies –

KING GORICE LOOKS DOWN FROM HIS CASTLE, IN E. R. EDDISON'S MASTERPIECE OF HEROIC FANTASY, *THE WORM OROBOUROS*

EVOCATIONS OF LANDSCAPE ARE ALL-IMPORTANT IN HEROIC FANTASIES SUCH AS *THE LORD OF THE RINGS*

are of less importance than the simple grandeur of the plot, the imaginary world and the story-telling dynamics. Tolkien continued to embroider his fantasies of Middle-Earth throughout his long life. The results have been published in *The Silmarillion* (1977) and many other posthumous volumes edited by the author's son, but, whatever their scholarly brilliance, these later books lack the central quality which vitalizes *The Lord of the Rings* – that sense of raw story, in all its glorious primitiveness.

Although he became a big seller in the 1960s and did much to create a space in the marketplace for all forms of fantasy – from the gothic weirdness of Mervyn Peake to the pulpy delights of Sword & Sorcery – another dozen years were to pass before Tolkien's direct legacy became apparent. The year 1977 marked the turning point. Not only did that year bring the long-awaited publication of *The Silmarillion*, but it saw the first appearance of big new instant bestsellers by two unknown American writers. Both would have been inexplicable (and probably unpublishable) without the example of Tolkien. Terry Brooks's *The Sword of Shannara* was condemned by some reviewers as a "rip-off" of Tolkien, but nevertheless it sold spectacularly well and set a pattern for many more novels to come, by Brooks and others. Stephen R. Donaldson's three-volume *The Chronicles of Thomas Covenant, the Unbeliever* was also a crowd-pleaser, but it was a more original and interesting work. There is no doubt that it belongs to the school of Tolkien. Donaldson gives us an entire sub-creation – the world of the Land, where the hero (magically displaced from our Earth) embarks on a mighty quest to defeat the corrupting powers of evil, as personified by Lord Foul the Despiser. Although the Land bears a resemblance to Middle-Earth, Thomas Covenant himself is a more modern hero than any of Tolkien's. He is depicted as an angst-ridden solitary who suffers extreme self-doubt, as well as the highly unpleasant physical disease of leprosy.

With the arrival of Brooks and Donaldson, we entered the era of the big commercial fantasy, a type of novel which has made its authors and publishers rich. For the sub-genre of Heroic Fantasy, this represents a vast change since the earlier part of the century (works such as *The Worm Ouroboros* did well to sell a few hundred copies on first publication). High Fantasy, which is to say Tolkien-esque fantasy, now leads the field: it is simply what fantasy *means* to most people. Other writers who have jumped successfully on the bandwagon include David Eddings (*Pawn of Prophecy*, 1982), Raymond E. Feist (*Magician*, 1982), Guy Gavriel Kay (*The Summer Tree*, 1984), Margaret Weis and Tracy Hickman (*Dragons of Autumn Twilight*, 1984), Janny Wurts (*Stormwarden*, 1984), Katharine Kerr (*Daggerspell*, 1986), Melanie Rawn (*Dragon Prince*, 1988), Tad Williams (*The Dragonbone Chair*, 1989), Robert Jordan (*The Eye of the World*, 1990), Mickey Zucker Reichert (*The Last of the Renshai*, 1992), Maggie Furey (*Aurian*, 1994–95), Terry Goodkind (*Wizard's First Rule*, 1994), Robin Hobb (*The Assassin's Apprentice*, 1995) and J. Gregory Keyes (*The Waterborn*, 1996). There are others. These writers vary in their talents – some produce clichéd secondary worlds which are examples of what Diana Wynne Jones has jokingly called "fantasylands" – but all enjoy careers which were made possible by Tolkien, and many of them will continue to give a great deal of pleasure to millions of readers.

THREE BRAVE HEARTS...
ADVENTURING IN A WONDER WORLD!
ADVENTURE OF
THE MASKED MEN!
ADVENTURE OF
THE WONDERFUL WEB!
ADVENTURE OF
THE ALL-SEEING EYE!
Alexander
KORDA
presents
THE
THIEF OF BAGDAD
In Magic Technicolor
with CONRAD VEIDT · SABU · JUNE DUPREZ
John Justin · Rex Ingram · Mary Morris
Released thru UNITED ARTISTS

FANTASY CINEMA

THE MAIN FEATURES

Although Fantasy has only recently been recognised as a distinct film genre, quite different in its motifs and methods from science fiction and horror, its extraordinarily rich tradition extends back to the earliest days of film-making. This chapter offers the first coherent and chronological account of the highlights of that tradition, looking at all the many and varied strands that make up the genre

Because film is an essentially artificial medium, whose apparent duplication of real experience is the result of extensive editing, it was always hospitable to the incorporation of "special effects". Unlike radio and TV, which both started out as "real time" media broadcasting live performances, the cinema was fantasized from the very beginning. The earliest film-makers took great delight in the magical effects of cutting and double exposure.

The ability to make characters vanish by splicing frames tracking their movements to frames of an empty set was lavishly exploited by early movie-makers, giving a literal edge to the notion of the cinema as a "dream factory". As techniques of film-making became more sophisticated, their users became more adept at producing illusions of reality, but throughout the silent era the artifice of film was so obvious that it remained a thoroughly fantasized medium. Elmer Rice's satirical novel *A Voyage to Purilia* (1930) insisted that the reflection of the world to be found in "realistic" Hollywood movies was so far removed from the original as to constitute an absurd utopia.

FEMME FATALE: THE IMMORTAL QUEEN IN *L'ATLANTIDE* MURDERED HER LOVERS WHEN SHE TIRED OF THEM

The advent of sound made it much easier to duplicate the texture of real experience on the screen, and that became the principal objective of most movie-makers, but the magic was never entirely banished to the peripheral fields of comedy and children's movies. Sentimental fantasy always remained an important cinema subgenre, and the aspects which were developed almost exclusively for children made rapid progress alongside cinematic realism.

The ability to animate cartoons created the opportunity to generate a fantasy world with its own conventional "laws of nature", such as the one which specifies that characters who run off the edge of a cliff will not begin to fall until they become aware of their danger. Making animated features was more time-consuming and at least as expensive as shooting the most lavish live action movies, but Walt Disney triumphantly demonstrated that it ws an economically viable enterprise, and set in train the development of a curious "parallel world" whose strange relationship to our own everyone now takes for granted.

The use of computers to manipulate image on film has recently breached the boundaries which once made it difficult to combine live action and animation, thus moving fantasy cinema into a new era. Every year that passes makes it easier to design worlds-within-films which are wonderfully exotic, and where all kinds of magic can be worked. The Golden Age of the silver screen is dawning now, and the fantasy tradition mapped out here constitutes the foundations on which future glories will be built.

1920 KORKARLEN

(THY SOUL SHALL BEAR WITNESS!)

Sweden; dir. and scr. Victor Sjostrom; starring Sjostrom, Hilda Borgstrom, Astrid Holm; 70 min; b/w; silent; aka The Phantom Carriage.

A melodramatic adaptation of Selma Lagerlof's moralistic novella, based on a legend that the last man to die on New Year's Eve must drive Death's cart throughout the following year. It was remade as a talkie in France in 1939, and Arne Mattsen made a second Swedish version in 1958.

1921 L'ATLANTIDE

France; dir. and scr. Jacques Feyder; starring Jean Angelo, Stacia Napierkowska; 125 min; b/w; silent.

A fervent adaptation of Pierre Benoit's feverishly masochistic clone of Rider Haggard's *She*, in which two comrades-in-arms discover the last remnant of Atlantis in the Sahara, ruled by an immortal queen accustomed to murdering her lovers. The movie was extremely expensive (two million francs!) and extremely successful, inspiring G. W. Pabst to make a German version (1932; aka *Queen of Atlantis*) starring Brigitte Helm as the charismatic dominatrix. The US version starring Maria Montez, *Siren of Atlantis* (1948), was a hollow mockery, and the French/Italian remake of 1961 could not recapture the dark eroticism of the original.

THE GREAT PIONEER

All early film-makers were delighted by the ways in which film could be edited to make "impossible" events occur, but for George Méliès, who had worked as a stage illusionist, film *was* fantasy. As early as 1896 he produced *The Bewitched Inn*, whose flying candlesticks and disappearing bed were recapitulated in the more substantial *The Inn Where No Man Rests* (1902). The first of his adaptations of classic fairy tales, *Bluebeard* (1901), was followed by the hand-coloured *Kingdom of the Fairies* (1903), *The Witch* (1908) and the longest of his surviving films – at 26 minutes – *Cinderella, or the Glass Slipper* (1912). He made two brief versions of Faust in 1898 and 1899 before producing the proto-expressionist *Faust in Hell* (1904) and the more substantial *The Damnation of Doctor Faust* (1904). His other demonic romances include *The Treasures of Satan* (1902), *The Devil's Daughters* (1903), the bizarre *The Infernal Cake-Walk* (1903) and the more substantial *The Merry Frolics of Satan* (1906). His most original and extended fantasy works mixed fairy-tale motifs with elements of chivalric romance; they include *The Knight of the Black Art* (1908) and *The Knight of the Snows* (1912); the latter – which was the last film in which Meliès played his favourite character, the enchanter Alcofrisbas – vies with *Cinderella*, his early essays in science fiction and the marvellous *The Palace of a Thousand-and-One Nights* (1905) for the honour of being reckoned his masterpiece.

ESSENTIAL EQUIPMENT: KRIEMHILD POSES WITH SWORD IN *DIE NIEBELUNGEN*

1924 DIE NIEBELUNGEN

Germany; dir. Fritz Lang; starring Paul Richter, Margaret Schon; scr. Thea von Harbou; 2 parts, 115 min and 125 min; b/w; silent.

A calculatedly grandiose version of the legend of Siegfried. Wagner – who had used it as the basis for the Ring Cycle – and other German Romantics had gladly adopted the story as a defining allegory of national identity and ambition, and this was the spirit in which Lang and von Harbou conceived and shot the film. It was a significant morale-builder in the decade following Germany's defeat in World War I and helped to persuade Hitler (who loved it) that the cinema was an important medium of ideological persuasion.

THE THIEF OF BAGDAD

US; dir. Raoul Walsh; starring Douglas Fairbanks, Anna May Wong; c.135 min; b/w; silent.

This was Hollywood's first major venture into fantasy, conceived by Fairbanks as an ideal showcase for his talents. The special effects were state-of-the-art in 1924 and the ebullience of the project still comes across in the short version that was cobbled together from surviving fragments for TV use.

1926 FAUST

Germany; dir. F. W. Murnau; starring Gosta Ekman, Emil Jannings; scr. Hans Kyser; 100 min; b/w; silent.

The Faust story was one of the most popular subjects of silent cinema, featuring in the repertoire of British pioneer G. A. Smith as well as Meliès, but Murnau's extended version easily outshone all its briefer rivals. The arrival of Mephistopheles and the eventual damnation of Faust were scenes ideally suited to melodramatic dumbshow, and Murnau made the most of them.

THE SORROWS OF SATAN

US; dir. D. W. Griffith; starring Adolphe Menjou, Lya de Putti; 115 min; b/w; silent.

A melodramatic adaptation of Marie Corelli's best-selling Faustian fantasy, in which the repentant Devil – who hates it when mortals fall prey to his temptations, because their recalcitrance is holding back his own redemption – is bowled over by the saintly virtue of a female writer whose initials are MC. Her male counterpart is, of course, easier prey. The novel had earlier been credited as the source of Carl Dreyer's *Leaves from Satan's Book* (1919), which attempts a wide-ranging survey of the history of temptation.

1929 NOAH'S ARK

US; dir. Michael Curtiz; starring Dolores Costello, Noah Beery, George O'Brien; scr. Anthony Coldeway and Daryl F. Zanuck; 135 min.

An allegory planned as a silent film, into which some talkie sequences were awkwardly tipped. It attempts to draw explicit, if somewhat elastic, parallels between World War I and the Biblical Deluge, interweaving narratives after the fashion of D. W. Griffith's classic *Intolerance* (1916).

1930 ALF'S BUTTON

UK; dir. W. P. Kellino, starring Jimmy Nervo, Teddy Knox, Tubby Edlin, Nora Swinburne; 96 min; b/w.

W. A. Darlington's cockney Alf had been invented during World War I to provide morale-boosting light relief in an Ansteyesque magazine series. A bestseller when it was reprinted in book form once the war has ended, the story – in which a beleaguered Tommy finds that one of his uniform buttons is made from the brass of Aladdin's lamp and still has the power of command over an intellectually challenged genie – was made into a silent film in 1920; this was a straightforward talkie remake. Nervo and Knox were a popular music-hall comedy act later incorporated into the enormously popular Crazy Gang, and Edlin came from the same milieu. All six Crazy Gang members – including Bud Flanagan and Chesney Allen – got together to make the sequel *Alf's Button Afloat* (1938), directed by Marcel Varnel.

LILIOM

US; dir. Frank Borzage; starring Charles Farrell, Rose Hobart; scr. S. N. Behrman; 94 min; b/w.

A silent version of Ferenc Molnar's 1909 stage play – which was translated for Broadway production by Benjamin F. Glazer in 1921 – had been made in 1921 as *A Trip to Paradise*, directed by Maxwell Karger. The eponymous anti-hero is a hot-tempered fairground barker kicked out by his mistress and employer when he marries a younger woman; when his wife falls pregnant he embarks on an

WHEN VISITING EARTH, ADOLPHE MENJOU'S SATAN CUNNINGLY DISGUISED HIMSELF BY MAKING HIS MOUSTACHE AND EYEBROWS CURL DOWN AND PUTTING BRYLCREEM ON HIS HAIR

FASHION ALERT: WILL ROGERS'S OVERCOAT IS SOMEWHAT OUT OF PLACE IN KING ARTHUR'S COURT

armed robbery and is killed. After 16 years in Purgatory he is allowed to return to Earth for one day to see his family, but when his daughter refuses the stolen star he has brought as a gift he ruins his opportunity to atone for his sins. It was remade again in 1933 by Fritz Lang, then working in France, with Charles Boyer in the lead.

OUTWARD BOUND

US; dir. Robert Milton; starring Leslie Howard, Douglas Fairbanks Jr; scr. J. Grubb Alexander; 82 min; b/w.

This movie version of Sutton Vane's allegorical play became the definitive cinematic posthumous fantasy, far more influential than the original or the subsequent novel. The play was written with the horrors of World War I sharply in mind; like James Hilton's *Lost Horizon* it agonizes over the difficulty of moving into a historical moral vacuum. This version cuts short the discussions aboard the ocean liner heading for the Seat of Judgment, concentrating instead on the difficulty the lead characters have in accepting that they are dead. It was remade in 1944 as *Between Two Worlds*; the new version – directed by Edward A. Blatt and starring John Garfield and Edmund Gwenn – took fuller advantage of its potential as a morale-booster.

1931 A CONNECTICUT YANKEE

US; dir. David Butler; starring Will Rogers, Maureen O'Sullivan, Myrna Loy; scr. William Counselman; 96 min; b/w.

This version of Mark Twain's classic timeslip fantasy followed a silent version made in 1921, directed by Emmett J. Flynn and starring Harry Myers. Adapting it as a vehicle for popular comedian Rogers necessitated the removal of the sharp satire, thus smoothing the way for the idiosyncratic 1949 musical version directed by Tay Garnett and starring Bing Crosby, Cedric Hardwicke and William Bendix, which used the full title, *A Connecticut Yankee in King Arthur's Court*. It became the parent of a cinematic sub-genre of timeslip comedies, including several other items where the timeslips are "rationalized" as dreams, although its most obvious clone – *Fiddlers Three* (1944) – despatches Tommy Trinder and companions to Roman Britain by means of a lightning-bolt. *The Spaceman and King Arthur* (1980) replaced Twain's mechanic with an astronaut.

1932 DAS BLAUE LICHT

(THE BLUE LIGHT)

Germany; dir., scr. and starring Leni Riefenstahl; 68 min; b/w.

A curious *femme fatale* story, probably inspired by Gerhardt Hauptmann's play *The Sunken Bell*, although the man beguiled by the mysterious mountain-maiden is a painter, not a bell-founder. It offers a useful insight into the yearning spirit which led Hitler to believe that Leni Riefenstahl would make a valuable instrument of propaganda.

1933 ALICE IN WONDERLAND

US; dir. Norman Z. McLeod; starring Charlotte Henry, W. C. Fields, Cary Grant, Gary Cooper, Edward Everett Horton, Edna May Oliver; scr. Joseph L. Mankiewicz and William Cameron Menzies; 75 min; b/w.

Lewis Carroll's classic was probably the first literary fantasy to be adapted for the cinema, in Cecil Hepworth and Percy Stow's version of 1903, starring May Clark; American pioneer Edwin S. Porter also made a version in 1910. The costumes for this new production were closely based on John Tenniel's drawings, but the spirit of the original remained elusive. The star cameos – Cooper as the White Knight and Grant as the Mock Turtle – don't work, although Fields is an intriguing Humpty Dumpty. For all its faults, though, it is much better than either the 1950 British version employing Leo Bunin's puppets, or Disney's 1951 animated version.

OUT OF TIME: LESLIE HOWARD SAVOURS THE DELIGHTS OF TIME TRAVEL IN *BERKELEY SQUARE*

BERKELEY SQUARE

US; dir. Frank Lloyd; starring Leslie Howard, Heather Angel; scr. Sonya Levien and John Balderston; 87 min; b/w.

Balderston had co-written the play on which this film was based with J. C. Squire, completing and sentimentalizing the story begun in Henry James's unfinished timeslip romance *The Sense of the Past*. Howard plays an American whose consciousness is transplanted into the body of an 18th-century English ancestor, allowing him to obtain a better understanding of his roots, and of the delicate folly of nostalgia. It was remade in 1951 as *I'll Never Forget You* (aka *The House in the Square*), with Tyrone Power in the lead; the new version deploys the symbolic device – borrowed from *The Wizard of Oz* and *The Blue Bird* – of switching from monochrome to colour when the time-displacement occurs.

GABRIEL OVER THE WHITE HOUSE

US; dir. Gregory La Cava; starring Walter Huston, Franchot Tone; scr. Carey Wilson & Bertram Bloch 87 min; b/w.

A curious political fantasy based on Thomas F. Tweed's novel *Rinehart*, in which a crook who is elected president of the USA undergoes a miraculous moral transformation, wiping out organized crime and instituting an era of world peace. Tweed's carefully inoffensive novel must have seemed a much safer bet than the more radical dreams of political reform penned by Upton Sinclair, Jack London and other American socialists, which Hollywood let strictly alone.

THE WANDERING JEW

UK; dir. Maurice Elvey; starring Conrad Veidt; 111 min; b/w.

The second film version of E. Temple Thurston's play, following a 1923 silent directed by Elvey and starring Mathieson Long (who had made his reputation with his stage performance). Thurston's version of the story of the Jew who hurried Christ along the road to Calvary and was instructed to await the Messiah's return lets the accursed wanderer off the hook at the time of the Spanish Inquisition. Elvey followed it in 1934 with *The Clairvoyant*, about a fraudulent medium who issues a prophecy that comes true.

1934 BABES IN TOYLAND

US; dir. Gus Meins and Charles Rogers; starring Stan Laurel, Oliver Hardy; scr. Nick Grinde & Frank Butler; 77 min; b/w; aka Wooden Soldiers, March of the Wooden Soldiers, Laurel and Hardy in Toyland.

Victor Herbert's operetta is here revamped as a vehicle for Laurel and Hardy, who bumble through the defence of Toyland with the aid of oversized wooden soldiers. The quasi-expressionist sets give it an extra touch of class and it remains much better than the Disney remake of 1961 or the 1986 TV movie.

IN DREAMS

As well as serving as justificatory frames for fantastic narratives, dreams often intrude significantly into otherwise naturalistic films. Classic cinematic dreams include the vision of Hell vouchsafed to a carnival owner (Spencer Tracy) in *Dante's Inferno* (1935), the Dali-designed dream experienced by a psychiatric patient (Gregory Peck) in Alfred Hitchcock's *Spellbound* (1945), and the erotic dreams which drive a discontented housewife (Catherine Deneuve) to prostitution in Luis Bunuel's *Belle de Jour* (1967). A tolerantly condescending view of fantasizing is taken by *The Secret Life of Walter Mitty* (1947), based on James Thurber's classic story, and the very similar *Dream Girl* (1947), based on Elmer Rice's play. *The Magician of Lublin* (1979) is an allegory about dreams of flight based on Isaac Bashevis Singer's novel, Terry Gilliam's *The Fisher King* (1991) includes an allegory involving dreams of dragon-slaying and the Steve Martin vehicle *L.A. Story* includes visionary sequences featuring an oracular traffic-signal. The capacity of modern special effects to generate highly effective dream-sequences is demonstrated by Peter Jackson's *Heavenly Creatures* (1994), where strange dreams map the descent of two teenagers into a terrible folie *à deux*. Film makers who have gone to enormous trouble to recapitulate their own dreams cinematically include Federico Fellini in *8½* (1963) and *Juliet of the Spirits* (1965) and Akira Kurosawa in *Akira Kurosawa's Dreams* (1990).

DEATH TAKES A HOLIDAY

US; dir. Mitchell Leisen; starring Fredric March, Evelyn Venable; scr. Maxwell Anderson, Gladys Lehman & Walter Ferris; 78 min; b/w.

A careful version of Alberto Casella's earnest allegorical play – translated for Broadway by Walter Terris in 1930 – in which Death (March) enters the human world to find out why mortals fear him and discovers the bittersweet joys of love. The film inspired three TV versions, but its first substantial cinematic clone was the intriguing *On Borrowed Time* (1939), adapted from a play by Lawrence Edward Watkin, in which "Mr Brink" has to put his annihilation business on hold when he is trapped in a tree by the old man he has come to collect. *Meet Joe Black* (1998) was a successful contemporary remake with Brad Pitt as the not-all-that-grim reaper, and Claire Forlani as the girl who steals his heart.

1935 THE GHOST GOES WEST

UK; dir. René Clair; starring Robert Donat, Eugene Pallette, Jean Parker; scr. Robert E. Sherwood and Geoffrey Kerr; 85 min; b/w.

Commissioning a French director to make a film about a Scottish ghost transplanted – with the stones of his haunt – to America evidently seemed a perfectly sensible idea to the Hungarian founder of London Films. Clair's credentials as an important cinematic fantasist had been established by *Paris qui dort* (1923; aka *The Crazy Ray*), *Le Fantôme du Moulin Rouge* (1924) and his early exercises in cinematic surrealism, but this thoroughly commercial product was pure froth.

A MIDSUMMER NIGHT'S DREAM

US; dir. Max Reinhardt and William Dieterle; starring James Cagney, Dick Powell, Olivia de Havilland, Mickey Rooney; scr. Charles Kenyon & Mary C. McCall, Jr; 133 min; b/w.

The mind might boggle at the thought of Cagney playing Bottom but he was at least as good as Benny Hill in the second TV version. Rooney, as Puck, was more like Benny Hill playing Benny Hill. Everyone involved tried *really hard* to make this unlikely project work; it remains watchable despite its conspicuous inauthenticity.

THE NIGHT LIFE OF THE GODS

US; dir. Lowell Sherman; starring Alan Mowbray, Florine McKinney; scr. Barry Trivers; 75 min; b/w.

The economy of the special effects required ensured that Hollywood attempted the most extravagantly licentious of Thorne Smith's comedies before the more suitable *Topper*, but this account of the bacchanal which follows the animation of a set of classical statues is too restrained for its own good.

PETER IBBETSON

US; dir. Henry Hathaway; starring Gary Cooper, Ann Harding; scr. Vincent Lawrence., Waldemar Young, Constance Collier, John Meehan & Edwin Justus Mayer; 88 min; b/w.

George du Maurier's tortured allegory about the wonderful and terrible power of romantic dreams had previously been filmed as *Forever* (1921) with Wallace Reid in the lead. Cooper is, alas, woefully miscast as the meek hero, who constructs an elaborate consolatory fantasy to make imprisonment bearable and is reunited in his dreams – which outlast life itself – with the childhood sweetheart whose brutal husband he has killed.

THE SCOUNDREL

US; dir. and scr. Ben Hecht and Charles MacArthur; starring Noel Coward, Alexander Woolcott; 74 min; b/w.

Hecht and MacArthur gave further exercise to the mordant wit they had incorporated into *The Front Page* – first filmed in 1931 – in this "second chance" fantasy, in which a dead writer, Coward, is allowed to return to Earth so that he might learn from his mistakes.

SCROOGE

UK; dir. Henry Edwards; starring Seymour Hicks; scr. Hicks and H. Fowler Mear; 78 min; b/w.

A cinema version of Hicks's stage version of Dickens's *A Christmas Carol*. As with most such exercises in self-promotion, the central performance comes across as pure ham. Alastair Sim made a better job of the role in the remake of 1951, which was directed by Brian Desmond Hurst and scripted by Noel Langley. The first US talkie,

PRAISE THE LORD: GOD TAKES A STROLL DURING A FISH FRY IN *THE GREEN PASTURES*

directed by Edward L. Marin in 1938, used Dickens's title in the US but clung to cinematic tradition in the UK; Reginald Owen put in a respectful and sober performance which made the movie preferable to most of the reconfigured versions which came after it. The British musical *Scrooge* (1970), directed by Ronald Neame, followed hot on the heels of the Dickensian hit *Oliver!,* but trashed the moral fable without discovering the least hint of a compensating virtue. The best of the updated versions is *Scrooged* (1988), directed by Richard Donner and starring Bill Murray; its effectiveness is partly based in Murray's performance as an ambitious executive warmly embracing the newly fashionable dictum that "Greed is Good" and partly in the slickness of the enterprisingly revamped Spirits. *A Muppet Christmas Carol* (1992) is not without charm.

SHE

US; dir. Irving Pichel and Lansing G. Holden; starring Helen Gahagan, Randolph Scott; 89 min; b/w.

The first movie version of Rider Haggard's novel had been a 1925 silent film directed by Leander de Cordova and starring Betty Blythe. This remake moved the setting from the dark heart of Africa to the Arctic wastes, perhaps to accentuate the icy temperament of its anti-heroine. It was easily outshone by the two versions of *L'Atlantide* which went before it, the frank masochism of the imitation translating better into visual form than the awkward Victorianism of the original. The British version of *She* made in 1965 could not overcome the stringent limitations of Hammer's budget, although Ursula Andress did look the part – more so, at any rate, than Gahagan.

1936 THE GREEN PASTURES

US; dir. William Keighley and Marc Connelly; starring Rex Ingram, Oscar Polk, Eddie Anderson; 88 min; b/w.

Marc Connelly scripted as well as co-directed this adaptation of his stage play, derived from Roark Bradford's painstaking attempts to describe the hopes and beliefs of black Christians. It is utterly serious in its contrived light-heartedness, rather difficult to watch because it is so horribly condescending, but cleverly done in cinematic terms. The film version of Lyn Root's all-black musical stage show *Cabin in the Sky* (1943), directed by Vincente Minnelli and staring Eddie Anderson, Lena Horne, Ethel Waters, Louis Armstrong and Rex Ingram, is in the same tradition; the fight between God and the Devil for the soul of a gambler is used as a framing device for the story.

IF I RULED THE WORLD: THE POSTER NEATLY CAPTURES THE SUBSTANCE OF THE CLASSIC FANTASY

THE MAN WHO COULD WORK MIRACLES

UK; dir. Lothar Mendes; starring Roland Young, Ralph Richardson, Ernest Thesiger; scr. Lajos Biro; 82 min; b/w.

Although not so quintessentially Wellsian as *Things to Come* (1936), this version of Wells's modern fable, similarly made by Alexander Korda's London Films, does not shy away from social criticism. The evocation of an experimentally minded godling (George Sanders) who bestows the fatal gift on Young's humble Everyman establishes that the story is to be viewed as a Voltairean *conte philosophique*; in that respect the film is a fascinating pioneering venture and a fine period piece as well. Another classic Wellsian fable was the basis of an effective short film directed by Glenn H. Alvey Jr: *The Door in the Wall* (1956).

1937 LOST HORIZON

US; dir. Frank Capra; starring Ronald Colman, Jane Wyatt, Thomas Mitchell, Sam Jaffe, Edward Everett Horton; scr. Robert Riskin; 133 min; b/w.

James Hilton's bestselling novel captured the bleak mood of those prescient souls who saw that the 1930s were drawing the world inexorably closer to a second World War. Its hero is a diplomat on the brink of despair, its central image – the Tibetan valley overlooked by the lamasery of Shangri-La – a haven of peace where a man might wait out the coming holocaust in perfect safety, miraculously preserved from ageing. The tragedy, brilliantly captured by Capra, is that the diplomat is too worldly to believe the fantasy – but Capra, unlike Hilton, was determined that he should be able to repent his wisdom. Although Capra's later films – especially *It's a Wonderful Life* – also move towards conclusive moments of triumph against the odds, they are quite different in asserting that fulfilment can only be found within the boundaries of a society riven by injustice and conflict; he too lost his faith in Shangri-La (as have we all). The 1972 musical version directed by Charles Jarrott is a dire travesty to which Peter Finch and John Gielgud add a fugitive touch of dignity.

THE MAN IN THE MIRROR

UK; dir. Maurice Elvey; starring Edward Everett Horton, Genevieve Tobin; scr. F. McGrew Willis & Hugh Mills; 82 min; b/w.

A deft comedy in which a timid man's reflection becomes tired of his inadequacy and emerges from the mirror to help himself sort out his affairs – a rare cinematic deployment of the *doppelgänger* motif.

SNOW WHITE AND THE SEVEN DWARFS

US; dir. David Hand et al; animated; voices of Adriana Caselotti, Harry Stockwell, Lucille La Verne; scr. Ted Sears et al; 82 min.

This was Disney's first feature-length cartoon, which seemed at the time to be a tremendous risk tackled with awesome boldness. The spectacular success of the eventual product was a triumphant vindication, but it was also a mixed blessing, in that the strictly sanitized, conspicuously cute and teasingly tuneful adaptation of the Grimm original established a formula that is still being slavishly copied to this day. Even if *Snow White* had not been the ground-breaker, it would still have strong claims to be reckoned the star of the subgenre, thanks to the dwarfs, the wicked queen, "Hi ho, hi ho, it's off to work we go" and the casual artistry of its animation. The movie deserves respect as a turning point in the history of the cinema, and admiration as a work of art in its own right, but the consequent Disneyfication of the entire culture of modern childhood is a prospect that the sensitive adult mind can only contemplate with gritted teeth and sinking heart.

TOPPER

US; dir. Norman Z. McLeod; starring Cary Grant, Constance Bennett, Roland Young, Billie Burke; 96 min; b/w.

Thorne Smith's All-American Ansteyan fantasies were sly celebrations of the liberating power of booze, but it was not until Prohibition had been repealed in 1933 that they were brought to the cinema. The attempts made by the ghosts of a hellraising couple (Grant and Bennett) to liven up the life of their erstwhile banker (Young) are necessarily less subversive than they were in the original, but the amiable slapstick worked well enough. *Topper Takes a Trip* (1939) was based on Smith's own sequel, but it suffered considerably from the fact that Grant – who had moved on to better things – was replaced by a dog; Topper's unruly wife (Burke) was saved nevertheless from a seductive conman. *Topper Returns* (1941), directed by Roy del Ruth, is pure cinematic froth in much the same vein as the comedy thriller *The Cat and the Canary* (the best version of which had been a great success in 1939) but with real ghosts; Young and Burke were supported by Joan Blondell and Carole Landis.

THE DESCENDANTS OF FAUST

Before and after Murnau's celebrated version of 1926 starring Emil Jannings, the story of Faust was remade repeatedly, often in updated versions which made further strategic changes to the classic literary formulations of Marlowe and Goethe. John Farrow's *Alias Nick Beal* (1949), starring Ray Milland and Thomas Mitchell, Americanized the plot more straightforwardly than the classic *All That Money Can Buy* (1941) and more adeptly than *Mister Frost* (1990), representing the corruption of politics by organized crime as a literally diabolical process. René Clair's *La Beauté du Diable* (1949) offered a more intriguing variant in which Mephistopheles exchanges places with the questing scholar and sets forth upon a glittering political career. In Claude Autant-Lara's *Marguerite de la Nuit* (1955), starring Yves Montand, the Faust-figure is an old man who trades his soul for youth. Michael Suman's 1964 *Faust*, starring Robert Towner, is carefully surrealized. Marlowe's play was straightforwardly filmed in 1967 by Nevill Coghill with Richard Burton in the lead and Elizabeth Taylor as Helen of Troy; this presumably inspired the eccentrically modernized *Hammersmith is Out* (1972), directed by Peter Ustinov, which also starred Burton and Taylor. *The Spanish Faustina* (1967) switched the sex of the central figure. Jan Svankmajer's 1994 *Faust* employed a mixture of live-action and animation.

1939 GULLIVER'S TRAVELS

US; animated; dir. Dave Fleischer; voices Lenny Ross, Jessica Dragonette; scr. Dan Gordon et al; 74 min.

Paramount producer Max Fleischer reacted quickly to the success of Disney's *Snow White and the Seven Dwarfs,* but his riposte was less successful in every respect. The songs were unmemorable and once the satire had been eliminated from Swift's account of Gulliver's adventure in Lilliput the plot was too thin; the substitution of a Romeo-and-Juliet subplot (with a happy ending, of course) did not help. The 1977 UK version, which mixed live action and animation, also tried unsuccessfully to make the episode into a musical romp. Fleischer's second animated feature, *Mr Bug Goes to Town* (1941; aka *Hoppity Goes to Town*), was even less successful than *Gulliver's Travels*; audiences were unable to work up any real indignation about the threat posed to a community of insects by urban developers.

THE WIZARD OF OZ

US; dir. Victor Fleming (and King Vidor); starring Judy Garland, Frank Morgan, Ray Bolger, Jack Haley, Bert Lahr, Margaret Hamilton; scr. Noel Langley, Florence Ryerson, Edgar Alan Woolf; 102 min.

A silent version of L. Frank Baum's novel had been made in 1925 by Larry Semon (who played the Scarecrow as well as producing and directing), starring Dorothy Dwan as Dorothy and Oliver Hardy – a year before teaming up with Stan Laurel – as the Tin Woodman. The production troubles afflicting the new version have become legendary, and one can only wonder what it would have been like had 20th Century Fox been willing to release Shirley Temple to take the lead, but nothing can take away the fact that this became the most famous of all fantasy movies. It is the only one to be so universally familiar that any reference to it is instantly recognizable in any company; it established such terms as "Somewhere Over the Rainbow", "Munchkin" and "Wicked Witch of the West" – as well

IT'S RUDE TO POINT: THE WICKED WITCH OF THE WEST DISPLAYS HER CONTEMPT FOR ETIQUETTE

as "Oz" itself – as key referents of popular culture, available for all manner of ironic modification. Judy Garland was so comprehensively defined by her role that the iconic significance of Dorothy's ruby slippers and the Yellow Brick Road had some curious extensions. Baum would not have approved of the way in which the movie turned his gentle consolatory fantasy into a nightmarish melodrama – whose subtext is that the imagination is a direly dangerous thing whose indulgence is to be resisted – but it made his posthumous fame absolutely secure. Oddly enough, its achievement was so quintessential that it had relatively little influence on other movies. Even its sequels, the 1974 animated feature *Journey Back to Oz* and *Return to Oz* (1985), make no attempt to capture its mercurial spirit. *The Wiz* (1978), directed by Sidney Lumet and starring Diana Ross and Michael Jackson – a Motown-inspired adaptation of an all-black hit Broadway musical – gently parodied the original's set-pieces.

1940 THE BLUE BIRD

US; dir. Walter Lang; starring Shirley Temple, Johnny Russell, Gale Sondergaard; scr. Ernest Pascal; 98 min.

After refusing to release Shirley Temple to star in *The Wizard of Oz* Fox decided to do their own supercharged children's fantasy, using the same monochrome-to-technicolor switch to signal the crossing of the boundary between reality and fantasy. Maurice Maeterlinck's symbolist allegory – which had established the Belgian writer's international celebrity virtually overnight when it premiered in New York in 1909 – had been filmed in the UK in 1910 and in Russia in 1911, and there had been a US silent version directed by Maurice Tourneur in 1918. Unlike Baum, Maeterlinck really had advised his readers that chasing the Blue Bird of Happiness into the manifold realms of fantasy is a waste of time – because the only true happiness is to be found in hearth and home – and the darker side of his morbid imagination helped to ensure that this dream-fantasy was even more deeply nightmare-tinged than its rival. The surviving version is considerably shorter than the original, which was cut for re-release when it struggled at the box office, but most of the lost footage belonged to the monochrome prologue. A second adaptation was attempted in 1976 by George Cukor, loudly hailed as the first ever US/Soviet co-production; the star-studded cast was headed by Elizabeth Taylor (who provided the allegorical symbols of both good and bad motherhood as well as Love and Light) and also featured Ava Gardner and Jane Fonda, but the story never began to come to life.

EARTHBOUND

US; dir. Irving Pichel; starring Warner Baxter, Lynn Bari, Andrea Leeds, Henry Wilcoxon; scr. John Howard Lawson and Samuel Engel; 67 min; b/w.

A remake of a 1920 silent film directed by T. Hayes, which set in place one of the most frequently repeated fantasy motifs. The spirit in question is earthbound because the man whose ghost it is has been framed for murder; it must do what it can to assist the unfortunate widow to bring the real murderer to justice.

FANTASIA

US; dir. Ben Sharpsteen et al; animated; narrator Deems Taylor; 135 min.

Having pulled off one coup, Disney went all the way with this bold attempt to enliven a classical concert (performed by the Philadelphia Orchestra, with Leopold Stokowski conducting) by providing cartoons to illustrate works by Bach, Tchaikovsky, Stravinsky, Beethoven, Schubert and others. The result is a masterpiece of sorts, in that no other work of art has ever wrought such a peculiar amalgam of high and low culture. The most famous sequence – deservedly – stars Mickey Mouse as Dukas's "The Sorcerer's Apprentice", but the mind-boggling spectacle of balletic hippos and alligators performing Ponchielli's "Dance of the Hours" is also unforgettable and Mussorgsky's "Night on the Bare Mountain" is embellished in suitably nightmarish fashion. This was the first movie to come equipped with stereophonic sound, and the use of multiplane cameras added new depth to the animation.

PINOCCHIO

US; dir. Ben Sharpsteen et al; animated; voices of Dickie Jones, Christian Rub, Cliff Edwards; scr. Ted Sears et al; 77 min.

Disney's other feature-length cartoon of 1940 was much more closely akin to *Snow White* and helped to turn the formula of the first film into a straitjacket for future endeavours. Carlo Collodi's cautionary tale about an animated puppet in quest of true humanity is not entirely stripped of its threatening *grotesquerie,* but the authentic voice of the Disney oracle is introduced as a counterweight, in the chirpy form of Jiminy Cricket. "Always Let Your Conscience Be Your Guide" and the Oscar-winning "When You Wish Upon a Star" became classic songs. Many critics prefer this movie to *Snow White* because the melodramatic quality of the more disturbing sequences gives it a sharper edge, and the quality of the animation work (supervised by Ben Sharpsteen) is superb. The belated "sequel", *Pinocchio and the Emperor of Night* (1987) – which owes nothing to Collodi or to Disney – is a tawdry ripoff.

THE THIEF OF BAGDAD

UK; dir. Michael Powell, Ludwig Berger and Tim Whelan; starring John Justin, Conrad Veidt, Sabu, Miles Malleson, Rex Ingram; scr. Malleson and Lajos Biro; 109 min.

This remake of the Douglas Fairbanks' silent classic was the most ambitious project ever attempted by Alexander Korda's London Films, and the boldest venture in the entire history of British

FOLLOWING THEIR DREAM: THE CHILDREN HAVE NO IDEA HOW TORTUOUS THEIR JOURNEY WILL BE

cinema. Sabu is excellent as Abu the thief, Ingram magnificent as the giant genie and Veidt wonderfully sinister as the villain. The set-pieces involving the liberation of the genie, the vast spiderweb and the flying horse still look superb, and the extensively mimicked script moves the action along at a breakneck pace. *The Thief of Bagdad* was twice remade, very feebly, once as a Steve Reeves "sword and sandal" adventure (1960) and once in a version intended for TV (1978) that was granted a theatrical release in the UK for old time's sake.

TURNABOUT

US; dir. Hal Roach; starring John Hubbard, Carole Landis, Adolphe Menjou, Mary Astor; scr. Mickell Novak, Berne Giler & John McLain; 83 min; b/w.

Thorne Smith's variant of *Vice Versa* was the first to bite the bullet and allow a married couple to switch. Even Smith had been forced to be coy in exploring the idea, and the US cinema's Production Code put restrictive limits on the opportunities for naughtiness.

LIVING ON CREDIT: THE DEVIL'S ACCOUNT HAS YET TO BE SETTLED IN *ALL THAT MONEY CAN BUY*

1941 ALL THAT MONEY CAN BUY

US; dir William Dieterle; starring Walter Huston, Edward Arnold, James Craig, Anne Shirley; scr. Dan Totheroh; 106 min; b/w; aka The Devil and Daniel Webster, Daniel and the Devil, Here is a Man.

A magnificent adaptation of Stephen Vincent Benet's "The Devil and Daniel Webster", a classic item of Americana in which the legendary lawyer (Arnold) takes on Mr Scratch (Huston) to appeal against the damnation of a desperate farmer who has been seduced into selling his soul for seven years' good luck. Scratch rigs the jury by summoning the greatest villains in American history to serve as the farmer's peers, but Webster's spirited appeal to their patriotism overrides the bitter legacy of their past sins. The cinematography and state-of-the-art special effects helped to make the film remarkable in every respect; none of the later works following in its footsteps came close to matching it. An 85-minute version re-released in 1952 is more likely to be encountered on TV than the original, but the full version was restored for video and laser-disc release.

DUMBO

US; dir. Ben Sharpsteen; animated; voices of Sterling Holloway, Edward Brophy, Verna Felton; scr. Joe Grant & Dick Huemer; 64 min.

The long decline of Disney began here, with this excessively cute "Ugly Duckling" tale of the baby elephant whose enormous ears prove to be capable of doubling up as wings. The slide was still so gradual as to be only just perceptible when *Bambi* (1942) carried the message forward without the support of the slapstick and the songs; no one could have guessed then how much steeper it would eventually become. A clever dream sequence and the crows' chorus could not compensate for the weak main narrative.

HERE COMES MR JORDAN

US; dir. Alexander Hall; starring Robert Montgomery, Evelyn Keyes, Claude Rains, Edward Everett Horton; scr. Sidney Buchman & Seton I. Miller; 93 min; b/w.

A movie version of *Heaven Can Wait*, in which a saxophone-playing prizefighter collected before his appointed time by an over-zealous agent of Heaven cannot be returned to his own cremated body. He finds the proffered replacement less than satisfactory, but adapts to his new circumstances with a gritty cheerfulness that came to seem all the more admirable when the USA was forced into full participation in World War II. The compassionately dignified Mr Jordan (Rains) and the bumbling agent (Horton) provided a key model of Heavenly bureaucracy for later movie-makers, setting important precedents for the sub-genre – which never tried to be serious but must have played a part in encouraging so many contemporary Americans to believe in the reality of angels. The movie was remade in 1978 as *Heaven Can Wait*, with a football player and a car accident substituted for the boxer and plane crash. The remake starred Warren Beatty, Julie Christie and Dyan Cannon, with James Mason as Mr. Jordan. Beatty – who was credited as co-director and co-writer – was surprisingly effective, but the new version inevitably lacked the freshness and timeliness of the original.

THE SHADOW OF A DREAM: VERONICA LAKE'S SECRET IS SUBTLY LET OUT IN *I MARRIED A WITCH*

1942 I MARRIED A WITCH

US; dir. René Clair; starring Veronica Lake, Fredric March, Cecil Kellaway, Robert Benchley, Susan Hayward; scr. Robert Pirosh, Marc Connelly & Dalton Trumbo; 82 min; b/w.

When Thorne Smith died he left behind a fragment of a comedy of magical liberation. The novel developed from it by Norman Matson, *The Passionate Witch,* adopted a censorious moral viewpoint flatly opposed to Smith's, but this film restored something of the original author's anarchic spirit. The lovely witch is here deflected by love from the vengeful mission on which she is sent by her malevolent father (Kellaway). The pattern was further softened by the derivative TV series *Bewitched*. The musical *I Married an Angel* (1942) directed by W. S. van Dyke, released in the same year as *I Married a Witch*, was much tamer; it was the last film in which Nelson Eddy and Jeanette MacDonald appeared together.

THE JUNGLE BOOK

UK; dir. Zoltan Korda and Andre de Toth; starring Sabu, Joseph Calleia; scr. Laurence Stallings; 109 min.

The last of the four films Sabu made for London Films cast him as Rudyard Kipling's Mowgli. He was ready-made for the part and played it with far more enthusiasm than he brought to any of his subsequent American ventures, but the difficulties of supplying him with a believable cast of animal tutors proved insuperable. The animated version of the stories made by Disney in 1967 wisely ignored the slender story-lines and concentrated on the "Bare Necessities" – the didactic elements – of the basic situation, dramatized in songs and lively "dance routines"; the actors' voices are also used to good effect in characterizing the leading players. The 1994 *Rudyard Kipling's Jungle Book*, directed by Stephen Sommers, added an inappropriately action-loaded plot.

THE REMARKABLE ANDREW

US; dir. Stuart Heisler; starring William Holden, Ellen Drew; scr. Dalton Trumbo; 80 min; b/w.

One of many comedies in which an innocent man in difficulties is "de-framed" by a helpful phantom – in this case the ghost of President Andrew Jackson, who is sympathetic to the troubled hero's crusade against crooked politicians. It acquired additional interest when Trumbo – who went on to script *A Guy Named Joe* – became one of the "Hollywood Ten" blacklisted during the witch-hunt which made Joseph McCarthy a star of sorts. Where was Andrew Jackson then?

LES VISITEURS DU SOIR

(THE DEVIL'S ENVOYS)

France; dir. Marcel Carne; starring Arletty, Alain Cuny, Jules Bery, Marie Dae; scr. Jacques Prevert and Pierre Laroche; 110 min; b/w.

The Devil sends his emissaries to prepare two medieval lovers for damnation, but the lovers resist all the misfortunes heaped upon them. The frustrated demons turn the luckless pair to stone, but their stout hearts continue to beat regardless. The film was made while France was under occupation, with extraordinary care devoted to the dangerously sensitive implications of the allegory. Someone surely ought to have arranged a screening for Hitler and Goebbels to help them while away the long hours they spent in their bunker in the early months of 1945.

... AND THEN I WOKE UP

The most prolific of all Méliès's fantasy devices was the dream fantasy. In *The Astronomer's Dream* (1898) an observatory is visited by a Moon which turns into a fairy; his other hallucinatory fantasies include *The Temptation of Saint Anthony* (1898), *Christmas Dream* (1900), *The Melomaniac* (1903), *The Dream of a Clockmaker* (1904), *Rip van Winkle's Dream* (1905), *Dream of an Opium Fiend* (1908), *Pharmaceutical Hallucinations* (1908) and *Baron Munchausen's Dream* (1908). Other early films of a similar stripe include *Dream of a Rarebit Fiend* (1906) by Edwin S. Porter. The cop-out ending "...and then I woke up" had already fallen out of favour in novels but hallucinatory fantasy retained some significance as a sub-genre of cinematic fantasy, partly because it was regularly employed in such classic adaptations as the many versions of *Alice in Wonderland*; its cinematic legitimacy was renewed by the 1939 version of *The Wizard of Oz*. It was frequently used to "justify" timeslip stories, as in the Eddie Cantor musical *Roman Scandals* (1933), *Dubarry was a Lady* (1943) and *Lilacs in the Spring* (1954). Other notable examples include the identity-exchange fantasy *Turn Back the Clock* (1933), the anti-TV satire *Meet Mr Lucifer* (1953), the Freudian fantasy *Valerie and Her Week of Wonders* (1970) and the quirky supernatural love story *Somewhere Tomorrow* (1983). Serious literary dream-fantasies have not, however, been well-served by cinematic adaptations: Wocjciech Has's *The Saragossa Manuscript* (1965) does no favours to Jan Potocki's original, the movies derived from *The Neverending Story* undermine the didactic import of Michael Ende's fable and *Paperhouse* (1988) utterly ruins Catherine Storr's sensitive *Marianne Dreams*.

1943 THE ADVENTURES OF BARON MUNCHAUSEN

Germany; dir. Josef von Baky; starring Hans Albers, Wilhelm Bendow; scr. "Berthold Burger" (Erich Kästner); 103 min.

This lavish version of the classic tall tales first put about by Rudolph Erich Raspe was commissioned by Joseph Goebbels, purely as an entertainment (presumably he never imagined that anyone might be so foolish as to see the aggressively boorish and monstrously ridiculous compulsive liar as a symbol of the Reich). Goebbels entrusted the execution of this eccentric coup to the famous author of *Emil and the Detectives*, whose work had been banned since 1933; Kästner dutifully complied, but the ungrateful Führer re-imposed the ban immediately afterwards. Another version of the stories, in which the old reprobate turned up on the moon, was made in Czechoslovakia as *Baron Prasil* in 1962; director Karl Zeman made the most of a moderate budget by employing cartoonish sets whose artwork was based on illustrations by Gustave Doré. A joint British/German effort recovering the original title was made in 1989 by Terry Gilliam, starring John Neville as the Baron; it outclassed the other two, easily qualifying as one of the quirkiest films ever made.

A GUY NAMED JOE

US; dir. Victor Fleming; starring Spencer Tracy, Irene Dunne, Ward Bond, Van Johnson, Lionel Barrymore; scr. Dalton Trumbo; 120 min; b/w.

This was the best of the wartime moral rearmament movies cloned from *Here Comes Mr Jordan*. An Army Air Corps pilot killed in combat is allowed to return briefly to Earth in order to complete a thoroughly altruistic romantic quest. Trumbo's script borrowed something of the heartfelt spirit of Robert Nathan's classic fantasy romances, while Tracy struck exactly the right note of heroic innocence. Very few Hollywood movies celebrate the virtues of generosity and humility so openly, because they are slightly subversive of the acquisitive American Dream – as evidenced by the fact that the writer of this one was hounded out as a dirty commie once the war was over. Steven Spielberg's decision to remake it as *Always* in 1989 might, therefore, have been slightly brave.

HEAVEN CAN WAIT

US; dir. Ernst Lubitsch; starring Don Ameche, Gene Tierney, Laird Cregar, Charles Coburn; scr. Samson Raphaelson; 112 min.

A movie version of a play by Laszlo Bus-Fekete. The drama of a long-enduring marriage is set in a fantasy frame in which the philandering but well-meaning husband is given a generous hearing by the Devil, thus overlaying a stylish exercise in nostalgia with a piquant icing of wit and moral generosity.

1944 THE CANTERVILLE GHOST

US; dir. Jules Dassin; starring Charles Laughton, Margaret O'Brien, Robert Young; scr. Edwin Blum; 95 min; b/w.

A misconceived attempt to turn Oscar Wilde's classic sentimental comedy into a propaganda piece, with Laughton's unhappy phantom learning to be more tolerant of the American soldiers billeted at Canterville Hall. Having lost the charm and point of the original, it attempts to compensate with silly slapstick and ends up a complete mess. The contemporary French film *Sylvie et la Fantôme* (1944; aka *Sylvia and the Phantom*) directed by Claude Autant-Lara did a much better job of adapting Arthur Adam's highly derivative play, which emphasized the sentimental aspects of the relationship between its heroine and a regretful ghost.

IT HAPPENED TOMORROW

US; dir. René Clair; starring Dick Powell, Linda Darnell, Jack Oakie; scr. Clair and Dudley Nichols; 84 min; b/w.

A reporter obtains tantalizing glimpses of tomorrow's newspaper, but the wonderland of opportunity thus opened up turns distinctly sour when he obtains news of his own imminent demise. A nice balance of comedy and drama helps to set up a suitably hectic climax.

HELL HATH NO FURY: REX HARRISON FAILS TO PLACATE THE NOT-SO-*BLITHE SPIRIT* OF HIS DEAD WIFE

1945

BLITHE SPIRIT

UK; dir. David Lean; starring Rex Harrison, Kay Hammond, Constance Cummings, Margaret Rutherford; 96 min.

Noel Coward wrote the stage version of *Blithe Spirit* to provide a little light relief from the rigours of morale-building war-work and Lean filmed it in order that it might have the same effect on its audience, adding an extra twist to soften the underlying cynicism of the original's flippant misogyny. Margaret Rutherford is magnificent as the medium Madame Arcati.

THE ENCHANTED COTTAGE

US; dir. John Cromwell; starring Dorothy McGuire, Robert Young; 92 min; b/w.

An earnestly sentimental adaptation of a slightly unsettling play by Arthur Pinero, in which the eponymous dwelling allows a disfigured man and a plain woman to perceive one another as beautiful.

THE HORN BLOW AT MIDNIGHT

US; dir. Raoul Walsh; starring Jack Benny, Alexis Smith; scr. Sam Hellman and James V. Kern; 80 min; b/w.

Jack Benny plays the incompetent angel sent to Earth to sound the Last Trump, whose distraction from his appointed task gives humankind a second lease of life. Benny got a lot of mileage out of the film, but not until afterwards, when he incorporated sarcastic references to its intrinsic silliness into his stand-up routines.

THE PICTURE OF DORIAN GRAY

US; dir. & scr. Albert Lewin; starring Hurd Hatfield, George Sanders, Donna Reed; 115 min; b/w.

An earnestly mannered adaptation of Oscar Wilde's classic moralistic fantasy, which soft-pedals the decadent aspects of Dorian's ill-fated attempt to live his life according to the doctrine of art for art's sake, relishing every new sensation. Hatfield was so comprehensively typecast by the central role that the rest of his career was eclipsed.

WHERE DO WE GO FROM HERE?

US; dir. Gregory Ratoff; starring Fred MacMurray, June Haver, Joan Leslie; scr. Morrie Ryskind; 77 min.

A propaganda piece in which a loyal American (MacMurray) deemed unfit for military service has only one wish to ask of the genie of Aladdin's lamp. Unfortunately, the genie's magic timepiece is out of kilter, so he winds up in George Washington's army and trips through several absurdly reconfigured highlights of American history – continually breaking out into comic song – before getting his heart's desire. In the mean time, he learns that the kind of girl who is likely to remain loyal to an absent soldier is infinitely preferable to a flirt who makes eyes at everyone available.

ANDRÉ PAULVÉ
PRÉSENTE
UN FILM DE
Jean Cocteau
JEAN MARAIS
JOSETTE DAY
dans
la BELLE et la BÊTE
HISTOIRE, PAROLES, MISE EN SCÈNE DE JEAN COCTEAU D'APRÈS LE CONTE DE MADAME LEPRINCE DE BEAUMONT
illustré par
CHRISTIAN BÉRARD
avec
MILA PARELY, NANE GERMON, MICHEL AUCLAIR et MARCEL ANDRÉ
CONSEILLER TECHNIQUE: R. CLÉMENT
MUSIQUE DE GEORGES AURIC
DIRECT. DE PRODUCT. EMILE DARBON
UNE SUPERPRODUCTION ANDRÉ PAULVÉ

MORE THAN JUST A PRETTY FACE: BEAUTY ENRAPTURED BY THE BEAST IN MAN

1946 ANGEL ON MY SHOULDER

US; dir. Archie Mayo; starring Paul Muni, Claude Rains, Anne Baxter; scr. Harry Segall; 101 min; b/w.

Following the success of *Here Comes Mr Jordan,* Harry Segall produced this sharper variant on the theme, in which the Devil offers a dead gangster a second chance at life if he will take over the career of a crusading judge. The outcome is, of course, not what either of them intended. The casting of Rains had the interesting effect of making it seem that the agencies of Heaven and Hell were virtually interchangeable within the afterlife's unified bureaucracy. It was remade as a TV movie in 1980.

LA BELLE ET LA BETE

(BEAUTY AND THE BEAST)

France; dir. and scr. Jean Cocteau; staring Jean Marais, Josette Day, Mila Parly, Marcel Andre; 96 min; b/w.

Cocteau had earlier worked with Serge de Poigny on *Le Baron Fantôme* (1943), where he had served as the narrator of a much more downbeat folk-tale, and had tackled the legend of Tristan and Iseult in *L'Eternal retour* (1943; aka *Love Eternal*). That experience laid the groundwork for this beautiful and sensitive film, which converts the famous folk-tale into a surreal post-Freudian psychodrama. Unfortunately, the excellent example had little effect on subsequent live-action adaptations of folk-tales. Jacques Demy's *Peau d'Ane* (1970; aka *The Magic Donkey*), had the benefit of a fine cast – led by Catherine Deneuve and Jean Marais – but the tale of a donkey whose dung turns to gold did not translate well into a merry musical. Subsequent versions of "Cinderella", including *The Glass Slipper* (1954) and Bryan Forbes's musical *The Slipper and the Rose* (1976), starring Richard Chamberlain and Gemma Craven, were equally tedious. Cocteau did, however, help to pave the way for such allegorical reconstructions of folkloristic materials as *The Company of Wolves* (1984).

IT'S A WONDERFUL LIFE

US; dir. Frank Capra; starring James Stewart, Henry Travers, Donna Reed, Lionel Barrymore, Thomas Mitchell; scr. Frances Goodrich, Albert Hackett and Capra; 129 min; b/w.

The war was over, but moral rearmament fantasies like *A Guy Named Joe* had made a mark which Capra was ambitious to extend to a much wider stage, taking in the lingering after-effects of the Depression and the continuing decay of small-town America. Although it was nominated for four Oscars, including best picture, contemporary audiences were unimpressed by this account of James Stewart's miraculous rescue from terminal frustration. Perhaps Clarence the guardian angel (Travers) was too whimsical, or perhaps the film built up too harrowing a catalogue of thwarted ambition before the final turnaround. Its reputation grew enormously, however, as it came to be considered definitive of Capra's unique artistry and crusading zeal. Stewart's heart-rending performance is less subtle than his other great roles, but remains a masterpiece nevertheless. Recent critics have attacked the tacit conservatism of the film's "Be content with what you have" message, just as they have attacked the use of "There's no place like home" as a mantra in *The Wizard of Oz*, but the movie's insistent plea is concerned with the subtle rewards of duty, not the folly of ambition. It spawned several clones, including the TV movie *It Happened One Christmas* (1977), *One Magic Christmas* (1985) and *Mr Destiny* (1990).

A MATTER OF LIFE AND DEATH

UK; dir. and scr. Michael Powell and Emeric Pressburger; starring David Niven, Roger Livesey, Kim Hunter, Marius Goring, Raymond Massey; 104 min; aka Stairway to Heaven.

Britain's contribution to the sub-genre of wartime moral rearmament fantasies arrived way too late for VE-Day, but it provided a neat summary of the propagandist intention of such movies and incorporated a distinctively British dignity. Niven is excellent as the pilot who cannot accept that he has been killed; Livesey plays the doctor who becomes his defence lawyer in a Heavenly trial whose prosecuting attorney is a virulently anti-British American lawyer (Massey). This sequence must have been inspired by *All That Money Can Buy*, and the whole enterprise owes something to *Outward Bound*, but Powell and Pressburger ingeniously adapted the messages of the earlier films to their own ends.

STAIRWAY TO HEAVEN: THE EFFECT IS NOW FAMILIAR BUT IT WAS SPECTACULAR IN ITS DAY

SONG OF THE SOUTH

US; dir. Harve Foster and Wilfred Jackson; starring James Baskett, Bobby Driscoll, Ruth Warrick; scr. Dalton Raymond; 94 min.

The naturalistic live-action frame takes up far too much of this dramatization of Joel Chandler Harris's tales of Uncle Remus; Brer Rabbit is confined to animated sequences lasting just over half an hour in total. Baskett won an Oscar, though – and so did "Zip-a-Dee-Do-Dah", whose catchiness allowed it to transcend its origin.

1947 THE BISHOP'S WIFE

US; dir. Henry Koster; starring Cary Grant, Loretta Young, David Niven, Monty Woolley; scr. Robert E. Sherwood and Leonardo Bercovici; 108 min; b/w.

This was the first attempt to translate Robert Nathan's unique brand of sentimental fantasy to the screen, wisely using a story which did not require the kind of emotional censorship that was to ruin the following year's *Portrait of Jennie*. An angel (Grant) is distracted from his mission to aid an out-of-touch clergyman by the lucky man's lovely wife (Young). The movie has depth, although it could not match the delicate pathos or the scrupulous subversiveness of the original. It was remade in 1996 as *The Preacher's Wife*, directed by Penny Marshall, starring Denzel Washington as the angel and Whitney Houston as the wife of a pastor; the casting of the new version had more to do with the desire to import some rousing gospel music than any commentary on racial politics.

SURREAL CINEMA

The most famous surrealist film is *Un Chien Andalou* (1928) directed by Luis Buñuel and co-scripted by Salvador Dali, but Man Ray had made *La retour à la raison* in 1923 and René Clair had followed it with *Entr'acte and Le voyage imaginaire* in 1924. Buñuel and Dali carried the cause forward in the more sustained and overtly satirical *L'Age d'Or* (1930), and Buñuel was to retain a surreal element in much of his later work, most notably *El Angel Exterminador* (1962; aka *The Exterminating Angel*) and *The Discreet Charm of the Bourgeoisie* (1972). Later French film-makers profoundly influenced by surrealism include Jean Cocteau, whose *Le sang d'un Poète* (19 3) had been another pioneering exercise, and Alain Resnais, whose *L'Année dernière à Marienbad* (1961; aka *Last Year at Marienbad*) was scripted by Alain Robbe-Grillet, the inventor of the *nouveau roman* – which insisted upon the immutable objectivity of the world and the hopelessness of attempts to "humanize" it. Cocteau's *La Belle et le Bête* and *Orphée* are the finest of all surrealist films. The first significant American surrealistic film was Hans Richter's painstakingly didactic *Dreams that Money Can Buy* (1946), but resonant echoes of the movement can be found in the work of such American film-makers as Kenneth Anger and Ed Emshwiller and the Australian Susan Dermody.

DOWN TO EARTH

US; dir. Alexander Hall; starring Rita Hayworth, Larry Parks, Roland Culver, Edward Everett Horton; scr. Edwin Blum & Don Hartman; 101 min.

A trivial sequel to *Here Comes Mr Jordan*, with Horton reprising his part as an incompetent heavenly messenger. The muse of dance, Terpsichore, descends to the mortal plane to help a troubled Broadway producer. He really needed Busby Berkeley. *Xanadu* (1980), directed by Robert Greenwald and starring Gene Kelly, is a bad carbon-copy in which Terpsichore – played by Olivia Newton-John – gets involved with roller-derby disco.

THE GHOST AND MRS MUIR

US; dir. Joseph L. Mankiewicz; starring Gene Tierney, Rex Harrison, George Sanders; scr. Philip Dunne; 104 min; b/w.

A deft and effective adaptation of Josephine Leslie's novel (originally published under the pseudonym R. A. Dick) about a widow who refuses to be frightened away from her dream cottage by the ghost of an old sea captain, eventually seducing his consent to her tenancy.

LES JEUX SONT FAITS
(THE CHIPS ARE DOWN)

France; dir. Jean Delannoy; starring Marcel Pagliero; scr. Jean-Paul Sartre; 91 min; b/w.

Two lost souls meet in Purgatory and fall in love. This entitles them to a second chance at life, which they fritter away. "If Cocteau can do it", Sartre must have thought, "why can't I? I can lighten up." Unfortunately, substituting Purgatory for Hell in the adage "Hell is other people" isn't what most people would call lightening up.

MIRACLE ON 34TH STREET

US; dir. and scr. George Seaton; starring Edmund Gwenn, Maureen O'Hara, Natalie Wood; 94 min; b/w.

An old man (Gwenn) hired as a late substitute for a department store Santa Claus befriends a sceptical little girl (Wood), but his insistent claim that he is the one and only Kris Kringle, the *actual* Father Christmas, leads to his being committed to Bellevue psychiatric hospital. His battle against incarceration takes him to court, where he proves his claim, at least to the satisfaction of the girl whose sense of wonder he has restored. The movie jerked the tears with such miraculous efficiency that the film became a modern American myth. It was remade for TV in 1973 and for the cinema in 1994; the latter version was directed by Les Mayfield and starred a woefully unconvincing Richard Attenborough. Only a curmudgeon would point out that the film is neither an authentic fantasy nor something deserving of moral approval. The one good thing to come out of its enshrinement as *the* Christmas movie is that it discouraged

Yes Virginia, there *is* a Santa Claus: the young Natalie Wood is doubtful, and who can blame her?

MIRANDA

UK; dir. Ken Annakin; starring Glynis Johns, Griffith Jones, Googie Withers, Margaret Rutherford; scr. Peter Blackmore; 80 min; b/w.

Peter Blackmore got a lot of mileage out of his stage-play, following this movie adaptation with a TV version. The eponymous heroine (Johns) is a mermaid fished up by a holidaymaker in Cornwall, who causes complications typical of those stage farces whose spirit was eventually to be summed up in the nostalgic *No Sex, Please, We're British*. Johns and Rutherford returned to their roles in a sequel, *Mad About Men* (1954), directed by Ralph Thomas and scripted by Blackmore, but it was a poor copy. The 1946 novel from which Blackmore may well have lifted his plot, *Mr Peabody and the Mermaid* by Guy and Constance Jones, was also filmed in 1948; it was directed by Irving Pichel and starred William Powell and Ann Blyth. The Americans did it on a more lavish scale; whereas Miranda was confined to a bathtub, Peabody's Caribbean captive got a whole swimming pool.

would-be competitors from devising further atrocities, at least until the days of *Santa Claus: The Movie* (1985), in which a superheroic Santa Claus embarks upon a mission to rescue an elf entrapped by a demonic toymaker, and *The Santa Clause* (1994), in which an advertising man who volunteers to fill in temporarily for the injured Santa finds himself stuck with the job.

1948 THE BOY WITH GREEN HAIR

US; dir. Joseph Losey; starring Dean Stockwell, Pat O'Brien, Robert Ryan; scr. Ben Barzman and Alfred Lewis Levitt; 82 min.

Losey's first film is a curious anti-war allegory in which a boy whose hair turns green after he hears of his parents' death in an air raid is put on public display as a symbol of the need for peace. It is difficult to believe that something as innocent and well-meaning as this could be held against a man in the days of the McCarthy witch-hunt, but Losey would probably have had to leave America anyway.

THE LUCK OF THE IRISH

US; dir. Henry Koster; starring Tyrone Power, Anne Baxter, Cecil Kellaway; scr. Philip Dunne; 99 min.

A romantic comedy in which a cynical reporter (Power) is lucky enough to meet up with a leprechaun (Kellaway), but is irritated by the little man's determination to set him on the right moral track.

ONE TOUCH OF VENUS

US; dir. William A. Seiter; starring Ava Gardner, Robert Walker, Eve Arden; Dick Haymes; scr. Harry Kurnitz and Frank Tashlin; 81 min; b/w.

Although it is ultimately based on F. Anstey's comedy *The Tinted Venus*, the immediate source of this movie was a saucy Broadway play by the famous humourists S. J. Perelman and Ogden Nash. It had to be toned down considerably, and seems staid even when compared with the 1935 movie of Thorne Smith's riotous variation on the same theme, *The Night Life of the Gods*. Ava Gardner plays the animated goddess in a manner which verges on the soppy.

VICE VERSA

UK; dir. and scr. Peter Ustinov; starring Roger Livesey, Anthony Newley, Kay Walsh, James Robertson Justice; 111 min; b/w.

A scrupulously faithful version of F. Anstey's classic, in which a Victorian schoolboy and his pompous father are allowed to exchange social situations by a wish-granting talisman, so that both can learn the folly of envy. By 1948, of course, it had become a period piece which required such sophisticated understanding that it was not of much interest to the young – a circumstance which drastically limited its appeal. The American "remake" of 1988 was updated and the plot was augmented by two comic villains of a kind never glimpsed outside calculatedly silly movies, but it actually worked quite well thanks to spirited performances by Judge Reinhold and Fred Savage.

MIRROR, MIRROR ON THE WALL: JEAN MARAIS PRACTISES THE TANGO ALONE.

1949 ORPHEE (ORPHEUS)

France; dir. and scr. Jean Cocteau; starring Jean Marais, Maria Casares, Marie Dae; 112 min; b/w.

Cocteau's striking reconfiguration of the legend makes Orpheus a modern poet, who descends into a vividly surreal underworld in search of his dead love, aided by a female personification of Death. The languorous original was cut to 95 minutes for US release, but retained its essential strangeness and intensely personal quality. The personal element was heavily emphasized when Cocteau chose to title his subsequent gnomic extravaganza of self-exploration *Le Testament d'Orphée* (1959), using most of the same actors again. Another significant reconfiguration is the musical *Orfeu Negro* (1958; aka *Black Orpheus*), directed by Marcel Camus and scripted by Vinitius de Moraes; set against the backcloth of the Rio carnival, it moves from a gaudily phantasmagoric real world to a surreally sombre Underworld, where the decision facing the hero is brutally uncompromising.

PORTRAIT OF JENNIE

US; dir. William Dieterle; starring Jennifer Jones, Joseph Cotten, Ethel Barrymore, Lillian Gish; scr. Paul Osborne, Peter Berneis & Leonardo Bercovici; 86 min; b/w.

Robert Nathan's original novel is a heartfelt exercise in romanticized paedophilia whose tragic ending – which brings a sequence of timeslips to a tragic culmination – is a harrowing concession of the impossibility as well as the immorality of the erotic dream. The movie can hardly be blamed for de-emphasizing the paedophilic element of the story, but the final scene is still a betrayal.

1950 CINDERELLA

US; dir. Wilfred Jackson et al; animated; voices of Ilene Woods, William Phipps, Eleanor Audley, Rhoda Williams; scr.Bill Peet et al; 75 min.

Disney made a tentative return to animated features with *The Adventures of Ichabod and Mr Toad* (1949), which had uncomfortably juxtaposed two half-length tales by Washington Irving and Kenneth Grahame, but this version of *Cinderella* – which had been filmed several times between Meliès's pioneering version and Ludwig Berger's version of 1923 but had been neglected for some while – was a calculated attempt to recapture the success of *Snow White and the Seven Dwarfs*, with the customary carbon copy accoutrements: the supporting cast of talking animals, the tinkling tunes and the winsomely feminine heroine.

HARVEY

US; dir. Henry Koster; starring James Stewart, Josephine Hull; scr. Mary Chase and Oscar Brodney; 104 min; b/w.

An earnest adaptation of Chase's play, which suggests that fantasies should be judged by the effect they have on the fantasizers, not their inherent plausibility. If only it were that simple! Although the giant invisible rabbit does open and shut a few doors, the film belongs to the marginal sub-genre of delusional fantasy; it was remade for TV in 1972.

FRANCIS

US; dir. Arthur Lubin; starring Donald O'Connor, Patricia Medina; scr. David Stern; 90 min; b/w.

Although F. Anstey did write "The Talking Horse", this Ansteyan farce about an army private and his talking mule is far more reminiscent of the work of his downmarket imitator W. A. Darlington. Just as Darlington outsold his model, so Stern outdid such rivals as Thorne Smith, extrapolating this cinematic adaptation of his novel through six equally stupid and equally successful sequels: *Francis Goes to the Races* (1951); *Francis Goes to West Point* (1952); *Francis Covers Big Town* (1953); *Francis Joins the WACS* (1954); *Francis in the Navy* (1955); and *Francis in the Haunted House* (1956, with Mickey Rooney replacing Donald O'Connor). When Francis had been laid to rest, TV invented Mister Ed.

MR DRAKE'S DUCK

UK; dir. and scr. Val Guest; starring Douglas Fairbanks Jr, Yolande Donlan; 85 min; b/w.

An adaptation of a successful radio play by Ian Messiter which updated the famous folk-tale about the goose that laid golden eggs into a tale of bureaucratic bumbling following the discovery of a duck that lays uranium eggs. Disney's *The Million Dollar Duck* (1971) was a less effective attempt to work the same trick.

SCRIPTURAL FANTASIES

Many Biblical epics of the 1920s and 1930s – most notably Cecil B. de Mille's 1923 version of *The Ten Commandments* and Watson and Webber's *Lot in Sodom* (1934) – included some spectacularly fantastic episodes, but the fact that these were supported by Holy Writ meant that they were not being employed as fantasy. *Samson and Delilah* (1949) launched a new wave of technicolor Biblical epics which included De Mille's remake of *The Ten Commandments* (1956), starring Charlton Heston. The supernatural element was muted in such movies as *Salome* (1953) and *The Story of Ruth* (1960) but had to be given freer rein in Robert Aldrich's *Sodom and Gomorrah* (1963) and John Huston's *The Bible–In The Beginning* (1966). The same wave of fashionability produced the all-star abomination *The Story of Mankind* (1957), in which a Heavenly Tribunal hears the case for abandoning the species to self-annihilation. The scriptures of other religions inevitably seem to Western audiences to be fantasies – examples include *The Light of Asia* (1925), *Shakuntala* (1943) and *The Mahabharata* (1989) – but it would be unreasonable to treat them as such.

1951 ANGELS IN THE OUTFIELD

US; dir. Clarence Brown; starring Paul Douglas, Keenan Wynn, Janet Leigh; scr. Dorothy Kingsley and George Wells; 99 min; b/w.

It is difficult for non-Americans to believe that angels could not be dispatched on worthier missions than helping bad baseball teams to win a few games, but baseball is a key element of American culture and the thriving sub-genre of baseball fantasies continually generates symbol-saturated allegories of the American dream. One can understand the temptation which led Disney to remake it more elaborately – with angels you could actually *see* – in 1994. The new version was directed by William Dear and starred Tony Danza, Danny Glover, Ben Johnson and Christopher Lloyd.

PANDORA AND THE FLYING DUTCHMAN

UK; dir. and scr. Albert Lewin; starring James Mason, Ava Gardner, Nigel Patrick; 123 min.

An emotionally unawakened American woman falls in love with a handsome but mysterious seaman. He turns out to be the legendary accursed wanderer, now allowed occasional shore leave in order that he might seek redemption by self-sacrificing love. The film is rather portentous, but remains one of the better cinematic attempts at supernatural romance. The legend of the Flying Dutchman was updated rather differently in John Frankenheimer's weak comedy-drama *The Extraordinary Seaman* (1969) starring David Niven, Faye Dunaway and Mickey Rooney.

1952 IT GROWS ON TREES

US; dir. Arthur Lubin; starring Irene Dunne, Dean Jagger; 84 min; scr. Leonard Praskins & Barney Slater; b/w.

A cautionary fable which expands a common wish-fulfilment fantasy, following the misadventures of a housewife who discovers that a tree in her backyard is producing dollar bills .

1953 THE FIVE THOUSAND FINGERS OF DOCTOR T

US; dir. Roy Rowland; starring Hans Conried, Tommy Rettig; scr. Theodore Geisel and Alan Scott; 88 min.

As "Dr Seuss", Geisel became one of the most successful American writers for children, partly because his insistently catchy rhymes on bizarre themes aided verbal development. His work forms the basis of some very effective animated shorts, including a 1966 version of *How the Grinch Stole Christmas* featuring the voice of Boris Karloff, but this visionary fantasy – in which a boy who hates his piano lessons imagines his stern teacher's ideal world – was far more ambitious. The vivid strangeness of Dr T's instrument-filled castle is far more impressive than the silly songs.

PETER PAN

US; dir. Hamilton Luske et al; animated; voices Bobbie Driscoll, Kathryn Beaumont, Hans Conried; scr. Ted Sears et al; 76 min.

Like *Cinderella*, this free adaptation of J. M. Barrie's play – supervised by Ben Sharpsteen – was solid Disney mid-period work, lacking the brilliance and magnificence of the best early productions, but retaining a certain flair and zest that no one else had yet contrived to duplicate. Captain Hook's encounters with his nemesis, the ticking crocodile, provide the most memorable moments. The play had been more faithfully filmed in 1924, in a silent version directed by Herbert Brenon, starring Betty Bronson as Peter and Ernest Torrence as Hook.

UGETSU MONOGATARI

Japan; dir. Kenji Mizoguchi; starring Masayuki Mori, Machiko Kyo, Sakae Ozawa; scr. Matsutaro Kawaguchi; 94 min; b/w; aka Ugetsu.

A cleverly wrought adaptation of a 17th-century collection of traditional tales by Akinara Ueda, in which two villagers set off to find their fortunes in a time of civil war, one in the big city and the other as a Samurai warrior. The "magic realism" mix of comedy, drama and the supernatural impressed the judges at the Venice Festival, where it repeated the success of *Rashomon* (1951).

1954 BRIGADOON

US; dir. Vincente Minnelli; starring Gene Kelly, Cyd Charisse, Van Johnson; scr. Alan Jay Lerner; 108 min.

An adaptation of Lerner and Frederick Loewe's Broadway hit, a musical romance in which two American tourists stumble into a ghostly village that is accessible to the outside world only once in every century.

AN INSPECTOR CALLS

UK; dir. Guy Hamilton; starring Alastair Sim; 79 min.

An effective dramatization of J. B. Priestley's theatrical fable about the extended teasing of the consciences of a prosperous family by a phantom policeman. Priestley's *Dangerous Corner* – in which a chance remark leads inexorably to revelations which shatter the contentment of a group of friends until a twist in time saves the situation – had been effectively filmed in 1934.

1955 ANIMAL FARM

UK; prod., dir. & scr. John Halas & Joy Batchelor; animated; 75 min.

The satire in this Halas and Batchelor version of George Orwell's scathing allegory on the failure of the Russian revolution is considerably softened, presumably in the hope of making it more entertaining for kids who have never heard of Trotsky and Stalin, but it ends up in a kind of comic limbo.

ULYSSES

Italy; dir. Mario Camerini; starring Kirk Douglas, Silvana Mangano, Anthony Quinn; 103 min.

Among the seven writers credited for this Homeric epic were Ben Hecht and Irwin Shaw, but their influence is not obvious in a story whose style is more reminiscent of a *Classics Illustrated* comic book. Some of the fantasy sequences – involving the hero's encounters with the Cyclops, Circe and the Sirens – are quite effectively done, especially by comparison with later "sword and sandal" movies which replayed the same motifs. The early history of Italian cinema had been dominated by such epics; the first full-length Italian feature film was Piero Fosco's *The Fall of Troy* (1912).

1956 THE BESPOKE OVERCOAT

UK; dir. Jack Clayton; staring Alfie Bass, David Kossoff; scr. Wolf Mankowitz; 33 min; b/w.

A fine but very free adaptation of a surreally paranoid story by Gogol which had been more accurately filmed in 1926 by Grigori Kozintsev as *The Overcoat*. Here, the employers of a downtrodden clerk in a clothing warehouse refuse to let him have a coat and he freezes to death before a tailor can run one up for him; his ghost exacts a curious poetic justice.

MIRACLE IN THE RAIN

US; dir. Rudolph Mate; starring Jane Wyman, Van Johnson; scr. Ben Hecht; 107 min.

The misery of a heartbroken girl is alleviated when she receives a supernatural token of the love of her fiancé, who was killed in the war.

SWORDS AND SANDALS

The strange sub-genre kick-started by Camerini's *Ulysses* (1955), Robert Wise's *Helen of Troy* (1955) and Francisci's *Hercules* (1957) mainly consisted of historical "epics", but did include some noteworthy fantasies. The less imaginative tended to multiply musclemen by bringing classical heroes together, as in *Ulysses and Hercules* (1961) and *Hercules, Samson and Ulysses* (1965). Much more interesting is *Le Baccanti* (1961; aka *The Bacchantes*) directed by Giorgio Ferroni, a version of Euripides' *Bacchae*, in which Dionysus visits poetic justice upon the apostate city of Thebes. Mario Bava's *Hercules in the Haunted World* (1961), starring Reg Park and Christopher Lee, is an enjoyable tongue-in-cheek adventure in the Devil's realm, but Piero Pierotti's *Hercules Against Rome* was leadenly dull. The "sword and sandal" merchants must have watched with dismay as "Arnold Strong", star of the idiotic ripoff *Hercules in New York* (1969), turned into Arnold Schwarzenegger and became a huge star, so "Lewis Coates" (Luigi Cozzi) retaliated by making a new version of *Hercules* (1983) starring ex-Incredible Hulk Lou Ferrigno; it was quickly followed by *Hercules II* (1985; aka *The Adventures of Hercules*).

MAN IN MANACLES: STEVE REEVES FLEXES HIS MUSCLES AND SHOWS OFF HIS LEGS IN *HERCULES*, THE PIONEERING "SWORD AND SANDAL" EPIC

Hecht presumably wrote this script more than 10 years earlier, as a cynical imitation of the ultra-schmaltzy consolatory fantasies which were in vogue in the war years; it was past its sell-by date in 1956.

1957 LE FATICHE DI ERCOLE

(HERCULES)

Italy; dir. & scr. Pietro Francisci; starring Steve Reeves, Sylva Koscina, Gianna Maria Canale; 107 min.

Although the ground had been prepared by *Ulysses*, this was the film which launched the "sword and sandal" sub-genre – by taking a surprising amount of money at the US box office – and made ex-Mr Universe Steve Reeves a star, of sorts. The script started out as the story of Jason and the Golden Fleece, with Hercules roped in as extra muscle, but that "extra muscle" was the key to the movie's success with the same audience that sustained the demand for magazines like *Health and Efficiency*. Francisci, Reeves and Koscina followed it up with *Ercole e la Regina di Lidia* (1960, aka *Hercules Unchained*), whose supporting cast included Sylvia Lopez as the Queen of Lydia and boxing champion Primo Carnera as yet more extra muscle.

BETWEEN DEATH AND THE DEEP BLUE: THE CHAMPION OF MANKIND PLAYS THE GAME IN BERGMAN'S CLASSIC ALLEGORY

DET SJUNDE INSEGLET
(THE SEVENTH SEAL)

Sweden; dir. and scr. Ingmar Bergman; starring Max von Sydow, Bengt Ekerot, Gunnar Bjornstrand, Bibi Andersson; 95 min; b/w.

A classic movie whose central motif – a doomed knight delaying fate by engaging Death in a game of chess – has been extensively parodied, deflecting attention away from the point of the exercise. The knight is actually playing on behalf of all mankind, and the game is a procrastination whose pieces are symbolic of human virtue and worth; its moves are reflected in the action which surrounds the game – but Death is implacable and the moral order painstakingly constructed by human endeavour goes unrewarded. Although it owes something to Fritz Lang's silent classic *Destiny* (1921), which features a similarly implacable grim reaper, this is the greatest of all cinematic moralistic fantasies, standing in sharp contrast to all those American movies which serve up casual miracles with the same grace, artistry and philosophical sophistication that McDonald's has brought to the preparation and serving of food. Bergman followed it up with *Anstiket* (1958; aka *The Face* and *The Magician*), a murkier allegory about the social role of Christian faith, in which a mesmerist exposed – perhaps mistakenly – as a fraud strikes back at his doubters.

1958 BELL, BOOK AND CANDLE

US; dir. Richard Quine; starring James Stewart, Kim Novak, Jack Lemmon, Hermione Gingold; scr. Daniel Taradash; 103 min.

This film of John van Druten's excellent stage-play was truer to the spirit of Thorne Smith than its august predecessor *I Married a Witch*. A magically beguiled publisher (Stewart) comes perilously close to avoiding the liberation he so desperately needs when the conscience-challenged witch who has enchanted him (Novak) has second thoughts. Her fellow coven-members (including Lemmon and Gingold) try hard to resist her unfortunate tendency to virtue. The idea that witches might have adapted themselves seamlessly to urban life was not new, but this movie was the first to deploy the idea with a measure of common sense and satirical sensibility.

DAMN YANKEES

US; dir. George Abbott and Stanley Donen; starring Gwen Verdon, Tab Hunter, Ray Walston; scr. Abbott; 110 min; aka What Lola Wants.

A musical version of Douglass Wallop's best-selling Faustian comedy *The Year the Yankees Lost the Pennant*, which neatly inverted the premise of *Angels in the Outfield*. Well, if God refuses to send angels to aid a loyal fan's ailing baseball team, what can he do but turn to the opposition? The substitute title was used in the UK in the halcyon days when it was perfectly acceptable to watch funny films about the Devil's wiles, but not to utter or display the word "damn".

NOT-SO-STARRY ARABIAN NIGHTS

A prolific sub-genre was built on the foundation stones laid by the thrice-filmed *Kismet* (1930/1944/1955) and the classic versions of *The Thief of Bagdad*, although its run-of-the-mill products were mostly risible. When Sabu went to America he was put into the carefully de-fantasized *Arabian Nights* (1942); his co-stars Jon Hall and Maria Montez followed up with the very similar *Ali Baba and the Forty Thieves* (1943) but Sabu wisely decided to become a war hero instead. *A Thousand and One Nights* (1945) was the first of many silly spoofs, with Rex Ingram playing a distinctly downmarket genie. *Sinbad the Sailor* (1947) was one of Douglas Fairbanks Jr's more determined attempts to follow in Daddy's footsteps, and it was enjoyable enough to found a whole dynasty of Sinbad movies, including the adventurous but rather tacky *Son of Sinbad* (1955). *The Magic Carpet* (1951), *Aladdin and His Lamp* (1952) and *The Golden Blade* (1953) were far less impressive. Although Ray Harryhausen's special effects in *The Seventh Voyage of Sinbad* (1958) injected some much-needed class into the sub-genre, the Italian/French remake of *The Thief of Bagdad* (1960), *The Wonders of Aladdin* (1961), *Captain Sinbad* (1963), *The Sword of Ali Baba* (1965) – which borrowed great chunks of footage from the 1943 *Ali Baba and the Forty Thieves* – and the Spanish *A Thousand and One Nights* (1968) failed to take any significant inspiration from it. Better use of special effects was made by Kevin Connor's *Arabian Adventure* (1979) starring Christopher Lee, Oliver Tobias and Mickey Rooney. The animated *1001 Arabian Nights* (1959) was a feature-length vehicle for Mr Magoo.

SINBAD IN TROUBLE: RAY HARRYHAUSEN'S SATYRICAL CYCLOPS WAS NO JOKE

THE SEVENTH VOYAGE OF SINBAD

US; dir. Nathan Juran; starring Kerwin Mathews, Kathryn Grant, Torin Thatcher; scr. Kenneth Kolb; 89 min.

This was the first of the production-line *Arabian Nights* fantasies to be enlivened by dramatic special effects using Ray Harryhausen's "Dynamation" technique. The plot – in which Sinbad's *inamorata* is reduced to Lilliputian dimensions by an evil sorcerer and he must find a *roc*'s egg to reverse the effects of the curse – is constructed around the effects, according to what subsequently became a standard method. It remains one of the best of its sub-genre.

TOM THUMB

US; dir. George Pal; starring Russ Tamblyn, Alan Young, Peter Sellers, Jessie Matthews; scr. Ladislaw Fodor; 98 min.

A musical for children based on the folk-tale about the boy who contrives to delight his parents' hearts – and outwit a couple of stock comic villains – in spite of his minuscule size. A very different treatment of the theme can be found in the surreally updated *The Secret Adventures of Tom Thumb* (1993) directed by Dave Borthwick.

1959 DARBY O'GILL AND THE LITTLE PEOPLE

US; dir. Robert Stevenson; starring Albert Sharpe, Jimmy O'Dea, Sean Connery, Janet Munro; scr. Lawrence Edward Watkin; 90 min.

A pleasant exercise in exaggerated Irish blarney – as reconstituted by the folks at Disney – in which a caretaker addicted to the telling of tall tales falls down a well and is granted three wishes by the King of the Leprechauns. Not unnaturally, nobody believes him, until he sets about making use of his gift. The film is slicker and slightly less sugary than most Disney live-action fantasies.

GREEN MANSIONS

US; dir. Mel Ferrer; starring Anthony Perkins, Audrey Hepburn; scr. Dorothy Kingsley, 104 min.

The whole point of W. H. Hudson's classic exercise in ecological mysticism is that the romance between the disaffected soldier-of-fortune and the magical bird-girl Rima can only end in tragedy. Grafting a happy ending on betrays the enterprise as thoroughly as *Portrait of Jennie* was betrayed – but who could have expected Hollywood to do anything else?

THE SHAGGY DOG

US; dir. Charles Barton; starring Fred MacMurray, Jean Hagen, Tommy Kirk; scr. Bill Walsh and Lillie Hayward; 104 min.

A Disney children's adventure story – based on *The Hound of Florence* by Felix Salten – about a boy transmogrified into a big hairy dog. who finds his new form convenient for thwarting crooks. The belated sequel, *The Shaggy D.A.* (1976), directed by Robert Stevenson and starring Dean Jones and Suzanne Pleshette, employed echoes of Watergate to obtain a rather un-Disneyish depth. Other notable doggy fantasies include *Oh Heavenly Dog* (1980), in which a private eye is reincarnated as a dog, and the animated *All Dogs Go to Heaven* (1989), in which a dog returns to Earth to play avenging angel and guardian angel.

RELIGIOUS ALLEGORY

The only religious fantasies which really belong to the fantasy genre are those which are sceptical and calculatedly subversive of conventional scriptural allegory. American film-makers have mostly shied away from such controversial material; the key examples are Helmut Kautner's *Der Apfel ist Aub* (1949; aka *The Apple Fell*, in which Adam and Eve take their marital difficulties to a counsellor for expert analysis, and Georges Franju's *La Faute de l'Abbé Mouret* (1970; aka *The Sin of Father Mouret*) based on a Zola novel about a priest who discovers true innocence. Diplomacy also made American directors reluctant to allow God to take direct action on His own behalf, although William Wellman's pietistic *The Next Voice You Hear* (1950) imagined Him issuing new commandments through the medium of the radio; a much more interesting take on the same basic idea is the delusional fantasy *Static* (1986). It is a sad comment on the poverty of the American imagination that the most successful allegory of spiritual uplift ever produced in the USA is *Jonathan Livingston Seagull* (1973).

SLEEPING BEAUTY

US; dir. Clyde Geronimi et al; animated; voices of Mary Costa, Bill Shirley, Eleanor Audley; 75 min.

This was Disney's principal mid-period attempt to get back to the great days of *Snow White and the Seven Dwarfs*; it was designed for a widescreen "Technirama" format and supported by a budget far more lavish than Cinderella, but the standard formula was beginning to look stale. The three good fairies were no substitute for the seven dwarfs, although the witch Maleficent was a reasonable stand-in for the wicked queen. The music – borrowed from Tchaikovsky's balletic suite – is somewhat out of keeping with the animation.

THE THREE WORLDS OF GULLIVER

US/Spain; dir. Jack Sher; starring Kerwin Mathews, Basil Sydney, Mary Ellis; scr. Sher and Arthur Ross; 100 min.

Despite the title this only covers the first two parts of Swift's classic, using the same Harryhausen camera-tricks to depict a giant Gulliver in Lilliput and a tiny one in Brobdingnag. With the satirical bite eliminated, as per usual, it struggles to find enough excitement in the thin plot.

1961 LA RIVIERE DU HIBOU

(INCIDENT AT OWL CREEK)

France; dir. and scr. Robert Enrico; starring Roger Jacquet; 27 min; b/w; aka An Occurrence at Owl Creek.

A beautifully atmospheric version of Ambrose Bierce's definitive posthumous fantasy "An Occurrence at Owl Creek Bridge", highly effective even for viewers who know perfectly well how it will end. Movies making more open use of similar motifs include Paul Fejos's *The Last Moment* (1927) and *Two Seconds* (1932).

1962 JACK THE GIANT KILLER

US; dir. Nathan Juran; starring Kerwin Mathews, Judi Meredith, Torin Thatcher; scr. Juran and Orville Hampton; 94 min.

Juran re-employed the key cast-members of *The Seventh Voyage of Sinbad* for this striking version of the English folk-tale. Howard Anderson's special effects were slightly less effective than Harryhausen's, but they were still a trifle over-the-top for the intended juvenile audience. The film was re-released with songs added to the sound-track in the hope of increasing its kiddie-friendliness, but the result was an aesthetic atrocity.

THE WONDERFUL WORLD OF THE BROTHERS GRIMM

US; dir. Henry Levin and George Pal; starring Laurence Harvey, Karl Boehm; scr. David P. Harmon, Charles Beaumont & William Roberts; 129 min.

Dramatic versions of three folk-tales are inserted into a frame. The awkwardness of the format is made even more uneasy by the uncertainty of everyone involved as to how seriously the material ought to be taken. The film fails to build into any kind of coherent whole, although some action sequences in the tales are vividly executed.

ZOTZ!

US; dir. William Castle; starring Tom Poston; scr. Ray Russell; 87 min; b/w.

Walter Karig's 1947 novel about a man suddenly gifted with a remarkable talent for making things disappear was a satire on military and political fudging, but this belated adaptation is a gutless farce. The very similar *Modern Problems* (1981) in which an air-traffic controller (Chevy Chase) acquires telekinetic powers is just as weak.

1963 JASON AND THE ARGONAUTS

US; dir. Don Chaffey; starring Todd Armstrong, Nancy Kovack; scr. Jan Reed & Beverley Cross; 104 min.

Ray Harryhausen here transferred his Dynamation effects to "sword and sandal" territory, outshining the elementary effects employed in the Italian originals. The plot and dialogue are light-hearted, but the supernaturalized action sequences are played straight.

THE SWORD IN THE STONE

US; dir. Wolfgang Reitherman; animated; voices of Ricky Sorenson, Sebastian Cabot, Karl Swenson; scr. Bill Peet; 80 min.

Disney followed up their animated version of the quintessentially British story *One Hundred and One Dalmatians* (1961) with their version of T. H. White's exceedingly English fantasy about Merlin's education of the boy destined to become King Arthur. Because White's comedy is much more understated than Dodie Smith', it seems distinctly effete when robbed of its serious subtext; the addition of the superfluous villainess Madame Mim does not help.

1964 THE BRASS BOTTLE

US; dir. Harry Keller; starring Tony Randall, Burl Ives, Barbara Eden; scr. Oscar Brodney; 89 min.

F. Anstey had written a successful stage version of his classic novel about a young Victorian gentleman embarrassed by the generosity of the genie he liberates from imprisonment, but no one had attempted to film it while any slight trace of freshness or relevance remained within it. This updated version had no chance, although the presence of Barbara Eden in the cast suggests that it helped to provide the inspiration for the better-planned and more cleverly executed TV sitcom *I Dream of Jeannie.*

HAUNTED BY ANGUISH: A HEART-RENDING SCENE FROM KOBAYASHI'S *KWAIDAN*

GOODBYE CHARLIE

US; dir. Vincente Minnelli; starring Debbie Reynolds, Pat Boone, Walter Matthau, Tony Curtis; scr. Harry Kurnitz; 116 min.

An adaptation of a remarkably tasteless comedy by George Axelrod which had enjoyed some success on Broadway, in which a philandering crook is reincarnated as a luscious blonde after being shot by a vengeful husband. Reynolds was ludicrously miscast, but it's not easy to think of anyone who could have played the part with conviction; even Mae West would have struggled. An equally tasteless variation on the same theme directed by Blake Edwards, *Switch* (1991), starred Ellen Barkin as a boorish male philanderer reincarnated as a good-looking woman with firm instructions from Above to become truly lovable.

KWAIDAN

Japan; dir. Masaki Kobayashi; starring Rentaro Mikumi, Ganjiro Nakamura, Katsuo Nakamura; scr. Yoko Mizuki; 164 min.

Four Japanese ghost stories (three in the 125-minute US version), named for an anthology by American exile Lafcadio Hearn in which they were collected. Hearn was a master of economical prose whose style was perfectly suited to the tales, and Kobayashi set out to provide a visual equivalent based on traditional illustrations. The result is an extraordinarily delicate and expressive visual experience.

MARY POPPINS

US; dir. Robert Stevenson; starring Julie Andrews, Dick van Dyke, David Tomlinson, Glynis Johns; scr. Bill Walsh and Don da Gradi; 140 min.

The most successful of Disney's live-action fantasies, judiciously spliced with some nice animated sequences. It is based on P. L. Travers's novel about a magical nanny who transforms the lives and characters of two disaffected children. Dick van Dyke's appalling travesty of a Cockney accent became a legend, the Oscar-winning Julie Andrews went on to make *The Sound of Music* and the best songs – "Supercallifragilisticespiallidocious" and the Oscar-winning "Chim Chim Cheree" – became as irritatingly unforgettable as any of Disney's earworms. The movie is likely to remain the best of its kind now that its mid-60s cheerfulness seems as dated as its Edwardian setting. Similar reality-to-fantasy segues from live action to animation were used in *The Incredible Mr Limpet* (1964).

SEVEN FACES OF DOCTOR LAO

US; dir. George Pal; starring Tony Randall, Arthur O'Connell, Barbara Eden; scr. Charles Beaumont; 100 min.

Charles G. Finney's *The Circus of Dr Lao* – a blisteringly sarcastic erotic fantasy about the loosening-up of an uptight small town by a visiting carnival – could hardly be transferred to the screen without considerable censorship, but that hardly justifies its use as a vehicle for Randall to display his versatility by playing the eponymous Chinaman and most of his exhibits. The property-development subplot is completely out of keeping with the original, but the movie does have a few effective moments.

1967 BEDAZZLED

UK; dir. Stanley Donen; starring Peter Cook, Dudley Moore, Michael Bates, Raquel Welch, Eleanor Bron; scr. Cook; 96 min.

A vehicle for the popular comedy duo in which Cook plays the diabolical Mr Spiggott, who buys Moore's soul for seven wishes – which the incompetent wretch wastes, according to the customary pattern of cautionary fantasies. The calculated sacrilege and sarcastic banter fall flat; Cook did better with his fanciful political satire *The Rise and Rise of Michael Rimmer* (1970).

BLACKBEARD'S GHOST

US; dir. Robert Stevenson; starring Peter Ustinov, Dean Jones, Suzanne Pleshette, Elsa Lanchester; scr. Bill Walsh; 107 min.

A run-of-the-mill Disney comedy in which the notorious pirate is softened into a lovable old rogue, who returns from oblivion to help out the owners of his ancient home. The miscast Ustinov valiantly attempts to make something of his part, but the real Blackbeard would have been entirely in sympathy with the racketeers who want to turn the place into a casino.

DOCTOR DOLITTLE

US; dir. Richard Fleischer; starring Rex Harrison, Anthony Newley, Samantha Eggar; scr. Leslie Bricusse; 152 min.

A musical adaptation of Hugh Lofting's stories about a vet who can talk to his patients and their wild cousins. Here he travels to the South Seas in search of an exotic mollusc. Rex Harrison repeated his *My Fair Lady* demonstration that one does not actually have to be able to sing to star in a musical; his number "Talk to the Animals" won an Oscar anyway. The special effects are clever, but the film failed to provide convincing opposition to *Mary Poppins*.

THE GNOME-MOBILE

US; dir. Robert Stevenson; starring Walter Brennan, Matthew Garber, Karen Dotrice; scr. Ellis Kadison; 90 min.

A modest musical adaptation of Upton Sinclair's children's book – which Hollywood naturally considered far more suitable than any of his political fantasies – in which the family of a bad-tempered businessman become the protectors of a population of gnomes. Although less popular than many of Disney's other live-action fantasies, it is one of the most polished and accomplished.

UN-AMERICAN ANGELS

Angelic fantasies produced in the UK tend to feature more dignified and self-effacing angels, whose low-key missions are usually more effective. The pattern was set by *The Passing of the Third Floor Back* (1935), in which Conrad Veidt played Jerome K. Jerome's enigmatic visitor; *The Angel Who Pawned Her Harp* (1954), derived from Charles Terrot's very similar 1951 TV play, is cast in the same mould. The Australian *Harlequin* (1980) uses a similar but less subtle formula, and comedian Paul Hogan was even more up-front in *Almost an Angel* (1990) – although his commissioning vision seemed decidedly dodgy to viewers who observed that God was actually Charlton Heston. A more striking contrast can be seen in the Italian *Miracle in Milan* (1951), directed by Vittorio de Sica, which was an adaptation of Cesare Zavattini's politicized parable *Toto il Buono* (1944), in which the guardian of a foundling descends from Heaven to help an entire population of poor folk to fly away to a better place.

1968 THE ADDING MACHINE

UK; dir. and scr. Jerome Epstein; starring Milo O'Shea, Phyllis Diller, Billie Whitelaw, Raymond Huntley; 99 min.

Elmer Rice's 1923 satire – a baroque posthumous fantasy in which a clerk named Mr Zero, driven beyond the limits of his endurance on Earth, is so thoroughly institutionalized that Heaven is unbearable – had been adapted for US TV, but Hollywood had steered clear of it. It might have made an intriguing item of expressionist cinema had it been sympathetically filmed in the 1930s, but this considerably rewritten version fails to cope with the problems inherent in trying to do it more than 30 years too late.

CHITTY CHITTY BANG BANG

UK; dir. Ken Hughes; starring Dick van Dyke, Sally Anne Howes, Lionel Jeffries, Robert Helpmann, Benny Hill; scr. Hughes and Roald Dahl; 145 min.

Britain's answer to *Mary Poppins*, *Doctor Dolittle* and *The Gnome-Mobile* was co-scripted by Roald Dahl, but the Ian Fleming novel on which it is based is an embarrassingly condescending atrocity. The worst features of the book are here reproduced with appalling fidelity, only slightly ameliorated by the catchy tunes and Helpmann's bravura performance as the Child-catcher. Given that Fleming once named a heroine Pussy Galore, the appearance here of Truly Scrumptious is almost forgivable.

YOU'RE NEVER TOO OLD TO DANCE: THE VETERAN FRED ASTAIRE IN *FINIAN'S RAINBOW*

FINIAN'S RAINBOW

US; dir. Francis Ford Coppola; starring Fred Astaire, Tommy Steele, Petula Clark; scr. E. Y. Harburg and Fred Saidy; 145 min.

A screen adaptation of Harburg and Saidy's 1947 musical comedy about a leprechaun whose crock of gold is carried off to the American Deep South, leaving him no alternative but to go with it. The political edge of the original – whose commentary on race relations was daring in its day – is inevitably lost, but the director and cast work hard to salvage something of its mildly anarchic spirit.

YELLOW SUBMARINE

UK; animated; dir. George Dunning; scr. Lee Minoff, Al Brodax, Erich Segal & Jack Mendlesohn; 87 min.

A vehicle for the music of Lennon and McCartney, using songs mostly derived from the classic *Sergeant Pepper* album. Pepperland, where Sergeant Pepper's Lonely Hearts Club band do their thing, is attacked by hordes of Blue Meanies; an emissary escapes in the eponymous sub, summoning the Beatles to aid the cause. The animation is calculatedly primitive, but it supplies effective backcloths for the various tracks. It was inevitable, given that the film was made in 1968, that the finale would be "All You Need is Love"; "Happiness is a Warm Gun" had, alas, yet to be written.

1969 THE LOVE BUG

US; dir. Robert Stevenson; starring Dean Jones, Michele Lee, David Tomlinson; scr. Bill Walsh and Don da Gradi; 107 min.

The Disney comedy which introduced Herbie, the Volkswagen "Beetle" with a mind of its own. Effortlessly outshining its human co-stars (*never* work with children, animals or beetles, darlings), the car went on to make three equally daft and cheerful sequels: *Herbie Rides Again* (1974), *Herbie Goes to Monte Carlo* (1977) and *Herbie Goes Bananas* (1980). Rumours concerning body-doubles are, of course, entirely false; Volkswagens last forever.

THE PHANTOM TOLLBOOTH

US; dir. Chuck Jones; animated; voice of Butch Patrick; scr. Chuck Jones & Sam Rosen; 90 min.

This adaptation of Norton Juster's unusually sophisticated children's novel was the brainchild of Chuck Jones, who relished the opportunity to raise his sights. He paid scrupulous attention to the adult-orientated aspects of the original, carefully preserving Juster's neat allegory pleading the cause of Rhyme and Reason.

1970 THE ANGEL LEVINE

US; dir. Jan Kadar; starring Zero Mostel, Harry Belafonte, Ida Kaminska, Milo O'Shea, Eli Wallach; scr. Bill Gunn & Ronald Ribman; 105 min.

This dramatization of a story by Bernard Malamud deploys a good cast but cannot translate Malamud's stylishly dark wit. The black angel answering the self-pitying prayers of an elderly Jewish tailor is a welcome variation on the theme, but the downbeat original leaves the movie with no alternative but to peter out tamely.

BREWSTER McCLOUD

US; dir. Robert Altman; starring Bud Cort, Sally Kellerman, Shelley Duvall; scr. Doran William Cannon; 105 min.

A subtle and delicately executed allegory in which a youth (Cort) hides out in the Houston Astrodome while perfecting the apparatus that will bring his dreams of flight to fruition. Before his wings are ready, however, he is deflected from his noble dream by the claims of a more down-to-earth romance – whose effects are, of course, heartrendingly lethal. Disney-corrupted audiences failed to see the point and could not sympathize with an ideological thrust which flatly contradicted one of the central myths of Hollywood. Had it not come immediately after *M*A*S*H* Altman might not have got the money to make it, but this remains one of the classics of cinematic fantasy, drastically underrated by the majority of critics.

BROTHER JOHN

US; dir. James Goldstone; starring Sidney Poitier, Bradford Dillman, Will Geer; scr. Ernest Kinoy; 94 min.

If Christ ever did return he'd probably be black, and he probably wouldn't be treated any better the second time around – but you have to be careful about saying things like that in a movie, so the point has to be made so softly that it could easily be ignored or misinterpreted. On the other hand, a little ambiguity isn't a bad thing; it helps to make people wonder.

HERCULES IN NEW YORK

US; dir. Arthur Allan Seidelman; starring "Arnold Strong" (Arnold Schwarzenegger), Deborah Loomis, Taina Elg; scr. Aubrey Wisberg; 91 min.

Although Hollywood reclaimed the spirit and substance of the "Spaghetti Western" within five years, it is hardly surprising that its minions steadfastly ignored the "sword and sandal" sub-genre. What, then, were they to do with a *mittel*-European Mr Universe with a thick accent and an unpronounceable name? "Hey, guys, how about we bring Hercules to New York, and do the thing as a *comedy?* As for the guy's voice, we can dub that." From little acorns, great oaks sometimes grow – but natural selection certainly moves in mysterious ways.

1971 BEDKNOBS AND BROOMSTICKS

US; dir. Robert Stevenson; starring Angela Lansbury, David Tomlinson, Sam Jaffe; scr. Bill Walsh and Don DaGradi; 117 min.

This musical children's fantasy based on two novels by Mary Norton never came close to capturing the charm of *Mary Poppins*. Set during the early years of World War II, it offers a highly fanciful account of the frustration of a German invasion by three children equipped with a magic bedstead. The Oscar-winning special effects and animated sequences have a certain charm, but the whole remains rather incoherent.

FRITZ THE CAT

US; animated; dir. and scr. Ralph Bakshi; 78 min.

Robert Crumb's classic "underground" comics broke the mould of that medium, inspiring a whole new generation of animators with a satirical, splenetic and scatological spirit of revolt. Bakshi's animation is forced to simplify Crumb's style and the film is by no means as savagely sarcastic as the original strips, but it still sent shockwaves through audiences accustomed to Disney and Chuck Jones. It now seems dated, being so firmly anchored in the 1960s' counterculture, but it was a landmark. The sequel, *The Nine Lives of Fritz the Cat* (1974) – made by Robert Taylor – callously subverted the thrust of the original by portraying the once-rebellious libertine cat as a burned-out, married pothead who has retreated into escapist fantasies; it seemed to many Crumb fans to be a calculated betrayal.

MALPERTUIS

France; dir. Harry Kumel; starring Mathieu Carrière, Susan Hampshire, Orson Welles; 124 min.

An intriguingly stylized adaptation of a bizarre novel by the Belgian writer Jean Ray, in which a young man is incarcerated in a Gothic pile, ultimately deducing (not necessarily correctly) that his fellow-inhabitants are the last remnant of the once-proud Greek pantheon. Hampshire showed unprecedented versatility in playing three contrasting parts.

TAM-LIN

UK; dir. Roddy MacDowall; starring Ava Gardner, Ian McShane, Stephanie Beacham; scr. William Spier; 106 min; aka The Devil's Widow, The Ballad of Tam-Lin.

A curious movie which scrupulously de-fantasizes the Scottish folktale – best-known nowadays in Robert Burns' poetic version – about the beguiling of Tam-Lin by the queen of the fairies and Janet of Carterhaugh's quasi-Orphean quest to reclaim him. It is interesting to those who can compare it with other versions, but perhaps only to them.

WILLY WONKA AND THE CHOCOLATE FACTORY

US; dir. Mel Stuart; starring Gene Wilder, Jack Albertson, Peter Ostrum; scr. Roald Dahl; 100 min.

Dahl's adaptation of his bestselling *Charlie and the Chocolate Factory* could not overcome the difficulties arising from the fact that the grotesque and witty violence which drives the plot so effectively on the page seems far more horrifying in visual form. Wilder's amiable presence fails to soften what becomes, when shorn of its anarchic humour, a moral tale in the terrorist tradition of Heinrich Hoffman's *Struwwelpeter*.

1972 ALICE'S ADVENTURES IN WONDERLAND

UK; dir. and scr. William Sterling; starring Fiona Fullerton, Michael Crawford, Robert Helpmann, Dudley Moore, Spike Milligan, Peter Sellers, Dennis Price, Flora Robson, Michael Hordern, Ralph Richardson; 101 min.

Arriving six years after Jonathan Miller's TV reinterpretation of the text, this version offered a straightforward and calculatedly innocent dramatization. Fullerton made a decent job of the central role, but the strategy of filling the cameo roles with great actors and comedians produced the usual effect: everyone overacted madly in the hope of stamping his or her personality more firmly on the product than the other contenders. The coherency of the whole suffered as a result and the music didn't help at all.

REACHING OUT FROM THE PAST: *THE AMAZING MR BLUNDEN* OFFERS THE INHABITANTS OF A WAR-TORN WORLD A CHANCE TO MAKE A GENUINE DIFFERENCE

THE AMAZING MR BLUNDEN

UK; dir. and scr. Lionel Jeffries; starring Laurence Naismith, Diana Dors, James Villiers, David Lodge, Lynne Frederick; 99 min.

This elaborate development of Antonia Baker's story *The Ghosts* is set solidly within the British TV tradition of timeslip fantasies for children, although the bigger budget permitted more lavish effects than any BBC serial had ever been able to deploy. The main story is set in 1918, in a Britain exhausted by World War I, where ghosts strayed from a happier past offer the opportunity to ameliorate an old tragedy. The climax is highly effective, building considerable tension before the heart-warming resolution is allowed to emerge.

THE PIED PIPER

UK; dir. Jacques Demy; starring Donovan, Donald Pleasence, Michael Hordern, Jack Wild; scr Demy, Andrew Birkin &Mark Peploe; 90 min.

A rather pedestrian dramatization of the legend of the Pied Piper of Hamelin, best-known in Robert Browning's poetic version. Demy's unprettified vision of 14th-century life collaborates with the rats to produce a nightmarish effect whose impact the actors labour in vain to soften.

1974 CELINE ET JULIE VONT EN BATEAU

(CELINE AND JULIE GO BOATING)

France; dir. Jacques Rivette; starring Juliet Berto, Dominique Labourier, Bulle Ogier; scr. Rivette, Berto, Labourie & Ogier; 192 min.

A languidly mannered film very loosely based on two ghost stories by Henry James, although the improvisations of the main actors and the director (all of whom got writing credits) resolutely commingle slapstick comedy, sentimentality and suspense. The two heroines contrive to interrupt and eventually subvert the endlessly reiterated phantom record of a tragic event played out in a haunted house, but not in the conventional manner.

IL FIORE DELLA MILLE E UNA NOTTE

(ARABIAN NIGHTS)

Italy; dir. & scr. Pier Paolo Pasolini; starring Ninetto Davoli, Franco Merli, Ines Pelegrini; 155 min.

This was the third element of Pasolini's admirably ambitious "trilogy" of lushly erotic portmanteau pieces, following *The Canterbury Tales* and *The Decameron*. It was less well received than its predecessors and was quickly cut to 130 minutes by omitting some of the framed material. Although the source-materials must have seemed more promising than those employed in its predecessors the visualization is less convincing; it includes some extraordinarily vivid moments but the whole is less than the sum of the parts.

THE GOLDEN VOYAGE OF SINBAD

UK; dir. Gordon Hessler; starring John Phillip Law, Caroline Munro, Tom Baker; scr. Brian Clemens and Ray Harryhausen; 105 min.

Since making *Jason and the Argonauts* in 1963, Harryhausen had applied his Superdynamation technique to several undistinguished science-fiction films; this was essentially a reprise of his 1958 success *The Seventh Voyage of Sinbad* but time had made the trickery familiar and he had to work harder to obtain a similar effect. Harryhausen stayed in Britain to make *Sinbad and the Eye of the Tiger* (1977), directed by Sam Wanamaker, with Patrick Wayne in the lead and Jane Seymour in support, but it proved even more of a struggle to rekindle a flicker of the old excitement.

AMERICAN ANGELS

It is easy to understand how the American sub-genre of angelic fantasies became firmly established during World War II but less easy to sympathize with the subsequent missions of Hollywood-despatched angels. In *Heaven Only Knows* (1947; aka *Montana Mike*) Robert Cummings is sent to the Wild West to reform a hard-bitten gambler. In *For Heaven's Sake* (1950) Clifton Webb and Edmund Gwenn have to keep a quarrelsome Broadway couple together until their baby arrives. In *Forever Darling* (1956) James Mason had to steady Lucille Ball's rocky relationship with Desi Arnaz. Harry Morgan brings Fred MacMurray news of his impending demise in *Charley and the Angel* (1973) and then grows impatient when the forewarned storekeeper misses several appointments with death. In *Two of a Kind* (1983) angels of destruction agree to spare mankind a second Deluge if two randomly selected humans (John Travolta and Olivia Newton-John) prove capable of self-sacrificing altruism – and never suspect that the ballot was rigged! In *Date with an Angel* (1987) an angel with a broken wing who falls into a swimming pool while a stag party is in progress walks off with the groom. In *Heart and Souls* (1993) the car-crash victims appointed as guardian angels to a baby whose parents survive the tragedy prove distinctly incompetent.

THE UNPREDICTABLE IN HOT PURSUIT OF THE UNATTAINABLE

LE GRAAL

(LANCELOT DU LAC)

France/Italy; dir. and scr. Robert Bresson; starring Luc Simon, Laura Duke Condominas, Humbert Balsan; 85 min; aka The Grail.

An allegorical account of the withering of faith in which the disillusioned Lancelot – one of few survivors of the grail quest – gives up and returns to his old ways, providing a feast of conscience-wringing fun for masochistically-inclined highbrow Catholics. Eric Rohmer's *Perceval le Gallois* (1978) is a more faithful rendering of French grail mythology, explicitly based on Chrètien de Troyes' medieval epic.

THE LITTLE PRINCE

US; dir. Stanley Donen; starring Richard Kiley, Steven Warner, Bob Fosse, Gene Wilder; scr. Alan Jay Lerner; 89 min.

A rather disappointing musical version of Antoine de Saint-Exupéry's posthumously published allegory (1944) in which a small boy from another planet learns about human life from anthropomorphized animals. Bob Fosse's sinuous snake upstaged the rest of the cast.

MONTY PYTHON AND THE HOLY GRAIL

UK; dir. Terry Gilliam; starring John Cleese, Eric Idle, Graham Chapman, Terry Jones, Michael Palin; scr. dir. & starring actors; 90 min.

A gleefully absurdist, Protestant antidote to Bresson's epic of despondency, exceedingly patchy but very funny in parts. It lacks the savage satirical bite of its superior successor, *Monty Python's Life of Brian* (1979), but its amiable silliness conceals an element of subversive mockery directed at the last British vestiges of the chivalric ideal.

1976 DONA FLOR E SEUS DOIS MARIDOS (DONA FLOR AND HER TWO HUSBANDS)

Brazil; dir. Bruno Barreto; starring Sonia Braga, José Wilker, Mauro Mendonca; scr. Barreto and Jorge Amado; 110 min.

Amado's 1966 novel was hailed as an example of "magic realism", although its plot is that of Noel Coward's *Blithe Spirit* with the sexes of the protagonists reversed and a great deal of intimate erotic detail added. The US remake *Kiss Me Goodbye* (1982), directed by Robert Mulligan and starring Sally Field, James Caan and Jeff Bridges, had to be toned down very considerably.

FREAKY FRIDAY

US; dir. Gary Nelson; starring Barbara Harris, Jodie Foster, John Astin; scr. Mary Rodgers; 100 min.

Mary Rodgers's screen adaptation of her feminized version of *Vice Versa* was one of the slickest Disney films of its era. Harris and Foster put in exceptionally well-matched performances as the mother and daughter who recklessly wish that they could change places for a day. Although the script now seems rather dated – the 1994 TV remake was careful to substitute a divorced career-orientated mother for the original harassed homemaker – the film holds up well as a period piece.

1977 JABBERWOCKY

UK; dir. Terry Gilliam; starring Michael Palin, Max Wall, Deborah Fallender, Warren Mitchell; scr. Gilliam and Charles Alverson; 101 min.

Gilliam used the experience gained in making *Monty Python and the Holy Grail* to good effect in this uneasy comedy, which superimposes a fairy-tale plot about a humble apprentice pressed into service as a dragon-slayer upon a distinctly unlovely view of the muddy ignominy of medieval life. The juxtaposition did not please contemporary critics, but it established the basis for Gilliam's uniquely cutting brand of dystopian comedy. The title, taken from Lewis Carroll's famous poem, underlines the implication that determined nonsense can be profoundly disturbing and strangely meaningful.

THE LAST WAVE

Australia; dir. Peter Weir; starring Richard Chamberlain, Olivia Hamnett; scr. Weir, Tony Morphett and Peter Popescu; 106 min.

A visionary fantasy based in Aboriginal folklore, in which a spell of freak weather triggers dreams of an impending Deluge while a lawyer defends an Aborigine accused of murder. Weir makes good use of evocative settings and sinister tribal rituals, building considerable suspense.

SWORDS AND SORCERY

When the paperback Conan series heated up sword-and-sorcery's market position in the late 1960s, movies like Bert Gordon's *The Magic Sword* (1962) began to look like bold pioneers, but the Conan movies of the early 1980s demonstrated that the sub-genre was woefully unsuited to cinematic adaptation at that time. *Conan the Destroyer* and *Red Sonja* were bad, but they were an order of magnitude better than the lower-budget imitations which flooded forth in their wake – many of them de-fantasized to the point of marginality. These included *The Sword and the Sorcerer* (1982), *Krull* (1983), *Ator: The Fighting Eagle* (1983) – which became the first of a series extending to *Quest for the Mighty Sword* (1989) – *Wizard of the Lost Kingdom* (1985) – whose sequel was *Wizard of the Lost Kingdom II* (1989) – and *The Barbarians* (1987). *The Warrior and the Sorceress* (1984), directed by John Broderick and starring David Carradine, was a sword-and-sorcery version of the Japanese classic *Yojimbo*, Westernized as *A Fistful of Dollars*. *Deathstalker* (1984) was depressingly earnest but its tongue-in-cheek sequels, *Deathstalker II: Duel of the Titans* (1987) and *Deathstalker III: The Warriors from Hell* (1988) saved them from utter triviality. The exploitation element of *Red Sonja* was further extrapolated in *Barbarian Queen* (1985) and *Amazons* (1986). *Quest of the Delta Knights* (1993) featured a quest for the lost treasure of Archimedes!

THE MOUSE AND HIS CHILD

US; animated; dir. Fred Wolf; voices of Peter Ustinov, Cloris Leachman, Andy Devine; 83 min.

Wolf's worthy but weak-kneed animated version of Russell Hoban's brilliant novel was unfortunately unable to capture the literary grace, pathos or satirical bite of the original while failing to substitute any action or suspense.

OH, GOD!

US; dir. Carl Reiner; starring George Burns, John Denver, Teri Garr; scr. Larry Gelbart; 104 min.

Hollywood sensitivity was cast aside in this tasteless adaptation of Avery Corman's 1971 novel. God (Burns) cruelly commissions a hapless supermarket manager (Denver) to put the world to rights; when summoned to court to prove his powers, he teases all present before performing a few casually contemptuous miracles. *Oh God Book Two* (1980) tried sentimentality instead of humour, proving that there is no limit to crassness and stupidity. *Oh God, You Devil* (1984) completed a joky "trilogy" with a feeble Faustian fantasy.

PETE'S DRAGON

US; dir. Don Chaffey; starring Helen Reddy, Jim Dale, Mickey Rooney; scr. Malcolm Marmorstein; 134 min.

A run-of-the-mill Disney musical about a lonely small boy and his unimaginary friend. The star of the film is the animated dragon, with whom the actors struggle to compete. A lukewarm audience reaction resulted in the film being cut down, initially to 121 minutes and then to 104 minutes. A superior film of similar ilk is *Little Monsters* (1989) directed by Richard Alan Greenberg and starring Fred Savage, in which a boy and his monstrous friend cross and re-cross the boundary between their two worlds.

THE RESCUERS

US; dir. Wolfgang Reiterman et al; animated; voices of Bob Newhart, Eva Gabor, Geraldine Page; scr. Ken Anderson et al; 77 min.

A pleasantly unassuming Disney feature based on stories by Margery Sharp about the heroic endeavours of the mice who make up the membership of the Rescue Aid Society. Here, with the aid of various other kindly creatures, they secure the release of a kidnapped girl. *The Rescuers Down Under* (1990) similarly benefits from a more robust plot than Disney's writers generally supplied, and also from the advent of computer-assisted animation techniques. The video-led renaissance of Disney as a maker of big-budget animated features was still some way off but they were keeping the children's cinema market reasonably well-fed; 1977 also saw the release of *The Many Adventures of Winnie-the-Pooh*, a portmanteau of three shorts made between 1966 and 1974.

WIZARDS

US; animated; dir. & scr. Ralph Bakshi; voices of Bob Holt, Jesse Wells, Richard Romanus; 80 min.

Bakshi's second attempt to break into animated films (following *Fritz the Cat*) was a concerted attempt to develop Secondary World fantasy for the cinema, making careful strategic use of a technique whereby silhouette figures were traced from live-action footage. The result is visually effective and the laid-back narration works well enough in the early phases, but the climactic *deus ex machina* is an unforgivable betrayal of the whole exercise.

1978 LORD OF THE RINGS

US; animated; dir. Ralph Bakshi; voices of Christopher Guard, John Hurt, William Squire; scr. Chris Conkling and Peter S. Beagle; 133 min.

The good work which Bakshi put into *Wizards* helped him tune up for this mammoth task, and he made further use of the technique of overlaying artwork on live-action footage to make the villains seem sinister, but the result was so disappointingly sluggish that no one was surprised when the project was aborted after this dramatization of volume one of Tolkien's classic three-decker. Tolkien's sonorous prose descriptions, however rich and atmospheric they may be, rarely specify what things actually look like, and Bakshi's improvisations seem distinctly tawdry. Peter Jackson's 2001 masterpiece was a far better evocation of Tolkien's Middle Earth, showing what could be done with a bit of vision – and free run of New Zealand. Following the failure of *The Lord of the Rings* Bakshi moved back to more modest fare in *Fire and Ice* (1983), a routine sword-and-sorcery adventure with character designs by Frank Frazetta, but could not reproduce the panache which made the early phases of *Wizards* so effective.

THE WATER BABIES

UK/Poland; dir. Lionel Jeffries; starring James Mason, Billie Whitelaw, Bernard Cribbins, Joan Greenwood; scr. Michael Robson; 92 min.

The substance of Charles Kingsley's classic moralistic fantasy is here relegated to a lacklustre animated insert into a rather tedious frame belatedly criticizing the Victorian institution of child labour.

WATERSHIP DOWN

UK; animated; dir. and scr. Martin Rosen; voices of John Hurt, Richard Briers, Ralph Richardson, Zero Mostel, Denholm Elliott; 92 min.

Richard Adams's surprise bestseller was presumably rejected by commercial publishers because it was too cartoonish in its anthropomorphization, its political allegorizing and its egregious sentimentality, so this dim-wittedly portentous version is an unusually faithful adaptation. The overheated song "Bright Eyes" captures the lachrymose mood perfectly.

1979 THE TEMPEST

UK; dir. and scr. Derek Jarman; starring Toyah Willcox, Heathcote Williams, Karl Johnson; 95 min.

Avant-garde director Jarman followed up his punk timeslip romance *Jubilee* (1977) by cutting Shakespeare's dialogue to ribbons in order to adapt it to the capabilities of anti-Establishment poet Williams and aspirant rock star Willcox, but they rose to the occasion magnificently and the film is an extraordinary visual experience. Jarman was later unable to explain why he decided to end it with the diva Montserrat Caballé singing "Stormy Weather", but it brought the film to a bizarrely fitting conclusion. This movie presumably inspired Peter Greenaway's equally free and equally enigmatic adaptation of the same original, *Prospero's Books* (1991), which had the benefit of Sir John Gielgud and included some magnificent phantasmagorical sequences.

1980 THE DEVIL AND MAX DEVLIN

US; dir. Steven Hilliard Stern; starring Elliott Gould, Bill Cosby, Susan Anspach; scr. Mary Rodgers; 95 min.

Disney must have needed some persuading to allow Rodgers to follow up the success of *Freaky Friday* with this highly atypical Faustian

HARRYHAUSEN'S LAST STAND: *CLASH OF THE TITANS*

comedy, whose plot seems to be based on Heinrich Marschner's 1827 opera *Le Vampyr* (which was bizarrely updated in a five-part TV version by the BBC in 1992). An unscrupulous businessman is offered a second chance at life if he can procure three souls for Satan; he fails.

HAWK THE SLAYER

UK; dir. Terry Marcel; starring Jack Palance, John Terry, Cheryl Campbell; scr. Marcel and Harry Robertson; 93 min.

This routine sword-and-sorcery adventure was an early attempt to cash in on the new generation of special effects, chiefly represented by the flying sword over whose custody and use two brothers violently disagree. It deserves credit for its pioneering spirit.

RESURRECTION

US; dir. Daniel Petrie; starring Ellen Burstyn, Sam Shepard, Eva LeGallienne; scr. Lewis John Carlino; 103 min.

An earnest miracle-working fantasy in which a woman's brush with death confers healing powers upon her, for no apparent reason. Burstyn's central performance gives the film considerable backbone but stories of this kind tend to hover uneasily between the morally suspect and the downright sick, because it is far easier for writers – who have godlike power over the worlds within their texts – to work casual miracles than it is for the charlatans who pose as healers in the real world. The trick becomes all the more offensive when it is employed to turn around such initially cynical plots as that of *Leap of Faith* (1992), which stars Steve Martin as the proprietor of a travelling gospel show. The deceptively amiable 1996 John Travolta vehicle *Phenomenon*, directed by John Turteltaub, is of a similar ilk, but American films of this kind tend to contrast sharply with European cinematic parables about people with strange powers, which include Werner Herzog's *Heart of Glass* (1976).

SOMEWHERE IN TIME

US; dir. Jeannot Szwarc; starring Christopher Reeve, Jane Seymour; scr. Richard Matheson; 104 min.

Matheson's earnest adaptation of his heartfelt timeslip romance *Bid Time Return* is competently visualized by Szwarc and the leading actors, maintaining the tradition according to which all great romances written by women end with marriage and happiness, while all great romances written by men end with loss and misery.

1981 CLASH OF THE TITANS

UK; dir. Desmond Davis; starring Harry Hamlin, Judi Bowker, Burgess Meredith, Laurence Olivier, Claire Bloom, Maggie Smith, Ursula Andress; scr. Beverley Cross; 118 min.

The story of Perseus is revamped with the aid of Superdynamation, here at its most effective – but it was to be Harryhausen's last film. The big-name actors play mannered Olympian cameos while the routine blood-and-thunder is left to the slightly uncomfortable Hamlin. Although it is played perfectly straight, its depiction of the relationship between gods and men establishes this movie as the closest in method and spirit to the new generation of mythological fantasies which came to TV with *Hercules: The Legendary Journeys*, on which it was probably a significant influence. It is, at any rate, an interesting period-piece which is very effective on a full-sized screen.

Danger in the small print: Indy's search for the Lost Ark of the Covenant is only just beginning

CONAN THE BARBARIAN

US; dir. John Milius; starring Arnold Schwarzenegger, James Earl Jones, Max von Sydow, Sandahl Bergman; scr. Milius and Oliver Stone; 129 min.

Even with a Hollywood budget the no-holds-barred approach of Robert E. Howard's classic sword-and-sorcery stories proved fiendishly difficult to translate into visual terms. The evil sorcerer's transformation into a gargantuan snake is well done, but is isolated from the action as a set piece, and the relative paucity of fantastic embellishments in the climax makes the whole enterprise ring false. Milius tried to take aboard the imagery of Frank Frazetta's paintings, which were done for the covers of 1960s paperbacks but became best-sellers in their own right; this required Schwarzenegger to strike defiant poses at the centre of tableaux while the camera studied his muscles and scowl. In the less stylized sequel directed by Richard Fleischer, *Conan the Destroyer* (1984), Grace Jones effortlessly out-scowled Arnie but their posturing could not redeem the tawdry plot. Fleischer's follow-up, *Red Sonja* (1985), employed George Macdonald Fraser as one of its scriptwriters but even he could not contrive a half-way plausible plot and the pairing of Schwarzenegger and Brigitte Nielsen was profoundly uncomfortable.

DRAGONSLAYER

US; dir. Matthew Robbins; starring Peter MacNicol, Caitlin Clarke, Ralph Richardson; scr. Robbins and Hal Barwood; 110 min.

This attempt to utilize new special effects in bringing the newly-fashionable sword-and-sorcery genre to the screen was more effective than average by virtue of moving the dragons to centre-stage; the plot written around them – in which a sorcerer's apprentice takes up magical arms which he is not yet competent to use – is, however, undistinguished.

RAIDERS OF THE LOST ARK

US; dir. Steven Spielberg; starring Harrison Ford, Karen Allen, Ronald Lacey, Denholm Elliott; scr. Lawrence Kasdan; 115 min.

This hectic action/adventure film was one of Spielberg's greatest triumphs, bringing the spirit of classic boys' books into the cinema with a tremendous flourish – although its actual source appears to have been the matinée serial *Lost City of the Jungle* (1940). The fantasy element involving the Ark of the Covenant is carefully hoarded until the climax, when it allows the melodramatic stakes to be raised to the limit. The equivalent McGuffins in *Indiana Jones and the Temple of Doom* (1984) and *Indiana Jones and the Last Crusade* (1989) are similarly kept in reserve but don't actually do much, presumably because any spectacular display on their part would detract from the hero's brave endeavours; the process of de-fantasization continued in the didactically-inclined spinoff TV series *The Young Indiana Jones Chronicles*, launched in 1992. The formula was subsequently applied to other action/adventure films aimed at a young audience, many of which thus acquired a slight element of fantasy. *The Goonies* (1985) and *Sky Pirates* (1986) are typical examples. Three clones which chose – perhaps unwisely – to exaggerate the fantasy element were *Big*

Trouble in Little China (1986), starring Kurt Russell and Kim Cattrall, *The Golden Child* (1986), starring Eddie Murphy and Charles Dance, and *Vibes* (1988), starring Jeff Goldblum and Cyndi Lauper. Russell's philosophical lorry-driver, Murphy's offbeat social worker and Goldblum's laid-back psychic had no chance to match the heroic élan of Ford's unorthodox archaeologist.

TIME BANDITS

UK; dir. Terry Gilliam; starring Ralph Richardson, David Warner, Sean Connery, Ian Holm, John Cleese, Shelley Duvall, Michael Palin, David Rappaport; scr. Gilliam and Palin; 116 min.

This wildly anarchic combination of action/adventure story and comedy follows the course of a hectic race through time undertaken by a party of dwarfs and a schoolboy, in the course of which they meet God (Richardson), the Devil (Warner), Agamemnon (Connery), Robin Hood (Cleese) and Napoleon (Holm). The whole is less than the sum of its parts, which are brilliantly bizarre, but the dizzying pace of the film makes it hugely enjoyable. It was the obvious inspiration for the scrupulously Americanized *Bill and Ted's Excellent Adventure* and its sequel.

1982 THE BEASTMASTER

US; dir. Don Coscarelli; starring Marc Singer, Tanya Roberts, Rip Torn; scr. Coscarelli and Paul Pepperman; 118 min.

A less ambitious sword-and-sorcery adventure than *Conan the Barbarian* or *Dragonslayer*, which combines old and new clichés in the hope of finding a viable alloy. A highborn child hijacked by sorcery becomes skilled in the martial arts and learns to communicate with the local wildlife in order that he might reclaim his heritage. Still casting around for a winning formula, the 1991 sequel *Beastmaster 2: Through the Portal of Time*, directed by Sylvio Tabet, brought Singer to present-day Los Angeles to continue his crusade against evil wizardry. In 1999, the films finally spawned a short-lived and abominably ill-conceived television series, which managed to be both duller and less coherent than the original.

SHOW US THE WAY TO GO HOME: THE *TIME BANDITS*

THE DARK CRYSTAL

UK; dir Jim Henson and Frank Oz; scr. David O'Dell; 94 min.

A vehicle for the products of Jim Henson's Creature Shop, employing designs supplied by the Arthur Rackham-esque illustrator Brian Froud. Thanks to Froud's input the majority of the figures inhabiting the Secondary World are a far cry from the regular staff of *Sesame Street* and *The Muppet Show*, and they confront the young heroes with a magnificently sinister set of opponents as well as providing them with some beautifully surreal helpers. The plot – involving a race to replace the missing fragment of the eponymous device before Evil extends its empire over the world – is rather banal but the film remains an impressive visual experience.

THE LAST UNICORN

UK; dir. Arthur Rankin & Jules Bass; animated; voices of Alan Arkin, Jeff Bridges, Mia Farrow; Christopher Lee, Angela Lansbury; scr. Peter S. Beagle; 93 min.

Peter Beagle was not entirely happy that film rights to his brilliantly heartfelt novel went to Rankin-Bass because no one else would take it on, but he did his best to provide an adequate script. The characters are too cutesy and the animation too primitive to do justice to the story, and the simple-minded songs are woefully inappropriate.

1983 SOMETHING WICKED THIS WAY COMES

US; dir. Jack Clayton; starring Jason Robards, Jonathan Pryce, Diane Ladd, Vidal Peterson; scr. Ray Bradbury; 95 min.

The fact that Ray Bradbury had worked with Disney on Epcot may help to explain why they adopted this highly atypical enterprise. Anyone else would have wanted to do it as a horror story, but Bradbury had written the novel as a moralistic fantasy, paying explicit homage to Charles G. Finney's *The Circus of Dr Lao* while resolutely substituting stern moral rearmament for the earlier novel's sly eroticism. This film comes as close as any visualization could to the texture of the original; its insistence that family values can not merely withstand but profit from the challenge of nightmarish threats is an ambitious extrapolation of the customary Disney credo.

1984

ALL OF ME

US; dir. Carl Reiner; starring Steve Martin, Lily Tomlin, Victoria Tennant; scr. Phil Alden Robinson; 91 min.

A comedy of transmigration based on Ed Davis's novel *Me Too*, in which the avaricious personality of a dying woman is magically transferred into the body of her idealistic lawyer instead of the intended target. Martin puts in one of his best performances as the two rival souls battle for mastery over their shared body, attempting to follow very different corrective agendas. This was one of the best of the 1980s glut of neo-Ansteyan comedies, carrying a sharper edge than most and cleverly gathering narrative pace as it progressed.

THE COMPANY OF WOLVES

UK; dir. Neil Jordan; starring Sarah Patterson, Angela Lansbury, David Warner, Graham Crowden; scr. Jordan and Angela Carter; 95 min.

A wonderfully atmospheric visualization of Angela Carter's radio play (based on two stories in *The Bloody Chamber*) exploring the sexual symbolism embedded in such traditional tales as "Little Red Riding Hood" and transfiguring their cautionary element with a celebration of female sexuality. The film includes some fine set-pieces of lycanthropic metamorphosis. Carter was one of the most significant fantasists of the 20th century and this film conserves as much of her literary grace and complexity as is cinematically possible; she also adapted her allegory *The Magic Toyshop* for the 1986 film.

GHOSTBUSTERS

US; dir. Ivan Reitman; starring Bill Murray, Sigourney Weaver, Dan Aykroyd, Harold Ramis, Rick Moranis; scr. Aykroyd and Ramis; 105 min.

A spirited and refreshingly original comedy about parapsychologists who perfect a machine for hoovering up ghosts and set themselves up in business just in time to cope with a crisis in the affairs of a comprehensively cursed apartment building. The state-of-the-art special effects are very effective, although the climax – in which the Earthly manifestation of Ultimate Evil turns out to be an analogue of the Pilsbury doughboy – is perhaps a little too silly. The chart-topping theme song is an unforgettable earworm. The whole team reassembled for the sake of an equally energetic but rather slavish repetition of the formula in *Ghostbusters II* (1989), which is invigorated by a more earnestly melodramatic climax.

GREMLINS

US; dir. Joe Dante; starring Zach Galligan, Phoebe Cates, Hoyt Axton; scr. Chris Columbus; 106 min.

Like *Ghostbusters*, this film deployed brand-new special effects to devastating effect with the aid of a beautifully offbeat plot. A cute "mogwai" is sold as a Christmas pet with earnest warnings as to the necessity of observing certain rules in its care. When the rules are broken the pet reproduces, producing a horde of monstrous variants which terrorize a small town. A gleefully gruesome antidote to traditional Hollywood Christmas fantasies, it was the most significant foundation-stone of a new era in cinematic fantasy, which blurred the boundary between fantasy and horror. *Gremlins 2: The New Batch* (1990) moved the setting to a hi-tech office building, where the pitch of the action was increased in step with the satirical black comedy. The exercise spawned numerous clones, including several science-fictional examples; the other fantasies include the substandard series begun with *Ghoulies* (1985) and the more interesting *Troll* (1986), in which a young girl is taken over by a nasty troll, who turns the entire neighbourhood into a troll breeding-ground.

THE NEVERENDING STORY

1984; West Germany; dir. and scr. Wolfgang Peterson; starring Noah Hathaway, Barret Oliver, Gerald McRaney; 92 min.

The first phase of an adaptation of Michael Ende's bestselling novel, in which an unhappy young boy takes refuge in the attic of his school with a strange book, and (literally) loses himself within it. The special effects are excellent, and this deserves credit as the first live-action film set in a half-way convincing Secondary World. Unfortunately, the film only covers the first half of the book, and provides a stopgap ending totally out of keeping with the remainder of the text; the mediocre *The Neverending Story II: The Next Chapter* (1990) and the frankly awful *The Neverending Story III* (1994) lost contact with the book and its message as well as skimping on

GETTING TO GRIPS WITH ADULTHOOD: TRANSFORMATION IN *THE COMPANY OF WOLVES*

the effects that made the first part so good. *The Pagemaster* (1994), directed by Joe Johnston – with animated sequences supervised by Maurice Hunt – and starring Macaulay Culkin, was an American didactic fantasy of similar ilk, in which a harassed boy who takes refuge in a library meets up with a series of famous fictional characters while cultivating a modicum of courage.

SPLASH

US; dir. Ron Howard; starring Daryl Hannah, Tom Hanks; scr. Lowell Ganz, Balaboo Mandel & Bruce Jay Friedman; 110 min.

This updated version of *Mr Peabody and the Mermaid* doesn't really add much except for colour and a more convincing tail; the tale, alas, is every bit as unconvincing. Sound performances by the leading actors made it successful enough for a 1988 TV sequel.

1985 THE BLACK CAULDRON

US; animated; voices of Freddie Jones, Nigel Hawthorne, John Hurt, John Huston; scr. David Jones et al; 80 min.

Disney's writers and animators struggled long and hard with this adaptation of Lloyd Alexander's *Chronicles of Prydain*, eventually frittering away so much money (reportedly $25 million) that they abandoned all thought of tackling any more modern classics. Together with Bakshi's *Lord of the Rings* (1978) – similarly aborted with only a fraction of the story told – this project conclusively demonstrated that the awesome difficulties of translating serious Secondary World fantasy into a visual medium would not be overcome until the new millennium. The result is certainly not without merit but it has to be reckoned as a noble failure.

LADYHAWKE

US; dir. Richard Donner; starring Matthew Broderick, Rutger Hauer, Michelle Pfeiffer; scr. Edward Khmara, Michael Thomas & Tom Mankiewicz; 124 min.

A folk-tale fantasy in which two young lovers become shape-shifters – their *alter egos* being a wolf and a hawk – who cannot assume human form simultaneously. The interesting idea is wasted by the uneasily organized storyline which leads to their eventual liberation.

LEGEND

US; dir. Ridley Scott; starring Tom Cruise, Mia Sara, Tim Curry; scr. William Hjortsberg; 109 min.

A good-looking but slow-moving tale of a beautiful innocent (Sara) entrapped by an impressively-horned demon of darkness (Curry) when she tries to catch a glimpse of the last unicorns. No one who saw Cruise's performance as the loutish hero could understand how he went on to become such a big star. The US version was only 89 minutes long but the distributors figured that Brits have more patience.

INCONVENIENT APPARITIONS

The success of *Ghostbusters* and *Gremlins* in 1984 rejuvenated the sub-genre of comic fantasy, unleashing a whole fleet of inconvenient supernatural events upon hapless mortals. The revenant starlet in *Maxie* (1985) – Paul Aaron's visualization of Jack Finney's *Marion's Wall* – is more benign than most, but when the hero screws her while she is in possession of his wife's body the situation becomes too hot to handle. When a dead housewife (Shelley Long) is belatedly brought back to life by her dippy sister in *Hello Again* (1987) her presence is an embarrassment to all concerned. The *Vice Versa* clones which suddenly glutted the marketplace all strove for extra sharpness; in *Like Father, Like Son* (1987) the adult body (Dudley Moore) possessed by the child mind is a busy surgeon, *18 Again!* (1988) carefully exaggerated the age-difference of the exchangers and *Dream a Little Dream* (1989) employed erotic complications – which reached further depths of tastelessness in the 1994 sequel *Dream a Little Dream 2*. Like *Gremlins* and *Ghostbusters II* many such movies strayed into the borderlands of horror-comedy, one notable example being *Those Dear Departed* (1987), in which the unlucky victims who fall to murderous traps laid for her husband by an unhappy wife (Pamela Stephenson) return to haunt her. *Drop Dead Fred* (1991) features Rik Mayall as an imaginary friend who puts on rather repulsive flesh.

THE PURPLE ROSE OF CAIRO

US; dir. and scr. Woody Allen; starring Mia Farrow, Jeff Daniels; 82 min.

A fine sentimental fantasy in which a downtrodden housewife seeks escapist solace in the movies and finds fiction overflowing into reality, initially illuminating her existence but ultimately proving inconvenient. A beautifully wrought and delicately balanced film, considered the best of Allen's films by those who think the ones in which he stars are overly self-obsessed. He went on to write the even more delicate but less fantastic *Alice* (1990) as a further vehicle for Farrow, imbuing the same message with a slightly more upbeat thrust.

RETURN TO OZ

US; dir. Walter Murch; starring Fairuza Balk, Nicol Williamson, Jean Marsh; scr. Murch and Gill Dennis; 110 min.

This belated sequel – in which poor Dorothy is incarcerated in an asylum for insisting that Oz is real, only to find on escaping harsh reality that the Secondary World has also been comprehensively blighted – is even further from the cheerful and consolatory spirit of L. Frank Baum than the original, but it is a very effective dark fantasy. The sinister Wheelers are magnificent, and the corridor of staring heads is seriously creepy. The movie was awarded a PG certificate in the UK, but the fact that it is likely to frighten nervous children should not be reckoned a disadvantage; it insists that children have the wit to overcome their nightmares and shows them how.

Be careful what you wish for...: Jennifer Connelly has a hard road to follow in *Labyrinth*

1986 HIGHLANDER

US; dir. Russell Mulcahy; starring Christopher Lambert, Roxanne Hart, Sean Connery; scr. Gregory Widen et al; 111 min.

A heroic fantasy in which a potentially immortal Scottish clansman is pitched into a fatal knockout contest that will decide who is to be heir to an unspecified destiny. No one could have guessed that the idea would run and run, but it did, perhaps helped by the Queen soundtrack. The first sequel, *Highlander II: The Quickening* (1990) carried the action into the future but further sequels, *Highlander III: The Sorcerer* (1994) and *Highlander: The Final Dimension* (1996), returned to more convenient locations. By then the TV series was under way and the last two movies with Lambert in the lead had to compete for space in video shops. *Highlander: Endgame* (2000) brought Lambert together with stars of both derivative TV series. However, none of the subsequent work has lived up to the stylish flair of the original.

LABYRINTH

US/UK; dir. Jim Henson; starring David Bowie, Jennifer Connelly, Toby Froud; scr. Terry Jones; 101 min.

The follow-up to *The Dark Crystal* received a mixed reaction from the critics – many disliked Bowie's laid-back Goblin King and thought the story-line – a young girl rescuing the brother she had carelessly wished away – too slight. However, its endearingly quirky charm and fine monsters may turn *Labyrinth* into the kind of cult movie that will still command affection when its contemporaries have been forgotten.

PEGGY SUE GOT MARRIED

US; dir. Francis Ford Coppola; starring Kathleen Turner, Nicholas Cage; scr. Jerry Leichtling and Arlene Sarner; 104 min.

A timeslip fantasy in which a messed-up woman on the brink of divorce is flipped back to her schooldays. Presented with a chance to start over, she decides to make all the same mistakes again, even though she has far less reason than Dorothy to think that there's no place like home. You might think that anyone who wouldn't do things differently if they had their time over – even if their lives had been idyllic – is an arrant coward with no imagination, but that's not the official position in Hollywood.

1987 THE BRAVE LITTLE TOASTER

US; animated; voices of Jon Lovitz, Tim Stack, Timothy E. Day; scr. Jerry Rees and Joe Ranft; 90 min.

Thomas M. Disch's original story is a subtle and graceful satire on anthropomorphic animal fantasies, which instead uses anthropomorphic household devices to illuminate the absurdity of such button-pushing exercises as Disney's *The Incredible Journey* (1963). Parody can, however, be so subtle that it can be consumed as if it were that which it is sending up; one hopes and presumes that Disch laughed all the way to the bank when they bought the rights, and was suitably impressed by the fact that the result is actually rather good.

DER HIMMEL UBER BERLIN

(WINGS OF DESIRE)

Germany; dir. Wim Wenders; starring Bruno Ganz, Solveig Dommartin, Otto Sander; scr. Wenders and Peter Handke; 130 min.

A subtle, serious and altogether admirable cinematic *conte philosophique*, partly shot in monochrome, in which one of two angels visiting Berlin falls in love with a circus artiste and decides that he wants to be human. He and his companion spend a lot of time discussing the implications of such a decision but the movie never gets bogged down because the visualization is so good. In the sequel, *Faraway, So Close* (1993) the second angel (Sander) follows the example of the first (Ganz), who is now running a pizza parlour; the even more extended length of the second film (164 minutes) did stretch the patience of audiences who found its meditations repetitive and its quality less magical.

MADE IN HEAVEN

US; dir. Alan Rudolph; starring Timothy Hutton, Kelly McGillis, Maureen Stapleton; 103 min.

This enterprisingly odd tale begins in Heaven, where a bored young man falls in love with a spirit as yet unborn and applies to be reincarnated as her contemporary. Unfortunately, neither reincarnated soul knows that it can only find true happiness with the other and chance seems determined to keep them apart – which puts an undue strain on the boy's guardian angel (Debra Winger, in drag).

MANNEQUIN

US; dir. Michael Gottlieb; starring Andrew McCarthy, Kim Cattrall; scr. Gottlieb and Edward Rugoff; 89 min.

A dull Ansteyan fantasy which evidently owes its inspiration to the movie *One Touch of Venus* rather than the book on which that movie was based. The department store dummy is a poor substitute for the goddess Aphrodite. In the sequel, *Mannequin Two: On the Move* (1991), William Ragsdale and Kirsty Swanson struggle with an even duller script.

THE PRINCESS BRIDE

US; dir. Rob Reiner; starring Carey Elwes, Mandy Patinkin, Chris Sarandon; scr. William Goldman; 98 min.

Goldman presumably wrote his wonderfully exaggerated and very clever spoof folk-tale to get away from the frustrating rigours of movie work, intending it as a deftly moralistic meditation on the art and craft of story-telling, but the inevitable happened. The movie is slighter than the book but it is fun, and some of the sly sarcasm survives.

THE WITCHES OF EASTWICK

US; dir. George Miller; starring Jack Nicholson, Cher, Susan Sarandon, Michelle Pfeiffer; scr. Michael Cristofer; 118 min.

A slick and sharp adaptation of John Updike's Faustian satire, in which the aspirations of three sophisticated women sadly disappointed by their discarded husbands can only be met – on a strictly temporary basis – by the Devil himself (Nicholson). The lurid ending, in which the Devil tries to raise Hell after being judged wanting in his turn, is more overstated than the conclusion of the book, but effectively so; the three leading actresses contribute deftly contrasted but equally fine performances.

YANZI KOU

(ROUGE)

Hong Kong; dir. Stanley Kwan; starring Anita Mui, Leslie Cheung; scr. Li Bihua & Qui-Dai Anping; 93 min.

A beautiful and delicately executed adaptation of a novel by Lee Bihua, in which the ghost of a courtesan who killed herself in the 1930s returns to Earth in the present day, intent on searching out the lover who failed to honour his part in their suicide pact. It is much more effective than the Hong Kong-produced comedy ghost story *Esprit d'Amour* (1983), which had attempted to adapt a similar motif to the Hollywood formula.

1988 ALICE

UK/Switzerland/West Germany; dir. and scr. Jan Svankmajer; starring Kristyna Kohoutova; 85 min.

An interesting interpretation of Lewis Carroll's classic fantasy which superimposes live action on animation to surreal effect. It is claustrophobic and rather nightmarish, taking aboard some of the psychoanalytic affectations of recent UK TV versions of the story and the Dennis Potter-scripted *Dreamchild* (1986). Czech animator Svankmajer went on to make a similarly intriguing version of *Faust* (1994).

... YOU MIGHT JUST GET IT: *THE WITCHES OF EASTWICK* ARE IN FOR THE DEVIL OF A TIME

A HEAD FOR BUSINESS: *BEETLEJUICE* GETS ON WITH THE JOB

BEETLEJUICE

US; dir. Tim Burton; staring Alec Baldwin, Geena Davis, Michael Keaton, Winona Ryder; scr. Michael McDowell and Warren Skaaren; 92 min.

A recently-deceased married couple appeal to the Celestial Bureaucracy for help in keeping their dream house out of the clutches of its obnoxious new owners but get no joy from the harassed time-servers. They turn instead to the renegade spirit Beetlejuice, whom they release from the imprisonment visited upon him for his former sins. A bold and vivid modernization of the theme of Oscar Wilde's *The Canterville Ghost*, replete with the Gothic touches that were to become Burton's chief stock-in-trade. Keaton struck a neat balance between mischief and menace, a year before he and Burton hit the big time with *Batman*.

BIG

US; dir. Penny Marshall; starring Tom Hanks, Elizabeth Perkins, John Heard, Robert Loggia; scr. Gary Ross and Anne Spielberg; 102 min.

An effective modern Ansteyan fantasy, in which a young boy on the threshold of his teenage years wishes that he were big and has his wish granted. He finds life as a child in an adult's body confusing and challenging, but not unrewarding. It is very difficult to convey authentic innocence in these cynical times but Hanks's fine central performance tuned him up nicely for *Forrest Gump*.

HIGH SPIRITS

UK; dir. and scr. Neil Jordan; starring Peter O'Toole, Steve Guttenberg, Beverly D'Angelo, Daryl Hannah; 96 min.

Hoping to attract tourists, the owner of an Irish castle decides to fake a few supernatural manifestations, but his plans are disrupted by the appearance of real ghosts. Jordan's plans for a subtle and meaningful comedy were scuppered by the producers, who wanted broad farce and got it, comprehensively ruining the movie.

THE NAVIGATOR: A MEDIEVAL ODYSSEY

New Zealand; dir. Vincent Ward; staring Hamish McFarlane, Bruce Lyons, Chris Haywood; scr. Ward and Kelly Lyons; 91 min.

A heartfelt and carefully understated allegory in which medieval English villagers endangered by the plague undertake a subterranean pilgrimage in response to a prophecy uttered by an innocent, ultimately emerging – uncomprehendingly and temporarily – in modern Auckland, New Zealand. The film is beautifully shot, using the now-familiar device of moving from black-and-white to colour to signal the transition between worlds, and very effective.

WHO FRAMED ROGER RABBIT?

US; dir. Robert Zemeckis; starring Bob Hoskins, Christopher Lloyd, Joanna Cassidy; scr. Jeffrey Price and Peter S. Seaman; 103 min.

A ground-breaking adaptation of Gary K. Wolf's novel *Who Censored Roger Rabbit?*, which mixes live action and computerized animation more completely than had ever been possible before – although some notable precedents had been put in place by Yoram Gross after he moved to Australia in 1977. Audiences were ready to overlook the thin plot – in which a world-weary private eye (Hoskins) has to solve a mystery set in Toontown, the ghetto where Hollywood's two-dimensional second-class citizens hang out – but it only required one more movie (*Cool World*) to make such interactions seem silly.

WILLOW

US; dir. Ron Howard; starring Val Kilmer, Joanne Whalley, Warwick Davis, Jean Marsh; scr. Bob Dolman; 126 min.

A quest fantasy cast in the mould of Tolkien's *The Hobbit*, although George Lucas took credit for the "original" story – in which a diminutive hero (Davis) must obtain taller and better-looking help to save a mislaid baby from a wicked sorceress (not nicked from the one in Narnia - honest, guv!). It works quite well, considering.

1989 ALWAYS

US; dir. Steven Spielberg; starring Richard Dreyfuss, Holly Hunter, Brad Johnson, Audrey Hepburn, John Goodman; scr. Jerry Belson; 123 min.

Spielberg's abiding love of feel-good fantasy sometimes led him astray, and his decision to remake the wartime morale-booster *A Guy Named Joe* seemed slightly ill-judged, given the absence of a war. Fighting forest fires is a noble cause, but it doesn't require the same involvement of the larger society. The movie is, however, saved by fine performances from Dreyfuss and the ever-reliable Hunter, and by the canny casting of Hepburn as the angel who supervises the dead pilot's final romantic mission. The movie had no chance of matching the delicate poignancy of the original but it does as well as could be expected.

ERIK THE VIKING

UK; dir. and scr. Terry Jones; starring Tim Robbins, John Cleese, Mickey Rooney, Eartha Kitt; Imogen Stubbs; 108 min.

An uneasy comedy in which a Viking who feels that there ought to be more to life than looting and pillaging sails off to set the world to rights. The plot was presumably suggested by William Morris's *The Earthly Paradise* but it swiftly moves on from an island Utopia to Valhalla, where the gods are revealed to be wanton boys whose sport is killing.

FIELD OF DREAMS

US; dir. and scr. Phil Alden Robinson; starring Kevin Costner, James Earl Jones; 107 min.

A ponderous adaptation of W. P. Kinsella's allegorical novel *Shoeless Joe*, about a farmer who cuts a baseball diamond in his crop, in which the ghosts of great players stage a classic game. "If you make the movie," some kindly spirit must have whispered in Costner's ear, "people will come" – and, gorblimey, they did! Only in America....

HOW TO GET AHEAD IN ADVERTISING

UK; dir. and scr. Bruce Robinson; starring Richard E. Grant, Rachel Ward; 94 min.

A deliberately crude satire in which a man psychologically ill-fitted for his job in advertising grows a new head equipped with an appropriately cynical and conscienceless brain.

THE LITTLE MERMAID

US; dir. & scr. Ron Clements & John Musker; animated; voices of Rene Auberjonois, Christopher Daniel Barnes, Jodi Benson; 83 min.

This carefully calculated return to the formula standardized in the glory days marked the beginning of Disney's modern period. Hans Christian Andersen's story is one of the best of all imitation folk-tales, resilient enough to retain some of its charm and substance even after comprehensive Disneyfication by John Musker. The final product is hardly a match for *Snow White* but it can certainly compare with *Cinderella*.

1990 EDWARD SCISSORHANDS

US; dir. Tim Burton; starring Johnny Depp, Winona Ryder, Dianne Wiest, Vincent Price; scr. Caroline Thompson; 98 min.

A magnificently bizarre and gloriously sentimental modern fable in which an artificial boy (Depp) with scissors instead of hands leaves the seclusion of his Gothic castle with an Avon lady to seek his fortune in suburbia. His skills win friends among the homemakers, but they all turn against him when the going gets rough – and so does the girl he loves (Ryder). The film established Burton as a highly original cinematic artist.

GHOST

US; dir. Jerry Zucker; starring Patrick Swayze, Demi Moore, Whoopi Goldberg; scr. Bruce Joel Rubin; 127 min.

A confused mix of comedy, drama and romance, in which the ghost of a murdered man has a hard time bringing himself to the attention of his widow – which he desperately needs to do if he is to protect her and bring his killer to justice. It was a surprise hit, presumably because fans of Swayze and Moore stubbornly refused to notice that its metaphysical framework is a crude affair patched together for momentary convenience, without the least trace of moral or logical coherence.

JACOB'S LADDER

US; dir. Adrian Lyne; starring Tim Robbins, Elizabeth Pena; scr. Bruce Joel Rubin; 113 min.

It is amazing that the man who scripted the cheesy *Ghost* could also come up with this defiantly grim and taut posthumous fantasy, which dexterously updates Ambrose Bierce's *Occurrence at Owl Creek Bridge* to the Vietnam war. Robbins contributes an excellent central performance and the metaphysical framework, though somewhat stretched, is both morally and logically coherent.

LITTLE NEMO:
ADVENTURES IN SLUMBERLAND

Japan; dir. Misami Hata & William T. Hurtz; animated; voices of Gabriel Damon, Mickey Rooney, Rene Auberjonois; scr. Chris Columbus & Richard Outten; 85 min.

This exuberant adaptation of Winsor McCay's classic cartoon strip was treated with suspicion in the US, even though it had been re-shaped for the screen by Ray Bradbury. It had been preceded by several *manga* films, including *Akira* (1988), but may have done more than those products to spread the news that Japanese animation was possessed of an energy and enterprise that Hollywood had long since given up.

TRULY, MADLY, DEEPLY

UK; dir. and scr. Anthony Minghella; starring Juliet Stevenson, Alan Rickman, Michael Maloney; 107 min.

An unusually sensitive moral fable in which a young woman

devastated by the death of her lover is allowed to keep his ghost around until she learns to let go. The delicate balance of wit and sentimentality is the closest cinematic fantasy has ever come to capturing the deft artistry of such novelists as Robert Nathan. It inspired a near-clone in *Heaven's a Drag* (1994), directed by Peter Mackenzie, in which one half of a gay couple returns to console his partner after dying of AIDS.

WINGS OF FAME

Netherlands; dir. Otakar Votocek; staring Peter O'Toole, Colin Firth; scr. Votocek and Herman Koch; 109 min.

A thoughtful, clever and highly original posthumous fable in which the newly dead are accommodated in a luxury hotel for as long as their fame lasts; the story tracks the peculiar relationship which develops there between a writer and the young man who assassinated him in order to win a moment's celebrity. It is the best modern successor to *Outward Bound*.

THE WITCHES

US; dir. Nicolas Roeg; starring Anjelica Huston, Mai Zetterling, Jasen Fisher; scr. Allan Scott; 91 min.

Roald Dahl's novel posed as many problems for its adaptors as *Charlie and the Chocolate Factory*, and the baroque ending seems slightly ill-fitting, but the mid-section, where the small boy stumbles upon the witches' convention and is turned into a mouse, is excellent. Most of Dahl's other fantasies could only be done as animated features; the most notable of these is *James and the Giant Peach* (1996), which was Henry Selick's follow-up to *The Nightmare Before Christmas*.

1991 THE ADDAMS FAMILY

US; dir. Barry Sonnenfeld; starring Anjelica Huston, Raul Julia, Christopher Lloyd; scr. Caroline Thompson & Larry Wilson; 99 min.

A big-screen adaptation of the cult TV series, in which Huston and Julia work hard to recapture the stylish Gothic irony of Carolyn Jones and John Astin. The reappearance of Uncle Fester (Lloyd) after long being presumed dead provides the basis of the rather slender plot. Nostalgia and the louche surrealism of some of the set-pieces helped the film to box-office success, resulting in the 1993 sequel *Addams Family Values*, also directed by Sonnenfeld, in which a new baby excites envious feelings and murderous intent in the existing children. Despite the best efforts of daughter Wednesday (Christina Ricci) and the serial killer hired as a nanny (Carol Kane), the new arrival flourishes. The second film is better than the first, bucking the trend, partly because it cleverly amplifies those aspects of the first film that worked best and partly because of the rivetingly menacing performance of Ricci, who fitted into her part with uncanny skill and conviction.

AMA

UK; dir. and scr. Kwesi Owusu; starring Thomas Baptiste, Anima Misi; 100 min.

An interesting attempt to employ African folklore in dramatizing the plight of Africans living in exile, in a society very different from the one sanctified by their traditions. The ancestral spirits are compelled to make themselves heard via modern information technology, and their appointed messenger suffers inevitable confusion as to the nature and purpose of her mission.

BEAUTY AND THE BEAST

US; dir Gray Trousdal & Kirk Wise; animated; voices of Paige O'Hara, Robby Benson, Angela Lansbury, David Ogden Stiers; scr. Linda Wolverton; 85 min.

A spirited rendering of the classic fairy tale, with the customary songs. Disney's saccharine sentimentality erases all the subtlety recognized and amplified by Cocteau's classic version, although a couple of scenes are casually lifted therefrom, but the final product is quite effective – more so, at any rate, than the 1976 live-action version directed by Fielder Cook and starring George C. Scott.

BILL AND TED'S BOGUS JOURNEY

US; dir. Peter Hewitt; starring Alex Winter, Keanu Reeves, Jeff Miller, David Carrera; scr. Ed Solomon and Chris Matheson; 93 min.

This sequel to the blithely absurd science-fictional comedy *Bill and*

EARTHBOUND SPIRITS

The spirits of the departed may be held back from further progress by the need to obtain justice or by quasi-angelic protective duties. Movies routinely conflate the two purposes, as in *The Uninvited* (1944), based on Dorothy Macardle's best-selling supernaturalized romance, and *Wonder Man* (1945), in which the ghost of a murdered night-club entertainer (Danny Kaye) has to help his bookish twin set matters to rights. Explicit terms for further progress are laid down in *The Time of Their Lives* (1946), an Abbott and Costello vehicle about two American patriots unjustly condemned as traitors, and *The Ghosts of Berkeley Square* (1947), an adaptation of *No Nightingales* by Caryl Brahms and S. J. Simon, in which the ghosts of two old military men witness a series of historical catastrophes. As with many Hollywood traditions, this one deteriorated into cynical silliness in the modern era. *The Heavenly Kid* (1985), in which a dead teenager has to aid a nerd in order to qualify for Heaven, *My Boyfriend's Back* (1993), in which a nerd killed saving a girl's life is allowed to accompany her to the prom anyway, and *Chances Are* (1989), in which a widow realizes that her daughter's boyfriend is a reincarnation of her dead lover, are all calculatedly trivial – but *Ghost* (1990) and *Truly, Madly, Deeply* (1990) managed to breathe some real spirit back into the sub-genre. As with most other sub-genres, European films tend to be more earnest; a notable example is Krzystof Kieslowski's Polish political fantasy *No End* (1984).

Ted's Excellent Adventure (1988) crosses genres by virtue of including an episode of posthumous fantasy, after which Death – having failed to retain Bill and Ted in the Afterlife – returns with them to Earth, joining their epoch-making rock band.

THE BUTCHER'S WIFE

US; dir. Terry Hughes; starring Demi Moore, Jeff Daniels, George Dzundza, Mary Steenburgen; scr. Ezra Litwak and Marjorie Schwartz; 105 min.

A curious lightweight romance, too earnest to be reckoned a comedy, in which the premonitions of a clairvoyant (Moore) complicate the lives of her husband's customers but eventually begin to draw some order out of the chaotic froth of their emotional problems.

DEAD AGAIN

US; dir. Kenneth Branagh; starring Branagh, Emma Thompson, Andy Garcia, Derek Jacobi, Hanna Schygulla; scr. Scott Frank; 108 min.

A tricky romance of reincarnation in which a present-day private eye (Branagh) discovers that he and his amnesiac client are in grave danger of being caught up in the recapitulation of a 40-year-old murder. The crucial plot-twist is difficult to swallow, but it adds a welcome element of complexity to a fragile plot.

DEFENDING YOUR LIFE

US; dir. and scr. Albert Brooks; starring Brooks, Meryl Streep, Rip Torn, Lee Grant; 112 min.

An enterprising posthumous fantasy in which the newly dead mark time while awaiting a hearing in Judgment City. An advertising executive (Brooks) is distracted from his own case by an inappropriate romantic attachment, but his advocate (Torn) remains cheerfully confident. Brooks's downbeat humour lacks the style and casual profligacy of Woody Allen's but one could argue that it has more depth.

HOOK

US; dir. Steven Spielberg; starring Robin Williams, Dustin Hoffman, Julia Roberts, Bob Hoskins, Maggie Smith; scr. Jim V. Hart & Malia Scotch Marmo; 144 min.

Spielberg's sequel to *Peter Pan* is unmistakably self-referential and self-indulgent. A middle-aged man who never wanted to grow up is allowed back into Neverland to meet his old playmates and get to grips with his revitalized nemesis. Tinkerbell, who used to be played in the theatre by a spotlight, is now Julia Roberts, while Captain Hook, who used to be an old Etonian, is now pure ham – but that's Hollywood.

1992 ALADDIN

US; dir. & scr. Ron Clements & John Musker; animated; voices of Scott Weinger, Robin Williams, Linda Larkin; 90 min.

One of the most successful of the new wave of Disney adaptations of children's favourites, doggedly but energetically proceeding along the deep rut established by its forebears. The songs are undistinguished but Robin Williams's thoroughly modern wisecracking genie has enough panache to carry the plot along. *Return of Jafar* (1994) was a patchwork pilot for a run-of-the-mill animated TV series in which Dan Castellaneta of *The Simpsons* provided the genie's voice, but Williams returned in *Aladdin and the King of Thieves* (1996).

LILIOM'S CHILDREN

The basic formula of *Liliom* – in which the dead are allowed to return to Earth to attend to family matters – became the template of an entire sub-genre of cinematic fantasy. The most famous example was based on the original's Broadway spinoff, the Rodgers and Hammerstein musical *Carousel*, which was filmed in 1956 by Henry King, starring Gordon Macrae and Shirley Jones. David Belasco's very similar but carefully softened play *The Return of Peter Grimm* (1911) was likewise filmed in both silent (1926) and talkie (1935) versions. *Beyond Tomorrow* (1940) was the first of several movies to soften the formula even further in moulding it to the purposes of sentimental Christmas fantasy. During the war years the dead were permitted to offer effective comfort to their hard-pressed families in such movies as Irving Pichel's *Happy Land* (1943), and when the war ended the theme remained available for comedy treatment, as in *That's the Spirit* (1945) and *The Cockeyed Miracle* (1946; aka *Mr Griggs Returns*). Comedy continued to outweigh sentimentality thereafter, although the two were usually compounded, as they are in *O'Hara's Wife* (1983), the hectic Bill Cosby vehicle *Ghost Dad* (1990) and *And You Thought Your Parents Were Weird* (1991).

COOL WORLD

US; dir. Ralph Bakshi; starring Kim Basinger, Gabriel Byrne, Brad Pitt; scr. Michel Grais and Mark Victor; 102 min.

Another attempt to marry live action and animation, less successful than *Who Framed Roger Rabbit?* A comic-book artist discovers a way into the parallel world inhabited by his creations; he enables a sexy "doodle" to put on flesh and escape to the real world, where she takes up with a sceptical private eye. The hysterical and wildly implausible plot serves to set up some sight-boggling morph sequences but always seems like much ado about next-to-nothing.

DEATH BECOMES HER

US; dir. Robert Zemeckis; starring Meryl Streep, Goldie Hawn, Bruce Willis, Isabella Rossellini; scr. Martin Donovan and David Koepp; 104 min.

A black comedy of female rivalry in which two ageing socialites (Streep and Hawn) obtain access to the elixir of life and are unwise enough to allow their conflict to escalate. The two harridans fight over the meek man-in-the-middle (Willis) with single-minded malice, unfazed by the horrific injuries they inflict upon one another, but once the point has been made the joke has nowhere to go but on and on, ending up way beyond the limits of sense and sensitivity.

HOLLYWOOD'S CAMELOT

After World War II Arthurian fantasy became a thriving cinematic sub-genre, although its paradigm examples were mostly devoid of supernatural content. The matinée serial *The Adventures of Sir Galahad* (1949), starring future Superman George Reeves, sent Galahad in search of Excalibur, but *Knights of the Round Table* (1953), starring Robert Taylor, had not even a quest to ennoble it. *The Black Knight* (1954), the comic-strip-derived *Prince Valiant* (1954) and *Lancelot and Guinevere* (1963; aka *Sword of Lancelot*) gradually established a standardized version of Arthurian England that was eventually taken to full stretch by the bizarrely misconceived musical *Camelot* (1967). John Boorman's *Excalibur* (1981) cast Nicol Williamson as Merlin and Helen Mirren as Morgan le Fay, but neither performed much magic and the good example of its ugly battle-scenes had little influence. *Sword of the Valiant* (1984), directed by Stephen Weeks, could not figure out how to make sense of the steadfastly enigmatic medieval allegory *Sir Gawain and the Green Knight*. Hollywood's Camelot reasserted its dominion in the ponderous *First Knight* (1995) and the remake of *Prince Valiant* (1997). The influence of the Hollywoodized ideal of chivalry even began to spread to Europe, being clearly reflected in Giacomo Battiato's *Hearts and Armour* (1985), based on Ariosto's Italianization of the "Song of Roland," *Orlando Furioso*.

FERNGULLY: THE LAST RAINFOREST

Australia; animated; voices of Tim Curry, Samantha Mathis, Christian Slater; scr. Jim Cox; 68 min.

A musical allegory featuring fairy folk who live deep in the heart of a magical forest; its heavy-handed message – which established it as a key work of modern ecological mysticism – is more radical than anything Disney would have countenanced, although Hanna-Barbera produced the earnestly lacklustre *Once Upon a Forest* (1992). *Ferngully* extrapolated a tradition of quirkily intelligent Australian animated films whose previous highlights had been *Grendel, Grendel, Grendel* (1981) and Yoram Gross's *Epic* (1985) and *The Magic Riddle* (1991).

ORLANDO

UK; dir. and scr. Sally Potter; starring Tilda Swinton; 93 min.

The producers obtained technical support from Russia, France, Italy and the Netherlands in making this episodic version of Virginia Woolf's sly decadent romance of immortality and transsexualism, so it's hardly surprising that the bits don't fit together into any kind of coherent whole. Quentin Crisp contributes a fine cameo as Queen Elizabeth I.

PRELUDE TO A KISS

US; dir. Norman Rene; starring Meg Ryan, Alec Baldwin, Kathy Bates, Ned Beatty; scr. Craig Lucas; 106 min.

An adaptation of Lucas's blackly comic play, in which a young man on honeymoon gets the strange impression that his new wife isn't the person with whom he fell in love. The solution to the mystery is hard to swallow and the saving *deus ex machina* is even more indigestible.

THE PRINCESS AND THE GOBLIN

UK/Hungary; dir. Jozsef Gemes; animated; voices of Joss Ackland, Claire Bloom, Roy Kinnear; scr. & prod. Robin Lyons; 111 min.

A faithful adaptation of George MacDonald's Victorian classic. It is, alas, too long and slow-paced – and perhaps too old-fashioned – to appeal to a modern juvenile audience.

STAY TUNED

US; dir. Peter Hyams; starring John Ritter, Pam Dawber, Jeffrey Jones; scr. Tom S. Parker and Jim Jennewein; 98 min.

An enterprising Faustian satire in which a couch potato (Ritter) who buys a satellite TV dish from the Devil is sucked into his set along with his wife. They are forced to participate in rigged game shows and risk death in sadistic soaps while their TV-wise son and his older sister try to figure out a way to get them out before the deadline for their damnation elapses.

1993 GROUNDHOG DAY

US; dir. Harold Ramis; starring Bill Murray, Andie MacDowell; scr. Ramis and Danny Rubin; 101 min.

A cynical TV reporter (Murray) finds himself repeating the same day over and over again; after making every possible attempt to escape and instituting every possible strategy for making the most of the unusual opportunities presented by the situation he finally gets it right. The rapid cutting, which eventually casts the audience adrift upon the endless but depressingly finite sea of possibility, allows the film a significant triumph of form over content.

HOCUS POCUS

US; dir. Kenny Ortega; starring Bette Midler, Sarah Jessica Parker; Kathy Najimy, Omri Katz; scr. Neil Cuthbert & Mick Garris; 96 min.

In this reasonably effective Disney comedy inquisitive children inadvertently reanimate three Salem witches on Hallowe'en. The revenants suffer considerable culture-shock, and barely begin to get their nasty act together before they are rendered harmless again.

THE LAST ACTION HERO

US; dir. John McTiernan; starring Arnold Schwarzenegger, Austin O'Brien, Charles Dance; scr. Shane Black and David Arnott; 131 min.

NO SUBSTITUTE FOR A HORSE: *LES VISITEURS* CONSIDER A MODERN MARVEL

A young boy obtains a magic ticket that will take him into the world-within-the-text of his favourite movie; unfortunately, the arch-villain (Dance) pinches the ticket and the hero (Schwarzenegger) has to follow him into the "real" world: a world where villains can win – except, of course that they can't, because the whole enterprise is caught in a self-referential loop whose parodic insults return like vindictive boomerangs. The enterprise was generally reckoned to be a fearfully expensive folly, but hindsight reveals that the finished product is ironically acceptable as the very action movie it is trying hard not to be.

THE NIGHTMARE BEFORE CHRISTMAS

US; dir. Henry Selick; animated; voices of Danny Elfman, Chris Sarandon, Catherine O'Hara; scr. Caroline Thompson and Michael McDowell; 75 min.

This blackly humorous account of the Pumpkin King's attempt to add Christmas to his Hallowe'en empire is usually billed as *Tim Burton's Nightmare Before Christmas*, although he only provided the story on which the script is based and acted as co-producer; the very striking stop-motion animation was supervised by Henry Selick. The parody of Christmas musicals is affectionate as well as inventive, providing a sound basis for the admirably bizarre visualization.

LES VISITEURS

France; dir. Jean-Marie Poire; starring Christian Clavier, Jean Reno; scr. Clavier and Poire; 107 min.

A timeslip fantasy in which a knight and his squire are displaced by magic from the 12th century to the present day. Once they have found their bearings – after gleaning the usual quota of laughs from their confusions – they react very differently to the reality of life in republican France. The noble crusader can hardly wait to reverse the spell and get home to his native time, but his companion has other ideas. The film was hugely successful in its native land, outgrossing *Jurassic Park* there by a vast margin.

1994 THE LION KING

US; dir. Roger Allers & Rob Minkoff; animated; voices of Matthew Broderick, Rowan Atkinson, Jeremy Irons, James Earl Jones, Whoopi Goldberg; scr. Irene Mecchi, Jonathan Roberts & Linda Woolverton; 88 min.

Although you might think that *Bambi* wouldn't work nearly as well with teeth and claws, this picture was a huge hit at the box office, easily outscoring Disney's other recent, far more orthodox, offerings. It is reputed to have done particularly good business in South Africa, where it was assumed to be a political allegory. Adolf Hitler was said to have adored *Snow White and the Seven Dwarfs*, so this may not have been the first time that an unintended meaning was discovered in a Disney film, but one inevitably has far more sympathy for those who cast Nelson Mandela as the Lion King.

THE MASK

US; dir. Chuck Russell; starring Jim Carrey, Cameron Diaz, Amy Yasbeck; scr. Mike Werb; 101 min.

A satirical comic-book-derived caper exploiting as well as satirizing the formula by which an innocent klutz can be turned into a superhero by some arbitrary narrative device. The flashy special effects fit Carrey's frenetic style like a well-tailored glove, albeit one with six fingers and no thumb.

THE SWAN PRINCESS

US; dir. Richard Rich; animated; voices of Jack Palance, Michelle Nicastro, John Cleese; 89 min.

Former Disney animators teamed up under Richard Rich to make this slavish imitation of the standard product, proving that they could do it just as formulaically without the studio breathing down their necks. Although it was distantly based on the folk-tale best known via Tchaikovsky's ballet *Swan Lake*, the story could hardly expect to carry much conviction featuring a prince called Derek.

THUMBELINA

US; dir., prod. and scr. Don Bluth; animated; voices of Jodi Benson, Gary Imhoff, Gino Conforti; 86 min.

The other Disney renegades who set up Don Bluth Productions did a little better than the animators of *The Swan Princess* with this spirited version of the Hans Christian Andersen story, which is strong enough to survive embellishment by Barry Manilow songs.

1995

CASPER

US; dir. Brad Silberling; starring Christina Ricci, Bill Pullman, Cathy Moriarty, Eric Idle; 100 min.

Poor Christina Ricci moved from the sublime to the ridiculous in following *Addams Family Values* with this lavish but rather ill-conceived adaptation of a long-established cartoon character usually known as Casper the Friendly Ghost. It was successful enough with its intended audience to spawn a sequel, *Casper: A Spirited Beginning* (1997).

LA CITE DES ENFANTS PERDUS
(THE CITY OF LOST CHILDREN)

France; dir. Jean-Pierre Jeunet and Marc Caro; starring Ron Perlman, Judith Vittet, Dominique Pinon, Daniel Emilfork; scr. Jeunet, Caro and Gilles Adrien; 112 min.

A vivid hallucinatory allegory in which a circus strongman (Perlman) and a runaway orphan (Vittet) go in search of the strongman's adopted brother, who has been kidnapped by cyclopean cyborgs. The child has been taken to an oil-rig where freakish relics of experiments in genetic engineering are controlled by a man incapable of dreaming; he is trying to make good this lack by stealing the dreams of children – but the ones he kidnaps usually have nightmares. The inhabitants of the phantasmagorical mainland are even more freakish than the population of the oil-rig; they include an ultra-decadent hit man whose instruments are trained fleas. This is the most outstanding cinematic fantasy of the new *fin-de-siècle*.

THE INDIAN IN THE CUPBOARD

US; dir. Frank Oz; starring Hal Scardino, Litefoot, David Keith; scr. Melissa Mathison; 96 min.

A thoughtful and effective adaptation of a Lynne Reid Banks novel, in which a young boy finds that the battered cupboard his brother has given him as a birthday present can convert toys into real people. The 18th-century Iroquois brave who is the first to emerge therefrom eventually makes peace with a 19th-century cowboy, but for one of his diminutive size a pet rat poses a less tractable problem.

JUMANJI

US; dir. Joe Johnstone; starring Robin Williams, Jonathan Hyde, Kirsten Dunst; scr. Jonathan Hensleigh, Greg Taylor & Jim Strain; 104 min.

A spectacular adaptation of a novel by Chris van Allsburg, which makes use of the same computer-assisted special effects as *Jurassic Park*, allowing the hypothetical world to invade the real world in no uncertain terms. A hapless player trapped in the magical game long before its discovery by two contemporary children tries to help them set things to rights, but things get out of hand. The real stars of the film are the stampeding animals which trash the neighbourhood.

MORTAL KOMBAT

US; dir. Paul Anderson; starring Robin Shou, Linden Ashby, Christopher Lambert; scr. Kevin Droney; 101 min.

This live-action version of the video game lifted its plot from the martial-arts film *Enter the Dragon* and was successful enough to generate the even less plausible sequel M*ortal Kombat: Annihilation* (1997). *Mortal Kombat: The Animated Movie* (1995) was more authentic. New computer games borrow so avidly from the cinema that films-of-the-games have become a significant sub-genre. Other such crossovers include *Dragon Knight* (1991), *Super Mario Brothers* (1993), the excellent animation *Street Fighter* (1995) and the dreadful 1994 Jean Claude Van Damme live action film of the same name, *Final Fantasy: The Spirits Within* (2001), *Tomb Raider* (2001), and *Resident Evil* (2002).

THE PROPHECY

US; dir & scr. Gregory Widen; starring Christopher Walker, Viggo Mortensen, Eric Stolze, Elias Koteas; 98 mins.

An unusually dark look at angels returning to earth – this time, it's to help wage a second rebellion against God. Christopher Walken is excellent as a humanity-hating Gabriel, but he's upstaged by Mortensen's sinister Lucifer, who sides with mankind in order to help preserve his own power. Widen does a great job of making his angels suitably inhuman. The sequels (1998, 2000) have not been anywhere near as good.

THREE WISHES

US; dir. Martha Coolidge; staring Patrick Swayze, Mary Elizabeth Mastrantonio; scr. Elizabeth Anderson; 115 min.

A glossy but coy adaptation of the famous folk-tale, set in the 1950s. Swayze plays a peripatetic fairy godfather in a manner which makes the film reminiscent of an extended episode of *Highway to Heaven*.

TOY STORY

US; dir. John Lasseter; animated; voices of Tim Allen, Tom Hanks, Don Rickles; scr. Joss Whedon et al; 80 min.

The first film animated entirely by computer, by courtesy of John Lasseter, and the one which made a star of heroic spaceman Buzz Lightyear, whose plastic effigy became exceedingly scarce in the run-up to Christmas 1996. The cowboy he replaces as top man on the toy shelf is initially resentful, until a more serious threat to their secret life appears.The 1999 sequel *Toy Story II* managed to be just as charming – and just as successful.

ALL DONE WITH COMPUTERS: THE NEW FORM OF ANIMATION DISPLAYED IN *TOY STORY*

1996 THE CRAFT

US; dir. Andrew Fleming; starring Neve Campbell, Fairuza Balk, Robin Tunney, Rachel True; scr. Peter Filardi; 101 mins.

Teen movie taking a negative look at witchcraft. Balk is the new girl in school whose new friends are all interested in the occult. Together, the four of them develop spectacular magic powers, and get up to all sorts of increasingly serious mischief. Balk is reluctant to give in to the corruption, and things turn nasty. The sternly Christian warning not to mess with the occult dominates everything, but there's little more than teen froth to compete with anyway.

DRAGONHEART

US; dir. Rob Cohen; starring Dennis Quaid, Julie Christie; scr. Charles Edward Pogue; 106 min.

A tenth-century dragonslayer comes up against the last of the dragons. The plot makes a concerted attempt to cash in on the new attitude to dragonkind developed by recent fantasy fiction: a curious alloy of overweening sentimentality and nostalgic awe, which had first seen muted cinematic expression in the eccentric animated feature *The Flight of the Dragon* (1982).

THE FRIGHTENERS

NZ/US; dir. Peter Jackson; starring Michael J. Fox, Trini Alvarado, John Astin; scr. Jackson & Fran Walsh; 109 min.

A *Beetlejuice*-inspired comedy in which a man caught between this life and the next sets up a supernatural protection racket, recruiting scary haunters which he then tidies away for his helpless clients, *Ghostbusters*-style. As with so many would-be racketeers, he eventually finds that he is in need of protection himself.

MICHAEL

US; dir. Nora Ephron; starring John Travolta, Andie MacDowell, William Hurt, Bob Hoskins; scr. Nora Ephron et al; 105 min.

A comedy set solidly in the Hollywood tradition of angelic fantasy, in which the eponymous hero (Travolta) finds his final earthly mission – to reform two cynical journalists – more challenging than he expected. Their unscrupulous boss (Hoskins) needs no supernatural assistance to provide diabolical opposition.

PEAGREEN (TOM FELTON) CLINGS TO A LIGHTBULB FOR DEAR LIFE IN *THE BORROWERS*.

1997 THE BORROWERS

UK/US; dir. Peter Hewitt; starring John Goodman, Jim Broadbent, Ruby Wax; scr. Mary Norton, Gavin Scott; 98 mins.

A family of four-inch-high "little people" live under the floorboards of a house. When the owner dies, they have to get the help of his son to fight off the evil plans of real estate developer John Goodman, who wants to destroy the place and turn it into a luxury apartment block. Reasonable effects couldn't really compensate for a flimsy plot and crude gags, but some children enjoyed it.

HERCULES

US; dir. & scr. Ron Clements & John Musker; animated; voices of Tate Donovan, Danny DeVito, James Woods; 93 min.

This Disney feature attempts to do for Greek myth what *Snow White* did with the Brothers Grimm, but the action/adventure component jars with the standard Disney template. The Gerald Scarfe designs give the movie a distinctive look but the animation robs them of any

real style. As is usual in Disney features, the villain – Hades, with Woods's voice – easily upstages the half-hearted hero.

KULL THE CONQUEROR

US; dir. John Nicoella; starring Kevin Sorbo, Tia Carrere, Litefoot; scr. Charles Edward Pogue; 95 mins.

King Kull is another of Robert E. Howard's barbarian creations – Kull and Conan are closely related – but there's little in this film to remind the viewer of the fact. The plot was risible, and although much of the dialogue was taken from Howard's work, it still sounded ludicrous. The casting didn't help; Sorbo and Carrere were both far too nice for their roles. A sweepingly retro-80s glam rock score was the final nail in the film's coffin.

PHOTOGRAPHING FAIRIES

UK; dir. Nick Willing; starring Toby Stephens, Frances Barber, Ben Kingsley; scr. Willing & Chris Harrald; 106 min.

An adaptation of a novel by Steve Szilagi, in which a sceptic sets out to debunk photographs of children playing with fairies. He interprets the pictures as an attempt to exploit his grief in much the same way that the infamous Cottingley photographs exploited the hunger for miracles that afflicted the widows of World War I, but the truth is far more complicated. The Cottingley case is given forthright consideration in the inaptly-titled *FairyTale: A True Story* (1997).

THE POSTMAN

US; dir. Kevin Costner; starring Kevin Costner, Will Patton, Olivia Williams; scr. Eric Roth; 177 mins.

Apocalyptic post-holocaust America is divided into scattered groups of survivors. While an insane warlord with his own private army is trying to take control of the whole world, Kevin Costner's hobo hero finds an old US Postal Service van, and uses the letters inside it to pass himself off as the first harbinger of restored civilization. He quickly gains a band of followers of his own, and decides to do something about the warlord. The film was an embarrassing and expensive mess, and its abject failure at the box office was richly deserved.

YESTERDAY'S FAKE IS TOMORROW'S FABLE: A FAMOUS HOAX RENEWED IN *FAIRYTALE: A TRUE STORY*

THE WIND IN THE WILLOWS

UK; dir. Terry Jones; starring Jones, Eric Idle, Steve Coogan, Anthony Sher; 84 min.

A live-action version of Kenneth Grahame's classic, orientated – as such productions nowadays have to be – towards nostalgic adults rather than children.

1998 FALLEN

USA; dir. Gregory Hoblit; starring Denzel Washington, John Goodman, Donald Sutherland, Embeth Davitz; scr. Nicholas Kazan; 123 mins.

Surprisingly effective supernatural thriller in which Denzel Washington's honourable cop finds himself hunting a serial killer with the uncanny ability to jump from body to body. The bad guy turns out to be one of Hell's fallen angels, out and about for some recreational murder. Some of the extras must have found their acting abilities taxed – the killer follows Washington through crowds in a number of impressive sequences, surfing from one person to the next. Clever direction and writing make the very most of the premise, and some excellent acting from the cast helps to keep it all running smoothly. The film made little impact on release, and remains surprisingly poorly-known.

1999 ASTERIX AND OBELIX TAKE ON CAESAR

France/Germany/Italy; dir. & scr. Claude Zidi; starring Christian Clavier, Gerard Depardieu, Roberto Benigni, Michel Galabru; Eng. trans. Terry Jones; 109 mins.

Asterix and Obelix live in a small village on the very edge of Roman Gaul that forms the last pocket of resistance to Caesar's empire. The Romans, of course, are desperate to complete their conquest, but the heroes have a secret weapon in the form of their village druid's magic potion, which grants supernatural speed and strength. This is the premise for all of the many Asterix and Obelix books, and for the film as well. Many fans were nervous about moving the characters to live-action, but the cast – particularly Depardieu – did a good job, and the effects were reasonably impressive. The film was a big hit in Europe, its core territory, but made less of an impact elsewhere.

THE MUMMY

US; dir. & scr. Stephen Sommers; starring Brendan Fraser, Rachel Weisz, John Hannah, Arnold Vosloo, Kevin J. O'Connor; 124 mins.

A stylish remake of the old Universal Pictures horror classic starring Boris Karloff. The film leaps firmly into H. Rider Haggard territory almost immediately, and stays there gleefully. With a lost tribe of avenging Bedouin, a secret mystical society, all sorts of supernatural shenanigans, a replay of the seven plagues, reanimated corpses in all shapes and sizes and a number of impressive special effects, the film was never going to be aiming at a realist niche, but the cast keep it all suitably tongue-in-cheek. Weisz is particularly good as the plucky 1930s heroine. The film was a definite success, and spawned a sequel, *The Mummy Returns* (2001).

O'CONNELL (BRENDAN FRASER) SHIELDS EVIE (RACHEL WEISZ) FROM A FACE WORSE THAN DEATH – *THE MUMMY.*

HARD DAY AT THE OFFICE, DEAR? ANTONIO BANDERAS AND DENNIS STOHOI UNDER THE WEATHER IN *THE 13TH WARRIOR.*

THE THIRTEENTH WARRIOR

US; dir. John McTiernan; starring Antonio Banderas, Vladimir Kulich, Dennis Storhoi, Daniel Southern, Neil Maffin; scr. William Wisher Jr; 102 mins.

This was a rather incoherent version of Michael Crichton's novel *Eaters of the Dead*, itself a playful take on the Beowulf legend. Antonio Banderas is the Arab courtier banished to northern Europe for getting involved with the wrong woman. He falls in with a band of Viking warriors, and discovers that he is fated to accompany them on a quest to defeat a tribe of rampaging cannibal savages. Needless to say, he gets used to the Viking culture, discovers all sorts of heroic skills within himself, and saves the day.

2000 DUNGEONS AND DRAGONS

US/Czech Republic; dir. Courtney Solomon; starring Jeremy Irons, Bruce Payne, Justin Whalin, Zoe McLellan, Marlon Wayans; scr. Topper Lilien & Carroll Cartwright; 107 mins.

Dungeons and Dragons was the groundbreaking 1970s fantasy game that created the role-playing game industry, and still dominates it. Its millions of fans have long hoped for a big-screen adaptation, but they couldn't have anticipated this horrible mess. The film was dreadful. It had an incoherent plot, laughable writing and leaden direction, and the acting was simply pathetic. All of the more experienced actors seemed desperate to be elsewhere – even Payne, a veteran B-movie villain, just seems constipated. In a bizarre twist,

the director was apparently determined to copy the look and timing of every single scene from one or other of the *Star Wars* films – presumably on the basis that if it worked for Lucas, it would also work for him. The worst element of the film was probably Wayan's grossly offensive "comedy negro" character however, who only just stopped short of tripping over his own feet and saying "Please doan' hurt me, Massah". One to miss.

2001 ATLANTIS: THE LOST EMPIRE

US; animated; dir. Gary Trousdale & Kirk Wise; voices of Michael J. Fox, Claudia Christian, Corey Burton, James Garner, Leonard Nimoy; scr. Tab Murphy; 95 mins.

An unusually action-orientated offering from Disney, in which a mild archeologist sets out on a quest to complete his famous grandfather's work by discovering Atlantis, and falls in love with an Atlantean princess. The animation was suitably impressive, and owed a certain debt to Japanese anime, but the film felt rushed, and minor characters were whisked on and off with unseemly haste. The comparatively serious content helped ensure that the film ended up with a PG rating.

HARRY POTTER AND THE PHILOSOPHER'S STONE

US; dir. Chris Columbus; starring Daniel Radcliffe, Rupert Grint, Emma Watson, Robbie Coltrane, Richard Harris, Alan Rickman, Richard Griffiths; scr. Steven Kloves; 152 mins.

Harry Potter lives with his unpleasant, small-minded aunt and uncle. They treat him dreadfully, and it is only when he finally get admitted to an exclusive boarding school for young wizards that he discovers that magic is real, that his parents were wizards, and that he himself is already famous in the magical community. Over the course of his first year, Harry and his friends Ron and Hermione uncover a sinister plot to steal the elixir of life and bring the long-defeated Dark Lord, Voldemort, back to the height of his power. They have to face all sorts of dangers and challenges in order to foil the evil plan, from trolls and deadly giant chess-pieces right through to getting expelled. J. K. Rowling's superb books about the magical schoolboy have been a world-wide phenomenon, winning over both children and adults all over the world. The film stays very faithful to the book, recreating its rather complex plot in full, and rendering all the major scenes effectively. It's got a lot to live up to, but Columbus does an excellent job of keeping it all balanced. The movie, released in the US as *Harry Potter and the Sorcerer's Stone*, was a great success at the box office, and the sequels – *Harry Potter and the Chamber of Secrets* is due late in 2002 – look like being every bit as good.

Galadriel (Cate Blanchett) gives Frodo Baggins (Elijah Wood) her blessing in *The Fellowship of the Ring.*

LORD OF THE RINGS: THE FELLOWSHIP OF THE RING

New Zealand/USA; dir. Peter Jackson; starring Elijah Wood, Ian McKellen, Viggo Mortensen, Sean Astin, Liv Tyler, Cate Blanchett; scr. Frances Walsh; 178 mins.

After the relative failure of the Ralph Bakshi animation, expectations for a live-action film of Tolkien's masterwork were generally pessimistic. The fact that Peter Jackson had cut his directorial teeth on the crass alien-zombie flick *Bad Taste* didn't help settle people's nerves. When the buzz started, cynics dismissed it as hype... but the final film proved to be nothing less than majestic. The script was a sensitive and faithful adaptation. The actors were very well cast, and put in superb performances. Viggo Mortensen's Aragorn was a particularly impressive surprise. The computer effects pushed the absolute boundaries of available technology and were superlative – the actors were resized perfectly to hobbit, dwarf or human proportions, and supposedly "problem" characters like the demonic Balrog looked stunning. As befits the book, the scenery was particularly amazing. The stunning New Zealand landscapes required very little enhancement to become a perfect recreation of Middle Earth, and captured the mystical feel of the land perfectly. Filming a work the size of the *Lord of the Rings* was always going to require compression, and certain elements of the plot were altered to improve the cinematics of the final film, so a small number of die-hard purists were

disappointed, but everyone else was bowled over. The film has already been hailed as the *Star Wars* of a new generation in terms of its impact, and looks to be the first billion-dollar grossing movie; it has certainly shattered the boundaries of filmed fantasy, and set a challenge that is going to be very difficult to live up to. *The Two Towers* (due in 2002) and *The Return of the King* (due in 2003) are certain to be mammoth hits too.

MONKEYBONE

US; dir. Henry Selick; starring Brendan Fraser, Bridget Fonda, Chris Kattan, Giancarlo Esposito, Rose McGowan, Whoopi Goldberg; scr. Sam Hamm; 92 mins.

A darkly humorous adaptation of Kaja Blackley's graphic novel *Dark Town*. Fraser plays a cartoonist about to hit it big who suffers a freak accident just before he can propose to his girlfriend. While he lies in a coma, he finds himself transported to a bizarre purgatorial realm for the long-term comatose and brain-dead, where mythical gods and creatures delight in the nightmares of the living. The only way back is by outwitting Death, in the form of Whoopi Goldberg. To make matters even worse, Monkeybone – Fraser's cartoon creation – has malicious plans of his own. Unlike Selick's equally entertaining *The Nightmare Before Christmas* (1993), Monkeybone is really aimed at adults.

SHREK

US; animated; dir. Andrew Adamson/Vicky Jenson; voices of Mike Myers, Eddie Murphy, Cameron Diaz, John Lithgow, Vincent Cassel; scr. Ted Elliott; 90 mins.

An amusing big-screen adaptation of William Steig's gently satiric fairy tale. Mike Myers is the eponymous Shrek, a gruff, smelly ogre with a heart of gold whose peaceful swamp is disturbed by a huge load of refugee fairy-tale characters – particularly Eddie Murphy's motor-mouthed Donkey. Tiny, villainous Lord Farquaad is responsible, but agrees to move the refugees elsewhere if Shrek will go rescue a beautiful princess for Farquaad to marry... The film manages to be funny on a number of levels, so that adults and children alike can get plenty of laughs out of it, and the cast put in suitably entertaining performances. It's good fun, and a lot less saccharine than many Disney offerings.

IT ISN'T ALL ABOUT LOOKS, AS *SHREK* SO POINTEDLY DEMONSTRATES

2002 THE SCORPION KING

US; dir. Chuck Russell; starring Dwayne "The Rock" Johnson, Steven Brand, Kelly Hu, Michael Clarke Duncan, Grant Heslov; scr. Stephen Sommers, Jonathan Hales; 94 mins.

Originally conceived as a prequel to *The Mummy* (1999) – the working title was *The Mummy III – The Scorpion King* is firmly in the tradition of the sword-and-sandals fantasies. The hero is played by a popular WWF Wrestling champion, The Rock – chiefly noted for being able to arch an eyebrow and speak in the third person. While years as a professional wrestler have undoubtedly helped sharpen The Rock's acting abilities, his main job in this film is to flex his immense sword arm while stopping the evil king from using Hu's sorcerous powers to take over the world. It's entertaining enough as eye-candy, but it did look rather pathetic after *The Fellowship of the Ring* showed what could be done with the genre.

TELEVISION FANTASY

From its humble origins of painted backdrops and imaginative but obvious costumes to the advent of super-realistic computer-generated special effects, televised fantasy has long been one of the most popular genres on the small screen. What follows is a selection of the most important, interesting and, above all, entertaining fantastic programmes

1946 ALICE: SOME OF HER ADVENTURES IN WONDERLAND

1946; play; UK (BBC); starring Vivian Pickles (Alice), Erik Chitty; prod. George More O'Ferrall; from Clemence Dane's stage version of Lewis Carroll's novel; 40 min.

STUCK IN THE MIDDLE: VIVIAN PICKLES AS ALICE, IN THE BBC'S FIRST POST-WAR PRODUCTION

The first item plundered from the rich repository of stage versions of children's classics when the BBC resumed TV broadcasting after World War II. A 25-minute version of *Alice Through the Looking Glass* and a two-part version of *Alice in Wonderland*, both produced by George More O'Ferrall and starring Ursula Hanray as Alice, had been included in the *Theatre Parade* series – which borrowed actors and productions from London's West End – in 1937.

TOAD OF TOAD HALL

1946; play; UK (BBC); starring Alan Reid (Toad), Kenneth More (Badger); prod. Michael Barry; from A. A. Milne's stage version of Kenneth Grahame's The Wind in the Willows; 90 min.

The success of the previous item prompted this more ambitious follow-up, which was aimed at an adult audience and succeeded in awakening the requisite sense of nostalgia. The production was repeated in 1950 with James Hayter substituting for Reid as Toad.

1949 MIRANDA

1949; play; UK (BBC); starring Peggy Simpson (Miranda), Emrys Jones; prod. John Glyn-Jones; from Peter Blackmore's stage play; 100 min.

Peter Blackmore's stage comedy had already been filmed in 1948 (perhaps in response to the success of the US film *Mr Peabody's Mermaid*) with Glynis Johns as the mermaid who finds the comforts of land-based civilization infinitely preferable to the rigours of the deep.

ALL AT SEA: MIRANDA THE MERMAID, PLAYED BY PEGGY SIMPSON IN 1949

WHITEHALL WONDERS

1949; play; UK (BBC); starring Edgar Chapman (The Minister), Henry Hewitt, William Mervyn; scr. J. B. Priestley; 90 min.

The first play written for TV by Priestley was a farce in which stuffy civil servants reluctant to implement the policies of Attlee's government are harassed by mischievous fairies, whose witchcraft curses them with asses' ears, elongated noses and other absurd embellishments. The camera had to pan away while the actors hastily donned these accoutrements and the derision of the critics was enough to discourage further experiments along these lines.

A BICYCLE BUILT FOR THREE: TOPPER LEARNS TO LOOSEN UP IN THE FIFTIES SITCOM

1951 FIVE CHILDREN AND IT

1951; 6-part serial; UK (BBC); starring Thomas Moore (the Psammead); 30-min episodes.

This adaptation of E. Nesbit's classic novel enclosed the smallest of its juvenile leads in a woolly suit which must have been distinctly uncomfortable. The dearth of fantasy elements made Nesbit's *The Story of the Treasure Seekers*, serialized in 1953 and 1961, much easier to adapt.

PUCK OF POOK'S HILL

1951; 6-part serial; UK (BBC); starring Georgie Wood (Puck), Carole Lorimer, Barry Macgregor; prod. Matthew Forsyth; scr. Vere Shepstone; 30-min episodes.

Rudyard Kipling's episodic fantasy of history, in which Puck allows two children to witness scenes from various past ages, was ready-made for adaptation into a TV serial.

1952 THE SILVER SWAN

1952–53; serial; UK (BBC); starring Carole Maybank (Lucy), Robert Irvine; prod. Rex Tucker; scr. C. E. Webber; 30-min episodes.

The first fantasy specially written for TV took its inspiration from the previous item, presenting a similar six-part multiple-timeslip fantasy in which a young girl is displaced from the present into eras ranging from Cromwellian times to World War II. She meets various ancestors, all played by Irvine. Scriptwriter Webber followed up with the next item but one and "The Gift" (1954), a marginal fantasy for adults in which John Slater played a clerk who begins to "speak in tongues" after a ledger falls on his head.

1953 TOPPER

1953–54; sitcom; US (CBS); starring Leo G. Carroll (Cosmo Topper), Robert Sterling, Anne Jeffreys; prod. Bernard L. Schubert; 25-min episodes.

The American tradition of "Ansteyan" comedies – in which magical devices disrupt the formalities of everyday life to wildly comic effect – arose from the work of the novelist Thorne Smith. The 1937 movie *Topper* was based on Smith's *The Jovial Ghosts*, in which a hellraising married couple killed in a car crash decide to use their afterlife to liberate the henpecked ultra-conformist banker Cosmo Topper from his social shackles. The book spawned one sequel, the movie two, and this pioneering fantasy sitcom ran to 78 episodes. Because it was on film it could be re-run – and was, by both ABC and NBC. It set a standard for wit and ingenuity that few of its immediate successors matched. CBS made a TV movie of *Topper* in 1979, directed by Charles Dubin, with Jack Warden in the title role and Kate Jackson and Andrew Stevens as the two ghosts, in which Topper became a lawyer; it failed to kick-start another series.

VICE VERSA

1953; 3-part serial; UK (BBC); starring Anthony Valentine (Dick Bultitude), George Benson (Paul Bultitude), Raymond Rollett (Dr Grimstone); prod. Joy Harington; scr. C. E. Webber; 30-min episodes.

The first of several TV adaptations of F. Anstey's "lesson for fathers", in which a smug businessman finds himself imprisoned in his son's body (and, of course, vice versa). The father learns the hard way that one's schooldays are definitely not the happiest of one's life, while the son learns that adult life involves responsibilities as well as privileges. The performances were praised by critic Harold Hobson, who was not noted for his generosity to TV fantasy. Webber's script was re-shot by the BBC in 1961 with William Mervyn as Paul Bultitude and Graham Aza as Dick. A more substantial six-part version was made in 1981 by ATV starring Peter Bowles as Paul Bultitude and Paul Spurrier as Dick; Jeremy Burnham's script – having much better resources to draw upon – was considerably slicker, and Bowles played the child in the man's body with admirable panache.

1954 MANDRAKE THE MAGICIAN

1954; series; US; starring Coe Norton (Mandrake), Woody Strode (Lothar); 25-min episodes.

An early TV children's series shot on film, modelled on similar cinema serials adapted from popular comic strips. The eponymous young hero had been tutored in the secret wisdom of ancient Tibet – which had been conserved in a secret College of Magic since the days of Genghis Khan – by the Master Theron (presumably no relation of the Master Therion); assisted by the ever-loyal Lothar, he used his powers to defeat miscellaneous villains. NBC's 1979 TV movie directed by Anthony Falk and starring Anthony Herrera as Mandrake had a certain nostalgia appeal to Americans of the relevant generation.

1955 PETER PAN

1955; play; US (NBC); starring Mary Martin (Peter), Cyril Ritchard (Captain Hook), Kathleen Nolan (Wendy); prod. Fred Coe; dir. Jerome Robbins; 110 min.

This musical version of J. M. Barrie's classic play initially went out live as a prestige "Producers' Showcase" item (Coe had been the producer of the legendary Philco Television Playhouse). It was so well received in the US – one leading critic described it as "television's happiest moment" – that the cast was reassembled early in 1956 to do it all again. The encore was taped and frequently repeated thereafter, although it was slated by the British critics when the BBC finally deigned to show it in 1965. A musical version of *Cinderella* shown in the same series was less successful. Given the response of the British critics to the original, it seems odd that anyone in the UK would commission another musical version using American stars, but ITV did exactly that in 1976, employing Mia Farrow as Peter and Danny Kaye as Captain Hook. The new version was directed by Dwight Hemion from a script by Andrew Birkin and Jack Burns.

1956 THE ADVENTURES OF SIR LANCELOT

1956–57; series; UK (Rediffusion); starring William Russell (Lancelot), Jane Hylton (Guinevere), Cyril Smith (Merlin); prod. Bernard Knowles; 25-min episodes.

Although the fantasy elements were minimal, this pioneering adaptation of the "Matter of Britain" was an interesting experiment. As with its companion show *The Adventures of Robin Hood,* executive producer Hannah Weinstein hired blacklisted American writers Ian McLellan Hunter and Ring Lardner to write pseudonymous scripts of unusual quality and enterprise. The series eventually ran to 30 episodes and established Russell as an early TV sex-symbol.

1958 AMPHITRYON-38

1958; play; UK (BBC); starring Alec Clunes (Jupiter), Googie Withers (Alkmena), Patrick Barr, Judy Campbell; scr. S. R. Behrman; 90 min.

A TV version of a French comedy-drama by Jean Giradoux whose title refers ironically to the number of times that the story of the divine conception of Herakles/Hercules had supposedly been told. The crucial role that the hero was ultimately to play in the rejuvenation of fantasy TV was, of course, impossible to anticipate.

THE GREEN PASTURES

1958; play; UK (BBC); starring William Marshall (De Lord), Nadia Cattouse; prod. Eric Fawcett; 105 min.

This version of Marc Connelly's excruciatingly patronising stage play about the American Negro version of Heaven was surprisingly well received by the critics, who praised Barry Learoyd's sets and found the performances rather moving. The seriousness of the project was reflected in its unusual length.

FANTASY ON RADIO

In Willy Russell's play *Educating Rita* the hard-pressed hairdresser, finding herself with little time to answer an essay question on "How would you overcome the problems of staging Ibsen's *Peer Gynt?*" offers the succinct reply "Do it on the radio." This answer shrewdly acknowledges that the business of visualizing fantastic beings and settings is fraught with problems of credibility. The BBC's 1943 radio version of *Peer Gynt* was hailed as a classic, but the two-part TV version broadcast in 1949, with Peter Ustinov in the lead, was derided for the poor quality of its trolls and the woeful inadequacy of its Great Boyg. The fact that radio need only supply sound effects has occasionally helped it to attract fantasists of the highest quality; Angela Carter's radio plays *Come Unto These Yellow Sands* (1978), *Vampirella* (1980) and *Puss in Boots* (1982) are among the finest products of a tradition which began with a wartime series of Heaven-set comedies by Eric Linklater, launched by *The Cornerstones* (1941). Radio dramatizations also helped to popularize some of the 20th century's more abstruse fantasy classics; the Third Programme's version of *The Childermass* (1951) was so well received that the BBC commissioned Wyndham Lewis to write the sequels *Monstre Gai* and *Malign Fiesta.*

1959 BERKELEY SQUARE

1959; play; UK (BBC); starring David Knight, Daphne Slater; prod. John Harrison; 90 min.

This version of the classic 1928 stage-play by John L. Balderston and J. C. Squire (based on an unfinished novel by Henry James which had been the basis for two successful movies) was quickly followed by Harrison's version of J. M. Barrie's *Mary Rose*, also starring Daphne Slater. Both items are earnest timeslip fantasies which strike a fine balance between sentimentality and distress, ideal for TV dramatization – but the critics found both of them unconvincing.

THE SAGA OF NOGGIN THE NOG

1959–65; animated series; UK (BBC); scr. Oliver Postgate; drawn by Peter Firmin; 10-min episodes.

A mock-Icelandic saga in which the heir to the Nog throne battles against his uncle Nogbad the Bad and the non-aggressive Ice Dragon, redeemed from triviality by the subtlety of its humour. Under the influence of BBCs radio's *The Goon Show*, briefly adapted to TV as *The Telegoons* (1963–4), and its TV successor Michael Bentine's *It's a Square World* (1960–64) this British animated series aimed at younger viewers often acquired a quirkily sophisticated element of the surreal, of which Postgate's *Noggin* was a key pioneer.

CHAMBER OF HORRORS: THE SMILING ROD SERLING KNOWS THAT WAXWORKS ARE HARMLESS, EVEN IN THE TWILIGHT ZONE

THE TWILIGHT ZONE

1959–64; anthology series; US (Coyuga); creator Rod Serling; 25- and 50-min episodes.

A long-running and influential series filmed at MGM studios, which gave Serling – a highly respected veteran writer of original TV drama – a significant niche within the new world of production-line series. He supplemented his own scripts with material by Richard Matheson, Charles Beaumont and others. The 156 episodes (18 of which are double-length) were constantly re-run in the US even before the advent of cable guaranteed them a kind of immortality. Although most celebrated for its pioneering endeavours in TV science fiction, the show presented a good deal of slick fantasy, usually of a stern-but-sentimental moralistic stripe perfectly exemplified by the early episode "One for the Angels", in which a canny salesman makes a deal with Death which he is forced to honour in spite of his carefully drafted get-out clause. The new episodes made and broadcast in 1985–87 were considerably better than those included in the rival series of *Steven Spielberg's Amazing Stories*, the stories having a greater range and mostly being far more ingenious in construction, but the second-season episodes were cut back in number and size. A further run of episodes was produced in 1996. Significant fantasy items in the newer series included the dramatizations of Harlan Ellison's surreal "Shatterday" and Roger Zelazny's "The Last Defender of Camelot".

1960 THE ADVENTURES OF ALICE

1960; play; UK (BBC); starring Gillian Ferguson (Alice), Geoffrey Bayldon (White Knight), Marian Spencer (White Queen); scr. Charles Lefeaux; 69 min.

This version of *Through the Looking Glass* was the first to be specifically designed for TV rather than borrowing a previous adaptation for the stage. Like the 1959 TV production of H. G. Wells' "The Truth About Pyecraft" it made use of "trick photography" to obtain a few meagre special effects, but the British critics were deeply suspicious of such innovations; *The Listener*'s reviewer also slated a 1960 BBC production of Josef and Karel Capek's satirical fantasy *The Insect Play* and it was not until John Cooper's version of *The Three Princes* in December of that year – starring Laurence Harvey, Ann Sears and Paul Whitsun-Jones – was widely praised that such devices seemed to have won acceptance as a significant element of the standard repertoire of TV production.

THE LOST HERITAGE

Early TV, broadcast live from tiny studios, vanished into the ether. The entire "Golden Age of American Television Drama" pioneered by the *Kraft Television Theater* (1947–58) and *Philco Television Playhouse* (1948–55) – in the days when TV was a medium consumed by the affluent rather than by the masses – is lost to us. Because early productions could not be taped Margaret Rutherford's legendary performance as *Miss Hargreaves* in the BBC's 1950 version of Frank Baker's novel is gone forever, as is Kevin Sheldon's 1951 BBC production of J. M. Barrie's classic "if only" fantasy *Dear Brutus*. We can only imagine what the young Kenneth Williams made of the role of the angel in the BBC's 1952 version of H. G. Wells's *The Wonderful Visit*, or how the original version of Charles Terrot's *The Angel Who Pawned Her Harp* (BBC, 1951) compared with the novel issued in 1953 or the 1954 feature film. The first TV versions of America's favourite fantasy classic, *Death Takes a Holiday* – the 1952 Broadway TV Theater production starring Nigel Green and the Kraft TV Theater version starring Joseph Wiseman – are also lost, along with many other items of fantastic Americana, including the 1953 Kraft production of *Rip van Winkle*. There is a certain unfortunate irony in the fact that the arrival of "immortal TV" coincided with the social saturation that turned it into a mass medium and had the effect of virtually killing off upmarket TV drama.

AN ARABIAN NIGHT

1960; musical play; UK (Rediffusion); starring Orson Welles (The Storyteller), Stanley Holloway, Martin Benson; prod. John Macmillan; music Muir Mathieson; choreography Philippe Perottet; 85 min.

A "spectacular" commissioned to celebrate the opening of Rediffusion's new Wembley studios, then considered the most advanced in Europe. The story was adapted from *The Arabian Nights*, but the real focus was on the music and dance routines.

MISTER ED

1960–66; sitcom; US (CBS); starring Alan Young and Connie Hines; prod. Al Simon; 25-min episodes.

An amiable comedy borrowing an idea from a popular movie series about Francis the talking mule. It employed the cheapest imaginable "special effect" – a voice-over! – to create a supposedly witty talking horse, who caused his owner endless frustration by refusing to reveal his gift to anyone else. The series was popular enough to run for 143 episodes, using a standard farcical formula by which Ed's shenanigans would bring initially simple matters to a fever-pitch of complication before whipping the chestnuts out of the fire in the nick of time.

THE STRANGE WORLD OF GURNEY SLADE

1960; sitcom; UK (ATV); starring Anthony Newley; prod. Alan Tarrant; scr. Sid Green and Dick Hills; 30-min episodes.

A pioneering exercise in TV surrealism in which a grumpily diffident young man fights shyness and insignificance by fantasizing, the camera obligingly reproducing the substance of his fantasies for the viewer. The first series of six episodes was always likely to be the last, given that it left a substantial fraction of the audience utterly mystified, but its techniques were carried forward into more conventional sitcoms as well as Pythonesque comedy sketches.

1964 THE ADDAMS FAMILY

1964–66; sitcom; US (Filmways/ABC); starring John Astin (Gomez), Carolyn Jones (Morticia), Jackie Coogan (Fester), Ted Cassidy (Lurch); 25-min episodes.

The TV adaptation of Charles Addams's offbeat cartoons preserved enough of the originals' piquant flavour to become one of the most stylish shows of the period. The Grouchoesque Astin and the sultry Jones were magnificent as the contentedly decadent and eccentrically romantic couple. Cassidy was superb as their butler, establishing the sepulchral enquiry "You rang?" as a key 1960s catch-phrase. The plots of the 64 episodes were never as fantastic as the characters (who included hairy Cousin Itt and the box-dwelling disembodied hand named Thing), but that was the essence of the joke; from the point of view of the inhabitants of Cemetery Ridge, it was the mores and customs of the rigorously sanitized "average Americans" of TV-land that were absurdly and inexplicably eccentric. NBC's animated version of 1973, in which the family took off in a camper to tour America, was a travesty. Although the theatre movies of 1991–93 paid proper homage to the originals, the fact that Gomez and Morticia were comprehensively upstaged by their daughter Wednesday (played by Lisa Loring in the original) proves that the TV series will remain an unsurpassable classic.

NEIGHBOURS FROM HELL: THE ADDAMS FAMILY ALWAYS TRIUMPHED OVER THE INTOLERANCE OF OTHERS

BEWITCHED

1964–72; sitcom; US (ABC); starring Elizabeth Montgomery (Samantha), Agnes Moorehead (Endora), Dick York (Darrin); cr. Sol Saks; exec. prod. Harry Ackerman; 25-min episodes.

This TV series took up where the 1942 movie *I Married a Witch* – based on *The Passionate Witch*, a 1941 novel which Norman Matson completed after Thorne Smith's death – left off. An advertising executive married to a witch tries hard to persuade her to forsake magic and fall in with the conventional routines of American suburban life. He is relentlessly opposed by his mother-in-law, Endora – a character seemingly inspired by Hermione Gingold's performance in the 1958 movie *Bell, Book and Candle* and played with some style by Moorehead – who does her level best to subvert his schemes and woo Samantha back to a freer and easier way of life. Even viewers without a flicker of feminist sympathy are bound to side with Endora against the insufferably pusillanimous Darrin; Dick York eventually abandoned the role to Dick Sargent, who was similarly defeated by its intrinsic inadequacy, but Montgomery and Moorehead had charm enough to extend the series to a record 252 episodes.

Samantha's daughter – who was played in the show's early stages by three different sets of twins – became the star of the short-lived spinoff series *Tabitha* (1977), in which she was played as a grown-up by Lisa Hartmann. Samantha was also the model for *Sabrina the Teenage Witch*, who first appeared on TV along with other characters from the popular comic strip in *The Archie Show* (CBS 1968–69); Sabrina's two slightly mischievous aunts played Darrin's civilizing role rather than Endora's subversive one.

A NOSE FOR TROUBLE: SAMANTHA ONLY HAD TO WRINKLE HERS TO WORK MAGIC IN *BEWITCHED*

A MIDSUMMER NIGHT'S DREAM

1964; play; UK (Rediffusion); starring Benny Hill (Bottom), Peter Wyngarde (Oberon); dir. Joan Kemp-Welch; 78 min.

This was the second British TV version of Shakespeare's fairy play, the BBC having broadcast a production by Rudolph Cartier in 1958. ITV's attempt to demonstrate that it too could be serious was a fascinating experiment in popularization, with marvellous sets by Michael Yates, weird mock-Victorian costumes and balletic fairies. Benny Hill's Bottom was surprisingly good in spite of the ridiculousness of his ass's head. There was also a 1969 version funded by CBS, starring Judi Dench as Titania and directed by Peter Hall, before the supposedly definitive version produced for the prestigious *BBC Shakespeare* series in 1981 by Elisha Moshinsky, starring Helen Mirren and Peter McEnery, with Brian Glover as Bottom.

THE MUNSTERS

1964–66; sitcom; US (CBS); starring Fred Gwynne (Herman), Yvonne de Carlo (Lily), Al Lewis (Grandpa); cr. Joe Connelly and Bob Mosher; 25-min episodes.

This blatant ripoff of *The Addams Family*, featuring the inhabitants of 1313 Mockingbird Lane, never had the style of the original. This was largely due to the inspired clowning of Gwynne, playing a dead ringer for Karloff's Frankenstein monster who never figures out why ordinary folk find him intimidating. Its 70 black-and-white episodes eventually outstripped its model, suggesting that viewers felt slightly more comfortable with its broader and more amiable style of comedy; they were supplemented by two 96-minute TV movies shot in colour: *Munster Go Home* (NBC 1966), in which Herman inherits an English castle, and the unfortunately belated *The Munsters' Revenge* (1981). An attempted revival, *The Munsters Today* (1988–89), benefited from colour and longer episodes, but Gwynne, de Carlo and all the charm were gone.

1965 ALICE

1965; play; UK (BBC); starring George Baker (Lewis Carroll), Deborah Watling (Alice); prod. James MacTaggart; dir. Gareth Davies; scr. Dennis Potter; 75 min.

A contribution to the landmark *Wednesday Play* series which pioneered the rich tradition of psychoanalytic studies speculating as to the hidden significance of Carroll's fantasies. It cleared the way for Jonathan Miller's 1966 production and sowed a crop of speculation that was still bearing fruit in a 1998 *Omnibus* documentary "celebrating" the centenary of the Rev. Dodgson's death, "Curiouser and Curiouser: Lewis Carroll 1898–1998". A similar spirit of psychoanalytical inquiry infused several of the biographical films which Ken Russell made for the BBC in the same period; *The Debussy Film*

ADAPTING FOLKLORE

The difficulty of staging fantasies posed particularly awkward problems for producers adapting traditional folk tales for children. Such works were central to the culture of childhood, but children's TV had to work with the tightest budgets of all. Early BBC productions made some use of shadow play (*The Happy Prince*, 1951) and puppetry (*Rumpelstiltskin*, 1951) but the fact that *The Princess and the Pea* became the tale most often dramatized with real actors had more to do with the ease of so doing than its merit as a story.

The BBC Christmas pantomime became an annual event after the successful broadcast of *Dick Whittington* in 1949 but more earnest treatments of traditional themes did not become a regular fixture until 1953, when enterprising versions of *Cinderella* and Thackeray's *The Rose and the Ring* were broadcast. The standard method of using such tales, however, remained the "*Jackanory* method" of putting an actor in front of the camera to read the story aloud. This was augmented by slow degrees, first by the insertion of still pictures and eventually by the filmic inserts and make-up effects used in such shows as *The Storyteller* (C4/TVS, 1988), for which Jim Henson's Creature Shop provided additional visual support.

EVERY MAN'S FANTASY (EXCEPT FOR THE SEX – *I DREAM OF JEANNIE* WAS A FAMILY SHOW)

(1965) was the only one which qualified as a fantasy in its own right, although the magnificently graphic *Dante's Inferno* (1967) – which similarly had Oliver Reed in the central part (this time as Dante Gabriel Rossetti) – included some nightmarish dream sequences.

I DREAM OF JEANNIE

1965–70; sitcom; US (NBC); cr. Sidney Sheldon; starring Barbara Eden (Jeannie), Larry Hagman (Tom Nelson), Bill Daily (Roger Healey), Hayden Rorke (Bellows); 25-min episodes.

Although it was an attempt to cash in on the success of *Bewitched*, this series actually came closer to capturing the essentially anarchic spirit of Thorne Smith. Trainee astronaut Tom Nelson coyly exploits the talents of the sexy genie he liberates from a bottle which he found in the wake of a slightly misguided splashdown. The suspicious psychiatrist Bellows, who compiles an extensive dossier on Nelson's "delusions", is a suitably stupid representative of the forces of repressive normality and the winsome Eden deftly supplied her own Endora-equivalent by donning a brunette wig to become her wayward sister-cum-alter-ego Jeannie II. Hagman's laid-back performance never pretended for a moment that the show was anything but amiable nonsense, and helped the hard-working Eden to carry it through a very respectable 139 episodes.

A spinoff animated series, *Jeannie* (CBS 1973–75), which switched the setting to a high-school, was tasteless and pointless. Two rather feeble TV movies were belatedly spun off from the series as vehicles for the typecast Eden. *I Dream of Jeannie: 15 Years Later* (1985), directed by William Asher, had Wayne Rogers as Tom Nelson, now safely married to his little treasure. *I Still Dream of Jeannie* (1991), directed by Joseph Scanlan, left Nelson off-stage, absent on a "secret mission" – thus facing Jeannie with a race against time to find a "temporary master" lest her place in the sun be taken by the still-scheming Jeannie II; the only real joke in the script was that Hagman's old Dallas rival Ken Kercheval was drafted to fill in for him. Another attempt to recapitulate the formula was the ABC sitcom *Just Our Luck* (1983–84), starring Richard Gilliland and T. K. Carter, in which the genie was a black man. Although it was closer in spirit to the original of modern variants on the theme – F. Anstey's *The Brass Bottle* (1900) – it had no chance in a world that had been changed by the Civil Rights Movement.

MY MOTHER, THE CAR

1965–66; sitcom; US (NBC); cr. Allan Burns and Chris Hayward; starring Jerry Van Dyke, Maggie Pierce; 25-min episodes.

A lawyer buys a classic car (a 1928 Porter) which turns out to be the reincarnation of his mother. His wife and children, unable to hear Ann Sothern's censorious voice emanating from the car radio, cannot understand his affection for what seems to them to be an obsolete wreck. Most of the viewers sympathized, but the show ran 30 episodes before it was axed. Although it was more a role-reversed *Bewitched* than a hi-tech *Mister Ed*, the writers never had the courage to exploit the psychoanalytic potential of their central motif; Dr Bellows would certainly have found more productive employment here than in *I Dream of Jeannie*.

BRAVE NEW WONDERLAND: ANNE-MARIE MALLIK AS ALICE IN JONATHAN MILLER'S EXPERIMENTAL PRODUCTION

1966 ALICE IN WONDERLAND

1966; play; UK (BBC1); starring Anne-Marie Mallik (Alice), Ralph Richardson, John Gielgud, Michael Redgrave, Malcolm Muggeridge, John Bird, Peter Sellers, Leo McKern and Peter Cook; dir. Jonathan Miller; 80 min.

This highly experimental adaptation of Carroll's classic by Jonathan Miller, which presents the events of the book as an absurd version of Victorian adult life as seen through a child's eyes, was a landmark in the history of television. The sly reinterpretation of the familiar set-pieces made many of them rather sinister instead of pleasantly nonsensical, ensuring that the production would be deeply controversial; it colluded with Dennis Potter's 1965 play to sensitize British programme-makers to the underlying implications of fantasy texts, affecting future productions for children as well as those intended for adult consumption. The all-star cast assembled by Miller relished the opportunity to ham it up in the noble cause of adding new depth to old lines; Gielgud won most plaudits as a supremely dignified Mock Turtle, although McKern's performance in drag (as the Duchess) was magnificently bizarre.

1967 THE FLYING NUN

1967–69; sitcom; US (ABC); cr. Harry Ackerman and Frank Wylie; starring Sally Field (Sister Bertrille), Marge Redmond, Madeleine Sherwood; 25-min episodes.

A novice in a convent in San Juan, Puerto Rico, discovers that she can fly, but her attempts to use her gift to help the disadvantaged people of the surrounding region are not wholly appreciated by her Mother Superior. Ackerman had previously been in charge of *Bewitched*, which might help to explain how he came by the bizarre notion that this might be a good idea, and why ABC gave him the go-ahead. Nothing, however, can explain the popularity that sustained it through 82 episodes.

THE SILVER AGE

TV fantasy for children and adults alike was heavily dependent on adaptations of classic tales that had already been made for the stage. Telecine film-inserts were hardly used at all until 1959, when loudly-advertised "trick photography" was used in a dramatization of H. G. Wells' *The Truth About Pyecraft* to provide the illusion that Pyecraft really was weightless. Although editable videotape had first become available in 1956, it was so expensive in the early days that it was used very sparingly; even in the USA economic restrictions helped the weight of tradition to extend the "Golden Age of Live Drama" until the end of 1958. It was not until the mid-60s that the Silver Age of cut-and-paste video editing enabled vanishing tricks to become routine in TV shows on both sides of the Atlantic. Split-screen effects allowing actors to appear twice in the same frame remained primitive until the advent of colour-separation in the mid 1970s, which also facilitated apparent increases and decreases in size. Even so, the disparity in budgeting between TV shows and movies remained so vast as to create a marked "generation gap" between TV and cinema special effects. Only when that gap was substantially narrowed by computer-aided effects could this Silver Age could give way to the Age of Heroes whose dawn we have witnessed in the 1990s. Throughout that Silver Age, however, the uphill struggle to make the most of limited resources was conducted with good grace and commendable vigour – and its triumphs are to be treasured in spite of the fact that everything was bigger and brighter in the movies.

THE PILGRIM'S PROGRESS

1967; 3-part serial; UK (ABC); starring William Squire, George Innes (Christian), Philip Locke, Colette O'Neil, Michael Robbins; scr. Trevor Preston; 50-min episodes.

ITV's initial terms of operation obliged it to supply a quota of religious programming, and this commandment inevitably generated some ingenious attempts at popularization. Preston's ambitious dramatization of Bunyan's classic allegory couched it as a visionary fantasy in which Squire played a prisoner whose dreams of liberation and redemption featured appropriate transfigurations of his various persecutors.

SHAZZAN!

1967–69; animated series; US (Hanna Barbera/CBS); voices Barney Phillips (Shazzan), Janet Waldo, Jimmy Dexter; 25-min episodes.

A magic ring shifts two non-identical twins into the world of the Arabian Nights, where they obtain command of a 60-foot-tall genie. This was one of the more extravagant offerings by the prolific Hanna-Barbera team, who were a major supplier of animated series to US TV until it became cheaper to use non-resident animators. The title is nowadays easy to confuse with *Shazam!* another long-forgotten CBS animated show which ran from 1974–77, in which radio broadcaster Billy Batson was selected by the Immortal Elders (Solomon, Mercury, Zeus, Achilles and Atlas) to serve mankind as Captain Marvel, aided by his trusty assistant Mentor.

1968 THE GHOST AND MRS MUIR

1968–70; sitcom; US (NBC/ABC); cr. Jean Holloway; starring Edward Mulhare (Captain Gregg), Hope Lange (Carolyn Muir); 25-min episodes.

The central theme of this comedy – lifted from the 1947 movie of the 1945 novel by "R. A. Dick" (Josephine Leslie) – is the attempts made by the ghost of an old salt to retain sole tenancy of Gull Cottage. Like Oscar Wilde's Canterville Ghost, on whom the original had presumably been modelled, Captain Gregg is more bark than bite, and his half-hearted mischievousness is tempered by the growth of a redeeming affection. The show had a pragmatic proto-feminist ambience which contrasted as markedly with the languid unadventurousness of *I Dream of Jeannie* as with the stubborn conventionality of *Bewitched*, but the idea was not infinitely extendable; ABC were unwise to pick it up after NBC dropped it and 50 episodes took it some way past its sell-by date.

1969 HERE COMES THE GRUMP

1969–71; animated series; US (NBC); 25-min episodes.

This was the less successful of NBC's two 1969 ventures into Secondary World fantasy – the other being *H. R. Pufnstuf* – but it was equally interesting in its own Doctor Seuss-influenced way. Terry and his dog Bib must search for the Cave of Whispering Orchids, in which the Grump has hidden the Crystal Key which can lift the Curse of Gloom.

LITTLE BOY LOST: JACK WILD MAKES HIS WAY THROUGH THE WILDERNESS OF LIVING ISLAND

H. R. PUFNSTUF

1969–73; series; US (NBC/ABC); starring Jack Wild (Timmy), Billie Hayes (Miss Witchiepoo); prod. Sid and Marty Krofft; 22-min episodes.

An interesting attempt to juxtapose human actors with "life-sized" puppets like those subsequently developed by Jim Henson for *Sesame Street* (1971–87) and *The Muppet Show* (1976–81). H. R. Pufnstuf is mayor of Living Island, to which Timmy is transported by his talking flute Freddie – a magical object which the wicked Miss Witchiepoo is very anxious to possess. Although it only lasted 17 episodes and was never more than a pale shadow of its model (*The Wizard of Oz*), it deserves credit for pioneering enterprise.

MY WORLD – AND WELCOME TO IT

1969–70; sitcom; US (NBC/CBS); starring William Windom, Lisa Gerritsen; cr. Sheldon Leonard; 25-min episodes.

A series which mixed live action and animation in presenting the story of a Walter Mitty-like cartoonist who continually retreats into his – or, strictly speaking, James Thurber's – private fantasy-world in order to escape the stresses of everyday existence. An interesting and engaging attempt to bring Thurber's quirky humour to the small screen; CBS picked it up for a second 13-part season after NBC dropped it, but had no greater success with it.

THE OWL SERVICE

1969–70; 8-part serial; UK (Granada); starring Francis Wallis, Gillian Hills, Michael Holden; dir. Peter Plummer; scr. Alan Garner; prod. and dir. Peter Plummer; 25-min episodes.

A breakthrough project which established ITV as a source of high-quality children's fantasy. Garner's script was a fine adaptation of his brilliant novel, although collaboration with the production team put such a strain on him that he eventually had to be restrained from attacking a misbehaving actor and had a nervous breakdown thereafter. The male actors – who play the two friends locked in competition for the affections of Roger's sister Alison, while their re-enactment of an ancient Celtic myth proceeds inexorably towards a tragic conclusion – are in fact the only weak elements in what is otherwise a *tour de force*.

RANDALL AND HOPKIRK (DECEASED)

1969–70; series; UK (ATV); starring Kenneth Cope (Marty Hopkirk), Mike Pratt (Jeff Randall), Annette Andre; cr. Dennis Spooner; prod. Monty Berman; 55-min episodes.

The most extreme of several off-beat crime-fighting series devised by Spooner and Berman, who had already strayed from familiar techno-thriller territory in chronicling the adventures of the psi-powered *The Champions* (1967). This was the series that set a limit to their adventurism; many viewers considered that the irredeemably chirpy but conveniently dematerialized Marty made detective work far too easy. Spooner and his fellow-scriptwriters tried hard to produce plot-worthy complications, but the principal result of their ingenuity was to generate storylines so bizarrely contrived as to be virtually definitive of what was later to be dignified as "cult TV". The curmudgeonly Pratt was oddly effective, after his own quaintly mulish fashion, although it was all-too easy to understand why he could never get it together with his partner's widow. The show only just lasted out the 26 episodes requisite to constitute a season in the US, where it was shown as *My Partner the Ghost*, but the second lease of life that it enjoyed on cable TV in the mid-1990s generated six new episodes in 2000. Despite the best efforts of comedians Vic Reeves and Bob Mortimer and ex-*Dr Who* Tom Baker, it bombed.

LIFE AND DEATH: MELVYN DOUGLAS IS CAPTIVATED IN *DEATH TAKES A HOLIDAY*

1970 ACE OF WANDS

1970–72; series of serials; UK (Thames); starring Michael MacKenzie (Tarot), Tony Selby, Judy Loe; scr. Trevor Preston; 25-min episodes.

Preston's follow-up to his version of *The Lion, the Witch and the Wardrobe* attempted to create a hero to rival the BBC's then-earth-bound Doctor Who: an illusionist with real magic powers who battled run-of-the-mill supervillains. Fourteen stories were broadcast over three seasons, each running 2–4 episodes; they mingled elements of science fiction, fantasy and horror. Selby and Loe jumped ship after the second series, following the pattern set by the Doctor's sidekicks, but their perfectly adequate replacements (Roy Holder and Petra Markham) couldn't get the same mileage out of their parts.

CATWEAZLE

1970–71; sitcom; UK (LWT); starring Geoffrey Bayldon (Catweazle), Robin Davies (Carrot); scr. Richard Carpenter; 25-min episodes.

A comic timeslip fantasy about a ragged 11th-century wizard displaced into the 20th century. In the first 13-part series he was befriended by a farmer's son, whose attempts to explain that modern technology is not really magical were unsuccessful. A second 13-part series, in which the unlucky but better-prepared Catweazle contrived to strand himself again, retained the zestful Bayldon in the lead but changed everything else; Carrot was replaced by the aristocratic Cedric (Gary Warren) and the much stronger supporting cast included Moray Watson and Elspeth Gray as Cedric's parents and Peter Butterworth as the family butler. The built-in obsolescence of the theme ensured that the second series would be the last, but the oddly endearing central character is fondly remembered.

1971 THE BLUE-EYED HORSE

1971; play; US (NBC); starring Ernest Borgnine (Melvyn Feebie), Joan Blondell; 50 min.

A rare fantasy broadcast in the *NBC Comedy Theatre* series, in which a compulsive gambler's wife is turned into a horse, bringing him under suspicion of having murdered her. The effect is akin to *My Mother the Car* than Thorne Smith, but overacted with commendable zeal.

DEATH TAKES A HOLIDAY

1971; TV movie; US (ABC); starring Melvyn Douglas, Myrna Loy, Monte Markham, Yvette Mimieux; dir. Robert Butler; 78 min.

The third US television version of Alberto Casella's play, which had made a considerable impact in a 1934 movie version starring Fredric March. The allegory – in which Death adopts human form in order to visit Earth, curious to know why humans are so terrified of him – requires quieter and more patient handling than it is given here. This is one fantasy classic which needs no special effects at all, and the existential stasis which follows Death's brief captivation by love does not require dramatic overemphasis.

JAMIE

1971; 13-part serial; UK (LWT); starring Garry Miller (Jamie), Aubrey Morris (Mr Zed); scr. Denis Butler; 25-min episodes.

Another in the long series of multiple-timeslip fantasies, this time involving a young boy who acquires a magic carpet from a junk shop. Under the tutelage of the enigmatic Mr Zed (a Doctor Who-clone) Jamie makes numerous attempts to avert famous historical disasters, but the scriptwriters never had the guts to let him succeed and face the resultant paradoxes.

THE PLOT TO OVERTHROW CHRISTMAS

1971; play; US (PBS); starring John McIntire (The Devil), Allen Reed (Santa Claus), Karl Swenson (Nero), Jeanette Nolan (Lucrezia Borgia); 50 min.

A TV adaptation of a famous radio play by Norman Corwin, in which the Devil recruits a crack team of all-time-great villains to help him assassinate Santa Claus. He fails. Broadcast in the *Hollywood Television Theatre* series.

1972 HAUNTS OF THE VERY RICH

1972; TV movie; US (ABC); starring Lloyd Bridges, Cloris Leachman, Ed Asner, Anne Francis; dir. Paul Wendkos; scr. William Wood; 73 min.

A teasing posthumous fantasy modelled on Sutton Vane's classic play *Outward Bound*, with a tropical leisure resort replacing the Judgement-bound ocean liner. As with most stories of this type, it never begins to work as a mystery and it has insufficient depth of character analysis to have any real weight as a moralistic fantasy, but given those limitations it is both interesting and watchable.

THE WISDOM OF THE EAST: FIRST SHAVE YOUR HEAD, THEN KICK SOME ASS

KUNG FU

1972–75; series; US (ABC); starring David Carradine (Kwai Chang Caine); cr. Ed Spielman; 75-min pilot/50-min episodes.

A calculatedly half-hearted attempt to adapt the newly fashionable martial arts movie to the TV medium, adding the plot-formula of *The Fugitive* and the settings of the obsolescent Western genre to the central idea of *Mandrake the Magician*. Carradine was surprisingly effective, given the inherent absurdity of his task, which required him to be a mystically inspired but thoroughly pragmatic violent pacifist. The show ran for 72 episodes on style alone, and repaid its debt to the cult movies which inspired it by helping to move the sub-genre into the mainstream of American entertainment. There were two spinoff TV movies in 1986 and 1987 and the series made a belated return to TV in 1993 in *Kung Fu: The Legend Continues*, by which time it was hopelessly corny.

POOR DEVIL

1972; TV movie; US (Paramount); starring Sammy Davis Jr, Christopher Lee, Jack Klugman; dir. Robert Scheerer; scr. Arne Sultan, Earl Barrett and Richard Baer; 73 min.

A comedy in which one of the Devil's minions tries hard to persuade a downtrodden book-keeper to sign away his soul but fails to get his name on the dotted line. It was difficult to sympathise.

SANDCASTLES

1972; TV movie; US (CBS/Metromedia); starring Bonnie Bedelia, Herschel Bernardi, Jan-Michael Vincent; dir. Ted Post, scr. Stephen and Elinor Karpf and James M. Miller; 73 min.

A sentimental fantasy – one of the earliest American TV endeavours in that sub-genre – tracking the relationship between a young woman and the ghost of a man killed in a road accident. It is of some further historical interest by virtue of being the first such movie shot entirely on videotape – and the one which proved that the picture quality was not yet satisfactory.

1973 THE GIRL WITH SOMETHING EXTRA

1973–74; sitcom; US (NBC); starring Sally Field, John Davidson; 25-min episodes.

An attorney's wife who can read thoughts is continually tempted to meddle in his affairs. The potential which it had to develop into something with a sharper cutting edge than *Bewitched* was never exploited, ensuring that nothing Field did on TV between *The Flying Nun* and her infamous Oscar acceptance speech would be remembered.

1974 THE CANTERVILLE GHOST

1974; play; UK (HTV); starring David Niven, Flora Robson, James Whitmore, Audra Lindley; dir. Walter Miller; scr. Robin Miller; 50 min.

An unusually sensitive version of Oscar Wilde's classic story, scrupulously faithful to the character of the original. An exceptionally fine performance by Niven, neatly counterpointed by Lindley, balanced the comic and pathetic elements of the role with a grace and conviction that no other actor has yet been able to match. The US TV movie version of 1986 directed by Paul Bogart went so far as to draft John Gielgud for the part, but he had become a relic of a legendary past himself by that time, and it was rather as if the poor ghost had been condemned to play him rather than vice versa. The UK TV movie version of 1997 directed by Crispin Reece for Carlton and scripted by Olivia Hetreed created cameos for various comedy turns, including Pauline Quirke and Rik Mayall, but the added complications did the plot no favours; Ian Richardson was miscast as the phantom and Sarah Jane Potts was unconvincing as his saviour.

WONDER WOMAN

1974; TV movie; US (Warner/ABC); starring Cathy Lee Crosby (Princess Diana/Diana Prince), Ricardo Montalban; dir. Vincent McEveety; scr. John D. F. Black; 75 min.

This pilot for a series based on the long-running comic book, in which the daughter of the queen of the Amazons leaves Paradise Island to explore the world of men, never came remotely close to

SILICONE VALLEY: WONDER WOMAN'S CLEAVAGE HAD MORE DEPTH THAN THE PLOTS IN WHICH SHE STARRED

being plausible – but that was hardly the point. When it proved unsatisfactory a second movie-length pilot was made under the ridiculously cumbersome title of *The New, Original Wonder Woman* (1975), moving the setting back to World War II and having pilot Steve Trevor (Lyle Waggoner) cast away on Paradise Island, where Princess Diana (Lynda Carter) falls in love with him while nursing him. The series of 50-minute episodes which eventually materialized in 1976–79 kept the cast of the second pilot but reverted to a modern setting and a standard "enhanced secret agent" formula; astonishingly, Carter's low-cut costume and glossy Miss America smile won it a second series.

1975 THE GEORGIAN HOUSE

1975; 7-part serial; UK (HTV); starring Spencer Banks, Adrienne Byrne, Brinsley Forde (Ngo); prod. Leonard White; scr. Jill Laurimore and Harry Moore; 25-min episodes.

An interesting and unusually enterprising timeslip fantasy in which two modern children are drawn back to 1772, when their Bristol home was owned by a family involved in the slave trade. Ngo, a psychically gifted slave-boy, has recruited them to help prevent him from being shipped westwards to labour on a plantation.

THE GHOSTS OF MOTLEY HALL

1976–77; sitcom; UK (Granada); starring Freddie Jones, Arthur English, Sheila Steafel; scr. Richard Carpenter; 25-min episodes.

The resident ghosts in a stately home like their privacy and deploy the customary tricks of their trade to deter unwelcome visitors, including those who think they own the place.

THE PHOENIX AND THE CARPET

1976–77; 8-part serial; UK (BBC 1); starring Tamzin Neville (Anthea), Max Harris (Robert), Jane Forster (Jane), Gary Russell (Cyril); dir. Clive Doig; scr. John Tully; 30-min episodes.

This was the most difficult of E. Nesbit's classic children's novels to adapt for TV, requiring a talking phoenix and a magic carpet to effect its otherwise straightforward displacements in time and space. The phoenix never looked convincing, but the production was otherwise well up to standard.

COSTUME DRAMA: VICTORIAN CHILDREN LOOKED EQUALLY ABSURD IN REALITY AND FANTASY

PINOCCHIO

1976; TV movie; US (Vidtronics); starring Sandy Duncan (Pinocchio), Danny Kaye; dir. Ron Field and Sidney Smith; scr. Herbert Baker; 74 min.

Having put in a mediocre performance in *Peter Pan*, Kaye did better playing three parts in this musical version of Carlo Collodi's classic, including the author (who might well have been spinning in his grave regardless). The original had been so conclusively eclipsed by the Disney film that this rather faint-hearted attempt to recover the authentic spirit of the tale was probably attempting the impossible. A better but still inadequate attempt was made in 1978 by a 4-part BBC serial starring Derek Smith as Geppetto, directed by Barry Letts and scripted by Alec Drysdale. It combined live actors and puppets – Pinocchio naturally being one of the latter – and made good pioneering use of the colour-separation technique which allowed actors to be inserted into separately filmed sets.

FANTASY ISLAND: IF YOU COULD MAKE DREAMS COME TRUE WOULD YOU WEAR THOSE OUTFITS?

1977 FANTASY ISLAND

1977–82; series; US (ABC); starring Ricardo Montalban (Mr Roarke), Herve Villechaize; exec. prods. Aaron Spelling and Leonard Goldberg; two 95-min pilots/50-min episodes.

The oddest product of Spelling's long-term fascination with luxurious lifestyles. In its early days the fantasies of the people who paid the permanent cast to grant their wishes were usually fulfilled in a mundane *Jim'll Fix It* fashion – although the fantasizers usually got more than they bargained for – but as the show staggered towards its 120th episode the supernatural aspects of Roarke's role became increasingly explicit. The ambivalence of Roarke's value as an instrument of education was displayed in an episode in which he had to fight his own personal battle against the Ultimate Master of Temptation.

THE HOBBIT

1977; animated TV movie; US (NBC); voices of John Huston, Orson Bean, Richard Boone, Otto Preminger; dir. Arthur Rankin and Jules Bass; scr. Romeo Muller, from J. R. R. Tolkien's novel; 74 min.

A visually interesting and atmospheric version of Tolkien's novel. The scriptwriters could not contrive to increase the early pace of Tolkien's languidly extended story; one can only wonder whether their disinclination to move swiftly on to the big battle scenes arose from respect for the original or anxiety about the ability of their animators.

KING OF THE CASTLE

1977; 7-part serial; UK (HTV); starring Philip da Costa (Roland), Fulton Mackay, Talfryn Thomas, Jamie Foreman; prod. Leonard White; scr. Bob Baker and Dave Martin; 25-min episodes.

An intriguing and enterprising visionary fantasy in which the unhappy Roland falls down a lift-shaft in the tower block where he lives and enters a fantasy world in which everyone he knows is transformed into an enigmatic figure of menace. He carries forward his private symbolic struggle while the race is on in the real world to save his life. This tense serial brought the tradition of such children's classics as Catherine Storr's *Marianne Dreams* and William Mayne's *A Game of Dark* into the TV medium with a considerable flourish.

1978 CHILD OF GLASS

1978; TV movie; US (Disney); starring Barbara Barrie, Biff McGuire, Anthony Zerbe, Nina Foch, Katy Kurtzman; dir. John Erman; scr. Jim Lawrence; 96 min.

A stickily sentimental but defiantly dignified Disney adaptation of Richard Park's novel *The Ghost Belonged to Me*, in which the resident ghost of an old house – a young girl who died in Victorian times – and her phantom dog befriend her modern counterpart.

DR STRANGE

1978; TV movie; US (CBS/Universal); starring Peter Hooten (Stephen Strange), Jessica Walter, John Mills; dir. Philip de Guere; 96 min.

Part of a package of pilots adapting various Marvel Comics superheroes, its basic formula was eventually adapted into the more earnest *Poltergeist: The Legacy*, but that show wisely employed it as a straightforward horror vehicle, whereas this deployment – in which Walter's Morgan le Fay serves as the villain – was far more mannered.

THE MOON STALLION

1978; 6-part serial; UK (BBC 1); starring James Greene (Professor Purwell), Sarah Sutton (Diana); prod. Anna Home; dir. Dorothea Brooking; scr. Brian Hayles; 30-min episodes.

An intriguing story in which an archaeologist's daughter becomes involved with the Matter of Britain, here augmented by the eponymous phantom. Much of it was filmed on location in the Vale of the White Horse, which gave it a useful touch of authenticity; Hayles's script was one of the most accomplished fantasies specially written for television. Home and Brooking swiftly followed up with a five-part dramatization of Alison Uttley's *A Traveller in Time* scripted by Diana de Vere Cole and starring Sophie Thompson, but the tale of a young girl's dabbling in Elizabethan politics lacked the originality and flair of *The Moon Stallion*. In the following year they offered an ambitious six-part version of E. Nesbit's *The Enchanted Castle* scripted by Julia Jones and starring Simon Sheard, Candida Beveridge, Marcus Scott-Barrett, Gill Abineri and Georgia Stowe. The original novel had been the best of E. Nesbit's fantasies, but also the least popular, because it allowed the children toying with powerful magic to run into real trouble and forced them to face up to some hard questions of moral responsibility. The adaptation was successful in purely artistic terms, but even the modern audience found it less comfortable than the more familiar Nesbit items.

THE MOON STALLION: THE APPEARANCE OF THE GHOST SPREADS ALARM AND CONSTERNATION

1979 THE LEGEND OF KING ARTHUR

1979; 8-part serial; UK (BBC1); starring Andrew Burt (King Arthur), Robert Eddison (Merlin), Felicity Dean (Guinevere), David Robb (Lancelot); prod. Ken Riddington; dir. Rodney Bennett; scr. Andrew Davies; 30-min episodes.

HTV had effectively de-fantasized the story of Arthur for the notable *Arthur of the Britons* (1972–73) starring Oliver Tobias, but the BBC were enjoying such a good run with their fantasy serials that the temptation to take the Matter of Britain back to Maloryesque basics must have been overwhelming. Morgan le Fay – played as a child by Patsy Kensit and as an adult by Maureen O'Brien – was built up into an effective villain, and Davies's script showed off his soon-to-be-legendary ability to condense complicated stories into lean and sinewy form.

MONKEY

1979–81; series; Japan (NTV/Kosukai Hoei); dir. Yusuke Matanabe; English adaptation for the BBC by David Weir; 50-min episodes.

Mythological fantasy based on an epic novel by Wu Cheng-en in which the ebullient Monkey, expelled from Heaven as a mischief-maker, must become one of the aides of Tripitaka, a pioneering Buddhist missionary. The special effects were minimal, but the production effected a neat combination of comedy, action and moralism. The philosophical pretensions were never overdone – at least in the English versions – and the built-in strangeness of the exotic mythos helped to make it intriguing as well as enjoyable.

THE THIEF OF BAGDAD

1979; TV movie; US (NBC); starring Peter Ustinov, Roddy McDowall, Terence Stamp, Kabir Bedi; dir. Clive Donner; scr. A. J. Carothers; 96 min.

The first-rate cast worked hard, but could not begin to eclipse the memory of the Douglas Fairbanks' silent classic and the brilliant Alexander Korda movie. A lacklustre script and feeble special effects ensured that it could not enter into meaningful competition with the sweep and spectacle of its predecessors.

TIME EXPRESS

1979; series; US (CBS/Warner); starring Vincent Price, Coral Browne; cr. Ivan Goff and Ben Roberts; 50-min episodes.

A train carries people back in time so that they might try to repair

OF COURSE IT ISN'T STOLEN – IT'S MAGIC: THE TV VERSION OF *THE THIEF OF BAGDAD* HAD FEW SPECIAL EFFECTS

the mistakes they made; the first attempt to adapt the rich tradition of American "second chance" fantasies to the series format. It was quickly followed by a TV remake of the 1946 movie *Angel on My Shoulder* (1980) directed by John Berry and starring Peter Strauss, Barbara Hershey and Richard Kiley, in which the character granted a second chance is a gangster reincarnated as a district attorney, who must outwit Satan's attempts to damn him all over again. *Time Express* was aborted after only four episodes and the movie was a pale shadow of its predecessor, but other attempts were inevitably made. Wes Craven made the most impressive stab at it in the short-lived *Nightmare Café* (1995), starring Robert Englund as the enigmatic and acidic Blackie. The sequence of failures demonstrates exactly what the individual shows asserted: that only those who contrive to learn from history can be reprieved from having to repeat it.

TURNABOUT

1979; sitcom; US (Universal/NBC); starring John Schuck and Sharon Gless; prod. Sam Denoff; scr. Steven Bochco; 25-min episodes.

The Thorne Smith novel in which husband and wife exchange identities was always the most daring and dangerous variation on the *Vice Versa* theme, and it turned out to be far too risqué for American TV even in the 1970s. Only Steven Bochco would have dared to try it; his involvement with the hastily cancelled show gave it whatever historical interest it retains.

THE TWO WORLDS OF JENNIE LOGAN

1979; TV movie; US (CBS); starring Lindsay Wagner, Alan Feinstein, Marc Singer, Linda Gray; scr. and dir. Frank de Felitta. 96 min.

A timeslip fantasy of a heavily-romanticized kind very common in the US – although Jack Finney's *Time and Again* and Richard Matheson's *Bid Time Return*, both of which feature male protagonists, are much better than David Williams's *Second Sight*, on which this script is based. Wagner was effective as the transtemporal adulteress.

MIRROR, MIRROR: LINDSAY WAGNER REALISES THAT SHE REALLY MUST DO SOMETHING WITH HER HAIR

WORZEL GUMMIDGE

1979–81; sitcom; UK (Southern); starring Jon Pertwee (Worzel), Una Stubbs (Aunt Sally), Geoffrey Bayldon (Crowman); scr. Keith Waterhouse and Willis Hall; 25-min episodes/50-min Christmas special.

The animated scarecrow who became a children's TV favourite had made an earlier appearance in *Worzel Gummidge Turns Detective*, a four-part serial shown by the BBC in 1953, starring Frank Atkinson as Worzel, with a script by Worzel's creator, Barbara Euphan Todd. Jon Pertwee's rendition was, however, the definitive TV Worzel. The prestigious writing team of Waterhouse and Hall did a sterling job of transferring the flavour of Todd's books to the TV medium and their scripts were beautifully realized by the cast. Pertwee was the prime mover in getting the series made and for some inexplicable reason he played the babbling scarecrow with more zest and conviction than he ever felt able to bring to the part of Doctor Who. The series might well have lasted longer than 52 episodes had Southern TV not lost their franchise; the adventures of *Worzel Gummidge Down Under*, produced in 1987 by a New Zealand company, cannot really count as a continuation of it.

1980 THE GIRL, THE GOLD WATCH AND EVERYTHING

1980; TV movie; US (Paramount); starring Robert Hays, Pam Dawber, Jill Ireland; dir. William Wiard; scr. George Zateslo; 96 min.

This adaptation of John D. MacDonald's highly atypical novel about the adventures of a young man armed with a watch that can stop time was stitched together from pilot episodes of an aborted series, and was as messily incoherent as most such salvage jobs. The more coherent "sequel," *The Girl, the Gold Watch and Dynamite* (1981), used a different cast but still failed to get the series off the ground. The central idea was used in a slightly more mature fashion in the UK children's serial *Bernard's Watch* (1997), scripted by Andrew Norris and Richard Fegen.

1981 AN AMERICAN CHRISTMAS CAROL

1981; TV movie; US (ABC); starring Henry Winkler (Benedict Slade), David Wayne, Chris Wiggins; dir. Eric Till; scr. Jerome Coopersmith; 100 min.

This Americanization of Dickens's archetypal Christmas fantasy replaces Scrooge with Benedict Slade, the ruthless president of a New Hampshire finance company. Henry Winkler was an odd choice for the part.

ARTEMIS 81

1981; TV movie; UK (BBC); starring Hywel Bennett, Sting (Helith), Roland Curram (Asrael) Dan O'Herlihy, Anthony Steel;

ARTEMIS 81: VARIOUS CAST MEMBERS ATTEMPT TO UPSTAGE A TREE, WITHOUT MUCH SUCCESS

dir. Alastair Reid;-scr. David Rudkin; 185 min.

The plot of this striking phantasmagoric fantasy – featuring a crucial battle, raging across various worldly stages, between the Angel of Life (Helith) and his dark counterpart (Asrael) – left most of its viewers utterly bewildered. The critics felt that its stunning imagery and bravura performances – the minor players included Daniel Day-Lewis and Hammer veteran Ingrid Pitt – could not begin to make up for its incipient incomprehensibility and extraordinary length, but it remains the most adventurous endeavour in adult fantasy ever to use the resources of the TV medium and deserves more respect than it received.

INTO THE LABYRINTH

1981–83; three 7-part serials; UK (HTV); starring Ron Moody (Rothgo), Pamela Salem (Belor), Simon Beal (Phil), Simon Henderson (Terry), Lisa Turner (Helen); 25-min episodes.

Three teenagers are summoned to release the white magician Rothgo from long captivity so that he might search through time for his protective talisman, stolen by the sorceress Belor. The first serial involved them with both historical and mythological figures, including Robin Hood and the Minotaur. In the second Belor struck back, using her own talisman to shatter Rothgo's; the search for the fragments took in various melodramatic highlights of history. The third series, which replaced Rothgo with an inferior copy and got rid of Terry and Helen, borrowed most of its melodramatic settings from literary works, including *Treasure Island*, *Dr Jekyll and Mr Hyde* and *The Phantom of the Opera* and building to a climax in Arthurian

England. Bob Baker wrote the first episode of each serial but turned the remainder over to others; the resultant unevenness detracted from the narrative tension but the imaginative sweep of the enterprise was admirable.

MR MERLIN

1981–82; sitcom; US (CBS); starring Clark Brandon, Barnard Hughes (Max Merlin); exec. prods. Larry Rosen and Larry Tucker; 30-min episodes.

A lacklustre comedy in which Merlin, now a San Francisco garage-owner, takes on a teenage apprentice who has his own ideas about the uses of magic. It died after 21 episodes.

1982 DEAD ERNEST

1982; sitcom; UK (Central); starring Andrew Sachs (Ernest); scr. John Stevenson and Julian Roach; 25-min episodes.

A sitcom set in a mist-beset Heaven, designed as a vehicle for Sachs (who had attained a peculiar fame playing Manuel in *Fawlty Towers*). Ernest had died – alongside many others – when a freak tidal wave hit the beach at Blackpool. There was nothing unusual in its own demise after 6 episodes.

FANTASIES READY-MADE FOR TV

Such fantasy classics as TV contrived during the era of live drama and the early days of videotape were victories won against tremendous odds. Almost all of them were facilitated by the fact that there is a handful of fantasy devices which make minimal demands on special effects technicians. Timeslip fantasies only require movement from one set to another and a change of costume; TV's investment in historical costume-dramas had produced the expertise necessary to create such artefacts, and actual materials which could be borrowed. Magical disruptions of the kind that are often called "Ansteyan" – after the great Victorian humorist F. Anstey – also tend to be economical, the most economical of all being the identity exchange, which merely requires two actors to trade mannerisms. Talking animals only require the invocation of voice-overs, although the problems of working with animals are themselves so vexatious that one can easily understand why the only notable follow-up to *Mister Ed* was *My Mother the Car*. The ready adaptability of these sub-genres – supplemented, once videotape arrived, by elementary vanishing tricks – greatly assisted the inbuilt tendency which TV production already had to indulge in endless repetition.

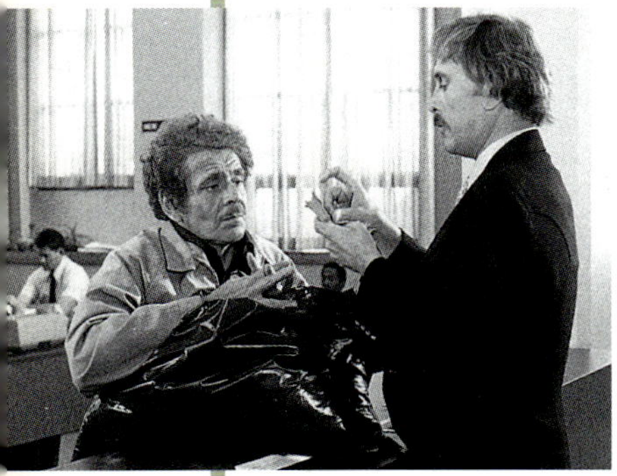

COSTUME-LED FANTASY: TIME EXPRESS

GULLIVER IN LILLIPUT

1982; 4-part serial; UK (BBC1); starring Andrew Burt (Gulliver), Jonathan Cecil, Jenny McCracken; dir. and scr. Barry Letts; 30-min episodes.

As with all dramatizations of the first part of Jonathan Swift's satire, this one had to milk the comic potential of the situation while disregarding the obsolete political concerns of the original, but Letts's script came closer to capturing the abrasive flavour of the original than most modern adaptations.

1983 DUNGEONS AND DRAGONS

1983–87; animated series; US (CBS); prod. Gary Gygax and Bob Richardson; 30-min episodes.

Notwithstanding the involvement of D&D supremo Gygax, this attempt to transpose the roleplaying game to TV never came close to capturing the essence of the original. Given that the whole appeal of the game is the active involvement of the players – it has nothing to offer spectators – the failure was unsurprising, although it lasted 27 episodes. CBS made a further attempt in the short-lived live-action series *Wizards and Warriors*, starring Jeff Conaway and Clive Revill, which provided a perfect illustration of all the reasons why TV was not yet ready or able to accommodate Secondary World fantasy.

MANIMAL

1983; series; US (CBS); starring Simon MacCorkindale, Melody Anderson; cr. Glen A. Larson; 70-min pilot/50-min episodes.

An "enhanced secret agent" series whose protagonist is a shape-shifter capable of transforming himself (while fully clad) into various creatures, including some which must have weighed a lot less than he did. Axed after seven regular episodes, the only surprise being that it ever got past the pilot stage.

THE WIND IN THE WILLOWS

1983; animated film; UK (Thames); voices Michael Hordern (Badger), Richard Pearson (Mole), Ian Carmichael (Rat), David Jason (Toad); prod. Brian Cosgrove and Mark Hall; scr. Rosemary Anne Sissons; 90 min.

A musical version of Kenneth Grahame's classic whose producers went on to make a very substantial contribution to the development of British TV animation. This version connected effortlessly with the seemingly infinite reservoir of nostalgia which the British audience maintains for the chosen few children's classics; a series of 25-minute "sequels" followed, running from 1984 to 1988, with

THE ARCHER AND HIS COMPANIONS FIGHT TO ESCAPE THE WORLD OF *DUNGEONS AND DRAGONS* IN THE ANIMATED TV SERIES

Peter Sallis substituting for Ian Carmichael. The American animated movie made for TV in 1984 by Rankin-Bass was hopelessly inauthentic by comparison.

1984 THE BOX OF DELIGHTS

1984; 6-part serial; UK (BBC1/Lellia); starring Devin Stanfield (Kay Harker), Robert Stephens (Abner Brown), Patrick Troughton; prod. Paul Stone; dir. Renny Rye; scr. Alan Seymour; 30-min episodes.

John Masefield's classic children's novel – subtitled "When the Wolves Were Running" – had been a great success when it was adapted for radio in the 1940s but the BBC wisely waited until adequate special effects were available before attempting a visualization. Using a co-production deal to set up a million-pound budget they lavished such exquisite care upon it – employing brand-new "electronic paintbox" and Quantel image-shrinking techniques as well as the now-familiar colour-separation overlays – that the result set new standards for TV fantasy. The performances were excellent, especially Stephens' portrayal of the arch-villain, and the serial built up considerable tension with the aid of some neat cliff-hangers. Kay's attempts to keep the magic box out of the hands of the villains bring him into contact with Herne the Hunter and the Matter of Britain, linking this serial to many other endeavours central to the development of British TV fantasy.

CHANCE IN A MILLION

1984–86; sitcom; UK (C4/Thames); starring Simon Callow (Tom Chance), Brenda Blethyn (Alison); prod. and dir. Michael Miles; scr. Andrew Norris and Richard Fegen; 25-min episodes.

A meek but quietly passionate librarian becomes engaged to a "coincidence-prone" man who bears his affliction bravely and philosophically. Exceptionally well acted and cleverly scripted, this very funny show never got the critical attention it deserved, although it was among the most popular of Channel 4's early offerings and a spectacular justification of the Channel's original brief. It was much better than serious variations of the same theme, which include an unsuccessful NBC pilot starring Valerie Perrine as *Lady Luck* (1973) and *Strange Luck* (1996–).

A CHRISTMAS CAROL

1984; TV movie; US; starring George C. Scott (Scrooge), Nigel Davenport, Frank Finlay, Edward Woodward, Lucy Gutteridge; dir. Clive Donner; scr. Roger O'Hirson; 100 min.

Dickens' definitive Christmas story had been read on screen many times and there had been several animated versions (the best of them featuring the voice of Alastair Sim as Scrooge in 1971) but this was the first dramatization to have a sizeable budget. Shot in Shrewsbury, it contrived to avoid many of the pitfalls usually afflicting American Victoriana and Scott put in a stirring performance.

HIGHWAY TO HEAVEN

1984–88; series; US (NBC); starring cr./exec. prod. Michael Landon (Jonathan Smith), Victor French (Mark Gordon); 50-min episodes.

Landon took up the torch of Carl Reiner's *Good Heavens* and its hastily-aborted successors, deciding that the idea would work better if it were played dead straight, after the fashion of *It's a Wonderful Life* and its clone-movies. No fantasy motif had yet been successfully adapted to the series-drama format and relatively few attempts had been made; none seemed readily adaptable to the infinitely repeatable templates such series required, unless it were carefully trivialized after the fashion of F. Anstey and Thorne Smith. Inserting a novice angel into the standard "wandering vigilante" template and taking the idea seriously was daring, but the formula worked as a generator of plots and it was in tune with the ever-more-clamorous insistence by Bible-belt Fundamentalists that angels are every bit as real as the Garden of Eden and Noah's Ark. Most importantly of all, it allowed the didactic moralism typical of American TV shows to obtain a uniquely explicit and authoritative voice.

Highway to Heaven was unashamedly sentimental but it involved the kind of schmaltzy sweetness which had Disneyfied most one-off

ENTERTAINING ANGELS

In the world of American TV it is not the road to Hell which is paved with good intentions but the road from Heaven. Americans have long been fascinated with the notion of guardian angels and TV has both reflected and amplified this fascination. Early shows like *Nanny and the Professor* (ABC, 1969–71) used purely metaphorical "angels" but *Good Heavens* (ABC, 1975–76), starring Carl Reiner as Mr Angel, began a process of literalization which continued in *Out of the Blue* (ABC, 1979), which starred James Brogan as Random, a guardian angel assigned to watch over two orphaned children. NBC made plans for a similar show whose pilot footage was assembled into the TV movie *The Kid with the Broken Halo* (1981); Gary Coleman played a novice angel who had to help a series of families in order to win promotion. *It Happened One Christmas*, a 1977 TV movie made for ABC, had already attempted to clone the classic Frank Capra movie *It's a Wonderful Life*, substituting a female protagonist for the James Stewart character. NBC's response to that experiment had been *Human Feelings* (1978), in which God despatches an angel (Billy Crystal) to Las Vegas in search of six souls sufficiently virtuous to warrant its deliverance from the fate of Sodom and Gomorrah. ABC retaliated with *For Heaven's Sake* (1979), in which Ray Bolger was the angel despatched to assist a hopeless baseball team. It was not until *Highway to Heaven* was made, however, that all this hectic activity finally paid off, and opened the road from Heaven to serious traffic.

Look homeward, angel: Michael Landon searches for inspiration

exercises in this vein – and was, in consequence, much better than the unusually protracted TV movie *It Came Upon the Midnight Clear* directed by Peter H. Hunt, released in the same year, which starred Mickey Rooney as an ex-cop angel who gets compassionate leave from Heaven so that he can show his grandson what an old-time Christmas was like. For these reasons *Highway to Heaven* not only succeeded where its predecessors had failed but became a significant model for other shows, including *Quantum Leap* and *Early Edition*. Among the earlier attempts to imitate it was *Ghost of a Chance* (1986), a failed pilot released as a TV movie, in which a piano player shot before his allotted time by an over-eager policeman has to readjust to the moral and existential requirements of a life in the margins of society. It was directed by Don Taylor and starred Redd Foxx and Dick Van Dyke.

MR STABS

1984; play; UK (Thames); starring David Jason (Mr Stabs), David Rappaport, Lorna Heilbron (Polandi), John Woodnut (Melchisedek); scr. Trevor Preston; 30 min.

The first (and best) of several fantastic contributions to the *Dramarama* series, employing a character spun off from *Ace of Wands*. An uninhibited sword-and-sorcery tale in which Stabs must secure the Raven Stone from the evil Polandi in order to open a gateway to Earth and fight a magical duel against Melchisedek.

ROBIN OF SHERWOOD

1984–86; series; UK (HTV); starring Michael Praed (Robin), Clive Mantle (Little John), Ray Winstone (Will Scarlett), Nickolas Grace (Sheriff of Nottingham), Judi Trott (Marian); cr. Richard Carpenter; 100-min pilot/50-min episodes.

Carpenter's brainchild – for which he also wrote many of the scripts – went bravely against the grain of TV tradition by *adding* to the fantasy element of a British legend, further dignifying Robin's rearguard fight for honour and justice with the support of Herne the Hunter, the enmity of powerful Druids (including Richard O'Brien's sinister Gulnar), and various other mystical accoutrements. The show was wonderfully atmospheric – an effect aided by Clannad's excellent theme music – and the performances were first-rate. The uncannily handsome Praed made such a deep impression that his Robin was martyred when the actor set off to conquer the strange new world of American supersoaps at the end of series two; although Jason Connery was a perfectly adequate replacement acting-wise, it just wasn't the same thereafter. Cable repeats and video release (including an omnibus containing a five-hour version of the entire first series) won the enterprise a new generation of fans in the 1990s.

1985 ALICE IN WONDERLAND

1985; 2-part mini-series; US (CBS/Columbia); starring Natalie Gregory (Alice). Lloyd Bridges, Red Buttons, Sid Caesar, Carol Channing, Imogen Coca, Sammy Davis Jr, Karl Malden, Roddy McDowall, Robert Morley, Anthony Newley, Martha Raye, Telly Savalas, Patrick Duffy; dir. Harry Harris; scr. Paul Zindel; 95-min episodes.

A remarkable illustration of the values and attitudes of US TV. Alice had been subjected to such scrupulous psychoanalysis in British productions that it had become difficult to do the story straight, but in the US there was no hint of any such compromise, and the makers gleefully followed the standard method of dealing with "classics": they hired lots of big stars to play themselves playing characters in funny hats (the costumes were so absurdly elementary that in this case the phrase can be taken literally). Paul Zindel's reverent script had no chance of getting past the monumental follies of the production; Sammy Davis boggled more minds than most as the Caterpillar, but Telly Savalas as the Cheshire Cat was an equally remarkable casting decision. Patrick Duffy played the Goat, to the astonishment of all those who had never realized that there was a Goat in *Alice in Wonderland*. The proper way to go about it was demonstrated the following year by a four-part serial version made by the BBC, which starred Kate Dorning as Alice, with careful support from Jonathan Cecil, Pip Donaghy and others. Barry Letts – who produced and directed it – offered a low-key, easy-paced and reverent dramatization which succeeded in restoring the innocence and buoyancy of the primal text.

ANGELS RUSHING IN

Highway to Heaven placed angels at the centre of the American tradition of TV fantasy, but the road from Heaven was still prone to the occasional traffic accident. As Capra's *It's a Wonderful Life* continued to gain in popularity and critical esteem it was only natural that someone should wonder why the first All-American guardian angel shouldn't have his own series, so *Clarence* (1990) materialized as yet another hopeful pilot, starring Robert Carradine as a rejuvenated Clarence Oddbody conveniently gifted with shapeshifting powers. He was assigned to a typical TV family, but he wasn't as sexy as Michael Landon – which led other experimenters to deploy Scott Bakula and Kyle Chandler in metaphorical angelic roles which would allow them a little more freedom to display their frustrations. The experiments worked, but they didn't meet the growing audience hunger for the real thing; nor did shows which tried to play it for laughs, like *Teen Angel*. The answer was to go back to the basics of *Nanny and the Professor* and send forth the winsome heroine of *Touched by an Angel*. Rival programme-makers – knowing how easy it is for writers to work casual miracles and alarmed by the series' tacit assertion that people who don't get saved by miracles don't really want to be saved – began a belated backlash in the horror series *Buffy the Vampire Slayer*, whose heroine is human through and through while Angel, who lends Buffy a helpful crucifix in the first episode, is an arrant coward. In *Buffy*, fighting real evil requires metaphorical balls.

ARTHUR THE KING

1985; TV movie; US (CBS/Comworld); starring Malcolm McDowell (Arthur), Candice Bergen (Morgan le Fay), Edward Woodward (Merlin), Dyan Cannon (The Tourist), Rupert Everett (Lancelot); dir. Clive Donner; scr. J. David Wyles and David Karp; 142 min.

An American tourist falls down a Carrollian rabbit-hole while visiting Stonehenge and finds herself in Camelot. As one might expect of a US production, this has more in common with *A Connecticut Yankee at King Arthur's Court* (with all the satire taken out) than with Malory. It was shot in 1983 – before *Alice in Wonderland* – but CBS were so affrighted by what they had paid for that they shelved it for a couple of years; it was cut to 94 minutes and retitled *Merlin and the Sword* for video release. In the interests of having a second stab at an idea which must have seemed good to somebody Paul Zindel was hired to rescript the whole thing for kids, with a younger female lead; this version, directed by Mel Damski and starring Keshia Knight Pulliam, was released as *A Connecticut Yankee in King Arthur's Court* in 1989. Unfortunately, Mark Twain could not contrive the timeslip which would have allowed him to sue for defamation of character – he would have won enormous damages.

STEVEN SPIELBERG'S AMAZING STORIES

1985–87; series; US (NBC/Amblin/Universal); cr. Steven Spielberg; 25-min/a few 50-min episodes.

Despite the sf title this series mostly consisted of wish-fulfilment fantasies in which sympathetic characters in tough spots are saved by casual miracles. The series did its level best to demonstrate that if you push the right moral and emotional buttons the audience will not only accept but welcome any contrivance, however absurd. "The Mission," a double-length showcase episode in which a stricken World War II bomber captained by Kevin Costner eventually lands on wheels drawn by an amateur cartoonist, was an archetypal example. H. L. Mencken famously remarked that nobody ever lost money by underestimating the taste of the public; in failing to find a sizeable audience or win any critical acclaim for this series Spielberg demonstrated that the TV audience really does have an intelligence capable of insult, and perhaps we should be thankful to him for that.

1986 BABES IN TOYLAND

1986; TV movie; US; starring Drew Barrymore, Richard Mulligan; dir. Clive Donner; scr. Paul Zindel; 150 min.

An elaborate TV remake of the 1934 Laurel and Hardy movie (which had already been remade in 1961), removing the plot even further from Victor Herbert's original operetta. There is an extraordinarily rich tradition of fantasy opera and ballet, classic folk tales having long been established as a key resource for scenarists, but attempts to adapt it to the TV medium – as opposed to merely photographing stage performances – have always come unstuck, even defying the talents of writers as able as Zindel.

BORN OF FIRE

1986; TV movie; UK (C4); starring Peter Firth, Suzan Crowley, Stefan Kalipha, Nabil Shaban; prod. and dir. Jamil Dehlavi; 90 min.

Though far from being the most successful of the feature films commissioned by Channel 4, this may well qualify as the most daring. It is based on the Arabic legend of the djinn Iblis (the Islamic counterpart of Lucifer), who defied Allah's instruction to bow down before Adam and was cast out of Paradise. Here, celestial

SHE-DEVIL WITH BIG HAIR: JULIE T. WALLACE MASTERS THE ART OF POWER-DRESSING

music heard by a flautist and an astronomer is a prelude to apparitions which demand that its mystery be elucidated. Many viewers found it every bit as confusing as *Artemis 81*, but it is similarly stunning as a visual experience and equally heroic in its attempt to place reality within an aesthetically apt metaphysical frame.

THE LIFE AND LOVES OF A SHE-DEVIL

1986; 4-part mini-series; UK (BBC2); starring Julie T. Wallace, Patricia Hodge, Dennis Waterman; prod. Sally Head; scr. Ted Whitehead; 60-min. episodes.

A BAFTA Award-winning dramatization of Fay Weldon's deliciously cruel satire, in which an ugly housewife who loses her husband to a lovely romantic novelist is magically empowered to exact an appropriate revenge. Wallace was superb in the lead and the supporting performances were first-rate.

MR PYE

1986; 4-part serial; UK (C4); starring Derek Jacobi, Judy Parfitt; dir. Michael Darlow; scr. Donald Churchill; 50-min episodes.

An excellent dramatization of Mervyn Peake's wry sentimental comedy about a man whose plan to bring news of the wonderful generosity of the "Great Pal" to the isle of Sark is subverted by the embarrassment of the angelic wings which sprout from his back. When he attempts to get rid of them by dabbling in small evils he begins to grow horns instead. A fine performance by Jacobi as the hapless Pye deftly captured the essence of a challenging role, and the beautiful locations provided a very effective backcloth to the special effects. The serial deserves recognition as one of the classics of TV fantasy (and an omnibus release on video).

THE SINGING DETECTIVE

1986; 6-part serial; UK (BBC1); starring Michael Gambon, Patrick Malahide, Janet Suzman, Imelda Staunton, Joanne Whalley; prod. Kenith Trodd; scr. Dennis Potter; episodes varied in length, averaging c70 min.

Potter often used surrealizing devices in his dramas, only occasionally spilling over into explicit supernaturalism – as in the brilliant *Brimstone and Treacle* (1976), which the BBC initially refused to broadcast. In this painful serial about a hospitalized writer whose superficial psoriasis echoes and intensifies a parallel unease of the soul, an idiosyncratic method of stylization involving the use of popular songs – which came equipped with a ready-made conventionality by virtue of its use in Potter's classic *Pennies From Heaven* (1978) – explodes into wholesale hallucinatory fantasy, unashamedly gaudy and intricately paranoid. Although foreshadowed by *King of the Castle*, this was one of the most original of all TV dramas, and one of the finest.

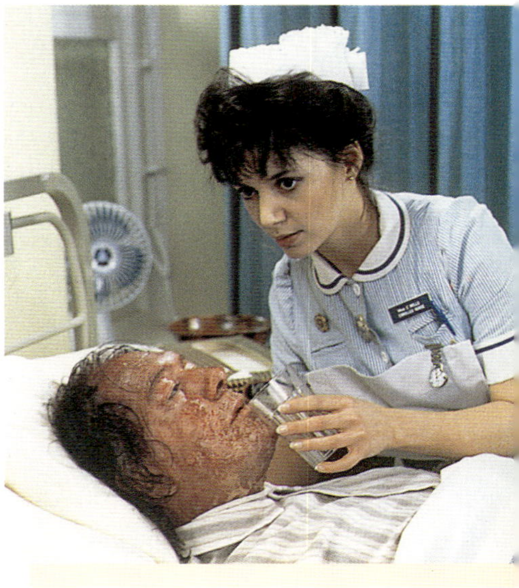

CARRY ON, NURSE: MICHAEL GAMBON FAILS TO RAISE A SMILE

1987 BEAUTY AND THE BEAST

1987–90; series; US (CBS); starring Ron Perlman (Vincent), Linda Hamilton, Roy Dotrice; cr. Ron Koslow; 50-min episodes.

Once *Highway to Heaven* had shown what might be done with fantasy variants of the "wandering vigilante" format, it was open season on daft-but-dignified ideas. This clever alloy of the famous folk tale and *The Phantom of the Opera* paired off a dewy-eyed assistant DA with a leonine inhabitant of a secret underworld beneath the city of New York. Vincent is a modern Cyrano de Bergerac: witty, macho and positively dripping with panache. When Linda Hamilton quit, presumably having found Terminators even sexier than big cats, she was replaced by Jo Anderson, but the most basic tenet of Grand Passion is that the participants aren't supposed to be interchangeable and it was all downhill from there to the 55th and final episode. The show was popular with female viewers who figured that if even if all men are beasts, there must be one somewhere with a heart of gold.

THE CHARMINGS

1987–88; sitcom; US (ABC/Embassy); starring Christopher Rich, (Prince Eric Charming), Caitlin O'Heaney (Snow White Charming), Judy Parfitt (Queen Lilian); cr. Prudence Fraser and Robert Sternin; 25-min episodes.

After sleeping for centuries, beautiful Snow White and her Prince awake to find the world much changed – and the wicked queen, who cast the spell, still around. They adjust well enough, assisted by the fact that they keep bumping into the leftovers of other classic fairy tales, although the rule about participants in Grand Passion not being interchangeable went by the board again when Carol Huston replaced O'Heaney half-way through the series (which managed a near-respectable 21 episodes before being axed).

THE SECRET WORLD OF POLLY FLINT

1987; 6-part serial; UK (Central); starring Katie Reynolds (Polly), Don Henderson (Old Mazy), Brenda Bruce (Granny Porter); dir. David Cobham; scr. Helen Cresswell; 25-min episodes.

An intriguing timeslip fantasy about a village cut adrift from the time-stream in the 16th century, condemning its inhabitants to become "time gypsies" until 20th-century Polly contrives to make contact with them and repair the rift. It was shot on location in and around Rufford Park, benefiting considerably from the authenticity of the settings.

1988 THE LION, THE WITCH AND THE WARDROBE

1988; 6-part serial; UK (BBC1); starring Richard Dempsey (Peter), Sophie Cook (Susan), Jonathan R. Scott (Edmund), Sophie Wilcox (Lucy), Barbara Kellerman (White Witch), voice of Ronald Pickup (Aslan); scr. Alan Seymour; 30-min episodes.

This was the third TV version of C. S. Lewis's children's fantasy, which had gone up in the public's estimation since BBC's 10-part version starring Zuleika Robson, Elizabeth Crowther, Edward McMurray, Paul Waller and Bernard Kay (as Aslan) had been aired in 1967. That version, produced by Pamela Lonsdale and scripted by Trevor Preston, had worked hard to overcome the limitations imposed by the primitive special effects available at the time, deserving respect for its bravery as well as its ingenuity, but it failed to overcome the handicaps afflicting all TV versions of Secondary World fantasy. The animated TV movie version of 1978 directed by Bill Melendez for the Children's Television Workshop was much more effective and deservedly won an Emmy. British critics were less fond of the US/UK joint production than their American counterparts, but those valiant heretics who continue to prefer it to the supposedly definitive BBC serial have an arguable case. The techniques which had helped to make *The Box of Delights* a masterpiece did so because they were intrinsically well adapted to the presentation of magical intrusions in an otherwise-real world; the task of using them to realize an entire Secondary World was a different kettle of fish. The attempt was undeniably heroic, but the result was an expensive mess. Lewis's reputation as a writer and part-time saint had been so comprehensively established, however, that the goodwill of the audience overrode the defects in the production and this serial gave rise to *The Chronicles of Narnia*, further comprising a six-episode dramatization which combined *Prince Caspian* and *The Voyage of the Dawn Treader* (1989) and a six-episode dramatization of *The Silver Chair* (1990). The effects grew even less convincing as budgetary

ASLAN: SAVIOUR OR SOFT TOY?

restrictions tightened, and all thought of attempting *The Last Battle* was wisely set aside. This project proved that Secondary World fantasy would have to await the next generation of computer-generated special effects before it could be accommodated to TV budgets.

MOONDIAL

1988; 6-part serial; UK (BBC1); starring Siri Neal, Tony Reid, Helen Avallano; prod. Paul Stone; scr. Helen Cresswell; 30-min episodes.

Cresswell had previously adapted her Lizzie Dripping stories for the BBC but it was ITV which presented her adaptation of the more ambitious *Secret World of Polly Flint* in 1987; the BBC were quick to reclaim her by offering an opportunity to adapt the best – or at least most melodramatic – of her timeslip fantasies. The three children who form a transtemporal alliance are forced into urgent confrontation with supernatural maleficence; the deployment within the plot of explicitly Satanic witchcraft caused some disquiet among the audience, but failed to provoke the kind of moral panic that it might well have triggered in America.

THE SNOW SPIDER

1988; 4-part serial; UK (HTV); starring Sian Phillips, Osian Roberts; dir. Pennant Roberts; 25-min episodes.

An ambitious but cleverly accomplished dramatization of a novel by Jenny Nimmo, in which a young boy who receives five unusual birthday gifts is led thereby to set out on a quest for a mythical land. The same production team followed it in 1990 and 1991 with similarly well wrought dramatizations of the novel's two sequels, *Emlyn's Moon* and *The Chestnut Soldier*. The TV serials provided a considerable service in publicizing a series which can stand comparison with the very best children's fantasies.

1989 TOM'S MIDNIGHT GARDEN

1989; 6-part serial; UK; starring Jeremy Rampling (Tom Long); prod. Paul Stone; scr. Julia Jones; 30-min episodes.

Philippa Pearce's heartfelt and unusually subtle timeslip fantasy had previously been seen in 1974, in a three-part BBC serial starring Nicolas Bridge and Margot MacAlaster, but this more substantial version did far more justice to the complexity and subtlety of the text. Young Tom, who is in quarantine while his brother is ill, makes psychic contact with the nostalgic dreams of the dying Mrs Bartholomew and obtains a unique educational experience. Jones's script artfully captured the moving qualities of the original novel.

1990 A MOM FOR CHRISTMAS

1990; TV movie; US (Disney); starring Olivia Newton-John, Doug Sheehan, Aubrey Morris; dir. George Miller; 100 min.

A typically excessive dose of sugary Disney sentimentality in which a department-store mannequin comes to life in response to a little girl's Christmas wish.

1991 EARTH ANGEL

1991; TV movie; US; starring Cindy Williams, Mark Hamill, Erik Estrada, Alan Young; dir. Joe Napolitano; scr. Nina Shengold; 100 min.

Thirty years after she was killed in a prom-night road accident the angelic heroine returns to Earth to help sort out the problems of her former classmates. The basic idea was presumably borrowed from Christopher Morley's classic *Thunder on the Left*, which employed it in a heart-rending parable of lost innocence, but the makers of this film – who clearly hadn't learned any lessons from *Highway to Heaven* – couldn't resist the cheap laughs.

WEIRD: OMRI KATZ FINDS SMALL TOWN AMERICA EERIE

EERIE, INDIANA

1991–2; series; US (Unreality Inc); starring Omri Katz (Marshall Teller). Justin Shenkarow (Simon Holmes); cr. Karl Shaefer and Jose Rivera; 25-min episodes.

Joe Dante directed the pilot episode of this marvellously uninhibited show about a small town where anything and everything can happen, and he remained a creative consultant. Incomer Marshall Teller and his new pal Simon are the only people who realize that Eerie is the "centre of weirdness for the entire USA"; everyone else thinks that it's a perfectly normal – and therefore literally perfect – small town. The show mixed sf, fantasy and occult motifs with a blithe disregard for consistency. Several of the episodes were absolute gems, including the one where Marshall forgets to put his watch back for daylight saving time and gets stuck in a time-warp. In the best one of all Marshall suddenly finds that real life has turned into a TV show in which he is an actor named Omri and his friends and family members are vain and patronising *stauchspielers* – especially the one who is sucking up to the writer with a view to having Marshall killed off so that he can take over the lead. Unfortunately, the show was far too whimsical for its target audience and it was axed – a tragic loss.

IT'S ALIVE: THE 1991 VERSION OF *FIVE CHILDREN AND IT* WAS A VAST IMPROVEMENT OVER ITS PREDECESSORS

FIVE CHILDREN AND IT

1991; 6-part serial; UK (BBC1); starring Tamzen Audas, Simon Godwin, Nicole Moway, Charlie Richards; prod. Richard Callanan; scr. Helen Cresswell; 25-min episodes.

This second BBC attempt at E. Nesbit's classic cautionary tale had the benefit of a sophisticated puppet, which looked a great deal older than the besuited child of the 1951 version. Cresswell was by now a past master at TV adaptation and her scripts were supported by strong performances. The major participants were deservedly rewarded with a second six-part serial, *The Return of the Psammead*, likewise scripted by Cresswell, broadcast in 1993.

HI HONEY, I'M DEAD

1991; TV movie; US (Fox); starring Curtis Armstrong, Catherine Hicks, Kevin Conroy, Joseph Gordon-Levitt; dir. Alan Myerson; 100 min.

A greedy property developer given to using cheap materials is killed by an accident on one of his building sites and finds his consciousness transplanted into the body of a vagrant – a fate he brought on himself by virtue of his conviction that society's losers deserve their fate. He obtains work as a servant in his old family home, learning for the first time what his nearest and dearest thought of him, and the true value of what he had.

MERLIN OF THE CRYSTAL CAVE

1991; 6-part serial; UK (BBC1); starring Robert Powell, Jon Finch, Jody David (young Merlin), George Winter (adult Merlin); prod. Hilary Bevan Jones & Shaun Sutton; scr. Steve Bescoby; 25-min episodes.

Although it was an adaptation of Mary Stewart's conscientiously de-fantasized account of the boyhood of Merlin, *The Crystal Cave* (1970) and its sequels, Bescoby's script restored just enough magic to qualify this serial as a fantasy. The historical interpretation of the Arthurian legends is reasonably convincing and the whole is effective in spite of covering so much ground that almost all the subtlety of the original novels is sacrificed.

1992 ARCHER'S GOON

1992; serial UK; (BBC); starring Annette Badland; dir. Marilyn Fox; scr. Jenny McDade.

An artful adaptation of Diana Wynne Jones's highly original novel, in which the eponymous heavyweight is sent to the home of a writer who cannot maintain his wordage quota. The visitation is an educative experience for the writer's son, who was previously unaware of his family's secrets and its special relationship with the town's wizard elite.

THE BORROWERS

1992; 6-part serial; UK (BBC1); starring Ian Holm (Pod), Penelope Wilton (Homily), Rebecca Callard (Arrietty); prod. Grainne Marmion; scr. Richard Carpenter; 30-min episodes.

The tiny heroes of Mary Norton's much-loved series of novels had previously been brought to the small screen by a 1973 TV movie starring Eddie Albert and directed by Walter C. Miller from a script by Jay Presson Allen. That version had removed the Clock family to New England and had not come close to reproducing the piquant humour of the original, although it had compensated for these failings with some neat special effects. The BBC serial – likewise embodying the first two volumes of the series – had to be more economical in its use of special effects but overcame its limitations cleverly. Beautifully designed sets and excellent performances helped this version win two awards, although Mary Norton – who died on the final day of filming – did not live to enjoy its success. The production team went on to make an equally fine six-part sequel, based on the third and fourth books, which was broadcast as a continuation of the series, under the same title, in 1993.

GROWING RICH

1992; 6-part serial; UK (Anglia); starring Rosalind Bennett (Carmen), Claire Hackett, Caroline Harker, Martin Kemp (The Driver), John Stride; prod. Brian Farnham; dir. Roger Gregory; scr. Fay Weldon; 50-min episodes.

Needs must when the Devil drives, and when the Mephistophelean driver promises to deliver the luscious Carmen to his plutocratic employer he puts pressure on her by making her two best friends very needy indeed. It seems as if she must sacrifice herself to redeem them – but the time has come for all women to rebel against the curse visited upon them by that serpent in Eden. A first-rate dramatization of the sharpest and most extravagant of Weldon's feminist fairy tales.

HIGHLANDER

1992– ; series; US; starring Adrian Paul (Duncan MacLeod); exec. prod. Peter Davis and Bill Panzer; cr. Gregory Widen. 50-min. episodes.

A surprisingly durable spinoff from the 1985 movie, in which a whole series of Immortals arrives, one after another, to challenge the 400-year-old MacLeod for the right to be the Last and Best. In the first two seasons the scriptwriters were content to recruit perfectly ordinary villains to keep the sword-wielding vigilante occupied between these definitive supernatural encounters, but they eventually capitulated to the rule which says that every superhero requires at least one personalized ultra-villain to provide him with an adequate challenge. The basic situation was complicated by the addition of Hunters dedicated to the extermination of all Immortals (who are themselves renegades from a benign organization of Watchers) and ultimate evil was then stirred into the plot in the shape of the ancient Sumerian anti-god Ahriman. In the meantime, Paul went through several female sidekicks, including those played by Tessa Noel and Elizabeth Gracen, before winding up with only a censorious Watcher (played by Jim Byrnes) to keep him company. Although the 1997–98 series of 13 episodes was commissioned – as a Canadian/French co-production made by Gaumont TV and Rysher Entertainment – on the assumption that it would be the last, TV movies and a further spin-off series with a female protagonist, *Highlander: The Raven*, continued to keep the licence alive.

NORTHERN EXPOSURE

1992–4; series; US (Universal); starring Rob Morrow (Joel Fleischman), Janine Turner (Maggie O'Connell), Barry Corbin (Maurice Minnifield), John Corbett, Darren E. Burrows, John Cullum, Cynthia Geary; cr. Joshua Brand and John Falsey; 50-min episodes.

A Jewish doctor from New York signs a contract with Maurice Minnifield to work for two years in the tiny town of Cicely, Alaska, which the *nouveau riche* ex-astronaut hopes to develop into a more substantial outpost of civilization. Only a few of the episodes were overtly supernatural, but these adopted a highly effective kind of "magic realism" which mingled elements borrowed from Inuit folklore with other equally *recherché* items. Much more sophisticated than *Eerie, Indiana* (and, for that matter, anything else on TV at the time), the show had a similar blithe uninhibitedness and it developed a touching streak of understated sentimentality. The team attempted to carry on regardless when Morrow began to ease himself out, but eventually capitulated to inevitability, after giving him a fine send-off which took its inspiration from Jessie Weston's classic account of how myths develop *From Ritual to Record*. With luck, the precedents it set will bear further fruit.

THERE CAN BE ONLY ONE: TWO FILMS AND THREE TV SERIES LATER, *HIGHLANDER* IS STILL BATTLING THE FORCES OF EVIL

SO HAUNT ME

1992–94; sitcom; UK (BBC1); starring Miriam Karlin (Yetta Feldman), George Costigan, Tessa Peake-Jones; cr. and scr. Paul A. Mendelson; 30-min episodes.

The members of a family who move into a new house when the breadwinner quits advertising to be a "real writer" capitulate by degrees to the unfortunate awareness that it is haunted by the ghost of a stereotypically overbearing Jewish mother. One by one they learn to see her, to tolerate her, and eventually to welcome her – well, almost – as a valued addition to their own family. Done with a calculated lack of sophistication, although there is probably no comedy so low that it could not be dignified by the ever-graceful Peake-Jones.

1994 HERCULES: THE LEGENDARY JOURNEYS

1994–1999; series; US (MCA); starring Kevin Sorbo; cr. Christian Williams; exec. prods. Sam Raimi and Robert Tapert; co-exec. prod. John Schulian; 80-min pilot/50-min episodes.

This show ushered in a whole new era of TV fantasy. It was not the deployment of computer-generated monsters *per se* which provided the vital precedents, but the development of an ambience and attitude that made their lack of realism seem unimportant. Even in the very best heroic fantasy movies up to that time, the special effects had never been entirely convincing, one result of this being that their makers had felt obliged to aim them at a supposedly uncritical juvenile audience. Thanks to the ever-inventive Raimi this series arrived with a tacit nudge and wink that said to the audience: "Hey, we aren't trying to pretend that all this is real, we're just having fun – but it is a whole lot of fun, isn't it?" – and it certainly was. Kevin Sorbo, whose charm is an order of magnitude greater than that acquired by any of his contemporary rivals among Hollywood's action heroes, struck exactly the right balance of wide-eyed innocence and knowing cynicism in playing Hercules. His co-starring sidekicks did not always rise to the challenge with equal aplomb, but Michael Hurst was good as Iolus and Bruce Campbell's occasional guest spots as Autolycus, the so-called King of Thieves, demonstrated the expected understanding of Sam Raimi's cock-eyed world-view. The show's deployment of special effects was initially modest, but its makers took full advantage of the increased budgets generated by the show's success over its five-year lifespan. The pilot movie, *Hercules and the Lost Kingdom*, was supplemented on video by other full-length stories initially shown as two-parters, including *Hercules and the Amazon Women* and *Hercules and the Circle of Fire*.

HEROISM IN THE AGE OF HEROES

In *Hercules: The Legendary Journeys* there is a humorous edge to everything: the blithely anachronistic recruitment of fantastic motifs, ranging all the way to Jack's beanstalk; the unrepentantly modern dialogue laden with slick one-liners and pert moral homilies; the preposterously stunt-crammed fights; and the mock disclaimers in the credits. All of these devices refer back to the sins and failings of previous TV series, explicitly marking the determination to begin a new era. The ridiculous stylization of TV fight scenes began with a 1970s moral panic that imposed strict limitations on the injuries that could be inflicted on characters. Even in shows like The A-Team the harmlessness of the spectacular violence took on a certain surreality, but Hercules goes all the way and a bit more besides, making the artifice blatantly ridiculous. In much the same way, *Hercules*'s ironically punctilious moral-mongering has a cutting edge whose implication is summed up in the blurb overlaying the opening credits. This informs viewers that the show is set in a world whose gods are "petty and cruel," deliberately overturning a familiar adage by assuming a moral universe in which error is divine (or at least divinely sanctioned) and forgiveness (a key indicator of moral wisdom) purely human. This conspicuously modern assumption – and the accompanying insistence that we are entirely responsible for our own ethical development – gives the show's contentedly absurd plots a subversive sharpness that has transformed the moral landscape of contemporary TV fantasy.

1995 ELIDOR

1995; 6-part serial; UK (BBC1); starring Damian Zuk, Suzanne Crowshaw, Gavin J. Morris, Alexandra Trippier; prod. Paul Madden and Mairede Thomas; scr. Don Webb; 25-min episodes.

Because it is partly set in a Secondary World this Alan Garner novel was markedly less suitable for TV adaptation than *The Owl Service* but the early phases – in which strays from Elidor intrude upon the grounds of a ruined church – were effective, as was the final phase when the harassed children return from the other dimension. A good attempt to add a visual dimension to a particularly fine book.

JOHNNY AND THE DEAD

1995; 4-part serial; UK (LWT); starring Andrew Falvey (Johnny), George Baker, Brian Blessed, Jane Lapotaire; prod. and dir. Gerald Fox; scr. Gerald Fox and Lindsey Jenkins; 30-min episodes.

An adaptation of the second (and best) novel in Terry Pratchett's series chronicling the adventures of Johnny Maxwell. When the local council plans to develop a cemetery site Johnny begins to see the ghosts of the people buried there and alerts them to their plight. The plot neatly sidesteps all the expected clichés, providing a moral far more sophisticated than any US TV fantasy had yet contrived. The script could not reproduce all the brilliance of the original but it made every effort to capture its essence.

SABRINA THE TEENAGE WITCH

1995; TV movie; US (Showtime); starring Melissa Joan Hart, Sherry Miller, Charlene Fernetz; dir Tibor Takacs; 90 min.

In the years following her first appearances as a bit-part player in *The*

HERCULES GETS READY TO STRUT HIS STUFF

Archie Show (1968–69) Sabrina had also featured in the unhappily-titled animated series *Sabrina and the Groovie Goolies* (1970–71) and in her own animated show (1971–73). This attempt to develop her as a live-action heroine was one of the few successful fantasy movie pilots, giving rise to a sitcom in which Melissa Joan Hart again took the lead (although the parts of her two aunts were recast). The irrepressibly charming Hart is the strongest element in both the movie and the series as she blithely deploys elementary magical tricks to cope with the usual travails of teenage life, inevitably discovering that many of them misfire. The whole enterprise is distinctly old-fashioned, blissfully unaware of the fact that the stereotyped and sanitized image of high-school life had been severely scorched by the acidic commentary of *My So-Called Life*. For this reason, it contrasts sharply, and entirely to its own detriment, with *Buffy the Vampire Slayer*, which offers a much more sarcastic commentary on the rigours of adolescence to complement its gaudy horror-comic motifs. Perhaps for that very reason, though, Sabrina quickly attracted her own fan base and the show achieved surprisingly good ratings.

TOUCHED BY AN ANGEL

1995– ; series; US (CBS/Moonwater); starring Roma Downey (Monica), Della Reese (Tess); cr. John Masius; 50-min episodes.

This show presumably became the most successful of *Highway to Heaven*'s imitators by being brutally frank about its own nature and purpose. Its longevity may be partly due to its popularity with devout American viewers. Apprentice angel Monica – who has carried her Irish accent into the afterlife – is given a series of assignments by her black mentor Tess, which continue her own education as well as providing people in need with moral rearmament. Unlike the modest heroes of previous series she is always willing to confess, when the time comes for her to work small miracles for those who have seen the light, that yes, she is an angel, sent by God! A white-clad Angel of Death named Adam, played by Charles Rocket, makes occasional guest appearances.

1996 THE ADVENTURES OF SINBAD

1996–97; series; US (Atlantic); starring Zen Gesner (Sinbad), Jacqueline Collen (Maeve), George Buza, Tim Progosh; cr. Ed Naha; 50-min episodes.

When the race to leap on the *Hercules* bandwagon began, Sinbad must have seemed a natural candidate, all the more especially because Fred Wolf's better-than-average animated series *The Fantastic Voyages of Sinbad* was already running. The importation of a busty Celtic white witch with a pet falcon called Dermott was licensed by the general ambience of free-and-easy wackiness, but did not serve to raise the scripts much above the juvenile level of the animated series. After a hesitant beginning, however, the project gained confidence and energy. A second and final season was commissioned, although Collen was replaced by a more sinister sorceress (played by Mariah Shirley).

EARLY EDITION

1996–2000; series; US (CBS); starring Kyle Chandler (Gary), Fisher Stevens (Chuck), Shanesia Davis (Marissa); 50-min episodes.

Gary Hobson's life is disrupted – and, in effect, taken over – when a mysterious cat begins delivering tomorrow's newspaper every morning. Resolutely resisting the pleas of his best friend Chuck, who wants to make a fortune on the horses, the stock market or the lottery, he allows himself to be guided by the blind and saintly Marissa, who suggests that his is a sacred mission to save people threatened with awful misfortune. Every time he changes the "future" the pages of the newspaper reprint themselves – often complicating the plots by replacing the averted misfortunes with urgently looming catastrophes. The scriptwriters were so conscientious in refusing to face up to the logical problems inherent in the premise that the show never came remotely close to making sense, but the plots did take some interesting sidesteps and the formula was a productive source of melodramatic countdowns; it is not surprising that four seasons were produced before the show was canned.

GULLIVER'S TRAVELS

1996; mini-series; US/UK (KH1/C4); starring Ted Danson, Mary Steenburgen; prod. Duncan Kenworthy for Jim Henson Productions; dir. Charles Sturridge; 2 x 90 min.

A bold attempt to tackle the whole of Swift's satire – including the third and fourth parts, from which previous adaptors had steered clear. The script even tried to take aboard some of the satirical aspects of the original, although the allegories contained in some passages – especially that dealing with the Struldbruggs – were changed so utterly as to work in frank defiance of Swift's intentions. The reformatting of the story as a maliciously prejudiced enquiry into the returned Gulliver's fragile sanity was also un-Swiftian, but it did lend the adaptation an extra – and very effective – melodramatic dimension, and the state-of-the-art visual effects helped make the endeavour something of a *tour de force*. Danson was surprisingly good in the lead.

NEVERWHERE

1996; 6-part serial; UK (BBC2); starring Gary Bakewell, Laura Fraser, Peter Capaldi, Freddie Jones, Hywel Bennett (Croup), Clive Russell (Vandemar); prod. Clive Brill; scr. Neil Gaiman; 30-min episodes.

Neil Gaiman transferred the artistry and melodrama of his exceptionally fine graphic novels into this adaptation of an idea that originated with comedian Lenny Henry (whose Crucial Films produced the series for the BBC). London is credited with an underworld akin to – but far more fantastic than – the one visited upon New York in *Beauty and the Beast*. Its inhabitants are invisible to the people of London Above, who have been desensitized to their existence by their habitual refusal to see homeless beggars and buskers, and access to it is regulated by a series of magical portals. As soon as the hero takes notice of the beleaguered heroine, he is detached from the routines of his own life and plunged into a nightmarish adventure. The serial was a bold and intriguing experiment but, despite persistent rumours and a certain cult status, the much-anticipated big-screen adaptation has not materialised. There have also been whispers of a possible follow-up television serial or a sequel to the novelisation – but these have not yet appeared either.

SMALL TALK: TED DANSON'S GULLIVER LISTENS ATTENTIVELY TO WHAT THE KING OF LILLIPUT HAS TO SAY

POLTERGEIST: THE LEGACY

1996–1999; series; US (Trilogy); starring Derek de Lint (Derek Rayne), Martin Cummins, Robbi Chong, Helen Shaver; cr. Richard Barton Lewis; 50-min episodes.

Derek de Lint plays a brooding modern magus in charge of the San Francisco cell of The Legacy, an ancient and secretive mystical order devoted to guarding the world from evil. He is assisted by his fellow Legacy cell members, who include an all-action former SEAL, a strangely sceptical psychiatrist mom and her fey child, a psychic archaeologist, and an Irish priest with a truly ludicrous accent. The protagonists live in a small castle-like manor on an isolated island in the bay, and come up against a wide selection of demons, malevolent ghosts and evil humans out to wreak havoc, resulting in a range of horrific and fantastical scrapes. The plots all have a strong overtone of biblical mythology. Despite its shortcomings – not the least of which were the accent and hair-style that de Lint had to work with – the show did occasionally manage to be genuinely creepy, and collected a hard-core of dedicated enthusiasts.

THE PRETENDER

1996–2000; series; US; starring Michael Weiss (Jarod), Andrea Parker, Patrick Bauchau; cr. Craig W. Van Sickle & Steven Long Mitchell; 50-min episodes.

The wandering hero of the title is a super-genius with the uncanny power of being able to assume the skills and personality traits of any profession or type of person. Having been kidnapped as a child and held prisoner for thirty years by a mysterious and ruthless organisation known as The Center – and used as some sort of human

The Pretender (Michael T. Weiss).

simulator – he finally escapes for the start of the show. His unsurprising self-imposed quest is to help the needy, find out what really happened to his allegedly dead parents, and remain one step ahead of his former captors, who never quite manage to track him down in time to stop him skipping town. The ambivalence and sexual tension between Jarod and his sexy female former captor helped give things an edge, as did Jarod's moral ambiguities. The series managed four seasons and two telemovies before it finally collapsed under the weight of its own internal mythology.

STRANGE LUCK

1996; series; US (Fox); starring D. B. Sweeney (Chance Harper), Pamela Gidley, Cynthia Martells, Frances Fisher; cr. Karl Schaefer; 50-min episodes.

Chance Harper's intensively-studied coincidence-proneness is supposed to lend plausibility to plots in which the scriptwriters carry intricately interwoven chains of odd events towards near-miraculous resolutions. Although it didn't really succeed on that level – it always looked like cheating – the idiosyncratic direction of approach took some of the saccharine out of the soft-centred "wandering vigilante" formula and Schaefer carried some useful inspiration forward from his work on *Eerie, Indiana*. Its good audience figures might not have been unconnected with the fact that it preceded *The X-Files* in the schedule, but they were not undeserved.

XENAPHILIA

Xena: Warrior Princess is even more subversive than *Hercules*. The involvement of a woman makes the parodic fight scenes even more effective, all the more so when Xena deploys her un-phallic rebounding ring or the carotid-squeezing "pinch" that allows her to refrain from more brutal tortures. The best of her party tricks is the somersault which brings her down astride some luckless male's shoulders, allowing her to render him unconscious by tweaking his head (symbolic, or what?) between her copious thighs. Whatever Hercules may do to spread the good news of Californian humanism he can only operate within a macho tradition perilously close in spirit to that of the myths his writers are plundering. In striking contrast, the achievements of Xena and Gabrielle cannot help but constitute a radical revision of that tradition. When Xena teaches Helen of Troy that the choice is not between Menelaus and Paris but between being a slave to "love" and an independent woman she wipes out the ideological basis of the ancient and enduring myth of romance. When Gabrielle outshines the boys at the Academy of the Performing Bards in the art of story-telling (matching her clips of Xena in action against their clips from *Spartacus* and Steve Reeves movies) she is cutting the heart out of the myth of heroic machismo. When Xena deduces that she, like Hercules, is tainted by divine blood (Ares being her true father) her sense of being a divided self is sharper than his, and the challenge facing her – to maintain the control acquired by her rational, human self over her brutal and divinely-inspired passions – is greater. Hers is the quest that is taking contemporary TV fantasy further and further into unexplored territory.

TARZAN:
THE EPIC ADVENTURES

1996– ; series; US (Keller Siegel); starring Joe Lara; exec. prods. Henry and Paul Siegel; 90-min pilot/50-min. episodes.

Previous TV dramatizations of the Tarzan stories, including one series broadcast in 1966–68 starring Ron Ely and another in 1991–92 starring Wolf Larson – and, for that matter, the 1955–56 comic-book-based ripoff *Sheena, Queen of the Jungle* starring Irish McCalla – steered clear of any fantasy elements beyond the grown-up feral child's rapport with animals, but once the pilot was out of the way the team in charge of this series was anxious to make use of the new special effects techniques. Because it drew more heavily than any of its predecessors on actual Edgar Rice Burroughs texts it was able to use the apparatus of *Tarzan at the Earth's Core* to introduce illusion-casting *mahars*, and the scriptwriters were careful to introduce equally *outré* motifs whenever they could. Unfortunately, the South African locations could not add any authenticity to what was always a wholly imaginary world and the hard-working Lara could not contrive to import any plausibility to his part. Surprisingly, a second series was commissioned, with new cast, but was immediately embroiled in contractual wrangles and never materialised.

XENA:
WARRIOR PRINCESS

1996–2001; series; US (MCA); starring Lucy Lawless, Renee O'Connor; cr. John Schulian and Robert Tapert; exec. prod. Sam Raimi; 50-min episodes.

Just good friends: Gabrielle and Xena

This spinoff from *Hercules: The Legendary Journeys* was reckoned by many to be better than the original. It is, at any rate, a perfect counterpart. The Junoesque New Zealander Lucy Lawless was initially recruited as a bit-part player (both shows use locations in the Auckland Regional Park) but re-cast when her potential was fully appreciated; she was magnificent as the brooding Amazonian warrior trying to make amends for a recklessly murderous past. Renee O'Connor was equally good as Xena's deceptively feminine companion Gabrielle; she provided a better counterweight than any of the sidekicks to whom Hercules had been briefly hitched. Although it could never have come into being without its predecessor, *Xena* pushed back the frontiers of TV fantasy much further, and provided a far more eloquent illustration than *The Adventures of Sinbad* or *Tarzan: the Epic Adventures* of the potential that *Hercules* opened up. Much comment was passed regarding its manifestly lesbian subtext – a gallery to which the show's creators were delighted to play, in an appropriately teasing manner – but that does not detract in any way from its cavalier feminism. The series produced several episodes that rank as classics of TV fantasy; the best of all is one that takes the plot of the movie *Groundhog Day* one step further in terms of plot-complication and moral finesse. The show's increasing popularity and budget carried the series through six seasons, including a number of "feature" episodes and TV movies, before the production team finally decided to call it a day.

1997 THE NEW ADVENTURES OF ROBIN HOOD

1997–1999; series; US (TNT); starring Matthew Poretta/John Bradley (Robin), Anna Galvin/Barbara Griffin (Marion); cr. Tom Kuhn and Fred & Sandra Weintraub; 50-min episodes.

A self-consciously post-Hercules adaptation of the famous British folk hero, the New Adventures of Robin Hood mixed derring-do and a few very un-British accents with a thick helping of overt magic. Although the villainous Sheriff of Nottingham remained the major baddy, evil monsters from all sorts of mythic environments mysteriously abounded, providing the outlaws with some computer-generated challenges. The series was filmed in Lithuania, which added a certain something to the scenery of Sherwood, but the plots tended towards the formulaic, and the effects were generally unconvincing. Lead actor Matthew Poretta parted with the show after the second season, much to the dismay of enthusiasts, and the third season turned out to be the last.

MATTHEW PORETTA PREPARES TO LET RIP WITH SOME UNLIKELY *NEW ADVENTURES OF ROBIN HOOD*.

THE ODYSSEY

1997; TV movie; US; starring Armand Assante (Odysseus), Greta Scacchi (Penelope), Isabella Rossellini, Eric Roberts, Christopher Lee; dir. & scr. Andrei Konchalovsky; 173 min.

A fairly faithful reworking of Homer's epic poem about the great hero Ulysses, who is cursed to wander the seas for ten years on his way home from victory in the Trojan war. While the strangely-renamed "Odysseus" and his crew are busy overcoming a fair sampling of the original's legendary foes – including the witch Circe, the Cyclops, Poseidon and even Hades himself – faithful wife Penelope remains at home. She has her hands full holding on to the faint hope that Odysseus may make it back, and trying to fend off ever-more persistent suitors after the hero's property. The goddess Athene, patron of warriors, does what she can to even the score a little and help the hero get back to Ithaca in time to prevent Penelope marrying the kingdom off to someone else. Despite the changes required to bring the epic down to a manageable size, this was a reasonably good adaptation of the material.

WYRD SISTERS

1997; 6-part animated serial; UK (C4/Cosgrove Hall); voices Christopher Lee (Death), June Whitfield, Jane Horrocks, Eleanor Bron, Graham Crowden; exec. prod. Mark Hall; prod. and dir. Jean Flynn.

An adaptation of the sixth novel in Terry Pratchett's hugely popular Discworld series. Although the makers presumably began with this one because rights to the earlier ones – including *Equal Rites*, in which Granny Weatherwax and her associates had first appeared – were already tied up, it was a happy choice. Much of the humour in this wry recomplication of the plot of *Macbeth* derives from the verbal interplay between the witches, which can be transferred to the screen without overtaxing the animators. Much of the extraordinary richness and complexity of the original is inevitably lost, but what comes through is very amusing. The team followed up with an equally good seven-part version of *Soul Music*, in which the Discworld's own version of rock music (rocks with music in them, naturally) causes some aural distress to the more conservative witches.

1998 BRIMSTONE

1998–1999; series; US (Fox); starring Peter Horton (Ezekiel Stone), John Glover, Albert Hall, Lori Petty; cr. Ethan Reiff; 50-min episodes.

Supernatural drama series in which a dead cop is allowed out of Hell in order to hunt down and despatch 113 escaped evil-doers. If he can get all of them, the Devil promises to let Stone have a second chance at life. Stone was sent to Hell for killing the man who raped his wife, and remains a decent sort of chap despite fifteen years of post-mortal torment. Back on Earth, both Stone and the escaped souls are effectively invulnerable except to each other. The only way to banish the fugitives back to their infernal torment is by destroying their eyes – "the windows of the soul". Given the basic formulaic nature inherent in the set-up – Stone tracks villain, catches up with villain, despatches villain – it was no real surprise that the hero only got a short way through his hit list before the show was cancelled.

IN YOUR EYE! EZEKIEL STONE (PETER HORTON) LOOKING TRIGGER-HAPPY IN *BRIMSTONE*.

CONAN: ADVENTURER

1998; series; US (Threshhold); starring Ralph Moeller (Conan), Danny Woodburn, T.J. Storm, Robert McRay, Ally Dunne; cr. Robert E. Howard; 50-min episodes.

Another poor Hercules imitation. Robert E. Howard's barbarian hero should have been an easy automatic shoe-in for an episodic television series – the original books are already geared that way – but the production team couldn't leave well enough alone. A dazzling

range of politically correct sidekicks were added – a black spirit warrior, a wise dwarf, a staff-spinning mute, a beautiful woman thief, and an axe-wielding Viking. An evil sorcerer served as the over-arching series villain. As if that wasn't all bad enough, the show's producers seemed determined to avoid offending the moral majority, and made the series insipidly non-provocative. Conan was neutered into some sort of kind and gentle giant, and what little violence there was seemed almost entirely bloodless. Poor writing and effects sealed the show's swift doom, much to the relief of Robert E. Howard fans everywhere.

THE CROW: STAIRWAY TO HEAVEN

1998; series; Canada (Alliance); starring Mark Dacascos (Eric Draven), Marc Gomes, Sabine Karsenti, Katie Stuart; cr. Bryce Zabel; 50-min episodes.

ALL DRESSED UP AND NOWHERE TO GO – ERIC DRAVEN (MARK DACASCOS) IN *THE CROW: STAIRWAY TO HEAVEN*.

The Crow was a successful movie about murdered rock musician Eric Draven, who is returned to life a year later to avenge the death of his fiancée, with the assistance of a crow spirit guide. In the film, he kills all the baddies, and gets to fade away into his lover's ethereal arms. This tight closure ensured that any sequel or TV series spin-off was going to run into trouble right from the start, but the original's popularity made sure that someone would try. The series was contrived and under-resourced, and fans of the film greatly resented the way in which the hero's earlier efforts were dismissed in order to excuse his continuing adventures. The programme was not recommissioned.

MERLIN

1998; TV movie; US/UK; starring Sam Neill (Merlin), Helena Bonham Carter (Morgan le Fay), Miranda Richardson (Queen Mab), Rutger Hauer, James Earl Jones; dir. Steve Barron; scr. Edward Khmara, David Stevens; 182 min.

A stylish look at Merlin's role within the Matter of Britain. The first half of the film focuses on the wizard's early life, going into a lot of inventive detail about his childhood with the witch Nimue and his subsequent training in the faerie realm of Queen Mab, and his subsequent adventures. The second half then introduces the expected Arthurian cast, although things do not remain entirely true to the legendary cycle. Overall, the whole atmosphere is surreal and dreamy, with impressive visual impact, suitably etheric music, and a range of reasonably effective special effects. The film gets a bit camp in places, but overall it is an interesting and well-produced take on Merlin's life.

YOUNG HERCULES

1998; series; USA (Fox); starring Ryan Gosling (Hercules), Dean O'Gorman (Iolaus), Chris Conrad, Kevin Smith; cr. Robert G. Tapert; 23-min episodes.

A number of flashback episodes during regular episodes of *Hercules: The Legendary Journeys* established Ian Bohen as a popular teenage version of the hero, and a related TV movie also titled *Young Hercules* further cemented him in the role. When the time came for this spin-off series, however, the lead role ended up with the rather long-faced Ryan Gosling, which aggravated swathes of the potential fan-base. O'Gorman had done well as Bohen's sidekick, but Gosling's presence seemed to bring out a more loutish side to young Iolaus' character, and the resulting series had very little of the charm of the original. The effects and choreography were at least as good as the parent series, but they weren't enough to save the show, and even 23 minutes became something of a chore. The series only lasted a single season.

1999 ALICE IN WONDERLAND

1998; TV movie; US/UK; starring Tina Majorino (Alice), Robbie Coltrane, Whoopi Goldberg, Christopher Lloyd, Peter Ustinov; dir. Nick Willing; scr. Peter Barnes; 129 min.

Another production from the people behind *Merlin* and *The Odyssey*, *Alice in Wonderland* is a combination of both "Alice in Wonderland" and "Through The Looking-Glass". Although the production had an excellent cast and looked suitably spectacular, it was criticised for its handling of Lewis Carroll's material. In particular, purists objected to the way that scenes from both books were interwoven to make a single narrative based around helping Alice to get over stage fright. With that said, however, most of the memorable scenes from the books were recreated sympathetically, and the production was a reasonable introduction to Carroll's works.

BEASTMASTER

1999–; series; Canada/Australia (Coote/Hayes); starring Daniel Goddard (Dar), Jackson Raine, Monika Schnarre, Steven Grives, Grahame Bond; cr. Steve Feke; 50-min episodes.

The movie *Beastmaster* was released in 1982, and starred Marc Singer as a brooding exiled prince with the magic power to talk to animals. The film was never a huge success, and a number of increasingly dreadful sequels did little to help, so it was something of a surprise when the licence was picked up as the basis for Yet Another Bad Attempt at *Hercules*. Seemingly determined to alienate the fans of the original movies, the show's producers threw out almost all of the back-story of the film series, keeping only the hero's name and his special power. The acting was understated at best, and inconsistencies within the setting further served to weaken the show. However, skimpy costumes and a certain amount of bravery on the part of the show's writers helped to lift it above certain of its competitors, and gave it sufficient strength to survive at least three seasons.

PURGATORY

1999; TV movie; US; starring Brad Rowe ("Sonny" Dillard), Sam Shepard (Wild Bill Hickock), Eric Roberts (Blackjack Britton), Donnie Wahlberg (Billy The Kid); dir. Uli Edel; scr. Gordon Dawson; 94 min.

Trying to escape pursuers after a botched bank robbery in the wild west, Eric Roberts leads his gang of psychotic desperadoes through a dust storm and into the mysterious town of Haven. The new arrivals are made welcome, and given free board and lodging, but cautioned not to swear. While the rest of the band push the locals around, the youngest member of the team is a decent enough human to get to know the residents, and discovers that they are all famous dead outlaws, taking a last shot at redemption... The rather obvious plot twist has been done far more effectively many times over the years, from films like the superlative *Jacob's Ladder* all the way down to individual episodes of the *Twilight Zone*. The cast give it their best shot, but the film drags along formulaically to its predictable conclusion.

RELIC HUNTER

1999–; series; Canada/France/Germany/USA (Fireworks); starring Tia Carrere (Sydney Fox), Christien Anholt (Nigel Bailey), Lindy Booth (Claudia, 1999–2001), Tanja Reichert (Karen, 2001–); cr. Bill Taub; 50-min episodes.

Tia Carrere brings a certain touch of style to the role of Sydney Fox, a professor and adventuring archaeologist. Despite the obvious comparisons to the *Tomb Raider* character Lara Croft that the show is aiming for, Sydney Fox is really the direct descendent of Indiana Jones – she travels all over the globe recovering ancient and mysterious artefacts from under the noses of her villainous opponents, and returning them to their rightful owners. Fantasy elements are understated, mostly staying implicit in the artefacts, traps and trials that the cast find themselves up again. The locations are impressive, and although the writing is fairly lazy, the series doesn't take itself too seriously, and mixes a fair amount of good-natured humour and charm in with the action. Both plot and execution owe a fair amount to the 30s serials, but it's all done engagingly. It may not be mentally challenging, but it's good, solid entertainment that has lasted three series to date.

"IS IT HOT UP HERE, OR IS IT ME?" RELIC HUNTER SYDNEY FOX (TIA CARRERE) LEADS NIGEL BAILEY (CHRISTIEN ANHOLT) INTO ANOTHER STICKY SITUATION.

THE TRIBE

1999–; series; New Zealand (Cloud 9); starring Beth Allen, Meryl Cassie, Caleb Ross, Victoria Spence, Antonia Prebble, Michael Wesley-Smith; cr. Raymond Thompson; 50-min episodes.

A teen soap-opera set in a fantastic future in which all the adults have been wiped out by a mysterious virus, and the children are left to fend for themselves. They quickly organise into gangs – the Tribe of the title live in an abandoned shopping mall – and switch to bizarre hair styles and make-up reminiscent of war-paint. Despite its obvious superficial silliness and simplicity, and a tendency to trite melodrama, the show deals effectively and sympathetically with the usual spectrum of teen soap opera concerns, such as sex, religion, the future, relationships and more sex.

2000 ARABIAN NIGHTS

2000; TV movie; USA (Hallmark); starring Mili Avital (Scheherezade), Alan Bates, James Frain, Jason Scott Lee, John Leguizamo, Vanessa Mae; dir. Steve Barron; scr. Peter Barnes; 180 min.

An effective and entertaining reworking of some of the most famous stories from the Arabian Nights. The Sultan has gone mad from grief and trauma following an attempted assassination. During the attack, he kills his wife, who is one of the conspirators in the murder attempt. The Sultan then develops a paranoid suspicion of women, and decides to indulge himself by marrying one of his harem and then having her executed the following morning. In order to prevent this dreadful injustice, Scheherezade – here the Grand Vizier's daughter and a childhood friend of the deranged Sultan – decides to spare the women of the harem by offering herself up, gambling that her stories and long friendship can bring the Sultan back to his senses in time to defeat his villainous brother's plots. All the usual suspects from the Thousand and One Nights are featured, including Aladdin and Ali Baba and the Forty Thieves. The production is attractively filmed and the cast go about their business with enthusiasm.

THE MAGICIANS

2000; TV movie; US; starring Charlie O'Connell (Michael DeVane), Peter Firth (Simon Magus), Kimberly Davies, Sam Healey, Gabrielle Fitzpatrick; dir. Lorraine Senna Ferrara; wr. Kim LeMasters, Bennett Cohen; 97 min.

A cynical young street illusionist is astonished to discover that magic is real when a thousand-year-old wizard attempts to recruit him as new head champion of the forces of good. The evil side also wants to engage his services. Can he make the right choice, and master his powers in time to save the world from a thousand years of hell? Well, yes. The basic premise – of cabals of good and evil mages struggling secretly down through the ages – is workable if uninspired. The actors make a spirited go of it too; Firth is excellent as the wry wizard who knows his time is up. However, the writing lets the film down. The bad guys are bad just because, and no sense of menace ever develops. The end of the film makes it perfectly clear that this is a pilot test for a wandering hero series, leaving the new magician with no less than three different missions to drive him from town to town. The film was strangely retitled "Death By Magic" for some territories.

THE LOST EMPIRE

2001; TV movie; USA/Germany (NBC); starring Thomas Gibson (Nick Orton), Ling Bai (Kwan Ying), Russell Wong (Monkey), Ric Young (Confucius); dir. Peter MacDonald; prod. Robert Halmi; 180 min.

The classic story "Journey to the West" is one of the strongest, best-loved pieces of Chinoiserie to make it into western culture. Given the fondness with which the eccentric seventies Japanese series "Monkey" is still remembered, it should be a natural subject for effective conversion to a TV movie. Sadly, this particular reworking manages to be both confused and tedious. Rather than sticking to the original plot, *The Lost Empire* decided to pander to network executives by bringing the story to modern times, featuring an all-American guy as the hero, and a goddess as his implausible love interest. The original heroes of the story are relegated to sidekicks. Even so, the project might have been salvageable, but the writers combined ineptitude with a total disregard for any sort of research. All sorts of basic tenets of Chinese culture, history, spirituality and mythology are thrown out of the window, their elegance replaced with American pap. Poor Confucius, a famously materialist philosopher, gets a particularly bizarre treatment – the equivalent of portraying Ghandi as Rambo's sidekick. The action sequences are badly filmed, and the special effects unimpressive. With poor dialogue, ludicrous plot sequences and disappointing acting thrown into the mix, the only surprise is that this travesty wasn't spiked before release. As it was, it managed to attract some of NBC's worst-ever ratings, and even surpassed Halmi's previous disaster, *The Tenth Kingdom*.

2001 THE LOST WORLD

2001; TV movie; UK (New Line); starring Bob Hoskins (Professor George Challenger), James Fox, Tom Ward, Matthew Rhys, Elaine Cassidy, Peter Falk; dir. Stuart Orme; wr. Sir Arthur Conan Doyle; 150 min.

Bob Hoskins was an inspired choice to play the determined professor who discovers a long-hidden Amazonian plateau that still contains living dinosaurs. He returns to the area with a team of fellow scientists, researchers and sundry other adventurers. The dinosaurs are discovered, along with a race of highly-evolved ape men, and a tribe of native humans who assume Challenger is a god. Despite its relatively low budget, this is a sympathetic reworking of the original classic, and good performances by the cast help to add real drama to the production. The script isn't shy of addressing the moral issues of scientific investigation either – the characters have a profound impact on the world, with chequered consequences.

WITCHBLADE

2001–; series; USA (Warner Brothers); starring Yancy Butler (Sara Pezzini), David Chokachi, Anthony Cistaro, Eric Etebari, Laila Robins, Kim De Lury; cr. David Wohl; 50-min episodes.

An adaptation of the comic book of the same name, about a tough-but-sexy New York cop who accidentally acquires a magical artefact. The Witchblade is a glove that enhances strength, agility and toughness, and can deflect bullets. It can also turn into other items – such as a full suit of armour, and a large sword – when the plot requires. Life duly gets complicated for Sara; an evil syndicate wants to try to manipulate her into using the Witchblade's power on their behalf, and on top of that the artefact itself has something of a mind of its own. The show made heavy use of the *Matrix*-style "bullet time" special effect, which pleased some and irritated others, but the first series of 11 episodes went down well enough for a second season to be commissioned.

JANE YOLEN
HERE THERE BE
UNICORNS
ILLUSTRATED BY DAVID WILGUS

Who's Who of Fantasy

This chapter consists of short entries, alphabetically arranged, on the creators of fantasy fiction. A few important editors and critics have been given entries, but the overwhelming majority of the people listed here are the creative writers – of fantasy short stories, novellas and novels

The creators of fantasy are as various as it is possible for any group of people to be. They come from all branches of writing, ranging from Oxford academics like C. S. Lewis to market-place "pulpsters" like Edgar Rice Burroughs (two men whose intellectual ambitions and circumstances in life may have been very different but whose works of fiction, at the end of the day, seem not so very far apart in quality). Some of them are literary novelists who would not have acknowledged the label "fantasy writer" even if they had been aware of it, while others – particularly among the more recent writers – are full-time fantasy professionals, and proud of the fact.

There is insufficient space here to give details of everybody who might merit inclusion. In particular, the older, classic writers of world literature are omitted – Aesop, Apuleius, Ariosto, Aristophanes, Basile, Beckford, Chaucer, Chretien de Troyes, Coleridge, Collodi, Dante, de la Motte Fouque, Dickens, Fielding, Joel Chandler Harris, Galland, Geoffrey of Monmouth, Homer, Washington Irving, Dr Johnson, Kafka, Lucian of Samosata, Malory, Meredith, Montalvo, Ovid, Rabelais, Raspe, Shakespeare, Spenser, Straparola, Swift, Mark Twain, Virgil, Voltaire and Wu Ch'eng-en are among those who are mentioned in this book – but their biographical and bibliographical details can be found in most standard encyclopedias.

Among the more recent "creators" others who are missing from this section but who have passing mentions elsewhere in this book are a large body of children's writers – among them Elisabeth Beresford, W. J. Corbett, Tove Jansson, Astrid Lindgren, John Masefield, A. A. Milne, Anna Sewell, Dodie Smith, Edward L. Stratemeyer, Barbara Euphan Todd and P. L. Travers – and a similar body of cartoonists, illustrators and comic-strip writers – Charles Addams, Alfred Bestall, Raymond Briggs, Steve Ditko, Will Eisner, Lee Falk, Hal Foster, Herge, Winsor McCay, Peyo and Elzie Crisler Segar among them. Also passed over here are some of the better-known pulp-magazine writers of the first half of the century, whose works are largely out of print nowadays but who nevertheless are important to the history of the genre – Frank Aubrey, H. Bedford-Jones, Guy Boothby, William L. Chester, James Francis Dwyer, Walter B. Gibson, Talbot Mundy, Norvell W. Page, Sax Rohmer, Charles B. Stilson, E. Charles Vivian and so many others.

EDGAR RICE BURROUGHS WORE A SUIT, BUT CREATED ONE OF THE KEY FIGURES OF UNBUTTONED FANTASY

Many of the above, along with other significant creators of fantasy, are mentioned in our sections on Types of Fantasy, Fantasy Films, Fantasy Television and in the A–Z of Fantastic Characters and Entities. Even Gilbert & Sullivan and P. G. Wodehouse merit brief mentions elsewhere in the text of this book, but not here.

Finally, my apologies to any reader whose favourite happens to be missing – and also to those living writers who have been passed over for lack of space. An attempt has been made to include a number of very new people, whose first books have appeared just in the last two or three years, and as a result some of the "less new" authors of the past two or three decades are omitted.

Richard Adams

British novelist
BORN: 1920

Adams was a civil servant in the Department of the Environment when he published *Watership Down* (1972), a heartfelt ecological morality play which tells of the migration forced upon heroic rabbits by encroaching urban development; because the sub-genre of animal fantasy had long fallen into disuse it was initially rejected by commercial publishers, but it became a spectacular bestseller, winning a Carnegie Medal and the *Guardian* children's fiction prize. Its success precipitated a spectacular revival in animal fantasy. Adams was ambitious to diversify into other fields but *Shardik* (1974), a dark moral tale about the political manipulation of the symbolic figure of a giant bear, the sentimental ghost story *The Girl in a Swing* (1980) and the uneasily fantasized bodice-ripper *Maia* (1984) did not please fans of *Watership Down*. The animal fantasies *The Plague Dogs* (1977), about two escapees from a cruel programme of scientific experiments, and *Traveler* (1988), a dour historical satire whose eponymous Candide-substitute is Robert E. Lee's horse, were also a far cry from their predecessor, but the folk tales reformulated in *The Iron Wolf and Other Stories* (1980) and the children's poems *The Tiger Voyage* (1976) and *The Ship's Cat* (1977) retain something of its innocence, and *Tales from Watership Down* (1996) marked Adams's final capitulation to popular demand.

Joan Aiken

British novelist
BORN: 1924

Aiken has written fiction of many kinds, but is most celebrated in the fantasy field for her long series of marvellously inventive children's novels set in a 19th-century alternate history where King James III rules, a series which began with *The Wolves of Willoughby Chase* (1962), *Black Hearts in Battersea* (1964) and *Nightbirds on Nantucket* (1966). A recent fantasy quite outside that series, and one which has been marketed to adult readers in America, is *The Cockatrice Boys* (1996).

Lloyd Alexander

American novelist
BORN: 1924

Highly regarded in children's fantasy for his "Chronicles of Prydain" sequence, whose first two books were the basis of Disney's animated movie *The Black Cauldron* (1985). The novels, whose Land of Prydain draws on the old Welsh myths collected as *The Mabinogion*, are: *The Book of Three* (1964), *The Black Cauldron* (1965), *The Castle of Llyr* (1966), *Taran Wanderer* (1967) and *The High King* (1968). Related story collections include *Coll and His White Pig* (1965).

Young hero Taran is a pig-keeper of unknown parentage; but his pig Hen Wen has oracular powers and his protector Dallben is a Merlin-like wizard. They and others – notably savage-tongued Princess Eilonwy – become involved in struggles to save Prydain from the menacing Horned King, hordes of undead warriors given unnatural life by the cursed Black Cauldron and eventually Arawn himself, King of the Underworld.

Alexander presents vivid characters, both good and evil, and often defies young-fantasy expectations ... by having the "wrong" people die or shockingly turn traitor, by subjecting would-be warrior Taran to humiliating apprenticeships in small crafts, and by refusing to reveal him as being nobly born after all. Happy endings are approached by harrowing paths and come at high cost.

The slightly odd-looking Hans Christian Andersen, one of the world's finest writers of short fantasy tales

Hans Christian Andersen

Danish short-story writer
BORN: 1805 DIED: 1875

Hans Christian Andersen's six novels and several volumes of autobiography are now forgotten, although they helped secure the international reputation which gave him the means to travel widely throughout Europe. His enduring fame was based on the fairy tales which he began to write in 1829 and to publish in 1835. Almost all of them were original, although they captured the spirit of authentic folklore so well that the brothers Grimm reproduced one which had been told to them as a "traditional German tale". The most famous include the scathingly satirical "The Emperor's New Clothes" (1837), the sentimental allegory of self-sacrifice "The Little Mermaid" (1837) and the beautiful parable "The Nightingale" (1845). "The Ugly Duckling" (1845) is one of several which allegorize Andersen's perception of his own life. "The Snow Queen" (1846) is an extravagant *tour de force* and "The Little Match Girl" (1848) is a heart-rending celebration of the power of the imagination. His more solemn philosophical allegories are often omitted from child-orientated collections, but a 20-volume Hans Andersen Library issued in the UK between 1869 and 1887 is nearly complete. Andersen's tales had an enormous influence on modern writers of sophisticated fairy tales; Oscar Wilde's finest efforts in that vein are obvious extrapolations of Andersen originals.

Poul Anderson

American novelist
BORN: 1926 DIED: 2001

This author's Scandinavian descent shows in such bleak fantasies, steeped in Nordic fatalism, as *The Broken Sword* (1954) – whose hero wields a cursed sword in a Dark Ages England racked by elf/troll wars, and dies a grim death. Even more purely Nordic is *Hrolf Kraki's Saga* (1973), reworking actual Icelandic saga material.

But Anderson, a versatile writer, also produced popular fantasies in sunnier vein. *Three Hearts and Three Lions* (1961) transports its Danish hero to a medieval fantasyland where modern knowledge helps interpret magical effects. When a giant turns to stone at dawn, our man realizes the traditional curse on giant's gold is real: changing carbon to silicon (stone) means a nuclear transformation and consequent radiation hazard…

Operation Chaos (1971), a classic of its kind, shows an alternate Earth where magic and science coexist and World War Two is fought with unicorn cavalry, helms of invisibility, shape-shifting commandos, etc. The werewolf hero and his beloved witch must eventually raid Hell itself, precariously armed with both magic and mathematics.

Also of note are the delightfully Shakespearean *A Midsummer Tempest* (1974) with its blank verse dialogue and the Celtic-fantasy "King of Ys" sequence (1986–88), written with his wife Karen Anderson.

F. Anstey

British novelist
BORN: 1856 DIED: 1934

A stalwart of *Punch* magazine, Anstey wrote comic fantasies in which conventional Victorian lives are turned topsy-turvy by magic. Most famously, the twice-filmed *Vice Versa, or A Lesson to Fathers* (1882) introduces a charmed stone which grants a father's hypocritical wish to be young again, and his son's wish to be grown-up. So they swap places. The boy-bodied father is soon reminded forcibly of the hellishness of boarding-school life, and treats his son more sympathetically when both eventually return to normal.

Anstey kept trying vainly to recapture this first success. *A Tinted Venus* (1885) afflicts a young man with unwelcome attentions from a statue of Aphrodite which he's accidentally "married"; *A Fallen Idol* (1886) sees an artist bedevilled by a malevolent Indian idol with magical powers.

Tourmalin's Time Cheques (1885) uses a clever idea – a Time Bank where unwanted hours are deposited and later reclaimed, but in inconveniently random order: Anstey couldn't handle the ensuing complexities and resorted to making it all a dream. His best later novel, *The Brass Bottle* (1900) showers its hero with comically embarrassing gifts from a too-grateful released genie. Prospective in-laws are unimpressed by the belly-dancer…

Piers Anthony

American novelist
BORN: 1934

Piers Anthony Dillingham Jacob (British-born) writes under this short form of his name. Initially noted for sf, he is now identified with fantasy series of which the most famous is "Xanth".

Xanth is a magic-rich fantasyland that borrows its shape from Anthony's home state of Florida, and contains virtually every imaginable fantastic creature, spell and cliché. Freshness of approach and thoughtful consideration of logical, technical and environmental consequences of magic gained the initial books considerable adult popularity despite occasional twee moments: *A Spell for Chameleon* (1977), *The Source of Magic* (1979) and *Castle Roogna* (1979).

As Xanth continued, feedback from teenage fans apparently persuaded Anthony to aim towards a younger audience and increase the quota of whimsy and puns (including puns submitted by

ANTHONY'S "XANTH" NOVELS ARE SILLY BUT SEDUCTIVE – ESPECIALLY TO YOUNGER READERS

readers), to the detriment of narrative thrust. Many further novels have followed, roughly annually. The pun obsession is evident in titles like *Crewel Lye: A Caustic Yarn* (1984) and, 21st in the series, *Faun and Games* (1997); touches of sniggering adolescent titillation are epitomized by *The Color of Her Panties* (1992).

The "Apprentice Adept" series also started interestingly with *Split Infinity* (1980) and *Blue Adept* (1981) as hero Stile – a serf from a science-fictional planet of elaborately formalized competitive games – discovers he is also a potent magical adept in a linked fantasy world. *Juxtaposition* (1982) concludes the trilogy with a somewhat silly and over-whimsical struggle of magic; a second, weaker trilogy followed.

Anthony's best individual fantasy may be *On a Pale Horse* (1983), where a man in a technomagical future has to take on the soul-ushering duties of Death, and grows to be worthy of this role. The devices and mechanisms whereby Death handles his impossible schedule are lovingly worked out, as is the vast civil-service operation of Purgatory. This opens the "Incarnations of Immortality" series, in which all the Incarnations who run the mechanisms of life and afterlife are mortal recruits: Death, Time, Fate, War, Nature and – as it turns out – also Evil (Satan) and Good (God).

Further Incarnation books are *Bearing an Hourglass* (1984), *With a Tangled Skein* (1985), *Wielding a Red Sword* (1986), *Being a Green Mother* (1987), *For Love of Evil* (1988) and *And Eternity* (1990). The relish with which Anthony tackles Satan's sympathetic viewpoint in the sixth book, and picks the least likely candidate for the needed replacement God in the last, does not quite make up for earlier longueurs and repetitions. The Time novel, for example, is burdened with long passages of space-operatic psychodrama in the joky, kidding vein of later Xanth. Nevertheless this is Anthony's best-sustained fantasy series.

Repeatedly, Anthony shows impressive and even charming inventiveness, only to milk his initial notion dry through too many sequels.

Tom Arden

British novelist

BORN: 1966

One of the newest, youngest and perhaps brightest entrants into heroic fantasy, this Australian-born writer made his debut with *The Harlequin's Dance: Book One of The Orokon* (1997), the first of a five-volume set that its publishers hoped would enjoy a David Eddings-like success. The series continued with *The King and Queen of Swords* (1998), *The Sultan of the Moon and Stars* (1999), *The Sisterhood of the Blue Stone* (2000), and *The Empress of the Endless Dream* (2001).

Sarah Ash

British novelist

BORN: 1950

A music-teacher by profession, Ash is also a prose stylist who first made her mark with several dreamy short stories in *Interzone* magazine. With the novels *Moths to a Flame* (1995), *Songspinners* (1996) and *The Lost Child* (1998) she has been building a solid reputation.

Mike Ashley

British bibliographer and editor

BORN: 1948

Ashley is a national treasure, his many fantasy anthologies the fruits of real research and enthusiasm. Among the more notable are *The Pendragon Chronicles* (1990), *The Camelot Chronicles* (1992), *The Merlin Chronicles* (1995), *The Chronicles of the Holy Grail* (1996), *The Chronicles of the Round Table* (1997) and *The Mammoth Book of Fairy Tales* (1997), *The Mammoth Book of Comic Fantasy* (1998), *The Mammoth Book of Seriously Comic Fantasy* (1999) and *The Mammoth Book of Awesome Comic Fantasy* (2001).

Robert L. Asprin

American novelist
BORN: 1946

Inspired, he has said, by the "Road" films of Bob Hope and Bing Crosby, Asprin wrote one of the first best-selling humorous fantasy series in the USA: *Another Fine Myth* (1978), *Myth Conceptions* (1980), *Myth Directions* (1982), *Hit or Myth* (1983), *Myth-ing Persons* (1984), *Little Myth Marker* (1985), *M.Y.T.H. Inc. Link* (1986), *Myth-Nomers and Imp-ervections* (1987), *M.Y.T.H. Inc. in Action* (1990) and *Sweet Myth-tery of Life* (1994), M.Y.T.H.ion Improbable (2001) and Something M.Y.T.H. Inc., due in 2003. As the titles indicate, the humour is very dependent on puns. Asprin is also of importance to fantasy as creator and editor (latterly with his wife, Lynn Abbey) of one of the longest-lived shared-world anthology series, the "Thieves' World" sequence.

A.A. Attanasio

American novelist
BORN: 1951

Alfred Attanasio is a Hawaii-resident science-fiction writer whose work has always tended to be wildly imaginative, if a bit messy in the execution. He has turned to fantasy in a big way in recent years, with novels like Kingdom of the Grail (1992), The Moon's Wife (1993), The Dragon and the Unicorn (1994), Arthor (1995) and the "Dominions of Irth" *Dark Shore* (1996), *The Shadow Eater* (1998) and *Octoberland* (1999). The last three were published in the USA under the pseudonym "Adam Lee" – which suggests that the author is trying to relaunch a flagging career in the American marketplace.

James Barclay

British novelist
Born: 1965

A long-term fantasy gamer and London-based investment bank executive, Barclay launched his career with a gritty trilogy, "The Chronicles of the Raven" – *Dawnthief* (1999), *Noonshade* (2000) and *Nightchild* (2001) – about a small team of expert mercenaries. Barclay's facility with character interaction makes for entertaining reading, and the plot romps along. His particular version of magic – which feels a bit like programming reality – is interesting too, although it is somewhat reminiscent of the fantasy card game *Magic: The Gathering*. A new trilogy, starting where the last left off – "The Legends of the Raven" – began with *Elfsorrow* (2002).

J.M. Barrie

British playwright and novelist
BORN: 1860 DIED: 1937

James Barrie was a successful writer of Scottish "kailyard" sentimental fiction in the late 19th century, but he joined the immortals of fantasy when he created the unforgettable lead character of his play *Peter Pan; or, The Boy Who Would Not Grow Up* (1904). The ever-youthful Peter and the children who escape with him to the Neverland also feature in the associated novelization, *Peter and Wendy* (1911). Among Barrie's many other plays are several highly emotive fantasies, notably *Dear Brutus* (1917) and *Mary Rose* (1920).

Gael Baudino

American novelist
BORN: 1955

Baudino has written the feminist "Dragonsword" trilogy – *Dragonsword* (1988), *Duel of Dragons* (1991) and *Dragon Death* (1992) – as well as the more interesting "Strands of Starlight" sequence – *Strands of Starlight* (1989), *Maze of Moonlight* (1993), *Shroud of Shadow* (1993) and *Strands of Sunlight* (1994) – plus a few singletons, all of them marked by her concern for gender issues.

L. Frank Baum

American novelist
BORN: 1856 DIED: 1919

Frank Baum published novels for adults and non-fiction but his fame rests exclusively on his fantasies for children, particularly the long series begun with *The Wonderful Wizard of Oz* (1900), which achieved a further dimension of fame by virtue of the 1939 movie. Dorothy, having first been transplanted into Oz by a freak whirlwind, eventually took her family to live there permanently (flatly contradicting the film's dour message that "There's No Place Like Home").

The other books were *The Marvelous Land of Oz* (1904), *Ozma of Oz* (1904), *Dorothy and the Wizard of Oz* (1908), *The Road to Oz* (1909), *The Emerald City of Oz* (1910), *The Patchwork Girl of Oz* (1913), *Tik-Tok of Oz* (1914), *The Scarecrow of Oz* (1915), *Rinkitink in Oz* (1916), *The Lost Princess of Oz* (1917), *The Tin Woodman of Oz* (1918), *The Magic of Oz* (1919) and *Glinda of Oz* (1920). Baum also produced six volumes of short stories aimed at younger readers, whose contents were combined in the omnibus *Little Wizard Stories of Oz* (1939).

After his death other writers were assigned to continue the series, but the first six books had set a standard which even Baum

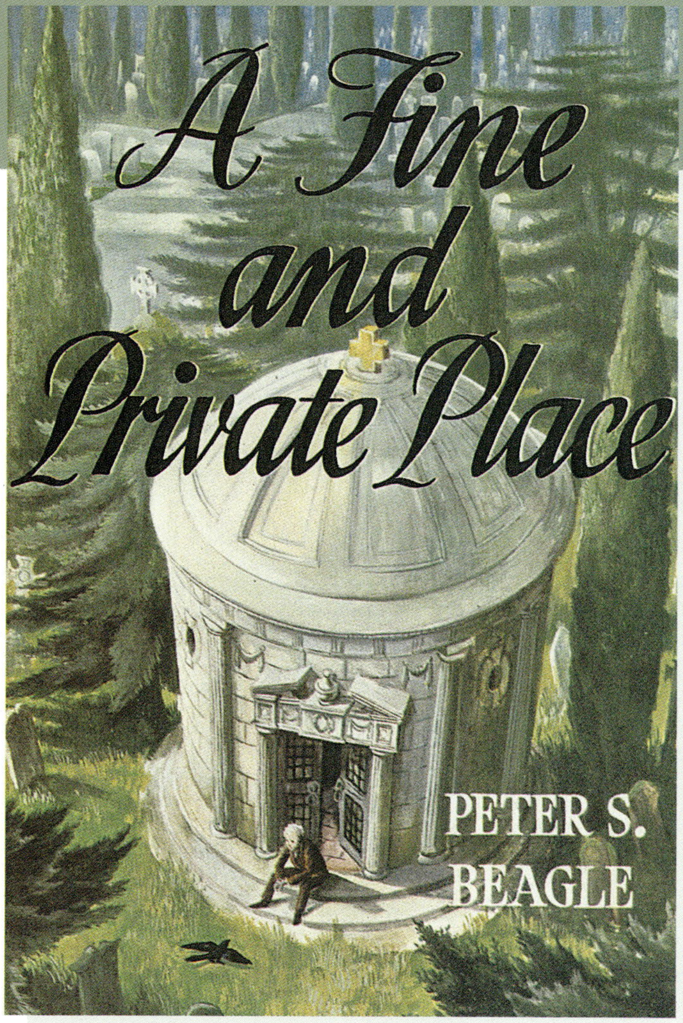

BEAGLE'S FIRST BOOK, WRITTEN WHEN HE WAS BARELY OUT OF HIS TEENS, WAS A HUMOROUS – AND TOUCHING – GHOST NOVEL

could not maintain, to which no one else even came close. They constitute a magnificently energetic consolatory fantasy which is unrepentantly escapist in the best sense of the word. The books with which Baum tried to broaden his range never found another trick to match it; the more interesting include *The Master Key* (1901), *The Life and Adventures of Santa Claus* (1902), *Queen Zixi of Ix* (1905) and *The Sea Fairies* (1911).

PETER S. BEAGLE

American novelist
BORN: 1939

Peter Beagle's precocious first novel was the elegiac *A Fine and Private Place* (1960), in which a young man who lives in a graveyard befriends the ghosts of the inhabitants and a smart talking raven. Its careful sentimentality echoes the work of Robert Nathan, although the short story "Come Lady Death" (1963) is a more obvious homage. *The Last Unicorn* (1968) is a delicate quest-fantasy which splices medieval allegory into a humorously edged adventure story more deftly than any other modern text. A long interval separated the novelette *Lila the Werewolf* (1969; book 1974) from *The Folk of the Air* (1986), in which the lifestyle fantasists of the League for Archaic Pleasures unwittingly conjure ancient beings into their midst.

Since then the flow of Beagle's works has increased considerably, with no loss of quality. *The Innkeeper's Song* (1993) is a quest fantasy with echoes of *The Last Unicorn; Giant Bones* (1997) collects six stories set in the same milieu. In *The Unicorn Sonata* (1996), a further branch nourished by the same root, a teenage girl follows music to the magical realm of Shei'rah, where unicorns are afflicted with a strange malaise. Beagle's latest work returns to ghostly themes – *Tamsin* (1999) is the story of a girl who meets a British ghost, and *A Dance For Emilia* (2000) is about a ghost who possesses a cat. *Peter S. Beagle's Immortal Unicorn* (1995), edited by Beagle, Janet Berliner & Martin H. Greenberg, is an anthology of stories on related themes. *The Rhinoceros who Quoted Nietzsche and Other Odd Acquaintances* (1997) collects seven miscellaneous stories and three essays, further confirming Beagle's status as one of the finest fantasists of his era.

JAMES BIBBY

British novelist
BORN: ?

A former TV comedy writer who hails from Merseyside, Bibby is one of the post-Terry Pratchett school of fantasy humorists. His debut, *Ronan the Barbarian: Translated from the Original Gibberish* (1995), was followed by the very similar (and very silly) sequels *Ronan's Rescue* (1996) and *Ronan's Revenge* (1998).

JAMES P. BLAYLOCK

American novelist
BORN: 1950

James Blaylock's first novels, *The Elfin Ship* (1982) and *The Disappearing Dwarf* (1983), employ a Tolkienesque setting but develop a distinctively light-hearted tone and manner; *The Stone Giant* (1989) belatedly completed the trilogy. *The Digging*

THE COIN OF BLAYLOCK'S TITLE WAS ONE OF JUDAS ISCARIOT'S PIECES OF SILVER

Leviathan (1984), a nostalgic mock-pulp romance, was followed by the masterful "steampunk" fantasy *Homunculus*, in which a band of Victorian heroes led by Langdon St Ives spoil the nefarious schemes of the evil magician Ignacio Narbondo; the conflict was renewed in the episodic *Lord Kelvin's Machine* (1992). Suburban Californian settings reflective of Blaylock's own neighbourhood predominate in a fine series of novels in which deceptively ordinary folk become involved in intricate supernatural mysteries: *Land of Dreams* (1987), involving a sinister carnival and trips through time which cause distortions of scale; *The Last Coin* (1988), describing a phase in the eternal search for the bounty paid to Judas; *The Paper Grail*, which draws on the same complex mythical wellsprings that inspire the work of Blaylock's close friend Tim Powers; and *All the Bells on Earth* (1995), which features an unusual diabolical pact. *Night Relics* (1994) and *Winter Tides* (1997) are more orthodox in their use of conventional hauntings. *The Magic Spectacles* (1991) was intended to be a children's novel, although it was not published as such.

Blaylock has also published a number of short stories in booklet form, including the World Fantasy Award-winning *Paper Dragons* (1985; book 1992) and *Doughnuts* (1997). "Thirteen Phantasms" (1996) also won a World Fantasy Award.

Elizabeth H. Boyer

American novelist
BORN: ?

Boyer has written a lengthy and fairly routine otherworldly fantasy series featuring the beings known as "The Alfar" (i.e. elves): *The Sword and the Satchel* (1980), *The Elves and the Otterskin* (1981), *The Thrall and the Dragon's Heart* (1982), *The Wizard and the Warlord* (1983), *The Troll's Grindstone* (1986), *The Curse of Slagfid* (1989), *The Dragon's Carbuncle* (1990), *The Lord of Chaos* (1991), *The Clan of the Warlord* (1992), *The Black Lynx* (1993) and *Keeper of Cats* (1995).

Ray Bradbury

American novelist
BORN: 1920

Bradbury is celebrated for his science fiction and his *Weird Tales*-type horror stories, but he has also written some notable short fantasies. A number of his fantastical stories were assembled in *Dandelion Wine* (1957), which remains one of his most satisfying books. Here "Green Town", Illinois, during the long hot summer of 1928, is made over in the feverish imagination of the 12-year-old hero so that it seems to become a realm of time-travellers and witches and magic, of enchanted tennis shoes and Rube Goldberg happiness machines. This is not a fantasy of the supernatural in any conventional sense, but it is a highly imaginative work which mines a deep vein of modern American folk-fantasy. There is much seductive whimsy here, combined with an obvious yearning for a simpler, old-fashioned way of life. Like all Bradbury's work it is very much about childhood and the child's-eye view of things.

Marion Zimmer Bradley

American novelist
BORN: 1930 DIED: 1999

Marion Bradley established her career with a long-running series of sf novels set on the planet Darkover, which extends from *The Planet Savers* (1958; book 1962) to *The Shadow Matrix* (1997). Although couched as planetary romance the series is essentially a fantasy, the

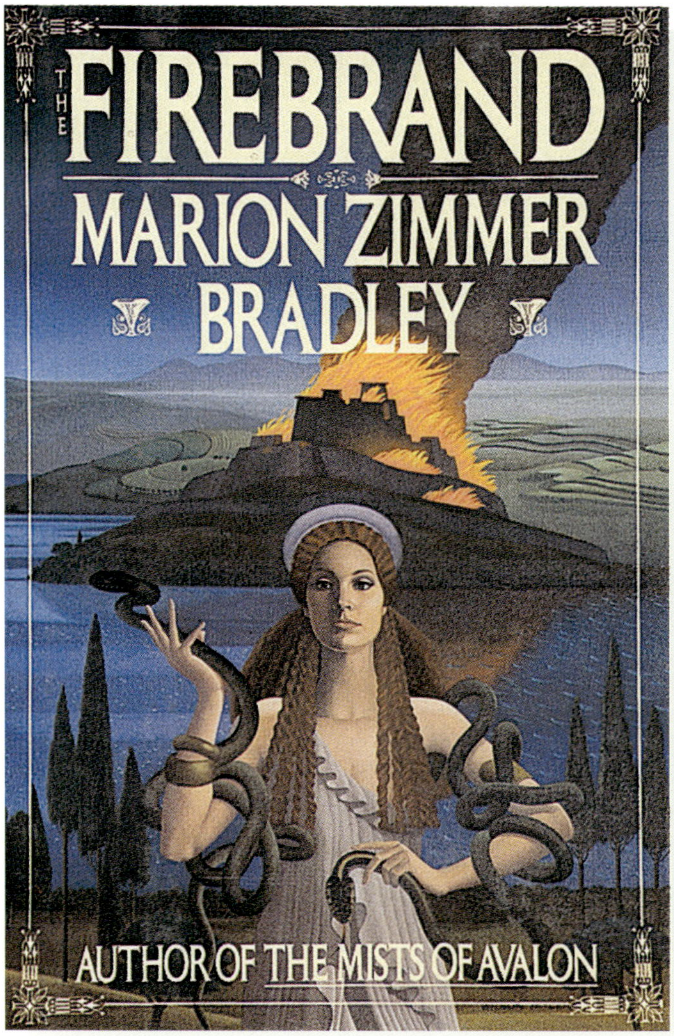

THE MATTER OF TROY IS REWORKED BY BRADLEY, WHO TELLS THE STORY OF KING PRIAM'S DAUGHTER CASSANDRA

"psi-powers" controlled by "matrices" being magic in all but name. Bradley attained far wider celebrity with the feminized Arthurian fantasy *The Mists of Avalon* (1982), which became one of the best-selling books of its era. Her early Sword & Sorcery novels were less successful, but her contributions to the "Thieves' World" shared-world scenario outgrew their origin, eventually extending from the stories collected in *Lythande* (1986) to *The Gratitude of Kings* (1997; with Elisabeth Waters). Bradley involved herself in many other collaborative endeavours, including her series of *Sword and Sorceress* (launched 1984), whose 15th volume was released in 1997, and *Marion Zimmer Bradley's Fantasy Magazine*, launched in 1988. She joined forces with Andre Norton and Julian May to produce the successful *Black Trillium* (1990), to which she added the sequel *Lady of the Trillium* (1995), and the same recipe was used to cook up *Tiger Burning Bright* (1995) whose other contributors were Norton and Mercedes Lackey.

The most ambitious of the solo fantasies which Bradley produced in the wake of *The Mists of Avalon* include *Night's Daughter* (1985), based on Mozart's *Magic Flute*, and *The Firebrand* (1987), about the Trojan seeress Cassandra. The conflict featured in *The Forest House* (1993) between the Roman conquerors of Britain and the Druidic religion, confused by a Romeo-and-Juliet scenario, is a striking version of her favourite theme; its sequel, *Lady of Avalon* (1997), connects it to *Mists of Avalon*. *Ghostlight* (1995), *Witchlight* (1996) and *Gravelight* (1997) ventured into new literary territory, featuring the contemporary exploits of the parapsychologists of the Bidney Institute. Only a small percentage of Bradley's work reaches her own highest standard, but she has been a crucial player in the establishment of fantasy as a popular genre and has worked tirelessly to widen the enclave occupied therein by female writers. Her influence will be missed.

Rebecca Bradley

Canadian novelist

BORN: 1952

A new writer who recently has been resident in Hong Kong, her first efforts, *Lady in Gil* (1996) and its sequel *Scion's Lady* (1997), have gained some praise.

Ernest Bramah

British novelist

BORN: 1868 DIED: 1942

The reclusive Bramah was the best of all English writers of "Chinoiserie", and he created that sub-genre's most memorable character, Kai Lung, for delightfully written books such as *The Wallet of Kai Lung* (1900), *Kai Lung's Golden Hours* (1922), *Kai Lung Unrolls His Mat* (1928) and *The Moon of Much Gladness* (1932; published in the USA as *The Return of Kai Lung*). He also wrote some rather good detective fiction.

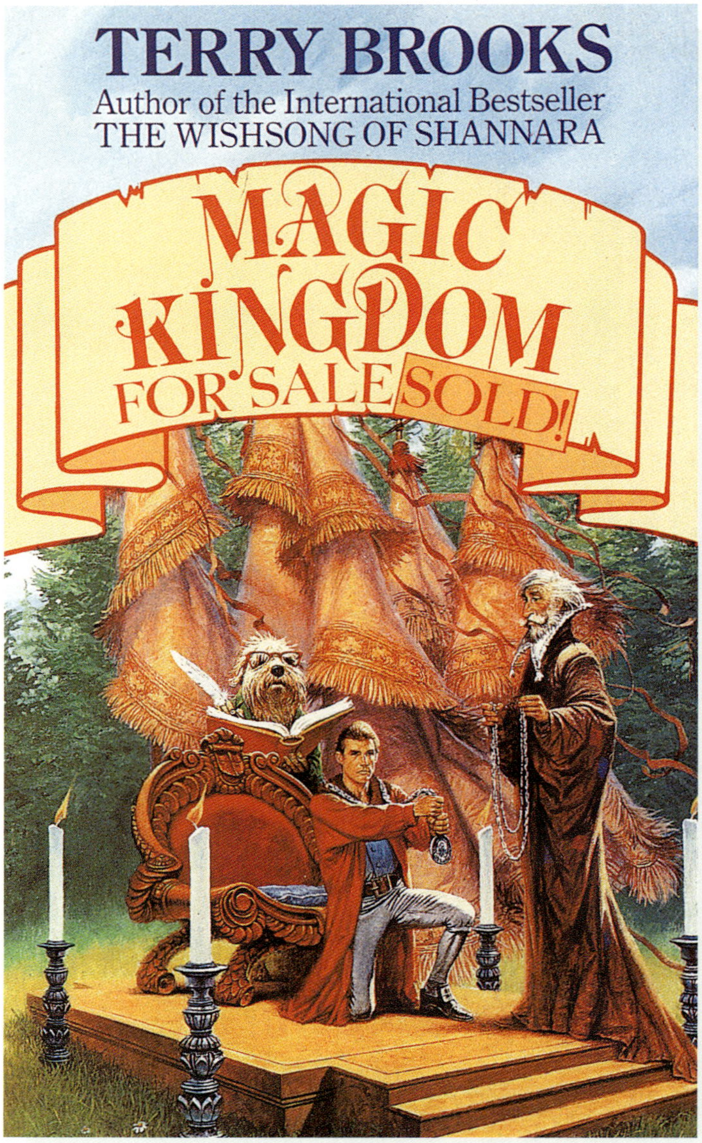

Brooks's "Landover" novels are popular examples of light fantasy. Ever wanted a magic kingdom of your own?

Terry Brooks

American novelist

BORN: 1944

Terry Brooks was one of the two writers (the other was Stephen R. Donaldson) who demonstrated in 1977 that the commercial success of Tolkien's *Lord of the Rings* had not been a fluke, and that fantasy really did have the potential to become a mass-market genre. *The*

Sword of Shannara was so closely imitative of Tolkien's masterpiece, and so careful in its dumbing-down, that Lin Carter was moved to describe it as "this war crime of a book", but Lester del Rey – who had recognized the marketability of Brooks' easygoing and unashamedly celebratory approach to the Tolkienian treasure-trove of motifs – made it the foundation stone of the Del Rey imprint which became the core of the new genre. Brooks extended the Shannara sequence through six sequels – *The Elfstones of Shannara* (1982), *The Wishsong of Shannara* (1985) and the trilogy consisting of *The Scions of Shannara* (1990), *The Druid of Shannara* (1991), *The Elf Queen of Shannara* (1992) and *The Talismans of Shannara* (1993), which carried the history of the setting through a further three centuries. Then – by which time he was following rather than establishing the freshly standardized practice of the new tradition – he added a prequel, *The First King of Shannara* (1996) and a further sequence, "The Voyage of Jerle Shannara", comprising *Isle Witch* (2000), *Antrax* (2001) and *Morgawr* (2002). Brooks's work became lighter in tone and manner as it progressed, although the manner of its inspiration continued to anchor the Shannara books with a certain earnest ponderousness. This was shed in the Landover series, begun with *Magic Kingdom for Sale – Sold!* (1986), a buoyant account of a jaded lawyer's purchase, in pursuit of escapist dreams, of a magical realm – which proves, of course, to be no Shangri-La. The series was continued in *The Black Unicorn* (1987), *Wizard at Large* (1988), *The Tangle Box* (1994) and *Witches' Brew* (1995), although the blithe spirit which had launched it became slightly unsteady as the sequence extended. A more radical new departure for Brooks was *Running with the Demon* (1997), an intriguing contemporary fantasy set in the Illinois town of Hopewell, in which Independence Day celebrations form the background to an epic struggle between the (good) Word and the (evil) Void. The sequence concluded with A *Knight of the Word* (1998), and *Angel Fire East* (1999).

Steven Brust

American novelist
BORN: 1955

Hungarian-American Brust (middle names Karl Zoltan) has used elements inherited from the mythology of his ancestors in his "Vlad Taltos" series of sophisticated fantasies: *Jhereg* (1983), *Yendi* (1984), *Teckla* (1987), *Taltos* (1988; also known as *Taltos and the Paths of the Dead*), *Phoenix* (1990) and *Athyra* (1993). Other books, such as *The Phoenix Guards* (1991) and its sequel *Five Hundred Years After* (1994), are pseudo-historical swashbucklers owing much to the (non-fantasy) influences of Alexandre Dumas and Rafael Sabatini. Brust has also co-written, with Emma Bull (below), the unusual historical fantasy *Freedom and Necessity* (1997).

Emma Bull

American novelist
BORN: 1954

Bull was married to Will Shetterly, also a fantasy novelist. Together they edited the "Liavek" series of shared-world anthologies; and a separate collection, *Double Feature* (1994), contains stories by both writers. Most of Bull's novels have been written solo, however, and at least three of them – *War for the Oaks* (1987), *Finder* (1994) and *The Princess and the Lord of Night* (1994) – are fantasies. Another, the highly praised *Bone Dance: A Fantasy for Technophiles* (1991) is, despite its subtitle, best classified as science fiction. Most recently, she has written, in collaboration with the preceding author Steven Brust, a long epistolary novel, *Freedom and Necessity* (1997), set in mid-19th-century England; this contains quotes from Hegel, Marx and Engels, and may well be regarded as the first Marxist steampunk fantasy.

Chris Bunch

American novelist
BORN: 1943

All Bunch's earlier work was written in collaboration with Allan Cole, notably the "Anteros" fantasy trilogy consisting of *The Far Kingdoms* (1993), *The Warrior's Tale* (1994) and *Kingdoms of the Night* (1995). Recently, however, the two have gone their separate ways, and Bunch's solo novels – *The Seer King* (1997) and *The Demon King* (1998), the first instalments in a "fantasy epic of empire, power and magic" – have tended to be the more substantial: Cole's principal solo efforts have been *When the Gods Slept* (1997) and *Wolves of the Gods* (1998), Arabian Nights-like fantasies inspired by *The Rubaiyat of Omar Khayyam*.

Edgar Rice Burroughs

American novelist
BORN: 1875 DIED: 1950

Edgar Rice Burroughs became a millionaire by developing a new sub-genre of fantastic adventure stories, which gave unprecedented freedom to the escapist imagination and took pulp fiction to a new extreme. Although the series begun with *Tarzan of the Apes* (1912; book 1914) was notionally set in Africa and the series begun with *A Princess of Mars* (1912; book 1917) on Mars, the settings were similar in all essentials and so were the fast-moving, cliffhanger-strewn plots. So successful did the template become that the later volumes of both series became tired exercises in repetition, but in the first phase of his career Burroughs produced several other works which were at least the equal of his first endeavours. These include the lost-race stories fixed up as *The Cave Girl* (1913–7; book 1925) and *The Land That Time Forgot* (1918; book 1924), and the early volumes of the "Pellucidar" series, launched with *At the Earth's Core* (1914; book 1922), set in a world within the hollow Earth. *The Moon Maid* (1923–5; book 1926), set in a similar world within the moon, was the last of his genuinely inventive works. Burroughs became one of the most widely imitated writers of all time and his influence remains powerful in spite of the relative sophistication of the contemporary audience. Tarzan is firmly established alongside Sherlock Holmes and Superman as one of the central hero-myths of the 20th century; its extrapolation continues in movies, on TV and in such spinoff texts as *Tarzan: The Lost Adventure* (1996), rewritten by Joe R. Lansdale from an unpublished Burroughs story.

JAMES BRANCH CABELL

American novelist
BORN: 1879 DIED: 1958

James Branch Cabell achieved brief notoriety when *Jurgen* (1919) was – absurdly – charged with obscenity on account of its humorous use of sexual symbolism. *The Cream of the Jest* (1917) had already reflected sarcastically on the absurd coyness of modern sexual mores, but Cabell was as interested in the asceticism of chivalry as he was in the urges of "gallantry" and the intoxications of artistry; his work is a celebration of the intricate interplay of the three motive forces. His series chronicling the history, influence and genealogy of the legendary hero Manuel, set in the imaginary French province of Poictesme, constitutes a unique literary endeavour. Its major fantasy inclusions are *Jurgen, Figures of Earth* (1921), *The High Place* (1923), *The Silver Stallion* (1926), *Something About Eve* (1927) and the stories in *The Witch Woman* (1926–9; omnibus 1948), but there are elements of fantasy in many others, including the chivalric romance *The Soul of Melicent* (1913; revised as *Domnei*, 1920).

Cabell usually shortened his signature to Branch Cabell for works outside this sequence, including the trilogy of dream fantasies *Smirt* (1934), *Smith* (1935) and *Smire* (1937), which are collected in *The Nightmare Has Triplets* (1972). His later work includes a number of relatively brief elegiac fantasies that lovingly revisit his favourite themes: *The First Gentleman of America* (1942; aka *The First American Gentleman*), *There Were Two Pirates* (1946) and *The Devil's Own Dear Son* (1949). Cabell stated his intention to "write perfectly of beautiful happenings", but was too honest to refrain from puncturing the illusions he thought most glorious; he had a better understanding of the true value of fantasy than any of his contemporaries.

ORSON SCOTT CARD

American novelist
BORN: 1951

Card became famous for his award-winning science fiction, but some readers believe his "Tales of Alvin Maker" sequence of fantasy novels to be the finest thing he has written – and among the finest things in American fantasy as a whole. The books to date are *Seventh Son* (1987), *Red Prophet* (1988), *Prentice Alvin* (1989), *Alvin Journeyman* (1995) and *Heartfire* (1998). The principal charm of the series is that it is so very American, set in an alternate 19th-century version of the Old West – one where magic works – and incorporating many details of US history and frontier folklore. There have been 1,001 fantasies set in mythical versions of Europe or Asia (or secondary worlds which resemble them): few fantasy writers have tackled America, and Card is among the most interesting of those who have. He has also produced a stand-alone fantasy not set in the world of Alvin Maker, *Enchantment* (1999).

JERRY JAY CARROLL

American novelist
BORN: ?

Author of an interesting debut novel, *Top Dog* (1996), in which a wheeler-dealer Wall Street businessman is transformed into a big dog and has to learn new kinds of survival skills. The sequel, *Dog Eats Dog*, was published in 1999.

LEWIS CARROLL

British novelist
BORN: 1832 DIED: 1898

Charles Lutwidge Dodgson, Oxford mathematics don, was so suffocatingly respectable that he felt Gilbert and Sullivan needed bowdlerizing; his transformation into nonsense author Lewis Carroll recalls that of Jekyll and Hyde. By posing as children's nonsense, Carroll's masterpieces *Alice's Adventures in Wonderland* (1865) and *Through the Looking Glass: and What Alice Found There* (1871) got away with turning Dodgson's Victorian respectability inside-out. Children should respect their elders: but every "adult" Alice meets in her travels is irrational or insane, with only the White Knight being dottily benevolent. Famous moral verses like Southey's "Father William" are replaced by amoral parodies. There are buried jokes about the great unmentionable, death.

The Alice books also contain much deft logical and mathematical byplay which requires adult appreciation: these are the children's books most tirelessly quoted by adults, especially politicians. Martin Gardner's *The Annotated Alice* (1960) usefully surveys the buried complexities.

The Hunting of the Snark (1876) may be the only successful long nonsense poem in English; its ship-of-fools theme and dark ending are unforgettable. Sadly, Carroll yielded to the moralizing tones of Dodgson in the late, fairy-infested *Sylvie and Bruno* (1889) and *Sylvie and Bruno Concluded* (1893), best left unread.

Lin Carter

American novelist and editor
BORN: 1930 DIED: 1988

As a writer Lin Carter specialized in derivative hackwork of no conspicuous merit, but he was enormously influential as an editor, playing a key role in the establishment of fantasy as a popular genre. His pastiches of Robert E. Howard include numerous Conan stories in collaboration with L. Sprague de Camp and the Thongor series, begun with *The Wizard of Lemuria* (1965). His more prolific imitations of Edgar Rice Burroughs include the "Callisto" series (1972–78), the "Green Star" series (1972–83) and the "Zanthodon" series (1979–82). The slightly less derivative "Gondwana Epic" begun with *Giant of World's End* (1969) and the "Terra Magica" series (1982–1988) are more interesting.

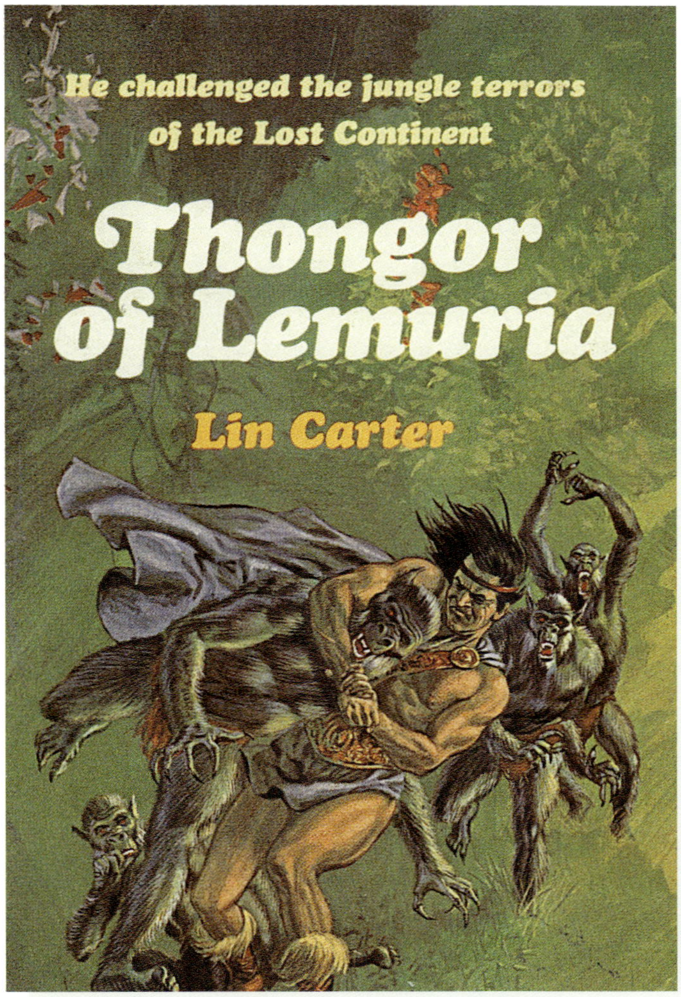

CARTER'S THONGOR WAS A CONAN IMITATION – THE MIGHTY WARRIOR OF A DAWN-AGE CIVILIZATION

As editor of the "Ballantine Adult Fantasy" series from 1969–74 he mingled 19th-and early 20th-century fantasy by George MacDonald, William Morris, Lord Dunsany and others with contemporary works by Evangeline Walton and Katherine Kurtz, marking out the territory of the genre. He provided context-setting anthologies, most significantly *The Young Magicians* (1969), *Golden Cities, Far* (1970) and *New Worlds for Old* (1971), and the non-fiction studies *Tolkien: A Look Behind the Lord of the Rings* (1969) and *Imaginary Worlds: The Art of Fantasy* (1973).

His interest in the Lovecraftian school of weird fiction – especially the work of Clark Ashton Smith – is reflected in the pastiches collected in *The Xothic Legend Cycle* (1997) edited by Robert M. Price, several anthologies and *Lovecraft: A Look Behind the Cthulhu Mythos* (1972). His other anthologies include the five-volume *Flashing Swords* series (1973–81), *Kingdoms of Sorcery* and *Realms of Wizardry* (both 1976) and the first six volumes of DAW's annual *Year's Best Fantasy* (1975–80).

His non-fiction was generally considered as shallow as his fiction, but no one could fault the breadth of his taste or the depth of his love for the genre whose renaissance he contrived.

Joy Chant

British novelist
BORN: 1945

Chant made her mark with *Red Moon and Black Mountain* (1970), a romantic fantasy epic, full of myth and passion and derring-do, in which three middle-class English children find themselves magically transported to an alien land. They arrive in the midst of an earth-shaking struggle between the forces of light and darkness: the Lord of the Black Mountain has fallen from the good, and has now returned from exile to challenge the legitimate forces of the Starlit Land; his nefarious power grows with the rising of this world's Red Moon; and the three young people must each learn to play a part in the coming battle.

The elements from which Chant constructed her exciting story were traditional, but they were deployed with skill and emotional conviction. Her works since have been few in number, consisting of *The Grey Mane of Morning* (1977), *When Voiha Wakes* (1983) and some retellings of old tales.

C. J. Cherryh

American novelist
BORN: 1942

Carolyn Cherryh is a prolific and much-lauded science-fiction author for whom fantasy has always been a sideline, although her very first books included a trilogy – *Gate of Ivrel* (1976), *Well of Shiuan* (1978) and *Fires of Azeroth* (1979); collected as *The Book of Morgaine* (1979) – which was essentially a blend of both science-fiction and fantasy.

Her pure fantasies since then have included *The Dreamstone* (1983), *The Tree of Swords and Jewels* (1983), *The Paladin* (1988), *Rusalka* (1989), *Chernevog* (1990), *Yvgenie* (1991), *The Goblin Mirror* (1992), *Faery in Shadow* (1993) and *Fortress in the Eye of Time* (1995), *Fortress of Eagles* (1998), *Fortress of Owls* (1999) and *Fortress of Dragons* (2000). She has proved herself a hard-headed, scientifically informed writer who can also turn on the Old Magic.

Deborah A. Chester

American novelist
BORN: 1957

Chicago-born Chester made her first reputation in the 1980s with historical romances and has also written a copious amount of science fiction as "Sean Dalton". Under her real name, she has penned a routine fantasy trilogy: *Reign of Shadows* (1996), *Shadow War* (1997) and *Realm of Light* (1997).

Jo Clayton

American novelist
BORN: 1939 DIED: 1998

As her publisher has expressed it, Clayton laboured "in the salt mines of paperback-original fiction for over 15 years, perfecting her craft with over 40 books", before achieving hardcover publication with *Drum Warning* (1996) and *Drum Calls* (1997) – Books One and Two of *The Drums of Chaos* – shortly before her untimely death from cancer.

James Clemens

American novelist
BORN: 1961

Potentially another wannabe Big Commercial Fantasist, the relatively young American Clemens (real name James Czajkowski) has made a very recent debut with "The Banned and the Banished" series, consisting of *Wit'ch Fire* (1998), *Wit'ch Storm* (1999), *Wit'ch War* (2000) and *Wit'ch Gate* (2002).

Brenda W. Clough

American novelist
BORN: 1955

Her early books, published under the genderless byline "B. W. Clough", were mostly paperback originals and included the "Averidan" series: *The Crystal Crown* (1984), *The Dragon of Mishbil* (1985), *The Realm Beneath* (1986) and *The Name of the Sun* (1988). The recent *How Like a God* (1997) is an attempt at a more serious kind of "realistic fantasy", and was followed up by the Suburban Gods sequence, *Doors of Death and Life* (2000), *Out of the Abyss* (2003), and *Off the Screen*, forthcoming.

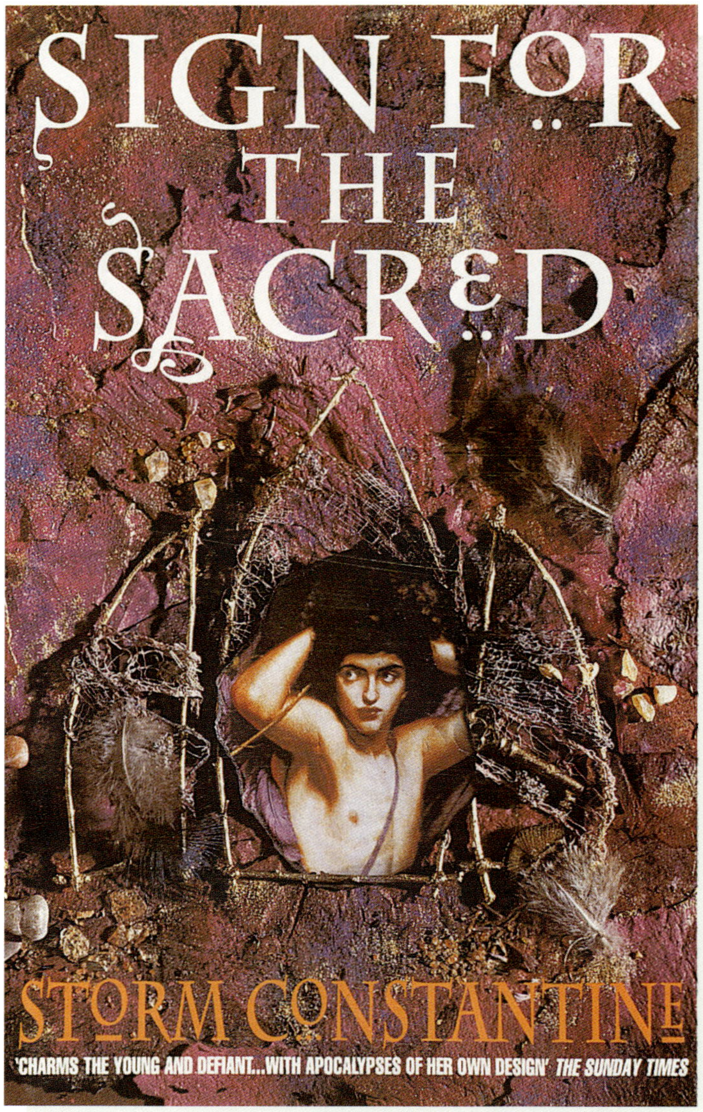

Constantine has taken to dealing with angels, in religiously-based but unorthodox fantasies such as this

Storm Constantine

British novelist
BORN: 1956

Storm Constantine's "Wraeththu" trilogy of futuristic fantasies, comprising *The Enchantments of Flesh and Spirit* (1987), *The Bewitchments of Love and Hate* (1988) and *The Fulfilments of Fate and Desire* (1989), extrapolated the affectations and visual style of the "Goth" subculture, combining its fascination with androgyny and ritual magic with a distinctive ecological mysticism.

Constantine's distinctive method and flamboyant mannerisms quickly established her as a key Decadent fantasist of the 20th century *fin de siècle*. She supplemented two feminist sf novels with a sequence of floridly fanciful and darkly erotic fantasies – the counter-cultural whimsy *Hermetech* (1991); the unorthodox vampire story *Burying the Shadow* (1992); the complex quasi-angelic romance *Sign for the Sacred* (1993); and the mock-apocalyptic extravaganza *Calenture* (1994) – before embarking on an ambitious trilogy of authentically apocalyptic fantasies based in the mythology of the apocryphal Book of Enoch, as extended and reinterpreted by the scholarly fantasist Andrew Collins. *Stalking Tender Prey* (1995) offers an account of the "reawakening" in England of the leader of the fallen angels Shemyaza, *Scenting Hallowed Blood* (1996) describes the first steps of his reclamation of his ancient heritage and *Stealing Sacred Fire* (1997) returns him to the newly rebuilt city of Babylon in order that the world's New Age might begin. A new sequence, "The Chronicles of Magravandias", was formed of *Sea Dragon Heir* (1999), *Crown of Silence* (2000) and *The Way of Light* (2001). A few of her short stories are collected in *Three Heralds of the Storm* (1997).

Louise Cooper

British novelist
BORN: 1952

Louise Cooper's debut novel was *The Book of Paradox* (1973), a mannered fantasy based in the imagery of the Tarot. Between the vampire novel *Blood Summer* (1976) and its sequel *In Memory of Sarah Bailey* (1978) she produced the heroic fantasy *Lord of No Time* (1977), whose plot – involving an intricate and eternal but human-centred conflict between Order and Chaos – was eventually expanded into the "Time Master" trilogy consisting of *The Initiate* (1985), *The Outcast* (1986) and *The Master* (1987). The sequence was extended in the "Chaos Gate" trilogy *The Deceiver* (1991), *The Pretender* (1991) and *The Avenger* (1992), and Cooper then supplied the "Star Shadow" trilogy of prequels consisting of *Star Ascendant* (1994), *Eclipse* (1994) and *Moonset* (1995). *Blood Dance* (1996), intended for teenage readers, is set in the same milieu. Fantasy novels written in parallel with this project include *Mirage* (1987) and the "Indigo" sequence, whose guilt ridden heroine is assisted by a sentient wolf in carrying forward a career as a demon-hunter: *Nemesis* (1988), *Inferno* (1989), *Infanta* (1989), *Nocturne* (1990), *Troika* (1991), *Avatar* (1991), *Revenant* (1992) and *Aisling* (1993). Cooper's subsequent work followed up the success of the "young adult" novels *The Thorn Key* (1988) and *The Sleep of Stone* (1991), mostly consisting of contributions to the Puffin "Dark Enchantment" series, including *Daughter of Storms* (1996), *Firespell* (1996), *Sacrament of Night* (1997) and *The Shrouded Mirror* (1997). Her work for adults continued in the convoluted conspiratorial dark fantasy *The King's Demon* (1996).

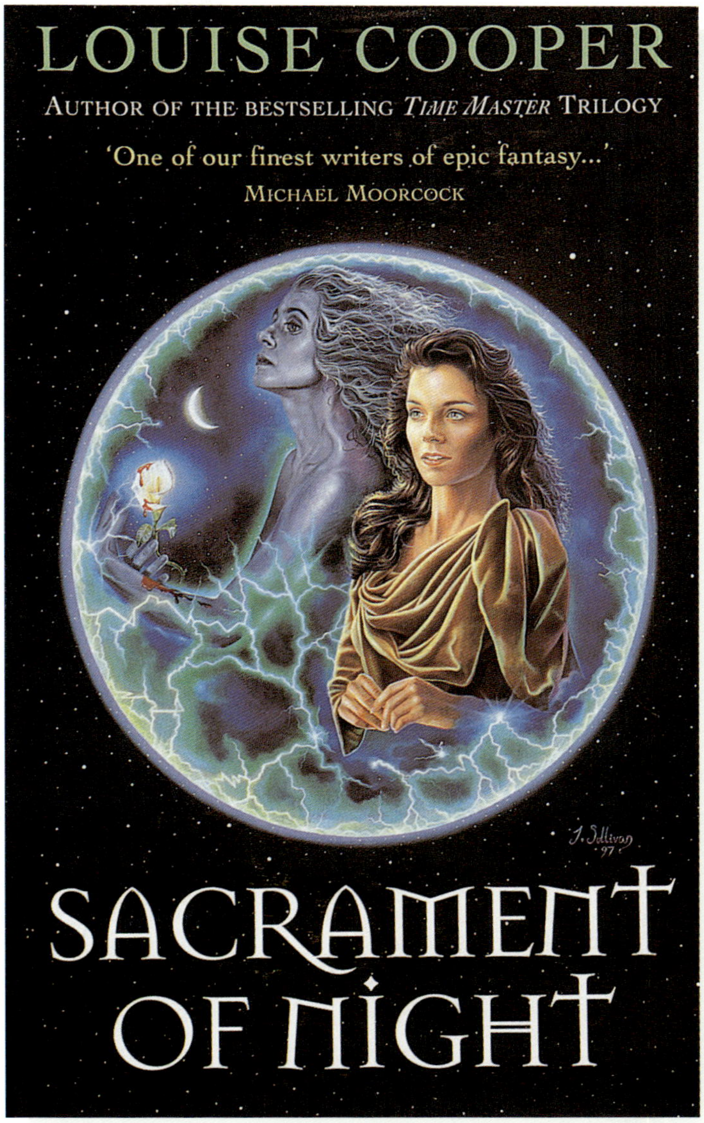

PROLIFIC AND COMPETENT, COOPER HAS WRITTEN FOR CHILDREN (THE ABOVE IS AN EXAMPLE) AS WELL AS WORKS FOR ADULTS

SUSAN COOPER

British novelist
BORN: 1935

Her five-volume sequence of novels known collectively as *The Dark is Rising* (1965–77) is regarded by many readers as one of the very best juvenile fantasies of recent decades.

MARY CORRAN

British novelist
BORN: 1953

Corran's novels, *Imperial Light* (1994), *Fate* (1995) and *Darkfell* (1996), are rich in ideas, despite their standard otherworldly settings, but tend perhaps to be a little preachy.

RONALD ANTHONY CROSS

American novelist
BORN: 1937

His "Eternal Guardians" series – *The Fourth Guardian* (1994), *The Lost Guardian* (1995) and *The White Guardian* (1998) – is an interesting fantasy involving a conspiratorial view of history, and in that respect slightly reminiscent of the "paranoia fictions" of Robert Anton Wilson and Robert Shea in their once-trendy "Illuminatus!" sequence.

JOHN CROWLEY

American novelist
BORN: 1942

Crowley's first novels were science-fiction – although *The Deep* (1976) eventually proves to have such an extraordinary setting that it crashes through into fantasy. His beautifully written *Little, Big* (1981) is probably the finest single fantasy of the 1980s.

This multi-generational story is set first in near-future America, then 25 years on when New York is in partial decay. Its pivotal character Smoky Barnable marries into the Drinkwater family, inhabiting the extraordinary country house Edgewood – built as an anthology of architectural styles. This family is aware both of elusive links with another world, Faerie, where "the further in you go, the bigger it gets", and of living an immense Story whose end approaches.

En route Crowley allows glimpses of magic, including fairies, changelings, a man turned into a trout and an extraordinary density of references to *Alice in Wonderland* creator, Lewis Carroll. The unsummarizable Story ends in transformations, sadness and triumph. Another powerful work, full of nested stories, angels and demons, remains incomplete.

Published volumes are *Aegypt* (1987), *Love and Sleep* (1994) and *Demonomania* (2001), revolving around secret histories of the world and the poignancy of lost alternate pasts. The 16th-century heretic philosopher Giordano Bruno is a key figure.

AVRAM DAVIDSON

American novelist
BORN: 1923 DIED: 1993

One of the oddballs of the American fantasy field, Davidson was an erudite author who drew his inspiration from obscure byways of historical knowledge. One of his finest novels, *The Phoenix and the Mirror* (1969), was based on medieval legends of the Roman poet Virgil (or "Vergil", as the author prefers to spell it). In this book, Vergil is commissioned against his will by the beautiful Queen Cornelia to construct a "virgin speculum" – a magical bronze mirror which has never reflected a face. He must obtain quantities of freshly mined copper ore, and so he sets out on a hazardous voyage to the east – to Cyprus, island of copper. The way is barred by brutal Hunnish pirates, but Vergil is able to win passage by playing off one of their hereditary kings against the others. Vergil's adventures on Cyprus prove to be equally memorable; and the detailed description of the actual making of the speculum, on his return to Naples, is a *tour de force*. The flurry of action at the end – when Vergil travels to Africa for a showdown with the Phoenix, the legendary bird of fire – seems a little rushed, but overall the novel is an eccentric masterpiece. It is a pity that Davidson, who began several abortive series, could not summon the energy to complete his projected "Vergil Magus" sequence: just one further novel appeared, after an 18-year gap: *Vergil in Averno* (1987). Also notable among his other fantasies are *The Island Under the Earth* (1969), *Peregrine: Primus* (1971), *Peregrine: Secundus* (1981) and the story-collection *The Enquiries of Dr Eszterhazy* (1975; expanded edition, 1991).

PAMELA DEAN

American novelist
BORN: 1953

Dean's first three novels formed a series intended for young-adult readers: *The Secret Country* (1985), *The Hidden Land* (1986) and *The Whim of the Dragon* (1989). Since then she has written *Tam Lin* (1991), a contemporary fantasy based on the ballad of that name, *The Dubious Hills* (1994) and *Juniper, Gentian and Rosemary* (1998), a stand-alone fantasy.

GREENMANTLE WAS MADE FAMOUS BY JOHN BUCHAN IN 1916, BUT CHARLES DE LINT HAS GIVEN IT A WHOLE NEW MEANING

L. SPRAGUE DE CAMP

American novelist
BORN: 1907 DIED: 2000

Sprague de Camp set the characteristic tone of the pulp magazine *Unknown*, which favoured works in which modern rationality was applied – usually with hilarious consequences – to premises borrowed from traditional fantasy. In "None But Lucifer" (1939, with Horace L. Gold) a young American employs modern marketing theory to revitalize Satan's temptation and punishment business. De Camp's long-standing literary partnership with Fletcher Pratt began in 1940 with the first of the "Harold Shea" stories, whose hero is displaced into a series of literary and mythical milieux.

In the first two novellas, collected in *The Incomplete Enchanter* (1941), Shea visits the worlds of Norse mythology and Spenser's *Faerie Queene*; in *The Castle of Iron* (1941; book 1950) he finds the Spenser-derived world of Ariosto's *Orlando Furioso* confusing. The two volumes were combined as *The Compleat Enchanter* (1975), but two further novellas had by then been issued in *Wall of Serpents* (1960), which had to be added to the larger omnibus *The Intrepid Enchanter* (1988; aka *The Complete Compleat Enchanter*). The series was further extended by the anthologies *The Enchanter Reborn* (1992) and *The Exotic Enchanter*, both co-edited by Christopher Stasheff; De Camp's contributions thereto – Pratt being long dead – were *Sir Harold and the Gnome King* (separately published 1991) and "Sir Harold of Zodanga".

De Camp and Pratt also collaborated on *The Land of Unreason* (1941; book 1942), in which an American tourist is mistaken for a changeling by drunken Irish fairies, the alternate-worlds story *The Carnelian Cube* (1948), and the tall tales collected in *Tales from Gavagan's Bar* (1953; expanded 1978). De Camp's solo fantasies for *Unknown* include *The Undesired Princess* (1942; book 1990 with a sequel by David Drake, "The Enchanted Bunny"), set in a fairy-tale world where subtle shades of colour and meaning are conspicuous by their absence, and *Solomon's Stone* (1942; book 1957), set on an astral plane inhabited by the dream-projections of ordinary men.

His subsequent humorous fantasies include those collected in *The Reluctant Shaman* (1970) and *The Purple Pterodactyls* (1979) and two novels written with his wife, Catherine Crook de Camp, *The Incorporated Knight* (1987) and *The Pixilated Peeress* (1991). De Camp played a crucial role in extending the career of Robert E. Howard's Conan, completing some fragments for *Tales of Conan* (1955) and revising Bjorn Nyberg's *The Return of Conan* (1957; aka *Conan the Avenger*) when the series was reissued in hardcover, then contributing many more pastiches for paperback publication in the late 1960s.

De Camp's own Sword & Sorcery stories are more light-hearted. *The Tritonian Ring and Other Pusadian Tales* (1953) collects his first such series; the more substantial "Novaria" series consists of *The Goblin Tower* (1968), *The Clocks of Iraz* (1971), *The Unbeheaded King* (1980) and *The Honorable Barbarian* (1989). *The Fallible Fiend*, set in the same quasi-Hellenistic milieu, is a broader comedy. De Camp edited an influential series of anthologies, beginning with *Swords and Sorcery* (1963), *The Spell of Seven* (1965) and *The Fantastic Swordsmen* (1967) which defined the sub-genre of heroic fantasy, supplementing their commentary with essays collected in *Literary Swordsmen and Sorcerers* (1976) and *Rubber Dinosaurs and Wooden Elephants* (1997).

STEPHEN DEDMAN

Australian novelist
BORN: 1959

Dedman is a bright new talent, best known for his short stories. His debut novel was *The Art of Arrow-Cutting* (1997), an urban fantasy. Its sequels were *Foreign Bodies* (1999) and *Shadows Bite* (2000).

Charles de Lint

Canadian novelist
BORN: 1951

Charles de Lint began publishing fantasy booklets through his own Triskell Press in 1979 – many of them in the "Cerin Songweaver" sequence, reflecting his strong interest in Celtic music – but his first full-length novel was the Tolkienesque *The Riddle of the Wren* (1984). With *Moonheart* (1984), de Lint began developing a distinctive species of contemporary fantasy, usually called "urban fantasy", in which modern cityscapes – initially those of de Lint's native Ottawa – overlap and merge with a magical realm populated by individuals drawn from several folkloristic traditions, including Native American mythologies. The apparatus of *Moonheart* was further elaborated in the tales in *Spiritwalk* (1992); *Yarrow* (1986) and *Greenmantle* (1988) are of a similar ilk. De Lint's more recent urban fantasies are mostly set in the imaginary city of Newford; they include the tales in *Dreams Underfoot* (1993), the novels *Memory and Dream* (1994), *Someplace to be Flying* (1998), *PaperJack* (2000), *The Onion Girl* (2001), *The Wishing Well* (2002) and the tales in *The Ivory and the Horn (1995).* These works frequently use artists or musicians as protagonists, and they have gradually honed to near-perfection a distinctive lyrical tone and deft sentimentality. De Lint has also written more orthodox fantasies based in traditional British folklore – including *Jack the Giant-Killer* (1987) and its sequel *Drink Down the Moon* (1990), *The Little People* (1991) and *The Wild Wood* (1994) – but it is urban fantasy that has allowed him to carve out his own niche within the field.

Gordon R. Dickson

American novelist
BORN: 1923 DIED: 2001

Primarily a science-fiction writer, Dickson produced a good-humoured fantasy novel, *The Dragon and the George* (1976), in emulation of the fantasies of his friend Poul Anderson. It is the tale of Jim Eckert, a college volleyball player and expert in medieval history, who is thrown into a magical world of knightly romance. But there is a humorous twist: unlike most Sword & Sorcery heroes, Eckert loses his human shape – and finds himself trapped in the form of a huge winged dragon. The story of Eckert and his friends and enemies has been continued in several belated sequels: *The Dragon Knight* (1990), *The Dragon on the Border* (1992), *The Dragon at War* (1993), *The Dragon, the Earl, and the Troll* (1994), *The Dragon and the Djinn* (1996), *The Dragon and the Gnarly King* (1997), *The Dragon in Lyonesse* (1998) and *The Dragon and the Fair Maid of Kent* (2000).

Stephen R. Donaldson

American novelist
BORN: 1947

Stephen R. Donaldson laboured for 10 years on "The Chronicles of Thomas Covenant", while it was rejected by 47 publishers, but when the trilogy – consisting of *Lord Foul's Bane*, *The Illearth War* and *The Power That Preserves* – finally appeared in 1977 it became a huge spontaneous bestseller. Thomas Covenant, who is afflicted with Hansen's disease (leprosy), is translocated into a Secondary World whose history, geography and metaphysics reflect his plight. His personal struggle for survival is thus transmuted, in spite of his unreadiness to believe in his experience, into a mission to save an entire world from the ravages of Lord Foul, the Despiser. "The Second Chronicles of Thomas Covenant", consisting of *The Wounded Land* (1980), *The One Tree* (1982) and *White Gold Wielder* (1983), returned the reluctant hero to the Land to find it blighted all over again, and to send him forth on a more confusing quest. The second trilogy introduced a major female character, Linden Avery, and much of Donaldson's subsequent work employs female protagonists, including the title-story of the collection *Daughter of Regals and Other Tales* (1984) and the two-volume epic *"Mordant's Need"*, consisting of *The Mirror of Her Dreams* (1986) and *A Man Rides Through* (1987), whose beleaguered heroine is Terisa Morgan.

The futuristic "Gap" series, consisting of *The Gap into Conflict: The Real Story* (1991), *The Gap into Vision: Forbidden Knowledge* (1991), *The Gap into Power: A Dark and Hungry God Arises* (1992), *The Gap into Madness: Chaos and Order* (1994) and *The Gap into Ruin: This Day All Gods Die* (1996) – which is a space opera in more than one sense of the word, being a version of the Germanic myths which provided the story of Wagner's "Ring" cycle – also places a female character, Morn Hyland, at centre-stage. The heroism of Donaldson's protagonists is perhaps more clearly manifest in grace under pressure than in chivalrous adventurism. Such power as his protagonists possess is usually beyond the reach of conscious control, evoked with great difficulty and problematic effect.

Few other writers are capable of reaching such a pitch of indignation at the harsh treatment of innocents, and few can sustain the resultant emotional intensity over such long distances. The passionate quality of Donaldson's work occasionally carries him into difficult territory, but it equips his stories with a powerful narrative drive. *Stephen R. Donaldson's Chronicles of Thomas Covenant: Variations on the Fantasy Tradition* (1995) by W. A. Senior is a scrupulous study of his first series.

David A. Drake

American novelist
BORN: 1945

For a while, Drake was known mainly as a writer of militaristic science fiction (*Hammer's Slammers*, etc), yet he has always been drawn to fantasy (as evidenced by *The Dragon Lord*, 1979, and *The Sea Hag*, 1988). So it came as no surprise when he attempted to relaunch his career with a big commercial fantasy, *Lord of the Isles* (1997), followed up by *Queen of Demons* (1998), *Servant of the Dragon* (1999) and *Mistress of the Catacombs* (2001).

Diane Duane

American novelist
BORN: 1952

Duane, who lives in Ireland and is married to writer Peter Morwood (see below), has written two principal fantasy series, the "Tale of the Five" sequence – *The Door into Fire* (1979), *The Door into Shadow* (1984) and *The Door into Sunset* (1992) – and, for younger readers, the "Wizardry" series – *So You Want to Be a Wizard?* (1983), *Deep Wizardry* (1985), *High Wizardry* (1990) and *A Wizard Abroad* (1993), *The Wizard's Dilemma* (2001). Her most recent effort is *The Book of Night with Moon* (1997), an "epic fantasy about super-intelligent cats", which was followed by *To Visit The Queen* (1998) and *The Big Meow* (2002). She has also written many novelizations and other media spinoffs, some of them fantasies.

Dave Duncan

Canadian novelist
BORN: 1933

The prolific Dave Duncan – who uses the familiar form of his name to distinguish himself from two other writers – made his genre debut with the mythological fantasy *A Rose-Red City* (1987) before launching himself into the first of three hectic action-adventure sequences, the "Seventh Sword" trilogy: *The Reluctant Swordsman* (1988), *The Coming of Wisdom* (1988) and *The Destiny of the Sword* (1988). This was followed by two four-volume sequences set in the lavishly populated land of Pandemia, the first comprising *Magic Casement* (1990), *Faery Lands Forlorn* (1991), *Perilous Seas* (1991) and *Emperor and Clown* (1991), and the second *The Cutting Edge* (1992), *Upland Outlaws* (1993), *The Stricken Field* (1992) and *The Living God* (1994). In parallel with the latter Duncan produced the amnesiac fantasy *The Reaver Road* (1992) and *The Hunter's Haunt* (1995). *Past Imperative* (1996), subtitled "Round One of the Great Game", began another sequence continued in *Present Tense* (1996) and *Future Indefinite* (1997), in which mysterious gateways – Duncan's favourite device – link alternate worlds that are on the brink of World War One. "The King's Blades" trilogy: *The Gilded Chain* (1998), *Lord of the Five Lands* (1999) and *Sky of Swords* (2000) was more medieval, and was produced at the same time as the parallel young adult series "The King's Blades: The King's Daggers": *Sir Stalwart* (1999), *The Crooked House* (2000) and *Silvercloak* (2001).

Lord Dunsany

Irish novelist
BORN: 1878 DIED: 1957

His full name was Edward John Moreton Drax Plunkett; his influence on later fantasy was remarkable. Using rich prose full of

MOST POETIC OF ALL FANTASISTS, DUNSANY WAS A GREAT COINER OF RESONANT NAMES AND PHRASES IN HIS EARLY COLLECTIONS

Biblical and poetic cadences, he defined his own imaginary pantheon in the collection *The Gods of Pegana* (1905) – then told stories of these gods and men in *Time and the Gods* (1906). *The Sword of Welleran* (1908) contains fine tales of high magic and deep irony which have been much imitated. Dunsany's novels are also important influences. *The King of Elfland's Daughter* (1924) definitively set the pattern for later works where Elfland or Faerie closely, if elusively, borders on "the fields we know", where the mixed blessings of elf/human intermarriage are realistically considered (cf. Tolkien), and where magical transformation of the whole world is possible. Less significant but exquisitely told, *The Charwoman's Shadow* (1926) uses human shadows as a metaphor for souls or essences. The old charwoman's shadow is held captive by a bad magician; when the hero restores it, her youth and beauty return. Further story collections include *The Travel Tales of Mr Joseph Jorkens* (1931) and its successors. These mostly outrageous yarns, told by clubman Jorkens when lubricated with whisky, contain Dunsany's best comic fantasy.

David Eddings

American novelist
BORN: 1931

David Eddings had written novels before turning his attention to the fantasy genre, but it was his first fantasy series – the five-volume "The Belgariad", comprising the trilogy *Pawn of Prophecy* (1982), *Queen of Sorcery* (1982) and *Magician's Gambit* (1983), and the two-volume extension *Castle of Wizardry* (1984) and *Enchanter's End-Game* (1984) – which enabled his career to take off. It follows the adventures of the magically gifted farm-boy Garion, whose gradually confirmed royal heritage is backed by 7,000 years of intricately worked-out history.

Although Garion's extended quest is set in a classical mould and his Secondary World is elaborately drawn, the exercise is distinguished by a lightness of tone and spirit which moves the narrative along with a swift and easy grace. Following the customary career-path of genre writers, Eddings was quick to supplement his first successful quintet with a second, "The Malloreon", consisting of *Guardians of the West* (1987), *King of the Murgos* (1988), *Demon Lord of Karanda* (1988), *Sorceress of Darshiva* (1989) and *The Seeress of Kell* (1991). Here Garion – now Belgarion, Overlord of the West – reassembles the band of brave companions who served him so well during his ascent to power to rescue his kidnapped son. Again, the richly detailed background and effortless style secure considerable narrative traction, the familiarity of the characters and their interplay having bred contentment among an increasing body of ardent fans.

The hero of Eddings' next series, the Elenium sequence – comprising *The Diamond Throne* (1989), *The Ruby Knight* (1990) and *The Sapphire Rose* (1991) – is a seasoned knight bearing the hereditary title Sparhawk whose quest combines elements borrowed from Don Quixote and Perrault with the high fantasy motifs of the earlier series. It too was followed by a carbon copy, the Tamuli sequence, comprising *Domes of Fire* (1992), *The Shining Ones* (1993) and *The Hidden City* (1994). Having completed this project, Eddings – now acknowledging the long-term involvement in his projects of his wife Leigh – returned to the world of the Belgariad, beginning a sequence of "prequels" with *Belgarath the Sorcerer* (1995) and *Polgara the Sorceress* (1997). *The Rivan Codex* (1998) is a "non-fictional" accessory.

The Redemption of Althalus (2000), about a morally bankrupt thief turned reluctant hero, was a stand-alone work, as was *Regina's Song* (2002), an urban fantasy about one of Jack The Ripper's descendants who lives in Seattle. Eddings' generous use of borrowed materials and linear plots consisting mostly of long journeys make his works seem straightforward, but he deploys both skill and artistry in maintaining their smooth flow and the quality of easy companionship that his followers relish.

E.R. Eddison

British novelist
BORN: 1882 DIED: 1945

A writer of brilliantly quirky, old-fashioned, vaguely Elizabethan prose which many readers find difficult. The rewards, however, are considerable. Eddison's major work *The Worm Ouroboros* (1922) is a deliberately grandiose, overstated epic. It chronicles war between the countries Demonland and Witchland – inhabited by humans despite those ill-chosen names, but humans of towering stature, mighty fighters all. Impossible journeys are undertaken, vast battles fought, unconquerable mountains climbed. The heroic Demons are nominally the good guys, while the Witches follow their magnificently villainous sorcerer-king Gorice ... but Eddison makes it clear that, as though this were Valhalla, it's the sheer joy of conflict that drives both sides. Thus, when Witchland is defeated, the victorious Demons beg for the turning-back of time so that the story – like the worm Ouroboros that bites its own tail – joins on to its beginning, with the Witches' first arrogant challenge. This *tour de force* is unique in fantasy. Linked works are the "Zimiamvia" trio, set in the after-life of the first book's world: *Mistress of Mistresses* (1935), *A Fish Dinner in Memison* (1941) and, uncompleted, *The Mezentian Gate* (1958). These are knottier, more philosophical narratives; it's *The Worm Ouroboros* which endures.

THE OPENING VOLUME OF EDDISON'S LATE, UNFINISHED TRILOGY – A DIFFICULT WORK, BUT MUCH ADMIRED BY CONNOISSEURS

PHYLLIS EISENSTEIN

American novelist
BORN: 1946

Eisenstein's most notable fantasy novel, *Sorcerer's Son* (1979), features a sorceress who lives alone in Castle Spinweb. She has the magical ability to manipulate all things woven, ranging from human-made fabrics to spiders' webs. She is able to view far scenes with the help of her gossamer webs, and even to listen to distant troubadours' songs through the medium of her tiny spider "spies". However, a fellow-sorcerer and summoner of demons feels threatened by her, and offers his hand in marriage – and is rebuffed. In pique, he summons a demon and commands it to take attractive human form in order to seduce the sorceress; for pregnancy will temporarily dampen her magical powers and enable him to prepare defences. Accordingly, a sorely wounded but handsome young knight arrives at Castle Spinweb and our heroine gladly takes him in, tends his injury, and allows him to dally for some weeks. She duly falls in love, and is heartbroken when he leaves. The fruit of her loins (and the demon's seed) is a baby who grows to be a strapping lad whose dearest wish is to be a knight-errant, just like his long-lost father. His mother tries to dissuade him, but as soon as he is able he leaves home and has picaresque adventures as he searches for his father, protected by his mother's spiders, and hindered along the way by the evil machinations of the sorcerer. At length he heeds his mother's advice and turns to sorcery as the only means to unravel the mystery of his parentage; he too learns how to summon demons, and with the help of these free beings he defeats the sorcerer and becomes reconciled with the demon who is his "father". It is a good tale written in pellucid style, as is its sequel *The Crystal Palace* (1988). Her other ongoing sequence, about a teleporting minstrel called Alaric, currently consists of *Born to Exile* (1978) and *In The Red Lord's Realm* (1989). The final volume, *City in Stone*, is still "forthcoming".

KATE ELLIOTT

American novelist
BORN: 1958

Under her real name, Alis A. Rasmussen, she has written a number of fantasies such as *The Labyrinth Gate* (1988) and the "Highroad" trilogy – *A Passage of Stars*, *Revolution's Shore* and *The Price of Ransom* (all 1990) – but latterly she has concentrated on her work as Kate Elliott, which includes one third of the massive novel *The Golden Key* (with Melanie Rawn and Jennifer Roberson, 1996) and the "Crown of Stars" pentalogy, currently consisting of *King's Dragon* (1997), *Prince of Dogs* (1998), *The Burning Stone* (1999), and *Child of Flames* (2000).

MICHAEL ENDE

German novelist
BORN: 1929 DIED: 1995

An important writer of children's fantasies, Ende is best known in translation for *Momo* (1973) and *The Neverending Story* (1979). *Momo* – also translated as *The Grey Gentlemen* – stars Momo, a ragamuffin girl who finds herself the last innocent in a world poisoned by parasitic Grey Gentlemen. These helpfully "organize" their victims' lives for adult, efficient use of time, but secretly steal the time for themselves. Only Momo's persistence can heal the world. The famous *The Neverending Story* is a fantasy about fantasy. In the

THE MOST CELEBRATED RECENT EXAMPLE OF GERMAN FANTASY, ENDE'S NOVEL TOOK THE WORLD BY STORM

eponymous book, young Bastian reads that the land of Fantastica is dying, its creative wellsprings drying up, its chosen hero unable to save the child Empress from encroaching "Nothing". Only Bastian can help, by entering the book and – in a symbolic act of creation – giving the Empress a new name. Fantastica is remade. But after joyously re-inventing Fantastica's primal forest and desert, Bastian steadily succumbs to his shortcomings of wisdom and imagination. Making himself an invincible warrior somehow fails to satisfy. His own inner wells come close to exhaustion. Eventually, humbled, he undergoes a resonant rite of passage into maturity. The 1984 movie adaptation unsatisfyingly omits this second half of the plot.

STEVEN ERIKSON

Canadian/British Novelist
Born: 1959

Toronto-born Erikson, now resident in the UK, trained as an anthropologist. His first publications, the story collections *A Ruin of Feathers* (1991) and *Revolvo and Other Canadian Tales* (1998) were under the name of Steve Rune Lundin. Erikson then switched to his birth name when he moved into sprawling commercial fantasy territory with his "Tales of the Malazan Empire" sequence, which started with *Gardens of the Moon* (1999) and *Deadhouse Gates* (2000).

DAVID FARLAND

American novelist
BORN: 1957

This apparently new author's five-book sequence"The Runelords", of which the first three books are *The Sum of All Men* (1998), *Brotherhood of the Wolf* (1999) and *Wizardborn* (2002), received general praise for its interesting system of magic and seemed to presage a commercially-successful career. It turned out that "David Farland" is a pseudonym for science-fiction novelist Dave Wolverton, who has been around for some years.

RAYMOND E. FEIST

American novelist
BORN: 1945

Raymond Feist's early novels drew on his experience of designing fantasy role-playing games. *Magician* (1982; revised 1992) cleverly deploys the standardized routines of game-scenarios in following the careers of two friends: Pug, whose latent talents emerge and flourish while he is schooled as a magician, and Tomas, whose ambitions as a warrior are much enhanced by his acquisition of a magical suit of armour from a friendly dragon. The "rifts" which open up between the two worlds of Midkemia and Kelewan are deployed as if by a games-master to move the plot through its various phases. As *Magician* progresses, however, it gradually moves away from game-like concerns as its author becomes more interested in the moral dilemmas of his characters, particularly those which arise from the question of the political legitimacy of monarchy.

Such issues were to become significant preoccupations of Magician's immediate "Riftwar" sequels, *Silverthorn* (1985) and *A Darkness at Sethanon* (1986) – which are two halves of a single story – and central concerns of *Prince of the Blood* (1989) and *The King's Buccaneer* (1992), whose plots push magic to the sidelines of swashbuckling tales of princely adventure reminiscent of classic "boys' books".

A game-like intricacy was retained in a series of Kelewan-set novels which Feist wrote with Janny Wurts, *Daughter of the Empire*

(1987), *Servant of the Empire* (1990) and *Mistress of the Empire* (1992), in which the use of a female protagonist requires more emphasis on diplomacy than derring-do. Feist also branched out into "dark fantasy", in *Faerie Tale* (1988), which follows the fortunes of a contemporary American family whose newly acquired house is subject to threatening intrusions from the Land of Faerie, into which the eight-year-old hero must eventually go in order to rescue his twin. Feist restored the epic sweep of potentially apocalyptic threats when he continued his Midkemian series with the "Serpent Wars" tetralogy, comprising *Shadow of a Dark Queen* (1994), *Rise of a Merchant Prince* (1996), *Rage of a Demon King* (1997) and *Shards of a Broken Crown* (1998). This sequence, unusually, builds towards a third-volume climax – in which the demon-led forces of the Emerald Queen invade the Kingdom, reuniting many characters from the earlier Midkemian books in its desperate defence – and then continues, displaying the aftermath of the great battle and the efforts required to mop up its leftovers.

The open-ended "Legends of the Riftwar" series of stand-alone novels set during the first Riftwar are all written by other authors "in collaboration with" Feist. In the meantime, he has been working on a lacklustre sequence of novelisations based on the "Krondor" computer games – *Krondor: The Betrayal* (1998), *Krondor: The Assassins* (1999), *Krondor: Tear of the Gods* (2000), *Krondor: The Crawler* (2002) and *Krondor: The Dark Mage*, forthcoming. A new sequence, "The Conclave of Shadows", which opened with *Talon of the Silverhawk* (2002), promised a return to epic form with the start of the third Riftwar.

John M. Ford

American novelist

BORN: 1957

Ford wrote the World Fantasy Award-winning *The Dragon Waiting: A Masque of History* (1983), set in an alternate 15th century in which Byzantium is the dominant power. Since then, alas, he has written little fantasy.

Alan Dean Foster

American novelist

BORN: 1946

Foster has been productive and popular, both in sf and in fantasy. His works in the latter mode include the "Spellsinger" series – *Spellsinger at the Gate* (1983), *The Day of the Dissonance* (1984), *The Moment of the Magician* (1984), *The Paths of the Perambulator* (1985), *The Time of the Transference* (1986), *Son of Spellsinger* (1993) and *Chorus Skating* (1994) – plus a few movie novelizations such as *Clash of the Titans* (1981) and *Krull* (1983), and the fantasy/Western collection *Mad Amos* (1996) which gathers together 10 tall tales of the frontier.

Esther M. Friesner

American novelist

BORN: 1951

Esther Friesner's career was launched by a quest fantasy set against a background derived from the Arabian Nights, *Mustapha and His Wise Dog* (1985). Although three more in the series were published – *Spells of Mortal Weaving* (1986), *The Witchwood Cradle* (1987) and *The Water King's Laughter* (1989) – it was allowed to die while she developed a

FRIESNER IS BEST KNOWN FOR FAIRLY ORTHODOX HUMOROUS FANTASIES, BUT THIS ONE IS A DELIGHT FOR SHERLOCKIANS

more extravagant kind of comic fantasy, first in the urban fantasy series *New York by Knight* (1986), *Elf Defence* (1988) and *Sphynxes Wild* (1989) and then in three even wilder trilogies, the first comprising *Here Be Demons* (1988), *Demon Blues* (1989) and *Hooray for Hellywood* (1999), the second *Gnome Man's Land* (1991), *Harpy High* (1991) and *Unicorn U* (1992), and the third *Majyk by Accident* (1993), *Majyk by Hook or Crook* (1994) and *Majyk by Design* (1994). All these series are repetitive; Friesner's better works are those which wring the best out of an idea within a single volume. *Harlot's Ruse* (1986) is half-hearted, but *Druid's Blood* (1988) is a marvellous steampunk-influenced fantasy starring a substitute Sherlock Holmes. *Yesterday We Saw Mermaids* (1991) tells of a 1492 landfall in an alternative America. *The Wishing Season* (1993; rev. 1995) is a juvenile tale featuring an over-generous genie. *The Psalms of Herod* (1995) and *The Sword of Mary* (1996), which are dark fantasies set in a post-holocaust dystopia, constitute a radical new departure. *Child of the Eagle* (1996) is an alternate world historical fantasy in which Caesar survives assassination. The flamboyantly subversive spirit of Friesner's best comedies is echoed by the contributors to her various anthologies, which include *Alien Pregnant by Elvis* (1994; with Martin H. Greenberg), *Blood Muse* (1995; with Greenberg), *Chicks in Chainmail* (1995), *Did You Say Chicks?*, *Chicks 'n Chained Mail* (1999) and *The Chick is in the Mail* (2000).

MAGGIE FUREY

British novelist
BORN: 1955

Aurian (1994), the first volume of Maggie Furey's "Artefacts of Power" sequence, features an eponymous heroine imbued with various magical powers who must learn to actualize, expand and control them. As in many other examples of feminized high fantasy, there is a conflict of interest between magic and sexuality; although she is not required to remain a virgin to develop her powers there are such powerful advantages in continence that Aurian's potentially immortal breed is on the brink of extinction. Her progress, extending through the sequels *Harp of Winds* (1994), *The Sword of Flame* (1995) and *Dhiammara* (1997) and the "Shadow League" series, *The Heart of Myrial* (1999) and *Spirit of the Stone* (2001), is neatly complemented by the author's growing assurance in handling her materials and her increasing skill as a literary craftsman.

NEIL GAIMAN

British comics writer and novelist
BORN: 1960

Although he has worked in numerous media, Gaiman is best known for scripting *The Sandman* (DC Comics, 1989–1996). This ran for 75 issues, and – indicating the writer's unusual degree of creative control – came to a planned, permanent end; the central character is not available for re-use. The original DC Sandman was a gas-masked vigilante who stunned villains with sleeping gas. Gaiman alludes to this cobwebbed figure, but his own Sandman – black-robed, dead white in complexion, with a shock of black hair – is altogether more cosmic. He is Dream, or Morpheus, lord of all dreams and therefore all stories: one of seven "Endless" beings personifying facets of the universe. His siblings are Death (a bubbly, Gothicaly attractive girl), Destiny, Despair, Desire, Delirium, and Destruction. The comics were reissued in graphic-novel format, titled as follows. Dream makes his entrance in *Preludes and Nocturnes* (1991), where his entrapment by black magic and his struggles against Hell and old DC supervillain Dr Destiny are not quite characteristic of the cold, aloof, sometimes strangely driven figure into which he matures. The story arc continues through *The Doll's House* (1990), whose complex action features G.K. Chesterton and reaches a peak of black comedy at a serial killers' convention uncannily like a science fiction event. *Season of Mists* (1992) expands the cosmology as Hell is emptied and Dream given its key – desperately coveted by Norse, Egyptian and Japanese gods, by Order, Chaos and Faerie, and by the exiled demons themselves. *A Game of You* (1993) pays homage to Jonathan Carroll's *Bones of the Moon* with its heroine's private dreamland of oversized talking animals, and to C.S. Lewis's *The Last Battle* when Dream, compelled by an ancient pact, shuts down the land forever. *Brief Lives* (1994) sees him helping sister Delirium hunt their lost brother. They are, literally, seeking Destruction; and Dream steps into a trap he avoided in *The Doll's House*, by spilling Endless family blood. Vengeance follows, deeply rooted in Dream's past acts, even of generosity...*The Kindly Ones* (1996) is titled for the Furies who harry him to an end which perhaps he had planned all along. He is mourned in the coda, *The Wake* (1997). Interspersed stories – some independent, some providing vital background history – are collected in *Dream Country* (1991), *Fables and Reflections* (1993) and *World's End* (1994). The first contains the Shakespearean episode "A Midsummer Night's Dream", a 1991 World Fantasy Award-winner. Death additionally appears in two effective graphic fables, *The High Price of Living* (1994) and *The Time of Your Life* (1997). Both Death and Dream have cameos in *The Books of Magic* (1993), a resonant story about a schoolboy magician's initiation, later continued by other hands.

Gaiman's novels are *Good Omens* (1990), written with Terry Pratchett – a hilarious spoof of the Omen movies – and *Neverwhere* (1996), novelizing his BBC TV series about a half magical otherworld beneath London, *Stardust* (1998), a characteristically quirky look at fairies; and *American Gods* (2001), a mythic urban fantasy of the sort associated with Tim Powers. *Angels and Visitations* (1993) collects some shorter prose work. Neil Gaiman's strength is to weave materials from multiple, often obscure, sources into stories with a mythic freshness.

Craig Shaw Gardner

American novelist
BORN: 1949

For a while, Gardner appeared to be the American equivalent of Terry Pratchett, with several cycles of would-be hilarious fantasy romps in the "Ebenezum" and "Wuntvor" and other series, but his star has faded in the area of broad comedy, and lately he has concentrated on movie novelizations – *Batman* (1989), *Batman Returns* (1992), etc. – and somewhat straighter fantasies such as the trilogy *Raven Walking* (1994; also known as *Dragon Sleeping*), *Dragon Waking* (1995) and *Dragon Burning* (1996).

Alan Garner

British novelist
BORN: 1934

Garner is one of Britain's most renowned writers of children's books. He began with *The Weirdstone of Brisingamen* (1960) and *The Moon of Gomrath* (1963), a pair of splendidly titled fantasies about a young brother and sister who have magical adventures in a legend-haunted district of Cheshire. These were followed by *Elidor* (1965), a tale of the supernatural set in Manchester, *The Owl Service* (1967), another effective blend of mythic fantasy and contemporary realism, set in Wales, and *Red Shift* (1973), a timeslip story involving Roman soldiers. His output since has been slim, much of it consisting of retold folk tales.

David A. Gemmell

British novelist
BORN: 1948

David Gemmell has become one of the most accomplished writers of action-adventure fantasy; his work comes closer than anyone else's to reproducing the fierce narrative drive and resolute masculinity of Robert E. Howard. Most of his work employs one of two imaginary histories. The Drenai series comprises *Legend* (1984; aka *Against the Horde*), *The King Beyond the Gate* (1985), *Waylander* (1986), *Quest for Lost Heroes* (1990), *Waylander II: In the Realm of the Wolf* (1992), the collection *The First Chronicles of Druss the Legend* (1993), *The Legend of Deathwalker* (1996) and *Winter Warriors* (1997); the earlier episodes were assembled in the omnibus *Drenai Tales* (1991). The loosely knit Sipstrassi series includes the post-holocaust Jerusalem Man sequence – *Wolf in Shadow* (1987; aka *The Jerusalem Man*), *The Last Guardian* (1989) and *Bloodstone* (1994); reprinted in *The Complete Chronicles of the Jerusalem Man* (1996) – the quasi-Arthurian "Stones of Power" novels *Ghost King* (1988) and *The Last Sword of Power* (1988), and two distantly related novels set in Ancient Greece, *Lion of Macedon* (1990) and *Dark Prince* (1991). *Ironhand's Daughter* (1995) and *The Hawk Eternal* (1995) launched a new sequence in which the "Hawk Queen" Sugarni passes through a dimensional gateway and encounters the last of the gate-builders; their use of a female hero does not compromise their toughness. Another unrelated sequence in Gemmel's grittily heroic style, the "Rigante" series consisted of *Sword in the Storm* (1998), *Midnight Falcon* (1999), *Ravenheart* (2001) and *Storm Rider* (2002). Gemmell's other works include *Knight of Dark Renown* (1989), *A Dark Moon* (1996) and *Echoes of the Great Song* (1997).

GEMMELL'S HEROIC FANTASIES ARE VIGOROUS, VIRILE AND ACTION-PACKED – BUT ARE BASED ON MORAL AND RELIGIOUS CONVICTIONS

Mary Gentle

British novelist
BORN: 1956

As if to belie her surname, Gentle is a fiercely imaginative writer. Although her debut novel, the children's fantasy *A Hawk in Silver* (1977), was a conventional piece, her later fantasies for adults such as *Rats and Gargoyles* (1990), *The Architecture of Desire* (1991) and the satiric *Grunts!* (1992) – the last is about a platoon of Orcs – are knotty, hard-headed and thoroughly individualistic. Unfortunately, she has published comparatively little in recent years.

Parke Godwin

American novelist
BORN: 1929

Godwin may be American, but he likes to write about Britain. He has produced one of the best Arthurian trilogies – *Firelord* (1980), *Beloved Exile* (1984) and *The Last Rainbow* (1985) – as well as two Robin Hood fantasies – *Sherwood* (1991) and *Robin and the King* (1993) – and a novel based on the Beowulf epic, *The Tower of Beowulf* (1995). He won a World Fantasy Award for his ghost story "The Fire When It Comes" (1981)

Lisa Goldstein

American novelist
BORN: 1953

Goldstein won an American Book Award for her children's fantasy *The Red Magician* (1982). Her next work, *The Dream Years* (1985), was in very different vein, an unusual timeslip romance in which the principal subject-matter – the antics of the members of the Surrealist movement in Paris during the 1920s – makes a welcome change from the more predictable stuff of most fantasies.

The hero, Robert St Onge, is a young acolyte of André Breton and those other poets and artists who believed in putting their lives at the service of the unconscious. Robert leads a Bohemian life, helping the Surrealists arrange their ill-attended readings and exhibitions. He encounters a young woman, and as he follows her through the streets of Paris he passes into another world. He finds himself among rioting students and armoured police, with the scent of revolution in the air: these are *les événements* of 1968, and somehow Robert has travelled over 40 years into the future. Thoroughly bewildered, he soon slips back to his own time; but in the following days he keeps glimpsing the girl and pursues her obsessively, making repeated visits to her frightening but heady future world. Good-humoured and engagingly written, *The Dream Years* is a playful work which deals with serious ideas; and much the same may be said of Goldstein's varied later novels such as the fine *Strange Devices of the Sun and Moon* (1993).

Terry Goodkind

American novelist
BORN: 1948

Terry Goodkind is the latest American writer to hit the best-selling jackpot with a series of quest fantasies set solidly in the post-Tolkienian mould of Terry Brooks and David Eddings. His "Sword of Truth" sequence began with *Wizard's First Rule* (1994) and continued in *Stone of Tears* (1995), *The Blood of the Fold* (1996) and *Temple of the Winds* (1997), *Soul of the Fire* (1999), *Faith of the Fallen* (2000) and *Pillar of Creation* (2001).

The customary formula, in which the young hero whose qualities are latent gathers a team of virtuous allies in order to challenge and eventually confront the spreading influence of a Dark Lord, is given a darker tint in Goodkind's version, not so much by virtue of the increased frequency of horrific incident – although there is no shortage of stomach-churning moments – as by a cold undercurrent of moral scepticism which wonders how much self-sacrifice can and ought to be required of heroes in a good cause. Like many such series – most especially the ones which sell hugely – the later volumes are more fluently composed, but the author's increasing skill has to engage the problem of the endless repetition of similar motifs and devices.

Kenneth Grahame

British novelist
BORN: 1859 DIED: 1932

Grahame's gentle English idyll *The Wind in the Willows* (1908) is one of the masterpieces of animal fantasy, appreciated by adults as much as by children. He is also remembered for his humorous short story "The Reluctant Dragon" (originally published in the collection *Dream Days*, 1898).

Simon R. Green

British novelist
BORN: 1955

Green's most notable fantasies have been *Blue Moon Rising* (1991), its sequel *Blood and Honour* (1992), and the separate *Shadows Fall* (1994). He has written numerous books besides these, many of them sf/fantasy crossovers.

A TURN-OF-THE-CENTURY ILLUSTRATION TO ONE OF THE BROTHERS GRIMM'S TALES

The Brothers Grimm

German folklorists
BORN: 1785 (Jacob), 1786 (Wilhelm) DIED: 1863 (Jacob), 1859 (Wilhelm)

Jacob Grimm was a pioneer in the scientific study of the German language, and it was from his enquiries into the history of that language that his interest in the folklore emerged. Whereas J.R.R. Tolkien found that the Anglo-Saxon heritage of Britain had been confused and all but eclipsed by the Gallic importations of the Norman conquest, and was therefore inspired to invent a mythology, Grimm found what seemed to be an almost-intact tradition whose breadth and texture could still be recovered and preserved. The more portentous elements – eventually summarized in his *Deutsche Mythologie* (1835) – were easily available, but the lightweight folklore of the common people seemed in danger of extinction; he enlisted his brother's support in collecting the "children's and household tales" which comprised the three-volume *Kinder-und Hausmärchen* of 1812–13. Later scholars – especially Jack Zipes, who prepared the definitive collection of 241 items, *Grimm's Fairy Tales* (1987) – have criticized the Grimm brothers' methods (they relied almost entirely on middle class informants and Wilhelm was particularly prone to rewriting tales in order to emphasize their moralizing and remove "offensive" material) but their versions of "Hansel and Gretel", "Snow White", "Rumpelstiltskin" and "Rapunzel" have become the bedrock on which thousands of modern revisions and adaptations to other media have been founded.

Stephan Grundy

American novelist
BORN: 1967

Swedish-resident Grundy strives to be as "Germanic" as the Grimms. His two big novels to date, *Rhinegold* (1994), *Attila's Treasure* (1996) and *Gilgamesh* (2000) are firmly based in Teutonic mythology, a subject the author studied at Cambridge University (his 1995 PhD thesis title was "The Cult of Odinn: God of Death?"). In a publicity handout which accompanied his second novel, he listed his hobbies as "brewing, classical singing, metalworking, woodcarving, and hunting".

H. Rider Haggard

British novelist
BORN: 1856 DIED: 1925

Henry Rider Haggard's hastily-written boys' book *King Solomon's Mines* (1885) provided his first commercial success and he was quick to follow up with the more extravagant and far more influential *She* (1886). *She* established a pattern for many of his later fantasies, introducing the theme of questing serial reincarnation which sustained an entire subgenre of imitative "karmic romance" and confronting its hero with a no-win choice between a sexually-arousing but dangerous woman and an insipid but serviceable one. This pattern was repeated in three sequels, *Ayesha* (1905), *She and Allan* (1921) and *Wisdom's Daughter* (1923) and several variants, most interestingly *The World's Desire* (1890, with Andrew Lang), whose hero is Odysseus, the pastiche Icelandic saga *Eric Brighteyes* (1891) and *The Wanderer's Necklace* (1914). Haggard became increasingly interested in "esoteric wisdom", but his credulous karmic romances – including *Love Eternal* (1918), *The Ancient Allan* (1920) and *Allan and the Ice-Gods* (1927) – are less exciting than their predecessors. His occult interests emphasized the fantastic elements with which most of his novels were framed – especially his lost-race stories, the most *outré* of which is *The Ghost Kings* (1908). The most fantastic of his other works are the tale of ancient Egyptian magic *Morning Star* (1910), the anti-hunting parable *The Mahatma and the Hare* (1911), *Red Eve* (1911) and the items collected in *Smith and the Pharaohs and Other Tales* (1920), whose title novella first appeared in 1912.

HAMBLY ALSO TURNED HER HAND TO A HUMOROUS HOLLYWOOD FANTASY, ABOUT A BEAUTIFUL SILENT-MOVIE STAR

BARBARA HAMBLY

American novelist
BORN: 1951

Hambly showed instant promise with her debut "Darwath" trilogy, where Lovecraftian horrors threaten a Tolkienian secondary world: *The Time of the Dark* (1982), *The Walls of Air* (1982) and *The Armies of Daylight* (1983).

Her best work includes the "dirty realist" sequence starring tough mercenary Sun Wolf. In *The Ladies of Mandrigyn* (1984) he's blackmailed into helping free a country from an unpleasant wizard who turns dissenters into eyeless, mindless cannibal horrors; victory comes at painful cost. Follow-ups are *The Witches of Wenshar* (1987), a murder mystery set at a school of magic, and the grimily atmospheric *The Dark Hand of Magic* (1990), where Sun Wolf's mercenaries are afflicted during routine siege-work by an elusive, all-pervading curse.

Dragonsbane (1986), *Dragonshadow* (1999), *The Knight of the Demon Queen* (2000) and *Dragonstar* (2001) seriocomically re-examine the roles of dragons and dragonslayers (who can win only by cheating), and, through transformation, whether it's better to be human or dragon. Opening the "Antryg Windrose" sequence, *The Dark Tower* (1986), *The Silicon Mage* (1988) and *Dog Wizard* (1993) feature clever intermixing of Earth science – including computers – with otherworld magic. In "Sun-Cross", comprising *The Rainbow Abyss* (1991) and *The Magicians of Night* (1992), wizards answering a call for magical aid chillingly find the callers are World War II Nazi occultists. *Bride of the Rat God* (1995) is an entertaining fantasy of Chinese magic and mayhem set in 1920s Hollywood. Hambly is pleasingly versatile.

ANDREW HARMAN

British novelist
BORN: 1964

Harman is one of the funny guys who have come to prominence in the wake of Terry Pratchett's astounding British success. His many farcical fantasies, which have been popular even if they are not a patch on the master's, include *The Sorcerer's Appendix* (1993), *The Frogs of War* (1994), *The Tome Tunnel* (1994), *101 Damnations* (1995), *Fahrenheit 666* (1995), *The Scrying Game* (1996), *The Deity Dozen* (1996) and *A Midsummer Night's Gene* (1997), *It Came From On High* (1998) and *The Suburban Salamander Incident* (2000).

Deborah Turner Harris

American novelist
BORN: 1951

Harris's fantasy output, which began with the "Mages of Garillon" series – *The Burning Stone* (1986), *The Gauntlet of Malice* (1987) and *Spiral of Fire* (1989) – includes the "Caledon Saga" – *Caledon of the Mists* (1994), *The Queen of Ashes* (1995) and *The City of Exile* (1995) – which are works of Americanized Scotticism, featuring characters with names like Jamie, Duncan and Ewart who converse "dourly" in the Highland mists.

M. John Harrison

British novelist
BORN: 1945

The unconventional Mike Harrison is a remarkable stylist whose main contribution to fantasy has been the "Viriconium" sequence of novels – one part Mervyn Peake, another part Jack Vance, and a third part the product of the author's own unique sensibility. *The Pastel City* (1971), a Sword & Sorcery adventure, is a colourful exercise in the packing-in of action. *A Storm of Wings* (1980) is a lush and involuted fantasy of far-future decadence. The third book, *In Viriconium* (1982), is slimmer, harder and sparer than the preceding two, and not futuristic in the least: here Viriconium, although a city in some alternative dimension, has all the grittiness of a present-day London or Manchester. Around his comical characters and their decaying world Harrison spins an amazing web of poetry. Later, non-Viriconium books such as *The Course of the Heart* (1992) and *Signs of Life* (1997), *Travel Arrangements* (2000) and *The Kephahuchi Discontinuity* (2002) are equally brilliant but still more demanding – "literary fantasies" of a high order.

Paul Hazel

American novelist
BORN: 1944

Hazel, a subtle writer, is known for his excellent "Finnbranch" trilogy – *Yearwood* (1980), *Undersea* (1982) and *Winterking* (1985) – plus a later singleton, *The Wealdwife's Tale* (1993). Unlike many fantasy novelists who have been too prolific for their own (and the reader's) good, he has not written enough.

James Hilton

British novelist
BORN: 1900 DIED: 1954

Hilton, who wrote all manner of things and ended up as a Hollywood screenwriter, is remembered for one well-loved fantasy, *Lost Horizon* (1933), the tale of a hidden valley in Asia where are to be found the secrets of immortality and peace of mind.

Robin Hobb

American novelist
BORN: 1952

Pseudonym of Megan Lindholm, who previously wrote several fantasies as Lindholm – notably the charming *Wizard of the Pigeons* (1986), in which magical talents are hidden among the street people of modern Seattle. Hobb first emerged with the bulky "Farseer" trilogy of intensely realized otherworld fantasies: *Assassin's Apprentice* (1995), *Royal Assassin* (1996) and *Assassin's Quest* (1997).

The competent, flawed hero Fitz – a continual victim of one cruel betrayal after another, all through the sequence – is a bastard sprig of royalty in an elaborately feudal world, and is trained in the twin trades of diplomacy and assassination. His land suffers from "Red Ship Raiders" who strip their victims of humanity and turn them loose as soulless predators. Defences include the prized Skill of farseeing – from which Fitz is excluded by jealous seers – and the forbidden Wit allowing mental contact with animals. Against all the rules, Fitz mindbonds with a young wolf...

After many plot convolutions and cruel betrayals, a legendary counterweapon against the Red Ships is launched – a weapon so devastating that the Raiders' terrible actions are almost justified as revenge for its past use. A grim, unsatisfying conclusion. A follow-up sequence, "Farseer: The Tawny Man", set ten years on, began with *Fool's Errand* (2001).

Ship of Magic (1998), *The Mad Ship* (1999) and *The Ships of Destiny* (2000) formed a separate sequence set in the same world, "The Liveship Traders", involving wooden ships that have literally come alive through magic.

Robert Holdstock

British novelist
BORN: 1948

Holdstock began his career as a science-fiction writer and dabbled in horror before obtaining a crucial artistic and commercial breakthrough with *Mythago Wood* (1984) – which won the first of his two World Fantasy Awards – and its sequel *Lavondyss* (1988), in which the seemingly-insignificant Ryhope Wood hides a dark and dense abysm of time where the archetypes of British mythology – the "mythagoes" – may still become manifest. Such figures as Arthur and Robin Hood mirror the superficial layers of the native collective unconscious, while the Green Man and the Wild Hunt represent a deeper layer and echoes of the earliest evolution of the human mind are contained in the fugitive manifestations of the Urcusmug. Although *Lavondyss* reaches a conclusion of sorts, Holdstock returned to Ryhope Wood in the title-story of *The Bone Forest* (1991), and then added *The Hollowing* (1993) before turning to the exploration of a similar wood located in Brittany in *Merlin's Wood* (1994). *Gate of Ivory, Gate of Horn* (1997) began a new cycle within the series, offering a version of Ryhope Wood whose fecundity is gaudier and less uniformly ominous and introducing a hero named Christian whose progressive pilgrimage is admirably wide-ranging. Although they are not part of the series, *The Fetch* (1991) and *Ancient Echoes* (1996) are rooted in a similar metaphysics, as is the World Fantasy Award-winning *tour de force* "The Ragthorn" (with Garry Kilworth, 1991). The various fantasy series which Holdstock wrote under house pseudonyms – including Chris Carlsen, Robert Faulcon and Richard Kirk – are shallow hack-work.

Tom Holt

British novelist

BORN: 1961

Generally regarded as Terry Pratchett's closest rival, Holt began his comic fantasies with *Expecting Someone Taller* (1987). This characteristically injects disruptive magic and myth into suburban England, as the Wagnerian Tarnhelm and Ring are inherited by a pleasant wimp who's soon pursued by Wotan, Valkyries, sexy Rhinemaidens, etc.

Who's Afraid of Beowulf? (1988) introduces a preserved longship full of magic-armed Norsemen, and also Holt's frequent motif of daft conspiracy theories. *Flying Dutch* (1991) stars the Flying Dutchman and *Ye Gods!* (1992) an infant suburban Hercules; *Overtime* (1993) sees Richard Lionheart's Blondel seeking him in all the wrong centuries; *Here Comes the Sun* (1993) shows a majestically inefficient cosmos whose Sun must be restarted each morning; *Grailblazers* (1994) spoofs the Grail Knights in modern England; *Faust Among Equals* (1994) features Faust and a comic theme-park Hell; *Odds and Gods* (1995) depicts an old folks' home for superannuated gods; *Djinn Rummy* (1995) explores the djinns-giving-wishes theme; *My Hero* (1996) is a writerly romp where fictions interpenetrate reality; *Paint Your Dragon* (1996) has a rematch between bad St George and the virtuous Dragon; and *Open Sesame* (1997) hilariously revamps Ali Baba in a metafictional tangle of fairy tales. Later books included *Only Human* (1998), *Snow White and the Seven Samurai* (1999), *Wish You Were Here* (2000), *Bitter Lemmings* (2001) and *Goat Song* (2002). Holt always produces good jokes; his narrative coherence varies wildly.

HOLT IS A GREAT SUBVERTER OF THE OLD, OLD STORIES – IN THIS CASE THE ONE ABOUT THE ACCURSED DUTCH SEA-CAPTAIN

Daniel Hood

American novelist

BORN: ?

This writer crosses light wizard'n'dragon fantasy with whodunnit mystery fiction, in his series consisting so far of *Fanuilh* (1994), *Wizard's Heir* (1996), *Beggar's Banquet* (1997), *Scales of Justice* (1998) and *King's Cure* (2000).

William Horwood

American novelist

BORN: 1944

Former journalist Horwood is perhaps the most successful of all those who jumped on the bandwagon set rolling by the success of Richard Adams's *Watership Down*. His best-known animal fantasies have featured moles, and include *Duncton Wood* (1980), *Duncton Quest* (1988), *Duncton Found* (1989), *Duncton Tales* (1991), *Duncton Rising* (1992) and *Duncton Stone* (1993).

Latterly, his work has gone in two slightly different directions, with sequels to Kenneth Grahame's *The Wind in the Willows*, including *The Willows in Winter* (1994), *Toad Triumphant* (1995), *The Willows and Beyond* (1996) and *The Willows at Christmas* (1999), and a new animal-fantasy series centring on wild wolves, which began with *Journeys to the Heartland* (1995) and *The Seekers at Wulfrock* (1997).

ROBERT E. HOWARD

American novelist
BORN: 1906 DIED: 1936

It still comes as a shock to remember that, although Howard and his creation Conan had such a tremendous influence on the future of Sword & Sorcery, the creator himself committed suicide at the age of 30. Short careers can cast long shadows.

Conan the ruthless Cimmerian barbarian was in fact established in a mere 20-odd original stories, most published in *Weird Tales* magazine between 1932 and Howard's death. Their luridly coloured, extremely violent mix of action-adventure and magic achieved rapid popularity, and after World War Two the stories were republished as the solitary novel *Conan the Conqueror* (1950; alias *The Hour of the Dragon*) and the collections *The Sword of Conan* (1952), *King Conan* (1953), *The Coming of Conan* (1953) and *Conan the Barbarian* (1954).

Already other hands were contributing revisions and extra passages of continuity: the next collection *Tales of Conan* (1955) was partly by L. Sprague de Camp. This heralded the later explosion of Conan titles, in which Howard's work was extensively reworked (for example, by deleting the lead characters of abandoned drafts and inserting Conan), retitled and pastiched. De Camp and Lin Carter re-edited the Hyborian Age series and wrote whole new stories into the gaps, to produce a neat chronology which Howard had never envisaged. One critic gloomily predicted its expansion to run as an unbroken narrative from *Conan the Toddler* to *Conan the Octogenarian*.

All 30-odd titles in the even newer Conan sequence that began with *Conan the Defender* (1982) are spinoffs using Howard's character but none of his text. Interestingly, the first seven of these are by Robert Jordan.

Other more or less Conan-like characters from Howard's pen are King Kull the brooding, violent exile from Atlantis, whose stories were collected as *King Kull* (1967); Bran Mak Morn the Celt fighting Rome's inexorable incursions into Britain, his exploits collected in *Bran Mak Morn* (1973); Turlogh Dubh, another Celtic outlaw; and Cormac Mac Art of Ireland, in four stories assembled as *Tigers of the Sea* (1977).

Other heroes have a rather different flavour. Howard's first-created fantastic series character, in 1928, was Solomon Kane. The voyages of this grim 16th-century Puritan, privateer and swordsman led to gory, often magic-ridden adventures all over the world. The definitive Kane collection is *Red Shadows* (1968). A sole novel of science fantasy, *Almuric* (1964 in book form), technomagically sends its hero Esau Cairn to the far-off planet of the title ... where his fights with fist and sword, and eventual winning of a gorgeous alien girl, are uncannily reminiscent of Edgar Rice Burroughs's *Barsoom*. Howard is also credited with inventing the important descriptive phrase "mighty-thewed", so essential to most Sword & Sorcery fantasy. His legacy is very considerable.

L. RON HUBBARD

American novelist
BORN: 1911 DIED: 1986

Hubbard, later famous (or notorious) as the founder of a religion, was one of the quintessential pulpsters – those American writers of the 1930s and 1940s who filled the garish pulp magazines with action fiction in every conceivable genre: crime, westerns, aviation, swashbuckling historicals, science fiction, horror and fantasy. His most notable work was in the last-named category, and mainly written for *Unknown* magazine. In book form, the best stories are to be found in *Slaves of Sleep* (1948) and *Fear and Typewriter in the Sky* (1951).

BARRY HUGHART

American novelist
BORN: 1934

Hughart is the American equivalent of Ernest Bramah – that is, another master of "Chinoiserie". His never-never China may be encountered in the humorous trilogy *Bridge of Birds* (1984), *The Story of the Stone* (1988) and *Eight Skilled Gentlemen* (1991).

BRIAN JACQUES

British novelist
BORN: 1939

Liverpudlian Jacques has become a big name in America, where his children's animal-fantasies in the "Redwall" series are marketed successfully for adults. The series consists of *Redwall* (1986), *Mossflower* (1988), *Mattimeo* (1989), *Mariel of Redwall* (1991), *Salamandastron* (1992), *Martin the Warrior* (1993), *The Bellmaker* (1994), *Outcast of Redwall* (1995), *Pearls of Lutra* (1996), *The Long Patrol* (1997), *Marlfox* (1998), *The Legend of Luke* (1999), *Lord Brocktree* (2000), *The Taggerung* (2001), *Triss* (2002) and *Loamhedge* (2003). The chief characters are mice.

Diana Wynne Jones

British novelist
BORN: 1934

Arguably the world's best writer of children's fantasy, especially in humorous vein; Jones has also published "adult" fantasies. Adults had been reading her all along.

This versatile, inventive author began to hit her stride with tales of magic afflicting realistic, semi-comically dysfunctional families. The difficulties of a merged family with many stepchildren are catalysed by alchemical chemistry sets in *The Ogre Downstairs* (1974). In *Eight Days of Luke* (1975), the young hero's position in a child-hating household is the background to complications with Loki and pursuing Norse gods.

The "Dalemark" series of secondary-world fantasies begins with *Cart and Cwidder* (1975) and includes the very remarkable *The Spellcoats* (1979), which builds to great intensity as its children emerge as avatars of the land's gods, their father being the great River who awaits cataclysmic release from bondage.

Particularly popular is the light-hearted "Chrestomanci" sequence, named for the enchanter and civil servant who polices misuse of magic in various parallel Earths. *Charmed Life* (1977) and *The Lives of Christopher Chant* (1988) are series highlights. More manically, the "Howl" fantasies offer copious, exuberant enchantments in a new otherworld: *Howl's Moving Castle* (1986) and the Arabian-nights romp *Castle in the Air* (1990). *Archer's Goon* (1984) is science fantasy of high, indescribable silliness.

Darker novels include the doom-laden *The Time of the Ghost* (1981), *The Homeward Bounders* (1981) with its realization of paranoid fears that we're all pieces on a gigantic gameboard, and a powerfully oblique reworking of the traditional Tam Lin story in *Fire and Hemlock* (1984). Comedy is convoluted with deliriously complex plotting in the distantly Arthurian masquerade *Hexwood* (1993), and the "adult" tale of multi-world magical conflicts intersecting at a British science fiction convention in *Deep Secret* (1997). *The Tough Guide to Fantasyland* (1996), a spoof tourist guide, is full of uncomfortably funny genre insights, and was followed by *The Dark Lord of Derkholm* (1998) and *Year of the Griffin* (2000).

Jenny Jones

British novelist
BORN: 1954

Jenny Jones (not to be confused with J. V. Jones, below) is a talented writer of individualistic fantasies, notably the "Flight Over Fire" trilogy – *Fly by Night* (1990), *The Edge of Vengeance* (1991) and *Lies and Flames* (1992) – and her children's novels *The Webbed Hand* (1994), *Firefly Dreams* (1995) and *House of Birds* (1998). Latterly, with books like *The Blue Manor* (1995), she has been tending more towards "dark fantasy", or horror.

J.V. Jones

British/American novelist
BORN: 1963

Julie Victoria Jones, who hails from Liverpool but now lives in California, achieved rapid success with her trilogy "The Book of Words": *The Baker's Boy* (1995), *A Man Betrayed* (1996) and *Master and Fool* (1996). She is a purveyor of "light" heroic fantasy. Her first book was praised for "a distinctive touch compounded largely of sadism and food". *The Barbed Coil* (1997) was a stand-alone novel, but *A Cavern of Black Ice* (1999) and *A Fortress of Grey Ice* (2002) began a new, unrelated sequence, quite considerably grimmer than the Book of Words.

Robert Jordan

American novelist
BORN: 1948

The chief pseudonym of Jim Rigney – in full, James Oliver Rigney Jr. He first became known in fantasy for a series of not greatly distinguished tie-in novels about Robert E. Howard's Conan: *Conan the Invincible* (1982), *Conan the Defender* (1982), *Conan the Unconquered* (1983), *Conan the Triumphant* (1983), *Conan the Destroyer* (1984), *Conan the Magnificent* (1984) and *Conan the Victorious* (1984).

Jordan achieved worldwide best-sellerdom with the immense "Wheel of Time" epic fantasy sequence. This, so far, runs to nine unusually hefty novels with at least two more to come: *The Eye of the World* (1990), *The Great Hunt* (1990), *The Dragon Reborn* (1991), *The Shadow Rising* (1992), *The Fires of Heaven* (1993), *Lord of Chaos* (1994), *A Crown of Swords* (1996), *The Path of Daggers* (1998) and *Winter's Heart* (2000).

Jordan has learned from Tolkien the narrative value of giving his world – the World of the Wheel – an extensive historical background whose details can be steadily revealed in a kind of counterpoint to the forward thrust of the narrative. The background may not be particularly original (it draws on numerous Creation, Golden Age, and Fall myths including Tolkien's, the sinking of Atlantis and Arthurian legend), and the foreground action is familiar in outline from many generic fantasy quests, but the narrative pace and tension still make for compulsive reading.

The young hero Rand al'Thor and his companions embark on a long quest to put the world to rights and prevent the freeing of the long-imprisoned Dark Lord by his incredibly powerful and moderately numerous minions, the Forsaken. Complications are provided not only by the intricacies of emerging back-story and by subclimaxes in which, repeatedly, further members of the Forsaken are defeated, but by elaborate tangles of magical, continental and world politics.

The Aes Sedai, manipulative female magic-users, are opposed on principle to men using the tainted and madness-inducing sources of male magic – and, indeed, resisting madness becomes one of Rand's many problems. The crusading Children of Light believe that all magic is evil. The kingdoms of the world's main continent are in strife, not to mention suffering problems of succession. Then there are the invaders from the western continent Seanchan... Matters would be complex enough even without the beastly hordes of Trollocs (corresponding to Tolkien's orcs) and other, worse, servants of the Dark.

Jordan's popularity derives from manipulating these and other strands with considerable storytelling power. Some readers admittedly feel that later volumes suffer from slackness and longueurs, but the most recent books have been back on top form. It is difficult to avoid the suspicion that the long-awaited series climax has been delayed by commercial considerations, though – the first book was clearly the first instalment of a trilogy, and even with the best will in the world, Jordan would need to go to eleven or twelve books now to resolve all the various complex plot threads playing through the series.

Nevertheless, the ongoing success of the Wheel of Time sequence is largely deserved. A spinoff "non-fiction" volume, giving much detail about the totally fictional world's convoluted history and present political affairs, is *The World of Robert Jordan's The Wheel of Time* (1997) written by Jordan and Teresa Patterson.

Guy Gavriel Kay

Canadian novelist

BORN: 1954

Guy Gavriel Kay helped Christopher Tolkien prepare *The Silmarillion* for posthumous publication and worked as a TV scriptwriter before embarking on his own epic fantasy trilogy, "The Fionavar Tapestry", comprising *The Summer Tree* (1984), *The Wandering Fire* (1985) and *The Darkest Road* (1986). Although the basic plot, which displaces five college students into a parallel world, is reminiscent of a grown-up version of C.S. Lewis's Narnia stories, the meticulously constructed, quasi-Platonic metaphysical frame that orchestrates the events in the fantasy world is highly idiosyncratic and deftly implemented. Despite working in a genre where originality is as hard to contrive as it is to find, Kay continued to produce works as distinctive in thought as they are in artistry.

Tigana (1990) selects one of the central argumentative threads of the Fionavar Tapestry – the replacement of matrilineal and matriarchal institutions by patriarchal ones – for further development, paying close attention to the costs which accrue when any social system is dismantled and replaced. *A Song for Arbonne* (1992) carries

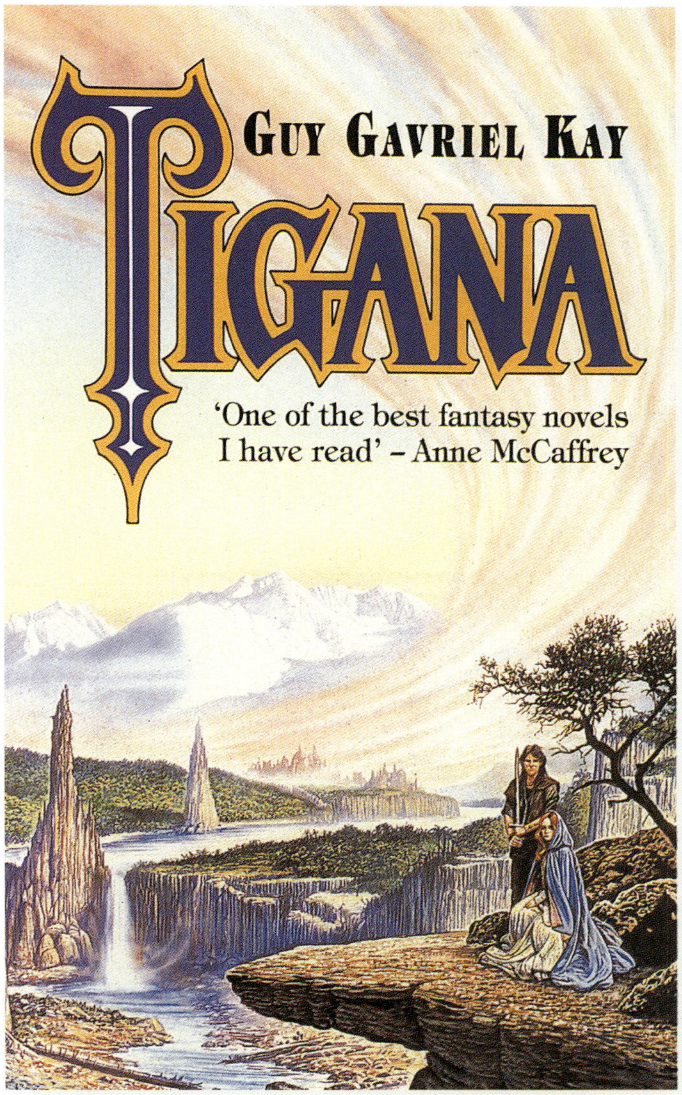

A SERIOUS FANTASY BY AN AUTHOR BETTER-QUALIFIED THAN MOST: HE STUDIED TOLKIEN'S MANUSCRIPTS AT FIRST HAND

the thread theme into yet another arena, emphasizing – in a manner more languid than its predecessors, but not inappropriately so – the role played by troubadours in the making of romantic mythology and the definition of sexual politics. *The Lions of Al-Rassan* (1995) is an elaborate historical fantasy set in a world more closely resembling our own, its settings recalling the milieu of the actual medieval troubadours; the religious conflicts that surrounded them and fuelled their mythologies are carefully duplicated and refined. The later "Sarantine Mosaic" series, so far standing at *Sailing to Sarantium* (1998) and *Lord of Emperors* (2000), is set in an alternate Holy Roman Empire.

Paul Kearney

British novelist
BORN: 1967

This young Irishman's first three novels, *The Way to Babylon* (1992), *A Different Kingdom* (1993) and *Riding the Unicorn* (1994) were fantasies intermixed with an impressive realistic grit. Recently, he has produced a more conventional otherworldly epic in sequence form, "The Monarchies of God", *Hawkwood's Voyage* (1995), *The Heretic Kings* (1996), *The Iron Wars* (1999), *The Second Empire* (2000) and *Ships From The West* (2002).

Patricia Kennealy–Morrison

American novelist
BORN: 1946

This author, who wrote initially as Patricia Kennealy (the "Morrison" was added in belated acknowledgment of her pagan marriage to the late rock star, Jim Morrison), has specialized in Celtic fantasies set on another planet: *The Copper Crown* (1984), *The Throne of Scone* (1986), *The Silver Branch* (1988), *The Hawk's Grey Feather* (1990) and *The Oak Above the Kings* (1994), *The Hedge of Mist* (1996), *Blackmantle* (1997) and *The Deer's Cry* (1999). More are promised, although evidently she is not a speedy writer.

Katharine Kerr

American novelist
BORN: 1944

The apparatus of Celtic myth and legend was quickly established as a favourite source of motifs for American fantasy writers and Katharine Kerr must have been very conscious of the fact that she was following in the footsteps of her near-namesake Katherine Kurtz when she began to develop her pseudo-Celtic kingdom of Deverry in *Daggerspell* (1986, revised 1993) and *Darkspell* (1987, revised 1994). Deverry is, however – and was doubtless carefully planned to be – very different from the quasi-medieval world of the Deryni, being far more liberally equipped with such Tolkienesque subspecies as the "Wildfolk" (gnomes), Elcyion Lacar (elves), dwarves and dragons. The extensive historical background of the Deverry series was further extended in *The Bristling Wood* (1989; aka *Dawnspell*) and *The Dragon Revenant* (1990; aka *Dragonspell*), intriguingly recomplicated by processes of reincarnation that link characters living in different centuries. In the great tradition of karmic romance launched by H. Rider Haggard and Edwin Lester Arnold, Kerr's secondary male lead Nevyn spends his exceedingly long life awaiting the rather frustrating returns of his one true love. The female lead, Jill, rejoices in her own mild temperament while relishing the fact that she was once the berserker warrior-princess Gweniver.

The ever-expanding time-scale of the next four volumes in the series, *A Time of Exile* (1991), *A Time of Omens* (1992), *A Time of War* (1993; aka *Days of Blood and Fire*) and *A Time of Justice* (1994; aka *Days of Air and Darkness*), allowed ample opportunity for Kerr to develop the key themes of her imaginary history: *dweomer* (innate magical power) and *wyrd* (fate), whose interplay complicates the karmic sequences linking the various incarnations of the central characters. This unusual emphasis distinguishes her work not merely from Kurtz and other practitioners of Celtic fantasy but also from other workers within the Tolkienesque tradition. A further Deverry series – the "Dragon Mage" sequence – was launched by *The Red Wyvern* (1997) and continued in *The Black Raven* (1998), *The Fire Dragon* (2000), *The Gold Falcon* (2002) and *The Black Shore* (expected 2004). The theme anthology *Enchanted Forests* (1995), edited by Kerr and Martin H. Greenberg, was followed by *The Shimmering Door* (1996; aka *Sorceries*), about the many kinds of magical practitioners.

J. Gregory Keyes

American novelist
BORN: 1963

Newcomer Keyes made a more-than-adequate splash with his "Chosen of the Changeling" diptych, *The Waterborn* (1996) and *The Blackgod* (1997), big commercial fantasies that seemed to do well. In his latest sequence, "The Age of Unreason", *Newton's Cannon* (1998), *A Calculus of Angels* (1999), *Empire of Unreason* (2000) and *The Shadows of God* (2001), he creates an intriguing alternate 18th century, where Sir Isaac Newton and Benjamin Franklin become involved with alchemical magic.

Garry Kilworth

British novelist
BORN: 1941

After long service in the RAF Garry Kilworth launched his writing career by winning a *Sunday Times* science-fiction competition; he followed up with several sf novels before branching out in several other directions. His principal fantasy productions are a series of earnest animal fantasies: *Hunter's Moon* (1989; aka *The Foxes of First Dark*), *Midnight's Sun: A Story of Wolves* (1990), *Frost Dancers: A Story of Hares* (1992) and *House of Tribes* (1995), whose protagonists are mice. The "Welkin Weasels" trilogy of *Thunder Oak* (1997), *Castle Storm* (1998) and *Windjammer Run* (1999) were for younger readers; his other, usually more darkly tinted, fantasies for teenagers include *The Wizard of Woodworld* (1987), *The Rain Ghost* (1989), the collection *Dark Hills, Hollow Clocks* (1990), *The Drowners* (1991), *Billy Pink's Private Detective Agency* (1993) – whose hero is a will-o'-the-wisp – and the timeslip romance *The Phantom Piper* (1994). In *A Midsummer's Nightmare* (1996) the faerie court of Oberon and Titania moves from Sherwood to the New Forest in the company of New Age travellers. The "Navigator Kings" sequence launched by *The Roof of Voyaging* (1996), *The Princely Flower* (1997) and *Land-of-Mists* (1998) is based in Polynesian myth. Kilworth's finely crafted short fantasies are very various; the best of them include the World Fantasy Award-winning "The Ragthorn" (with Robert Holdstock, 1991) and the bizarre title story of *Hogfoot Right and Bird-Hands* (1993).

Charles Kingsley

British novelist
BORN: 1819 DIED: 1875

Kingsley's place among the most influential 19th-century fantasists was secured by his children's novel *The Water-Babies: A Fairy Tale for a Land-Baby* (1863). Although aimed at kids and possessing many magical moments, it is also a curiously harsh satire – best appreciated in its full version by adults.

Rudyard Kipling

British novelist
BORN: 1865 DIED: 1936

Like many great writers before the hardening of genre boundaries, Kipling (a 1907 Nobel Prize-winner) wrote occasional fantasy without condescension. Examples are scattered through his many short stories, and collected in *Kipling's Fantasy* (1992) edited by John Brunner.

RUDYARD KIPLING – ONE OF THE GREATEST INFLUENCES ON 20TH-CENTURY POPULAR FICTION IN MOST OF ITS FORMS

His most famous fantasies are the intense, unforgettable tales of Mowgli, the Indian boy raised by wolves, in *The Jungle Book* (1894) and *The Second Jungle Book* (1895). These have the power of new-minted myths as Mowgli is claimed by a tiger, defended by a wolf, ransomed by a panther, educated by a bear, and asserts his manhood by mastering the "Red Flower" of fire which all animals fear. The oft-mentioned "Law of the Jungle" is shown not as a licence to shed blood but a grimly necessary social contract.

For younger readers, *Just So Stories* (1902) presents charmingly impossible "origin stories" for the elephant's trunk, camel's hump and other animal features. The framing narrative of *Puck of Pook's Hill* (1906) and *Rewards and Fairies* (1910) has Puck magically introducing children to folk from the past, whose finely told stories – most of them not fantastic – illuminate the history of England. Kipling repeatedly goes out of fashion, only to be rediscovered.

Katherine Kurtz

American novelist
BORN: 1944

Kurtz was one of the leaders of the fantasy revival in America, with her Welsh-flavoured epic *Deryni Rising* (1970) and its various sequels and spinoffs: *Deryni Checkmate* (1972), *High Deryni* (1973), *Camber of Culdi* (1976), *Saint Camber* (1978), *Camber the Heretic*

(1981), *The Bishop's Heir* (1984), *The King's Justice* (1985), *The Quest for Saint Camber* (1986), *The Harrowing of Gwynedd* (1989), *King Javan's Year* (1992) and *The Bastard Prince* (1994). and the "Childe Morgan" trilogy, leading up to events in Deryni Rising, which started with *In The King's Service* (2002). Long resident in Ireland, she has been less productive of late although she has participated in a number of collaborations and "sharecrops" with such writers as her husband, Scott Macmillan, and Deborah Turner Harris.

ELLEN KUSHNER

American novelist
BORN: 1955

"Fantasy of Manners" is a phrase that was coined to describe the none-too-prolific but talented Kushner's novels such as *Swordspoint* (1987) and *Thomas the Rhymer* (1990). The latter, based on an old ballad, was a co-winner of the World Fantasy Award.

HENRY KUTTNER

American novelist
BORN: 1915 DIED: 1958

A master pulpster, like Robert E. Howard and L. Ron Hubbard, Kuttner wrote copiously and widely before his premature death. Although he contributed Sword & Sorcery stories to *Weird Tales* in the 1930s, his works of most enduring fantasy interest are the highly coloured A. Merritt-like adventures which he wrote mainly in collaboration with his wife, C.L. Moore, during the 1940s (some of these originally appeared as by "Lewis Padgett"; some have been republished under Kuttner's name alone; exact attributions of authorship are tricky, and the dates given here are for first book publication): *Well of the Worlds* (1953), *Beyond Earth's Gates* (1954), *Valley of the Flame* (1964), *The Dark World* (1965) and *The Mask of Circe* (1971).

MERCEDES LACKEY

American novelist
BORN: 1950

The central thread in the work of the amazingly prolific Mercedes Lackey is a long series of novels set in the world of Valdemar, including several distinct trilogies: *Arrows of the Queen* (1987), *Arrow's Flight* (1987) and *Arrow's Fall* (1988); *Magic's Pawn* (1989), *Magic's Promise* (1990) and *Magic's Price* (1990); *Winds of Fate* (1991), *Winds of Change* (1992) and *Winds of Fury* (1993); *Storm Warning* (1994), *Storm Rising* (1995) and *Storm Breaking* (1996); and *The Black Gryphon* (1994), *The White Gryphon* (1995) and *The Silver Gryphon* (1996), written in collaboration with her husband Larry Dixon. Other Valdemar-set books are *The Oathbound* (1988) and its sequel Oathbreakers (1989), and the anthology *Swords of Ice and Other Tales of Valdemar* (1996).

The opening-up of the setting in the last-named volume reflects a trend by which Lackey has involved herself in numerous collaborative and shared-world endeavours, making her bibliography inordinately various and complex. The two novels combined as *Bedlam's Bard* (1992) were co-credited to Ellen Guon, while novels featuring the elvish South Eastern Road Racing Association are variously co-credited to Dixon, Mark Shepherd and Holly Lisle. She wrote the first "Bardic Voices" trilogy – *The Lark and the Wren* (1992), *The Robin and the Kestrel* (1993) and *The Eagle and the Nightingale* (1995) – and the associated *Four and Twenty Blackbirds* (1997) solo, but *A Cast of Corbies* was co-credited to Josepha Sherman, with whom she co-edited the anthology *Lammas Night*. Her other work with Dixon includes the trilogy *Owlflight* (1997), *Owlsight* (1998) and *Owlknight* (1999) and she has also contributed to collaborative projects with Marion Zimmer Bradley, C.J. Cherryh, Andre Norton, Piers Anthony and Anne McCaffrey.

Although she has an inevitable tendency to over-use her templates she has written some idiosyncratically interesting books, notably *Sacred Ground* (1994), the best of several occult detective stories; *The Fire Rose* (1995), a Gothic romance akin to "Beauty and the Beast", set in San Francisco in 1905; and *Firebird* (1996), based on the Russian fairy tale which inspired Stravinsky's ballet.

ANDREW LANG

British novelist and editor
BORN: 1844 DIED: 1912

Although he wrote some fantasy novels such as *The Gold of Fairnilee* (1888) and *The World's Desire* (1890), the latter a notable collaboration with Rider Haggard, Lang's principal importance to the genre resides in his extended editorship of a well-loved series of fairy-tale anthologies, beginning with *The Blue Fairy Book* (1889) and ending with *The Lilac Fairy Book* (1910). His wife, Mrs Leonora Lang, helped with these.

STEPHEN LAWHEAD

American/British novelist
BORN: 1950

Lawhead, who lives in Oxford, England, is perhaps the best-known of the current crop of committedly Christian fantasists. His main work to date has consisted of the "Dragon King" trilogy – *In the Hall of the Dragon King* (1982), *The Warlords of Nin* (1983) and *The Sword and the Flame* (1984); the "Pendragon Cycle" of Arthurian tales – *Taliesin* (1987), *Merlin* (1988), *Arthur* (1989), *Pendragon* (1994), *Grail* (1997) and *Avalon: the Return of King Arthur* (1998); the "Song of Albion" trilogy – *The Paradise War* (1991), *The Silver Hand* (1992) and *The Endless Knot* (1993); the "Celtic Crusaders" series – *The Iron Lance* (1998), *The Black Rood* (1999) and *The Mystic Rose* (2001); and a large, impressively researched singleton about the travels of a medieval monk, *Byzantium* (1996).

He has managed to combine his evangelical purpose with genuine popularity.

Tanith Lee

British novelist
BORN: 1947

Tanith Lee launched her career with the children's fantasy *The Dragon Hoard* (1971); her subsequent work for younger readers includes *Companions on the Road* (1975), *The Winter Players* (1976), *The Castle of Dark* (1978) and its sequel *Prince on a White Horse* (1982), and the trilogy comprising *Black Unicorn* (1991), *Gold Unicorn* (1994) and *Red Unicorn* (1997). Her first adult novel was the stirring and breezily erotic heroic fantasy *The Birthgrave* (1975), which was supplemented by the sequels *Vazkor, Son of Vazkor* (1978; aka *Shadowfire*) and *Quest for the White Witch* (1978). A similar trilogy comprises *The Storm Lord* (1976), *Anackire* (1983) and *The White Serpent* (1988). A more adventurous setting and a more varied cast were provided for the "Flat Earth" series comprising *Night's Master* (1978), *Death's Master* (1979), *Delusion's Master* (1981), *Delirium's Mistress* (1986) and *Night's Sorceries* (1987). Alongside these two series she wrote Volkhavaar (1977) and *Day by Night* (1980) and branched out into science fiction and horror; much of her subsequent work is on the fantasy/horror borderline, often involving unorthodox vampires or – as in the intriguing *Lycanthia* (1981) – werewolves. The eroticism of Lee's work became more heated and more stylized in an episodic series set in the Paris-inspired city of *Paradys*, comprising *The Book of the Damned* (1988), *The Book of the Beast* (1988), *The Book of the Dead* (1991) and *The Book of the Mad* (1993). The vampire novel *The Blood of Roses* (1990) is her most extravagantly Decadent fantasy. Her reconfigurations of literary texts include the Shakespearean fantasy *Sung in Shadow* (1983) and *Red as Blood; or, Tales from the Sisters Grimmer* (1983). She has made use of Hindu mythology in *Tamastara; or, The Indian Nights* (1984) and *Elephantasm* (1993) and Near-Eastern mythology in *Vivia* (1995). *Reigning Cats and Dogs* (1995) is a dark fantasy set in quasi-Dickensian steampunkish London. Recent work has included the lupine "Claidi" sequence of *Law of the Wolf Tower* (1998), *Wolf Star Rise* (1999) and *Queen of the Wolves* (2000), and the "Secret Isles of Venus" sequence, *Faces Under Water* (1998) and *Saint Fire* (1999). Lee's work is uneven but fitfully brilliant; some of her short fiction – the best of which is collected in *Forests of the Night* (1989), *Women as Demons* (1989), *Nightshades* (1993) and *When the Lights Go Out* (1996) – is very fine.

Ursula Le Guin

American novelist
BORN: 1929

One of those rare authors who are highly regarded not only in genre circles but in the larger world outside. All Le Guin's writing is

LE GUIN'S SOMEWHAT CONTROVERSIAL FOURTH VOLUME IN THE "EARTHSEA" SEQUENCE, A BELATED FOLLOW-UP TO THE CENTURY'S BEST JUVENILE FANTASY TRILOGY

marked by grace of style and clarity of thought. As her literary career progressed, her feminist concerns also became clear.

The early sf *Rocannon's World* (1966) hauntingly reworks a fairy-tale theme in its tragic introductory section – whose heroine travels with goblin folk and returns to find that, as in traditional visits to fairyland, 16 years have passed in a flash. Also nominally sf is *The Lathe of Heaven* (1971), where the gentle hero's dreams come true and, directed by a madly ambitious psychiatrist, repeatedly change the world. With nightmarish brilliance, this cautionary tale shows the dangers of getting what you wished for: each "correction" makes things worse.

Le Guin's most admired fantasy is the Earthsea trilogy, which like all the finest children's fantasies deals with adult concerns of light, dark, life, death, balance and morality: *A Wizard of Earthsea* (1968), *The Tombs of Atuan* (1971) and *The Farthest Shore* (1972). Here a compellingly believable system of magic commands the world through knowledge of its components' true names, their names not in common speech but in the original language of Earthsea's creation. Knowing things' true names – standing for their inner essences – gives wizards power over them, but limits that power because there are so many names to learn. If the trilogy hero Ged wished to lay a spell on the whole ocean of the Earthsea archipelago, he'd need to name every part of it: every body of water, every single bay, cove and strait. And regions of the Outer Sea have names that no wizard has ever learned.

Despite Earthsea's originality, certain tacit assumptions of fairy tales crept in and later irritated Le Guin's feminist sensibilities. Wizards are all male; women can only be witches. "Weak as women's magic" and "Wicked as women's magic" are common Earthsea proverbs. Wizards wield the ultimate powers of the universe, and witches give you warts.

This imbalance is redressed in Book Four, *Tehanu: The Last Book of Earthsea* (1990), which focuses on ordinary, magic-less people – particularly Ged, who sacrificed his power to save the world in *The Farthest Shore*, and Tenar, heroine of *The Tombs of Atuan*, both now twenty years older. Points are quietly made about the different strengths of non-wizards and especially women, in the grimy muddle of ordinary life. Some readers disliked this conscious rejection of the original books' clear, ringing simplicities. In the end, it is a disfigured young girl who proves to have a special relationship with the Old Speech and the dragons whose native tongue it is. Tehanu was later followed by a book of short stories, *Tales From Earthsea* (2001), and *The Other Wind* (2001), which explored the real identity of the Tehanu character, and examined the true nature of Earthsea's dragons.

A solo novel, *The Beginning Place* (1980; in the UK, *Threshold*) takes its adolescent American protagonists to and from a fantasy realm where they undergo significant and haunting rites of passage. Le Guin has also written wisely about fantasy in essay collections like *The Language of the Night* (1979).

Fritz Leiber

American novelist
BORN: 1910 DIED: 1992

Even without his huge and varied contributions to science fiction, some masterful horror stories and that fine novel of modern witchcraft *Conjure Wife* (1943), Leiber would be immortal for creating the heroic-fantasy duo of Fafhrd and the Grey Mouser.

FRITZ LEIBER WAS HONOURED DURING HIS LIFETIME BY *THE MAGAZINE OF FANTASY AND SCIENCE FICTION*

Fafhrd is a tall Northern barbarian, reminiscent of Conan but more introspective. The Mouser is small, tricksy, magniloquent, a little vain and always likely to over-reach. Both are deadly fighters, with vast appetites for high living and good sex, and well-developed senses of humour. Their stories can move seamlessly from wit, whimsy, badinage and even pratfalls to gripping scenes of real danger and horror.

The pair's adventures through the perilous world of Nehwon began in 1939 with the short story "Two Sought Adventure" (later retitled "The Jewels in the Forest") which explored the baffling riddle of "how, when there is no peril whatever inside a vast stone house, nor any sort of jeopardy anywhere outside it, there may still be vast danger". After which the saga of Fafhrd and the Mouser continued for almost half a century.

The resulting "Swords" series – some of which first appeared under other titles – was eventually packaged according to internal chronology: *Swords Against Deviltry* (1970), *Swords Against Death* (1968), *Swords in the Mist* (1970), *Swords Against Wizardry* (1968), *The Swords of Lankhmar* (1968), *Swords & Ice Magic* (1977) and *The Knight and Knave of Swords* (1988).

Of these, *The Swords of Lankhmar* is the only full-length novel and probably the high point of the series – a dashing Sword & Sorcery adventure shot through with mild eroticism and comic perversity. Our heroes are distracted from their task of saving Lankhmar City by unusual female charms: a lady Ghoul with invisible flesh but visible bones, so she seems a walking skeleton; an enigmatic slave who seems to be an air elemental; a lovely rat-human hybrid with improbably numerous nipples; and a bald maidservant whose kinky Overlord requires his female staff to be shaved all over. Only the Gods know how the pair find time to rescue their city at all.

Swords Against Deviltry introduces us to the young Fafhrd and Mouser, and contains the tragicomic story "Ill Met in Lankhmar" (1970) which describes their first, historic encounter – when they discover themselves committing the same robbery – and its dark aftermath. It's one of the rare stories of pure fantasy to have won the sf-biased Hugo and Nebula Awards.

There are many more fine tales of the duo's loves, perils and thefts, sometimes featuring their enigmatic wizard mentors Ningauble of the Seven Eyes and Sheelba the Eyeless. Leiber's own favourite was "Bazaar of the Bizarre" (in *Swords Against Death*), which rings witty changes on the old fantasy theme of the magic shop. New readers should perhaps avoid the late, sombre mini-novel *Rime Isle* (in *Swords & Ice Magic*) and the somewhat weary final volume. Fritz Leiber's masterful control of language – by turns understated, hilariously ironic and verging on poetry – is a continuing joy of the "Swords" series.

C.S. Lewis

British novelist

BORN: 1898 DIED: 1963

C. S. Lewis, a writer for adults and children. His fame seems set to endure

An author whose devout Christianity coloured all his fantastic fiction, Lewis produced several popular and very different fantasies. The "Cosmic Trilogy" or "Ransom Trilogy" begins as enjoyable science fiction in the vein of H.G. Wells – whom it also attacks. *Out Of the Silent Planet* (1938) describes the hero Ransom's kidnapping by amoral Wellsian scientist Weston, whose solar-powered spacecraft takes them on a marvellous journey to Mars. The Martian races include almost-invisible "eldils", which the sequels identify as angels.

In *Perelandra* (1943, alias *Voyage to Venus*) it's not a ship but an angel which carries Ransom to the lovingly described floating islands of Venus, there to witness a replay of the temptation in Eden. Venus's green-skinned Adam is elsewhere: Ransom watches helplessly as Weston – now directly possessed by Satan – tempts the green Eve to break a divine commandment. Since (according to Lewis) a mere woman cannot resist temptation, it's left to Ransom to sock the tempter on the jaw and fight him to the death.

That Hideous Strength (1945) sees Ransom back on Earth, organizing the last spiritual defence of Britain against an almost obscenely unpleasant organization, the NICE, whose facade of scientific research conceals Kafkaesque nightmare and alliance with Earth's dark eldils. Because Weston's space flights have at last broken our fallen planet's quarantine, the eldils of other worlds can now intervene. Ransom calls them to grant apocalyptic powers to the awakened sleeper Merlin, who infiltrates, disrupts and finally destroys the NICE. It's a powerful though very uneven novel.

Lewis's more directly didactic output of popular theology included two effective fantasies. *The Screwtape Letters* (1942) issues moral admonition in inverted form as the demon Screwtape advises his nephew on how best to entrap souls; the infernal "Lowerarchy" provides some amusing bureaucratic satire. In *The Great Divorce* (1946), daytrippers from the dreary suburbs of another Hell are taken to the dazzling foothills of Heaven. Ironically, most are frightened by the conditions of eternal bliss and decide to stick with the devils they know.

For children, the "Narnia" series has been enduringly successful. This consists of *The Lion, the Witch and the Wardrobe* (1950), *Prince Caspian* (1951), *The Voyage of the "Dawn Treader"*, (1952), *The Silver Chair* (1953), *The Horse and His Boy* (1954), *The Magician's Nephew* (1955) and *The Last Battle* (1956) – best read in this order. The earlier books in particular have patches of sloppy writing and inconsistencies, some later glossed over. For example, Book Six "explains" why there's a solitary modern lamp-post in the trackless medieval forest of Book One. Book Two introduces a Bacchanalian revel and (remembering the audience) hastily changes the wine to fresh grape-juice. Lewis's gift for telling phrases and imagery triumphs over these minor drawbacks.

Till We Have Faces (1956), a stand-alone novel using the myth of Cupid and Psyche to examine moral themes of possessiveness and suffocating jealousy, is highly regarded by many readers but lacks the inventive exuberance of Lewis at his best. The Ransom and Narnia books seem likely to be reprinted indefinitely.

David Lindsay

British novelist

BORN: 1878 DIED: 1945

David Lindsay's first novel, *A Voyage to Arcturus* (1920), is a masterpiece of allegorical fantasy which struggles to create and explicate a distinctive theory of universal and personal Creation; it remains unparalleled, and is one of the monuments of the genre. His other fantasies attempt to import an intense visionary element into more conventional plots. *In The Haunted Woman* (1922) a time-tilted stairway offers its users brief liberation from the burden of repression and constraint to which centuries of civilization have subjected human consciousness. *Sphinx* (1923) embeds muted images of a similar ilk in a conventional domestic drama. *The Violet Apple*, in which the taste of fruit from the Edenic Tree of Knowledge spoils two engagements, was not published until 1975. *Devil's Tor* (1932) employs a mystery-story frame to delay the reassembly of a powerful talisman which precipitates the quasi-apocalyptic return of a primal Earth-Mother. He left behind fragments of a more ambitious allegory, The Witch, which offers tantalizing glimpses of a world-view even richer and stranger than that of *A Voyage to Arcturus*; they were appended to the 1975 edition of *The Violet Apple*.

Jane Lindskold

American novelist

BORN: ?

Lindskold, who was Roger Zelazny's companion during his last years, is perhaps best known for completing that major writer's final novel, *Donnerjack* (1997). Prior to that, however, she had published a number of solo fantasies, including such titles as *Brother to Dragons*, *Companion to Owls* (1994) and *When the Gods Are Silent* (1997). She then moved on to the "Athanor" sequence, which started with *Changer* (1998) and *Legends Walking* (1998).

Holly Lisle

American novelist

BORN: 1960

Lisle, although little-known in Britain where she appears not to have been published at all, is one of the more popular of the newer US light-fantasy merchants. Her books include *Fire in the Mist* (1992), *Bones of the Past* (1993), *When the Bough Breaks*, with Mercedes Lackey (1993), *Minerva Wakes* (1994), *Mind of the Magic* (1995); the "Devil's Point" sequence, *Sympathy for the Devil* (1996), *The Devil and Dan Cooley* (1996, with Walter Spence), and *Hell On High* (1997, with Ted Nolan); and the "Secret Texts" sequence, *Diplomacy of Wolves* (1998), *Vengeance of Dragons* (1999) and *Courage of Falcons* (2000).

A.R. Lloyd

British novelist

BORN: 1927

Alan Lloyd, a naturalist, put his knowledge of wild life to good use in the "Kine Saga" animal-fantasy trilogy – *Kine* (1982; later retitled *Marshworld*), *Witchwood* (1989) and *Dragonpond* (1990). The hero is a weasel.

Hugh Lofting

British/American novelist and artist

BORN: 1886 DIED: 1947

Lofting created the memorable figure of Dr Dolittle, who could talk to the animals, in a long series of delightfully self-illustrated children's fantasies which extended from *The Story of Dr Dolittle* (1920) to *Dr Dolittle and the Green Canary* (1950). Although he is usually thought of as quintessentially English, Lofting emigrated to the USA and his books originated there; so the series may be regarded as an example of sentimental American Anglophilia. A non-Dolittle novel of particular interest is the E. Nesbit-like *The Twilight of Magic* (1930).

Anne Logston

American novelist

BORN: ?

Throughout the 1990s, Logston has quietly been building a successful career with romantic adventure fantasies. Her titles include *Shadow* (1991), *Shadow Hunt* (1992), *Shadow Dance* (1992), *Greendaughter* (1993), *Dagger's Edge* (1994), *Dagger's Point* (1995), *Wild Blood* (1996), *Guardian's Key* (1996) and *Firewalk* (1997).

ELIZABETH A. LYNN

American novelist
BORN: 1946

After publishing a science-fiction novel, Elizabeth Lynn produced a notable fantasy trilogy, the "Chronicles of Tornor", comprising *Watchtower* (1979) – which won a World Fantasy Award – *The Dancers of Arun* (1979) and *The Northern Girl* (1980). Unusually, the central characters of *Watchtower* are pacifists by inclination, and will not relinquish that principle even when they recognize that violence is inevitable whenever survival is at stake. The trilogy also makes good use of Lynn's interest in the arts and embodies an exhaustive discourse on gender politics. The final volume is unexpectedly inconclusive and downbeat, foreshadowing the fact that by the time she published her second sf novel and the collection *The Woman Who Loved the Moon and Other Stories* in 1981 Lynn was suffering from a writer's block whose oppression was only slightly alleviated during the next decade, by the juvenile fantasy *The Silver Horse* (1984) and the short stories in *Tales from a Vanished Country* (1990). A new beginning finally became possible with the production of the first volume of a new sequence, *Dragon's Winter* (1998), whose climactic battle is fought to release its imaginary world from magical glaciation.

A NOTABLE FEMINIST FANTASIST, LYNN GAINED THE FIELD'S HIGHEST AWARD FOR THIS EARLY NOVEL

R.A. MACAVOY

American novelist
BORN: 1949

In Roberta MacAvoy's debut novel, *Tea With the Black Dragon* (1983), Mrs Martha Macnamara, a middle-aged musician with an interest in Zen Buddhism, travels to San Francisco, where she meets a most unusual and compelling man. Mr Mayland Long, as he calls himself, is scholarly, golden-eyed, part-Chinese, apparently ageless – and as strong as an ox, though slimly-built. He tells wonderful stories, and hints that he is centuries old. He also claims to have begun life as the Black Dragon, a wise reptilian hoarder of treasure and *objets d'art* who has now given up material things in order to seek Truth. When Martha searches for her missing daughter, Mayland Long offers to help, and there follows a skein of events which encompasses computer fraud, embezzlement of bank funds, kidnapping and perhaps even murder. It is a charming novel – part fantasy, part love story, part whodunnit. Mayland Long and Martha Macnamara are fresh and engaging characters, far from the stereotyped hero and heroine of most genre fantasies, and their story is told with a pleasant lightness of touch. MacAvoy has since become a popular spinner of fantastic tales, her other books including the "Damiano" trilogy (1983–84), set in Renaissance Italy, *The Book of Kells* (1985), set in medieval Ireland, and *Twisting the Rope* (1986), a sequel to *Tea With the Black Dragon*, in which Martha and Mr Long become involved in another Californian caper. A later trilogy of high merit consists of *Lens of the World* (1990), *King of the Dead* (1991) and *Winter of the Wolf* (1993; published in America as *The Belly of the Wolf*).

George MacDonald

British novelist

BORN: 1824 DIED: 1905

Now mainly remembered for children's fantasies and his influence on C.S. Lewis, acknowledged in Lewis's *The Great Divorce*. MacDonald's adult novels are *Phantastes* (1858), a sprawling exploration of a whimsical fairyland or wonderland, and *Lilith* (1895), a more tightly constructed religious allegory featuring Adam, Eve, and Adam's legendary first wife, the evil Lilith. Both, though occasionally confused in their symbolism, are strongly Christian in tone; both display remarkable understanding of the strange almost-logic of dreams.

For children, *At the Back of the North Wind* (1871) gives its young hero edifying adventures with the North Wind – personified as a beautiful woman – and ultimately, in Victorian fashion, an edifying death. *The Princess and the Goblin* (1872) has a moralistic fairytale setting, with resourceful young miner Curdie saving his princess from scheming goblins; the less joyful sequel is *The Princess and Curdie* (1883). MacDonald also wrote several short fairy tales, notably "The Golden Key", "The Giant's Heart" and "The Light Princess".

Ian McDowell

American novelist

BORN: ?

This new writer's Arthurian trilogy, which begins with *Mordred's Curse* (1996) and *Merlin's Gift* (1997), is thoroughly iconoclastic and "revisionist". You can tell that it's revisionist when you notice the four-letter word in the first paragraph of the first book, or when you read the opening sentence of the second volume: "None of this would have happened if Guinevere's little sister hadn't grown a penis".

Patricia A. McKillip

American novelist

BORN: 1948

Patricia McKillip's earliest works were the juvenile fantasies *The House on Parchment Street* (1973) and *The Throne of the Erril of Sherill* (1973; reissued with "The Harrowing of the Dragon of Hairsbreath", 1984). *The Forgotten Beasts of Eld* (1974), a stylish moralistic fantasy about the sentimental education of an enchantress, was marketed as a juvenile but won a World Fantasy Award. The trilogy comprising *The Riddle Master of Hed* (1976), *Heir of Sea and Fire* (1977) and *Harpist in the Wind* (1979) is a thoroughly orthodox but uncommonly well-wrought heroic fantasy. After producing some novels in other genres and the juvenile fantasies *The Moon and the Face* (1985) and *The Changeling Sea* (1988), McKillip returned to adult fantasy with *The Sorceress and the Cygnet* (1991), which light-heartedly compares and contrasts the intellectual odysseys of a stigmatized boy, an assiduous but reckless female scholar and a pragmatic swordswoman in a world whose constellations embody a series of tutelary deities; *The Cygnet and the Firebird* (1993) is a sequel.

Something Rich and Strange (1994), an earnest and exquisitely detailed romance in which a female artist and her half-hearted lover are separately seduced by sea-spirits which turn out to be more powerful and more sinister than they had imagined, confirmed that McKillip had become one of the most accomplished prose stylists working in the genre. *The Book of Atrix Wolfe* (1995) tells the story of a fugitive mage hiding among wolves while searching for the lost daughter of the Queen of the Wood. *A Winter Rose* (1996), set in Victorian England and a parallel Fairyland, is a beautifully written and scrupulously modernized variant of the "Fairy Bridegroom" theme which underlies such classic folk tales as "Beauty and the Beast". Recent works include *Song for the Basilisk* (1998) which

AN ATTRACTIVE EXAMPLE OF THE WORK OF ONE OF AMERICAN FANTASY'S MOST HIGHLY-REGARDED WRITERS

featured an amnesiac hero, *The Tower at Stony Wood* (2000) about a knight's quest for truth in a land that blurs reality and illusion, and *Ombria in Shadow* (2002).

Robin McKinley

American novelist
BORN: 1952

Robin McKinley made her debut with *Beauty* (1978), one of the most interesting of many modern versions of "Beauty and the Beast". Other variants on classic folk tales are included, alongside folk-tale pastiches, in the collection *The Door in the Hedge* (1981). *Deerskin* (1993) is an adult version of a traditional tale which Perrault had had to censor in order to fit it to his own purpose. *Rose Daughter* (1997) is a further version of "Beauty and the Beast" intended for younger readers. *Spindle's End* (2000) was aimed at young adults. Another exercise in folkloristic revisionism is *The Outlaws of Sherwood* (1988), which has no fantasy elements. McKinley's other fantasies are mostly set in the imaginary kingdom of Damar; she won the Newbery Medal for *The Hero and the Crown* (1985), a prequel to the previously issued *The Blue Sword* (1982), and some other tales set in the same locale are included – with other items – in *A Knot in the Grain and Other Stories* (1994). Her anthology *Imaginary Lands* (1985) won a World Fantasy Award. She married fantasy writer Peter Dickinson in 1992.

George R.R. Martin

American novelist
BORN: 1948

Martin is yet another of the legion of established science-fiction writers who have taken a look at modern fantasy and seen a good thing (commercially speaking, at any rate). He entered the big-time stakes with his huge novel *A Game of Thrones: Book One of A Song of Ice and Fire* (1996). It was generally well received, and Martin followed it up with *A Clash of Kings* (1998), *A Storm of Swords* (2000) and *A Feast for Crows* (2002). The series will complete, we are told, with *A Dance for Dragons* and *A Time for Wolves*.

A. Merritt

American novelist
BORN: 1884 DIED: 1943

Abraham Merritt was a journalist, who became editor of William Randolph Hearst's *American Weekly*; the extraordinarily lush fantasies he wrote on the side took escapist exotica to even further extremes than Edgar Rice Burroughs, and Merritt became almost as popular within the arena of the pulp magazines. *The Moon Pool* (1919) is a fix-up of an effective 1918 novelette about an interdimensional doorway and its pedestrian sequel. A further sequel, *The Metal Monster* (1920; book 1946) is borderline science fiction, but employs the same lavishly purple prose style. *The Face in the Abyss* (1931) – which fixes up a fine novella published in 1923 with its belated sequel "The Snake Mother" (1930) but is decidedly inferior to the magazine versions – is also borderline sf. *The Ship of Ishtar* (1924; book 1926) is a spirited heroic fantasy. *Dwellers in the Mirage* (1932) is a marvellously melodramatic lost-race story whose downbeat conclusion was censored, only being replaced in the version reprinted in the pulp magazine *Fantastic Novels* in 1941. Although *Burn, Witch, Burn!* (1933) is a horror story its sequel, *Creep, Shadow!* (1934), has a greater fantasy component. Merritt left a number of fragments, two of which – *The Fox Woman and the Blue Pagoda* (1946) and *The Black Wheel* (1947) – were completed by the artist Hannes Bok; the former can also be found in *The Fox Woman and Other Stories* (1949); some other oddments were reprinted in *A. Merritt: Reflections in the Moon Pool* (1985) edited by Sam Moskowitz.

Haydn Middleton

British novelist
BORN: 1955

Middleton, who began as a mainstream novelist, has written a strikingly dark and anguished Arthurian sequence known as "The Mordred Cycle": *The King's Evil* (1995), *The Queen's Captive* (1996) and *The Knight's Vengeance* (1997).

L.E. Modesitt, Jr.

American novelist
BORN: 1943

Modesitt's popular "Recluce" fantasies have an underlying sf rationale and handle magic in terms of rigorous, physics-like conservation laws. Order and Chaos are precisely balanced: when masters of Order increase their overall power, the power of Chaos also increases ... and vice-versa.

Books to date are *The Magic of Recluce* (1991), *The Towers of the Sunset* (1992), *The Magic Engineer* (1994), *The Order War* (1994), *The Death of Chaos* (1995), the sf prequel *Fall of Angels* (1996), *The Chaos Balance* (1997), *The White Order* (1998), *The Colours of Chaos* (1999), *Magi'i of Cyador* (2000) and *Scion of Cyador* (2001). The harmony between order-magic, meticulous craftsmanship and engineering is attractively presented, the penalties of imbalance – like hysterical blindness when Order is misused – aren't shirked, and there are ingenious conceits like magic-driven military lasers. The series' chief flaws are unnecessary length, repetitiveness, and over-use of silly sound effects: "CRRRRRuuummmmmpppp!!!!"

A newer series opens with *The Soprano Sorceress* (1997) and *The Spellsong War* (1998). *Darksong Rising* (1999), *The Shadow Sorceress* (2001) and *Shadowsinger* (2002) transported a singer and music teacher to a secondary world where her singing ability equates with magical power.

Richard Monaco

American novelist
BORN: 1940

Monaco remains best-known for a dark-toned and ironical sequence of Arthurian novels: *Parsival; or, A Knight's Tale* (1977), *The Grail War* (1979), *The Final Quest* (1980) and *Blood and Dreams* (1985). His other works include two Romans-versus-Druids adventures – *Runes* (1984) and *Broken Stone* (1985) – and *Journey to the Flame* (1985), a pastiche sequel to Rider Haggard's *She*.

Elizabeth Moon

American novelist
BORN: 1945

Moon's service in the US Marine Corps provided some realistic underpinning for her "Deed of Paksenarrion" series of fantasies about a female warrior: *Sheepfarmer's Daughter* (1988), *Divided Allegiance* (1988), *Oath of Gold* (1989), *Surrender None: The Legacy of Gird* (1990) and *Liar's Oath* (1992). She has also written sf, some of it in collaboration with Anne McCaffrey.

Michael Moorcock

British novelist
BORN: 1939

More perhaps than any other fantasy writer, Moorcock is a protean genre-switcher who slips deftly between fantasy, "science fantasy", sf, straight mainstream novels and metafictional play. His bibliography is enormous and complex, fraught with revisions, rearrangements and alternative titles. Ambitious projects jostle with potboilers throughout. The key figure of Moorcockian fantasy is the "Eternal Champion", doomed to fight Chaos through countless reincarnations in every world and plane of the "multiverse". (See also the **Fantastic Worlds** section.) Of these incarnations, the best-known is Prince Elric, who lives in uneasy symbiosis with his demonic sword Stormbringer. Elric made his debut in 1961, and his first stories – slightly rough-hewn, but memorably colourful – were collected in *The Stealer of Souls* (1963). *Stormbringer* (1965) brought his career and his world to a spectacular end; *Elric of Melniboné* (1973) returns to his earlier days and first betrayals. There are many more Elric stories, the most recent being *The Dreamthief's Daughter* (2001).

Corum, the Prince with the Silver Hand (he has lost an eye and hand to the enemy), likewise battles the lords of Chaos, but with weary thoughtfulness rather than Elric's febrile, self-destructive energy. His first and best exploits appear in *The Knight of the Swords* (1971), *The Queen of the Swords* (1971) and *The King of the Swords* (1971). Their dates show Moorcock's headlong writing speed when in potboiler mode.

Elric's and Corum's worlds are purely magical. In Dorian Hawkmoon's, grotesque science crossbreeds with magic to produce horrors like the living, hungry Black Jewel which the technocrats of Granbretan set in the hero's forehead. Hawkmoon's "History of the Runestaff" – the Runestaff being one of rather too many magical plot coupons – comprises *The Jewel in the Skull* (1967), *The Mad God's Amulet* (1968), *The Sword of the Dawn* (1968) and *The Runestaff* (1969).

Further avatars of the Champion include Ereköse, who remembers his other lives and first appeared in *The Eternal Champion* (1970), and von Bek, the 17th-century soldier who seeks the Grail in *The War Hound and the World's Pain* (1981). Related figures who more or less parody the Champion include the ultra-hip Jerry Cornelius in the sf *The Final Programme* (1968) and its oblique sequels, later collected as *The Cornelius Chronicles* (1977); and the ineffectual, ultra-decadent Jherek Carnelian of "The Dancers at the End of Time", a far-future *fin de siècle* science-fantasy sequence beginning with *An Alien Heat* (1972).

Moorcock's finest single fantasy is surely the stand-alone novel *Gloriana, or the Unfulfill'd Queen* (1978), set in a richly detailed alternative Elizabethan England whose great queen Gloriana pursues copious, joyless sex in futile search of the orgasm that will spiritually heal her and perhaps her land. Gloriana's palace is a wonderful labyrinth, full of shades and echoes of Mervyn Peake's Gormenghast. When at last she turns from her father's grim legacy of Realpolitik to the lover who seemed least acceptable, the story reaches a joyous and literal climax.

Since 1992 Moorcock's work has been usefully assembled in many omnibus volumes as *The Tale of the Eternal Champion*. Deceitfully, these include both Champion and non-Champion work.

C.L. Moore

American novelist
BORN: 1911 DIED: 1987

Wife to Henry Kuttner, with whom she wrote much in collaboration, Catherine Moore established her reputation in the 1930s and 1940s with excellent stories such as "Shambleau" (*Weird Tales*), a planetary romance in Sword & Sorcery vein. Much of her later fantasy appeared under her husband's name in various pulp magazines (see the entry for Kuttner, above).

JOHN MORRESSY

American novelist

BORN: 1930

This author's first entry into fantasy, the "Iron Angel" series of quest-adventures – *Ironbrand* (1980), *Graymantle* (1981), *Kingsbane* (1982) and *The Time of the Annihilator* (1985) – was serious in tone. His second, the "Kedrigern" series about a reluctant wizard, was much more light-hearted; it consists of *A Voice for Princess* (1986), *The Questing of Kedrigern* (1987), *Kedrigern in Wanderland* (1988), *Kedrigern and the Charming Couple* (1990) and *A Remembrance for Kedrigern* (1990).

KENNETH MORRIS

British novelist

BORN: 1879 DIED: 1937

This Morris (not to be confused with his namesake William, below) is regarded by a few cognoscenti as one of the true geniuses of fantasy fiction. He lived and wrote in obscurity, but much of his work has been reprinted, and some of it published for the first time, since his death. There are two principal novels, *Book of the Three Dragons* (1930) and *The Chalchiuhite Dragon: A Tale of Toltec Times* (1992), and a fine collection, *The Dragon Path: Collected Stories of Kenneth Morris*, edited by Douglas A. Anderson (1995). A believer in the Theosophical brand of mysticism, he wrote some beautiful prose.

WILLIAM MORRIS

British novelist

BORN: 1834 DIED: 1896

The multi-talented Morris is remembered for furniture, fabric and wallpaper patterns, the Kelmscott Press and some poems. He also wrote pioneering fantasy novels, prefiguring the "secondary world" setting perfected by Tolkien. Morris's central fantasies are *The Story of the Glittering Plain* (1890), *The Wood Beyond the World* (1894), *The Well at the World's End* (1896), *The Water of the Wondrous Isles* (1897) and *The Sundering Flood* (1897).

The best is *The Well at the World's End*, tracing hero Ralph's long quest across an extensive medieval land with the fresh colours of newly woven tapestry ... a quest to the end of the known world, over the mountains beyond and the deathly desert beyond that, to the Ocean Sea and the magic Well that renews life. Its simple pleasures of endlessly unfolding landscape, and of a quest that comes full circle to a triumphant return home, have been influential.

IN THE OPINION OF MANY, MORRIS STARTED IT ALL. HIS LENGTHY PROSE ROMANCES BECAME TEMPLATES OF HEROIC FANTASY

The Water of the Wondrous Isles offers a different magic, of marvellous tableaux rather than plausible geography. Its heroine escapes a witch's enslavement to explore the islands of a great lake navigable only by the demon-driven "Sending-Boat"; she encounters wonders and, later, mildly silly excesses of knightly chivalry.

JAMES MORROW

American novelist

BORN: 1947

A sharp satirist by nature, Morrow first came to fame with the science-fantasy *This is the Way the World Ends* (1986), in which the survivors of a nuclear war are put on trial for genocide by the spirits of the unborn. His later novels, *Only Begotten Daughter* (1990) and

Towing Jehovah (1994; winner of the World Fantasy Award), move further into fantasy, of a kind which takes a rise out of organized religion and human folly in general.

Peter Morwood

British novelist

BORN: 1956

Married to fantasy writer Diane Duane, Morwood has lived in Ireland for many years. He has written various series of fairly routine adventure fantasies: the Japanese-flavoured "Alban Saga" – *The Horse Lord* (1983), *The Demon Lord* (1984), *The Dragon Lord* (1986) and *The Warlord's Domain* (1989); the Russian-flavoured "Prince Ivan" trilogy – *Prince Ivan* (1990), *Firebird* (1992) and *The Golden Horde* (1993), with a further extension, *The Blue Kremlin*, due soon; and the "Clan Wars" series – *Greylady* (1993), *Widowmaker* (1994), and *Firedrake* (forthcoming).

H. Warner Munn

American novelist

BORN: 1903 DIED: 1981

Munn was a pulpster who wrote a considerable amount of dark fantasy for *Weird Tales* in the 1930s, but is best remembered now for his "Gwalchmai" series of heroic-fantasy novels about the post-Arthurian age: *King of the World's Edge* (1966), *The Ship from Atlantis* (1967) and *Merlin's Ring* (1974). The former two were combined in the omnibus *Merlin's Godson* (1976).

John Myers Myers

American novelist

BORN: 1906 DIED: 1988

Although he wrote fantasy-tinged historical novels, among other works, Myers is remembered in fantasy circles for one book, *Silverlock* (1949), in which the hero is shipwrecked on the shore of a mysterious land of myths, legends and famous fictional characters made flesh. There he meets a beautiful sorceress who turns him into a pig; but he is rescued from Circe's swine-pen by a new-found friend, and together the pair go on to encounter Beowulf, Til Eulenspiegel, Manon Lescaut, Friar John, Anna Karenina, Prometheus, Don Quixote, Robin Hood, Raskolnikov, Sir Gawain and many others, plus sundry cannibals, Vikings and Red Indians. The story reaches its climax in the underworld, from which the hero emerges a wiser man, only to be carried away by the winged horse Pegasus and dumped once more in the ocean where all his adventures began. It is a strange, harshly whimsical and rumbustious book, "as live with incident as a beehive with buzz and as tirelessly busy" (in the felicitous words of one reviewer at the time of first publication).

Robert Nathan

American novelist

BORN: 1894 DIED: 1985

Largely forgotten now, Nathan was a slick fantasist whose work inspired a number of Hollywood films, his best-known titles being *The Bishop's Wife* (1928), about an angelic visitation, and *Portrait of Jennie* (1940), about a time-slipped love-affair. Long-lived, he continued to produce his own brand of sentimental fantasy in books as late as *The Elixir* (1971), *The Summer Meadows* (1973) and *Heaven and Hell and the Megas Factor* (1975).

E. Nesbit

British novelist

BORN: 1858 DIED: 1924

Edith Nesbit was a landmark author of children's fantasy, characterized by inventiveness, humour, and a lack of the dreary moralizing considered appropriate for young readers in Victorian times. Though containing elements of hackwork – she wrote fast, out of need – her books are often quietly subversive.

Following successful non-fantasies like *The Story of the Treasure Seekers* (1899), Nesbit found her own quirky vein of magic in *Five Children and It* (1902). The children are the young Bastables from earlier books; "It" is a Psammead or sand-fairy, a stalk-eyed and engagingly grumpy creature which they find in a sand-pit and which reluctantly grants wishes. The consequences, developed with remorseless common sense, are generally disastrous. Wish for beauty, and no one recognizes you; wish for gold, and be instantly suspected of theft ... Near the end, Nesbit tacitly acknowledges the influence of F. Anstey's comic fantasies.

The Bastables' lives are complicated by a magic carpet and a famous fabulous bird in *The Phoenix and the Carpet* (1904), leading to a tangle of backfiring wishes and carpet-flights to exotic destinations until the Phoenix departs in an appropriate blaze. The Psammead reappears in *The Story of the Amulet* (1906), whose Egyptian half-amulet opens doorways through time for adventures in the deep past: the Stone Age, Babylon, Atlantis, ancient Egypt. C.S. Lewis and others were influenced by the rich descriptions; Lewis's *The Magician's Nephew* contains an obvious homage to scenes where Nesbit's Queen of Babylon runs riot in London.

Different children feature in *The Enchanted Castle* (1907), which revolves around an unusual magic ring that has whatever power the wearer believes it to have. This convolutes the plot in a more adult way, as Nesbit saw (like Diana Wynne Jones long after) that writing for children needn't mean keeping everything simple. Again, time-limited wishes are granted, with results that now often go deeper than comic cautionary tales. When young Kathleen incautiously wishes to be a statue, the initial horror gives way to charming and effective scenes with classical statuary that comes alive to revel by moonlight.

Nesbit's own favourite children's books were the linked *The House of Arden* (1908) and *Harding's Luck* (1909), in which children journey into the past through the agency of another magical and slightly Psammead-like creature, the Mouldiwarp ... whose name is an old-fashioned, rustic word for "mole". A late and exuberant fantasy, *Wet Magic* (1913), escalates from the rescuing of a captive mermaid from fairground-sideshow display to a romping war between undersea factions, in which characters out of books take a hand. Unfortunately, it ends with a less than happy cliché of children's fantasy, the "memory wipe" which deprives young protagonists of any recollection of their adventures.

Nesbit's treatment of children has been seen by some as slightly condescending. She still deserves credit for pioneering work in portraying kids as small humans rather than stuffy miniature adults or prigs trailing alleged clouds of glory. Others have built on the foundations she laid.

Adam Nichols

British novelist

BORN: ?

This Canadian-born author has been touted as "a new star in British fantasy", and his work certainly has vigour. His debut novels were *The War of the Lords Veil* (1994) and *The Pathless Way* (1996). His latest series, "the Whiteblade Saga" – *The Paladin* (1998), *The Songster* (1999) and *The Curer* (2001) – is a Norse-flavoured fantasy.

Jenny Nimmo

British novelist

BORN: 1944

This Welsh writer has produced an acclaimed trilogy of fantasies for children – *The Snow Spider* (1986), *Emlyn's Moon* (1987) and *The Chestnut Soldier* (1989) – which won awards and formed the basis of three UK television serials (1988–91).

Andre Norton

American novelist

BORN: 1912

MANY YEARS A WRITER OF COMPETENT SF FOR BOYS AND GIRLS, NORTON BECOME A GRAND MISTRESS OF THE US FANTASY FIELD

Alice Norton was a librarian when she began writing in the mid-1930s, although the fantasies she produced then – including the two novellas making up *Garan the Eternal* (1972) – did not see print for many years. She adapted two medieval romances for young readers in *Rogue Reynard* (1947) and *Huon of the Horn* (1951) before turning to teenage sf novels, some of which were signed "Andrew North". When her work won popular approval she became extraordinarily prolific; her work edged back towards fantasy by degrees, crossing a significant border in *Witch World* (1963), about a parallel world where the magical psi-powers of the inhabitants are enhanced by talismanic "jewels". The series extending from it eventually became a shared-world scenario including anthologies and "collaborative" novels by other hands; Norton's solo contributions are: *Web of the Witch World* (1964), *Year of the Unicorn* (1965), *Three Against the Witch World* (1965), *Warlock of the Witch World* (1967), *Sorceress of the Witch World* (1968), *The Crystal Gryphon* (1972), *Spell of the Witch World* (1972), *The Jargoon Pard* (1974), *Trey of Swords* (1977), *Zarsthor's Bane* (1978), *Lore of the Witch World* (1980), *Gryphon in Glory* (1981), *Horn Crown* (1981), *Ware Hawk* (1983) and *The Gate of the Cat* (1987). The "Secrets of the Witch World" series, mostly written by others, includes Norton's *The Wardling of Witch World* (1996). Her other collaborative endeavours include novels written together with Phyllis Miller and Mercedes Lackey. She wrote *Black Trillium* with Julian May and Marion Zimmer Bradley, her own sequel being *Golden Trillium* (1993).

Norton's other substantial series is for younger readers, displacing children into a variety of historical and imaginary settings; it consists of *Steel Magic* (1965; aka *Gray Magic*), *Octagon Magic* (1967), *Fur Magic* (1968), *Dragon Magic* (1972), *Lavender-Green Magic* (1974) and *Red Hart Magic* (1976). The same pattern recurs in *Here Abide Monsters* (1973). Her most ambitious fantasies are among her most recent; they include the poignant quest fantasy *The Hand of Llyr* (1994); *Mirror of Destiny* (1995), in which a war between humanity and the inhabitants of Faerie is narrowly averted; and *The Monster's Legacy* (1996), in which an apprentice embroiderer flees to mountains which had formerly been guarded by a magical beast. Her fondness for cats is expressed in many of her works, especially *Mark of the Cat* (1994) and four *Catfantastic* anthologies (1989–96) edited with Martin H. Greenberg.

Mary Norton

British novelist
BORN: 1905 DIED: 1992

Norton was cherished by several generations of readers as the creator of the little people who live beneath the floorboards in *The Borrowers* (1952) and its sequels *The Borrowers Afield* (1955), *The Borrowers Afloat* (1959), *The Borrowers Aloft* (1961) and *The Borrowers Avenged* (1982).

Eric S. Nylund

American novelist
BORN: 1964

This new writer came to fantasy readers' attention with the novel *Pawn's Dream* (1995), and has since followed it up with such well-received books as *A Game of Universe* (1997), a sf/fantasy crossover in which the hero has "to scour the cosmos for the legendary *Holy Grail*", and the contemporary fantasy *Dry Water* (1997).

Patrick O'Leary

American novelist
BORN: 1952

O'Leary's well-received debut novel, *Door Number Three* (1995), was science fiction, but his second, *The Gift* (1997), is a very fine fantasy, and his third, *The Impossible Bird* (2002) is a sf/fantasy crossover. He is one to watch.

Mervyn Peake

British novelist and artist
BORN: 1911 DIED: 1968

As shown by his quirky and highly individual illustrations for his own work (some sombre and brooding, some comic), Mervyn Peake had an artist's eye for shapes and masses. His fantastical prose uses adjectives and phrases like heavy brush-strokes to build up scenes crammed and clotted with visual detail, like some crowded painting by Breughel or Bosch.

Peake's prose masterpiece is the Gormenghast trilogy … or rather, its first two volumes, *Titus Groan* (1946) and *Gormenghast* (1950), which are dominated by the monstrous sprawl of Gormenghast Castle and its strange social life. It is a dense, oppressive world, locked in stifling patterns of daily ritual – so we half-sympathize with the villainous kitchen-boy Steerpike who rebels and, like Macbeth, sets out to murder his way to the top of the heap.

Some of the results are simultaneously comic and horrific, like the Earl of Groan sliding into madness when his library is burned, and perching round-eyed on the mantelpiece in the belief that he is an owl. Or Steerpike's faked skull-on-a-stick ghost, uttering ridiculously melodramatic threats which would be hilarious if not for their devastating effect on the two silly women who are threatened. Elsewhere, grandiose gestures of Gothic horror are undermined by witty asides; and amid Gormenghast's majestic gloom there are some inset nonsense verses as good as Lewis Carroll's. Peake was a master of the unexpected.

Titus, heir of Groan, saves and then finally renounces his ancestral home in Gormenghast, to move onward through an odd, surreal refraction of England in the very different *Titus Alone* (1959). Here Peake was trying for fresh effects, some of them memorable – there's a nice trial scene where Titus truthfully informs a puzzled magistrate that his father was eaten by owls. But the book is sadly fragmentary, not so much by intention as because the author was already in the grip of his last illness. Some coherence was restored to the 1970 revision by its editor Langdon Jones.

A related episode is the short "Boy in Darkness" (1956), in which a boy who is clearly Titus escapes from castle rituals to encounter sinister talking animals – the Goat and Hyena who are partly transformed men, and the monstrous Lamb who means to work a similar change on the boy. This menacing *grotesquerie* is genuinely frightening.

Mr Pye (1953) is a rather more conventional fantasy, a comic morality fable set on the island of Sark, whose title character is alarmed to find his determined goodness and niceness rewarded with sprouting angel-wings. Embarrassed by this mark of grace, he tries the obvious remedy of doing bad deeds instead, only to develop horns…

A large and welcome selection of Peake's artwork, verse – both distinguished and nonsensical – and miscellaneous prose is *Peake's Progress* (1978), which includes "Boy in Darkness" and most of the frivolous rhymes from his *A Book of Nonsense* (1972). Meanwhile, there's nothing else in English literature like Peake's key works *Titus Groan* and *Gormenghast*, in which he achieved greatness.

Charles Perrault

French poet and story-writer
BORN: 1628 DIED: 1703

Charles Perrault was an influential administrator who threw himself into contemporary literary disputes with gusto, but is now remembered only for a collection of moralistic adaptations of folk tales published in 1697. It is known by various titles, most famously the one translated as *Tales of Mother Goose*. It was so successful that it unleashed a flood of similar adaptations and original tales in the same vein; its versions of "The Sleeping Beauty", "Little Red Riding Hood", "Bluebeard", "Cinderella", "Puss-in-Boots" and "Tom Thumb" became standard. Perrault's notion that traditional tales could (and should) be rewritten in order to provide an educative tool for the "civilization" of children has become one of the principal forces shaping modern fantasy fiction and the culture of childhood.

Tamora Pierce

American novelist
BORN: 1954

Pierce writes popular young-adult fantasies such as the series consisting of *Alanna: The First Adventure* (1983), *In the Hand of the Goddess* (1984), *The Woman Who Rides Like a Man* (1986) and *Lioness Rampant* (1988). A later series began with *Wild Magic: The Immortals* (1992) and has continued with *Wolf-Speaker* (1994), *The Emperor Mage* (1994) and *Realms of the Gods* (1996).

Rachel Pollack

American novelist
BORN: 1945

Pollack's *Unquenchable Fire* (1988), won the Arthur C. Clarke Award for science fiction despite the fact that it's really a fantasy of magic – although one of an unusual type, set in the future. The sequel is *Temporary Agency* (1994). Her other works, which have been few in number but always quirky and stylish, include a fantasy anthology, *Tarot Tales* (edited with Caitlin Matthews, 1989).

Tim Powers

American novelist
BORN: 1952

His genre debut, *The Drawing of the Dark* (1979), was justly described as the first real-ale fantasy novel. Powers claimed serious attention with *The Anubis Gates* (1983), an unfailingly inventive story of time-travel to a Dickensian "steampunk" London riddled with streetwise magic, and then deeper into the past. Next came *On Stranger Tides* (1987), adding voodoo lore and a surreal Fountain of

Powers uses historical settings, often quite delightfully as in this fantasy involving the Romantic poets

Youth quest to action-adventure among Caribbean pirates, and *The Stress of Her Regard* (1989), which rewrites the Byron/Shelley/Keats milieu in terms of horrific "lamias" – silicon-based vampire beings, both predators and demon lovers.

Later books are set in a hallucinated, magic-infested modern USA. *Last Call* (1992), following booby-trapped card games with souls at stake, sees the waste land of Las Vegas healed by the proper choice of Fisher King; *Expiration Date* (1995) spins its tortuous plot from the notion that ghosts can be literally snorted for a rejuvenating "high"; *Earthquake Weather* (1997) is a bizarre but effective combined sequel to both preceding books; and *Declare* (2000) is an alternate-world fantasy about British traitor Kim Philby's involvement in the supernatural elements behind the Soviet secret service. Powers's characters are notoriously liable to lose bodily parts (usually eyes or hands) as the price of victory or stalemate. His confidence, intensity, wit and rich erudition make for compelling reading.

TERRY PRATCHETT

British novelist
BORN: 1948

The author of the Discworld comedies – compared by some critics to P.G. Wodehouse – still seems slightly bemused by the runaway success of his creation. Besides the series' 27 novels (and counting), Discworld spinoff material looks set to outdo Tolkien's Middle-Earth and challenge the fantasy merchandising pinnacle of Winnie-the-Pooh...

It all began with *The Colour of Magic* (1983) and *The Light Fantastic* (1986), knockabout farces which spoofed innumerable fantasy clichés as Rincewind the inept, cowardly wizzard (he can't even spell it) escorted Twoflower, Discworld's first tourist, through shambolic adventures – accompanied by the implacable Luggage, a carnivorous magic trunk which follows its owner on lots of little legs.

Pratchett introduced other lead characters from Book Three, but still returns to Rincewind and his now highly developed theories of Practical Cowardice. *Sourcery* (1988) involved him in all-out magical wars. *Eric* (1990) toured Discworld's creation, Fall of Troy, Aztec Empire, and Hell. *Interesting Times* (1994) pitched Rincewind into the strife-torn Agatean Empire during its invasion by the Silver Horde – seven very aged barbarians led by the legendary Cohen. *The Last Continent* (1998) confronts him with every imaginable joke about old and new Australia.

Another sequence, beginning with the third book *Equal Rites* (1987), stars redoubtable witch Granny Weatherwax, a lady of stubborn virtue who knows the exact rules which should be followed by everyone except Granny Weatherwax. Having stormed the male-only bastions of the wizards' college Unseen University in *Equal Rites*, she joins coven-mates Nanny Ogg (aged reprobate) and Magrat (wet New Ager) to settle – Macbeth-style – the royal succession of their homeland, Lancre, in *Wyrd Sisters* (1988). *Witches Abroad* (1991) sees the trio in foreign parts, dealing with vampires, twisted fairy tales and voodoo. In *Lords and Ladies* (1992), Lancre suffers an invasion of singularly vicious elves. *Maskerade* (1995) takes Granny and Nanny to the great city of Ankh-Morpork, whose Opera House is troubled by a Phantom. In *Carpe Jugulum* (1998), a family of vampires arrive in Lancre and start a charm offensive...

Mort (1987) launched the "Death" subseries as the Grim Reaper himself – a much-loved character throughout – takes an apprentice ... gangling young Mort, who makes fateful mistakes. Death determinedly copes with involuntary retirement in *Reaper Man* (1991) and with Ankh-Morpork's rock-music craze in *Soul Music* (1994); *Hogfather* (1996) makes him step really out of character to replace the missing Discworld version of Father Christmas.

The final subseries features Samuel Vimes and his motley colleagues of the Ankh-Morpork Night Watch, defending their city with exasperated love – against cultists who summon an invincible dragon in *Guards! Guards!* (1989), serial killings with Discworld's first prototype rifle or "gonne" in *Men at Arms* (1993), a poison plot complicated by rampant golems in *Feet of Clay* (1996), full-scale war with the desert empire of Klatch in *Jingo* (1997), global disaster in *The Fifth Elephant* (1999), and the end of the world itself in *The Last Hero* (2001).

Further novels are *Pyramids* (1989), with sinister high jinks amid the oversized tombs and walking mummies of Discworld's ancient Egypt; *Moving Pictures* (1990), featuring a glitzy invasion of Hollywood fever; and the very fine *Small Gods* (1992), a darkly hilarious tale of the cruel fundamentalist religion of Omnia, which threatens gory worldwide crusades; *The Truth* (2000), about Ankh-Morpork's first newspaper; and *Thief of Time* (2001), which features a hidden temple of lethally dangerous but spiritually serene monks.

Pratchett's first novel *The Carpet People* (1971) also deserves mention: a children's fantasy of tiny creatures living in the weave of a carpet. The Omen movie spoof *Good Omens* (1990) is a collaboration with Neil Gaiman. Meanwhile, like an unstoppable comic juggernaut, Discworld rolls forever on... Pratchett's tough common sense and psychological realism give his best comedy a hard, sharp edge.

FLETCHER PRATT

American novelist
BORN: 1897 DIED: 1956

Pratt was noted for his collaborations with L. Sprague de Camp (see above), but he also wrote several fantasies on his own. Chief among them are *The Well of the Unicorn* (1948) and *The Blue Star* (1953).

CHRISTOPHER PRIEST

British novelist
BORN: 1943

Priest is another unclassifiable, in some respects like M. John Harrison (although completely different in style). His forte is the extremely cunning plot and the well-sprung surprise. It is his later novels which may be classed as fantasies, and indeed one of them, *The Prestige* (1995), won a World Fantasy Award. An earlier work of interest is *The Glamour* (1984), one of the oddest love-triangle stories ever penned, in which a TV news cameraman, recovering from injuries sustained in a terrorist bombing, becomes obsessed with a young woman who visits him in hospital (though initially he has no memory of her), and then recalls how their love-affair was "haunted" by the girl's former boyfriend – a sinister, unseen presence who gradually wedges himself between the two. The ex-boyfriend is perhaps the leading character of the novel, though he is invisible throughout: he is one of "the glams", those folk who have the Glamour, which is to say the ability to cloud normal people's minds and render themselves invisible. There are some extraordinary scenes in the latter part of the book; it is a compelling narrative, subtly constructed and full of strange turns.

PHILIP PULLMAN

British novelist
BORN: 1946

He began as a children's writer, but took the wider fantasy readership by storm with his novel *Northern Lights* (1995; published in the USA as *The Golden Compass: His Dark Materials, Book One*). Although it had a young (female) protagonist, this proved to be a rich blend of icy imagery with themes borrowed from Milton's epic poem *Paradise Lost*. In Britain, where it was ghettoized in the kids' section, it won the Carnegie Medal and the Guardian Children's Fiction Award; in America it was marketed successfully as an adult novel. The keenly awaited sequels are *The Subtle Knife* (1997) and *The Amber Spyglass* (2000) which won the Whitbread Book of the Year in 2001.

ROBERT RANKIN

British novelist
BORN: 1949

Robert Rankin is a humorist whose method involves importing all manner of fantastic materials into thoroughly mundane settings in order to generate bizarre situations and hectic action. The tone of his works was set by the trilogy comprising *The Antipope* (1981), *The Brentford Triangle* (1982) and *East of Ealing* (1984), but its content became much more extravagant when the series was extended with *The Sprouts of Wrath* (1988). *Nostradamus Ate My Hamster* (1996), *The Brentford Chainstore Massacre* (1997) and *Sprout Mask Replica* (1997) share the same milieu. The trilogy comprising *Armageddon: The Musical* (1990), *They Came and Ate Us* (1991) and *The Suburban Book of the Dead* (1992) juxtaposes a time-tripping Elvis Presley with B-movie sf motifs. The trilogy comprising *The Book of Ultimate Truths* (1993), *Raiders of the Lost Car Park* (1994) and *The Greatest Show Off Earth*

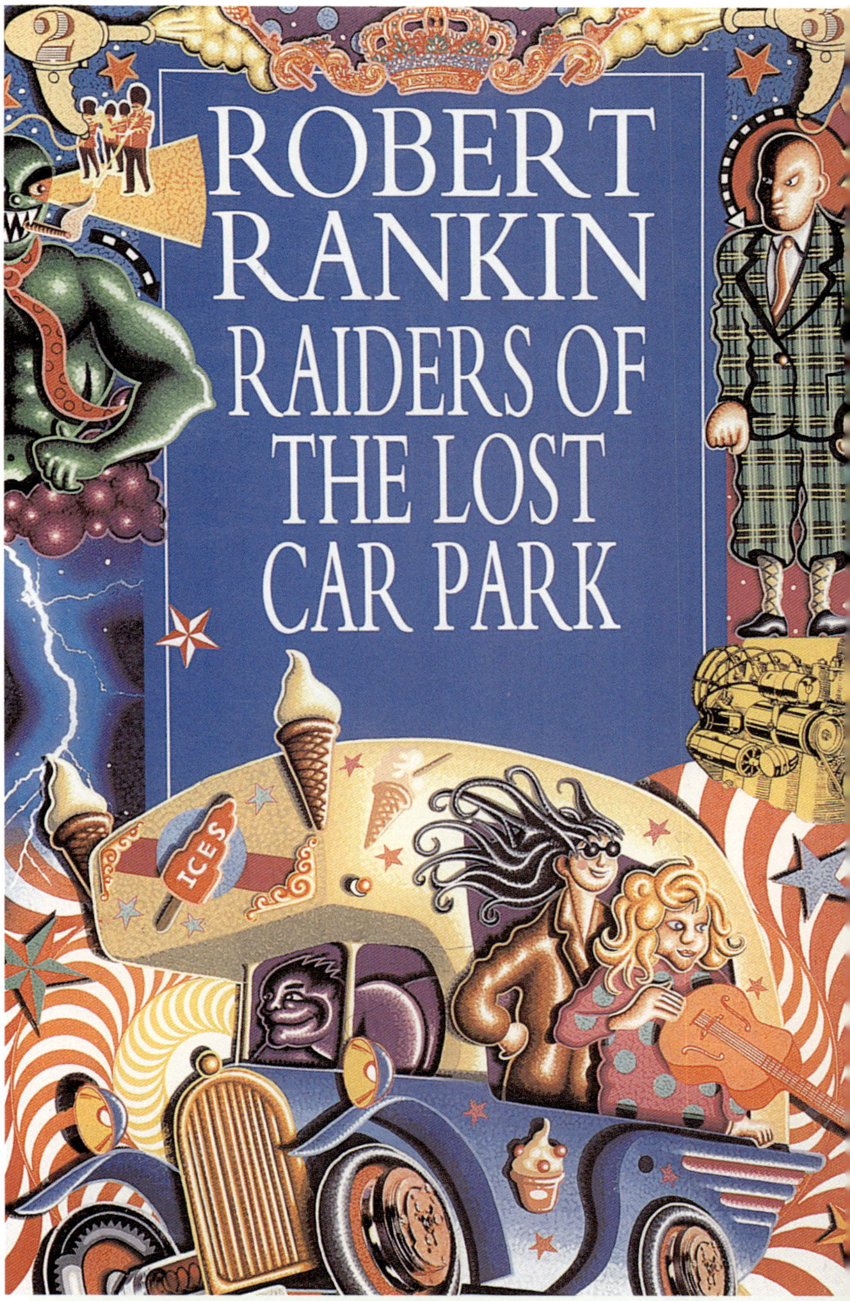

RANKIN IS SURELY THE LOONIEST: HIS BOOKS SHOULD APPEAL TO *GOON SHOW* AND *MONTY PYTHON* FANS

(1994) draws further inspiration from *Fortean Times* and the *Weekly World News*, as does *The Most Amazing Man Who Ever Lived* (1995). Rankin moved closer to the core of genre fantasy in *The Garden of Unearthly Delights* (1995), in which Earth enters a zone of non-causality where magic works and technology doesn't. *A Dog Called Demolition* (1996) was the story of Danny Orion, the world's first surreal killer. More recent works, which increasingly blend all sorts of elements from his various millieux, include *Apocalypso* (1998), *Dance of the Voodoo Handbag* (1998), *Sex and Drugs and Sausage Rolls* (1999), *Snuff Fiction* (1999), *Interpid Coitions* (2000), *Website Story* (2001) and *Hollow Chocolate Bunnies of the Apocalypse* (2002).

MELANIE RAWN

American novelist
BORN: 1953

Melanie Rawn is the most successful of several writers who have attempted to relocate dragons similar to those deployed by Anne McCaffrey within the tradition of high fantasy (to which they ought, in theory, to be far better adapted than to the realms of interplanetary romance). Although the dragons of Rawn's imaginary world are initially regarded as pests, and hence as the legitimate and appropriate target of murderous knight-errantry, her first trilogy, comprising *Dragon Prince* (1988), *The Star Scroll* (1989) and *Sunrunner's Fire* (1990), includes an account of the reconciliation of humankind and dragonkind, inspired by its hero's discovery that dragons' eggs can be alchemically converted into gold. The economic consequences of Prince Rohan's mastery of this new source of wealth allow him to pursue his personal as well as his political ends, the former attaining a near-soap-operatic melodramatic intensity while the latter obtain a near-Byzantine complexity.

Rawn followed the customary genre fantasy career path by supplementing her first trilogy with a second – the "Dragonstar" series – set some years later, comprising *Stronghold* (1990), *The Dragon Token* (1991) and *Skybowl* (1993). Rohan, having become High King – although his political problems continue – is faced with an invasion of his realm by barbarians whose iron-based technology nullifies the effects of the magic on which his realm has previously relied for defence. After this obligatory reprise, Rawn turned to fresher fields in the "Exiles" series, launched with *The Ruins of Ambrai* (1994) and continued in *The Mageborn Traitor* (1997). This series is set in a world of reversed sex-roles, developing a version of the conventional fantasy scenario in which magically talented individuals have become feared and hated, subject to continual and mostly unjust harassment by witch-hunters. *The Golden Key* (1996), a three-way collaboration by Rawn, Jennifer Roberson and "Kate Elliott" (Alis Rasmussen) – each author having contributed a distinct novel-length segment – is set in an alternative late-medieval Spain, Tira Verte, where all documentation is in the charge of an artists' guild, one of whose core families is magically talented.

MICKEY ZUCKER REICHERT

American novelist
BORN: 1962

Reichert's fat commercial fantasies include the "Bifrost" series – *Godslayer* (1987), *Shadow Climber* (1988), *Dragonrank Master* (1989), *Shadow's Realm* (1990) and *By Chaos Cursed* (1991) – and the "Renshai" trilogy – *The Last of the Renshai* (1992), *The Western Wizard* (1992) and *Child of Thunder* (1993). Her more recent works are *The Legend of Nightfall* (1993), *Beyond Ragnarok* (1995), *Prince of Demons* (1996) and *The Children of Wrath* (1998); the stand-alone *Flightless Falcon* (2000); and the "Books of Barakhai", about shape-shifters – *The Beasts of Barakhai* (2001) and *The Lost Dragons of Barakhai* (2002).

JENNIFER ROBERSON

American novelist
BORN: 1953

Much of Roberson's works fall into a long series known as "Chronicles of the Cheysuli" – *Shapechangers* (1984), *The Song of Homana* (1985), *Legacy of the Sword* (1986), *Track of the White Wolf* (1987), *A Pride of Princes* (1988), *Daughter of the Lion* (1989), *Flight of the Raven* (1990) and *A Tapestry of Lions* (1992) – but she has also written a separate sequence consisting of *Sword-Dancer* (1987), *Sword-Singer* (1988), *Sword-Maker* (1989) and *Sword-Breaker* (1991), *Sword-Born* (1998) and *Sword-Sworn* (2002), and one-third of the massive collaborative epic *The Golden Key* (1996, with Melanie Rawn and Kate Elliott) – about a world of magical paintings, and artists in search of the "golden key" to their craft. She is one of the reliable purveyors of standard otherworldly fantasy.

MARK E. ROGERS

American novelist and illustrator
BORN: 1952

Rogers is known for his self-illustrated humorous fantasies about a time-travelling feline hero: *The Adventures of Samurai Cat* (1984), *More Adventures of Samurai Cat* (1986), *Samurai Cat in the Real World* (1989), *The Sword of Samurai Cat* (1991), *Samurai Cat Goes to the Movies* (1994) and *Samurai Cat Goes to Hell* (1998). He has also written horror novels.

Michael Scott Rohan

British novelist
BORN: 1951

"The Winter of the World" trilogy is Rohan's most significant fantasy work, comprising *The Anvil of the Ice* (1986), *The Forge in the Forest* (1987) and *The Hammer of the Sun* (1988), and followed up by a prequel trilogy, *The Castle of the Winds* (1998), *The Singer and the Sea* (1999) and *Shadow of the Seer* (2001). Its background draws on both the real Ice Age and the Finnish *Kalevala* legends, whose witch-queen Louhi commands freezing cold. Elof, the hero whom Rohan pits against Louhi and other powers of advancing ice, is an avatar of Weland Smith and the Kalevala's smith-god Ilmarinen. He crafts marvellous devices, ranging from a magic sword and helm to functional wings and the equivalent of a tactical nuke.

ROHAN: ONE OF BRITAIN'S BEST FANTASY WRITERS

The "Spiral" books, where Earth is adjoined by magical and time-slipped regions accessible by ship, open with *Chase the Morning* (1990), *The Gates of Noon* (1992) and *Cloud Castles* (1993). A modern entrepreneur's adventures in Spiral realms involve ingenious crossbreeding of magic and technology, ultimately involving him with the Grail Knights. *Maxie's Demon* (1997), a singleton romp, shares the Spiral background.

Rohan's Scots heritage lies behind *The Lord of Middle Air* (1994), exploiting legends that the 13th-century scholar Michael Scot – the author's ancestor – had wizardly powers. Magical interventions in grisly Border wars follow, varied by a long trip to Faerie.

J. K. Rowling

British novelist
BORN: 1965

Joanne Kathleen Rowling suddenly became one of the world's best-known authors when she achieved spectacular (and richly-deserved) success with her sequence of children's books about a young wizard, Harry Potter. A single mother on income support living in Edinburgh for most of the time that the first book, *Harry Potter and the Philosopher's Stone* (1997) – retitled *Harry Potter and the Sorcerer's Stone* (1998) for the US market – was being developed and written, Rowling has said that she would often go into cafés and restaurants to write, so that she and her daughter could stay warm. The book was eventually finished with the assistance of a grant from the Scottish Arts Council, and was rejected several times before Bloomsbury bought the rights to it for around £2,500.

It wasn't until accolades started pouring in – including the British Book Awards Children's Book of the Year '97, and the coveted Smarties Prize for children's writing – and the American rights sold that Rowling actually received enough money to make writing her full-time occupation, a moment that she has described as the happiest of her life. Sequels were quickly forthcoming, and proved to be as excellent as the earlier books. *Harry Potter and the Chamber of Secrets* (1998), *Harry Potter and the Prisoner of Azkaban* (1999) and *Harry Potter and the Goblet of Fire* (2000) continued the sequence's runaway success, and the fifth book, *Harry Potter and the Order of the Phoenix* – delayed from 2001 to late 2002 or even 2003 due to Rowling's utter exhaustion – has pre-sold more copies than any other book to date. The books have all won multiple awards, and have sold more than 30 million copies worldwide in more than 35 languages. When *The Prisoner of Azkaban* was published, Rowling found herself in the unique position of occupying all of the top three slots on the *New York Times* bestseller list – a feat that prompted the paper to create a dedicated bestseller list for children's books, to the delight of children's authors everywhere.

The books tell the story of an orphan boy living with his horrible (and totally mundane) aunt and uncle who discovers, on his eleventh birthday, that his parents were wizards. He is invited to enrol at Hogwarts School of Witchcraft and Wizardry, a boarding school for children with magical powers. As soon as he escapes from his aunt and uncle and enters the wizarding world, he discovers that he's a major celebrity. His parents did not die in a car crash as he had believed, but were murdered by an incredibly powerful evil wizard, Lord Voldemort, who had been terrorizing the entire wizardly community. Voldemort then tried to kill the baby Harry, but the dark powers rebounded, and the dark lord was defeated, presumed destroyed. The novels focus on Harry's school life, and chart his progress through Hogwarts – each book takes place over the course of one school year – as he learns wizardry, develops his talent for the wizardly sport of Quidditch, and is faced with a huge array of dangerous plots, challenges and mysteries. In the meantime, Voldemort is slowly regaining his strength, and beginning to renew his reign of terror…

The books have been as popular with adults as they are with children. Rowling undoubtedly has a great talent; unlike most modern children's writers, she is neither patronising nor condescending, nor does she write as if for adults with a reduced vocabulary. The contrast with the dreadful would-be Potter cash-in "Artemis Rune" books by Eoin Colfer is a very pointed lesson in just how good Rowling is. Her world is wildly imaginative and superbly realised, yet manages to stay cosy and familiar – while also being exciting, and having the topsy-turvy element that most children cherish. Meanwhile, the plotting and characterisation in the books are strong enough to hold adult interest. A few cynical detractors have accused Rowling's success of being based on hype, but one can only assume that they haven't actually read the books. Rare as it may be nowadays, the story of Harry Potter's success is a genuine case of quality winning the recognition it deserves.

Kristine Kathryn Rusch

American novelist and editor
BORN: 1960

Known for her editorship (1991–1997) of the long-established *Magazine of Fantasy and Science Fiction*, Rusch has resigned that post to concentrate on her writing which, in addition to fantasy, consists of a number of sf novels, some of them in collaboration with her husband, Dean Wesley Smith. Her principal fantasy work to date has been an epic sequence, "The Fey": *Sacrifice* (1995), *Changeling* (1996), *Rival* (1997), *The Resistance* (1998) and *The Victory* (1998), and the separate "Black Throne" sequence – *The Black Queen* (1999) and *The Black King* (2000).

Geoff Ryman

British novelist
BORN: 1951

Although his fantasy novel *The Warrior Who Carried Life* (1985) reached book form first, Canadian-born Ryman really made his name with his World Fantasy Award-winning novella *The Unconquered Country* (1986). The latter deals movingly with the tragedy of Cambodia in the 1970s – as seen through a thin veil of the imagination which makes the pain and the pathos of the real events seem more bearable, without diminishing them. Cambodia is not actually mentioned in the text, although the author makes clear in an afterword that this is certainly the "unconquered country" he has in mind.

Of greatest fantasy interest among Ryman's diverse later novels is one entitled *Was...* (1992), which re-imagines the life in an all-too-real Kansas of Dorothy, the little girl from L. Frank Baum's *The Wizard of Oz*.

Fred Saberhagen

American novelist
BORN: 1930

Saberhagen is an old trooper of the sf field who has also produced competent and colourful adventure fantasies throughout his career. They include the "Empire of the East" trilogy – *The Broken Lands* (1968), *The Black Mountains* (1971) and *Changeling Earth* (1973) – and the lengthy "Swords" sequence – *The First Book of Swords* (1983), *The Second Book of Swords* (1983), *The Third Book of Swords* (1984), etc., etc., concluding with *The Last Book of Swords: Shieldbreaker's Story* (1994). A new series, "The Book of the Gods", is about the trouble that the Greek gods cause when they return to the modern world and take up where they left off – *The Face of Apollo* (1999), *Ariadne's Web* (2000), *The Arms of Hercules* (2000), *God of the Golden Fleece* (2001), and *Gods of Fire and Thunder* (2002).

R.A. Salvatore

American novelist
BORN: 1959

The popular Robert Salvatore began his career as a writer of TSR, Inc.'s game-based fantasy novels, producing many titles in the "Forgotten Realms" series, ranging from *The Crystal Shard* (1988) to *Siege of Darkness* (1994). He has also branched out with works of slightly more original inspiration such as the Bermuda Triangle mystery/fantasy *Echoes of the Fourth Magic* (1990), the "Spearwielder" trilogy – *The Woods Out Back* (1993), *The Dragon's Dagger* (1994) and *Dragonslayer's Return* (1995) – and a later series beginning with *The Sword of Bedwyr* (1995), *Luthien's Gamble* (1996) and *The Dragon King* (1996). He then followed this with the more sedately-turned out "Demon King" series, *The Demon Awakens* (1997), *The Demon Spirit* (1998), *The Demon Apostle* (1999), *Mortalis* (2000), *Ascendance* (2001) and *Transcendence* (2002). He novelized the Edgar Rice Burroughs-based TV series *Tarzan: The Epic Adventures* (1996).

Fay Sampson

British novelist
BORN: 1935

Apart from her many children's books, Sampson is known for her "Daughter of Tintagel" series of Arthurian fantasies: *Wise Woman's Telling* (1989), *White Nun's Telling* (1989), *Black Smith's Telling* (1990), *Taliesin's Telling* (1991) and *Herself* (1992). Her longest novel to date, *Star Dancer* (1993), is a historical fantasy based on Sumerian myth.

Felicity Savage

Irish/American novelist
BORN: 1975

The Irish-born and perhaps appropriately named Felicity Savage made her debut at the age of 19 with the remarkable *Humility Garden* (1995), a novel which was compared to the erotic fantasies of Tanith Lee. The immediate sequel is *In Human Country* (1996; published in Britain as *Delta City*). She followed this with the "Ever" sequence – *The War in the Waste* (1997), *The Daemon in the Machine* (1998) and *A Trickster in the Ashes* (1998).

Michael Shea

American novelist
BORN: 1946

Shea writes fantasies in the Jack Vance vein – his first novel, *A Quest for Simbilis* (1974), was a direct sequel to Vance's *The Eyes of the Overworld*. Yet in his picaresque World Fantasy Award-winning masterpiece *Nifft the Lean* (1982) Shea transcends the older writer's influence to produce a work which has more in common with the apocalyptic paintings of Hieronymus Bosch. The setting is a "Dying Earth" of the indeterminate future, and the hero is the eponymous trickster and thief, Nifft. In the book's most powerful and grotesque scenes he is obliged to visit various netherworlds of the afterlife. A sequel is entitled *In Yana, the Touch of Undying* (1985). His short stories, collected in *Polyphemus* (1987), are also memorable.

Lucius Shepard

American novelist
BORN: 1947

Lucius Shepard's works extend across the entire genre spectrum of imaginative fiction, the great majority being science fiction or horror. His major contribution to fantasy is the trilogy of novellas *The Man Who Painted the Dragon Griaule* (1984), *The Scalehunter's Beautiful Daughter* (1988) and *The Father of Stones* (1988), in which the immobile body of a 6,000-foot dragon is carefully explored within and without by its human neighbours. Most of his other relevant works involve remote regions of the world where fantastic encounters work a subtle alchemy of the soul; they include the title-story of the World Fantasy Award-winning collection *The Jaguar Hunter* (1987; revised 1988), the title-story of *The Ends of the Earth* (1989) and the novella *Kallimantan* (1990). "How the Wind Spoke at Madraket" (1985) and "Human History" (1996; reprinted in *Barnacle Bill the Spacer and Other Stories*, 1997) are set closer to home, but still occupy margins of civilization, The vampire novel *The Golden* (1993) is set in Castle Banat, a symbolic edifice several orders of magnitude greater than Mervyn Peake's Gormenghast.

Sharon Shinn

American novelist
BORN: 1957

Shinn, whose first fantasy novel was the accomplished *The Shape-Changer's Wife* (1995), has achieved sudden popularity with her romantic trilogy about the lives and loves of "angels" on an alien planet – *Archangel* (1996), *Jovah's Angel* (1997) and *The Alleluia Files* (1998). There may be a science-fictional rationale, involving a starship full of colonists, but the feel is of fantasy.

Susan Shwartz

American novelist
BORN: 1949

Dr Shwartz put her classical education to good use in the "Heirs to Byzantium" trilogy of historical fantasies, *Byzantium's Crown* (1987), *The Woman of Flowers* (1987) and *Queensblade* (1988). Since then, she has dabbled in Chinoiserie – *Silk Roads and Shadows* (1988) and *Imperial Lady: A Fantasy of Han China*, with Andre Norton (1989) – and Arabian Nights fantasy – two anthologies, *Arabesques: More Tales of the Arabian Nights* (1988) and *Arabesques II* (1989) – before returning to a more classically based kind of historical fantasy in *The Grail of Hearts* (1992) and *Empire of the Eagle*, with Andre Norton (1993). Her day job as a successful Wall Street wheeler-dealer has perhaps constrained her from writing more.

Clark Ashton Smith

American poet and story-writer
BORN: 1893 DIED: 1961

Clark Ashton Smith's poetry consciously continued the French traditions imported to the American West Coast by Ambrose Bierce and George Sterling. The short stories he wrote during a brief period of hectic productivity in the 1930s, during which time he was greatly encouraged by H.P. Lovecraft, developed the Decadent style and sensibility to their furthest extreme. Smith's vocabulary is extraordinarily rich, and his stories calculatedly set out to remove themselves as far as possible in setting, apparatus and attitude from the mundane world.

The "Dying Earth" scenario of Zothique allowed his imagination its most extravagant expression and his stories set there remain the ultimate examples of Decadent dark fantasy. Smith's stories were initially reprinted from the pulp magazines in the Arkham

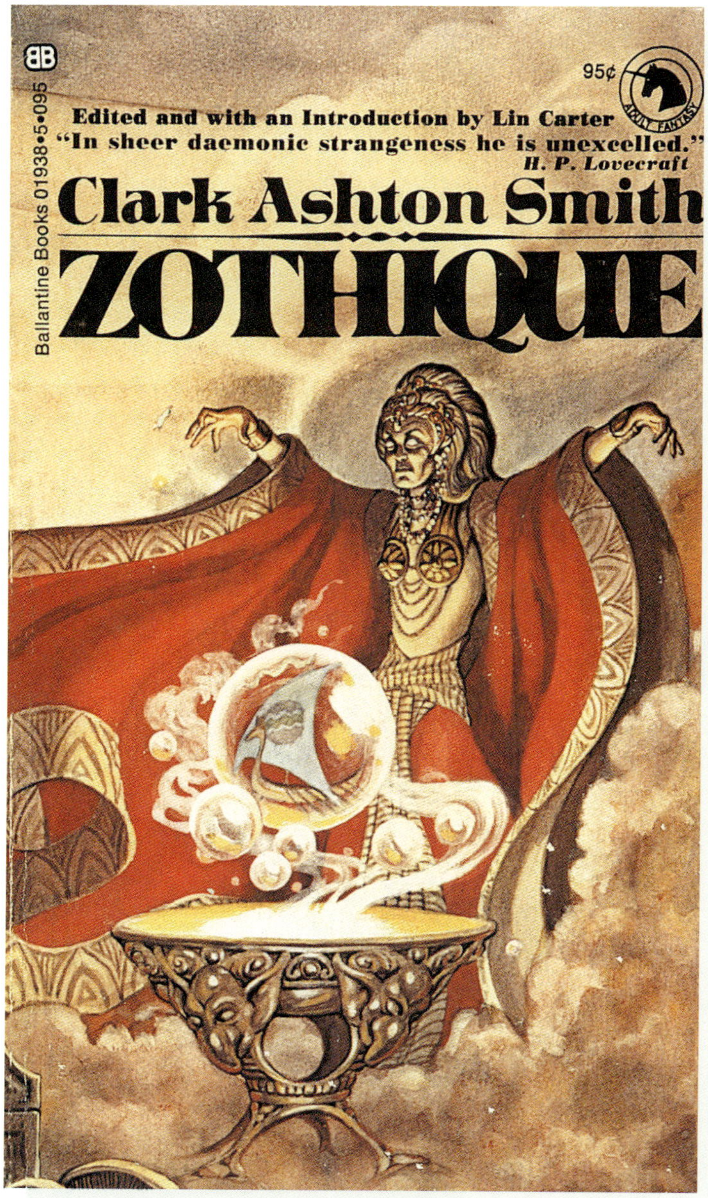

SMITH WAS A CALIFORNIAN RECLUSE WHO LIVED MOSTLY IN POVERTY BUT PRODUCED SOME REMARKABLE POETRY AND PROSE

House collections *Out of Space and Time* (1942), *Lost Worlds* (1944), *Genius Loci* (1948), *The Abominations of Yondo* (1960), *Tales of Science and Sorcery* (1964) and *Other Dimensions* (1970). His various series were separated out in four collections issued in Ballantine's Adult Fantasy series: *Zothique* (1970), *Hyperborea* (1971), *Xiccarph* (1972) and *Poseidonis* (1973); the first two were given definitive form by Necronomicon Press in *Tales of Zothique* (1995) and *The Book of Hyperborea* (1996), which used – wherever possible – unexpurgated texts.

THORNE SMITH

American novelist
BORN: 1893 DIED: 1934

Humorous novelist whose standard fantasy ploy was to shake up characters' lives with some magical affliction that forced them loose from what Smith saw as the stifling conventions of respectable America.

In the "Topper" books, *Topper* (1924; alias The Jovial Ghosts) and *Topper Takes a Trip* (1932) the initially staid hero is plagued by irresponsible ghosts, one a provocative, intermittently tangible female. *The Stray Lamb* (1929) subjects its protagonist to unlikely transformations; *Turnabout* (1931) updates F. Anstey's *Vice-Versa* with an identity swap between husband and wife; *The Night Life of the Gods* (1931) unleashes a pantheon of animated classical statuary on New York; *Rain in the Doorway* (1933), only mildly fantastic, contrasts the US depression with an alternate-world department store run on Marx Brothers principles; *Skin and Bones* (1933) transforms its hero at random intervals into a living skeleton; and *The Glorious Pool* (1934) complicates an ageing husband-wife-mistress triangle by rejuvenating them in turn. Both *Turnabout* and *The Night Life of the Gods* were filmed. Today, there's something touchingly old-fashioned about Smith's recipe for freedom and happiness, involving copious alcohol, uninhibitedly sexy women and easily shocked neighbours. But his jokes, though overly milked, are still funny.

ALISON SPEDDING

British novelist
BORN: 1962

Anthropologically trained Spedding, who has lived in Bolivia since 1989, is the author of a powerful fantasy trilogy called "A Walk in the Dark", based on the careers of Alexander the Great and his successors: *The Road and the Hills* (1986), *A Cloud Over Water* (1988) and *The Streets of the City* (1988).

NANCY SPRINGER

American novelist
BORN: 1948

Springer has written children's books and a wide variety of pleasing fantasies for adults. She likes to use the fantastic "to illuminate contemporary reality", and this approach is best exemplified in some of her more recent books: *The Hex Witch of Seldom* (1988), *Larque on the Wing* (1994) and *Fair Peril* (1996).

Christopher Stasheff

American novelist
BORN: 1944

Stasheff made a hit with *The Warlock in Spite of Himself* (1969), a humorous "planetary romance" type of fantasy which appeared at a time when fantasy novels were still fairly thin on the ground. Since then he has been bewilderingly prolific and has generally come to be regarded as a middle-of-the-road hack, though he has his keen followers.

Later titles, most of them entries in an endless intertwining series, include *King Kobold* (1971), *A Wizard in Bedlam* (1979), *The Warlock Unlocked* (1982), *The Warlock Enraged* (1985), *Her Majesty's Wizard* (1986), *The Warlock Heretical* (1987), *The Warlock Insane* (1989), *Warlock and Son* (1991), *A Wizard in Absentia* (1993), *The Oathbound Wizard* (1993), *The Witch Doctor* (1994), *The Secular Wizard* (1994), *A Wizard in Mind* (1995), *A Wizard in War* (1995), *My Son, the Wizard* (1997), *A Wizard in Chaos* (1997), *A Wizard in Midgard* (1998), *The Feline Wizard* (2000), *Wizard in a Feud* (2001), and many more.

Sean Stewart

American/Canadian novelist
BORN: 1965

American-born Stewart, who resided in Canada for many years and so has been regarded as a Canadian author (though he now lives in Houston, Texas), first attracted serious attention with his novel *Resurrection Man* (1995), set in an alternate world where magic works. Its sequel is *The Night Watch* (1997). He has since produced a range of stand-alone novels, including *Nobody's Son* (1998), about what happens after the "happily ever after"; *Cloud's End* (1999), about a land at the edge of reality; *Mockingbird* (2000); and *Galveston* (2001), about a magical-realist version of a small seaside town.

Amy Stout

American editor and novelist
BORN: 1960

A publishers' editor, married to the writer Alan Rodgers, Stout made her debut as a novelist with *The Sacred Seven* (1996), conventional light fantasy but well done. Its sequels are *The Royal Four* (1997), billed as "Book II of The One Land Saga", and *The Imperial Three* (1998).

Brad Strickland

American novelist
BORN: 1947

Strickland's principal fantasy work is the "Jeremy Moon" trilogy – *Moon Dreams* (1988), *Nul's Quest* (1989) and *Wizard's Mole* (1991) – in which an advertising copywriter finds himself plunged into an imaginary world.

Thomas Burnett Swann

American novelist
BORN: 1928 DIED: 1976

Thomas Burnett Swann's heartfelt mythological fantasies could not initially find a market in his homeland, many of them first appearing in the British magazine *Science Fantasy*. "Where is the Bird of Fire?" (1962; expanded as *Lady of the Bees* 1976; the 1970 book *Where is the Bird of Fire?* is a collection), based on the legend of Rome's founding and telling of a love-affair between Remus and a dryad, established the heart-rendingly poignant tone and beautifully polished style which became his hallmarks; *Queens Walk in the Dusk* (1977) and *Green Phoenix* (1972) are prequels to it. Swann's first book, the elegiac *Day of the Minotaur* (1966) depicts the world of classical mythology in terminal decline, giving way to known history; *Cry Silver Bells* (1977) and *The Forest of Forever* (1971) similarly provided prequels, all three being reprinted as *The Minotaur Trilogy* (1997). Three early novellas are collected in *The Dolphin and the Deep* (1968). Other novels in a classical setting are *The Weirwoods* (1967) and *Wolfwinter* (1972); *The Minikins of Yam* (1976) is set in an earlier period in Egypt. *Moondust* (1968) and *How Are the Mighty Fallen* (1974) are fantasies set against Old Testament backgrounds, and *The Gods Abide* (1976) is an allegory comparing the classical and Christian world-views. Novels set in later periods of history are the medieval fantasy *The Tournament of Thorns* (1976); *Will-o'-the-Wisp* (1976), featuring the poet Robert Herrick; *The Not-World* (1975), featuring Elizabeth Barrett Browning; and the 19th-century-set *The Goat Without Horns* (1971). Swann's mother commemorated his passing by sponsoring a series of academic conferences (he had taught English literature at Florida Atlantic University), which provided the seed of the International Conference for the Fantastic in the Arts.

Michael Swanwick

American novelist
BORN: 1950

Michael Swanwick established his reputation as a science-fiction writer before moving towards what he called, in a 1994 essay reprinted in *The Postmodern Archipelago* (1997), "hard fantasy". The move is symbolically recapitulated in the plot-development of the fine quest fantasy *The Iron Dragon's Daughter* (1993), whose heroine experiences a series of fantasized environments mapping

THE "IRON FANTASY" OF A SCIENCE-FICTION WRITER – AND ONE OF THE BETTER AMERICAN FANTASY NOVELS IN RECENT YEARS

the conventional spectrum of science-fantasy and urban fantasy milieux. *Jack Faust* (1997) is an equally brilliant modernized version of the Faust legend, in which the hero's Mephistophelean informant enables him to see the Industrial Revolution through from its beginning to its implicit end within the space of a single generation. Swanwick's short stories in the same vein are collected in *A Geography of Unknown Lands* (1997), which includes the World Fantasy Award-winning "Radio Waves", the Theodore Sturgeon Memorial Award-winning "The Edge of the World" and "The Changeling's Tale". Swanwick's deep suspicion of the conventional consolations of popular fantasy combines with a keen critical intelligence to make these works outstanding in every way.

ANTONY SWITHIN

British/Canadian novelist
BORN: ?

Swithin is author of the Atlantis fantasies in the "Perilous Quest for Lyonesse" series: *Princes of Sandastre* (1990), *The Lords of the Stoney Mountains* (1991), *The Winds of the Wastelands* (1992) and *The Nine Gods of Safaddne* (1993).

JUDITH TARR

American novelist
BORN: 1955

Like Susan Shwartz, Tarr has a PhD in medieval studies and has used her knowledge to good effect in historical fantasies (although latterly she has tended towards historical fiction *pur*). They include the "Hound and the Falcon" trilogy – *The Isle of Glass* (1985), *The Golden Horn* (1985) and *The Hounds of God* (1986); the "Avaryan Rising" series – *The Hall of the Mountain King* (1986), *The Lady of Han-Gilen* (1987), *A Fall of Princes* (1988), *Arrows of the Sun* (1993) and *Spear of Heaven* (1994); and such singletons as *A Wind in Cairo* (1989), *Ars Magica* (1989), *Alamut* (1989), *The Dagger and the Cross* (1991), *Lord of the Two Lands* (1993), *Throne of Isis* (1994), *Eagle's Daughter* (1995) and *Pillar of Fire* (1995).

SHERI S. TEPPER

American novelist
BORN: 1929

The clever and prolific Tepper, who only began publishing in middle age, has made a mark on science fiction, horror and crime fiction as well as on fantasy. Her fantasies range from the light-hearted "True Game" trilogy – *King's Blood Four* (1983), *Necromancer Nine* (1983) and *Wizard's Eleven* (1984) – through the similar "Jinian" series – *Jinian Footseer* (1985), *Dervish Daughter* (1986) and *Jinian Star-Eye* (1986) – and the "Marianne" books – *Marianne, the Magus, and the Manticore* (1985), *Marianne, the Madame, and the Momentary Gods* (1988) and *Marianne, the Matchbox, and the Malachite Mouse* (1989) – to such heavyweight works of high seriousness as *Beauty: A Novel* (1991), *A Plague of Angels* (1993), *Gibbon's Decline and Fall* (1996) and *The Family Tree* (1997). Hers is a considerable talent.

J.R.R. TOLKIEN

British novelist
BORN: 1892 DIED: 1973

It came as no surprise to readers that a nationwide British bookshop poll in 1997 voted *The Lord of the Rings* the century's most popular novel. Though drawing on established mythic sources, Tolkien virtually created the modern genre of commercial epic fantasy: the greatest problem for writers working in his gigantic shadow is how to assimilate or escape the influence of *The Lord of the Rings*.

JOHN RONALD REUEL TOLKIEN – THE FATHER OF THE FIELD

The tip of the iceberg of Tolkien's vast invented mythology emerged in his children's fantasy *The Hobbit, or There and Back Again* (1937), set in a Middle-Earth seen through childlike eyes. In the semi-comic opening, Bilbo the hobbit (a humanlike race now famed for being small, tough and hairy-footed) is persuaded to accompany the wizard Gandalf and a motley gang of dwarfs as the burglar who will steal for them the far-off dragon Smaug's hoard. The perilous adventure is beset by trolls, goblins, giant spiders and mistrustful elves, eventually approaching a Nordic hardness and darkness with the concluding Battle of the Five Armies. Meanwhile, *The Hobbit* hints at an immense back-story, the mythic history which Tolkien had been constructing since shortly after World War One: "things higher or deeper or darker than its surface: Durin, Moria, Gandalf, the Necromancer, the Ring".

Hence the seeds of *The Lord of the Rings* (1954–5), the mainspring of whose plot is that the magic ring of invisibility won by Bilbo in *The Hobbit*'s riddle-game is no mere trinket but the long-lost One Ring holding the colossal power of Sauron, Dark Lord of Mordor (alias the Necromancer). It is a weapon too dreadful for Gandalf and his good allies to use. Their agonizing decision at the Council of Elrond is that the Ring must be destroyed in the volcanic forge where Sauron created it, in shadowed Mordor. Bilbo's young cousin Frodo accepts the task.

The tremendous story that now unfolds is shaped by several ironies. Evil Sauron, preparing to conquer Middle-Earth by sheer force even without the Ring, is incapable of imagining that anyone could destroy rather than wield this weapon: good can understand evil, but not vice-versa. When Frodo's company splits up to fight in various theatres of the growing war, there's a potent contrast between the sweeping scenes of battle and heroism (enhanced by Tolkien's flair for sonorous description and ability to shift gears into archaic diction appropriate to an epic) and the tiny party of Frodo, his faithful servant Samwise and his faithful enemy Gollum, creeping into the heart of Mordor on a mission far more important than those great battles. Finally, there's a fruitful tension between the initially almost comic little "halflings" and Tolkien's noble, mythic figures of kings, knights and wizards: we identify with the flawed and very human hobbits.

When Sauron and his fortress are finally, satisfyingly destroyed by the unmaking of the Ring, lingering sadness clouds the celebrations. Frodo in particular has suffered too much ever to enjoy Middle-Earth again. Always, prices must be paid.

The jewelled heart of Tolkien's private mythos appeared in *The Silmarillion* (1977) and many posthumous books of his manuscripts. *The Silmarillion* carries poetic conviction, but lacks the fierce, driving power of story which gave such lasting popularity to *The Lord of the Rings*.

JACK VANCE

American novelist

BORN: 1916

Beginning as a minor writer of short sf (later to become a major sf novelist), Vance showed his talent for fantasy in his first published book, *The Dying Earth* (1950). Its linked stories described an enormously distant future Earth, lit by a fading red sun, where myths and magic flourish in the final twilight of civilization as they had at its dawn. Particularly unforgettable was the ironic, erudite tone of voice, cherishing exotic words for their own sake.

Later, witty follow-ups used the same setting and episodic format with slightly broader comedy. *The Eyes of the Overworld* (1966) introduced picaresque non-hero Cugel the Clever, whose efforts to outwit wizards and monsters generally lead to his over-reaching and tripping over his own ingenuity. A characteristically bizarre episode features a magician's grandiose attempt to gain control over TOTALITY – the entire universe – by incarnating it as a jellyfish-like blob; Cugel, finding this while desperately hungry, proceeds to eat it.

A quirk of fate gave *The Eyes of the Overworld* two contradictory sequels. *A Quest for Simbilis* (1974) was written with Vance's permission – and in a fair pastiche of his style – by Michael Shea. Later, Vance produced his own considerably more polished *Cugel's Saga* (1983), featuring some of the rogue's best exploits.

Rhialto the Marvelous (1984), set slightly earlier in the Dying Earth timescale, has an unscrupulous wizard as title character and includes the memorable story "Morreion", featuring a wonderful flight in a spacegoing palace to the literal edge of the universe, where a fellow-wizard has been trapped on a dead star.

Much of Vance's sf also has a flavour of fantasy, dealing with exotic and often obsessed cultures on strange worlds, and often featuring bizarre religions which are cynical confidence tricks. His one venture into conventional fantasy packaging – a trilogy of full-scale novels set in a bygone age of fable – is "Lyonesse", comprising *Suldrun's Garden* (1983), *The Green Pearl* (1985) and *Madouc* (1989).

The Lyonesse sequence takes place on the "Elder Isles" (west of France and the English Channel, now sunk like Atlantis) in pre-Arthurian times, and partly foreshadows the Arthur legend. Tensions between the isles' 10 kingdoms lead to polished diplomacy, smiling cruelties, strategic manoeuvres and outright war, complicated by various magicians who would like to intervene but are theoretically forbidden to do so; by the volatile and malicious fairy folk; by sinister prophecies, curses and magical devices; and by a monstrous sleeper who lies chained beneath the sea, awaiting his hour. It's a heady narrative mixture, beautifully told if not always entirely plausible.

Vance has been criticized for the unwavering polish of his dialogue, in which even enraged kings express themselves with deadly *politesse*, as in Ernest Bramah's Chinese fantasies, and children are as flawlessly articulate as their elders, as in the novels of Ivy Compton-Burnett. Like the authors just mentioned, Vance deliberately cultivates this deadpan fluency as one of his chief vehicles of humour.

ROBERT E. VARDEMAN

American novelist
BORN: 1947

A writer of enormous productivity, Vardeman has written action-packed but routine fantasy adventures, including the "Cenotaph Road" series – *Cenotaph Road* (1983), *The Sorcerer's Skull* (1983), *World of Mazes* (1983), *Iron Tongue* (1984), *Fire and Fog* (1984) and *Pillar of Night* (1984); the "Jade Demons" series – *The Quaking Lands* (1985), *The Frozen Waves* (1985), *The Crystal Clouds* (1985) and *The White Fire* (1986); the "Keys to Paradise" trilogy – *The Flame Key* (1987), *The Skeleton Lord's Key* (1987) and *The Key of Ice and Steel* (1988); and the "Demon Crown" trilogy – *The Glass Warrior* (1989), *Phantoms of the Wind* (1989) and *A Symphony of Storms* (1990). He has also written many other fantasy novels in collaboration with Victor Milan or Geo. W. Proctor.

PAULA VOLSKY

American novelist
BORN: ?

Volsky's entertainingly titled books include *The Curse of the Witch-Queen* (1982) and *The Luck of Relian Kru* (1987), as well as a more standard trilogy – *The Sorcerer's Lady* (1986), *The Sorcerer's Heir* (1988) and *The Sorcerer's Curse* (1989). Her biggest novel, *Illusion* (1991), deals with a fantastical version of the French Revolution; and *The Wolf of Winter* (1993) is a fine, dark-toned, otherworldly fantasy of good and evil magic. More recent offerings include *The Gates of Twilight* (1996), *The White Tribunal* (1997) and *The Grand Ellipse* (2000).

KARL EDWARD WAGNER

American novelist and editor
BORN: 1945 DIED: 1994

Although he moved mainly to horror fiction in later life, Wagner was identified primarily with Sword & Sorcery fantasy in the 1970s. His series about a moody hero called Kane included *Darkness Weaves With Many Shades* (1970; revised as *Darkness Weaves*, 1978), *Death Angel's Shadow* (1973), *Bloodstone* (1975), *Dark Crusade* (1976), *Night Winds* (1978) and *The Book of Kane* (1985). He also wrote one of the better "Conan" pastiches, *Conan: The Road of Kings* (1979), and edited some useful anthologies of pulp-magazine fantasy: *Echoes of Valor* volumes 1–3 (1987–1991). An active promoter of fantasy and horror, he has been sorely missed since his sad death at the age of 48.

EVANGELINE WALTON

American novelist
BORN: 1907 DIED: 1996

Walton, who produced her first fantasy in the 1930s and then languished unpublished for several decades until literary fashion caught up with her, is best known for her excellent series of novels based on *The Mabinogion*, a collection of medieval Welsh tales: *The Virgin and the Swine* (1936; reissued as *The Island of the Mighty*, 1970), *The Children of Llyr* (1971), *The Song of Rhiannon* (1972) and *Prince of Annwn* (1974).

WALTER WANGERIN, JR.

American novelist
BORN: 1944

Wangerin is a religious fantasist who wrote a bestseller called *The Book of the Dun Cow* (1978), designed as an allegory. It concerns Chauntecleer the rooster and his barnyard friends, and how they face a terrible threat to their world. The less effective sequel is *The Book of Sorrows* (1985).

Paul Ware

British novelist
BORN: 1960

This new fantasist debuted with *Flight of the Mariner* (1997), described by its publishers as an "epic novel of conflict and adventure in an astounding otherworld". The world in question seems like an old-fashioned cross between Edgar Rice Burroughs's Barsoom and C.S. Lewis's Narnia.

Freda Warrington

British novelist
BORN: 1956

Warrington spent the 1980s writing traditional fantasy novels – *A Blackbird in Silver* (1986), *A Blackbird in Darkness* (1986), *A Blackbird in Amber* (1987), *A Blackbird in Twilight* (1988) and *The Rainbow Gate* (1989) – and then in the 1990s turned to vampire horror with works such as *A Taste of Blood Wine* (1992). In both spheres she is a writer of high competence.

Margaret Weis & Tracy Hickman

American novelists
BORN: **Weis, 1948; Hickman, 1955**

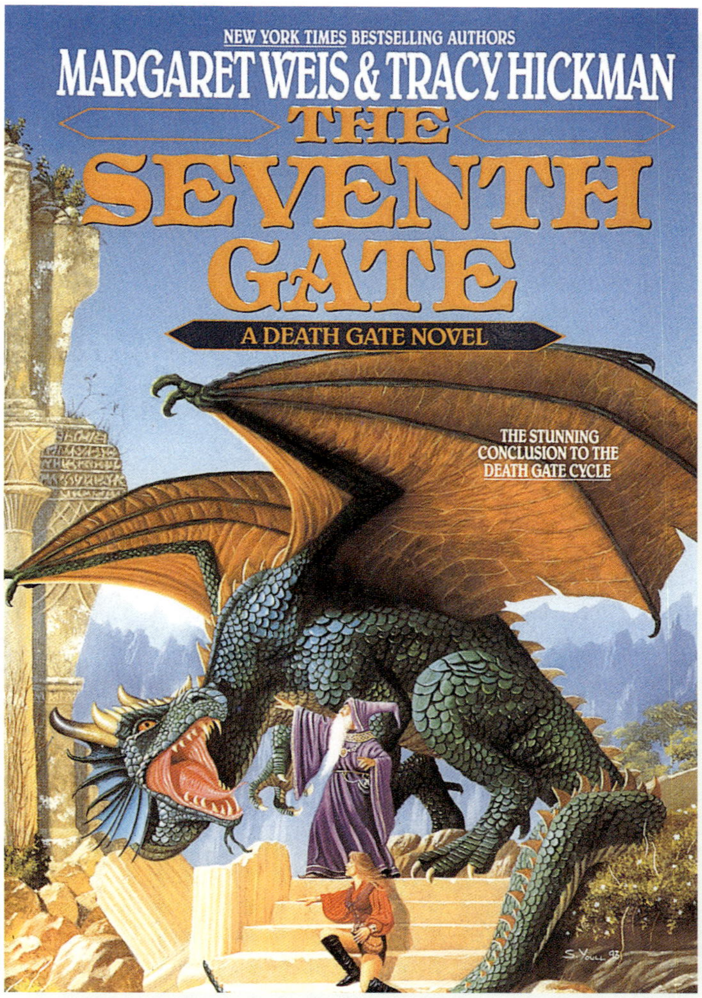

THE LEADING WRITERS OF GAMESTER FANTASY: THEIR LIGHT TOUCH HAS BEEN APPRECIATED BY MILLIONS

Weis and Hickman owe their awesome success to having been in the right place at the right time; when TSR, the manufacturers of the Dungeons & Dragons role-playing game, decided to branch out into publishing, game-designer Hickman teamed up with Weis, who turned his grindingly mechanical plots into slightly less mechanical prose. With the popularity of the game at its height, the ready-made audience boosted their early endeavours to spectacular best-sellerdom. The "DragonLance Chronicles" initially comprised *Dragons of Autumn Twilight* (1984), *Dragons of Winter Night* (1985) and *Dragons of Spring Dawning* (1985); it was subsequently extended by the anthologies *DragonLance: The Second Generation* (1994) and *DragonLance: The Dragons of Krynn* (1994), and the novels *Dragons of Summer Flame* (1995) and *The Dragons at War* (1996). The trilogy collected as *Dragon Lance Legends* (1988) consists of *Time of the Twins*, *War of the Twins* and *Test of the Twins* (all 1986) and the recent "DragonLance: War Of Souls" sequence – starting with *Dragons of a Fallen Sun* (2000) and *Dragons of a Lost Star* (2001); many other associated volumes – mostly anthologies – were released between 1987 and 1994. Weis and Hickman then began to produce non-tie-in novels of a similar stripe, including two trilogies – one comprising *Forging the Darksword*, *Doom of the Darksword* and *Triumph of the Darksword* (all 1988), further augmented by *Legacy of the Darksword* (1997), the other the Arabian Nights-influenced *The Will of the Wanderer*, *The Paladin of the Night* and *The Prophet of Akhran* (all 1989) – and the much more extended "Death Gate Cycle", comprising *Dragon Wing* (1990), *Elven Star* (1990), *Fire Sea* (1991), *Serpent Mage* (1992), *The Hand of Chaos* (1993), *Into the Labyrinth* (1994) and *The Seventh Gate* (1994). The pair are currently embarking on a new sequence, "The Sovereign Stone" – so far consisting of *Well of Darkness* (2000) and *Guardians of the Lost* (2001). Weis has since branched out into space opera, alone and in collaboration with Don Perrin, with whom she also produced *DragonLance: The Doom Brigade* (1996). She has also been active as an anthologist, producing *Fantastic Alice* (1995) and *A Magic-Lover's Treasury of the Fantastic* (1997) in collaboration with Martin H. Greenberg and *Treasures of Fantasy* (1997) with Hickman and Greenberg. She is credited as "creator" (with David Baldwin) of the episodic *Margaret Weis' Testament of the Dragon* (1997). TSR was taken over by leading US fantasy games company Wizards of the Coast, Inc. in 1997, but those who struck while the iron was hot retained its warmth.

JANE WELCH

British novelist
BORN: 1964

Yet to become a big name in the field, Welch showed considerable promise with her "Runespell Trilogy": *The Runes of War* (1995), *The Lost Runes* (1996) and *The Runes of Sorcery* (1997). This was followed with the "Runespell: Book of Ond" trilogy – *The Lament of Abalond* (1998), *The Bard of Castaguard* (1999) and *The Lord of Necrond* (2000) – and the "Runespell: Book of Man" trilogy, beginning with *Dawn of a Dark Age* (2001).

H.G. WELLS

British novelist
BORN: 1866 DIED: 1946

The master of scientific romance also wrote several fantasies, among them *The Wonderful Visit* (1895), about an angel from another dimension, and *The Sea Lady: A Tissue of Moonshine* (1902), which features a mermaid. Many of his short stories are also classifiable as fantasies.

JOHN WHITBOURN

British novelist
BORN: 1958

Although he had published some earlier small-press material, Whitbourn's career was fairly launched when he won the BBC/Gollancz First Fantasy Novel Prize for his interesting alternate-world fantasy *A Dangerous Energy* (1992). The follow-ups were *Popes and Phantoms* (1993) and *To Build Jerusalem* (1994), and a new novel, *The Royal Changeling,* was released in 1998. This was followed with the "Downs-Lord Trilogy": *Downs-Lord Dawn* (1999), *Downs-Lord Day* (2000) and *Downs-Lord Doomsday* (2002).

T.H. WHITE

British novelist
BORN: 1906 DIED: 1964

Despite its broadly comic elements, this author's much-loved omnibus volume *The Once and Future King* (1958) has become the definitive 20th-century retelling of the tale of King Arthur.

White's original books – heavily revised for the omnibus – were as follows. *The Sword in the Stone* (1938) contains the parts everyone best remembers: young Wart growing up in a richly-detailed period England; becoming the pupil of Merlyn, who educates him by magical transformation into animal forms; and claiming the crown of England by drawing Excalibur from the stone. The weaker *The Witch in the Wood* (1939; retitled "The Queen of Air and Darkness") carries the story forward and features the grisly witch Queen Morgause. *The Ill-Made Knight* (1940) tells of Lancelot and his eventual fatal adultery with Guenever. *The Once and Future King* ends with "The Candle in the Wind", wherein Arthur's realm tumbles into darkness but one gleam of future hope remains.

WHITE WAS A RATHER TORTURED INDIVIDUAL

The Book of Merlyn (1977), written to conclude the omnibus, was rejected for both pacifism and artistic weariness: its finest passages, describing Wart's experiences as an ant and a goose, were instead transplanted into *The Sword in the Stone.* Less famous is *Mistress Masham's Repose* (1946), whose child heroine discovers and, briefly, maltreats a colony of Gulliver's tiny Lilliputians in England.

OSCAR WILDE

British playwright and novelist
BORN: 1854 DIED: 1900

This legendary wit wrote some of the most beautiful short fantasies in the English language, mainly collected in *The Happy Prince and Other Tales* (1888) and *Lord Arthur Savile's Crime and Other Stories* (1891). His horror-fantasy novel *The Picture of Dorian Gray* (1891), about a man whose magical portrait ages while he remains young, is also world-famous.

CHARLES WILLIAMS

British novelist
BORN: 1886 DIED: 1945

The third important member of the "Inklings" group of Christian fantasists dominated by Tolkien and C.S. Lewis, Williams wrote theological thrillers which have gained cult status.

These include *War in Heaven* (1930), featuring a Grail hunt in modern England and effective depiction of black magic's sheer nastiness; *The Place of the Lion* (1931), in which Platonic archetypes – like the one Lion, Serpent and Butterfly which are the patterns for all others – disturb the world; *Many Dimensions* (1931), revolving around the miraculous powers of the holy Stone of Solomon and their blasphemous misuse; *The Greater Trumps* (1932), which credits the "original" Tarot pack with cataclysmic powers that soon threaten disaster; and, written before the others, *Shadows of Ecstasy* (1933).

Descent into Hell (1937) offers a complex interplay of fantastic elements – *doppelgängers*, ghosts, time dislocation, a succubus, some genuinely frightening final scenes of damnation – and is Williams's most powerful novel. *All Hallows' Eve* (1945) is also of note, particularly for bleak scenes where a woman's ghost roams an "empty" postwar London, unable to see its living people.

Michael Williams

American novelist and poet
BORN: 1952

Like Weis & Hickman and so many others, Williams began as a writer of "DragonLance" game tie-ins for TSR, Inc., his titles including *Weasel's Luck* (1989), *Galen Beknighted* (1990) and *The Oath and the Measure* (1991), about the adventures of the hero Galen Pathwarden. An independent trilogy, "From Thief to King", consists of *A Sorcerer's Apprentice* (1990), *A Forest Lord* (1991) and *The Balance of Power* (1992), and is about the education into magic and spiritual kingship of another hero. There seems to be a religious subtext, which surfaces again in his most ambitious novel to date, *Arcady* (1996), based on the mythology of the poet William Blake, and its sequel *Allamanda* (1997).

Tad Williams

American novelist
BORN: 1957

Tad Williams launched his literary career with the whimsical animal fantasy *Tailchaser's Song* (1985), whose characters are cats. He followed it up with the ambitious "Memory, Sorrow and Thorn" trilogy, comprising *The Dragonbone Chair* (1988), *Stone of Farewell* (1990) and *To Green Angel Tower* (1993; the two-volume UK edition consists of *Siege* and *Storm*), which sets out carefully to criticize and correct certain aspects of Tolkien-descended fantasy which he considered problematic: the racist undertones of the conventional characterization of quasi-human races and the moral absolutism of the easy separation of powers of Good and Evil. Like the USA, the Osten Ard in which the trilogy is set has been founded by genocidally inclined colonists, and the High King's castle, Hayholt, is a complicated edifice whose murky symbolism is comparable to that of Peake's Gormenghast. The plot, involving a search for a series of magical artefacts, is superficially conventional but is stocked with unsettling resonances. Although it does not flow as smoothly as the works of other best-selling fantasists Williams' stately narrative is potentially more rewarding to connoisseur readers, and he has so far resisted the temptation to produce a carbon copy.

Williams' other fantasies are much smaller in scale than his magisterial trilogy, but constitute similar considered responses to familiar patterns. *Child of an Ancient City* (1992), written in collaboration with Nina Kiriki Hoffman, is a vampire story whose conventional form is drastically altered by its removal into an Arabian Nights scenario. *Caliban's Hour* (1994) takes issue with Shakespeare in much the same iconoclastic spirit that the trilogy had employed in taking issue with Tolkien, presenting Caliban's account of the events leading up to the crucial encounters in *The Tempest* and their consequences. Although their close relationship with previous literary works limits their scope as *contes philosophiques* these tales carry forward – albeit idiosyncratically – the authorial quest begun in "Memory, Sorrow and Thorn". The four-book "Otherland" series begun with *City of Golden Shadow* (1996) and continued in *River of Fire* (1998) *Mountain of Black Glass* (1999) and *Sea of Silver Light* (2001) is science fiction, but it is mostly set in a fantastic virtual reality of cyberspace controlled by the avaricious and sinister Grail Brotherhood.

Philip G. Williamson

British novelist
BORN: 1955

Williamson's early satirical novels, written as "Philip First" and presented as mainstream fiction, were *The Great Pervader* (1985) and *Dark Night* (1989). Since then, he has turned fairly prolifically to genre fantasy – most of it belonging to the "Firstworld" series (which may be some kind of joke on his erstwhile pseudonym) – with the novels *Dinbig of Khimmur* (1991), *The Legend of Shadd's Torment* (1993), *From Enchantery* (1993), *Moonblood* (1994), *Heart of Shadows* (1994), *Citadel* (1995), *Enchantment's Edge* (1996), *Orbus's World* (1997) and *The Soul of the Orb* (1998).

Terri Windling

American editor and novelist
BORN: 1958

Windling has become one of the field's best-known names in her capacity as the editor of numerous anthologies, notably the long-running *Year's Best Fantasy and Horror* series (with Ellen Datlow, who handles the horror). Her interesting debut novel, *The Wood Wife* (1996), is set mainly in the Arizona desert , and she followed it with *Voyage of the Bassett: The Raven Queen* (2001).

GENE WOLFE

American novelist
BORN: 1931

Wolfe's undoubted masterpiece "The Book of the New Sun" was initially acclaimed as exotic far-future fantasy – but on close inspection has sf underpinnings throughout. "Magic" swords are merely ingeniously crafted, a flying cathedral is a hot-air balloon, water-dwelling giants result from forced evolution, etc. Yet the sf rationale is in turn underlaid by tough theology…

The Book, magnificently written with impressive resources of language that can sometimes baffle through sheer clarity, describes the torturer Severian's initially haphazard-seeming journeys, leading into a quest for the New Sun that will bring both healing and ruin. It comprises *The Shadow of the Torturer* (1980), *The Claw of the Conciliator* (1981), *The Sword of the Lictor* (1982) and *The Citadel of the Autarch* (1983), plus a later pendant, *The Urth of the New Sun* (1987). This was followed by two further four-volume sequences, "The Book of the Long Sun" (1993–1996) and "The Book of the Short Sun" (1999–2001).

Contrasting with Severian's eidetic memory, the hero of Wolfe's fine ancient-Greek "Latro" sequence forgets everything within hours and must constantly take notes. Latro's *aide-memoire* scrolls form the text of *Soldier of the Mist* (1986) and *Soldier of Arete* (1989). His compensation for forgetting is that, movingly, he can see, touch and talk with the gods and spirits who abound in those classic days of myth.

JANNY WURTS

American novelist
BORN: 1953

Janny Wurts is an artist as well as a writer, and is married to the artist Don Maitz; her fantasy novels reflect this other allegiance in that she usually pays more attention to visual imagery than to narrative drive. *Sorcerer's Legacy* (1982) was followed by *Stormwarden* (1984), but before completing the story whose foundations are established therein – which she eventually did in *Keeper of the Keys* (1988) and *Shadowfane* (1988) – she teamed up with Raymond Feist to produce *Daughter of the Empire* (1987), which was also expanded into a trilogy by *Servant of the Empire* (1990) and *Mistress of the Empire*

YET ANOTHER OF THE POPULAR FANTASY WORLDS OF RECENT TIMES, CREATED BY AMERICAN WRITER AND ILLUSTRATOR WURTS

(1992). The episodic *The Mistress of Whitestorm* (1992), which tracks the making of a legendary fortress-builder, was followed by the languorous *The Curse of the Mistwraith* (1993), whose two sequels *The Ships of Merior* (1994) and *Warhost of Vastmark* (1995) appeared separately in the UK but were combined into a single volume, under the former title, in the US edition of 1995.

A further continuation of the series – which tracks the fortunes of two half-brothers who overcome a curse which made them enemies – was launched by *Fugitive Prince* (1997), *Grand Conspiracy* (1999) and *Peril's Gate* (2001). *That Way Lies Camelot* (1994) is a short-story collection.

Jonathan Wylie

British novelist(s)
BORN: 1952, 1955

"Jonathan Wylie" is a pen-name that conceals a husband-and-wife team, Mark and Julia Smith. While working for a publishing house they established themselves as competent writers of fantasy with the "Servants of Ark" trilogy – *The First Named* (1987), *The Centre of the Circle* (1987) and *The Mage-Born Child* (1988) – and the "Unbalanced Earth" trilogy – *Dreams of Stone*, *The Lightless Kingdom* and *The Age of Chaos* (all 1989). Going freelance, they produced two large singletons, *Dream-Weaver* (1991) and *Shadow-Maze* (1992), which showed an increase in originality. Then came the "Island and Empire" trilogy – *Dark Fire* (1993), *Echoes of Flame* (1994) and *The Last Augury* (1994) – and several more singletons, including *Other Lands* (1995), *Across the Flame* (1996), *Magister* (1997) and *Ice-Mage* (1998). The last-named is unusual in that it was inspired by the life of the composer Arnold Bax.

Laurence Yep

American novelist
BORN: 1948

San Francisco-born Yep is known for fiction about the Chinese experience in America, mainly juvenile books. His "Shimmer and Thorn" sequence – *Dragon of the Lost Sea* (1982), *Dragon Steel* (1985), *Dragon Cauldron* (1991) and *Dragon War* (1992) – features the adventures of a shape-changing dragon called Shimmer and a boy called Thorn.

Jane Yolen

American novelist
BORN: 1939

Since her career was launched in 1963 Jane Yolen has become an extremely prolific writer of fantasies for readers of all ages. She is particularly adept at adapting and devising material for very young children, but she also produces excellent material for teenagers and – occasionally – adults. Harcourt Brace introduced a young-adult imprint called Jane Yolen Books under her guidance in 1990. The bulk of her work consists of short stories, and many of her longer works are episodic. Her most substantial works include the cautionary fantasy *The Magic Three of Solatia* (1974), the poignant parable of difficult communication *The Mermaid's Three Wisdoms* (1978) and the interplanetary fantasy *Cards of Grief* (1984). Among the best of her works are the remarkable Messianic fantasies *Sister Light, Sister Dark* (1988) and its sequel *White Jenna* (1989), the longest of her several variants on the Sleeping Beauty theme, *Briar Rose* (1992), and the legendary fantasy *The Wild Hunt* (1995). Outstanding among her many short-story collections are *Tales of Wonder* (1983), *Dragonsfield and Other Stories* (1985), the series *Here There Be Dragons/Unicorns/Witches/Angels* (1993–6) and *Twelve Impossible Things Before Breakfast* (1997). Her strong interest in Arthuriana, reflected in the collection *Merlin's Booke* (1986), the novel *The Dragon's Boy* (1990) and the anthology *Camelot* (1995), is further extended in the "Young Merlin" trilogy comprising *Passager*, *Hobby* and *Merlin* (all 1997) – aimed at seven-to-10-year-olds, in which a falconer finds and "tames" a magical boy, who eventually returns to the wild folk of the woods before meeting a child-who-is-to-be-king. Yolen is also the editor of the three-volume *Xanadu* series of original anthologies (1995–97).

Roger Zelazny

American novelist
BORN: 1937 DIED: 1995

An ingenious muddler of genre boundaries, Zelazny relished the "science fantasy" form. Thus the fine *Lord of Light* (1967) uses lush descriptive prose to establish a world ruled by Hindu gods (wittily, the feared Dark Lord proves to be Christian) ... but bases the cycle of reincarnation on technology, and the gods' powers on psionic ability augmented by exotic weapons. *Creatures of Light and Darkness* (1969) makes similar but less substantial use of Ancient Egyptian myths.

His best-known fantasy is the "Amber" sequence, centred on the primal world Amber of which Earth and others are supposedly mere shadows. The five books beginning with *Nine Princes in Amber* (1970) evoke the tortuous betrayals of Jacobean drama as narrator Corwin and rival princes – and princesses – double-cross one another in tricky, gory and magical ways, all seeking the crown of Amber. *Trumps of Doom* (1985) opens an inferior follow-up starring Corwin's son Merlin.

Other works of note include *Jack of Shadows* (1971), the "Wizard World" sequence *Changeling* (1980) and *Madwand* (1981), the more conventional "Dilvish" fantasies *The Changing Land* (1981) and *Dilvish the Damned* (1982) and the wildly comic *A Night in the Lonesome October* (1993).

Jack Zipes

American academic and editor
BORN: 1937

Over the past couple of decades, Zipes has become "Mr Fairy Tale", his expertise in the Brothers Grimm revealed in several magisterial books and his wider knowledge of the fantasy tradition reflected in a number of definitive anthologies, including *Beauties, Beasts and Enchantment: Classic French Fairy Tales* (1989) and *Spells of Enchantment: The Wondrous Fairy Tales of Western Culture* (1991).

A-Z
OF FANTASY CHARACTERS & ENTITIES

Many creatures, characters and beings great and small from the huge world that is fantasy are covered in this chapter. Everybody has a favourite from their childhood or current fantasy novel or film

Most of us have been touched by the characters of fantasy at many points in our lives. They have moved or amused, horrified or inspired us since early childhood. In some cases these characters are scarcely human, and take the forms of supernatural beings or anthropomorphized animals. It is more usual however, the characters in fantasy stories are no more than simply imaginary human beings.

This section contains short entries which provide information on dozens of these fantastic characters and entities. They originate not only in novels, but in many other sources – poems, plays, short stories, comic-strips, films and television. With one or two partial exceptions (Alice, Baron Munchausen), we have tried to limit the entries to the strictly fictional. Actual persons – particularly historical heroes of one sort or another – have often been the subjects of fantasy novels and films, but such fictional treatments of the real are not listed here. This is a short Who's Who of people or things that never were: figments, phantasms, the dramatis personae of a fantasy "mythology."

CHILDREN'S FANTASY IN PARTICULAR IS FILLED WITH VERY SPECIAL CHARACTERS, FROM ALICE IN WONDERLAND (OPPOSITE) TO MARY POPPINS (ABOVE)

Some of the traditional characters of myth, legend and poetry, and those of the Classical, Medieval and Renaissance period – from Odysseus to King Arthur and Amadis of Gaul – are included, and so are some generic creatures such as Dragons, Elves and Unicorns. But the majority of the characters are modern, creations of the last hundred years or so.

It is an eclectic selection, in which Ebenezer Scrooge rubs shoulders with Wonder Woman. One important criterion for including a particular character is that he or she (or it) should have lived beyond the original source. That is to say, the majority of characters included here have been perpetuated by the original author from work to work, or have been perpetuated by other authors and by adaptations to different media, or have names which have entered the language for one reason or another.

Most of the entries attempt to give a brief outline of the character's fictional "career" over the years since their creation and their point or place of origin (if known) is noted.

The Addams Family

CREATOR: **Charles Addams**
SOURCE: **The New Yorker (magazine)**
DATE: **1938**

This spooky family – husband, wife, two kids, a live-in uncle and grandmother, and a most peculiar manservant – featured in single-panel cartoons by the artist of the comical-macabre, Charles Addams, who was a regular contributor to the weekly *New Yorker* from the late 1930s. Initially nameless, they soon became known by their creator's surname; but it was not until the characters were further developed by producers David Levy and Nat Perrin for a funny television series, *The Addams Family* (1964–66), that they gained first names. The smooth, uxorious Gomez Addams was played by John Astin, his gorgeous black-clad wife Morticia by Carolyn Jones, and their grotesque Uncle Fester by an ageing Jackie Coogan (ironically a former angelic child star). The characters also appeared in a novelization by Jack Sharkey (1965); an animated TV series (1973, revived 1992); and in a one-off TV movie, *Halloween with the Addams Family* (1977).

In the mid-1980s drawings of the Addams Family were used on London advertising posters to sell the telephone services of British Telecom. The fame of the creepy characters was further reinforced by two successful films, *The Addams Family* (1991) and *Addams Family Values* (1993), both featuring a superbly-picked all-new cast headed by Raul Julia as Gomez, Anjelica Huston as Morticia, Christopher Lloyd as Fester and Christina Ricci as Wednesday. The films could well have become a successful ongoing franchise, but Julia died tragically in 1994.

Alice

CREATOR: **Lewis Carroll**
SOURCE: **Alice's Adventures in Wonderland**
DATE: **1865**

A little girl of mid-Victorian times who has some very odd experiences in strange realms of the imagination. She appears in two slim books, the Wonderland volume and its sequel *Through the Looking-Glass and What Alice Found There* (1871), both by Lewis Carroll (real name Charles Lutwidge Dodgson). In these she encounters such delightfully (and sometimes disturbingly) memorable characters as the White Rabbit, the Cheshire Cat, the Mad Hatter, the Mock Turtle, Humpty Dumpty, and the Red Queen and White Queen. As is now well known, Alice was modelled on a real-life girl of Dodgson's acquaintance, Alice Liddell – but since the author never mentions her surname, and since her adventures are wholly fantastic, she counts as a fictional character. Indeed, she is one of the most famous characters in English-language fiction, an everlasting childhood favourite who retains an enormous appeal for adults. The literature on Alice is vast, ranging from the meticulous scholarship of *The Annotated Alice* (1960) by Martin Gardner, through such studies as *Alice in Many Tongues* (1964) by Warren Weaver (the Alice books have been translated "more often and into more languages than almost any other work except the Bible", it has been claimed) to the critical compendium *Aspects of Alice* (1972) edited by Robert Phillips. Recent attempts at sequels by other hands – often ingenious, though it is impossible fully to recapture the magic – include *Alice Through the Needle's Eye* (1984) by Gilbert Adair, the anthology *Fantastic Alice* (1995) edited by Margaret Weis and Martin H. Greenberg, and *Automated Alice* (1996) by Jeff Noon.

Our visualizations of Alice over the years owe a great deal to the illustrators of Carroll's books -which he illustrated himself to begin with – first and foremost among them John Tenniel. Other artists who have drawn distinctive pictures to accompany the texts include Arthur Rackham, Mabel Lucie Attwell, Mervyn Peake, Ralph Steadman, and even Salvador Dali. There have been countless stage adaptations of Alice's adventures, beginning with an operetta, *Alice in Wonderland* (1886), by Henry Savile Clarke.

There have also been many films since the first short silent version was made in 1903. (Unless otherwise indicated, all of the adaptations mentioned here are called *Alice in Wonderland*, although in fact many of them use material from *Through the Looking-Glass.*) Silent movies were produced in 1910, 1915 and 1927. The first Hollywood sound version (1933) starred Charlotte Henry as Alice. It was followed by a full-length Disney cartoon (1951); this almost coincided with a lesser-known British version (1950) which had Carole Marsh as Alice amidst a cast of puppets. Versions since then include a remarkable BBC television adaptation by Jonathan Miller (1966), starring Anne-Marie Malik, which reinterpreted the books as a child's-eye view of a nightmarishly threatening Victorian society; and an insipid musical film, *Alice's Adventures in Wonderland* (1972), with Fiona Fullerton.

A more recent five-part adaptation for British independent television (1985) had Giselle Andrews as Alice, with puppets as the other characters. An American mini-series version (also 1985), with Natalie Gregory as Alice, was described by one critic as "mind-boggling" and a "travesty". The film *Dreamchild* (1986) starred Coral Browne as the real-life Alice Liddell.

Alice is the favourite "mystery girl" of English literature, symbol of childhood innocence and at the same time of a certain youthful knowingness. There is a pleasing sharpness to her personality, and it seems at times as if she can see through all adult impostures.

GUSTAVE DORÉ'S WONDERFUL ENGRAVING OF THE ANCIENT MARINER BY SAMUEL TAYLOR COLERIDGE: "THE ALBATROSS ABOUT MY NECK WAS HUNG..."

Amadis of Gaul

CREATOR: **Garcia Ordonez de Montalvo**
SOURCE: **Amadis de Gaula (prose romance)**
DATE: 1508

A brave, handsome young man of confused (but ultimately royal) parentage who grows up to fight giants and to win the love of the beautiful Princess Oriana, whom he rescues from sorcerous captivity on an enchanted island. The knightly Amadis was the first great fantasy hero of post-Renaissance times. Medieval romances had been written in verse, as often as not, and had been based on history (Alexander the Great, or Charlemagne and his Paladins) or on mythical history (King Arthur and his Knights of the Round Table). By the 16th century, however, and particularly in Spain – then the dominant European country, thanks to the gold flowing in from the New World – the prose romance, which was something rather like the "novel" in the modern sense, had taken firm hold, and its subject-matter was as a rule unashamedly fictional rather than any sort of historical tradition real or unreal. The vogue for the particular type of lengthy fictions known as Chivalric Romances began with Montalvo's *Amadis* (first printed in 1508, although it may have been written in the late 15th century and based on a now-lost Portuguese original).

So hugely popular was this exciting work, with its long succession of knightly quests and magical encounters, that it was translated throughout Europe and provoked dozens of imitations (a phenomenon very like the modern fashion for large heroic fantasies, inspired by Tolkien). Garcia Ordonez de Montalvo himself wrote a sequel, *The Exploits of Esplandian* (printed in 1510), about the wild adventures of Amadis's son, and it was in this work that he coined the name "California" for an imaginary island peopled by Amazon-like women. A decade or so later, when Hernan Cortez conquered Mexico for Spain, his scouts reported the existence of a large island off the Mexican coast to the north-west (actually a peninsula) and Cortez (possibly as a joke?) named it California after the fantastic land in Montalvo's romance. Thus the modern-day American state of California (originally "Alta California", as opposed to the peninsular "Baja California" which is still a part of Mexico) derives its name from a fantasy novel – a source which many people may think peculiarly appropriate.

Popular imitations of Montalvo's sagas included *Palmerin de Oliva* (1511), possibly by Francisco Vazquez, and *Palmerin of England* by Francisco de Moraes (1547–48), both about a very similar chivalric hero called Palmerin. There was at least one direct continuation of Amadis, entitled *Amadis of Greece*, by Feliciano de Silva (1535). So the phenomenon of "sequels by other hands" proves to be nothing new – such books existed in 16th-century Spain, just as today they proliferate in the shape, for example, of the many further adventures of Robert E. Howard's *Conan the Barbarian* (there is even a series of illicit sequels to Tolkien's *The Lord of the Rings*, published in Russia but prevented from appearing elsewhere by copyright law). In a sense, Amadis and Palmerin and their kindred are the ancestors of Conan the Barbarian and Frodo Baggins and all the heroes of present-day "Sword and sorcery" or heroic fantasy.

The Ancient Mariner

CREATOR: **Samuel Taylor Coleridge**
SOURCE: **"The Rime of the Ancient Mariner" (ballad)**
DATE: 1798

An aged sailor with a hypnotic eye, who is compelled to tell his bizarre story over and over again – as recounted in Coleridge's magical poem first published in *Lyrical Ballads*, a joint volume of verse by Coleridge and William Wordsworth. The Mariner is sole survivor of a terrible voyage to the South Seas and the Antarctic ("And ice, mast-high, came floating by, As green as emerald"), during which he committed the crime of killing a friendly albatross (symbol of good fortune). The bird's carcass is hung around the Mariner's neck by his horrified shipmates; nevertheless every man on the voyage comes to woe. Written in the style of a traditional ballad, the poem is packed with wonderful romantic imagery and hauntingly memorable lines. The Mariner's influence has been immense – a great deal of English-language imaginative writing of the past two centuries abounds with references to him – and over the years the poem has been illustrated by Gustave Doré and Mervyn Peake among many others. Some of the Mariner's words seem almost prophetic: a vast under-ice lake was discovered recently in Antarctica, and a mechanical drill is cautiously probing its way down to the water which has been isolated there for millions of years; one can imagine the scientists, at the moment of breakthrough, chanting the Ancient Mariner's lines – "We were the first that ever burst/ Into that silent sea"!

King Arthur

"CREATOR": **Geoffrey of Monmouth**
SOURCE: **The History of the Kings of Britain**
DATE: 1136

Arthur, the high-born boy who is tutored by the wizard Merlin, who draws the magical sword from the enchanted stone, who accedes to the throne of Britain, who wins the hand of Guinevere and the enmity of his illegitimate son Mordred, who fights many wars and ushers in an era of peace and plenty, who presides over the Round Table at Camelot and the greatest body of chivalrous knights ever

RICHARD HARRIS AS KING ARTHUR IN ONE OF THE POPULAR CINEMATIC RENDITIONS OF THE STORY, THE MUSICAL *CAMELOT*, BASED ON T. H. WHITE'S NOVEL *THE ONCE AND FUTURE KING*.

gathered in one place, and who eventually is mortally wounded in battle, returns his sword Excalibur to the mysterious Lady of the Lake, and is carried away to the isle of Avalon ...this Arthur may have some small basis in history, and a rather larger one in Celtic myth, but essentially he was given to the world – in outline, at least – by Geoffrey of Monmouth and by all those who embroidered Geoffrey's story over the succeeding century, especially Robert Wace, Chrétien de Troyes, Layamon and Robert de Boron. Much later, his tale was given a definitive form for English-language readers by Thomas Malory in his *Morte D'Arthur* (first printed in 1485).

King Arthur's subsequent influence on fantasy literature is so vast that we cannot begin to recapitulate it here (see the section on "Arthurian Fantasy" in an earlier chapter). Likewise, there is insufficient space to list all the famous characters from Arthur's story and the cycles of tales associated with it such as those concerning the Quest for the Holy Grail – Bedivere, Galahad, Gawain, Guinevere, the Lady of the Lake, Lancelot, Merlin, Morgan Le Fay, Mordred, Perceval, Tristan and Isolde, and Uther Pendragon are just a few – so Arthur himself, as the linch-pin of them all, must stand as their representative. (See the fantasy films section of this book for mention of the many Arthurian movies such as *Camelot*, 1967, and *Excalibur*, 1981).

ASLAN

CREATOR: **C. S. Lewis**
SOURCE: **The Lion, the Witch and the Wardrobe (novel)**
DATE: **1950**

A magnificent lion who acts as a Christ-figure in Lewis's famous children's story. Aslan presides over the land of Narnia – which Peter, Susan, Lucy and Edmund reach by way of a magical portal in the back an old wardrobe. Aslan reappears in the later books of the series: *Prince Caspian* (1951), *The Voyage of the 'Dawn Treader'* (1952), *The Silver Chair* (1953), *The Horse and His Boy* (1954), *The Magician's Nephew* (1955) and *The Last Battle* (1956). He is a character who has made some adult critics uneasy due to his religious symbolism and his authoritative nature: "Virtue, in the Narnia books, is seen ultimately to lie in obedience and not in brave, hazardous free decision ..." Even so, the books have been perennially popular. Aslan loomed large in a ten-part serial of *The Lion, the Witch and the Wardrobe* which was shown on British television in 1967, and in an American animated TV-movie version (1978) which won an Emmy Award. Later, BBC TV undertook a large-scale cycle of serials based on the later novels, under the umbrella title *The Chronicles of Narnia* (1988–90).

AYESHA

CREATOR: **H. Rider Haggard**
SOURCE: **She (novel)**
DATE: **1886**

Also known as She Who Must Be Obeyed, the long-lived white queen of the lost city of Kor in central Africa. Ayesha's love for the Englishman Leo Vincey causes her to re-enter the Flame of Life in order to persuade him of its power to bestow immortality. The Flame will not accept her twice; she withers and dies in moments. The story is narrated by Ludwig Horace Holly, scholar and explorer, as presented to the world through the pen of Rider Haggard in his bestselling novel (first serialized in the weekly paper *The Graphic*). This potent tale of supernatural romance provoked numerous emulations, parodies and sequels – including three more books by Haggard himself: *Ayesha* (1905), in which She is reincarnated in central Asia; *She and Allan* (1921), in which a slightly younger Ayesha meets the famous hunter Allan Quatermain and the Zulu warrior Umslopogaas; and *Wisdom's Daughter* (1923), which tells of Ayesha's early life in the Egypt of more than 2,000 years ago.

Sequels by other hands include *The King of Kor*, or *She's Promise Kept* (1903) by Sidney J. Marshall, *The Vengeance of She* (1978) by Peter Tremayne and *Journey to the Flame* (1985) by Richard Monaco. The most famous parody was *He* (1887) by Andrew Lang and Walter H. Pollock. There were stage adaptations of the original story and at least seven silent movie versions, of which the most notable were made in 1916, with Alice Delysia in the lead, and in 1925, with Betty Blythe. Sound films include *She* (1935), which starred Helen Gahagen as Ayesha; and a Hammer Films remake (1965) with Ursula Andress in the leading role, plus its sequel *The Vengeance of She* (1968), with Olinka Berova. A loose Italian remake of the original story (1985) starred Sandahl Bergman. Ayesha has frequently been taken as some kind of symbol of the eternal feminine, even by commentators as serious-minded as the psychologist Carl Jung but, whatever her deeper meaning, she is certainly a fictional character who has haunted Western culture for a century and more.

Bilbo Baggins

Creator: J. R. R. Tolkien
Sources: The Hobbit (novel)
Date: 1937

Bilbo the hobbit is a small hairy-footed personage, a "halfling", apparently timid but with hidden reserves of intelligence and courage, a quick wit, and a hobby of writing poetry and prose. As the hero of Tolkien's first novel, *The Hobbit*, or *There and Back Again*, he helps slay a dragon and recover a treasure-hoard, in the company of the wizard Gandalf and a dozen dwarves. Bilbo's personal adventures have been dramatized on BBC radio and in the animated television movie *The Hobbit* (1977).

THE FELLOWSHIP OF THE RING: THE ONE RING SHOWS FRODO (ELIJAH WOOD) THAT IT HAS A MIND OF ITS OWN.

Frodo Baggins

Creator: J. R. R. Tolkien
Sources: The Lord of the Rings (novel)
Date: 1954

Frodo Baggins is a younger hobbit, cousin and heir to Bilbo. Although a mere halfling, with all the natural timidity and diffidence of his type, he plays the hero's role in Tolkien's epic fantasy *The Lord of the Rings*. With the aid of Bilbo, Gandalf and many other characters – including faithful servant Sam and the mysterious Aragorn, also known as Strider – and with the unwitting help of the corrupted Gollum, Frodo succeeds in destroying the One Ring which is sought by Sauron, the Dark Lord who wishes to spread his deathly rule over all Middle-Earth. Frodo rises to the grand occasion admirably, suffering from injuries, despondency and temptation, but ever pressing on. In the animated movie *Lord of the Rings* (1978) Frodo's voice was provided by Christopher

Guard. In the BBC radio serialization of the same story (1981), scripted by Brian Sibley, he was played by Ian Holm – who coincidentally went on to portray Bilbo magnificently in Peter Jackson's superlative 2001 big-screen adaptation *Lord of the Rings: The Fellowship of the Ring*. Frodo, meanwhile, passed to the competent American actor Elijah Wood. During the first great Tolkien boom of the late 1960s, the phrase "Frodo lives!" became a familiar graffito across America.

Belgarath

Creator: David Eddings
Source: The Pawn of Prophecy (novel)
Date: 1982

A disreputable old sorcerer who habitually dresses in a wrinkled, much-patched tunic and hose and mismatching boots, Belgarath is the most powerful figure – both politically and magically – in David Eddings' "Belgariad" and "Malloreon" sequences. Known and feared throughout his secondary world as the implacable "Eternal Man", Belgarath is more than seven thousand years old, and seems to devote a lot of time to ordering balky kings and emperors around. As the chief divine instrument against the evil machinations of the maimed dragon-god Torak, he is the one tasked with preserving a hidden royal bloodline, and making sure that its duly prophesied scion, Garion, is able to come into his own power and slay the dark god. One of the most complicated and fully-realised characters of Eddings' work to date, Belgarath is a pitiless crusader who reluctantly accepts the nastier side of his work because of his immense love of the world and its inhabitants. His extremely detailed personal history, which is woven throughout the ten books of the "Belgariad" and "Malloreon", was finally given its own showcase in *Belgarath the Sorcerer* (1995).

Bomba

CREATORS: **The Stratemeyer Syndicate**
SOURCE: **Bomba the Jungle Boy (novel)**
DATE: 1926

A jungle lad who has many fantastic adventures, discovering lost cities, etc. Bomba, who lives in the Amazon basin, was one of the best-known of all the pseudo-Tarzans (others include Tarzan's son Korak, Sheena – Queen of the Jungle, Otis Adelbert Kline's Jan of the Jungle, Marvel Comics' Ka-Zar, William L. Chester's Kioga of the Wilderness, and Republic Pictures' serial heroine Nyoka). He is the hero of many novels by "Roy Rockwood", a house name of Edward L. Stratemeyer's writing syndicate; the sequels include such titles as *Bomba at the Moving Mountain*, *Bomba at the Giant Cataract*, *Bomba at Jaguar Island* and *Bomba in the Abandoned City*. Bomba was played by Johnny Sheffield in the low-budget film *Bomba the Jungle Boy* (1949) and 11 sequels, ending with *Lord of the Jungle* (1955). These movies were later re-edited to make a television series. Bomba has also appared in comic books.

The Borrowers

CREATOR: **Mary Norton**
SOURCE: **The Borrowers (novel)**
DATE: 1952

Homily, Pod and little Arriety – a family of tiny people who live beneath the floorboards of a human house, in Mary Norton's highly-regarded children's book. Their further adventures are to be found in *The Borrowers Afield* (1955), *The Borrowers Afloat* (1959), *The Borrowers Aloft* (1961) and *The Borrowers Avenged* (1982). The first of these books formed the basis of an American television movie (1973), with Eddie Albert and Judith Anderson; and the first four were adapted as two BBC TV serials (1992–93), with Ian Holm as Pod and Penelope Wilton as Homily.

Eric Brighteyes

CREATOR: **H. Rider Haggard**
SOURCE: **Eric Brighteyes (novel)**
DATE: 1891

In many ways the first champion of Sword & Sorcery, Eric is the Icelandic hero of Haggard's rousing historical adventure novel, a bloodthirsty tale told in the manner of the Norse sagas. A modern sequel by another hand is *Eric Brighteyes 2: A Witch's Welcome* (1979) by Sigfriour Skaldaspillir (i.e. the American fantasy writer Mildred Downey Broxon).

Dick Bultitude

CREATOR: **F. Anstey**
SOURCE: **Vice-Versa (novel)**
DATE: 1882

An English schoolboy who, with the help of a magic stone, exchanges bodies with his father, Mr Paul Bultitude (a stern Victorian paterfamilias). Their story is told in the humorous fantasy classic *Vice-Versa, or a Lesson to Fathers* by F. Anstey (real name Thomas Anstey Guthrie). The novel was filmed by Peter Ustinov as Vice Versa (1947), with Anthony Newley as young Dick and Roger Livesey as Bultitude Senior, and has since been serialized on British television (1981), with Paul Spurrier as Dick Bultitude and Peter Bowles as his father.

CINDERELLA

CREATOR: Charles Perrault
SOURCE: Mother Goose Tales (story collection)
DATE: 1697

Poor working girl, dressed in rags, who is tormented by her wicked step-sisters but is nevertheless able to go to the ball and win the love of the handsome prince, thanks to the magical intervention of her Fairy Godmother. Cinderella is possibly the best-known heroine in the whole of fairy-tale fantasy, one "literary character" who is almost universally recognized. Her story is centuries, or rather millennia, old, a genuine folk tale which has come down the generations by word of mouth – but it was Monsieur Perrault who gave her the name and form we recognize, complete with pumpkin coach, rat coachmen and glass slippers. Perrault actually called her "Cendrillon", but that was translated as Cinderella in the 18th century, since when she has become the heroine of English-language pantomimes, plays, films and countless nursery books. She even crops up frequently in non-fantasy stories; an example is the Hollywood movie *Pretty Woman* (1990), whose heroine recapitulates Cinderella's tale (with hints of Rapunzel letting down her hair) in a very conscious way. There is insufficient space here to list all the other imperishable characters from fairy stories and folk tales –

CINDERELLA, BY THE FIRESIDE, IS TAUNTED BY HER CRUEL SISTERS BEFORE THEY LEAVE FOR THE BALL (ILLUSTRATION BY HENRY RICHTER)

Beauty (of "Beauty and the Beast"), Goldilocks, Hansel and Gretel, the many different Jacks (such as he of the Beanstalk), the Pied Piper, Puss in Boots, Rapunzel, Red Riding Hood, Rumpelstiltskin, Sleeping Beauty (also known as Briar Rose), Snow White and Tom Thumb are just a few – so Cinderella, as perhaps the most archetypal of them all, may stand as their representative. (See the fantasy films section of this book for mention of other Cinderella movies such as *The Slipper and the Rose*, 1976.)

Conan the Barbarian

CREATOR: **Robert E. Howard**
SOURCE: **"The Phoenix on the Sword" (short story)**
DATE: 1932

A mighty-thewed warrior from a land named Cimmeria (which now lies beneath the North Sea) in the so-called Hyborian Age (shortly after the fall of Atlantis). Conan is the archetypal Sword & Sorcery hero, long in brawn and short in brain (though his "dumbness" has been exaggerated), hacking his way through a pseudo-historical never-never world of magic, monsters and beautiful women. He first appeared in 17 short stories and novellas written for *Weird Tales* magazine between 1932 and 1936. The only novel-length Conan story that Howard wrote, "The Hour of the Dragon" (serialized 1935–36), eventually became the first Conan book, *Conan the Conqueror* (1950 – published well after its author's premature death). More Conan volumes followed, cobbled together by various editors (the most notable being L. Sprague de Camp) from Howard's magazine stories and unpublished fragments: *The Sword of Conan* (1952), *The Coming of Conan* (1953), *King Conan* (1953), *Conan the Barbarian* (1955), *Tales of Conan* (1955), and numerous later revisions and recombinations of the material contained in these books. When Howard's stories reached mass-market paperback, in the late 1960s, they became one of the two greatest influences on the nascent commercial genre of heroic fantasy, the other being the equally delayed impact of J. R. R. Tolkien's *The Lord of the Rings*.

The first of many sequels by other hands was *The Return of Conan* (1957; also known as *Conan the Avenger*) by Bjorn Nyberg and L. Sprague de Camp. Other sequels include *Conan of the Isles* by de Camp and Lin Carter (1969); *Conan the Buccaneer* by de Camp and Carter (1971); *Conan of Aquilonia* by de Camp and Carter (1977); *Conan the Swordsman* by de Camp, Carter and Nyberg (1978); *Conan and the Sorcerer* by Andrew J. Offutt (1978); *Conan the Liberator* by de Camp and Carter (1979); *Conan: The Sword of Skelos* by Offutt (1979); *Conan: The Road of Kings* by Karl Edward Wagner (1979); *Conan the Rebel* by Poul Anderson (1980); *Conan and the Spider God* by de Camp (1980); the aptly-titled *Conan the Mercenary* by Offutt (1980; on which the magazine *Locus* commented: "this is part of

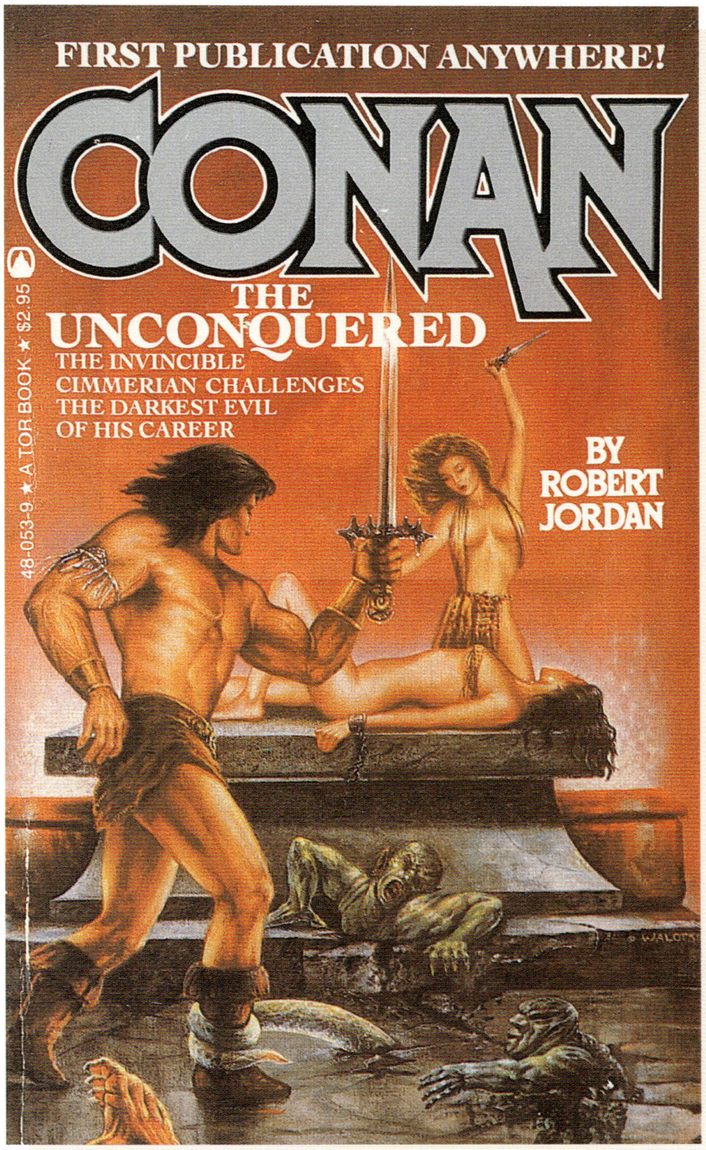

CONAN: COMMON PROPERTY OF NUMEROUS WRITERS, INCLUDING THIS ONE, OF WHOM L. SPRAGUE DE CAMP SAID: "NOBODY ALIVE WRITES CONAN BETTER THAN ROBERT JORDAN"

Ace's original Conan series, not to be confused with Bantam's original Conan series or de Camp's editing of Howard's original Conan series or the original Conan series comics, movies, or wind-up dolls"); *Conan the Invincible* by Robert Jordan (1982); *Conan the Defender* by Jordan (1982); *Conan the Unconquered* by Jordan (1983); *Conan the Triumphant* by Jordan (1983); *Conan the Magnificent* by Jordan (1984); *Conan the Victorious* by Jordan (1984); *Conan the Valorous* by John Maddox Roberts (1985); *Conan the Fearless* by Steve Perry (1986); *Conan the Renegade* by Leonard Carpenter (1986); *Conan the Raider* by Carpenter (1986); *Conan the Champion* by Roberts (1987); *Conan the Defiant* by Perry (1987); *Conan the*

Marauder by Roberts (1987); *Conan the Warlord* by Carpenter (1988); *Conan the Valiant* by Roland Green (1988); *Conan the Hero* by Carpenter (1989); *Conan the Bold* by Roberts (1989); *Conan the Indomitable* by Perry (1989); *Conan the Free Lance* by Perry (1990); *Conan the Great* by Carpenter (1990); *Conan the Formidable* by Perry (1990); *Conan the Guardian* by Green (1991); *Conan the Rogue* by Roberts (1991); *Conan the Outcast* by Carpenter (1991); *Conan the Relentless* by Green (1992); *Conan the Savage* by Carpenter (1992); *Conan of the Red Brotherhood* by Carpenter (1993); *Conan and the Gods of the Mountain* by Green (1993); *Conan the Hunter* by Sean A. Moore (1993); *Conan and the Treasure of the Python* by Roberts (1993); *Conan, Scourge of the Bloody Coast* by Carpenter (1994); *Conan at the Demon's Gate* by Green (1994); *Conan and the Manhunters* by Roberts (1994); *Conan the Gladiator* by Carpenter (1994); *Conan and the Amazon* by Roberts (1995); *Conan and the Mists of Doom* by Green (1995); and no doubt many more to come.

Conan seemed to reach the highest pitch of his popularity in the early 1980s, 50 years after his creation – and almost as long after the suicide of his creator (Robert E. Howard never lived to see what a monstrous figment he had unleashed on the world). The character has also appeared in comic books, with at least three different Marvel Comics series, *Conan the Barbarian* (from 1970), *The Savage Sword of Conan* (from 1974) and *King Conan* (from 1980). There have also been Conan role-playing games and choose-your-own-adventure game-books. The first Conan movie, John Milius's *Conan the Barbarian* (1982), was a blood-soaked fantasy made ponderous by references to Nietzsche. It starred body-builder Arnold Schwarzenegger in the title role – and no actor ever looked the part of an established fictional character more convincingly. He played the hero again in *Conan the Destroyer* (1984). Both films were novelized in their years of release, the first by the inevitable team of L. Sprague de Camp and Lin Carter, the second by the best of the latter-day Conan pasticheurs, Robert Jordan.

Hugh Conway

CREATOR: James Hilton
SOURCE: Lost Horizon (novel)
DATE: 1933

English man-of-affairs who, through a chapter of accidents, finds himself stranded in the hidden valley of Shangri-La, somewhere beyond the Karakorum Mountains in the wastes of still-mysterious Tibet. There he meets a wise Chinese gentleman called Chang, and a mysterious High Lama who is hundreds of years old; and with their aid he finds an inner peace. Conway receives a wonderful offer from the Lama, but is hesitant to accept; meanwhile his younger companion has fallen in love with a beautiful girl, and tragedy strikes when they all try to leave the valley together. "Shangri-La" has entered the language, to denote a tranquil haven far from the anxiety and violence of 20th-century life. In Frank Capra's exciting film of the book (1937) Conway was played by Ronald Colman. The movie was remade much less effectively in a musical version (1972), with Peter Finch. A sequel by another hand in book form is *Return to Shangri-La* by Leslie Halliwell (1987); in this, set 50 years after the events of Hilton's novel, a small expedition makes its way to the lost valley by a southerly route – there to find Hugh Conway, still living.

Thomas Covenant

CREATOR: Stephen R. Donaldson
SOURCE: "The Chronicles of Thomas Covenant the Unbeliever"
DATE: 1977

A present-day American, suffering from leprosy, who enters the magical world known simply as the Land, and there comes into conflict with its blighter (and the symbol of Covenant's own disease), Lord Foul the Despiser. In saving the Land, Covenant saves himself. He is the hero of Donaldson's odd, pretentiously written but best-selling fantasy series, the first three volumes of which were published simultaneously: *Lord Foul's Bane*, *The Illearth War* and The *Power That Preserves* (all 1977). The later titles in the sequence, under the umbrella title "The Second Chronicles of Thomas Covenant the Unbeliever", are *The Wounded Land* (1980), *The One Tree* (1982) and *White Gold Wielder* (1983). The latter trilogy introduces the heroine Linden Avery, who gradually takes over the lead role from Covenant.

Wendy Darling

CREATOR: J. M. Barrie
SOURCE: Peter Pan (play)
DATE: 1904

Daughter of Mr and Mrs Darling, who learns how to fly away to Never-Never-Land with Peter Pan, there to be substitute mother to the "Lost Boys". Her name (Barrie's coinage, which has since become popularly accepted as a girl's forename) is not short for Gwendoline but a lisping version of "friend" or "friendy".

Death

CREATOR: Terry Pratchett
SOURCE: The Colour of Magic (novel)
DATE: 1983

Skull-faced, dark-robed, scythe-carrying "anthropomorphic personification" of Mortality (and well aware that he is such) who always speaks hollowly in BLOCK LETTERS. Despite the essentially

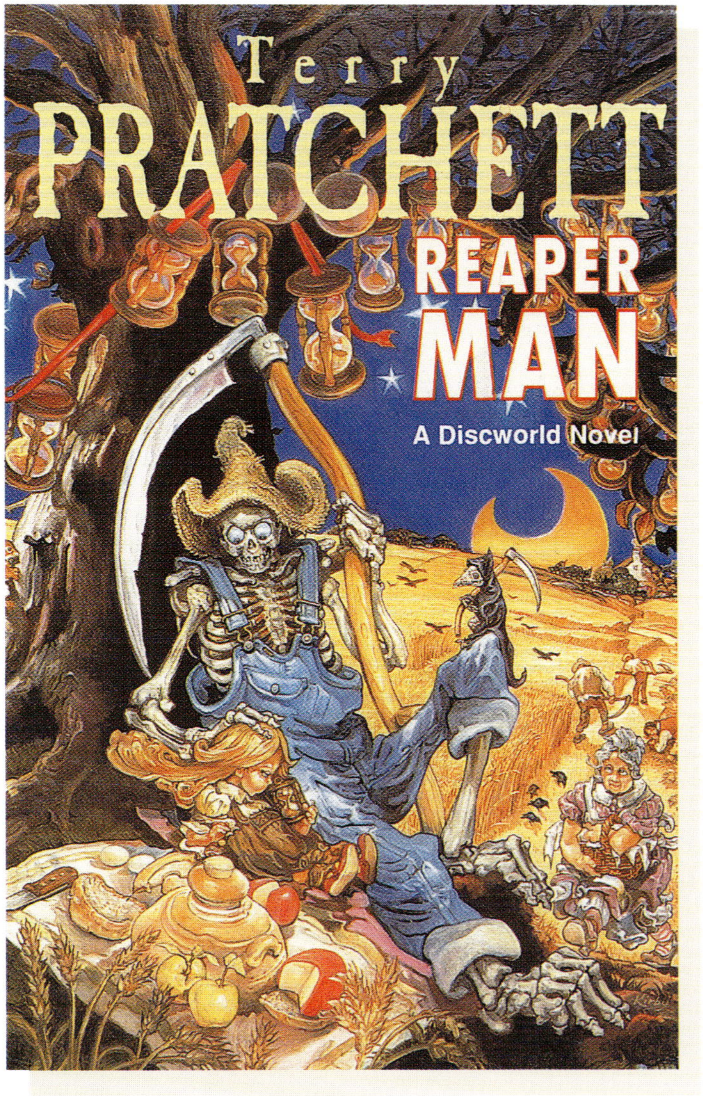

The guy with the scythe. Who would have thought that a humorous fantasy novelist would turn Death himself into a well-loved fictional character?

gloomy nature of his profession, he has a soft side – and a liking for curry. Perhaps appropriately, he is the nearest thing to a continuous character in Terry Pratchett's hugely popular "Discworld" sequence of humorous fantasies, the later volumes of which are *The Light Fantastic* (1986), *Equal Rites* (1987), *Mort* (1987), *Sourcery* (1988), *Wyrd Sisters* (1988), *Pyramids* (1989), *Guards! Guards!* (1989), *Eric* (1990; novella), *Moving Pictures* (1990), *Reaper Man* (1991) *Witches Abroad* (1991), *Small Gods* (1992), *Lords and Ladies* (1992), *Men at Arms* (1993), *Soul Music* (1994), *Interesting Times* (1994), *Maskerade* (1995), *Feet of Clay* (1996), *Hogfather* (1996), *Jingo* (1997), *The Last Continent* (1998), *Carpe Jugulum* (1998), *The Fifth Elephant* (1999), *The Truth* (2000), *Thief of Time* (2001) *and The Last Hero* (2001).

As in life, death appears throughout — although sometimes only in a "spear-carrying" (sorry, scythe-carrying) capacity.

Other recurring characters, such as the incompetent wizard Rincewind or the iron-willed witch Granny Weatherwax, pop in and out of the books, but Death is the only one who is present in them all. As their titles indicate, *Mort* and *Reaper Man* are those in which he takes centre stage. Although he now seems very much Terry Pratchett's creation, one may solemnly describe Death's origins as "traditional" (but it's likely he was inspired by the skeletal figure from Ingmar Bergman's film *The Seventh Seal* of 1957, see page 62).

The Discworld books have yet to be filmed (Pratchett has an anecdote about an American producer who wanted to make a deal for *Mort* but said, "first we'll have to get rid of this Death angle") although a number of them have been read or dramatized on BBC radio, released as talking books or adapted as graphic novels, and in 1997 two of them – *Wyrd Sisters* and *Soul Music* – were adapted as animated television serials. The Discworld cult will continue to grow and grow.

Cruella de Vil

CREATOR: **Dodie Smith**
SOURCE: **The Hundred and One Dalmatians (novel)**
DATE: 1956

Villainess whose plan to kidnap and skin a huge brood of puppies for fur coats provides the plot mechanism for Dodie Smith's children's fantasy. The story was made into an animated film by Disney (1961) – since when the name of Cruella de Vil has been a byword for female heartlessness. More recently, Glenn Close played Cruella in a live-action version of the story (1996) and its 2000 sequel, *One Hundred and Two Dalmatians*.

Dr Dolittle

CREATOR: **Hugh Lofting**
SOURCE: **The Story of Doctor Dolittle (novel)**
DATE: 1920

A "people doctor" who talks with the animals, and gives up his human practice to become an "animal doctor", he lives in the very English town of Puddleby on the Marsh, but his adventures take him all over the world and even as far as the Moon. His friends include Polynesia the parrot, Dab Dab the duck, Chee Chee the monkey and Gub Gub the pig (who has poetic aspirations and is author of a love-lyric beginning "Meet me on the compost heap/ When the Moon is hanging low"), as well as a few token humans such as Matthew Mugg, the cat's-meat man.

The hero of a series of books written and illustrated by Lofting – later volumes are *The Voyages of Doctor Dolittle* (1922), *Doctor Dolittle's Post Office* (1923), *Doctor Dolittle's Circus* (1924), *Doctor Dolittle's Zoo*

(1925), *Doctor Dolittle's Caravan* (1926), *Doctor Dolittle's Garden* (1927), *Doctor Dolittle on the Moon* (1928), *Gub Gub's Book* (1932), *Doctor Dolittle's Return* (1933), *Doctor Dolittle and the Secret Lake* (1948), *Doctor Dolittle and the Green Canary* (1950) and *Doctor Dolittle's Puddleby Adventures* (1952) – John Dolittle's charm lies in his total lack of pretension: he is a middle-aged, kind-hearted, rather overweight, West-Country bachelor, and impractical with money; but he always spreads a message of compassion and humane values. The middle volumes of the series are usually thought to be the best. A not-very-successful musical film, *Doctor Dolittle* (1967), starred Rex Harrison as the gentle Doctor; later film efforts included the unlikely casting of Eddy Murphy as an all-American madcap Dolittle, but the 1999 film did just about well enough to spawn an even poorer sequel in 2001.

DOROTHY

CREATOR: L. Frank Baum
SOURCE: The Wonderful Wizard of Oz (novel)
DATE: 1900

Full name Dorothy Gale, a little Kansas girl who is carried away by a cyclone to the magical land of Oz in Baum's tale for children (now accepted as an enduring classic, although it was long frowned upon by high-minded critics and librarians). In her journey down the Yellowbrick Road to the Emerald City, Dorothy meets the Scarecrow, the Tin Woodman, the Cowardly Lion, and eventually the Wizard of Oz himself. It proved an immensely popular story, America's most celebrated modern fairy tale. Baum went on to write 13 sequels: *The Marvellous Land of Oz* (1904), which has a curious trans-sexual theme – it is mainly about a boy called Tip who is changed into a beautiful princess; *Ozma of Oz* (1907), which reintroduces Dorothy along with such new characters as Billina the hen and Tik-Tok the mechanical man; *Dorothy and the Wizard in Oz* (1908); *The Road to Oz* (1909); *The Emerald City of Oz* (1910), in which Dorothy brings her Aunt Em and Uncle Henry from Kansas to Oz; *The Patchwork Girl of Oz* (1913); *Tik-Tok of Oz* (1914); *The Scarecrow of Oz* (1915); *Rinkitink in Oz* (1916); *The Lost Princess of Oz* (1917); *The Tin Woodman of Oz* (1918); *The Magic of Oz* (1919) and the posthumous *Glinda of Oz* (1920). All of these books except the first were illustrated by John R. Neill. At least three of the stories were turned into stage plays in Baum's lifetime, and the author himself experimented in making short films about the Oz characters.

By the time of Baum's death Oz had become an American institution, and his publishers swiftly commissioned another writer to continue the series. Ruth Plumley Thompson wrote 21 Oz books in all, of which the first half dozen are: *The Royal Book of Oz* (1921); *Kabumpo of Oz* (1922); *The Cowardly Lion of Oz* (1923); *Grampa in Oz* (1924); *The Lost King of Oz* (1925); and *The Hungry Tiger of Oz* (1926). After Thompson ceased writing in 1939 the illustrator John R. Neill wrote another three titles in the series. Since then there have been occasional sequels by other hands, including some by the original author's great-grandson, Roger S. Baum: *Dorothy of Oz* (1989) and *The Rewolf of Oz* (1990). A more bizarre example (intended for adults) is *A Barnstormer in Oz* (1982) by Philip José Farmer, which purports to be about the adventures of Dorothy's son, Hank. In movies, Dorothy has been immortalized by the young Judy Garland, who played her in the musical film *The Wizard of Oz* (1939; see page 47). "Over the Rainbow", and the other songs by Harold Arlen and E. Y. Harburg which were written for this colourful production have been used in stage versions of the story ever since. The animated film *Journey Back to Oz* (1974) featured the voice of Liza Minnelli (Judy Garland's daughter) to characterize Dorothy. *The Wiz* (1978) was based on a stage musical which transposes the action of the original Oz story to New York; it had an all-black cast, with Diana Ross as Dorothy. The later Disney blockbuster, *Return to Oz* (1985) starred a young actress called Fairuza Balk.

DRAGONS

CREATOR/DATE: traditional
SOURCE: Nordic and other mythologies

Huge lizardy monsters, usually be-winged and fire-breathing, and traditionally associated with hoards of treasure which they guard jealously, dragons have become the essential big beasts of fantasy

LEFT: DOROTHY (JUDY GARLAND) MEETS THE SCARECROW (RAY BOLGER) IN OZ – HE PROVES A CRAFTY COMPANION.
RIGHT: A DRAGON, BY VIRGINIA FRANCES STARRETT FOR NATHANIEL HAWTHORNE'S *TANGLEWOOD TALES*

fiction, ranging from the hideous "worms" of medieval romance to the sympathetic, almost cuddly, creatures of such recent novels as Graham Edwards's *Dragoncharm* (1995) – which last could be described as a piece of traditional dragon-lore crossed with Richard Adams's *Watership Down*. Despite recent attempts at animal-liberationist revisionism, dragons exist essentially to be killed – by heroes; and from the legends of Perseus and St George onwards that has been their normal fate. Modern fantasy has been quite varied in its use of dragons, however, and works which have featured them memorably include J.R.R. Tolkien's *The Hobbit* (1937), where Bilbo's task is to confront the dragon Smaug; Ursula Le Guin's *A Wizard of Earthsea* (1968) and sequels, where the dragons are wise; Gordon R. Dickson's *The Dragon and the George* (1976) and follow-ups, where the creatures are humorous; Laurence Yep's *Dragon of the Lost Sea* (1982) and sequels, where the dragon is Chinese; Lucius Shepard's "The Man Who Painted the Dragon Griaule" (1984) and sequel novellas, where the beast in question is petrified (literally); Melanie Rawn's *Dragon Prince* (1988) and follow-ups, where the dragons are tamed; Tad Williams's *The Dragonbone Chair* (1988) and sequels, where the throne named in the title is built from a monster's bones; and Michael Swanwick's *The Iron Dragon's Daughter* (1993), where the beast is a machine.

Druss the Legend

CREATOR: **David Gemmell**
SOURCE: **Legend (novel)**
DATE: 1984

No one better illustrates the distinction between the heavyweight pretensions of heroic fantasy as opposed to the moral and intellectual lightness of Sword & Sorcery than Druss, the hero of Gemmell's "Drenai" series, who first rose to prominence in *Legend*. That debut volume features the death of the ageing hero, fighting in what appears to be a doomed cause. Only in 1993 did Gemmell get round to publishing *The First Chronicles of Druss the Legend*, which describes how he comes to be as he is.

Druss is the grandson of a mad axeman, and made more aware of the taint in his blood because the axe is his own favoured weapon; *First Chronicles* opens with him using one (on a tree), and it's four feet long with a 10 pound head – but nothing to the two-headed battleaxe he comes by a little later. The attraction of Druss as a hero lies in his constant awareness, bordering on the morbid, of his own potential for evil, which inevitably grows in keeping with his skill as a warrior. He despises the gods, in whom he has no belief, but sees all around him the degradation which can come upon strong men who have compromised their ideals, whether to satisfy a passing craving or to assuage a deeper yearning for security. The only way for him is a moral code based on the categorical imperative and an existential drive to control all the aspects of his own nature which might conflict with it. It is summed up in appropriately simple language: "Never violate a woman, nor harm a child. Do not lie, cheat or steal. These things are for lesser men. Protect the weak against the evil strong. And never allow thoughts of gain to lead you into the pursuit of evil".

This formula is given to Druss by Shadak, one of his early influences. Shadak is a lone hunter who, since the murder of his family, has dedicated himself to the destruction of wicked men. Other influences are Borcha, a gigantic and highly experienced warrior whom Druss fights to a standstill over a bout of a single round (and who thereafter undertakes his training), and Sieben, a swordsman, poet, raconteur and lover of women very reminiscent of Fritz Leiber's Gray Mouser. It is typical of Druss and of Gemmell that Borcha's influence is the more enduring. Druss is attentive to Borcha but does not set up in partnership with Sieben – as Sieben remarks, he tends to fall asleep during his recitations – and he remains a countryman at heart. *Legend* opens with Druss retired from the wars and living the life of a simple farmer. He joins his last great adventure purely from a sense of duty. Because of the many prophetic insights typical of the Drenai books Druss is strongly inclined to fatalism. But he is also a believer in free will: a man always has two choices – to face his fate well or ill.

Dwarfs

CREATOR/DATE: **traditional**
SOURCE: **Nordic and Celtic mythologies**

Human-like beings very short of stature but usually immensely strong and sometimes wise, associated with caves, mine-workings and underground realms in general. Often bearded and axe-bearing, dwarfs (the plural "dwarves" belongs only to J. R. R. Tolkien), although earthy and fierce, are among the commonest "companions" in fantasy fiction: they make staunch allies, but sometimes also deadly foes. Gnomes, goblins and leprechauns are all variant kindred in the fantasy writer's imagination. Tolkien's dwarfs, such as Gimli, whose ancestors hewed out the deep dark Mines of Moria, are paradigmatic, but many others have appeared in the literature before and since. Two of this compiler's favourites are Otter, the four-foot-tall black warrior capable of crushing most men of normal stature, who plays a major role in Rider Haggard's African lost-race novel *The People of the Mist* (1894) – it turns out that he is the living image of the lost people's god, and they worship him accordingly; and M. John Harrison's Tomb the Iron Dwarf in *A Storm of Wings* (1980) – a tough, tinker-like scavenger of ancient technologies who feels obliged to remind himself from time to time that he is "a dwarf and not a philosopher".

Elric of Melnibone

CREATOR: **Michael Moorcock**
SOURCE: **"The Stealer of Souls" (novella)**
DATE: **1961**

The first and greatest avatar of the Eternal Champion, whose various guises and incarnations embrace much of Moorcock's oeuvre, Prince Elric is a complete decadent, very unlike the cheerfully amoral gallants, such as Fritz Leiber's Gray Mouser and Michael Shea's Nifft the Lean, who dominate Sword & Sorcery, and further still from such iron-thewed exemplars of the heroic virtues as David Gemmell's Druss. He is the last survivor of the royal line of Melnibone, a defunct empire which once dominated the world, and whose aristocracy has become both more and less than human, partly from copulating with demons but also through inbreeding. The consequences are manifest in Elric, a thin-blooded albino incestuously fixated on his sister and almost helpless without his magic sword, Stormbringer.

The blade Stormbringer is the physical embodiment of a demon, with a purpose of its own, and (as Elric well knows) drinks the souls of its victims. From their agony he draws superhuman vitality, but Stormbringer is as likely to turn on friend as on foe. When Elric, hoping to do without it by use of drugs, casts it away, it reappears in his armoury. Their relationship is not finished, and he will be needing it again.

Elric first appeared in the pages of *Science Fantasy* magazine. His adventures are collected in the books *The Stealer of Souls* (1963), *Stormbringer* (1965), *The Singing Citadel* (1970), *The Sleeping Sorceress* (1971; aka *The Vanishing Tower*), *Elric of Melnibone* (1972; aka *The Dreaming City*), *The Sailor on the Seas of Fate* (1976), *Elric at the End of Time* (1984), *The Fortress of the Pearl* (1989), *The Revenge of the Rose* (1991) and *The Dream-Thief's Daughter* (1999). Some of the contents of the earlier books have been recombined under different titles, including *The Weird of the White Wolf* and *The Bane of the Black Sword* (both 1977). Moorcock eventually tied the stories into his "Eternal Champion" cycle, which encompasses the adventures of other Sword & Sorcery heroes such as Erekose, Hawkmoon and Corum. Elric has also appeared in comic books and graphic novels; one of the latter is *Elric: The Return to Melnibone* (1973), illustrated by Philippe Druillet.

Elves

CREATOR/DATE: **traditional**
SOURCE: **Nordic and Celtic mythologies**

Human-like supernatural beings of slender build, graceful and good-looking, often conceived as small but sometimes taller than the human average, artistically and magically gifted, invariably mysterious in their ways, evasive, remote and – from the human point of view – "alien". They are associated with natural landscapes, with forests and with green living things in general. In most fantasy writers' imaginations elves (singular, "elf"; deriving from the Norse "alfar") are regarded as the opposite of dwarfs – they are ethereal, of the air rather than of the earth; in Shakespearean terms, they are Ariel rather than Caliban (see under Prospero, below); in more everyday domestic terms, they are cats rather than dogs. They may work with humans, or against them, but they rarely make loyal companions. Brownies and pixies and, indeed, nursery-tale fairies are all variant kindred, with the stress on the mischievous rather than the dignified attributes of elfdom. (In fact, elves could be defined briefly as "fairies for grownups".) They have taken many forms, but, as ever, it is J. R. R. Tolkien who has fixed the image of the elves most clearly for modern readers: his elven folk are tall, aristocratic and wise, custodians of old knowledge, and they live in beautiful realms, such as Rivendell, Mirkwood and Lothlorien – a paradise of Faerie which Tolkien invests with the emotions of yearning and nostalgia.

A Victorian nursery image of Elves, far removed from Tolkien's: the Elf King asleep beneath a toadstool, by Richard Doyle

Erekose

CREATOR: Michael Moorcock
SOURCE: "The Eternal Champion" (novella)
DATE: 1962

Also known as John Daker, the reluctantly sword-swinging hero of Moorcock's fantasy novel *The Eternal Champion* (1970) and its various sequels (a shorter version of the story had first appeared in the magazine *Science Fantasy*, 1962). It describes how the 20th-century John Daker is summoned by dream voices to serve as champion to a beleaguered people of the far future (or distant past). He takes the name Erekose, and eventually sides with humanity's enemies, the morally superior Eldren. His adventures are continued in *Phoenix in Obsidian* (1970; also known as *The Silver Warriors*), *The Quest for Tanelorn* (1975) and *The Dragon in the Sword* (1986). In the course of these books his destiny becomes entangled with those of other Moorcock heroes, including Elric of Melnibone, Dorian Hawkmoon and Prince Corum. It is revealed that all these (and others) are aspects of the same Eternal Champion, doomed to fight throughout the ages in the everlasting war of Law against Chaos.

Fafhrd & the Gray Mouser

CREATOR: Fritz Leiber
SOURCE: "Two Sought Adventure" (novelette)
DATE: 1939

A pair of swashbuckling adventurers in Leiber's series of Sword & Sorcery tales set in the imaginary world of Newhon. Fafhrd is a giant brawling barbarian, a good-humoured version of Robert E. Howard's Conan, while the Mouser is a small wily sneak-thief, expert with a knife. Both are practised killers, though they can appreciate a joke – not to mention the inevitable wine, women and song. Their first exploit was published in the pages of *Unknown* magazine in 1939, although their first book, *Two Sought Adventure* (1957), did not appear until almost two decades later. Leiber acknowledged the assistance of his friend, Harry Fischer, in the creation of the characters, and stated that the heroes were in fact versions of themselves – the tall, Nordic-looking Leiber, who had inherited his actor-father's handsome features, was Fafhrd, while the much shorter Fischer was the cat-like Mouser. Later books in the series are *The Swords of Lankhmar* (1968), *Swords Against Wizardry* (1968), *Swords in the Mist* (1968), *Swords and Deviltry* (1970), *Swords and Ice Magic* (1977) and *The Knight and Knave of Swords* (1988). When British writer Terry Pratchett wrote his first humorous fantasy, *The Colour of Magic* (1983), he peopled it with (among many others) two rapscallions called Bravd and the Weasel, clearly based on … guess who?

Dr Fu Manchu

CREATOR: Sax Rohmer
SOURCE: "Fu-Manchu" (short story)
DATE: 1912

Chinese master villain, head of the secret society known as the Si-Fan. A cold-eyed calculating expert in conspiracy, torture and murder, Fu operates all over the globe, his apparent aim the ultimate mastery of the world. He is described as having "a brow like Shakespeare and a face like Satan", and he uses rare poisons, unques-

CHRISTOPHER LEE, SPLENDIDLY THE PART, AS THE SINISTER DR FU MANCHU IN ONE OF A SERIES OF 1960S HAMMER FILMS

tioning human servants and a whole menagerie of strange animals to achieve his ends. However, his nefarious plans are repeatedly foiled by the stout Britishers Dennis Nayland Smith and Dr Petrie. Fu was created by Sax Rohmer (real name Arthur Sarsfield Ward) in a series of stories which ran in the UK pulp magazine *The Story-Teller* from 1912. These were soon cobbled together into bestselling novels: *The Mystery of Dr Fu Manchu* (1913; in the USA as *The Insidious Dr Fu Manchu*), *The Devil Doctor* (1916; in the USA as *The Return of Dr Fu Manchu*), and *The Si-Fan Mysteries* (1917; in the USA as *The Hand of Fu Manchu*). For several years Rohmer tried to escape from the loom of his most famous character, but following the success of Fu Manchu in the American "slick" magazine *Collier's Weekly*, and in silent films during the 1920s, he was driven to resume the series and to continue it throughout the remainder of his long writing career. The later novels are: *Daughter of Fu Manchu* (1931), *The Mask of Fu Manchu* (1932), *Fu Manchu's Bride* (1933; also known as *The Bride of Fu Manchu*), *The Trail of Fu Manchu* (1934), *President Fu Manchu* (1936), *The Drums of Fu Manchu* (1939), *The Island of Fu Manchu* (1941), *Shadow of Fu Manchu* (1948), *Re-enter Fu Manchu* (1957) and *Emperor Fu Manchu* (1959). By the end, Fu has become a kind of hero, fighting against communism – although these last books are distinctly weary. A posthumous collection of short stories is *The Wrath of Fu Manchu* (1973).

The Fu Manchu tales are among the leading examples of a subgenre which may be called the fantasy thriller – tales of crime and conspiracy which contain large elements of the supernatural, the quasi-science-fictional, or at very least the downright improbable. The whole concept of the "Eastern menace", the notion that the Chinese (or any Asian people) are inherently hostile to all Westerners and bent on a stealthy world-conquest, is itself a fantasy in the political sense, perhaps born out of an unconscious collective guilt for Western imperialism, and it is one which had a long life: it can be seen as late as the 1950s and 1960s, in Ian Fleming's James Bond thrillers *Dr No* (1958) and *The Man with the Golden Gun* (1965) – and in Kingsley Amis's pseudo-Bond novel, *Colonel Sun* (1968). Since World War Two Sax Rohmer has been much criticized for his racism, and the books have fallen out of fashion. Nevertheless, they were seductively written examples of pulp fiction, and there have been periodic revivals. (In the American pulp magazines, particularly the "hero-pulps" of the 1930s, there were many direct imitations: fantastic villains who bore names like Wu Fang and Yen Sin.)

The actor Harry Agar Lyons played Fu Manchu in the short silent movies of the 1920s. The first talkie to feature the Devil Doctor, *The Mysterious Dr Fu Manchu* (1929), starred Warner Oland, who repeated the part in two subsequent films. However, the most memorable Fu on celluloid proved to be Boris Karloff in *The Mask of Fu Manchu* (1932). He was followed by Henry Brandon, who took on the role in the serial *Drums of Fu Manchu* (1939). Decades later, a new series of five Fu Manchu films was made in Britain, with Christopher Lee filling the part splendidly; *The Face of Fu Manchu* (1965) was the first of these, and *The Castle of Fu Manchu* (1970) was the last. An unsuccessful spoof movie, *The Fiendish Plot of Dr Fu Manchu* (1980), starred Peter Sellers.

In the 1930s and '40s Fu Manchu was very popular on American radio and in comic-strip adaptations. He also appeared on Radio Luxembourg, broadcast to a British audience, from 1936 to 1938. An American television series, *The Adventures of Fu Manchu* (1955–56), starred Glen Gordon. Probably the most famous villain in 20th-century popular fiction, Fu Manchu has remained a byword: he is the "Yellow Peril incarnate", one of the best-known embodiments of an unpleasing racial stereotype. A new Fu Manchu novel appeared in 1984 – *Ten Years Beyond Baker Street* by Rohmer's erstwhile friend and biographer, Cay Van Ash. In this the deadly doctor is pitted against the great detective Sherlock Holmes, who has been summoned from retirement to help rescue the unfortunate Nayland Smith from the arch-fiend's clutches. A further sequel by Van Ash is *The Fires of Fu Manchu* (1987).

FUNGUS THE BOGEYMAN

CREATOR: Raymond Briggs
SOURCE: Fungus the Bogeyman (picture book)
DATE: 1977

The loveable but at the same time repulsive hero of Briggs's illustrated book for children, Fungus and his family live underground, in a dank smelly world where all things dry and clean are abhorred. The book is full of "dirty jokes" and horrid inversions which have made it appealing to adults as well as kids. Briggs reworked the material for his *Fungus the Bogeyman Plop-Up Book* (1982).

GANDALF

CREATOR: J. R. R. Tolkien
SOURCE: The Hobbit (novel)
DATE: 1937

An ageless wizard with a long white beard. He first appears in Tolkien's children's book, where he assists the hobbit Bilbo Baggins to retrieve a great treasure guarded by a dragon. He reappears in the author's lengthy masterwork *The Lord of the Rings* (1954–55) where he plays a crucial, super-heroic role in helping to defeat Sauron, the Dark Lord. It transpires that Gandalf is much more than a mere wizard, more of a demigod, and on his wise grey head depends the fate of a whole world, as the Ages turn...

Gandalf became a cult figure in the late 1960s, when a British "underground" magazine, *Gandalf's Garden*, was named after him. He appears in the animated television movie *The Hobbit* (1977) and the cartoon feature film *Lord of the Rings* (1978). In the BBC radio adaptation of the latter title (1981) he was voiced by Michael Hordern, and he was played to perfection by Ian McKellen in Peter Jackson's magnificent 2001 film.

GIANTS

CREATOR/DATE: traditional
SOURCE: Greek and other mythologies

Human-like supernatural creatures of vast dimensions, usually hostile and man-eating, giants have had a common role to play in many mythologies. The Greek word "cyclops" means one-eyed, but has also come to denote a giant, since Odysseus's monocular enemy Polyphemus was of huge size. Ogres and trolls are variant kindred, familiar from numerous fairy tales, romances and legends; and Arabian genies (more properly, jinni or djinns) are usually portrayed in fantasy fiction and film as enormous beings. Giants of various kinds, sometimes even benign, appear in such modern fantasy works as Poul Anderson's *Three Hearts and Three Lions* (1961), John Gordon's *The Giant Under the Snow* (1968), Piers Anthony's *A Spell for Chameleon* (1977) and Charles de Lint's *Jack the Giant-Killer* (1987). In J. G. Ballard's moving fantasy parable "The Drowned Giant" (1964), the giant is dead from the story's outset and the narrative concentrates on how he is dismembered – and his parts scattered – by those lesser beings, ourselves. (James Morrow's World Fantasy Award-winning satire *Towing Jehovah* [1994]similarly portrays God as a gigantic carcass.)

GREMLINS

CREATOR: modern traditional
SOURCE: Royal Air Force lore
DATE: late 1930s

Malicious imps who sabotage aircraft engines and other machinery. The legend of the Gremlins arose in the early years of World War Two, fed by anecdotes from British pilots and aircrew. (*Brewer's Dictionary of Phrase and Fable* attributes the coinage to members of a squadron of Bomber Command serving in India just before the war: "compounded from *Grimm's Fairy Tales*, the only book available in the mess, and Fremlin, whose beer was the only drink available"; but other dictionaries simply say "origin unknown".) Within a few years the imaginary creatures appeared as characters in a comic strip, "It's the Gremlins!" by Fred Robinson, which ran in the comic paper *Knockout* (1943–47). The ex-RAF pilot and writer Roald Dahl introduced the imps to America in his children's novella *The Gremlins* (1943), which was purchased by the Walt Disney company before publication; the intended animated feature film never materialized, but the book appeared with Disney-authorized illustrations (and is now a rare collectors' item). Dahl revived the imps in another now-hard-to-find book, his first adult novel *Some Time Never: A Fable for Supermen* (1948), in which a pilot discovers the secret underground city of the Gremlins. The 1984 comedy-horror film by Joe Dante, *Gremlins*, about fast-breeding little monsters who take over an American town, seems to owe almost nothing to Dahl or to RAF lore; it was followed by *Gremlins 2: The New Batch* (1990).

AN ARCHETYPAL FOLK-TALE GIANT WITH SOME OF HIS VICTIMS – FROM A 19TH-CENTURY ILLUSTRATION (ARTIST UNKNOWN) FOR "JACK THE GIANT-KILLER"

TITUS GROAN

CREATOR: Mervyn Peake
SOURCE: Titus Groan (novel)
DATE: 1946

The youthful 77th Earl of Groan, who inherits Gormenghast Castle and eventually leaves to seek the wider world, in Mervyn Peake's great fantasy trilogy, continued by *Gormenghast* (1950) and *Titus Alone* (1959). Titus is still a baby at the end of the first volume, and the action principally concerns the machinations of a villainous underling called Steerpike. The trilogy is full of memorably eccentric characters who are depicted in Dickensian fashion. The first two Titus novels were dramatized on BBC radio (1984), with Julian Firth as Titus Groan.

WORZEL GUMMIDGE

CREATOR: Barbara Euphan Todd
SOURCE: Worzel Gummidge (novel)
DATE: 1936

A scarecrow who stands in the Ten-acre Field at Scatterbrook Farm. He comes to life, much to the astonishment of the children. Worzel – who speaks with a ripe country accent, carries an old umbrella and has birds nesting in his pockets – becomes involved in many comical adventures which are recounted in Barbara Todd's sequels: *Worzel Gummidge Again* (1937), *More About Worzel Gummidge* (1938), *Worzel Gummidge and Saucy Nancy* (1947), *Worzel Gummidge Takes a Holiday* (1949), *Earthy Mangold and Worzel Gummidge* (1954), *Worzel Gummidge and the Railway Scarecrows* (1955), *Worzel Gummidge at the Circus* (1956), *Worzel Gummidge and the Treasure Ship* (1958) and *Detective Worzel Gummidge* (1963). Worzel's adventures became popular on BBC radio, and later on television, where a short series, *Worzel Gummidge Turns Detective* (1953), had Frank Atkinson as the scarecrow. Decades later, the books were freshly adapted to TV by Keith Waterhouse and Willis Hall: their series, *Worzel Gummidge* (1978–81), starred Jon Pertwee, and its success led to a new series of spinoff books by Waterhouse and Hall.

Kay Harker

CREATOR: **John Masefield**
SOURCE: **The Midnight Folk (novel)**
DATE: 1927

Young English lad who goes treasure-hunting at night, with the assistance of some supernaturally endowed animal friends. In a second story, *The Box of Delights* (1935), he is given a magic box which enables him to shrink in size, travel in time, and conjure up people from the past. Other members of the Harker family had already appeared in Masefield's adult adventure novels *Sard Harker* (1924) and *Odtaa* (1926). In the expensively produced BBC television serial *The Box of Delights* (1984), Kay was played by Devin Stanfield.

Captain Hook (Dustin Hoffman) and a somewhat aged Peter Pan (Robin Williams) in Steven Spielberg's uninspired continuation of J. M. Barrie, *Hook* (1991)

Hazel

CREATOR: **Richard Adams**
SOURCE: **Watership Down (novel)**
DATE: 1972

A courageous, level-headed rabbit, who is the hero of Adams's best-selling children's tale, a book which soon formed a cult among adults. Hazel and his second-sighted brother Fiver lead a small band of rabbits from their doomed warren and go in search of a new home. It is an epic story, compellingly told. In the animated feature film, *Watership Down* (1978), Hazel's voice was provided by John Hurt.

Ludwig Horace Holly

CREATOR: **H. Rider Haggard**
SOURCE: **She (novel)**
DATE: 1886

An ugly, hairy, ape-like man who is the learned narrator of Haggard's adventure fantasies *She* and *Ayesha* (1905). He accompanies the golden-haired young Leo Vincey to the lost African city of Kor, where they both fall in love with Ayesha, the near-immortal white queen also known as She Who Must Be Obeyed. In film versions of *She,* Holly has been played by Nigel Bruce (1935) and Peter Cushing (1965), neither of whom seemed physically right for the part.

Captain Hook

CREATOR: **J. M. Barrie**
SOURCE: **Peter Pan (play)**
DATE: 1904

Pirate captain, whose lower right arm has been bitten off by a crocodile and replaced by a wicked steel hook, in J. M. Barrie's play and its associated novel *Peter and Wendy* (1911). The crocodile gets the rest of Captain Hook in the end, after he has done his utmost to make life miserable for Peter Pan, Wendy Darling and the other inhabitants of Never-Never Land. Notable actors who have relished the role of Hook on stage include Gerald du Maurier, Charles Laughton, Alastair Sim and Boris Karloff. Dustin Hoffman played him in the film *Hook* (1991).

Iolanthe

CREATORS: **W. S. Gilbert and Arthur Sullivan**
SOURCE: **Iolanthe, or The Peer and the Peri (operetta)**
DATE: **1882**

A "peri", or fairy, who marries a mortal and gives birth to a semi-mortal son, Strephon, in Gilbert and Sullivan's oft-performed satirical light opera.

The Jabberwock

CREATOR: **Lewis Carroll**
SOURCE: **"Jabberwocky" (poem)**
DATE: **1871**

Monstrous creature, with "jaws that bite [and] claws that catch", in Carroll's mock-heroic nonsense poem which appears in *Through the Looking-Glass and What Alice Found There* (see Alice, above). As envisaged in the book's illustrations by John Tenniel, the Jabberwock is a winged, dragon-like beast.

Indiana Jones

CREATOR: **George Lucas**
SOURCE: **Raiders of the Lost Ark (film)**
DATE: **1981**

A rugged, whip-cracking American field-archaeologist of the 1930s who hunts various time-worn artefacts and sites of mystery around the world and then copes with the supernatural mayhem which invariably ensues. Created by Lucas for the movie directed by Steven Spielberg, he was played by the stubbly and laconic Harrison Ford, who portrayed Jones as a latter-day version of the omnicompetent heroes in the B-movies and cinema serials of the pre-war years. Jones reappears in two sequels, the rousingly titled *Indiana Jones and the Temple of Doom* (1984) and *Indiana Jones and the Last Crusade* (1989), both with the same producer, director and star. Indiana ("Indy" for short) has also appeared in film novelizations, a Marvel Comics series entitled *The Further Adventures of Indiana Jones*, and choose-your-own-adventure game-books. A spinoff series of paperback novels by Rob MacGregor consists of the titles *Indiana Jones and the Peril at Delphi* (1991), *Indiana Jones and the Dance of the Giants* (1991), *Indiana Jones and the Seven Veils* (1991), *Indiana Jones and the Unicorn's Legacy* (1991), *Indiana Jones and the Genesis Deluge* (1992) and *Indiana Jones and the Interior World* (1992). In these he runs the gamut of typical pulp-fantasy situations, discovering lost worlds, secret enclaves and terrifying conspiracies. Presumably MacGregor tired eventually, for other writers have continued the series of spinoffs, with novels like *Indiana Jones and the Sky Pirates* (1993) and *Indiana Jones and the White Witch* (1994), both by Martin Caidin, and *Indiana Jones and the Philosopher's Stone* (1995) by Max McCoy. Meanwhile, yet other hands have produced children's novels about Indy as a lad, to tie in with a television series, *The Young Indiana Jones Chronicles* (1992–93), which starred Sean Patrick Flanery as the 17-year-old hero and, in some episodes, Corey Carrier as an even younger incarnation (aged ten).

Clearly, Lucas will keep Jones alive as long as the franchise pays off: the major problem for him and his many collaborators is finding enough time-slots in the 1920s and 1930s to squeeze in all those fantastic adventures.

Joseph Jorkens

CREATOR: **Lord Dunsany**
SOURCE: **"The Tale of the Abu Laheeb" (short story)**
DATE: **1926**

A gentleman's-club-member, and sometime traveller, who now tells tall tales (well lubricated by alcohol) of strange doings and fantastic events from around the globe. If he is to be believed, Jorkens is forever running into magic, witches and monsters. He first appeared in a story by Dunsany published in *Atlantic Monthly*. Jorkens continued to spin his far-fetched yarns in a subsequent series of stories written for many leading slick magazines and newspapers on both sides of the Atlantic, and these were collected in the books *The Travel Tales of Mr Joseph Jorkens* (1931), *Mr Jorkens Remembers Africa* (1934), *Jorkens Has a Large Whiskey* (1940), *The Fourth Book of Jorkens* (1947) and *Jorkens Borrows Another Whiskey* (1954).

Jorkens is the most famous of the clubman storytellers in fantasy fiction. A later equivalent is Sterling E. Lanier's Brigadier Ffellowes, whose yarns are collected in *The Peculiar Exploits of Brigadier Ffellowes* (1972) and *The Curious Quest of Brigadier Ffellowes* (1986). Slightly more science-fictional, though laced with fantasy in the Jorkens spirit, are the stories to be found in L. Sprague de Camp and Fletcher Pratt's *Tales from Gavagan's Bar* (1953) and Arthur C. Clarke's very similar *Tales from the White Hart* (1957).

Isaac Asimov's *Tales of the Black Widowers* (1974) and its sequel volumes are predominantly crime-fiction variants of the form, though his *Azazel* (1988), consisting of anecdotes about a wish-granting demon told by a somewhat Jorkens-like character called George Butternut, is pure fantasy.

Jurgen

CREATOR: **James Branch Cabell**
SOURCE: **Jurgen**
DATE: **1919**

A middle-aged pawnbroker who is magically restored to the age of 21 and then sets out on an adventurous (and amorous) quest through the land of Poictesme and as far afield as Heaven and Hell. This story is told in Cabell's eccentric work of fantasy – a book which had the good fortune to be charged with obscenity by the New York Society for the Suppression of Vice, as a result of which it became a best-seller and made the author's name. The novel is just one of a series which runs to some 20 volumes, all set in the imaginary realm of Poictesme. The principal character of the series is not Jurgen but Dom Manuel, a pig-keeper turned prince. The other titles include *The Cream of the Jest* (1917), *Figures of Earth* (1921), *The High Place* (1923) and *The Silver Stallion* (1926).

Kai Lung

CREATOR: **Ernest Bramah**
SOURCE: **The Wallet of Kai Lung (story collection)**
DATE: **1900**

Chinese sage and tale-teller who is the hero of an amusing series of fantasies by the English author Bramah (real name E. B. Smith). These abound with mock-Chinese aphorisms, of the type also made popular in fiction and film by the detective Charlie Chan. Later tales are collected in *Kai Lung's Golden Hours* (1922), *Kai Lung Unrolls His Mat* (1928), *The Moon of Much Gladness* (1932; also known as *The Return of Kai Lung*) and *Kai Lung Beneath the Mulberry Tree* (1940). A selection of stories from the various Kai Lung books is *The Celestial Omnibus* (1963).

Korak

CREATOR: **Edgar Rice Burroughs**
SOURCE: **The Beasts of Tarzan (novel)**
DATE: **1916**

Real name Jack Clayton, the son of Tarzan (Lord Greystoke) and his wife Jane Porter. His adventures begin when he is a mere babe in arms: in *The Beasts of Tarzan* young Jack is kidnapped, and this action sets in train a particularly gruelling series of adventures for the boy's father. In *The Son of Tarzan* (1917) more than a decade has gone by, and Jack has grown into a muscular lad who senses the call of the jungle in his blood (although he has been kept ignorant of his father's true past). He befriends a captured ape, runs away from his over-civilized home in England and takes ship for Africa, where he spends several years learning the ways of the wild. He is dubbed Korak (apish for "Killer") by his great-ape friends. Eventually he is reunited with his family, and marries a beautiful French girl. In *Tarzan the Terrible* (1921), Korak returns from the First World War just in time to rescue Tarzan, who is in deadly peril in the lost land of Pal-ul-Don. He plays a very minor role in several of the Tarzan novels which follow.

Korak was played by Kamuela Searle in the cinema serial *Son of Tarzan* (1920); unfortunately, the young actor was killed during filming, and Korak made no further appearances in the serials. Later "sons of Tarzan" who appeared in the movies – for example, Boy, played by Johnny Sheffield in *Tarzan Finds a Son* (1939) and several subsequent films – were actually foundlings taken in by the Lord of the Jungle and his mate. Korak has continued to lead a vigorous independent life in the comic books, however. Philip José Farmer argues in *Tarzan Alive* (1972) that Korak is not really Tarzan's son at all (since Tarzan was born in 1888 it would have been impossible for him to have fathered a son who was old enough to fight in World War One). According to Farmer, Korak is actually the younger brother of Tarzan's cousin, Hugh "Bulldog" Drummond – and he was adopted by the Greystokes in 1912, at the age of 14. The writer J. T. Edson accepts this genealogy in his pseudo-Tarzanic *Bunduki* novels (from 1975), where Korak is referred to as Sir John Drummond-Clayton.

Doctor Lao

CREATOR: **Charles Finney**
SOURCE: **The Circus of Dr Lao (novel)**
DATE: **1935**

An aged Chinese circus-master who tours America with a menagerie of unicorns, sphinxes, werewolves, etc., in Finney's remarkable fantasy. In the film version, *The Seven Faces of Dr Lao* (1964), he was played by Tony Randall.

The Little Mermaid

CREATOR: **Hans Christian Andersen**
SOURCE: **"The Little Mermaid" (short story)**
DATE: **1836**

The youngest daughter of the Mer-King, in Andersen's latter-day fairy tale. She saves a human prince from drowning, falls in love with him, and longs to join him on dry land. At the price of losing her tongue, she has her fishtail changed into human legs by the Sea Witch. The Danish fabulist Andersen differs from earlier col-lators of fairy tales, such as Charles Perrault and the Brothers Grimm, in that most of his works were freshly invented fictions

THE MAGICAL WORLD OF *LITTLE NEMO IN SLUMBERLAND*, AS PORTRAYED IN THE 1990 ANIMATED FILM. THERE IS NOTHING ELSE QUITE LIKE IT IN FANTASY

rather than reworkings of oral traditions. Although a few of Andersen's stories were based on genuine folk tales, "The Little Mermaid" is largely his own creation (even if it does bear some resemblance to the novella "Undine" [1811] by the Baron de la Motte Fouque, and to earlier French and Italian tales about underwater temptresses).

Later stories about mermaids include H. G. Wells's novel *The Sea Lady: A Tissue of Moonshine* (1902); the British film *Miranda* (1947), which was based on a play by Peter Blackmore and starred Glynis Johns; the Hollywood movie *Mr Peabody and the Mermaid* (1948), with Ann Blyth; and the later American film *Splash!* (1984). The last-named, which starred Daryl Hannah as a sexy mermaid, followed the outlines of Andersen's fable quite closely. Andersen's original model came back into fashion in a big way with the full-length *The Little Mermaid* (1989), the Disney company's most successful animated film in many years. The derivative 2000 sequel was less well received.

Little Nemo

CREATOR: Winsor McCay
SOURCE: The New York Herald (newspaper)
DATE: 1905

A small boy who falls asleep to dream wonderful dreams, in McCay's ground-breaking comic strip, "Little Nemo in Slumberland" (1905–1914). This much-praised, phantasmagorical strip, which has been republished in book form, is regarded as the first great landmark in strip art. Little Nemo also appeared in early animated films (from 1911), and was revived for a comic book (drawn by McCay's son) in the 1930s. A full-length Japanese cartoon, *Little Nemo: Adventures in Slumberland* (1990), has kept the character in the public eye.

Pippi Longstocking

CREATOR: Astrid Lindgren
SOURCE: Pippi Longstocking (novel)
DATE: 1945

Gawky, red-headed, extremely athletic young girl in the Swedish children's book by Lindgren (the character is known as Pippi Langstrump in the original). Pippi is an orphan who believes that her father is a South Sea cannibal king. She is so strong that she can heft horses and policemen; she is also very untidy, and wears mismatching stockings. In the words of one critic she embodies "the dreams of small children who weave fantasies about total freedom from adult supervision, enormous physical strength, [and] escape from the conventions of a civilization invented by grownups". Sequels, also by Lindgren, are *Pippi Goes on Board* (1946) and *Pippi in the South Seas* (1948). Pippi has appeared in four Swedish films (1969–71), where she was played by Inger Nilsson, and in an English-language movie, *The New Adventures of Pippi Longstocking* (1988), which starred Tami Erin.

Mandrake the Magician

CREATOR: Lee Falk
SOURCE: "Mandrake the Magician" (comic strip)
DATE: 1934

Mesmerizing hero who has learned all manner of secret powers from a Tibetan guru. With the help of his black African sidekick Lothar, he uses his magical abilities to trap numerous villains in the strip, written by Falk and drawn by Phil Davis, which enjoyed a very long run in American newspapers. Mandrake became the hero of a cinema serial (1939), which starred Warren Hull, and also featured in various short-lived comic books of the 1950s and 60s. A television series, *Mandrake* (1954), had Coe Norton in the leading role. The TV movie *Mandrake the Magician* (1978) was an unsuccessful attempt to revive the character; it starred Anthony Herrera as Mandrake.

Walter Mitty

CREATOR: James Thurber
SOURCE: "The Secret Life of Walter Mitty" (short story)
DATE: 1939

The daydreaming hero of Thurber's funny short story, first published in the *New Yorker* and later collected in the book *My World – and Welcome to It* (1942). In the film *The Secret Life of Walter Mitty* (1947), where he was played by Danny Kaye, Mitty's character is elaborated: he works as a magazine proofreader, and, inspired by the pulp fiction he reads for a living, he spins extravagant fantasies within his own mind, projecting himself as a daring sea-captain, pilot, western outlaw, and so on – which episodes are dramatized in the movie. Thurber's original is not so much a fantasy as a clever story about fantasy, but Mitty's name has entered the language to refer to all dozy, fantasizing dreamers (as has that of another fictional character – Keith Waterhouse's "Billy Liar", 1959).

The Moomins

CREATOR: Tove Jansson
SOURCE: Comet in Moominland (novel)
DATE: 1946

Moomintroll is a bland-faced little creature, vaguely reminiscent of a pygmy hippopotamus, who lives with his Moominpappa and Moominmamma in the Valley of the Moomins, somewhere in Northern Scandinavia. The story of the Moomins and the bizarre creatures and events surrounding them has been told by the Finnish writer and illustrator Jansson in a series of highly imaginative books which have been compared to the work of Lewis Carroll (she has illustrated Finnish editions of Carroll, as well as Tolkien's *The Hobbit*). The principal later books are *Finn Family Moomintroll* (1948), *The Exploits of Moominpappa* (1950), *Moominsummer Madness* (1954), *Moominland Midwinter* (1958), *Tales from Moomin Valley* (1962), *Moominpappa at Sea* (1965) and *Moominvalley in November* (1971). The characters have gained world-wide popularity, and have appeared in newspaper comic strips and on television.

Hank Morgan

CREATOR: Mark Twain
SOURCE: A Connecticut Yankee at the Court of King Arthur (novel)
DATE: 1889

A resourceful Yankee who travels through time as a result of a blow to the head and wakes up to find himself a member of King Arthur's Round Table at Camelot, where he endeavours to change the course of history – with dubious results. Twain's amusing (but rather dark) novel is the archetype of all those comic fantasies, such as L. Sprague de Camp and Fletcher Pratt's *The Incompleat Enchanter* (1942), in which a present-day character is thrust into a "literary" secondary world. A silent movie version of the story (1921) starred Harry Myers; in the first talkie version, *A Connecticut Yankee* (1931), Hank the Yank was played by American folk-hero Will Rogers; in the musical remake, *A Connecticut Yankee in King Arthur's Court* (1949),

THE HAWAIIAN ACTOR JASON SCOTT LEE AS THE INDIAN WOLF-BOY MOWGLI IN THE 1994 VERSION OF *THE JUNGLE BOOK*. HE LOOKED GOOD IN THE PART, THOUGH THE FILM WAS A FLOP

he was embodied (and given a crooning voice) by Bing Crosby. A TV movie of the same title (1989) was a spoof with Keshia Knight Pulliam as a modern-day girl in the "Hank Morgan" role.

MOWGLI

CREATOR: **Rudyard Kipling**
SOURCE: **"In the Rukh" (short story)**
DATE: **1892**

A boy raised by wolves in the forests of India. Mowgli (which means "Frog") is saved by the wolves after he and his parents have been attacked by Shere Khan the tiger. He is reared as a wolf cub, and later learns the Law of the Jungle from Baloo the bear. His other main allies are Bagheera the panther and Kaa the python, and with the help of these beasts he survives many dangers, including several renewed encounters with the mighty Shere Khan. Eventually Mowgli reaches adulthood and returns, sadly, to the world of human beings. Prior to Tarzan (who resembles Mowgli in several ways) he is the most celebrated feral child in modern fiction. Kipling first invented him for an adult short story, collected in the book *Many Inventions* (1893); in this Mowgli appears as a grown-up, but there are references to his childhood in the jungle. Kipling went on to write a number of children's stories about Mowgli's strange upbringing, and these were included in *The Jungle Book* (1894) and *The Second Jungle Book* (1895). Neither volume is devoted entirely to Mowgli, and several decades went by before the tales of the wolf-boy were collected in one book as *All the Mowgli Stories* (1933).

Kipling's vividly written animal fantasies became immensely popular and influential. Lord Baden-Powell's cub scouts took their language and lore from the Mowgli stories. There have been several attempts to film Mowgli's adventures, none of which really succeeds in capturing the magic of Kipling's original. *The Jungle Book* (1942) had Sabu as Mowgli. A Disney-produced animated film of the same title (1967) depends mainly on its jazzy musical score, and comes a very long way after Kipling. A new live-action movie version, with Jason Scott Lee as Mowgli, was released in 1994 but failed to set the world afire. There have also been stage renditions of *The Jungle Book*.

BARON MUNCHAUSEN

CREATOR: **Rudolph Erich Raspe**
SOURCE: **Baron Munchausen's Narrative of His Marvellous Travels (novel)**
DATE: **1785**

A braggart military man who spins endless yarns about his exploits, which include a flight to the Moon. The mendacious Baron is not strictly a fictional character, in that he had a real-life original, the

THE GREATEST LIAR OF ALL TIME? JOHN NEVILLE AS BARON MUNCHAUSEN IN TERRY GILLIAM'S REMARKABLE 1989 FILM OF HIS FANTASTIC ADVENTURES

appropriately named Hieronymous von Munchausen(1720–1797), but Raspe's work was so gloriously over the top, so replete with the unbelievable and the fantastic, that Munchausen has been regarded as fictitious ever since. Raspe was a German (something of a fugitive hoaxer and rogue himself), but his book was published originally in English, and was much added to in subsequent editions, partly by other hands. It inspired an entire sub-genre of absurdist tall tales, and in the present century it has formed the basis of several films, notably *The Adventures of Baron Munchausen* (1943), which starred Hans Albers, and the similarly titled movie by Terry Gilliam (1989), with John Neville as the Baron. In 1996 the ever-untruthful Baron, seeming scarcely a day older, was revived by Ian McDonald for an amusing story, "The Further Adventures of Baron Munchausen: The Gulf War", published in *Interzone* 109; he is also the subject of a hilarious story-telling game of competitive yarn-spinning, *The Adventures of Baron Munchausen*, released in 1997 by British games company Hogshead Publishing.

THE MUNSTERS

CREATORS: **Joe Connelly and Bob Mosher**
SOURCE: **The Munsters (TV series)**
DATE: **1964**

A delightfully ghoulish family, based on characters from the 1930s horror films of Universal Studios. Head of the household is the amiable, peace-loving Herman Munster, a look-alike of Frankenstein's monster; his wife, Lily, is a vampire (Dracula's daughter, in fact), and his son, Eddie, is a werewolf – but they pose no threat to average citizens, since they just want to lead a normal suburban existence in the town of Mockingbird Heights. Herman was played by Fred Gwynne, and Lily by Yvonne DeCarlo, in the US television comedy series (1964–66) conceived by a committee and produced by Connelly and Mosher (possibly in imitation of the slightly more subtle *Addams Family*, although the opening episodes of the two shows were aired just a week apart). Subsequent TV movies with Herman and family were *Munster Go Home* (1966) and *The Munsters' Revenge* (1981), both starring Fred Gwynne. A revived series, *The Munsters Today* (1988–89), featured a wholly new cast, headed by John Schuck as Herman and Lee Meriwether as Lily.

DR NIKOLA

CREATOR: **Guy Boothby**
SOURCE: **A Bid for Fortune (novel)**
DATE: **1895**

An urbane, hypnotic cat-lover, with a brilliant mind like that of his contemporary Professor Moriarty (in Conan Doyle's Sherlock Holmes stories), Dr Nikola demands total obedience from his minions as he searches for the secret of immortality. A master villain who in some ways prefigures Sax Rohmer's Dr Fu Manchu (though without such racial overtones), Nikola plies his nefarious trade in the once-popular fantasy thrillers of the Australian-born writer Boothby, who died young: *A Bid for Fortune* (1895; also known as *Dr Nikola's Vendetta*), *Dr Nikola* (1896), *Dr Nikola's Experiment* (1899) and *Farewell, Nikola* (1901). Dr Nikola also plays a lesser role in Boothby's *The Lust of Hate* (1898).

HOMER'S ODYSSEUS, THAT MOST CUNNING OF GREEK HEROES, PLOUGHING THE SEASHORE IN AN ENGRAVING BY CONSEN, AFTER HARDY

ODYSSEUS

"CREATOR": **Homer**
SOURCE: **The Odyssey (epic poem)**
DATE: **c. 750 BC**

The wily hero – both soldier and sailor, and something of a trickster – who fights for the Greek cause in the Trojan wars and then makes his way home by sea to his wife Penelope on the island of Ithaca. It is that great return journey, a circuitous voyage of ten years around the Mediterranean and into mythical parts, which forms the subject-matter of Homer's poem, and it is a voyage replete with fantastic detail and supernatural incident, ranging from the meddlesome behaviour of the Olympian gods to the adventures involving the one-eyed giant Polyphemus and the sorceress Circe (who can change men to swine). Also known by his Roman name, Ulysses, Odysseus stands as the great archetype of the resourceful adventurer and explorer in Western literature. As such, his influence on the fantasy genre has been incalculable.

It has also been claimed, often enough, that Homer's *Odyssey* and its companion poem *The Iliad* represent the "beginning" of Western literature (and hence fantasy) as a whole. Nothing could be further from the truth: Homer's epics were the end-products of a tradition of oral poetry, or Heroic Song, which lasted for several centuries – possibly from the time of the semi-legendary Trojan wars themselves, around 1200 BC, until the epics took their "final" form in the 8th century BC (not so very final, since the texts we have date from many centuries later still, and were edited by a long line of Athenian and Alexandrian scholars). We know from references in later Greek literature that Homer's epics were just two among a large cycle of now-lost narrative poems – others dealt with other incidents in the long-drawn-out story of the wars (including the fall of Troy itself, not described by Homer), and with the return home of various other heroes. Homer's masterpieces were in fact "late" examples of their form, and have survived not because they were unique but because they were considered the best.

There is insufficient space here to list all the other marvellous heroes and fantastic beings from Greek and Roman myth, legend and literature – Aeneas, Achilles, the inventor Daedalus and his son Icarus (who flew too close to the sun on birds' wings), Heracles (also known as Hercules, whose 12 labours pitted him against all manner of monsters), Jason and the Argonauts (who voyaged in search of the Golden Fleece), Orpheus and his wife Eurydice (who entered the underworld), Perseus (who flew the winged horse Pegasus, killed a dragon to save the maiden Andromeda, and later cut off the Gorgon's head), Romulus and Remus (suckled by a wolf), and Theseus (who braved the labyrinth to slay the Minotaur) are just a few – so Odysseus, as one of the most fundamental of them all, must stand as their representative. (See also the fantasy films section of this book for mention of movies based on *The Odyssey* and other Graeco-Roman literature.)

The Wizard of Oz

CREATOR: **L. Frank Baum**
SOURCE: **The Wonderful Wizard of Oz (novel)**
DATE: **1900**

Ruler of the Land of Oz in Baum's children's book and its many sequels. In fact he is a charlatan who has arrived in the magical country of Oz by balloon. He befriends Dorothy Gale, the little girl from Kansas, although he is unable to help her to find her way home. In the famous musical film *The Wizard of Oz* (1939) the Wizard was played by Frank Morgan. An all-black movie version of the story, *The Wiz* (1978), had Richard Pryor in the part. The title of John Boorman's odd science-fiction film *Zardoz* (1973) is a veiled reference to the Wizard of Oz.

Peter Pan

CREATOR: **J. M. Barrie**
SOURCE: **The Little White Bird (novel)**
DATE: **1902**

A boy who never grows up. As a baby, he befriends the fairies in Kensington Gardens and they come to accept him as more-or-less one of their own. In Peter's best-known adventure he carries Wendy Darling and her two little brothers away to Never-Never Land, where they encounter the villainous Captain Hook. Peter was invented by Barrie in his novel *The Little White Bird*, the relevant chapters of which were later republished as a children's book with illustrations by Arthur Rackham, *Peter Pan in Kensington Gardens* (1906). Barrie's imagination was seized by the magical figure of the elfin boy, and he used him as the central character of an astonishingly elaborate stage play, *Peter Pan, or The Boy Who Wouldn't Grow Up* (1904). It was in this production that Barrie introduced the Darling children and their dog Nana, the fairy Tinker Bell, and the pirate leader Captain Hook. He later turned the play into a novel, *Peter and Wendy* (1911), which contained much new material. Because of its length and complexity the book has often been abridged or "retold" by other authors – just as the stage play has been through many adaptations during its frequent revivals.

The first film of the play was made in 1924, and starred Betty Bronson as Peter (it has become traditional practice for the boy to be played by an actress). Following this, J. M. Barrie added to the Peter Pan myth by writing his own film scenario (never produced) and by publishing a new book version of the play (1928), both of which contained fresh details that have been incorporated into later stage productions (notably, a Royal Shakespeare Company version of 1982 which was described by one critic as "a national masterpiece"). The best-known film is the Walt Disney animated feature, *Peter Pan* (1953). There have also been an American television production (1955), starring Mary Martin, and a British TV movie (1976), with Mia Farrow. In 1991 film-maker Steven Spielberg reincarnated Peter Pan and the pirate captain in his failed blockbuster, *Hook*; Robin Williams starred as a middle-aged American version of Peter, who rediscovers his magical boyhood when spirited away to Neverland. A statue of Peter Pan, erected at Barrie's expense in 1912, still stands in Kensington Gardens. In recent years, Peter Pan has become a fruitful subject for psychologists and psychologizing literary critics; he has lent his name to at least one "syndrome", and the critic Jacqueline Rose worries about him at length in her book *The Case of Peter Pan, or The Impossibility of Children's Fiction* (1984). A sequel by another hand in book form is *Peter Pan and the Only Children* (1987) by Gilbert Adair.

The Phantom

CREATOR: **Lee Falk and Ray Moore**
SOURCE: **"The Phantom" (comic strip)**
DATE: **1936**

Real name Kit Walker (or perhaps Christopher Standish), a costumed superhero of American newspaper fantasy-thriller strips, conceived by writer Falk and artist Moore. Also known as the Ghost Who Walks, the Phantom was the first of the masked-and-suited comic-strip heroes, an obvious inspiration for Batman and many others who have followed. The contemporary Phantom is supposed to be the heir to a 400-year line: a 16th-century ancestor was marooned in the land of "Bangalla"; protected by a tribe of pygmies, he created a secret home for himself in Skull Cave. From there he and his long line of sons have ventured forth as the Phantom, pursuing wrongdoers around the world. A cinema serial, *The Phantom* (1943), starred Tom Tyler as the hero. The Phantom has also appeared in comic books, and in a series of 12 novels by Frank S. Shawn and Lee Falk, beginning with *The Story of the Phantom* (1972).

Pinocchio

CREATOR: **Carlo Collodi**
SOURCE: **The Adventures of Pinocchio (novel)**
DATE: **1883**

A wooden puppet who eventually becomes a real flesh-and-blood boy, in the well loved classic of Italian children's literature by Collodi (real name Carlo Lorenzini). Pinocchio is carved by an old

THE MAGICIAN PROSPERO CONFRONTS THE WILD THING, CALIBAN, IN THIS UNATTRIBUTED ENGRAVING BASED ON SHAKESPEARE'S GREAT FANTASY PLAY *THE TEMPEST*

carpenter, Gepetto, and since he has been made from an enchanted piece of wood, he comes to life before Gepetto has even finished his shaping task. Pinocchio is endlessly mischievous and most reluctant to attend school. In a famous scene the good fairy who watches over the puppet causes his wooden nose to grow longer every time he tells a lie. After running off and having many frightening adventures, which include being swallowed by a whale, Pinocchio mends his ways and is at last transformed into a real boy.

The story has proved very popular in English translation, and has been adapted to the stage, film and television innumerable times. The most celebrated version is Walt Disney's animated feature film *Pinocchio* (1940) – which introduced the extraneous character of Jiminy Cricket. A TV movie of the same title (1976) had Sandy Duncan as Pinocchio; and a later animated feature was entitled *Pinocchio and the Emperor of the Night* (1987). On the celebration of Pinocchio's centenary it was reported that some 60,000 visitors a month were drawn to the Pinocchio Monumental Park in the village of Collodi, Tuscany.

POPEYE

CREATOR: **Elzie Crisler Segar**
SOURCE: **Thimble Theatre (comic strip)**
DATE: 1929

A pugilistic sailor-man with a unique way of talking ("I yam what I yam, an' tha's all I yam!"). He turns into a superhero whenever he eats a can of spinach, and is able to pound the living daylights out of his perennial enemy, the hulking Bluto (also known as Brutus). His girl-friend is the scrawny and screechy Olive Oyl, and another of his associates is the hamburger-eating J. Wellington Wimpy. Popeye, a great figure in 20th-century American mythology, was the happy creation of newspaper strip-cartoonist Segar, who introduced the character into his already well established strip *Thimble Theatre* at the end of the 1920s. Popeye soon became its leading figure, and from 1933 onwards he appeared in some 234 animated films produced by Max Fleischer. Noted for their vigour and inventiveness, most of these films were short, though several, such as *Popeye the Sailor Meets Sinbad the Sailor* (1936), were of "featurette" length. Jack Mercer was the longest-serving of the actors who gave voice to Popeye. Later (much inferior) series of Popeye cartoons were made for American television in the 1960s and 70s. There were also

Popeye comic books from the 1930s to the 1970s, as well as a series of "Big Little Books" about the sailor's antics. Robert Altman's rather ponderous live-action film *Popeye* (1980) starred Robin Williams as the tattooed sailor with the bulging forearms.

Mary Poppins

CREATOR: **P. L. Travers**
SOURCE: **Mary Poppins (novel)**
DATE: 1934

A London children's nanny who is gifted with magical powers, including the ability to slide up staircase banisters. She appears in Travers's children's book and its sequels: *Mary Poppins Comes Back* (1935), *Mary Poppins Opens the Door* (1944), *Mary Poppins in the Park* (1952) and *Mary Poppins in Cherry Tree Lane* (1982). In the highly successful musical film *Mary Poppins* (1964) she was played by Julie Andrews, who was suitably charming but rather too young for the part.

Harry Potter

CREATOR: **J. K. Rowling**
SOURCE: **Harry Potter and the Philosopher's Stone (novel)**
DATE: 1997

Harry Potter was still just a baby when his parents were murdered by the evil Lord Voldemort – a wizard so terrifying that the entire magical community refers to him as "You-Know-Who", just in case. Despite being next on the dark wizard's hit list, some special quality of Harry's made Voldemort's powers rebound, and the murderer was defeated. The young orphan was then raised neglectfully by his mean-spirited, muggle (ie non-magical) uncle and aunt, the Dursleys, having been told only that his parents died in a car crash. Everything changed on Harry's eleventh birthday, when he discovered the truth about his magical heritage and abilities, and was invited to enrol in Hogwarts School of Witchcraft and Wizardry.

Harry's adventures are all set against the backdrop of his ongoing education at Hogwarts school. Voldemort is trying to regain his lost power, and it repeatedly falls to the brave, resourceful young wizard and his best friends, Ron Weasley and Hermione Granger, to do what they can to thwart the evil plans, under the watchful eyes of sweet-natured half-giant gamekeeper Hagrid, and the wise, powerful Professor Dumbledore, headmaster of Hogwarts school. The books have been a world-wide phenomenon, and the sequence currently stands at *Harry Potter and the Philosopher's Stone* (1997), *Harry Potter and the Chamber of Secrets* (1998), *Harry Potter and the Prisoner of Azkaban* (1999), *Harry Potter and the Goblet of Fire* (2000), and *Harry Potter and the Order of the Phoenix* (expected late 2002). There will be just two more books in the sequence, taking Harry up to the age of 17 and the end of his school life – the last chapter of the last book is already written and is locked in a bank vault, where it has been since 1997. The excellent movie of the first book, starring Daniel Radcliffe as Harry, was released in 2001; the movie of the second book is due for release in 2002.

DRACO MALFOY (TOM FELTON) SNEERS ON AS HARRY POTTER (DANIEL RADCLIFFE) AND RON WEASLEY (RUPERT GRINT) HEAD INTO TROUBLE.

Prospero

CREATOR: **William Shakespeare**
SOURCE: **The Tempest (play)**
DATE: 1611

An exiled magus who, with his daughter Miranda, rules over an island of strange beings, including the sprite Ariel and the monstrous wild-man Caliban. Prospero can conjure the winds and cast illusions before men's eyes – as he does with the shipwrecked party whose arrival triggers the action of the play. Shakespeare's fantasy island (ostensibly in the Mediterranean, but its atmosphere probably inspired by the recently settled Bermuda) and its presiding genius have echoed through later works of the fantastic, Prospero himself providing one of the basic templates for the figure of the wizard. Modern fantasy novels inspired by the play include *Mrs Caliban* by Rachel Ingalls (1982), *Caliban's Hour* by Tad Williams (1994) and *A Sorcerer and a Gentleman* by Elizabeth Willey (1995).

The Psammead

CREATOR: **E. Nesbit**
SOURCE: **"The Psammead" (magazine serial)**
DATE: **1902**

A "sand fairy", which is to say a remarkably ugly creature with a fat furry body, bat-like ears and eyes on stalks. It is also ill-tempered, but it has the wonderful gift of being able to grant wishes. This magic beast was invented by Nesbit for her delightful children's books *Five Children and It* (1902) – first serialized in *The Strand Magazine* as "The Psammead" – and *The Story of the Amulet* (1906). In the first book the wish-granting results in comic mayhem; in the second novel the Psammead's magical abilities allow the children to travel backwards in time to ancient Egypt and Babylon – and even Atlantis. The books, which are among the best things in children's literature, and in humorous fantasy in general, have been serialized a number of times on BBC television.

Mr Pye

CREATOR: **Mervyn Peake**
SOURCE: **Mr Pye (novel)**
DATE: **1953**

Harold Pye, the eccentric hero of Peake's fantasy, who arrives on the Island of Sark determined to convert all its inhabitants to his religion of love – and ends up sprouting wings. A fine dramatized version on British independent television (1986) had Derek Jacobi in the leading role.

Allan Quatermain

CREATOR: **H. Rider Haggard**
SOURCE: **King Solomon's Mines (novel)**
DATE: **1885**

A grizzled hunter, small of stature but very brave, who is known to the natives of Southern Africa as "Macumazahn ... in vulgar English, he who keeps his eyes open". He is the hero and narrator of a series of adventure fantasies by Haggard, beginning with the ever-popular *King Solomon's Mines*. With his guide, the majestic Umbopa, and his companions, the sterling Englishmen Sir Henry Curtis and Captain John Good, Quatermain penetrates an unexplored region of Africa in search of the lost diamond mines of the Biblical king. In the sequel, entitled *Allan Quatermain* (1887), he visits the long-lost land of Zu-Vendis in the company of the heroic Zulu warrior Umslopogaas; and at the end of this novel the "editor" reports that Allan has died. Despite this early killing-off of his best-loved hero, Haggard went on to write a further 12 books about Quatermain's earlier adventures. Many of them are supernatural in flavour. The titles are: *Maiwa's Revenge* (1888), *Allan's Wife* (1889), *Marie* (1912), *Child of Storm* (1913), *The Holy Flower* (1915), *The Ivory Child* (1916), *Finished* (1917), *The Ancient Allan* (1920) – in which Quatermain "dreams" himself back to the Egypt of the Pharaohs – *She and Allan* (1921) – a notable crossover volume where he and Umslopogaas meet the immortal white queen Ayesha – *Heu-Heu* (1924), *The Treasure of the Lake* (1926) and *Allan and the Ice Gods* (1927) – another time-slip tale, which Rudyard Kipling helped Haggard to plot.

The first Allan Quatermain novel has been continuously in print for over a hundred years, though most of the others are now little read. In the film of *King Solomon's Mines* (1937) Quatermain was played by Cedric Hardwicke. In a 1950 remake he was impersonated none too convincingly by Stewart Granger. The disappointing centenary remake (1985) starred an even less convincing Richard Chamberlain – Allan Quatermain reimagined as an American adventurer in the mould of Indiana Jones. A poor sequel to the last film is *Allan Quatermain and the Lost City of Gold* (1986), also starring Chamberlain. There has also been a movie called *King Solomon's Treasure* (1977), with David McCallum in the Quatermain role. (With depressing regularity, in film reference books and the like, the character's name is mis-spelled "Quartermain"; note that there should be no "r" before the "t".)

Rasselas

CREATOR: **Samuel Johnson**
SOURCE: **The History of Rasselas, Prince of Abyssinia (novel)**
DATE: **1759**

A young man who escapes from the Happy Valley where he has been confined by his father, only to discover that the world has nothing better to offer him. His story is told in Dr Johnson's excellent philosophical fable, which he wrote in the space of a few days in order to pay his mother's funeral expenses (and it has rarely been out of print since) and which, along with William Beckford's *Vathek*, is one of the two best-known English-language examples of a widespread and significant 18th-century form of fantasy fiction – the "Oriental tale".

Uncle Remus

CREATOR: **Joel Chandler Harris**
SOURCE: **Uncle Remus: His Songs and His Sayings (story collection)**
DATE: **1880**

Old cotton-plantation slave who tells wonderful folk tales, blending African myth with American topography. His stories are animal fables, and involve such recurring characters as Brer Rabbit and Brer Fox. Remus was invented by Joel Chandler Harris for his many books, which include *Nights with Uncle Remus* (1883), *Uncle Remus and His Friends* (1892), *Told by Uncle Remus* (1905), *Uncle Remus and Brer Rabbit* (1907), *Uncle Remus and the Little Boy* (1910) and *Uncle Remus Returns* (1918). Remus was played by Edric Connor in the BBC radio series *Cabin in the Cotton* (1947). The character also appeared in the semi-animated Walt Disney film *Song of the South* (1947) where he was played by James Baskett.

Rima

CREATOR: **W. H. Hudson**
SOURCE: **Green Mansions (novel)**
DATE: **1904**

A South American jungle-girl, full name Riolama, who wins the love of the hero, Guevez de Argensola Abel, in Hudson's popular romance of the tropical forest. Obsessed with his "bird girl" (who can commune with animals), he tries to help find her people, but they become separated and Rima is sacrificed by Indians. The film *Green Mansions* (1959; directed by Mel Ferrer) starred Audrey Hepburn as the jungle waif; and a famous statue of Rima, by Jacob Epstein, stands in London's Hyde Park.

Rupert Bear

CREATORS: **Mary Tourtel and Alfred Bestall**
SOURCE: **The Daily Express (newspaper)**
DATE: **1920**

A small bear, invariably clad in check trousers, red pullover and scarf, who has magical adventures in an English rural setting. He is the most enduring newspaper comic-strip character in Britain. Books of Tourtel's drawings and stories about Rupert began to appear in the mid-1920s, but it was not until 1936 that the much-lauded and unbroken series of *Rupert Annuals* began. These were almost entirely the work of the outstanding artist Alfred Bestall, who had taken over responsibility for Rupert from the ailing Mary Tourtel in 1935. For some 30 years Bestall wrote and drew the bulk of the Rupert stories which appeared in the daily newspaper strip, the annual volumes and quarterly pamphlets. He created a world of enchantment, centred on the cosy village of "Nutwood" but ranging as far as the South Sea islands and the North Pole. Rupert's friends include Bill Badger, Algy Pug, Edward Trunk, Bingo the Brainy Pup, and a host of eccentric characters such as the Wise Old Goat and the Chinese Conjuror. At its height of popularity, in the 1950s, the *Rupert Annual* sold one-and-a-half million copies. Since the mid-1960s Rupert has been perpetuated by artists Alex Cubie, John Harrold and others. He also made an unauthorized and scandalous appearance in the "underground" paper *Oz*, which was prosecuted for obscenity in 1971.

Rupert's name and figure have long been exploited in merchandizing, and millions of Rupert dolls, mugs, towels and the like have been sold. In 1970 British commercial television began an animated Rupert series which lasted for seven years. A short animated film, *Rupert and the Frog Song* (1984) was produced by Paul McCartney, one of the little bear's most influential admirers. In the 1980s, Rupert's standing had never been higher. This was indicated by the publication of the celebratory book *Rupert: A Bear's Life* (1985) by George Perry, and by a long-drawn-out correspondence which appeared in the *Guardian* newspaper towards the end of 1985: this last concerned the important subject of what Rupert's father did for a living, and it culminated in a letter from the 93-year-old Alfred Bestall – who had done so much to make Rupert one of the best-loved children's heroes of the 20th century.

Gregor Samsa

CREATOR: **Franz Kafka**
SOURCE: **"The Metamorphosis" (novella)**
DATE: **1916**

A young man who wakes one morning to discover that he has been transformed into a large insect, and who then has to cope with the day-to-day consequences. The horrifyingly matter-of-fact tone of Kafka's disturbing psychological allegory has had a large effect on the subsequent literature of the fantastic – as in such stories as J. G. Ballard's "The Drowned Giant" (1964). Kit Reed's short story "Sisohpromatem" (1967) is a neat inversion of Kafka's tale: it is about a bug which changes into a human. A ballet by David Bintley is also based on "The Metamorphosis"; it was performed at Sadler's Wells in 1984.

The Sandman

CREATOR: **Neil Gaiman**
SOURCE: **The Sandman (graphic series)**
DATE: **1988**

The pale, supernatural Lord of Dreams who features in a series of highly praised comic books written by Gaiman, later collected in graphic-novel form. Volume titles include *The Doll's House* (1990), *Preludes and Nocturnes* (1991), *Dream Country* (1991), *Season of Mists* (1992), *A Game of You* (1992), *Fables and Reflections* (1993), *Brief Lives* (1994), *World's End* (1994), *The Kindly Ones* (1996) and *The Wake* (1997). The character had actually begun life many years earlier (1939), as a very minor member of DC Comics' stable of superheroes, but Gaiman was to re-imagine him totally and take him to extraordinary new heights of fantasy in tales that range through the whole of history, legend and mythology. (The figure of the Sandman, who throws sand or dust in a sleepy person's eyes, comes from nursery folklore, and was alluded to by German fantasist E. T. A. Hoffmann in his famous story "The Sandman" [1816].)

Santa Claus

"CREATORS": **Dutch settlers**
SOURCE: **New York folklore**
DATE: **17th–19th centuries**

The jolly "Santa" we have known throughout the past century-and-a-half, often confused in England with the more traditional, mysterious and even frightening figure of Father Christmas, is essentially a New York creation. The 17th-century Dutch founders of the city (then New Amsterdam) brought with them legends of Saint Nicholas, the gift-giver and protector of children (the historical St Nicholas is supposed to have lived in Asia Minor in the 4th century). This saint was known familiarly to the Dutch settlers as "Sinta Klaas", and in the 19th century his name was adapted by English-speakers as Santa Claus. The literary figure who above all others was responsible for reviving and sentimentalizing Christmas – hitherto a rural, Old-World, semi-pagan feast (the sort of thing frowned upon by the Puritans who founded America) – and for remaking it as a domestic, middle-class festivity suitable for the capitalist metropolis was the Manhattan-born Washington Irving.

Writing in his Diedrich Knickerbocker persona, in the comical *History of New York* (1809), Irving mentioned St Nicholas flying above the city's rooftops and distributing largesse. In later essays, collected in *The Sketch Book of Geoffrey Crayon, Gent.*, 1819, he also described the old English yuletide festival so memorably that a generation of urban readers on both sides of the Atlantic was moved to delight: one of its members was the young Charles Dickens, an Irving enthusiast who went on to create another figure closely associated with Christmas, Ebenezer Scrooge, in the 1840s. In 1823 another Irving admirer, his fellow New Yorker Clement Clark Moore, had published the poem "A Visit from St Nicholas" (opening line: "T'was the night before Christmas..."), and this much-reprinted piece introduced many of St Nick's salient features to the world – in particular, his flying sleigh pulled by magical reindeer, his descent via the chimney-flue while bearing gifts, his merriness and rotundity – and from there on the pattern was set.

Santa Claus's red-suited image was embellished by 19th-century American cartoonists and illustrators for gift-books, novelty

THE MOST FAMOUS OF FICTION'S MISERS: DICKENS'S EBENEZER SCROOGE, PLAYED BY GEORGE C. SCOTT (LEFT) WITH EDWARD WOODWARD, IN *A CHRISTMAS CAROL* (1984)

Christmas cards and advertising campaigns, and subsequently he found his way into fiction and film. He made notable appearances in L. Frank Baum's children's novel *The Life and Adventures of Santa Claus* (1902); in George Seaton's film *Miracle on 34th Street* (1947), appropriately set in Manhattan's Macy's department store, where he was played by Edmund Gwenn; in the children's movie *Santa Claus* (1985), where he was embodied by David Huddleston, and in its novelization by Joan D. Vinge. The New York basis of the Santa story is made very clear in this last film and novel: although Claus is depicted as a warm-hearted old Scandinavian woodcutter given immortality by the elves, the action of the tale soon moves to the hard streets of the great American city – Santa's true spiritual home.

Ebenezer Scrooge

CREATOR: **Charles Dickens**
SOURCE: **A Christmas Carol (short novel)**
DATE: 1843

A miser who mends his ways, in Dickens's well-loved fable. The most famous skinflint in fiction, Scrooge is haunted by the chain-rattling ghost of his late business partner, Jacob Marley. When shown the terrible future which awaits him if he remains selfish and heartless he repents, showers gifts on everybody he knows, and leads the Christmas revels. Other important characters in this heart-warming story are Scrooge's good-natured clerk, Bob Cratchit, and the latter's crippled son, Tiny Tim. There have been numerous stage adaptations of the tale, including an opera by Thea Musgrave (shown on British television in 1982, with Frederick Burchinal as

Scrooge). There were at least seven silent movie versions (usually entitled Scrooge). Sound films include *Scrooge* (1935), with Seymour Hicks in the title role; *A Christmas Carol* (1938), starring Reginald Owen; a remake of the same name (1951), with Alastair Sim; and the musical *Scrooge* (1970), in which Albert Finney gave a memorable performance in the title part. In addition, there has been an animated film version, *A Christmas Carol* (1971), in which Alastair Sim once more provided Scrooge's voice (this short production won an Academy Award). The TV movie *An American Christmas Carol* (1979) had Henry Winkler as an updated version of Scrooge.

There has, perhaps inevitably, also been a Walt Disney cartoon "featurette", *Mickey's Christmas Carol* (1983), in which Scrooge becomes "Scrooge McDuck", and Bob Cratchit is played by Mickey Mouse. Many other incarnations of Dickens's original are mentioned in the book *The Life and Times of Ebenezer Scrooge* (1990) by Paul Davis.

THE SHADOW

CREATOR: **Maxwell Grant**
SOURCE: **Detective Story Hour (radio show)**
DATE: 1930

Alias Lamont Cranston (alias Kent Allard), a cloaked-and-hatted crime-fighter who has the power to "cloud men's minds" and render himself effectively invisible. One of the leading lights of the fantasy thriller sub-genre, the Shadow was created originally as the fictitious "host" of a Sunday-night radio series, *Detective Story Hour*, but soon went on to feature in more than 280 short novels written by Maxwell Grant (real name Walter B. Gibson) for *The Shadow* magazine, a pulp periodical issued by Street & Smith from 1931 to 1949. Many of these stories have been reprinted as paperback books since the 1960s. The house pseudonym Maxwell Grant was also used by a few other writers who added about 40 more tales to the magazine saga at times when the prolific Gibson's inspiration flagged. With the success of the paperback reprints, crime novelist Dennis Lynds added yet more novels to the sequence, beginning with *The Shadow Strikes* (1964) and continuing with a further seven titles (again, all under the Grant pseudonym).

The Shadow also appeared in a revived radio show, to great acclaim, between the years 1936 and 1954. A generation of American listeners became familiar with the repeated homilies: "Who knows what evil lurks in the hearts of men? The Shadow knows" and "The weed of crime bears bitter fruit". For a few remarkable months in 1937–38 the Shadow was played on the air by Orson Welles. The character also featured in films, beginning with *The Shadow Strikes* (1937), in which he was portrayed by Rod La Rocque. A cinema serial, *The Shadow* (1940) starred Victor Jory, and later serials, including *The Shadow Returns* (1946), had Kane Richmond in the role. There was also a comic book devoted to the penumbral sleuth.

Recently, the character staged yet another comeback, this time impersonated by actor Alec Baldwin in the movie *The Shadow* (1994). The accompanying novelization was by James Luceno who dedicated his book, with appropriate grace, to "the late Walter Gibson (aka Maxwell Grant) ... who could turn out a Shadow novel of this size in five days, on a Smith-Corona portable".

SHEENA, QUEEN OF THE JUNGLE

CREATORS: **Will Eisner and S. M. Iger**
SOURCE: **Jumbo Comics**
DATE: 1938

Real name Janet Ames, a jungle girl who is very much the female equivalent of Tarzan – a white foundling reared by members of an African tribe who teach her martial arts and shamanistic skills. Sheena was created by Eisner and Iger for comic books, but she also appeared briefly in pulp magazines (1951–54) and a US television

TARZAN'S FEMALE RIVAL: TANYA ROBERTS MAKES AN ATTRACTIVE SHEENA, QUEEN OF THE JUNGLE, IN THE 1984 MOVIE BASED ON THE MUCH EARLIER COMIC BOOKS series, also called *Sheena, Queen of the Jungle* (1955–56), starred Irish McCalla as the tree-swinging heroine. A feature film, *Sheena* (1984), had Tanya Roberts in the part.

SINBAD

"CREATOR": **Antoine Galland**
SOURCE: **"The Seven Voyages of Sinbad" (story cycle)**
DATE: **1701**

Arab sea-captain whose daring voyages take him to various undiscovered islands where he encounters monsters such as the Roc, a giant bird which carries him away in its talons. The origins of the character of Sinbad (or Sindbad) the Sailor are lost in the depths of Arabian antiquity, but for the modern Western world he was effectively created by the French translator Galland. It is possible that Sinbad was based on real navigators of the Persian Gulf and the Indian Ocean, but it is equally possible that he derives from Homer's Odysseus or from an even older source, the "Shipwrecked Sailor" whose tale has been found in an ancient Egyptian papyrus. Originally, his cycle of seven tales was not a part of *The Arabian Nights* but a separate work, perhaps much older than the bulk of the *Nights.* Galland translated it into French and published it in Paris in 1701, some three years before he began producing his monumental *Les Mille et une nuits* (1704–17), within which the Sinbad cycle later found a home. There is insufficient space here to list all the other immortal characters from that work – Aladdin, Ali Baba and Scheherazade chief among them – so Sinbad, as the oldest, may stand as their representative. (For the many movie appearances of Sinbad see the section of this book devoted to fantasy films.)

THE SMURFS

CREATOR: **Peyo**
SOURCE: **Johan et Pirlouit (comic strip)**
DATE: **1957**

A race of blue pixie-like beings invented by the Belgian comic-strip artist Peyo (Pierre Culliford). In the French-language original the Smurfs are known as "Les Schtroumpfs". They first appeared in the 1950s, and were given a strip of their own from 1960. Since the 1970s they have become popular throughout Europe, have appeared in books and television series and pop songs, and have been much used in merchandising. In the early 1980s they also conquered America.

THE SPIDER

CREATOR: **R. T. M. Scott**
SOURCE: **The Spider Strikes (short novel)**
DATE: **1933**

Real name Richard Wentworth, the Spider is a mysterious avenger of a similar type to the Shadow, and as such is another of the leading lights of the fantasy thriller sub-genre. He adopts a hunched back and fangs, he carries a fine silk cord which is useful for climbing walls, and he stamps his dead enemies' foreheads with a red spider-shaped seal. His girl-friend is the elegant Nita Van Sloan. Among the monthly threats to New York that they fend off are mysterious-plagues, rampaging animals, a metal-eating virus, revived Neanderthals, and various cults and mad master-criminals, including a supernatural personification of Death in the January 1942 story "Death and the Spider". The pulp magazine *The Spider* ran from 1933 to 1943, and most of the 118 novellas it published were written by the flamboyant pulpsmith Norvell Page (under the house name "Grant Stockbridge") – the originator, R. T. M. Scott, wrote just the first couple of stories in the series. Two movie serials starred Warren Hull as the hero: *The Spider's Web* (1938) and *The Spider Returns* (1941). Philip José Farmer, the leading expert on the genealogy of fictional characters, once argued that the Spider, the Shadow and another pulp-fantasy hero, G-8, were one and the same person. In the Addendum to his book *Doc Savage: His Apocalyptic Life* (1973), Farmer withdraws this suggestion, saying that "Wentworth was far more bloodthirsty than the Shadow... The only good crook was a dead crook, according to Wentworth, and he saw to it that the streets and the backrooms of New York City were littered with good crooks".

STEERPIKE

CREATOR: **Mervyn Peake**
SOURCE: **Titus Groan (novel)**
DATE: **1946**

A murderous young machiavellian who upsets the cobwebby world of Gormenghast, in Peake's novel. He begins as a persecuted kitchen-boy, and ends as "His Infernal Slyness, the Arch-fluke Steerpike". His story continues in the sequel, *Gormenghast* (1950), which concludes with Steerpike's death at the hands of the castle's rightful heir, the youthful Titus Groan.

In Brian Sibley's BBC radio adaptations of the two books (1984) Steerpike was played by the rock singer Sting (who bought the movie rights to Peake's novels and has promised film versions of them).

SAMANTHA STEPHENS

CREATORS: **William Dozier and Harry Ackerman**
SOURCE: **Bewitched (TV sitcom)**
DATE: **1964**

An attractive, domesticated witch played by Elizabeth Montgomery in the American television comedy series *Bewitched*

(1964–72). An ordinary suburban housewife much of the time, she summons her magic powers by twitching her nose. This popular series was created by producers Dozier and Ackerman, and has been re-shown many times. A spin-off series, *Tabitha* (1977–78), was about the adventures of Samantha's equally talented daughter.

DR STRANGE

CREATORS: **Steve Ditko and Stan Lee**
SOURCE: **Strange Tales (comic book)**
DATE: **1963**

Full name Stephen Strange, a comic-book hero who is gifted with supernatural powers and a Cloak of Levitation. He is known as "The Master of the Mystic Arts". Strange was created by artist Ditko and writer Lee for Marvel Comics. The character has also appeared in a television movie, *Dr Strange* (1978), which starred Peter Hooten, and in a novel, *Nightmare* (1979), by William Rotsler.

SUMURU

CREATOR: **Sax Rohmer**
SOURCE: **Nude in Mink (novel)**
DATE: **1950**

An exotic villainess invented by Rohmer at a comparatively late stage in his blood-and-thunder writing career. This attempt at a female substitute for Dr Fu Manchu appeared in five fantasy thrillers: *Nude in Mink* (1950; also known as *Sins of Sumuru*), *Sumuru* (1951; also known as *Slaves of Sumuru*), *The Fire Goddess* (1952; also known as *Virgin in Flames*), *Return of Sumuru* (1954; also known as *Sand and Satin*) and *Sinister Madonna* (1956). She was played by Shirley Eaton in the film *Sumuru* (1967; also known as *The Million Eyes of Su-Muru*).

TARZAN

CREATOR: **Edgar Rice Burroughs**
SOURCE: **"Tarzan of the Apes" (magazine novel)**
DATE: **1912**

Also known as John Clayton, Lord Greystoke, an English foundling who is reared in the African jungle by great apes. A hero of enormous strength, agility and intelligence, he communes with animals, rescues damsels in distress (beginning with his first love, Jane Porter), and discovers sundry lost civilizations. Created by Chicago-born novelist Burroughs in 1912, Tarzan first appeared in *All-Story* pulp magazine, since when he has become perhaps the most famous 20th-century fictional character – a universal hero sprung from popularized versions of Rousseau's and Darwin's ideas. His adventures have featured in every medium – magazines, books, films, newspaper strips, radio, comic books and TV series (both live-action and animated) – but essentially there have been three major incarnations: the book Tarzan, the movie Tarzan, and the comic-strip Tarzan.

JOHNNY WEISSMULLER STARS IN *TARZAN'S SECRET TREASURE* (1941), WITH MAUREEN O'SULLIVAN AS JANE

The books by Burroughs are: *Tarzan of the Apes* (1914), *The Return of Tarzan* (1915), *The Beasts of Tarzan* (1916), *The Son of Tarzan* (1917 – chiefly about the adventures of Tarzan Junior, alias Korak the Killer), *Tarzan and the Jewels of Opar* (1918), *Jungle Tales of Tarzan* (1919), *Tarzan the Untamed* (1920), *Tarzan the Terrible* (1921), *Tarzan and the Golden Lion* (1923), *Tarzan and the Ant Men* (1924), *Tarzan, Lord of the Jungle* (1928), *Tarzan and the Lost Empire* (1929), *Tarzan at the Earth's Core* (1930 – in which he visits an underground world), *Tarzan the Invincible* (1931), *Tarzan Triumphant* (1932), *Tarzan and the City of Gold* (1933), *Tarzan and the Lion Man* (1934), *Tarzan and the Leopard Men* (1935), *Tarzan's Quest* (1936), *Tarzan and the Forbidden City* (1938), *Tarzan the Magnificent* (1939), *Tarzan and the "Foreign Legion"* (1947), *Tarzan and the Madman* (1964) and *Tarzan and the Castaways* (1965). The last two titles were posthumous, as is *Tarzan: The Lost Adventure* (1995), the completion of a Burroughs fragment by Joe R. Lansdale. Sequels by other hands include an illicit series of five novels by "Barton Werper" (Peter T. Scott and Peggy O. Scott). These are: *Tarzan and the Silver Globe*, *Tarzan and the Cave City*, *Tarzan and the Snake People* (all 1964), and *Tarzan and the Abominable Snowmen* and *Tarzan and the Winged Invaders* (both 1965). Sequels actually authorized by the Burroughs estate include *Tarzan and the Valley of Gold* (1966) by Fritz Leiber (loosely based on a film script by Clair

Huffaker) and *Tarzan: The Epic Adventures* (1996) by R. A. Salvatore (from a TV script). A more unusual piece of "apocrypha" is *The Adventure of the Peerless Peer* (1974) by Philip José Farmer, in which Tarzan meets Sherlock Holmes. Tarzan appears, in various guises, in a number of other books by Farmer, including the pornographic *A Feast Unknown* (1969) where he is called "Lord Grandrith" and does battle with "Doc Caliban" (i.e. Doc Savage). Farmer has also written *Tarzan Alive: A Definitive Biography of Lord Greystoke* (1972), which contains a family tree linking Tarzan to numerous other fictional characters. Taking his cues from Farmer, J. T. Edson (writer of Western stories) produced a short series of novels, beginning with *Bunduki* (1975), about the jungle adventures of Tarzan's adopted son.

The film *Tarzan of the Apes* (1918) starred strong-man Elmo Lincoln as the hero, and there were various other silent movie and serial versions throughout the 1920s. *Tarzan the Ape Man* (1932) was the first talkie to feature the hero – and the first to star Olympic swimming champion Johnny Weissmuller, who played Tarzan in a further 12 films, perhaps the best of which is *Tarzan and His Mate* (1934). Meanwhile, Buster Crabbe starred in *Tarzan the Fearless* (1933), and Herman Brix (Bruce Bennett) featured in *The New Adventures of Tarzan* (1935) and a sequel. After an ageing Weissmuller retired from the role with *Tarzan and the Mermaids* (1948), Lex Barker made a handsome lead in *Tarzan's Magic Fountain* (1949) and four subsequent films, while Gordon Scott was an over-muscled incarnation of the ape man in *Tarzan's Hidden Jungle* (1955) and five later movies. Denny Miller was a rather immature blonde Tarzan in the dire remake of *Tarzan the Ape Man* (1959). Jock Mahoney was a lean and mature hero in *Tarzan Goes to India* (1962) and one other film, while Mike Henry played the protagonist as a hulking brute in *Tarzan and the Valley of Gold* (1966) and two sequels. Miles O'Keefe played Tarzan as a pretty-boy nonentity in the second remake of *Tarzan the Ape Man* (1981), while Christopher Lambert was splendid in the leading role of *Greystoke: The Legend of Tarzan, Lord of the Apes* (1984). This last is the only film which comes close to doing justice to Burroughs's conception of Tarzan. In addition to all these English-language movies, there have been many Indian films based on the character, including such intriguing titles as *Tarzan and Delilah* (1964), starring Azad, *Tarzan and King Kong* (1965), starring Dara Singh, and *Tarzan in Fairy Land* (1968), starring Azad once again. Inevitably, there have also been pornographic additions to the Tarzan saga – for example, the little-known movie *Tarzan and the Valley of Lust* (1976).

The actor James H. Pierce, Burroughs's son-in-law, played Tarzan on the radio for many years. Ron Ely was an amiable television Tarzan in an American series made in 1966–69. An animated TV series, *Tarzan, Lord of the Jungle* (1976), featured the voice of Robert Ridgely. A TV movie, *Tarzan in Manhattan* (1989),starred Joe Lara while another TV series (1991–92) starred Wolf Larson and yet another, *Tarzan: The Epic Adventures* (1996–97), had Joe Lara returning to the part.

The comic-strip Tarzan is best represented by the work of Burne Hogarth, collected in the book *Tarzan, Jungle Lord* (1968) together with an essay in which he describes Tarzan as "a shimmering figment of myth and dream". In 1972 Hogarth published his *Tarzan of the Apes*, a graphic version of the first half of Burroughs's novel. In his book *Tarzan and Tradition: Classical Myth in Popular Literature* (1981) the classics professor Erling B. Holtsmark asserts: "the power that makes us respond to the wanderings of Odysseus is also at work in Burroughs' Tarzan, and the two great popular heroes speak openly to our most cherished fantasies".

TINTIN

CREATOR: **Hergé**
SOURCE: **Le petit vingtième (newspaper)**
DATE: **1929**

Plucky young adventurer, a cub reporter who has a quiff of red hair, and is accompanied in all his fantastic travels by a faithful dog, Milou (called Snowy in the English translations). A Francophone equivalent of the American hero Terry Lee (of Milton Caniff's 1930s strip *Terry and the Pirates*), Tintin appeared in comic strips by the Belgian artist and writer Hergé (Georges Rémi). Other immortal characters of the Tintin saga are the near-identical policemen, Dupond and Dupont (Thompson and Thomson, or the Thompson Twins, in English); and Captain Haddock, Professor Calculus, and many more. Tintin's exploits have been reprinted around the world in book form, selling over 100 million copies. The first of these was *Tintin in the Land of the Soviets* (1930), and the last complete new title to be published was *Tintin and the Picaros* (1976). The character also appeared in a French animated television series of the 1950s and in at least two feature-length cartoon films, *Tintin and the Temple of the Sun* (1969) and *Tintin and the Lake of Sharks* (1972). There is also a novel based on Hergé's creation, *Tintin in the New World* by Frederic Tuten (1993).

TOAD OF TOAD HALL

CREATOR: **Kenneth Grahame**
SOURCE: **The Wind in the Willows (novel)**
DATE: **1908**

A braggadocio toad, who drives a motor car, lives in the "finest house on the whole river", and has adventures with his more staid and thoughtful friends Mole, Rat and Badger. Toad is perhaps the best-known of the animal characters in Grahame's well loved children's novel. This beautiful, pastoral book was turned into a somewhat coarser musical play, *Toad of Toad Hall,* by A. A. Milne (1930), which gained enduring popularity on the stage and on British radio and TV. (This is probably why the absurd Toad has emerged as the "hero" of the novel in the general public mind, although lovers of the book have argued that he is far from the centre of the narrative's interest.) A later and very successful dramatization of *The Wind in the Willows*, which retains the book's original title as well as more of its flavour, is by Alan Bennett (1991). Recent sequels by other hands in book form are *Wild Wood* by Jan Needle (1981), *A Fresh Wind in the Willows* by Dixon Scott (1983), *If Only Toads Could Fly* by John Gilmore (1993) and *The Willows in Winter* by William Horwood (1993): the last two of these feature Toad as aviator rather than motorist. An animated film version of *The Wind in the Willows* was made by the Walt Disney company as half of the two-part feature *The Adventures of Ichabod and Mr Toad* (1949). Another animated version was broadcast on British television in 1983, and led to a subsequent series based on the characters (1984–85), with David Jason giving voice to Toad. There has also been an American-produced TV movie (1984). A BBC radio play, *The Killing of Mr Toad* by David Gooderson (1984), concerned the unhappy domestic life of Toad's creator, Kenneth Grahame.

Tom the Chimney–Sweep

CREATOR: Charles Kingsley
SOURCE: The Water-Babies, a Fairy Tale for a Land Baby (novel)
DATE: 1863

Young chimney-sweep who is ill-treated by his master, Mr Grimes. Shamed by the unexpected sight of himself in a mirror, Tom runs away, dives into a river and is transformed into a "water-baby". He travels out to sea, where he visits the magical Isle of St Brendan and meets the perfect teacher, Mrs Doasyouwouldbedoneby. Tom's fantastic story is recounted in Kingsley's book, which, fuelled by the author's Christian Socialism, became extremely popular and influential: it helped put an end to the practice of using children as chimney-sweeps. There have been many stage adaptations and several film versions of Tom's adventures. The most recent movie, Lionel Jeffries's *The Water Babies* (1978), had Tommy Pender in the leading role.

Cosmo Topper

CREATOR: Thorne Smith
SOURCE: Topper (novel)
DATE: 1926

A staid American banker whose life is transformed when he meets two mischievous ghosts. He is the unlikely hero of Smith's humorous novels *Topper* (also known as *The Jovial Ghosts*) and *Topper Takes a Trip* (1932). The film *Topper* (1937) starred Roland Young. It was followed by *Topper Takes a Trip* (1939) and *Topper Returns* (1941), also with Young. The American television series *Topper* (1953–54) had Leo G. Carroll in the lead role, and a TV movie of the same title (1979) had Jack Warden.

Tros of Samothrace

CREATOR: Talbot Mundy
SOURCE: Tros of Samothrace (novella)
DATE: 1925

Sword-swinging hero of fantastic historical adventures set at the time of Julius Caesar, by the English-born American writer Mundy (real name William Lancaster Gribbon). Tros, who is a literary forebear of Conan the Barbarian, first appeared in a series of novellas which ran in the pulp magazine *Adventure* in the 1920s (collected in book form as *Tros of Samothrace*, 1934). He reappears in the sequels *Queen Cleopatra* (1929) and *Purple Pirate* (1935). These books were re-edited for paperbacks under various titles during the 1960s and 70s.

Unicorns

CREATOR/DATE: traditional
SOURCE: travellers' tales

Magical white horses with long single horns projecting from their foreheads, unicorns traditionally have been associated with shyness

A TRADITIONAL UNICORN, WITH A PARTICULARLY LARGE HORN, AS PICTURED IN THE *MUNSTER COSMOGRAPHIA* IN 1543

and virginity – it is said that only an unsullied maid can touch one. Their horns have the power of healing, and more generally the very presence of the unicorn itself can somehow, mystically, "heal the land". The last notion is certainly present in the most famous of modern fantasy novels to feature this animal, Peter S. Beagle's *The Last Unicorn* (1968). Other books which have unicorns in their titles (although sometimes the usages are metaphorical) include Fletcher Pratt's *The Well of the Unicorn* (1948), Terry Brooks's *The Black Unicorn* (1987), Tanith Lee's young-adult trilogy consisting of *Black Unicorn* (1991), *Gold Unicorn* (1994) and *Red Unicorn* (1997), A. A. Attanasio's *The Dragon and the Unicorn* (1994), Jane Yolen's collection *Here There Be Unicorns* (1994), and Beagle's *The Unicorn Sonata* (1996), a novella which returns to the subject of that author's greatest success. If the dragon is fantasy's favourite big beast, then perhaps the unicorn is the genre's second-favourite species of megafauna.

Prince Valiant

CREATOR: **Hal Foster**
SOURCE: **newspaper**
DATE: 1937

A young adventurer in the days of King Arthur, hero of a celebrated American comic strip conceived and drawn by Foster. His travels take him from his birthplace, "Thule", to Arthur's Britain, and later across the sea to the mysterious New World. Prince Val is notable for being one of the few comic-strip characters who ages over the decades; in later episodes his son Arn takes the leading role. The film *Prince Valiant* (1954) starred Robert Wagner; a later production of the same title (1997) had Stephen Moyer in the part.

Rip Van Winkle

CREATOR: **Washington Irving**
SOURCE: **The Sketch Book of Geoffrey Crayon, Gent. (collection)**
DATE: 1819

Colonial who falls asleep in the Catskill mountains, after drinking a dwarf's magic potion, and awakes 20 years later to find himself a citizen of the United States. He appears in Irving's story "Rip Van Winkle". Said to be based on a folk tale from the Orkneys, Rip's tale has become a part of American lore. It was adapted to the stage many times in the 19th century: one actor, Joseph Jefferson, played Rip Van Winkle for nigh on 40 years, from the 1860s to the 1900s. The tale has also formed the basis of three operas – by G. F. Bristow (1855); by Robert Planquette (1882); and by Henry Louis Reginald de Koven (1920).

Vathek

CREATOR: **William Beckford**
SOURCE: **Vathek, an Arabian Tale (novel)**
DATE: 1786

Caliph who sells his soul to Eblis (the Devil) in Beckford's extraordinary Eastern tale. He is permitted to enter the underground halls of Eblis and view the treasures there, but is condemned to suffer evermore when his heart bursts into flame. Beckford wrote several more lengthy episodes which were included in a French edition of the story (1815), and these were first published in English a century later as *The Episodes of Vathek* (1912). One of Beckford's more famous admirers, Lord Byron, called *Vathek* his "Bible".

Remo Williams

CREATORS: **Warren Murphy and Richard Ben Sapir**
SOURCE: **Created, the Destroyer (novel)**
DATE: 1971

Known as "The Destroyer", hero of a lengthy series of fantasy thrillers initiated by Murphy and Sapir. Williams is a tough cop who becomes a master of unarmed combat, thanks to the mystical training he receives from an 80-year-old Korean guru. He now works as an agent for the USA, and is prepared to go anywhere and do anything. More than 90 novels about the Destroyer have been published. Later titles in the series are bylined Warren Murphy only, although in fact most of those after number 40 have been written by other hands, particularly those of Molly Cochran and Will Murray. The film *Remo Williams – The Adventure Begins* (1985; released in Britain as *Remo – Unarmed and Dangerous*) starred Fred Ward.

Winnie-the-Pooh

CREATOR: **A. A. Milne**
SOURCE: **When We Were Very Young (verse collection)**
DATE: 1924

A bear of very little brain, originally called Edward Bear, who first appeared in Milne's nursery verses. In the story books *Winnie-the-Pooh* (1926) and *The House at Pooh Corner* (1928) he has mild adventures with the boy Christopher Robin and their animal friends Eeyore, Piglet and Tigger. These were illustrated by Ernest Shepard and soon became established as oft-quoted children's classics, notable for their subtlety of humour and emotion at both infant and adult levels. The last chapter of *The House at Pooh Corner* has been described as "the saddest thing in literature". The little bear's adventures have been translated into Latin, and there have also been mock-scholarly studies: *The Pooh Perplex: A Freshman Casebook* (1963) by Frederick C. Crews and *The Tao of Pooh* (1982) by Benjamin Hoff. Pooh has appeared frequently on radio and television. Three short animated films produced by the Disney studios between 1966 and 1974 were collected with new interstitial material in the feature-length release known as *The Many Adventures of Winnie the Pooh* (1977).

The Wombles

CREATOR: **Elisabeth Beresford**
SOURCE: **The Wombles (novel)**
DATE: **1968**

Small, hairy bear-like creatures who live beneath Wimbledon Common, near London. They are dedicated conservationists, and make ingenious use of the litter left by human beings. These cuddly creatures first appeared in Beresford's book, and they soon became cult figures on BBC children's television, appearing in short animated films with puppets designed by Ivor Wood. In the mid-1970s the cult became a craze, when a Wombles pop group, clad in hairy costumes, sang: "The Wombles of Wimbledon Common are we..." Later books by Beresford include *The Wandering Wombles* (1970) and *The Wombles at Work* (1973).

Wonder Woman

CREATORS: **Charles Moulton Marston and Harry Peter**
SOURCE: **All-Star Comics**
DATE: **1941**

Inspired by Greek mythology, Princess Diana (also known as Wonder Woman, or Diana Prince) is a gorgeous Amazon from the lost Paradise Island, located in the mythical "Bermuda Triangle". Dressed in a star-spangled costume, and possessing various super-powers, a magical lasso, and marvellous bracelets that protect her against bullets, she travels to America in order to help the forces of good fight World War Two. Wonder Woman has been among the most successful of comic-book super-heroines, pursuing a long career as a vigilante for right, justice and even a kind of women's liberation – although she was created by a male writer and artist. She has been a member of the Justice League of America, along with the DC Comics male superheroes Batman and Superman. She appeared in the animated television series *Super Friends* (1973) and its follow-ups, and as a live-action character in the TV movies *Wonder Woman* (1974), starring Cathy Lee Crosby, and *The New Original Wonder Woman* (1975), with Lynda Carter. The subsequent TV series (1976–79) also starred Carter. A make-over of the DC Comics *Wonder Woman* title in the late 1980s, under artist George Perez, reduced the (very slight) science-fictional elements and increased the fantasy content.

Willy Wonka

CREATOR: **Roald Dahl**
SOURCE: **Charlie and the Chocolate Factory (novel)**
DATE: **1964**

Owner of the chocolate factory in Dahl's very popular children's book. He wears a top hat and goatee beard, and carries a cane. Mr Wonka's sweet factory is a wonderful and mysterious place for the young Charlie Bucket, winner of a competition set by Wonka. It is crammed with eccentric machinery, and staffed by a tribe of African pygmies known as the Oompa-Loompas (this detail has been criticized for its racism). In the sequel, *Charlie and the Great Glass Elevator* (1973), Mr Wonka takes Charlie and his long-suffering family into outer space. The musical film, *Willy Wonka and the Chocolate Factory* (1971), had Gene Wilder as the madcap factory-owner-cum-inventor.

Xena

CREATORS: **John Schulian and Robert Tapert**
SOURCE: **Hercules: The Legendary Journeys (TV series)**
DATE: **1994**

A beautiful but muscular Amazon warrior of ancient Greek times who is able to hold her own against any mere male. Played by Lucy Lawless, she first appeared as a secondary character in the *Hercules* TV show but soon was given a series of her own, *Xena: Warrior Princess* (from 1996); and in this she has full-blooded fantasy adventures along with her sidekick Gabrielle (played by Renée O'Connor). A series of spinoff novels about Xena, written in the main by Ru Emerson, includes such titles as *The Empty Throne* (1996), *The Huntress and the Sphinx* (1997) and *The Thief of Hermes* (1997).

Zadig

CREATOR: **Voltaire**
SOURCE: **Zadig, ou La Destinée (novella)**
DATE: **1748**

Ancient Babylonian hero of the satirical Eastern tale by Voltaire (real name François Marie Arouet). In search of happiness and prosperity for all, he eventually learns that good cannot exist without evil, and evil cannot exist without good. Armed with this wisdom, he becomes a benign king.

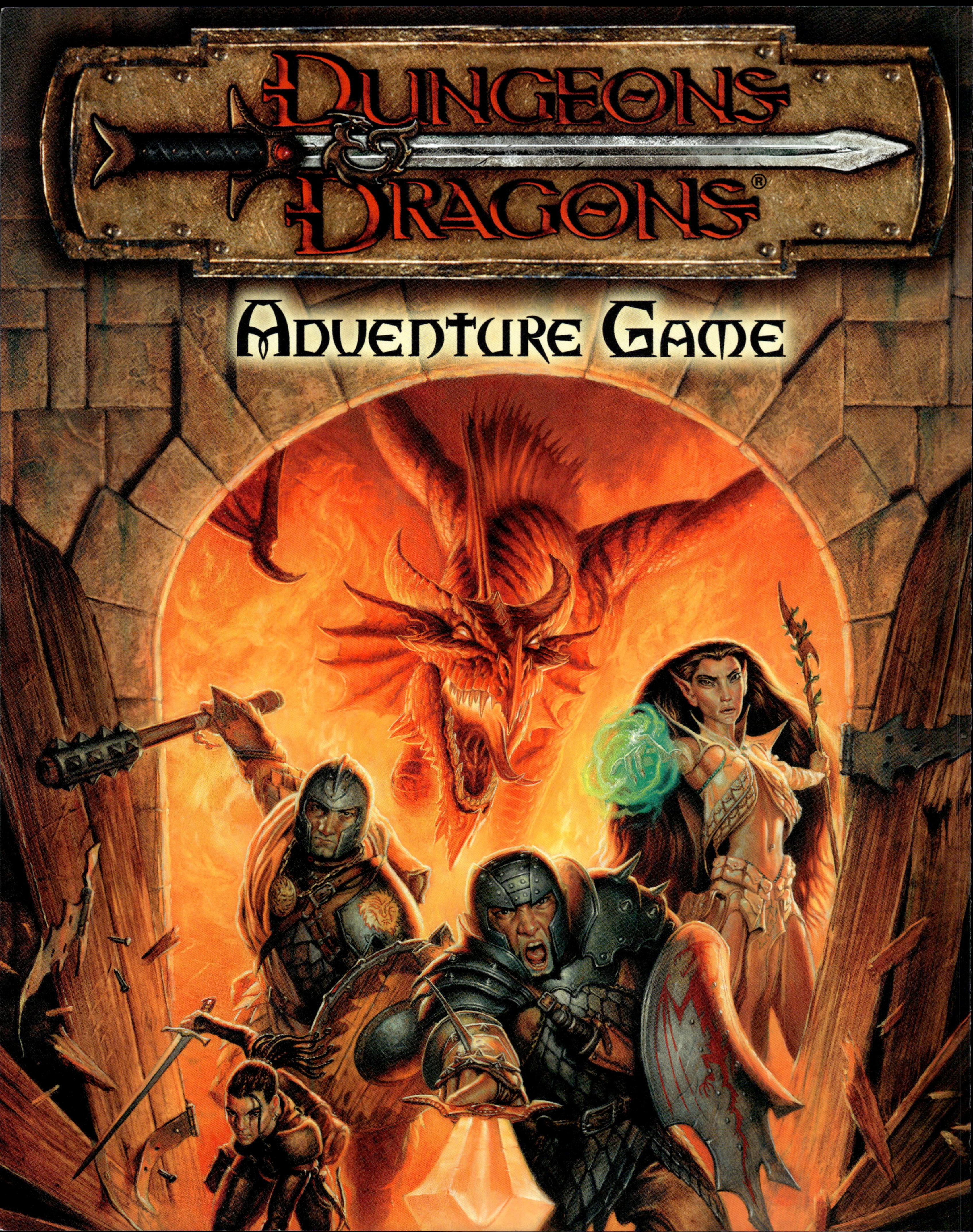
Dungeons & Dragons®
Adventure Game

Fantasy Games

The hobby of games-playing has grown beyond all recognition over the last thirty years. While gaming is one of the most ancient human traditions – some games still in common use are several thousands of years old – the pastime stayed more or less the same until recently

Board games, card games and battle simulations have all been around for a very long time. Newer games, like Monopoly, were not that far removed from more ancient ones. The complexity of the rules increased along with player literacy, and mass-production made the trappings of games more impressive, but at the heart of it all many of the ideas borrowed heavily from the past.

That situation has now changed completely. New technologies and intellectual innovations have greatly broadened the field. Computer games, in particular, are rapidly taking the place of many older forms of gaming, and the electronic games industry is far larger now than even the movies. There are several strong genres within the modern hobby, but perhaps the largest – larger even than science fiction – is fantasy.

In many respects, the whole modern games industry has been shaped by one single event: in 1973, a small Wisconsin company named Tactical Studies Rules, run by Gary Gygax and Donald Kaye, published a small game written jointly by Gygax and a colleague of his named Dave Arneson. Tired of the rigid rules inherent in war games and military simulations, Arneson had wanted to design a game that would allow its players to play fantasy warriors and wizards. The game took place in the imagination, so you could do absolutely anything you wanted to. You didn't need to measure the distance between metal miniatures with a tape-measure, or stay restricted to a certain board. Instead, you played the role of a hero designed according to your tastes – mighty warriors, subtle wizards, beautiful elf princesses and cunning thieves were all fair game. Along with other heroes controlled by your friends, you adventured through an imaginary world, pitting your wits against the opponents and puzzles described to you by the game's controller. Your hero could grow in personality and ability from game to game; the effects of one game lasted into the next. To provide fairness, consistency and excitement, conflict situations such as fighting and using skills were resolved randomly with the aid of several different dice. Sometimes you would hit your enemies; other times they would damage you. If you were unlucky, your hero would die, and you had to start another one from scratch. As the hero got more experienced, he or she would succeed more often, becoming rich and powerful. The effect was rather like simultaneously writing and reading a book, where the controller provided the plot and scenery, and the other players provided narrative and dialogue. It was creative, absorbing, exciting and sociable. Described as a "role-playing" game, because that was what the game was about, it was called *Dungeons & Dragons*.

POWERFUL SORCERERS AND TERRIFYING MONSTERS ARE THE ARCHETPYAL MOTIFS OF FANTASY GAMING

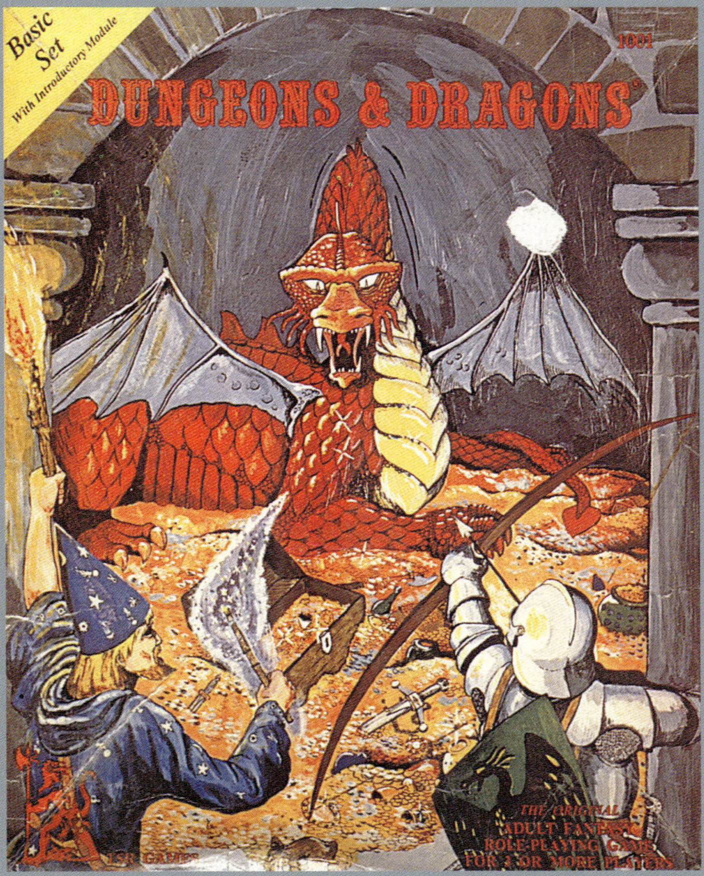

FROM TINY ACORNS... *DUNGEONS & DRAGONS* MOULDED AND SHAPED THE MODERN GAME INDUSTRY

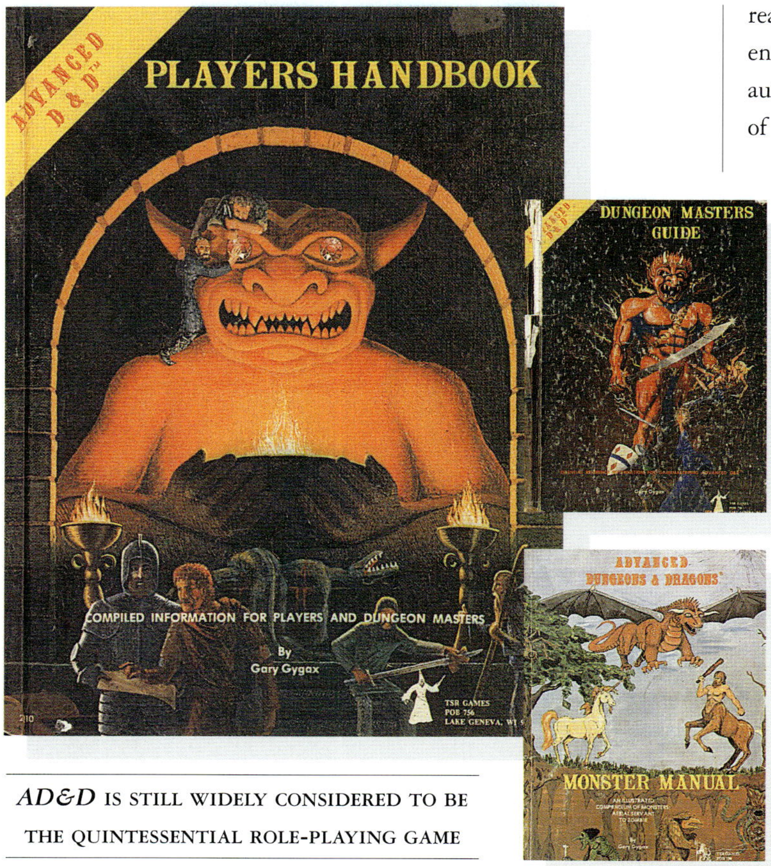

AD&D IS STILL WIDELY CONSIDERED TO BE THE QUINTESSENTIAL ROLE-PLAYING GAME

The Role-playing Game Phenomenon

The idea of the role-playing game – or RPG as it is now universally known – clearly owed more to the bardic traditions than it did to poker or chess. The innovation behind *Dungeons & Dragons* (*D&D*, for short) lay in fusing together elements from several different areas of traditional gaming. The field of fantasy fiction had received a major boost in 1965 when J. R. R. Tolkien's *The Lord of the Rings*, a previously little-known hardback work, was released in paperback. It suddenly became hugely successful, and the ideas and setting contained within it quickly spread.

The hobby of tabletop wargaming, in particular, contributed a lot to *D&D*. Before setting up Tactical Studies Rules, Gygax had, with Jeff Perrin, been part of a small wargaming company called Guidon Games. Guidon had released a game called *Chainmail* in 1971, a set of rules for wargaming with medieval miniatures. The second edition of *Chainmail*, printed in 1972, included rules for adding fantasy elements. Wargames had a long history – the first recorded military simulation game was *Kriegspiel*, written in 1824 by a Prussian staff officer named von Reisswitz, and it was quickly adopted for training new officers. While many games before had reflected military strategy – chess being the most notable example – this was the first time a game had been designed to model a battle realistically. The hobby had spread among military historians and enthusiasts, and grown to include strategy gamers, and a market for authentic miniature military figurines had grown up. The majority of wargames before 1970 had placed great store by authenticity. Fantasy was often unwelcome. Tolkien's influence soon led to a growing interest in fantasy battles, however.

Another thread that tied in to *D&D* was the practice of playing games by mail. Play-by-mail games had started as ways for geographically isolated people to play an everyday game – often chess – but several had grown into strategic games set in their own little universes, often fantastical. *Slobbovia*, a humorous *Diplomacy*-like game based very loosely on the comic strip *Li'l Abner*, began in 1969. *Slobbovia* finally closed in 1984, but some contemporary play-by-mail games, such as *Midgard*, are still active.

Dungeons & Dragons quickly became successful. By the end of 1974, it had spread across America, and at the start of 1975, Tactical Studies Rules – known now almost exclusively by its initials, TSR – started developing rules expansions and clarifications for *D&D*. The worlds of Greyhawk and Blackmoor were introduced as settings for *D&D*, and included extra rules, new types of available heroes to play – known as characters – and information to help the game controller, called the Dungeon Master (usually shortened to DM), to recreate the worlds concerned. TSR continued to publish more traditional wargames, along with other roleplaying games – a Wild West game called *Boot Hill* and a science-fiction game called *Metamorphosis Alpha* – and a board game named *War of Wizards*. This latter was set in a complicated fantasy world named Tekumel, the creation of Professor M. A. R. Barker, which would later spawn another roleplaying game, *The Empire of the Petal Throne*. None of these other games was as successful as *D&D*, however.

The first significant imitator of *D&D* was the rather cheekily named *Tunnels & Trolls*, published by Flying Buffalo, Inc. Players were amused and surprised to find that they could play a duck as a character (albeit a humanoid duck); where in *D&D* magic spells had names such as "Magic Bolt" and "Cure Light Wounds", the equivalents in *Tunnels & Trolls* were "Take That You Fiend!" and "Poor Baby". For all its humour, *Tunnels & Trolls* never really challenged *D&D*; the first game to do that was called *RuneQuest*.

RuneQuest differed from *D&D* in several important respects. The game mechanics were significantly different. The controller was referred to as a Game Master (GM), not a Dungeon Master, and the former title has more or less become industry standard. The most important difference, however, was that where *D&D* presented all the ingredients for controllers to make up their own fantasy settings, *RuneQuest* came with a complete world already built in, called

RuneQuest was set in a vivid secondary world

Glorantha. The land of Glorantha had gods, towns, cults, social structures, and provided the bones of an entire artificial society. While players were encouraged to change the world as they saw fit, the burden of creativity thrust on the controller was reduced. Glorantha was a cleverly thought-out world, and it worked well. This was not always the case with the worlds designed by *D&D* Dungeon Masters, and the players' experiences of role-playing were frequently improved by the addition of a coherent universe.

The role-playing market quickly expanded after this, with a succession of systems being released, generally with their own background. Among the fantasy games – and fantasy was by no means the only RPG genre – some of the most notable early games included *Chivalry & Sorcery* and *Pendragon*, both based loosely around the English myths of King Arthur. *Dungeons & Dragons* was released as a second edition, but more important was the release of a substantially expanded version, *Advanced Dungeons & Dragons*, or *AD&D*. This greatly expanded the game, although it still did not include a world background. *AD&D* was more like a hypermarket from which to stock a fantasy realm of your own design. It is still the best-known and best-selling RPG.

As the genre developed into the 1980s, several other games were released that set the characters inside fictional worlds based on novels. Amongst these, the most successful was to be *Call of Cthulhu*, developed by Sandy Petersen and published by Chaosium. Set in the parallel 1920s of horror writer H. P. Lovecraft, *Call of Cthulhu* was a bleak fantasy where ancient, evil gods waited to reclaim the earth and humanity was doomed. Despite this rather depressing outlook, many players regard *Call of Cthulhu* as the best-ever RPG. Another favourite was *Middle-Earth Role Playing (MERP)*, published by Iron Crown Enterprises and set firmly in Tolkien's world. It was a simple, amusing system, and Middle-Earth was extensively detailed in a range of high-quality supplements. Other notable games include a series of RPGs based on the work of Michael Moorcock, including *Stormbringer* and *Hawkmoon*. Less successful, *Amber Diceless Roleplaying* was based on the Amber novels by Roger Zelazny. This system is of interest for being the first RPG to do away with random event resolution; all gameplay is negotiated.

As the market expanded through the 1980s, TSR released a bewildering array of expansions for *AD&D*, then a second edition, and – early in the new millennium, after being acquired by Seattle games giant Wizards of the Coast – a substantially revised and improved *Dungeons and Dragons 3rd Edition*, making use of the so-named "d20 System". Uniquely, D&D3 has been published as an open license – all games companies are free to release settings, rules expansions and other material that is compatible with the d20 System. The effects are still to be seen, but more and more games are switching over from their own rules sets to the d20 System.

Many other fantasy RPGs have contributed to the hobby. *Warhammer Fantasy Role Play*, *Sky Realms of Jorune*, *Earthdawn*, *Harnmaster* and *Exalted* are all heroic fantasy games. *GURPS* and *Hero* are both generic role-playing systems, providing a rules framework to hang any type of game from. *Ars Magica* is a complex game of medieval wizardry. Other important games with fantasy elements include *Over the Edge*, a surreal game of magical realism, Dave Allsop's *SLA Industries*, an atmospheric dark-future urban fantasy, *Nephilim* and *In Nomine*, games with an occult flavour, *Kult*, a game of fantastic horror, and *Nobilis*, a truly beautiful, elegant game about the on-going battle to define reality.

Set in the dark fantasy world of HP Lovecraft, *Call of Cthulhu* is probably the best ever role-playing game

DRAGONLANCE, BASED AROUND THE SECONDARY WORLD OF KRYNN, IS ONE OF TSR'S MOST POPULAR *AD&D* GAME SETTINGS

Several RPG magazines exist worldwide, although this is a field where publications are notoriously short-lived. The longest-running RPG magazine is *Dragon*, a TSR vehicle for *D&D* and *AD&D*. Its sister magazine, *Dungeon*, concentrates on ready-made game scenarios. Steve Jackson Games, the producer of *GURPS*, publishes the excellent *Pyramid* e-zine, another in-house organ. The original independent RPG magazine was *White Dwarf*, and it is still going, but during the 1980s Games Workshop, the then-owners, converted it to an in-house-only magazine. Early issues remain the standard by which all other RPG magazines are judged. Two independent magazines are currently available: *Shadis* is published in the USA, and covers all aspects of the hobby games industry. *Valkyrie*, on the other hand, is a British magazine which has been going since 1994, and dedicates itself chiefly to supporting role-playing.

THE RPG FALLOUT: BOARD GAMES, GAME BOOKS AND LARP

Role-playing games have been the inspiration for a wide range of related gaming activities. Of these, perhaps the most obvious step was the move to fantasy board games. The major disadvantage of RPGs is that they take a lot of work for the GM to set up. Some fantasy board games attempted to provide a game where the rules and mechanics would replace the Games Master. Typically, in these games, sections of board depicting different rooms in a dungeon are selected randomly. There are several different pre-generated characters, which the players choose from. As the players explore the random dungeon, they have encounters with monsters and other notable events. Characters can get wounded in battles, or even killed, or can pick up better items of equipment, increasing their skill in battle. While these games can be quite fun, the most important elements of roleplaying – including much personal interaction – are all missing. On the other hand, they are quick and easy to play, and don't require hours of intensive preparation. Characteristic games of this type include *Talisman* and *HeroQuest*, both by Games Workshop.

Other RPG board games take a different approach. Rather than try to replicate the RPG experience, they instead reproduce the events of a more-or-less typical gaming session. With games such as these, there is usually a single printed board, and players have specific objectives to achieve. In TSR's *Knights of Camelot*, the aim of the game is to become a knight of the Round Table. The players travel the board from region to region, accumulating honour and skill. When they have enough, Arthur himself will give them a final test. In Chaosium's *Arkham Horror*, based on *Call of Cthulhu*, the players are not competing against each other, but against the game itself. They travel the board seeking portals where the Great Old Ones are breaking through, and closing them – or going mad in the attempt. A new portal appears every move or so, and there are many monsters, treasures and other such things scattered around the board. If at any time all portals have been closed, the players win.

There are of course many fantasy board games that have nothing to do with role-playing as such. *War of the Ring* is a strategy board game set in Tolkien's Middle-Earth, and it has no links to *MERP* or any other RPG system. There are many different fantasy board games available, but some of the more popular include *War of Wizards*, *Dungeon*, *Citadel*, *Sorcerer*, *Elfenroáds*, *Kings and Things*, and *Dungeonquest*.

DALMUTI – FANTASY MEETS RUMMY... WITH TEETH!

A different approach to fantasy gaming are the storytelling games. *Once Upon a Time* is a card-based game in which the aim is to spin a story out from the cards which you have been dealt, culminating in victory when you have set the story up so you can play your "Happily Ever After" card. Other players will interrupt with their own story threads, muddling things and trying to get closer to their own Happily Ever After.

Many fantasy games are purely card-driven. *The Great Dalmuti*, by Wizards of the Coast, is a game in which the aim is to empty your hand by accumulating multiples of a certain card; it is rather like a medieval version of gin rummy, but the leaders can force the other players to do their bidding. The microgame *Creatures and Cultists*, a card game produced by Pagan Publishing, involves lining up rows of cards representing the aforementioned creatures and cultists, and battling your opponents' forces.

But board games are not the only option. In the early 1980s, the founders of Games Workshop, Steve Jackson and Ian Livingstone, published a fantasy game novel. Billed as a "Fighting Fantasy" book, the work contained 400 numbered paragraphs. Each paragraph described a situation, and offered the reader several different alternative actions. Each possibility referred the reader to a new paragraph. In some paragraphs, the reader came across items of equipment and treasure, traps, riddles, monsters and so on. The book, called *The Warlock of Firetop Mountain*, was a huge success, selling 200,000 copies in eight weeks, and many more followed. Fourteen million *Fighting Fantasy* books have now been sold worldwide, and they are available in 23 different languages. Other series of *Fighting Fantasy*-style books were released, including Steve Jackson's *Sorcery*, Joe Dever's *Lone Wolf*, and the TSR *Endless Quest* series of *Dungeons & Dragons* tie-ins. Jackson and Livingstone's *Fighting Fantasy* series was the most successful and popular, however.

A ROLE-PLAYING BOARD GAME, *TALISMAN* PITS PLAYERS AGAINST MONSTERS AND TRAPS IN THE QUEST FOR TREASURE

Live-action role-playing, or LARP, is the name given to the physical enactment of role-playing games. Rather than sitting around a room, players find a quiet area outdoors and act out the game. In some systems, combat actually takes place using harmless latex weapons; others are no-contact. The game area is prepared beforehand by the Games Master. People are recruited to take the part of monsters and other incidental denizens of the world, and objects and other clues are placed as appropriate, out on the site. Everyone, players, monsters and GM, tends to be costumed. This takes far more preparation and equipment than other forms of role-playing, so it is usually done on a professional basis, by companies such as the UK firm Labyrinth. Some extremely impressive latex weaponry and armour is available for purchase, but it is not particularly cheap. The problems associated with LARP are reduced when there is no physical contact, but costuming and preparation are still costly and time-consuming.

Fantasy Wargaming

Despite the long history of historical wargames, the element of fantasy in this hobby is a fairly recent addition. After the release of *D&D*, the hobby games market became more receptive to fantasy battles, but it was not until a small English firm, Games Workshop, released a set of fantasy battle-rules called *Warhammer* that fantasy wargaming really started to catch on.

Steve Jackson and Ian Livingstone, who later became the authors of *Fighting Fantasy*, started Games Workshop in 1975, out of a small apartment. At that time, the company was dedicated to selling fantasy board games. The first Games Workshop shop was opened in London 1977, and when Jackson and Livingstone sold Games Workshop in 1992 it had grown to include 30 shops across Britain employing 250 staff.

Warhammer was a set of rules for engagements between armies of fantasy miniatures on tabletop battlefields. While the rules were fairly crude, they were easy to learn and relatively quick to play. Along with the core-game *Warhammer*, a classic fantasy wargame, they also produce several science-fiction wargames and many board games. The basic *Warhammer* set comes with rulebooks, dice, and two armies of miniatures. As players get more experienced, they purchase more miniatures from Games Workshop to expand their armies, along with painting supplies, terrain, and so on. Games Workshop's miniatures' label, Citadel Miniatures, is a major source of the company's revenue.

There are also several smaller fantasy wargame systems, of which the most popular is *Hordes of the Things*, based around the well-respected DBM/DBA rules for historical wargaming and battle simulation. *HotT*, as it is known, is more accurate than *Warhammer* in terms of recreating battlefield scenarios, but it is also slower to play. TSR's most recent attempt to move back into the wargames market, the *AD&D Battle System*, surprisingly failed to generate any interest at all.

THE ARMIES OF THE UNDEAD ASSAIL THE LIVING – A TYPICAL AFTERNOON IN THE WORLD OF *WARHAMMER*

The use of miniatures is not confined to wargaming. Most RPG controllers like to use miniatures to illustrate and clarify combat situations, and many people get a lot of pleasure from simply painting and collecting the figurines. Many of them are quite exquisite. Fantasy miniature firms like Ral Partha, Reaper and Fantasy Forge all produce ranges of individual fantasy characters and monsters for the RPG market, and Citadel also produce some figures more suited for role-playing than wargaming.

With the amount of effort associated with wargaming, it should be no surprise that computer wargaming is becoming increasingly popular. There are several good fantasy wargame programs available, and they all work in much the same way. The program models the terrain, populates it with troops, and supervises the movement of units, including measuring the distance – a big improvment on tape measures and marker counters in terms of playability. The computer plays one side, and the player controls the other. As a wargame can take anything up to an hour just to lay out ready for play, having it all done electronically is a definite bonus. On the negative side though, no computer is as ingenious an opponent as another human, and many of the programs are relatively narrow in the range of different scenarios they can play. Among the different fantasy programs available, *Warhammer: Shadow of the Horned Rat*, the *Command and Conquer* series, *Heroes of Might* and *Magic*, and *Warcraft I*, *II* & *III* are all well-regarded.

COMPUTERS IN FANTASY GAMING

The computer revolution has brought about great changes in many aspects of life, but one of the most strongly affected has been leisure and entertainment. The first fantasy gaming use of computers was for adventure games. These programs have been called interactive fiction, and they are close to that. Originally, the computer described a location to the player, along with objects in the area. The player would then tell the computer what to do next. By exploring the locations in the game, and performing the correct actions with the correct objects, the player would gain access to further areas and objects, finally completing the game when a number of specific actions had been carried out.

The first adventure game was called *Colossal Cave*. Programmer Will Crowther and his wife explored and mapped a cave in Kentucky in 1972, and later Crowther produced a textual computer simulation of the cave. In 1976, a colleague of Crowther's named Don Woods expanded the model, adding mythic elements, objects, puzzles, and a greater range of actions, converting the simulation into a game. This was then converted to a more common computer language, C, later in 1976 by Jim Gillogly, and the game spread across the world.

With the advent of home computing, the market for adventure games became obvious. Early home computers had fairly basic graphical capabilities at best, so a text-only interface was not much of a detriment for a game. A range of companies released adventure games in the 1980s, many of which were fantasy-based, including Scott Adams Adventures and Level Nine, but the most influential fantasy adventure game – in fact, the most influential adventure game full stop – was *Zork*, by Infocom. With a range of fiendish puzzles and a versatile user interface, *Zork* was a big hit. Over the years, it has spawned several sequels. Infocom released a whole range of adventures across different genres, and dominated the market in the early-to-mid-1980s.

As computers have continued to grow in power, text has been done away with almost completely, and the graphics have become more sophisticated, with cartoon graphics replaced with complex, beautifully rendered three-dimensional imagery. The best-known are *Myst* and its sequels, *Riven* and *Exile*, all excellent, but other popular games in the genre include *The Crystal Key 2*, *Syberia*, *Ico*, *The Omega Stone* and *Ring 2*. Despite the switch from text to graphics, gameplay remains much the same, though – the player has to locate objects and perform the correct actions with them.

A different strand of computer gaming has been computer RPGs. In these largely strategic games, the player controls characters, moving them around to explore dungeons, kill monsters, complete quests and grow in power and ability. The first computer RPG was *Rogue*, and it involved an overhead view of a lone player running around a random dungeon killing monsters and picking up treasure. The "graphics" were all made up of ASCII text characters, which is still a common feature of this family of game. *Rogue* is a good game even today, and many people still play it. Several derivative games have been developed over the years, the most important – and best – of which are *Moria*, *Angband* and *Omega*. Others include *Rogue* itself, *Hack*, *Nethack*, *Ragnarok* and *Larn*. All of them are free, addictive, and easily available over the Internet or as shareware. They are collectively known as Roguelike games.

WITH STUNNINGLY-RENDERED GRAPHICS AND ABSORBING GAMEPLAY, *MYST* WAS A BIG HIT

More sophisticated software was quickly made available commercially. Based on the same principle as the Roguelike games but featuring several player characters and, usually, first-person perspective views, early RPG computer games were important staples of the industry. The best known is probably *The Bard's Tale*, set in the city of Skara Brae. The field has continued to develop, however, and current computer RPGs (known as CRPGs) are almost as sophisticated as the full pen-and-paper games. The best released to date is easily *Baldur's Gate II: Shadows of Amn*, which is a very close recreation of the experience of playing D&D3. Other excellent games in the field include *Dungeon Siege*, *Baldur's Gate: Dark Alliance* (not actually a direct relation of *Shadows of Amn*), *Final Fantasy X*, and *Morrowind*.

In the mid–late 90s, CRPGs received a boost with the release of Bullfrog's *Dungeon Keeper*. Breaking from all previous styles of computer roleplaying, *Dungeon Keeper* allowed the player to take the role of an evil DM, building a dungeon, laying tempting treasures, hiring monstrous creatures, and waiting for unwary heroes to come blundering in. The game was a huge hit. Another very significant game, released at roughly the same time, was *Eidos's Diablo*. A direct tribute to *Moria* and the other Roguelike games, this was a dungeon-bash game in top-down view – little roleplaying, but lots of slaughtering hapless zombies and demons. *Diablo* was extremely impressive visually, with 3D graphics, rich textures and stunning sound. Its sequel, *Diablo II*, was even prettier. Both games featured a huge range of objects, monsters, spells, treasures and several specific quests to be completed.

These two separate threads of computer fantasy gaming – adventure games and role-playing games – united explosively in ID Software's fantasy/horror/sci-fi crossover, *Doom*. With a sophisticated first-person real-time graphical interface and pre-designed levels, *Doom* redefined the industry. It was the inspiration for a number of high-quality clones. The next step was a game called *Quake*. Like *Doom*, it was a fantasy/horror/sci-fi hybrid, similar in concept, but with greatly improved graphics, sound and gameplay. Playable over the Internet, *Quake* provided the opportunity to run around castles blowing up friends with a rocket-launcher. On-line players even organize into clans. Like *Doom* before it, *Quake* was incredibly successful, and spawned a number of sequels and similar imitators – *Quake II, Quake III Arena, Unreal* (and *Unreal Tournament*, the on-line version), *Half-Life*, and a whole slew of others.

Not all online gaming is about killing people, though. A relatively recent development is the Massively Multiplayer On-line Role Playing Game or MMORPG, which is a mouthful, however you say it. These games allow thousands of people to play together at the same time in the same computer world. They can meet in the

DESPITE APPEARANCES, *WARCRAFT III* WAS SURPRISINGLY SOPHISTICATED.

FANTASY, SCI-FI, HORROR AND BIG GUNS COME TOGETHER IN *DOOM*

virtual realm, talk, trade, fight, build properties, co-operate, complete quests, slay monsters, and grow in power and influence. Some couples have even met, fallen in love and married – both in the games and in real life. The most famous MMORPG is *EverQuest*, but there are many other fantasy games, including *Asheron's Call* and *Ultima Online*.

There are plenty of computer games with a fantasy setting unrelated to roleplaying games or adventure games. These range from strategy games such as the fantasy chess variant of the mid-1980s, *Archon*, through to platform games such as *Ghosts and Goblins* or, more recently, *Malice*, *Abe's World*, *Grim Fandango* and many more. Among the most historically interesting fantasy-based games are *Populous*, in which the player takes the part of a god shepherding his followers and encouraging them to wipe out the followers of a rival god, *Sabre Wulf* and *Knight Lore*, *Chaos* (a game of duelling wizards), *Shadow of the Beast* and, in arcades, *Venture*, *Mr Do*, *Black Tiger*, *Altered Beast*, *Rastan Saga* and others.

The Internet is becoming a valuable resource for all aspects of fantasy, of course. Amateur World Wide Web pages tend to change fairly swiftly, so for fantasy information in general the best place to start is with your favourite search engine. Try putting in the name of an author or RPG. For information on getting started, you might like to turn to the following newsgroups: rec.games.frp.misc for role-playing information; rec.games.mud.misc for MUDs; rec.games.miniatures.misc for information on figurines; rec.games.roguelike.misc for the free *Rogue* family of games; rec.games.trading-card.misc for information about Collectable Card Games; alt.fantasy for general fantasy chit-chat; the numerous alt.fan groups and alt.games groups for specific games or authors, or rec.arts.books for books in general.

TRADING CARD GAMES

The most recent development in fantasy gaming took everyone by surprise. In 1993, a small Seattle role-playing company named Wizards of the Coast developed and released a card game based on fantasy gaming. The idea was that the players would take the part of duelling wizards, summoning creatures and mighty sorceries with which to attack the other player. This would be done through a deck of cards: each player would draw cards from his or her deck, and could then cast the spells that they had the cards for. In order to make it a bit more exciting, they borrowed a leaf from football-sticker manufacturers, and designed several hundred cards. Some cards were common, some were uncommon, and some were rare. Each pack purchased would contain a random assortment of cards. This meant that you'd never know what cards your opponent was playing with, and you'd need a flexible strategy. You wouldn't play with all your cards at the same time; instead, you'd select 60 or so that worked well together. If you wanted a complete set, you'd have to trade with friends, just as with baseball cards. That way, you could have fun getting ready to play as well as when playing. The game, set loosely in the fantasy universe of Dominaria, was called *Magic: The Gathering*.

The initial print-run of 2.5 million cards, known as Alpha, was supposed to provide enough stock to last six months. It sold out completely in just a few weeks. Before the remainder of the contracted 10-million card-run was printed, a few corrections were made, and this became the Beta set. Stocks quickly ran out again and, not even four months after the game first hit the shelves, a third printing had to be done. That was known as the Unlimited print, and was a run of 35 million cards. It sold out in a further five months. In the years since then, the game has been translated into at least nine different languages, and tens of billions of cards have been printed in over 30 separate releases, both revisions of the core set and entirely new expansions. Over 3000 different cards make up the game, and there are millions of players.

Several other trading-card games (or TCGs for short) have been released since *Magic: The Gathering* – including *Pokemon*, which was wildly successful for a short time – but *Magic* is by far the dominant market leader. The game's popularity hinges on a number of things. To start with, the game appeals to collectors, even those who do not play it. The artwork on the cards is often very interesting, and there is a robust second-hand card market, which means that purchasing cards can be seen as an investment. While fairly complicated, the game plays well, and is fluid. The variety of the cards you encounter means that it doesn't get boring – there are always new strategies to try. There is very little set-up time involved, aside from originally selecting a deck to play with, so it is convenient. Perhaps most importantly, though, the rarer cards tend to be the most useful for advanced strategies, so as players get better they find themselves needing more cards to construct more efficient decks. Perhaps unsurprisingly, repeat sales of *Magic: The Gathering* are very high.

At the heart of the game is the idea of summoning creatures from the cards in your hand to the play area. These creatures have a certain amount of attack strength and a certain amount of defence strength. On your turn, you send your creatures rampaging over to attack your opponent, who intercepts them with his or her creatures, if possible. You also have a range of other spells available that can enhance your creatures or weaken enemy ones, deal damage to your opponent directly or to opposing creatures, or affect other areas of gameplay, such as the cards you have in your hand. You start with seven cards, and generally draw another one each turn. The first player to knock the other from 20 points of health down to zero is the winner. There are different colours of cards, and different colours specialize in different areas, representing different types of magic. Green, for example, is the colour of nature and specializes in big, fierce creatures, while red is the colour of destruction and specializes in spells that blow things up. The overall effect is surprisingly intricate.

There is a wide range of other TCGs available, some of which have greater or fewer fantasy components. *On the Edge* is a surreal game of influence in the magical-realist world of the roleplaying game *Over the Edge*. In it, the idea is to gain political power rather than to damage your opponent. *Shadowfist* is a game based on Oriental mythology, past, present, and future, and is a blend of fantasy, horror and sci-fi. Like the Hong Kong cinema tradition it stems from, games often finish in huge, sprawling conflicts. *Mythos* is based on *Call of Cthulhu*, and recreates the dark horror fantasies of Lovecraft's work. *Legend of the Five Rings* is another game with Oriental overtones, this time more narrowly a feudal Japanese fantasy. It, too, is linked with a roleplaying game of the same name. TSR's trading-card game, *Spellfire*, was loosely based on *AD&D*, but it proved unpopular and has little market presence. Another product of theirs, *Dragon Dice*, has met with greater acclaim. Unlike TCGs it is, as the name suggests, a collectible trading dice game. While this means the game mechanics are far more restrictive than for TCGs, it can still be entertaining.

THE FIVE BASIC LAND VARIETIES IN *MAGIC: THE GATHERING* EACH PROVIDE A DIFFERENT TYPE OF POWER – MANA – FOR CASTING SPELLS WITH

RAMPAGING CREATURES AND DEVASTATING SPELLS ARE THE WEAPONS USED IN A *MAGIC: THE GATHERING* DUEL

Because of the value of having the cards you want at your disposal, all TCGs have second-hand markets, but none is as strong as that surrounding *Magic: The Gathering*. Wizards of the Coast – now a division of Hasbro – do not formally recognize this market, holding themselves aloof. It's probably a good thing. The single most expensive *Magic: The Gathering* card, Black Lotus, has been out of print since the middle of 1994. One of these cards, in good condition, can cost upward of a week's pay; staggering when you consider that each card costs just a little more than a boiled sweet, new. While it is definitely the most expensive card, and has been since the second-hand market first arose, there are hundreds of other cards that cost more that a hardback book.

Part of the strength of *Magic: The Gathering* can be attributed to the lively tournament scene surrounding the game. The DCI (or Duelists' Convocation International) is a free organization run by Wizards of the Coast to promote the competitive play of *Magic: The Gathering*. The DCI sponsors open tournaments, and authorizes many more according to certain strict rules of fair play. Scoring for a *Magic* tournament is calculated in much the same way as it is for chess, and the DCI calculate player ranks. The highest-ranked players are invited to participate in the annual World Championships in Seattle, for a substantial cash prize. There is also a Pro Tour, for which players have to qualify to enter at special tournaments; top prize for winning a Pro Tour tournament is $25,000. Even small tournaments tend to provide a relatively generous prize, though. It is a sign of *Magic: The Gathering*'s growing respectability that it recently received accreditation as one of the Mind Games of Mensa, the international High IQ society. Further information on Magic: The Gathering, the DCI, and TSR products (as Wizards of the Coast now own TSR) can be obtained from the Wizards of the Coast Web pages at http://www.wizards.com.

FANTASY WORLDS

In the epic fantasy tradition popularised by Tolkien, vast and colourful lanscapes are major characters of the story. They invite us to explore

MIDDLE-EARTH

There is no more famous or imitated fantasy world than J. R. R. Tolkien's Middle-Earth, whose map shows the most recognizable geography in modern fiction. To devotees of *The Lord of the Rings*, this land has the strange quality of seeming more real than reality.

"There is good rock here. This country has tough bones", says Gimli the dwarf at Helm's Deep. Just so, Tolkien – an expert in languages and mythology – built up the structure of Middle-Earth from tough bones of language and myth.

Unusually, language came first. Tolkien had always loved playing with artificial languages, and for his own amusement invented the various dialects of Elvish, a "high" and formal speech with the stateliness of classical Greek or Latin. The earthy horse-riders of the Land of Rohan speak a rougher language which is essentially Old English. Other races – the dwarves, the Ents, even the Orc soldiers of the Enemy – have their own more or less secret languages, painstakingly worked out by Tolkien. One result of all this careful linguistic scaffolding is that the names of Middle-Earth ring true.

A landscape needs more than just the country's granite bones. Tolkien fleshed out Middle-Earth with skilful, conscientious evocations of unspoilt countryside with its endless shades of green ... and, later, of landscapes made barren or horribly polluted by the works of the Dark Lord and his minions.

Both Bilbo's expedition in *The Hobbit* and the great quest of the Ring begin in the Shire, a quaint and slightly comic version of rustic England not all that long ago. The idyllic surroundings change and darken as Frodo and the Ring travel east, but with splashes of sunlight and even comedy amid growing danger.

So the claustrophobic horror of the Old Forest, whose paths slyly shift to lead unwary visitors to their doom, is relieved by good-humoured Tom Bombadil with his babble of nonsense syllables (making him a literary forerunner of the Teletubbies). Gloom, fog and supernatural peril on the spooky Barrow-Downs give way to lamplight, beer and song in the Prancing Pony inn at Bree, where the worlds of men and hobbits touch and a more tangible danger lurks. The terror of pursuit by phantom Black Riders reaches its peak near Elrond the half-elf's great house of Rivendell, but here Frodo and his companions find healing, fire, good talk and a pause to plan for worse things ahead.

Much more of Middle-Earth remains to be explored now that this first leg of the journey has ended at the approach to the vast, sky-dominating barrier of the Misty Mountains. Bilbo in *The Hobbit* ventures through and eastward into the dismal shades of Mirkwood, hung about with cobwebs woven by giant spiders. In its desperate expedition to destroy the fateful Ring, the Fellowship in *The Lord of the Rings* goes underground through the darkness of the dread Mines of Moria – long ago excavated by dwarves, now abandoned to evil creatures.

The dwarves, tireless miners, craftsmen and fighters, are one of Middle-Earth's most secretive races, and we see little of their real homes. Tolkien is careful, though, to give more detail about the three most important peoples of the West.

First come the remote and magical elves, the lesser descendants of near-angelic races of old. They represent an earlier world, and are slowly fading from Middle-Earth.

Their chief remaining stronghold is in the trees of Lothlórien the Golden Wood, a place charged with magic and feared by ordinary mortals. Here the Fellowship of the Ring takes refuge and recuperates after its terrible loss in Moria.

Further south lies Gondor (meaning the Stone Land), separated from Mordor (the Black Land) in the East by the Great River Anduin, the unpopulated wilderness of Ithilien, and the awful Mountains of Shadow. Gondor's people are supposedly the highest race of men, descended from the ancient nobility of sunken Númenor – Middle-Earth's version of Atlantis – and to some extent from intermarriages with elves. But they also are gradually dwindling. In Gondor's great citadel Minas Tirith, there's lots of beautifully carved stone but a shortage of defenders for the walls ... and too few children.

The youngest, most vital inhabitants of Middle-Earth are the horse-loving Rohirrim in the nearby land of Rohan. King Théoden holds court in an Anglo-Saxon hall of joyously decorated pillars and tapestries, contrasting significantly with the cold black marble and bleak statuary of the chamber where the gloomy Steward of Minas Tirith sits on his cold stone chair. The Rohirrim are exuberant, violent, noisy, quarrelsome, in fact not far removed from barbarism – but they are the race of the future, the ultimate inheritors of the coming Fourth Age.

The most interesting minority peoples of the West, the dwarves and the tree like Ents, are also passing away – though almost imperceptibly, thanks to their great longevity. Dwarves suffer from a low birth-rate, while the Ents no longer have children at all owing to the mysterious disappearance of all their females in the mythic past. Another elusive tribe, the Woses or wild men of the woods, have already almost disappeared into legend.

Orcs or goblins, the main troops of Mordor, are supposedly an artificial and debased people, bred by Sauron the Dark Lord as a twisted imitation of elves. They are likely to be hunted down and wiped out, after the War of the Ring has been brought to an end by the Ring's final destruction in the fiery "Cracks of Doom" within Mordor's volcano Orodruin. This act, which topples the Dark Tower and ends Sauron's power, is made possible by the hobbits Frodo and Samwise, and by the once-hobbit Gollum, long warped and debased by the Ring.

It is the story's final irony that repulsive, murderous Gollum, whom everyone has long wished dead, inadvertently completes the Quest when others cannot – and saves Middle-Earth.

CONAN HAS LITTLE INTEREST IN DIPLOMACY

THE HYBORIAN AGE

Back in some uncertain era of the deep past, after the sinking of legendary Atlantis but before the dawn of modern history, the lands of the Hyborian Age are the setting for the gory exploits of the most celebrated individual Sword & Sorcery hero of all time: Conan the Cimmerian, created in 1932 by Robert E. Howard.

The essence of Sword & Sorcery is open-ended heroic adventure, like a long-running TV series. In the next story, the next district or the next land, there will always be another arrogant warlord who needs humbling ... another scheming sorcerer to be defied ... another ranting high priest whose temple is clearly overstocked with treasure as well as supernatural horrors ... another fair maiden to be rescued and then roughly treated by mighty-thewed Conan. Born a blacksmith's son in the frozen North, Conan is the classic barbarian adventurer whose escapades we expect to continue forever, world without end. Although he eventually wins through to the throne of Aquilonia at the heart of the Hyborian lands – the chief civilized country of the time – his repeatedly expressed contempt for effete civilization is a sure indication that he will always break out again.

Howard describes Hyboria with great if slapdash conviction, like fragments from a vivid dream. One of his devices for underpinning this bygone world's reality is to hint that the polyglot ragbag of place names in Conan's glory days is echoed in later names and mythologies. The countries Argos, Ophir and Corinthia all have a familiar ring. The Egypt-like sorcerer-kingdom of Stygia is bordered by the River Styx. Nearby is Punt, an old Egyptian name for part of Africa, south of which is Zembabwei ...

North of the Styx, the land of Shem recalls Noah's son Shem and the linked word "semitic". In the far north are the obviously Nordic regions Vanaheim and Asgard; to their east is Hyperborea, which is the mythical land "beyond the North Wind" mentioned by the ancient writers Pindar and Herodotus. The Hyborian country of Brythunia suggests later ages' Brythonic (pre-Celtic) languages like Welsh and Cornish, while for Irish and Scots there is the "Pictish Wilderness".

Introducing a collection of Howard's tales, *Skull-Face and Others*, August Derleth suggested that the only way to convey the Conan stories' lurid intensity would be to print them on blood-red paper with an accompanying soundtrack of thunderclaps. Our hero fights his way through larger-than-life temples of vile and ancient gods, thieves' kitchens, the decks of swashbuckling pirate vessels, the armed clash of open medieval war, etc. Although the world map has a superficial plausibility (one published version is overlaid with a map of modern Europe to indicate how the shape of coastlines has since altered), the main function of the variegated Hyborian Age lands is to provide an inexhaustible succession of dramatic settings for Conan's ruthless exploits.

Conan's world is distantly linked to that of two other warlike series heroes created by Howard. King Kull, the exile from Atlantis, flourished in the even more ancient continent of Thuria; owing to general upheaval when Atlantis and Lemuria sank beneath the sea, Thuria was reshaped and eventually became Hyboria. Further continental changes led to the early modern world in which Howard set the few adventures of Celtic barbarian Cormac Mac Art – descended from Picts and Conan's people the Cimmerians, themselves descended from Kull's Atlanteans.

With Kull, Conan, Cormac and similar heroes outside this Hyborian lineage, Robert E. Howard created the crude but vigorous template of modern Sword & Sorcery. He has been much imitated.

Gormenghast Castle

The enormous sprawl of Gormenghast Castle is the real hero of Mervyn Peake's strange, Gothic, intensely imagined and darkly witty novels *Titus Groan* and *Gormenghast*. (A third volume, *Titus Alone*, explores a surreal version of England far away from the castle itself.) Or is Gormenghast the villain?

To some of the bizarrely named cast, the endless labyrinths of stone represent the one and only possible way of life. Sourdust, Gormenghast's Master of Ritual, is concerned only with the castle's complex patterns of absurd daily ceremonial, which are gloomily accepted by melancholic Lord Sepulchrave (76th Earl of Groan) and angrily defended by both his wife the Countess and his cadaverous, fiercely loyal manservant Flay.

Other characters are less devoted to the ancient ways. Fuschia, adolescent daughter of the Earl and Countess, finds Gormenghast life oppressive without knowing quite why. Intelligent but maddeningly quirky Dr Prunesquallor looks amusedly askance at the whole social scene. The brutal chef Swelter is interested only in his kitchen tyranny and bitter feud with Flay. Steerpike the kitchen-boy escapes from Swelter's realm and, rising fast by murderous ambition, intends to grab power for himself.

The backdrop of Gormenghast itself is huge and varied. There are barbaric remnants like the ugly Tower of Flints whose denizens are flesh-eating owls. There are internal mazes, like the bleak corridors of the Stone Lanes where Flay stalks. There are wholly nonsensical follies, such as a region entirely filled with pillars that one can just squeeze between. There is the Earl's exquisite library, doomed to be burnt as part of Steerpike's plotting. Fuschia's secret attic, crammed with old toys, furniture and everything from a baboon's skin to a complete stuffed giraffe, is the perfect hidey-hole of any child's dreams. By night in the web-hung Hall of Spiders, angular Flay and bloated Swelter fight to the death at last.

A journey across the high roofscape reveals more and more towers, a huge quadrangle of flagstones hidden from everywhere but the sky, a full-grown but dead tree emerging horizontally from a wall (on whose trunk the two Aunts of the Groan family take afternoon tea, high above the ground), a horse and foal swimming in the top of a tower filled with rainwater...

There is no end to Gormenghast's nooks and crannies. To educate its hordes of children, it contains a complete school which

Young Titus Groan and his headmaster

outdoes even fictional English public schools in eccentricity. To feed the family and staff requires the Great Kitchen, so large that eighteen members of a hereditary caste known as the Grey Scrubbers are required for daily cleaning-up.

By the end of the first book, the new heir Titus Groan is only two, but already a catalyst for change. *Gormenghast* sees him grow up with conflicting feelings. He hates Steerpike, the secret enemy of Gormenghast, who is now entrenched. But he also shares the spirit of rebellion against the castle's pointless ceremonial, against having his whole life orchestrated by each day's instructions from the voluminous Books of Ritual.

Eventually a great flood converts the castle to a jagged stone archipelago, and Steerpike – unmasked at last as a multiple murderer – is hunted through towers which have temporarily become islands. Titus does his duty to the enormous hulk of Gormenghast by killing Steerpike, and his duty to his own free spirit by leaving home to explore a wider world.

The atmosphere of Gormenghast is heavily brooding, oppressive, and unforgettable, and Peake describes it in prose to match ... but with a wit and irony which transmute many of the sinister doings into black comedy.

NARNIA

C. S. Lewis's land of Narnia has been beloved by children for nearly half a century. It is one of those rare worlds of fantasy which we see from beginning to end – from Creation to the Day of Judgement.

When first visited in *The Lion, the Witch and the Wardrobe*, Narnia offers a cheerful jumble of fantasy ingredients. There are fauns, centaurs and unicorns from Greek mythology. There are giants and dwarfs, with a more Nordic flavour, and a fairytale wicked witch. Even Father Christmas puts in an appearance. Lastly and most famously – since this is Narnia's trademark – the land contains many engaging talking animals, from moles and mice to horses and lions.

One very special talking lion is Aslan (from the Turkish for "lion"), Narnia's saviour and redeemer, who is sacrificed and resurrected in this first book. As the series continues it becomes increasingly clear that Aslan is another aspect of Christ.

The geography and population grow from book to book. *The Voyage of the Dawn Treader* takes readers to marvellous islands out in the eastern seas, including the terrifying Island Where Dreams Come True – and so do all nightmares. *The Silver Chair* travels to the giant-infested North and reveals the fiery underworld of Bism and its misshapen gnomes; the show is stolen by lugubrious Puddleglum the Marsh-Wiggle, a manlike though slightly froggy creature.

THE WHITE WITCH IS THE SERPENT IN NARNIA'S EDEN

FROZEN SEA
CLAWS
BONES OF THE OLD ONES
COLD WASTE
TROLLSTEP MTS.
STEPPES
BARRIER MTS
Mo-Ombrlusk
Illik-Ving
GREAT FOREST
MANGRISHIK RIVER
Kvarch Nar
Kleg Nar
City of Ghouls
DESERT
DRAGON ROCKS
INNER SEA
Sarheenmar
Lankhmar
Ilthmar
DIKE
GRAIN FIELDS
RIVER HLAL
SALT MARSH
SINKING LAND
Ningauble's Cave
Earth's End
CANAL
OUTER SEA
SEA

Narnia and Earth run on different clocks. The visiting children in *The Lion, the Witch and the Wardrobe* live long lives as kings and queens of Narnia, before returning to home and childhood to find that only minutes have passed.

Thanks to these timeflow differences, Narnia's aeons-past Day of Creation took place while, on Earth, "Mr Sherlock Holmes was still living in Baker Street". So, in *The Magician's Nephew*, hapless travellers from Victorian London find Aslan singing Narnia into existence, causing its animals to sprout from a soil so fertile that even gold and silver coins grow into appropriate trees, and bestowing speech on his chosen Talking Animals.

In Earth time, Narnia's end comes not many years after *The Lion, the Witch and the Wardrobe*. The country has gone to the bad; Aslan is no longer seen; and an imitation Aslan appears, in the form of a foolish donkey disguised in a lionskin – Narnia's Antichrist. Indeed, this is a very Christian finale, in which night falls forever on the beloved land, everybody dies and is judged by Aslan, and a better Narnia on the far side of death proves – of course – to be a province of Heaven.

Narnia contains many wonderful things, despite Lewis's occasionally slapdash invention. The deep notes sounded by the world's birth and death make the series unforgettable.

LANKHMAR

Fritz Leiber invented an entire world, Nehwon, for his Sword & Sorcery heroes Fafhrd and the Gray Mouser to adventure in. But Nehwon itself – an anagram of "no-when", as Samuel Butler's *Erewhon* is "nowhere" – is a witty medley of standard ingredients, most of them found in Robert E. Howard's earlier Hyborian Age stories. It is Lankhmar, City of the Black Toga, which is Leiber's enduring creation.

Lankhmar, sprawling, exotic and sleazy, is the first meeting-place of the tall northern barbarian Fafhrd (trained as a singer and tale-teller) and the quicksilver-nimble Gray Mouser (trained, none too successfully, as a hedge-wizard's apprentice). There they meet, and lose, and avenge, their first foolish young loves. It is the city of too many memories which they repeatedly leave "forever", vowing never to come back ... but as Sheelba the wizard taunts them on their first departure, "*Never and forever are neither for men. You'll be returning again and again*". And they do.

Many feats of derring-do are plotted in Fafhrd's and the Mouser's favourite Lankhmar tavern, the Silver Eel between Dim Lane and Bones Alley. Beyond, the street names show this is a functioning city, alive with commerce and villainy: not only Cash Street, Silver Street, Gold Street, Crafts Street, the Street of the Silk Merchants and Wall Street (which, logically, runs along the city wall) but also Pimp Street and Whore Street.

For more exotic pleasures and assignations, visit the Plaza of Dark Delights. Thieves' House, ancient headquarters of the Thieves' Guild, lies amid Murder Alley, Death Alley and Plague Alley. The long Street of the Gods contains a hundred brightly coloured temples of the many rival "Gods in Lankhmar" ... but no sensible citizen ever approaches the one sullen, square, lightless church of the "Gods of Lankhmar".

North of the city, on the shore of the Inner Sea, the city's Overlord lives in the Rainbow Palace. The Overlords are rarely useful or sensible men: dotty Glipkerio Kistomerces in *The Swords of Lankhmar* has a regrettable taste for seeing his nubile young servant girls regularly whipped, and duly comes to a sticky end.

In the same book, Lankhmar meets its greatest threat. It's not so much that barbarian hordes – outrageously called Mingols – are threatening to invade across the Sinking Land, a piece of Nehwon

LANKHMAR LIES AT THE HEART OF THE EXOTIC NEHWON

FAFHRD AND THE MOUSER PLOTTING TROUBLE

which regularly rises from the sea and sinks again. The real menace is from Lankhmar Below, an underground city of tunnels which mirrors Lankhmar Above, but whose inhabitants are intelligent rats and rat-human hybrids. Fafhrd and the Mouser save the day despite overwhelming odds and powerful distractions (mostly involving sex), and get little thanks for it.

Fafhrd is based slightly on Conan, but also on the very tall Leiber himself; and, unlike Conan, he has a sense of humour. So does the small, tricky Mouser: his mercurial personality is largely that of Leiber's friend Harry Fischer, who originally suggested the characters.

Over the years the pair have had comic and dramatic adventures all over Nehwon (and once, via wizardly portal, on Earth in the heyday of Sidon and Tyre). The dread Bleak Shore, the foulness of the drowned land Simorgya, the sorcerous subterranean realm of Quarmall, the sky-grazing mountain Stardock, the land of Death himself ... they survive them all, and in later life settle into near-domesticity on Rime Isle far to the north. But they are always most at home when carousing or fighting – with torchlight glittering on Fafhrd's great sword Graywand, on the Mouser's blade Scalpel and dagger Cat's Claw – in the rich, exuberant and deadly streets of Lankhmar.

Discworld

"In a distant and second-hand set of dimensions, in an astral plane that was never meant to fly ... " The opening of *The Colour of Magic* sets the scene of Terry Pratchett's Discworld. Paying homage to various legends, especially Indian ones, Discworld is roughly flat and is supported on the broad shoulders of four gigantic elephants named Berilia, Tubul, Great T'Phon and Jerakeen, which in turn stand on the shell of the world-sized star turtle Great A'Tuin that swims ponderously through the void. Astrozoologists have yet to determine A'Tuin's sex ...

Somehow Discworld revolves like a gramophone record on the elephants' shoulders; enquiries into the precise mechanics are inadvisable. It has a tiny sun and moon travelling in flattish elliptical orbits about A'Tuin, leading to a complicated and silly calendar which features two summers and two winters in each year of approximately 800 days (divided into 13 months – seven with familiar names, plus Offle, Grune, Spune, Sektober, Ember and Ick). The main compass points are Hubward, Rimward, Turnwise – that is, in the direction of the Disc's rotation – and Widdershins. All this information is fascinating to wizards and astrologers, tedious in the extreme for anyone else.

Beginning as a semi-parodic setting in which Pratchett could poke fun at fantasy clichés, Discworld took on an uncanny life of its own. It was some time before its geography – still not guaranteed as fixed – settled down enough to be mappable.

At the Hub is the great mountain-spire of Cori Celesti, where the gods dwell in their ancient home Dunmanifestin and play dice (or any other game that permits sufficient cheating) with human lives.

Along a large arc of the Rim, the empire of Krull salvages valuables drifting towards the edge as the sea pours off in the endless Rimfall. Enquiries about how this lost water is replenished are inadvisable. "Arrangements are made".

In between are numerous lands, most forming part of a single central continent. Discworld, "world and mirror of worlds", has its own versions of many familiar countries. Its classical Greece is Ephebe, where philosophers experimentally test axioms by shooting arrows at tortoises. Its ancient Egypt is the mummy- and pyramid-infested land of the river Djel, named "Child of the Djel" or Djelibeybi. (Another land somehow reminiscent of confectionery is the nearby Hersheba.) The Tezuman Empire is approximately Aztec. Llamedos is suspiciously Welsh and, like Dylan Thomas's village of Llareggub, demands to be spelt backwards.

Elsewhere, the Agatean Empire mixes old and new China, with tyrannical emperors, terracotta armies, the Red Guard and competitive literary examinations for such jobs as nightsoil collector. Genua, that fairy-tale city of good eating and strong voodoo, seems uncannily reminiscent of New Orleans. And the huge, remote island of XXXX (alias *Terror Incognita*) offers a repertoire of canned lager, drag queens, kangaroos, the Dreamtime and corks dangling round hats.

But Discworld mirrors imaginary as well as real worlds. High up in the magic-rich Ramtop Mountains, the indomitable witch Granny Weatherwax lives in the tiny kingdom of Lancre (a name which nods to the famous Lancashire Witches). Granny and her coven of three are constantly struggling against the power and momentum of stories that are alarmingly more real than Discworld's rather thin and tenuous reality. When events fall comically but insidiously into the pattern of *Macbeth*, of *A Midsummer Night's Dream*, of dangerously simple fairy tales, or of modern myths like *The Phantom of the Opera* ... Granny Weatherwax & Co try to put the story right and give it a common-sense ending. For example, despite the machinations of the ruthless Godmother (who's made Destiny an offer it can't refuse) Discworld's Cinderella doesn't *want* to marry the Prince. Just as well, since he's really a frog.

The same mirror-effect is at work in Discworld's greatest and smelliest city, Ankh-Morpork – which, first and foremost, looks gratefully back to Fritz Leiber's city of Lankhmar. Versions of Fafhrd and the Gray Mouser have bit parts in *The Colour of Magic*. The Crimson Leech inn, Street of Small Gods and Plaza of Broken Moons recall Leiber's Golden Lamprey, Street of the Gods and Plaza of Dark Delights. The Thieves' Guild of Lankhmar is elaborated into Ankh-Morpork's wild medley of 300-odd guilds: Alchemists, Assassins, Bakers, Beggars, Butchers, Conjurers, Embalmers, Fools, Plumbers and Dunnikindivers (a touch of realism there), and so on, and on. There is even the Dead Rights Society, which leaves little cards inside coffin lids explaining that "You Don't Have To Take This Lying Down!"

Instead of a Wizards' Guild, though, we find the great campus of

IN *SOURCERY*, PRATCHETT SENDS UP WIZARDS AND HEROES (MALE AND FEMALE) – AND THEIR LUGGAGE

Unseen University – playing on the "Invisible College" of occult lore — where overweight, donnish wizards consume enormous dinners while students pursue worrying research in the High Energy Magic building.

Ankh-Morpork's streets have been mapped in detail, and include many further jokes and allusions. The filth-choked river Ankh flows round the central Isle of Gods, and is crossed by (among others) the Bridge of Size, Maudlin Bridge and Contract Bridge. The over-the-top Chrononhotonthologos Street is genuinely named after an exaggeratedly satirical real-world play of 1734, by Henry Carey. Much more lies buried....

Keeping Ankh-Morpork under control is a full-time effort for the city's Machiavellian ruler, Lord Vetinari the Patrician – who is unloved, but tolerated for preserving reasonable order and having street mimes thrown into the scorpion pit.

Despite his efforts, strange ideas and thought-patterns from outside keep running riot in Ankh-Morpork. Early in *The Colour of Magic*, the underworld's delighted reaction to the amazing new concept of fire insurance soon has the city ablaze. *Moving Pictures* sees a violent outbreak of movie fever when a magic-powered cinema industry – with tiny demons painting *very fast* inside each camera – takes off in nearby Holy Wood. In *Soul Music*, the craze that sweeps madly through Ankh-Morpork is the hot new sound of "Music with Rocks In", leading even respectable wizards to make themselves leather robes with slogans picked out in studs on the back. LIVE FATS DIE YO GNU ... the Dean of Unseen University is not terribly good at stud-work.

Meanwhile, gloomy Captain Vimes of the Ankh-Morpork Night Watch, a quintessentially hard-bitten, cynical detective, walks the mean streets of police-procedural fantasy whose risks include having to put the cuffs on dragons. Vimes repeatedly tackles plotters obsessed with overthrowing the Patrician and restoring the city's long-gone monarchy – whose nasty aspects have been forgotten in the warm glow of royalism. In the words of *1066 and All That*, this persistent notion is Wrong but

Wromantic ... while Lord Vetinari is Right but Repulsive.

For all its madcap invention and wild incongruities, Discworld is a background not only for romps involving the ultra-cowardly wizard Rincewind but for comedy with a serious edge – usually featuring the grim determination of Vimes or Granny Weatherwax. Indeed the most popular Discworld character is Death, the eternal, skeletal straight-man who invariably speaks in HOLLOW, DOOM-LADEN CAPITALS and regularly performs his melancholy duty of taking life as it comes. It's a characteristically Pratchettian achievement to establish Death as sympathetic, ponderously comic (he sympathizes with but can't quite grasp mortals' emotions) and somehow, in spite of everything, *on our side.*

THE YOUNG KINGDOMS

The world in the Age of the Young Kingdoms exists mainly as a flamboyant backdrop for the career of Michael Moorcock's doomed prince Elric. Elric is an enfeebled albino; a sorcerer and trafficker with demons; a melancholy, Byronic hero or antihero of fantasy. His fate is to bring the violent end of the world's present age and usher in a new one.

Elric comes of ancient and elf-like lineage. He is among the last of a decadent, aristocratic elder race on the island of Melniboné, who foolishly scorned the mere coarse humans of the new-born Young Kingdoms. It is Elric himself, doomed to perpetual betrayals, whose revenge on Melniboné's usurper Yyrkoon leads to the destruction of his own home of Imryrr, the Dreaming City, and the end of his own people's power. He is left to roam the Young Kingdoms, an accursed wanderer living in evil partnership with his demonic sword Stormbringer. This black sword painfully drains the souls of its victims and passes some of the unholy energy to Elric as remedy for his natural physical weakness. Another part of the curse is Stormbringer's malign tendency to strike down his friends and lovers ...

The geography of the Young Kingdoms is full of appropriately melodramatic yet entirely descriptive placenames: the Sighing Desert, the Weeping Waste, the Fortress of Evening, the Boiling Sea, the Dragon Sea, the Straits of Chaos, the Marshes of the Mist, the City of the Screaming Statues, and World's Edge. In his non-English names Moorcock, perhaps influenced by Lord Dunsany, is fond of rather alien double-vowel sounds: Yyrkoon, Kaneloon, Ashaneloon, Gromoorva, Yeshpotoom-Kahlai, Karlaak, Hwamgaarl, Bakshaan, and the slightly over-the-top lizard god Haaashaastaak ... . Elric's journeys through these multicoloured lands, wielding the evil of Stormbringer against a succession of still worse evils, make for heady, spicy travelogues.

All the Kingdoms' garish splendours are doomed to fade in the last battle between the gods of Chaos, to whose service Elric has long been sworn, and Law – whom, instead, he aids. After this apocalyptic struggle, the Cosmic Balance between Law and Chaos is righted at last, and the world is remodelled in the paler colours of today.

But this is far from being the whole picture. It is Moorcock's favourite conceit that the worlds of all his fiction are riddled with portals, transfer points and places of contact (like the eternal city of Tanelorn), linking them into an overarching "multiverse". As Elric works against the Chaos gods in the Young Kingdoms, another and differently maimed version of him – Corum, the Prince with the Silver Hand – is fighting other incarnations of the Chaos gods in his own separate world. Elsewhere, Dorian Hawkmoon battles the Chaos-infected hordes of future "Granbretan" (Great Britain). Somewhere else again, the hero Erekosë fights the good fight on other dimensional planes, and is uniquely blessed or cursed with memories of past or future lives as Elric, Corum, Hawkmoon, Count Brass and many more ... all aspects of the Eternal Champion.

Thanks to slippages between the "Million Spheres" of the multi-

FLEE THE CITY! ELRIC IS COMING...

verse, Elric meets some of these brother-heroes on more than one occasion, fighting side by side with them in the world-hopping Vanishing Tower and in timeless Tanelorn. In *Elric at the End of Time* he finds himself a plaything of the futile, *fin de siècle* aristocrats in Moorcock's *Dancers at the End of Time* comedies; this is perhaps the only story which invites us to laugh a little at Elric's melancholic and self-pitying excesses.

Most authors invent a world: Moorcock offers a whole gaudy universe.

Earthsea

Earthsea, setting of Ursula Le Guin's best-known fantasies, has one important difference from traditional fantasy lands. Its known world is a large archipelago of separate islands with their own histories and traditions, surrounded by endless sea. So in place of that endless walking or riding that pads out the typical fantasy quest, the skills of sailing and navigation are necessary for journeys of any length – and a Windkey, a wizard who can influence wind and weather, is always in demand.

In *A Wizard of Earthsea* the hero Ged begins his long journey through life on Gont, a flinty name for a flinty island renowned for goats and wizards. His precocious talent soon leads him to a magical education on sophisticated Roke Island at the heart of the Inmost Sea, under the nine masters of Roke's legendary school of wizardry. As expected, learning the magic of True Names is long and hard. Not so expected is the Taoist flavour of Earthsea's magical lore, whose ultimate wisdom is that the balance of the world is a fragile, precious thing and that a great mage uses magic only when he must. Too proud to take this in, Ged shows off with a forbidden summoning of the dead that brings something dreadful into the world and sends him fleeing into exile.

His flight brings him to the western isle of Pendor, where he confronts dragons; then north to gloomy Osskil, where an Old Power of the world is trapped and eager for his soul; next, via a desperate escape in falcon's shape, to his first teacher on Gont; and finally out into the uncharted eastern seas to confront the horror that can't be defeated but only accepted, since it is his own shadow.

Another unusual quest, this time for a lost rune that promotes peace and harmony, takes Ged north-east to the warlike theocracy of the Kargad Lands in *The Tombs of Atuan*. (Dwellers in Atuan and its sister islands Atnini, Karego-At and Hur-at-Hur are unusual in being white rather than Earthsea's normal brown or black.) Nine standing-stone "tombs" and an underground labyrinth are the focus of a grim religion that worships more life-hating Old Powers of earth and darkness. Tenar, the girl priestess who supposedly rules but in practice is enslaved by this cult, is more prominent than Ged in this book. Both her sympathy and assistance, and Ged's own strength to hold back the jealous Powers' destroying earthquake, are needed for their escape.

The action of *The Farthest Shore* shows why wizards' teachings stress the importance of balance, which here goes badly askew. A much older

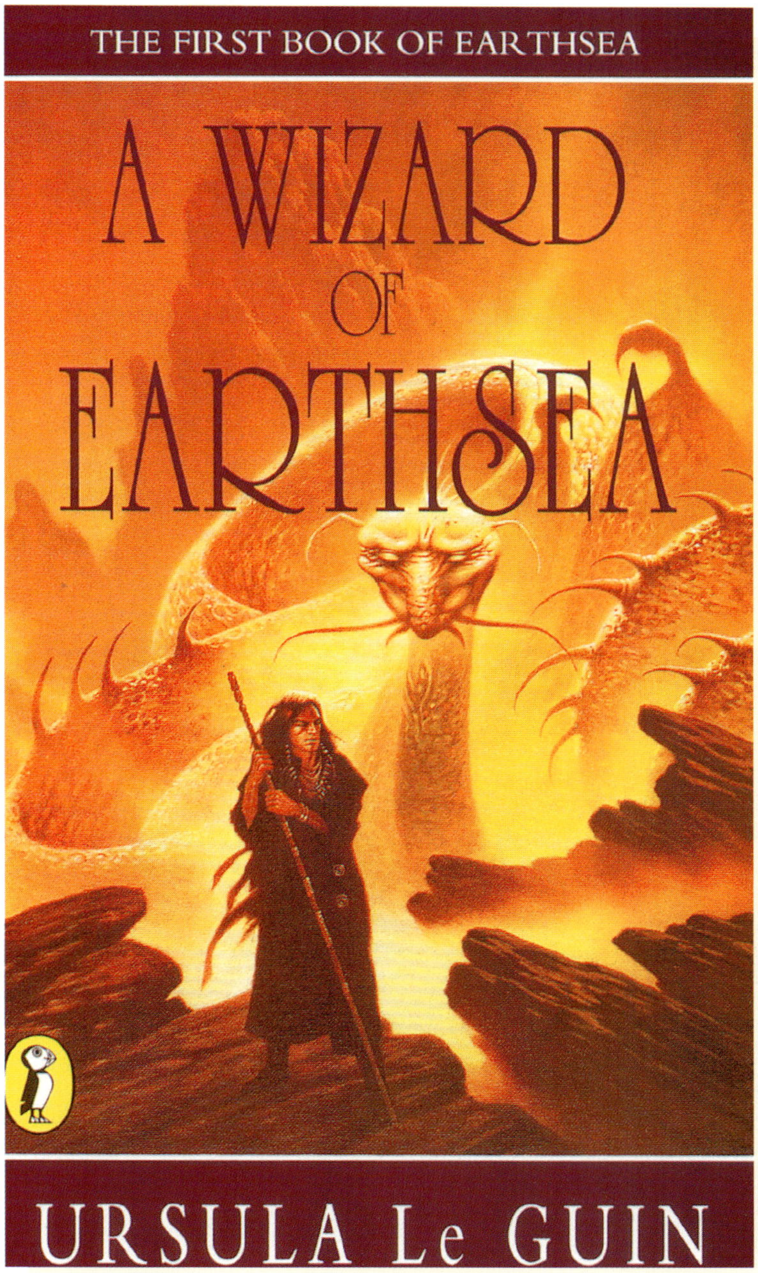

Earthsea's dragons are dangerous, subtle and talkative – only wizards dare chat with them

Ged, now Archmage in Roke, learns that the wellsprings of Earthsea's magic, craftsmanship and song are drying up. After a long voyage under evil stars, he finds the "hole in the world" through which the light and luck are running out, reducing even wise dragons to dumb beasts. Why? A misguided mage has upset the balance between life and death, allowing his dupes an ugly return from the grave at the expense of all that's good in life. Ged must travel beyond mere geography into the arid land of the dead, and spend the very last of his power to seal the fatal breach between the worlds.

The philosophy of Earthsea is that this one precarious life is all we get, and that death is necessary to give it value. As Ged himself puts it: "There is no safety. There is no end. The word must be heard in silence. There must be darkness to see the stars ... "

The World of the Wheel

The world of Robert Jordan's immense (and, as this book went to press, still incomplete) "Wheel of Time" saga follows the example of Middle-Earth in having a lengthy, complicated history which stretches back to an ancient golden age and its fall.

In this Age of Legends, war was unknown and life was made easy by both advanced technology and use of the magical One Power. The rare men and women able to channel and wield the separate male and female aspects of this power were known as Aes Sedai, "servant of all". Their channelling could boost crops without fertilizers or pesticides, through "seed singing"; extract metal ores from the earth without the need for digging; and heal almost any injury or illness without medicine. But then a huge mistake was made.

Magical researchers detected a new source of this power somewhere outside the known world. Like Adam and Eve unwisely eating the forbidden apple or Pandora opening her box, they bored a hole in the fabric of reality to exploit this power-source ... and, disastrously, opened the way to the baleful influence of the "Dark One" (also known as Shai'tan, Father of Lies, etc.) who had been locked outside since time began.

The golden age went steadily downhill over the next century as many people, including powerful Aes Sedai, listened to this being's promises of power and immortality and were tempted to join the Dark. There followed the War of the Shadow, in which the One Power was perverted into a weapon and hordes of magical-biological horrors were loosed on the world.

This war ended, in one sense, when the Light forces of the Aes Sedai warlord and mage nicknamed The Dragon succeeded in a grand *coup*. They sealed up the "borehole" to the Dark One's prison with seven seals carrying the yin-yang symbol of the channellers, and simultaneously entrapped the feared and powerful leaders of Dark-corrupted humanity, known as the Dreadlords or Forsaken.

Already, though, the Dark One had struck back devastatingly, by poisoning one of the twin wellsprings of Power – the male half. All male magic was now tainted, and, quickly or slowly, the minds and bodies of male Aes Sedai decayed. Their uncontrolled, insane use of the Power led rapidly to the "Breaking of the World": magic-spawned floods, storms, volcanoes, earthquakes, even the raising and levelling of mountain ranges and sundering of continents. The lands were remade and their populations vastly reduced.

Over the next millennium, there were several regroupings and struggles to restore civilization, with many lesser conflicts like the Trolloc Wars and the War of the Hundred Years, and more than one would-be conqueror who hoped to cash in on a certain prophecy by proclaiming himself the Dragon Reborn. Early on, in 98 AB (After the Breaking), the now all-female Aes Sedai established their stronghold of learning, the White Tower in the city of Tar Valon – a rare fixed point as borders shifted over the following centuries. Various potent devices from the Age of Legends are preserved in this and other repositories of the past, and hidden in secret places of the land. Most of these are tools to help channel the One Power, known as *angreal* or – if very powerful – *sa'angreal*, reminding us of the Sangreal or Holy Grail.

In the "modern" world where the story of the new and true Dragon Reborn begins in 998 AB, the central lands are bordered on the north by the imaginatively named Mountains of Dhoom, beyond which lies the Dark-ruined, monster-ridden region called the Blight; on the east by another straight-line mountain range, the Spine of the World; to the west by the Dead Sea and Aryth Ocean; and to the south by the Ocean of Storms.

The long legacy of the War of Shadow is most evident at the northern "Blightborder", where unpleasant things are apt to come creeping from the Blight. These Shadowspawn include the giant, raging beast-men known as Trollocs; their more intelligent overseers, the humanoid but eyeless Fades or Myrddraal, who project an aura of cold dread reminiscent of Tolkien's Black Riders; and the winged, vampiric Draghkar, who lure their victims with siren songs and then suck out souls with a deadly kiss. There are other varieties of Shadowspawn, like the relentless packs of pony-sized Darkhounds with their poison fangs.

All these horrors are made far worse by the evil directing intelligence of the once-human Forsaken, who one by one have been freeing themselves from their imprisonment by the steadily weakening Seals in the central bad place of the Blight. This place is the volcanic mountain Shayol Ghul, containing the Pit of Doom (another nod to Tolkien) from which the sealed Bore leads to the otherworldly confinement of the Dark One – for whose complete release the Forsaken are forever struggling.

Nonhumans on the side of Light are rare. The only such people to be both natural and sentient are the gentle Ogier. These are large, slow, long-lived, furry and have a deep rapport with plant life and nature in general. Since they are also guardians of historical record and famous stonemasons, it could be said that they combine the best features of Tolkien's elves, dwarves and Ents. Ogier also built the Ways, secret and now Dark-tainted short cuts outside normal space, like the "wormholes" of sf. Another race of plant-lovers, the Nym, were an artificial creation in the Age of Legend. The last surviving Nym, the Green Man, guards the Eye of the World: a precious pool of untainted male magic preserved in an enchanted grove somewhere deep inside the unholy heat of the Blight.

The World of the Wheel contains other significant countries over the mountains and across the sea. Beyond the Spine of the World to the east of the central lands lies the Aiel Waste, whose human inhabitants,

CAN YOU SPOT THE FOREORDAINED SAVIOUR AND DESTROYER OF THE WORLD IN THIS PICTURE?

the Aiel, are deadly nomadic warriors. Still further west is mysterious and sandy Shara, home of a secretive, veiled people who are masters of deceit but still valued for their exports of silk and ivory. Over the Aryth Ocean is the western continent of Seanchan, long conquered by invaders from the central lands, and boasting a variety of bizarre, alien animals imported from Elsewhere as fighters against Shadowspawn. Based on islands in the Aryth Ocean, the wandering, tattooed Seafolk trade with all these lands.

Back at the heart of the world, the greatest of the "home" lands is Andor with its mighty capital city of Caemlyn. Its most obscure village, perhaps, is out near the Mountains of Mist which form the country's western border: Emond's Field. Here the young village lad Rand al'Thor (whose parentage is not as he supposes, and whose heron birthmark and heron-marked sword are fraught with significance) receives his first intimations of a dangerous future as the slayer of the Forsaken, the true Dragon Reborn.

All this is wrapped around with prophecies about his being both the destroyer and saviour of the World of the Wheel in the foreordained Last Battle against the Shadow – saving but a remnant of a remnant, as the Aiel say. It's a tough job, but someone has to do it.

Hogwarts School of Witchcraft and Wizardry

Hogwarts school, hidden somewhere in the north of England, provides the fascinating backdrop for Harry Potter's various adventures. It was started over a thousand years ago, by the four greatest wizards of the time, Godric Gryffindor, Helga Hufflepuff, Rowena Ravenclaw and Salazar Slytherin. The founders were concerned with the way that the peoples of the time were turning against wizardry, and used special magics to hide the school from the rest of the world. Now it does not appear on any map, and only another wizard can even see it; to normal people, it looks like a ruined heap in a patch of wasteland. The truth is very different, though. In reality, the school is a huge gothic castle perched on top of a rocky crag, the school looks out over a large, mysterious lake to the front, and has a dark, threatening wood located to the rear. It's packed with all sorts of magical and mysterious features – staircases that don't go anywhere or that have steps that disappear when you tread on them, corridors that change destination, secret tunnels galore, hidden luxury bathrooms, dank dungeons, massive kitchens crewed by House Elves, an ancient Sorting Hat that can psychically divine the best House for a new pupil to be placed in, and a general assortment of wonders of all shapes and sizes. Modern technology even stops working within its boundaries.

The heart of the school, once you get in past the huge, sweeping entrance with its impressive staircases, is the Great Hall — a huge dining room cum assembly area whose ceiling is enchanted to look like the sky above the school, so it appears open-air. Each of the four student houses has its own tower, with dormitories, central lounge, password-protected entry door, and patron ghost. No one other than Hagrid, the gigantic gamekeeper, is allowed into the forest, which is just as well, because it's crammed full of werewolves, man-eating spiders, fey centaurs and all sorts of other creatures. The students aren't too restricted though — lessons take place all over the rest of the school grounds. They study the stars with Professor Sinistra from the top

Hermione Granger (Emma Watson) shows she's top of the class in *Harry Potter and the Philosopher's Stone.*

NEVILLE LONGBOTTOM (MATTHEW LEWIS) GETS ALL BENT OUT OF SHAPE DESPITE EXPERT TUITION FROM MADAME HOOCH (ZOE WANAMAKER) IN *HARRY POTTER AND THE PHILOSOPHER'S STONE.*

of the tower of Astronomy, the highest point of the school, and out of bounds at all other times. Professor Sprout teaches herbology from a series of greenhouses. The Potions Master, Snape, lectures on his art from down in the dungeons – a location that he himself has surely picked to suit his forbidding personality. Care of Magical Creatures takes place out and about in the grounds. The headmaster of the school, Professor Dumbledore, lives and works up at the top of a mysterious tower that almost no one can get into. Flying, though, is taught within the school's Quidditch stadium. Quidditch is the wizardly version of football – and it's the only sport that any real wizard cares about. There are seven players on each side, four balls, six goals, and at least two different ways of scoring points.

For all the magical touches around Hogwarts – and every corner seems to hide some fascinating new mystery or magical innovation – it is a very familiar place. The look and feel of it evoke a nostalgic, idealized version of traditional British private education. It is a wild blend of the colleges of Oxford and Cambridge, the manorial school at Eton, the beautiful settings of St Andrews and countless other establishments — a zany dream of the perfect boarding school, eccentric and sprawling and never quite staying constant, full of mystery, danger and excitement, yet still somehow safe and comforting. There's always huge platters of good food to eat, and the four-poster beds are deliciously soft and warm. Even the issues of wealth and privilege, which lurk uncomfortably near the surface of any such private school setting, are idealized; Ron, who comes from a poor family, is far too proud to let his (rich) best friend Harry help bail him out, and only the occasional bully has anything negative to say regarding status. Hogwarts is a gentle homage to private education, not a barbed satire, which is why it is so successful as a charming, quirky setting. Hogwarts reminds us of how it was supposed to be ... and that is what the best fantasy is all about.

FANTASY MAGAZINES

Apart from books and the theatre, magazines were once the most important medium for fiction. Short stories, novellas and serialized novels – many of them fantasy – filled the popular magazines of the late 19th century and the first half of the 20th century.

Until the time of the World War One the cinema offered little competition, and radio and television were merely the dreams of a future yet to be realized. Even after Hollywood had established itself, magazines remained a potent medium for fiction; it was the coming of radio to most homes by the 1930s, followed by the arrival of TV a couple of decades later, that finally killed off the majority of fiction magazines – although, even then, a few lingered on. Some continue to exist to the present day, and although read by comparatively small numbers of people they remain significant as breeding-grounds for new writers and for new styles of story-telling.

Broadly speaking, there have been four different types of fiction-carrying magazine – differentiated by their size, their shape, the type of paper they were printed on, and the audiences they were designed to appeal to. Initially, there were what one might call the "standard" late-Victorian magazines, of which *The Strand Magazine* remains the best-remembered example. These were shaped rather like large paperback books, with spines, and printed on book-quality paper. With their black-and-white line illustrations and photographs (printed photography was a newfangled thing in the 1890s), these appealed to a broad middle-class, middlebrow readership. As the new century began, however, two types of magazine diverged from the standard model, the split occurring mainly in the decade between 1910 and 1920.

On the one hand, there were the "slicks", tending to larger formats, glossier paper and copious advertising: *The Saturday Evening Post* was the best-known American example of this kind (although there were smaller-circulation equivalents in Britain), and at its height in the late 1920s the *Post* would carry alongside its non-fiction contents as many as eight short stories and two or three serial segments per weekly issue – some of them by the finest writers of the day (the stylish F. Scott Fitzgerald, for example, who wrote several fantasies though he is best remembered for his social novels). The slicks eventually would prevail, providing the normal format for late 20th-century magazines, although ironically most such magazines have dropped, or at any rate drastically reduced, their fiction content.

On the other hand, there were the "pulps", lower-class periodicals which retained the normal size and shape of the turn-of-the-century standard magazines but which were printed on the cheapest, roughest, woodpulp paper: *All-Story, Weird Tales* and *Fantastic Adventures* are examples of the kind, all carrying comparatively little advertising and non-fiction content, and all designed to entertain the common reader simply by the exciting and frequently sensational qualities of their fiction – flagged by their garish cover illustrations, the front cover being the only part of these magazines printed in colour.

An old copy of FFM, a good fantasy magazine, which last published in 1953

Finally, in the wake of World War Two paper-shortages, and in competition with the rise of TV and modern paperback books, there were the fiction "digests" – magazines of a shrunken type, borrowing their small format (and hence their name) from *The Reader's Digest*. These carried few illustrations and had comparatively sober covers, priding themselves on being "a cut above" the pulps, and often the fiction they published was of slick-magazine quality: *The Magazine of Fantasy and Science Fiction* is one well-known post-war example, still publishing to this day. The digests have fought a losing battle, however: they never could attain the high circulations of the major pre-war slicks and pulps, and such readerships as they attracted have declined over the years. Although some survive, no new digests have been founded successfully since the 1970s. The very infrequent new fiction magazines of recent years, such as *Realms of Fantasy*, tend to adopt a larger, slicker format.

Here are brief descriptions, in chronological order, of some of the major magazines which have carried fantasy fiction over the past century. Not all of them specialized in fantasy, although some did, but each of them published significant work in the field – stories which might not otherwise have come into existence had it not been for the encouragement of these magazines. All the titles discussed are American unless otherwise stated.

THE STRAND MAGAZINE *(British, 1891–1950)* is most famous for having published several series of Sherlock Holmes stories by A. Conan Doyle – in fact, so popular were these that they pushed its circulation to over half a million copies per month. But in addition to its services to crime fiction (and to humorous fiction: P. G. Wodehouse was another favourite in *The Strand*), this well-loved magazine, edited for many years by Herbert Greenhough Smith, also published a considerable amount of fantasy. E. Nesbit's dragon stories ran there throughout 1899 (later collected as *The Book of Dragons*); then, in 1900, there appeared F. Anstey's memorable comic serial about an Arabian genie, *The Brass Bottle*. That in turn was followed by E. Nesbit's delightful Anstey-influenced children's fantasy The Psammead (1902; later published in book form as *Five Children and It*), and all its various follow-ups such as *The Phoenix and the Carpet* (1903–1904) and *The Story of the Amulet* (1905–1906). Additionally, there were short stories by H. G. Wells ("The Inexperienced" Ghost", 1902, "The Magic Shop", 1903, etc) and Rudyard Kipling (*Puck of Pook's Hill*, in 10 parts, 1906).

If you were a lover of the light fantastic, the 1900s were a good time to be a reader of *The Strand Magazine*.

THE STRAND HAD A STANDARDIZED COVER IN ITS EARLY YEARS, SHOWING A VIEW OF THE STREET AFTER WHICH IT WAS NAMED

THE ALL-STORY MAGAZINE *(1905–1929)* was one of the first great pulps, published by Frank Munsey (the man who is credited with inventing pulp magazines) and edited by Robert H. Davis and others. Initially monthly, later weekly, it merged with its sister magazine *The Argosy* (from June 1920) to become *Argosy All-Story Weekly* during its last decade. A general pulp, with the emphasis firmly on adventure fiction, it is most famous for discovering Edgar Rice Burroughs and for publishing his *Tarzan of the Apes* (complete in one issue, October 1912). Many other Burroughs fantasies followed, including the timeslip-to-the-Stone-Age yarn *The Eternal Lover* and the first of the "Pellucidar" lost-in-the-bowels-of-the-Earth series, *At the Earth's Core* (both 1914). Fantasy master A. Merritt made his debut in *All-Story* with Through the Dragon Glass (1917), swiftly followed by *The Moon Pool* (1918–1919) and other lushly written tales. Western writer Max Brand contributed fantasies – John Ovington Returns (1918) and That Receding Brow (1919) – as did numerous other pulpsters ranging from Ray Cummings and John U. Giesy to Francis Stevens and Charles B. Stilson. *All-Story* distilled the gaudy essence of pulp fiction.

THE *ARGOSY* IN THE 1930S, AFTER ITS SISTER MAGAZINE, *ALL-STORY*, HAD CEASED PUBLICATION

WEIRD TALES *(1923–1953)* is the most legendary of the fantasy pulps. Edited monthly by Farnsworth Wright, and later by Dorothy McIlwraith, it is perhaps best remembered as the principal home of horror writer H. P. Lovecraft and offbeat poetic fantasist Clark Ashton Smith. However, of greater heroic-fantasy relevance were the many swashbuckling tales contributed by Robert E. Howard, whose extravagant "Conan" yarns began to appear there in 1931. *Weird Tales* can claim to be the

WEIRD TALES NOW SEEMS ONE OF THE MOST ENDURING PRODUCTS OF PULPDOM

magazine which created Sword & Sorcery fiction, a tradition carried on in its pages after Howard's premature death by writers such as Clifford Ball, Nictzin Dyalhis (a real name!), Henry Kuttner, C. L. Moore and H. Warner Munn. A short-lived sister magazine which specialized in exotic "Eastern" fantasy and to which many of the same writers contributed was *Oriental Stories* (1930–1934; later retitled *Magic Carpet*). Perhaps the final achievement of *Weird Tales*, in the 1940s, was to nurture the distinctive talent of Ray Bradbury (a writer who went on to become tremendously successful in the "slicks" such as *Collier's Weekly* and *Mademoiselle*). Bradbury's fine collection *The October Country* (1955) contains a number of memorable stories from *Weird Tales*.

UNKNOWN *(1939–1943; later retitled Unknown Worlds)* was another pulp, and another legend. Edited monthly by John W. Campbell (best known for his work in science fiction), its speciality was intelligent "rationalized fantasy" crossed with good humour. The writing team of L. Sprague de Camp and Fletcher Pratt shone in this area of expertise (their entertaining books *The Incomplete Enchanter* and *The Castle of Iron* began life in *Unknown*); but many other writers had their memorable moments in this magazine, including Robert Bloch, Anthony Boucher, Fredric Brown, Lester del Rey, Robert A. Heinlein, L. Ron Hubbard, Fritz Leiber (who introduced his Sword & Sorcery duo Fafhrd and the Gray Mouser here), Norvell W. Page, Theodore Sturgeon and A. E. van Vogt. The wartime paper-squeeze killed *Unknown*, and some long-lived fans have mourned the magazine ever since.

This issue features a sequel to Jonathan Swift's satirical masterpiece *Gulliver's Travels*

FANTASTIC ADVENTURES *(1939–1953)* was a much more average pulp product, but quite a long-lived one (128 issues) and fondly remembered by some readers. Edited by Raymond Palmer, then Howard Browne (and not to be confused with the similarly titled *Fantastic* and *Fantastic Universe*, both of which were digests), it specialized in lost-race or other-dimensional adventures, leavened with a considerable amount of punning silliness – titles like Time Wounds All Heels (Robert Bloch, 1942) were not uncommon. Among leading contributors to *FA* were Edgar Rice Burroughs (with some of his last stories), John Jakes (long before he became famous as an historical novelist), Theodore Sturgeon (whose first novel, *The Dreaming Jewels*, appeared there) and Robert Moore Williams – whose *Jongor of Lost Land* (1940) and its sequels were *echt*-heroic fantasy of the pulpiest sort.

FAMOUS FANTASTIC MYSTERIES *(1939–1953)*, whose life-span was almost identical to that of *Fantastic Adventures* although it came from a completely different publisher, was a wonderful pulp magazine of quite another stamp. It was mainly a reprint publication, drawing initially on old Munsey titles like *All-Story* but also including some new material and much British fiction taken from obscure books. Editor Mary Gnaedinger did a great deal to retrieve the legacy of pulp fantasy, especially the stories of A. Merritt, and she also encouraged some outstanding illustrators such as Hannes Bok and Virgil Finlay. Sister publications of much the same type were *Fantastic Novels* (1940–1941, revived 1948–1951) and the short-lived *A. Merritt's Fantasy Magazine* (1949–1950).

THE MAGAZINE OF FANTASY AND SCIENCE FICTION *(launched 1949)* was the first, and the greatest, of the fantasy digests (it took its cues from another genre's leading digest, *Ellery Queen's Mystery Magazine*). In order to establish "literary" credentials superior to those of the pulps, it reprinted a certain amount of slick-magazine and book-published fiction in its first decade, but has concentrated on original stories since. The editors have changed over the years, the earliest being Anthony Boucher and J. Francis McComas, and the most recent being Kristine Kathryn Rusch and Gordon Van Gelder. Produced monthly over a span of nearly five decades now, it has published hundreds of notable authors, but on the fantasy side (as opposed to the science-fiction side) major contributors have included Poul Anderson (who revived "*Unknown*-style fantasy" with his amusing *Three Hearts and Three Lions*, 1953), Gordon R. Dickson (who began his similar *Dragon and the George* sequence in this mag-

A Brit mag of glorious memory, it published early stories by many UK writers

azine in 1957), Avram Davidson (numerous stories, plus a spell in the editor's chair), Harlan Ellison, Stephen King, Sterling E. Lanier, Fritz Leiber, Ursula Le Guin, C. S. Lewis, Thomas Burnett Swann, Jack Vance, Manly Wade Wellman and Roger Zelazny. A magazine to be cherished: long may it continue to thrive.

SCIENCE FANTASY *(British, 1950–1967; retitled Impulse in its last year)* was edited in the main by John Carnell, and later by Kyril Bonfiglioli and others. A bimonthly digest for most of its existence, it published notable fantasy by leading English authors such as Brian Aldiss, John Brunner (the outstanding *"Traveller in Black"* sequence), J. G. Ballard (some of his moody *"Vermilion Sands"* tales, from 1956) and Keith Roberts (his "Anita" stories, about a lively witch, and his haunting alternative-timestream novel *Pavane*, 1966). This was the magazine that brought Michael Moorcock to the fantasy scene, with his early 1960s Sword & Sorcery tales of the albino prince Elric and his fated sword Stormbringer. It also published the debut story of a bright teenager named Terry Pratchett.

FANTASTIC *(1952–1980)* was a digest-sized spinoff from the pulp *Fantastic Adventures* (see above), initially edited by Howard Browne, and later by Cele Goldsmith and Ted White, on a bimonthly basis. Its period of greatest acclaim was in the 1960s and early 1970s when, among many other achievements, it persuaded Fritz Leiber to resume his Fafhrd and Gray Mouser Sword & Sorcery series, and also ran contributions from other veteran fantasists such as L. Sprague de Camp. Among the newer writers the magazine encouraged at that time were Piers Anthony, Lin Carter, Ursula Le Guin, Michael Moorcock and Roger Zelazny.

INTERZONE *(British, launched 1982)* is primarily a science-fiction magazine, though open to other things. Beginning quarterly, then bimonthly, and then monthly since 1990 under the editorship of David Pringle and Lee Montgomerie, it is slick in format, though fairly small in circulation. Its moments of fantasy glory have included the publication of two original stories by the late Angela Carter (1982) and the World Fantasy Award-winning novella "The Unconquered Country" (1984) by Geoff Ryman. Latterly its occasional fantasy stories have included edgily disturbing adult fairy tales by Gwyneth Jones, Garry Kilworth and Tanith Lee, and some of the strange, atmospheric, dark fantasies of American author Darrell Schweitzer.

MARION ZIMMER BRADLEY'S FANTASY MAGAZINE *(launched 1988)* is, despite its bestselling editor-publisher's name, very much a small-press publication (though large in format, with colour covers), appearing quarterly. It has encouraged many newer writers, mainly American and mainly female, among the better-known being Jo Clayton, Phyllis Ann Karr, Mercedes Lackey, Diana L. Paxson and Jennifer Roberson.

REALMS OF FANTASY *(launched 1994)* is the newest kid on the fantasy-magazine block – large, slick, full of colour, and probably the most wholehearted attempt yet to produce a magazine devoted to genre fantasy as it is understood by most readers of paperback novels at the end of the 20th century. Edited by Shawna McCarthy, it appears bimonthly and already its contributor list looks like a roster of the more popular and talented current writers – Louise Cooper, Charles de Lint, Alan Dean Foster, Lisa Goldstein, Tanith Lee and Jane Yolen among them. Terri Windling contributes interesting non-fiction regularly, and the magazine also takes advantage of internal colour printing to showcase the work of a respected fantasy artist in each issue.

CHINA MIEVILLE TALKS ABOUT FANTASY THAT BITES BACK TO LEADING SCI-FI MAG *LOCUS*.

BLACK GATE: ADVENTURES IN FANTASY LITERATURE *(launched 2000)* is the newest member of the fantasy magazine community. At well over 200 pages, the quarterly magazine is packed full of fiction, book reviews, articles and fantasy gaming. The brief set by editor John O'Neill is to publish original adventure-orientated fantasy fiction, from sword and sorcery through to dark fantasy, urban fantasy and magical realism. The magazine is distributed across North America, and available globally by subscription, which can be purchased from the detailed web site. Although the magazine is very new, it has received excellent reviews in publications right across the industry, including *Locus*, *Interzone* and *Science Fiction Chronicle*. So far, Black Gate has been extremely impressive, and hopefully it will flourish.

GLOSSARY

Achilles' Heel It's unsporting for heroes to be completely invulnerable, so there's always a weak spot. Achilles had his heel; Superman has green kryptonite.

Adult Fantasy Not pornography, as you might imagine, but a publisher's phrase once used to distinguish "serious" fantasy from children's fairy tales.

Alchemy A sometimes-magical, sometimes-scientific discipline using primitive chemical apparatus and mindbogglingly abstruse theories.

Alternative World One where history took another turning. Often the difference from Earth is that scholars researched magic instead of science.

Amulet Any magical or protective item of jewellery.

Antichrist The false Christ who will supposedly appear in the run-up to Armageddon.

Apocalypse The end of the world, as predicted in the Bible.

Armageddon In Christian fantasy, the final battle of good and evil.

Arthurian To do with King Arthur, who repeatedly pops up in modern as well as historical fantasy.

Asgard Home of the Norse gods.

Astral Plane Spiritual realm where the souls of dreamers, magical adepts and the dead tend to wander.

Atlantis The most famous of once-great but now sunken lands. Others include Lemuria, Mu, Tolkien's Númenor and Pratchett's Leshp.

Balance There are endless struggles of good vs evil, light vs dark, order vs chaos; the Cosmic Balance (Moorcock's phrase) shows the state of play.

Beast Fables Moral fantasies, like Aesop's, which are acted out by animals.

Birthmark If interesting enough in shape (e.g. a crown), a sure sign that the marked person is a Hero or otherwise Special.

Broomstick Trademark symbol and personal air transport of witches.

Camelot King Arthur's legendary court.

Cantrip (or cantrap) A spoken or written spell.

Cauldron Traditional stewpot of witches. In Welsh myth and Lloyd Alexander's Prydain series, the Black Cauldron reanimated the dead as mindless warriors.

Cauldron of Story Tolkien's phrase for the mythic stockpot in which countless myths boil together and become confused, like the older legends absorbed into King Arthur's story.

Changeling Unsatisfactory substitute left in exchange when fairies steal a human baby.

Chaos Anarchy The formless matter before creation began; the force (not necessarily evil) which works against order.

Clairvoyance "Clear sight", the magic talent of seeing what mere eyes can't.

Companions Essential company for any Quest in Fantasyland, whether you want them or not.

Crystal Balls Used in place of mobile phones, spy cameras or Internet access.

Cthulhu Mythos A background of dreadful gods and elder races invented by H. P. Lovecraft for his supernatural stories, and elaborated by many other authors.

Dark Lord Generic bad guy of many trilogies, who controls overwhelming forces and wants to rule or destroy the world. Tolkien's

Sauron is the classic example.

Dark Tower Home of either a Dark Lord or a Nameless Evil.

Dis The inner city of Hell.

Dreams A popular route for messages sent by gods and mages.

Dying Earth Jack Vance's name for a far distant future Earth where the Sun is fading and science and magic seem indistinguishable. Clark Ashton Smith and Gene Wolfe used similar settings.

Elementals Living and usually very dangerous incarnations of the alchemical elements earth, water, air and fire.

Excalibur King Arthur's sword, also known as Caliburn; a frequent fantasy prop.

Eucatastrophe "Good catastrophe", a word coined by Tolkien to describe the fairy-tale ending which is a happy surprise.

Faerie Posh word for fairyland.

Fantasyland We know the place by heart: that stereotyped land of dragons, elves and heroes that's been worn smooth by countless Tolkien imitators. See Diana Wynne Jones's *The Tough Guide to Fantasyland.*

Fates The three sinister ladies of Greek myth who spin, assign and finally cut the thread of everyone's life.

Fimbulwinter The unnatural winter leading up to Ragnarok.

Fire-Starting A minor magical talent, the ability to set things alight.

Fisher King The wounded guardian of the Grail.

Fountain of Youth Magic spring that restores youth; dangerous both to seek and to find, since an overdose reduces you to babyhood.

Four Horsemen Traditionally War, Plague (he's Conquest in the Bible), Famine and Death, who ride out to mark the Apocalypse or whenever else they feel like it.

Geas (Irish geis) A binding spell whose victims are forced to perform or avoid specified actions.

Glamour The magic of false appearances, causing people to seem beautiful, unrecognizable or invisible.

Golden Bough Sir James Frazer's classic (but much-disputed) *The Golden Bough: A History of Myth and Religion* includes "rules of magic" adopted by many fantasy writers.

Golem Legendary Hebrew clay man animated by magic; a sort of early robot.

Grail Holy vessel that once held Christ's blood; therefore, a coveted McGuffin in Arthurian and other quests.

Gramarye, or grammarie An old word for magic, connecting it to learning (grammar), grimoires and glamour.

Grimoire A book of spells, usually black magic.

Heroic Fantasy Much the same as sword-&-sorcery.

High Fantasy Usually fantasy with a "lofty" or "noble" style, following James Branch Cabell's aim: "to write perfectly of beautiful happenings".

Identity Swap What happens when two people exchange souls, like the father and schoolboy in F. Anstey's *Vice-Versa.*

Immortality "Eternal" life; rare, coveted and usually purchased at great expense from dubious gods or demons. May wear off at embarrassing moments; see H. Rider Haggard's *She.*

Inklings The 1930s–40s Oxford discussion group to which Tolkien, C. S. Lewis and others read their work in progress.

Kalevala Finnish oral-tradition legends about the age of magic and heroes.

Lethe One of the rivers of Hell, whose water brings amnesia.

Levitation Raising oneself into the air by magic or (in the case of saints) general holiness.

Limbo Part of the afterlife which is neither Heaven nor Hell; often, in fantasy, a celestial waiting-room or civil service HQ.

Lycanthropy Posh word for what werewolves do, i.e. shape-shifting into wolf form.

Mage High-class term for wizard.

Magic Words Condensed mini-spells, like the famous "Abracadabra" or "Open Sesame".

Mabinogion Collection of old Welsh legends on which several authors have based their fantasies. Example: Alan Garner's *The Owl Service.*

Mana, or sometimes manna Raw magical or spiritual force; the power-source of magic in Larry Niven's fantasies.

Map All too often found at the front of fantasy novels. Some interesting maps are gathered in J. B. Post's *An Atlas of Fantasy.*

McGuffin Alfred Hitchcock's word for any highly desirable object which kick-starts the plot by luring everyone to chase it: the Ring, the Grail, the Maltese Falcon.

Mindspeech (or farspeaking) The fantasy word for telepathy.

Mooreeffoc "Coffee-room" seen in a mirror; used by G. K. Chesterton for stories that discover the fantastic in familiar things.

Mythopoeic Awards Annual fantasy awards, leaning towards Christian fantasy and the tradition of the Inklings.

Necromancy Literally, fortune-telling by summoning the spirits of the dead; also, other sorts of sinister and grisly magic. Necromancers are usually evil wizards.

Necronomicon "Book of Dead Names", the famous imaginary grimoire of the Cthulhu Mythos; it crops up in many other writers' works.

Norns Nordic equivalents of the Fates.

Olympus The Greek gods lived on Mount Olympus.

Oz The magic land of L. Frank Baum's *The Wizard of Oz* and its sequels.

Pacts Magically enforced contracts, less easily broken than business promises (especially pacts with the Devil).

Pentacle A five-sided star within a circle, usually drawn on the floor as a barrier against demons.

Philosophers' Stone Sought after by alchemists: the substance that can transmute base metals into gold.

Plot Coupon Term used by critics when a lazy writer's heroes win not so much by plausible effort and courage as by collecting a set of magical coupons ("the Nine Components of the Chaos Runefork") which automatically bring victory.

Plot Voucher Emergency "Get Out of Jail Free" card issued to any fantasy protagonist. "Take this", the wizard says: "When the proper time comes you will know its use ..."

Poltergeist German for noisy ghost; invisible but tiresome spirit that throws around furniture and crockery.

Portals Handy magical doorways of all shapes and sizes, which transport protagonists from Earth to adventures in a Secondary World.

Possession The state of having one's body taken over by a stronger-minded human or demon.

Prophecies In fantasy, these always come true ... but often in unexpected ways.

Quest Approved fantasy word for any purposeful journey. One doesn't go to the newsagent's but embarks on the Quest of *The Sun.*

Ragnarok The Norse myths' version of Armageddon.

Recursive Fantasy Critical term for fantasy that makes play with other authors' worlds or characters. Many such stories feature Sherlock Holmes and/or Dracula.

Reincarnation Return of the soul after death, in a new-born body.

Ring In the tradition of Aladdin, fairy tales and the legend of the Nibelungs, fantasy rings are always magical. Well, almost.

Runes Old-fashioned, angular lettering; spells written in such letters.

Salamander Another name for a fire elemental.

Secondary World Tolkien's phrase for an imagined fantasy land which isn't simply set on some remote island or medieval land of fable, but occupies a separate creation from ours.

Shape-shifting Changing between human and other forms, usually animal shapes and usually voluntarily. Werewolves shape-shift into wolves, vampires into bats, and wizards into whatever they choose.

Spell The words and/or gestures by which magic-users do their stuff.

Staff Wizard's equivalent of the witch's broomstick; not generally airworthy, but can usually store spells, emit fireballs, etc.

Sub-creation Tolkien's word for inventing fantasy worlds (as a Catholic he felt that true "creation" was reserved for God).

Sword The basic weapon of fantasy heroes, usually magical or accursed or with its own name. Stormbringer, in Michael Moorcock's fantasies, is all three.

Sword-&-Sorcery "Low" adventure fantasy in the pulp-fiction tradition of Conan. Fritz Leiber's Lankhmar stories showed that S&S could be done with style and polish.

Sympathetic Magic A Frazerian (see Golden Bough) principle of magic in which effects resemble causes: e.g., sticking pins in a wax image of your victim causes stabbing pains or wounds.

Talisman Any portable object with magical properties.

Talking Animals Often found in children's fantasy, like C. S. Lewis's Narnia books.

Theriomorphy Posh word, favoured by respectable critics, for shape-shifting.

Three Wishes A famous fairy-tale plot device. Usually two go wildly wrong and the third is needed to cancel them.

Time Out of Joint Timeslips and time distortions are common in fantasy. Visitors to Faerie may spend a night there and find a century has passed on Earth ... or vice-versa.

Transmutation Changing one lifeless material into another. See Philosopher's Stone.

True Names Magic-users can gain power over dragons, demons or people by learning their true names (shorthand for deep understanding of their natures).

Undead Generic name for the vitality-challenged or differently alive, especially vampires and zombies.

Unknown Fantasy The "science fantasy" popularized by *Unknown* magazine, which applies scientific or engineering logic to fantastic ideas.

Valhalla The Viking Heaven, with endless feasting, hunting and fighting.

Wandering Jew Ahasuerus, who offended Christ and was cursed with immortality until the Second Coming. Like the Flying Dutchman, he appears in numerous historical and modern fantasies.

Wards Magical protection, like an intangible electric fence.

Waste Land In many fantasies, the land itself sickens and dies if not ruled by its true King.

White Goddess Robert Graves's *"The White Goddess",* a poetic and unreliable interpretation of many myths, has influenced several fantasies.

Wild Hunt Legendary pack of supernatural hounds which in fantasy is usually led by stag-horned Herne the Hunter and is all too often summoned to chase the bad guys.

Witches Traditionally evil, hag-like women with warts, broom-sticks and pointy hats. Modern fantasy, influenced by feminism, allows witches to be benign, good-looking and sometimes even male.

Wizards Traditionally dignified, scholarly old men with beards, grimoires and pointy hats. Modern fantasy allows wizards to be comic buffoons (see Terry Pratchett) or sometimes even female.

Wonderland Magic land visited by Lewis Carroll's Alice; used to describe other imaginary lands that operate by arbitrary or eccentric rules.

World Fantasy Awards Presented annually by the World Fantasy Convention to the novel, story, etc. judged best of the year.

Year King Rules for a year and is then sacrificed for the good of the land. Not a coveted position.

Yin-Yang Old Chinese symbol of perfect balance between light and dark, male and female, etc.

INDEX

Page numbers in *italics* refer to illustrations; (f) after an entry refers to a film, (m) to a magazine, (c) to a fictional character (g) to a game and TV to a television show.

Picture Credits

The publishers would like to thank the following sources for their kind permission to reproduce the pictures in this book:

AKG, London 10, 13/Erich Lessing 9
BBC 89l,r, 94b, 95b, 100b, 102, 105, 111t, b, 112, 114, 187, 235
Blizzard Entertainmant 241
Courtesy Broderbund 227t
Jean Loup Charmet 18, 19, 21, 26, 144, 219
Corbis UK 152/Bettmann/UPI 121, 122, 156, 173, Everett Collection 27, 38, 46, 53, 100, 101, 106, 107, 109, 113, 115, 117, 118, 119, 203, 204, 212, 213/*Addams Family* 1964 UIP/Paramount 93, *The Amazing Mr Blunden* 1972 Hemdale/Hemisphere 69, *Baron Munchausen* 1962 Ceskoslovensky Film 205, *Beetlejuice* 1988 Warner Bros/Geffen 80, *La Belle et la Bete* 1946 Discina (Andre Paulve) 54, *Berkeley Square* 1933 Fox 43, *Bewitched* 1964 MGM 94t, *The Blue Bird* 1940 TCF 49, *Camelot* 1967 Warner 185, *Clash of the Titans* 1981 MGM/Charles H. Schneer, Ray Harryhausen 73,*The Company of Wolves* 1984 ITC/Palace 76, *Conan*, Dino de Laurentiis 34, *A Connecticut Yankee*1931 Fox 42, *Death Takes a Holiday* 1971Paramount 98, *Fairytale a True Story* 1997 87, *Le Fatiche di Ercole* 1957 Oscar/Galatea 61, *Finian's Rainbow* 1968 Warner Seven Arts 67, *The Green Pastures* 1936 Warner 45, *Hercules* 1957 Oscar/Galatea 88, *Hook* 1991 Columbia TriStar/Amblin 200, *I Dream of Jeannie* 1965 Republic 95, *Labyrinth* 1986 Tri-Star/Eric Rattray, George Lucas 78, *Les Visiteurs* 1993 Arrow/Gaumont/France 3/Alpilles/Amigo 85, *Lost Horizon*, 1937 Columbia 30, *Mary Poppins* 1964 Walt Disney 181, *I Married a Witch* 1942 UA/Cinema Guild/Rene Clair 51, *A Matter of Life & Death* 1946 GFD/Archers 55,*Miracle on 34th Street* 1947 TCF 57, *Pufnstuf* 1969 Universal/Krofft Entreprises 97, *Raiders of the Lost Ark* 1981 Paramount/Lucasfilm 74, *The Seventh Seal* 1957 Svensk Filmindustri 62, *The Seventh Voyage of Sinbad* 1958 Columbia/Morningside 63, *The Sorrows of Satan* 1926 Famous Players/Paramount 41, *Tarzan's Secret Treasure* 1941 MGM 215, *Time Bandits* 1981 HandMade Films 75, *Topper* 1953 MGM/Hal Roach 90, *Toy Story* 1995 86, *Twilight Zone* 1959 Warner 92, *The Wizard of Oz* 1939 MGM 48 Corbis UK/Richard T. Nowitz 1
Courtesy Eidos 227
Mary Evans Picture Library 3, 23, 180, 183, 188, 193, 195, 198, 206, 208, 217/Explorer 24, Arthur Rackham Collection 22
Games Workshop Ltd. 220, 225, 226
Courtesy GT Interactive 228
Roger Garland 7, 37, 186, 230
Ronald Grant Archive 14, 104/*All That Money can Buy* 1941 RKO/William Dieterle (Charles L.Glett) 50, 1921 *L'Atlantide* 39, 1924 *Die Niebelungen* 40, *Kwaidon* 1964 Ninjin Club/Bungei 65, *Orphee* 1949 Andre Paulve I/Films du Palais Royal 58, *Monty Python and the Holy Grail* 1975 EMI/Python 70, *TheWitches of Eastwick* 1987 Warner/Guber-Peters/Kennedy Miller 79
Victor Gollancz 239
Hasbro/Wizards of the Coast 234
The Kobal Collection 99, 196/*Thief of Baghdad* 1978 Columbia/Palm Films/Victorine 103, *The Wizard of Oz* 1939 MGM 192
LFI 123tl, 124, 128/Polygram TV 126/Warner Bros 125.
Locus 263
©The Estate of Mervyn Peake, *Gormenghast,* The Overlook Press, Woodstock, New York 233
Penguin 241
Photostage/Donald Cooper 32
Return to Lankhmar , White Wolf Publishing, Tim Kirk, Owlswick Press 236
Return to Lankhmar , White Wolf Publishing,
Rex Features: 89l, 89r, 90r, 91, 200, 223, 258, 259/Fotos International 87.
Mike Mignola 237
Darryl K Sweet 17, 243
Wizards of the Coast, Inc. 224b, 229

Additional photography: Chris Lobina

Every effort has been made to acknowledge correctly and contact the source and/copyright holder of each picture, and Carlton Books Limited apologises for any unintentional errors or omissions which will be corrected in future editions of this book.